BY CALEB CARR

SURRENDER, NEW YORK

SURRENDER, NEW YORK

A NOVEL

CALEB CARR

RANDOM HOUSE
NEW YORK

Copyright © 2016 by Caleb Carr

Published in the United States by Random House, an imprint and division of Penguin Random House LLC, New York.

RANDOM HOUSE and the HOUSE colophon are registered trademarks of Penguin Random House LLC.

Library of Congress Cataloging-in-Publication Data
Names: Carr, Caleb, author.
Title: Surrender, New York : a novel / by Caleb Carr.
Description: First Edition. | New York : Random House, [2016]
Identifiers: LCCN 2016004992 | ISBN 9780679455691 (hardback) |
ISBN 9780812989311 (ebook)
Subjects: | BISAC: FICTION / Mystery & Detective / General. | FICTION / Literary. |
GSAFD: Mystery fiction. | Suspense fiction.
Classification: LCC PS3553.A76277 S87 2016 | DDC 813/.54—dc23 LC record available
at http://lccn.loc.gov/2016004992

Printed in the United States of America on acid-free paper

randomhousebooks.com

9 8 7 6 5 4 3 2 1

First Edition

Book design by Diane Hobbing

For:
Jim Monahan and Dennis Whitney
and everyone at Thorpe's in Hoosick Falls:
They have fought to preserve a way of life
and business that has kept many people
going, most of all this author

And for:
Arnie Kellar, whether he likes it or not.

PART ONE

THE CURSE OF KNOWLEDGE

Once we know something, we find it hard to imagine what it was like not to know it. Our knowledge has "cursed" us. . . . Reversing the process is as difficult as un-ringing a bell. You can't unlearn what you already know. There are, in fact, only two ways to beat the Curse of Knowledge reliably. The first is not to learn anything. The second is to take your ideas and transform them.

—CHIP HEATH AND DAN HEATH, *MADE TO STICK*

For in much wisdom is much grief; and he that increaseth knowledge increaseth sorrow.

—ECCLESIASTES 1:18

CHAPTER ONE

"You Cannot Escape It, in This Country"

{i.}

The case did not so much burst upon as creep over Burgoyne County, New York, just as the sickness that underlay it only took root in the region slowly, insidiously, and long before the first body was found. My own initial indication that at least one crime of an unusual and quite probably violent nature had been committed came in the form of a visit from Deputy Sheriff Pete Steinbrecher, in early July of that summer. I was then living, as I had been for about five years, at Shiloh, a dairy farm belonging to my spinster great-aunt, Miss Clarissa Jones. Shiloh is centered on a large Italianate farmhouse that is the sole residence in Death's Head Hollow, one of a half-dozen valleys that lead down from the high ground of the northern Taconic Mountains into the small town of Surrender.

Despite my having spent some seven or eight years working as a criminal psychologist (primarily with the New York City Police Department) prior to relocating to the pastoral severity of the Taconics, I had only occasionally interacted with what passes for local law enforcement during my time up north. Due to severe budget cuts at every level of government, there was and remains precious little law in Burgoyne County. Communities like Surrender long ago lost their town constabularies, as well as their county sheriff's substations, and what little regular patrolling the latter department can still do is focused primarily on the county seat of Fraser. The residents of the many small communities in the region have thus been left to see to their own safety, which they are happy to do: for Burgoyne County is gun country, and only in cases involving extreme disturbances are either the sheriff's office in Fraser or the New York State Police contacted.

For these and other reasons, my main criminological efforts since relocating to my great-aunt's farm (where I'd spent nearly every weekend and summer vacation as a boy) had been less applied than academic. I'd been establishing an online course of study in various controversial aspects of forensic science under the aegis of the State University of New York at Albany. That institution's first-rate School of Criminal Justice had long offered a range of classes in forensics, both at the undergraduate and the graduate levels; but its senior faculty and officials, wisely taking into account the scandals that have rocked both federal and regional crime laboratories as well as the field of forensic science generally during the last twenty years, had decided, just before my own relocation to their area, to offer complementary courses that would explore the well-documented weaknesses of forensics. Mine had been one of the most outspoken voices attempting to expose those weaknesses; and because my work (and the methods that underlay them) had led to a series of widely publicized conflicts with the NYPD's crime lab that had ultimately made me *persona non grata* in the metropolis where I was born, I was not altogether surprised, but was entirely grateful, when SUNY-Albany offered me the chance to help structure their balancing course of study.

Partnering with my closest co-worker in New York, Mike Li—an expert in trace and DNA evidence who had spent years vociferously pointing out the widespread and often fatal flaws that marred the gathering, handling, and courtroom use of such evidence—I gladly accepted the university's offer, provided Mike's and my own courses could be taught online. (The lingering effects of a childhood bout with osteosarcoma on my left femur and pelvis had recently made extended travel, even the fifty miles or so to Albany and back, increasingly difficult for me.) The administrators of the School of Criminal Justice, already anxious to expand their presence in the burgeoning world of online teaching, had readily agreed to this condition; and soon Mike and I had established a virtual lecture hall inside a rickety old airplane hangar that sat on a hill behind two large green barns built in the mid-nineteenth century that were the centerpieces of the farm that my great-aunt oversaw with an iron will.

To be more precise, Mike and I had built our Skype-operated classroom inside the fuselage of a pre–World War II Junkers JU-52/3m, a classic German civilian aircraft, the care and maintenance of which had been the passion of my great-aunt's father. After piloting it from Germany to Senegal in 1935 via a circuitous European and North African route, the old lunatic had shipped the plane to Brazil and flown it north: an adventure that was apparently as colorful—and expensive—as it sounds. But the tri-engine beast was now immobile, the ghostly occupant of nearly every inch of the large hangar; and inside it Mike and I worked to disabuse our students, first, of the widely accepted idea that forensics (not only trace and DNA collection, but such far older practices as fingerprinting and ballistics, as well) were the "gold standard" of evidentiary analysis and courtroom argument and, second, of the equally popular and pernicious notion that forensics had made criminal psychology, and especially profiling, somehow obsolete.

On the afternoon in question, I had just given a long and fairly impassioned summer term lecture explaining precisely how damaging this last set of beliefs had become, asking that my students—representatives of the coming generation of criminal investigators—restore both psychology and profiling to the positions of respect that they had largely lost when the purportedly more precise areas of forensics had begun to monopolize criminal investigation in the early 1990s. Stepping away from the half-dozen large video monitors that dominated the interior of the JU-52 when I was finally finished, I then descended slowly into the hangar via a set of steel steps that my great-grandfather had built up and over the starboard wing of the plane to the forward hatch, and went outside to lean on my cane and smoke a cigarette. From there, I caught sight of Pete Steinbrecher's patrol car moving quickly up the hollow, lights flashing but siren mute: Pete was well enough acquainted with both Shiloh and my diminutive yet fiery great-aunt to know that the sound of the siren would bring Clarissa swiftly from the farmhouse, to which she would not return until she had delivered a stern lecture to the deputy on the effects of such sounds on dairy cattle. For this and other reasons, Pete did not brave the hollow on minor errands—indeed, his presence almost certainly indicated just one thing:

"Mike," I called, stepping back toward the great maw that was the open hangar door, "Pete Steinbrecher's on his way up." I could hear Mike cut short his preparations for a seminar as I added flatly, "Looks like someone's been murdered..."

In the time it took Pete to park his patrol car beside one of the milking barns below the hangar, Mike shot out of the plane and down the steel steps, his mood characteristically brightened. "Excellent!" he called as he joined me, his eyes—narrowed by years of examining often microscopic pieces of evidence—widening with enthusiasm. "Should I cancel my next class?" He looked up at me eagerly (Mike stands about five foot six, even when excited, while I, despite my usual stooped posture, am a good half-foot taller), and grinned almost fiendishly as he accepted a cigarette from the pack I held out to him.

"Not yet," I said, pulling a pocket watch from my vest and popping it open. "You've got a good twenty minutes—let's hear him out, first."

"Ah," Mike noised in disappointment. "How did I know you were going to say that, *gweilo*?" (When irritated with me, it was Mike's custom to use the Cantonese phrase for "white devil.")

"Easy, there, Yellow Peril," I answered, replacing my watch, producing a Zippo lighter, and offering its flame to my partner.

"Damn it, L.T.," Mike replied. "I've told you, 'Yellow Peril' refers to the Japs—and the Chinese have a lot more fucking reasons to hate them than you do. So dibs."

I turned to him, amused. "'Dibs'?"

"On hating the Japanese," Mike said, with a wave of his cigarette.

"Ah," I replied with a nod; but I could not help another chuckle. "'Dibs,'" I murmured. "You often have a whimsical way of putting things, Michael . . ."

"Yeah, yeah, yeah—come on, Trajan, I'm half-crazed for a real case."

"You're always half-crazed. And we don't know that this *is* a real case: he may just want advice."

"Sure," Mike said dubiously, as we smoked and watched the deputy walk up a dirt pathway toward us. "Pete's risking a nasty run-in with your aunt for *advice*."

"Just give the man a chance to talk," I said.

Pete held up a hand in greeting as he neared us, then removed his grey Stetson when he arrived to shake each of our hands. "Doc," he said to me. "Mike. I, uh—I'm wondering if you're in the mood to help the county out." Pete was a big man, with solid German features typical of the many waves of immigrants from that country who had come to upstate New York during the nineteenth century. In addition, he possessed the kind of even, sonorous voice that I admired in honest, hardworking first responders, which in his case was lightly tinged with the not-quite-definable but appealing accent of the area, a sound that was very unlike the affected redneck twang that younger locals had adopted: ironically, only *after* farming had ceased to be their chief occupation.

"Cigarette, Pete?" I said, holding out the pack. I noted, as did he, that my hand was trembling, slightly but uncontrollably, in anticipation of his news.

"You know damn well my wife made me quit, Dr. Jones," Pete answered, drawing out a handkerchief and wiping his brow. "I come home smelling like smoke and she'll crease my skull with a socket wrench."

I did indeed know this; but it was the nature of our relationship, just as it was of my interactions with Mike, to push each other's buttons with abandon. Returning the pack to my jacket pocket, I loosened my tie and asked, "So—who's dead?"

"Jesus . . ." Pete's smile suddenly disappeared and his visage darkened— but it was what he'd said that was the more important indication that something very unusual was up. Burgoyne County may be gun country, but it is not, for the most part, church country; and those few who, like Pete, fight to keep its sprinkling of multi-denominational Christian churches alive take their work and its details seriously—yet the matter at hand, and my light reference to it, had permitted him to utter what he considered a genuine blasphemy. "You don't half tread lightly, do you, Doc?" he went on, mournfully. Putting his hat back on his head, which was now free of the sweat drawn out by the July heat, Pete next assumed an uncharacteristically official air. "Truth be told, I'd rather you see it for yourself."

I eyed this one of my few good friends in county law enforcement closely. "Pete? What is it?"

"You want to come inside, have a beer, Pete?" Mike asked, also studying the deputy's face and seeing the unusual amount of concern—even bewilderment—on it. Pete had of course handled deaths before, and even murders; but at just that moment the man was clearly rattled.

He shook his head to Mike, smiling briefly in gratitude. "I gotta get back. Hopefully with the Doc, here. You're welcome to come along, too, Mike. We could use you."

Mike turned to me and tried to suppress a smile of deep satisfaction. "Well—an official invitation. So it's none of your fucking business, anymore, L.T." Quickly stamping out his cigarette, Mike told Pete, "Just give me five minutes to tell my class. Maybe give them some extra homework. Can you spare it?"

"Sure," Pete answered, visibly relieved. "If it's really just five minutes, no problem."

"I could use a few minutes, too," I said, turning toward a pasture that stretched away on a hill behind and above the hangar. About ten acres in size, the enclosure occupied ground that led to a small foothill at the base of a steep, heavily wooded mountain. It was surrounded by an especially strong and, at ten feet, exceptionally tall, high-tensile box wire fence, reinforced by tight chicken wire. "I've got to take care of something . . ."

"You going to feed your 'dog'?" Pete asked, finally easing up and smiling freely.

"I am. You want to tag along?"

"Doc—no disrespect, but, uh, you know that thing—"

"That 'rare African hunting dog'?" I quickly interjected.

"Yeah, yeah, I'll keep playing along with the story, don't worry. But you know the thing makes me nervous."

"The more time you spend around her, the less reason you'll have to *be* nervous. Besides, she likes you. A little."

"Yeah, well—a little ain't enough, thanks all the same. I'll just wait here." As I walked toward a nearby gate in the fencing that was covered on each side with several additional layers of wire, I heard Pete shout, "What's the damned thing's name again?"

"Marcianna!" I called back to him. "The favorite sister of the Roman emperor Trajan."

"And he wonders," I heard Pete tell Mike, "why I can't remember it . . ."

When I reached the enclosure gate and issued a very particular call— almost a chirp, in its way, and a sound that usually brought my favorite sister running—I discovered that Marcianna was nowhere to be seen. From long experience I knew that she had likely caught some large bird—a raven or crow, in all probability, or perhaps even a hawk that had spotted some small rodent within her enclosure—and was enjoying the kill inside the large stone den that I had designed for her, using flat and oblong boulders brought down from high on the mountain by several of the farmhands with a tractor and sledge. The hands had not known, at the time, what they were building, or what it might be intended to house; and when they subsequently found out, they played along with my request that they not reveal the secret of what lived inside the enclosure, just as Pete and a few others would later do. As time went by, it became something of a speculative legend, in Surrender, and I think everyone in the know got a kick out of not revealing the answer. At any rate, certain that I knew Marcianna's whereabouts, I opened a nearby cooler in which I had that morning placed a good-sized slab of frozen beef, along with her nutritional supplements. By now the meat was nicely melted and warmed, and, after pushing the soluble supplements deep inside the red, bloody tissue, I tossed the meal over the fence onto a bare patch of earth near the gate.

"Marcianna!" I called, for she knew her name perfectly well. "I'm going to the store—I'll be back very soon!" *Store* and *soon* were words she also understood, although she didn't like them; but I had no doubt that she wouldn't worry while I was gone, and so turned back around and returned to the hangar door.

Mike had made short work—undoubtedly too short—of his students, and was standing next to Pete once again, his evidence kit at his feet. Together we walked quickly down to the patrol car, Mike reluctantly agreeing to play the prisoner and be locked into the rear as I opened the passenger-side door up front. Waiting for Pete to open his own door, I said, with transparent nonchalance:

"You know, Pete—you've never refused to give us at least the victim's sex and age before. What's going on?"

"Fifteen-year-old girl," Pete said, visibly troubled again. "And that's all you're getting out of me, for now."

As I entered the car, I glanced back at Mike and saw him raise his eyebrows with irrepressible anticipation. He had wanted a real case; and apparently we were about to get one.

As I settled into my seat, Pete handed me a small pillow that he had brought along, with characteristic decency. "Here," he said uneasily. "For your—hip, or whatever."

"Very good of you, Deputy," I said gratefully, attempting to bolster the left side of my lower back and pelvis into as comfortable a position as possible. "And may we also know where we're going?"

"West Briarwood," he answered. "But that really is *it*. Just hang on till we get there." And with that we headed back down the hollow, Pete once more turning his spinning roof lights on and leaving his siren alone, while driving faster than was his custom. In addition, I noticed that he had turned his radio off: a highly unusual move for any officer, and one plainly intended to prevent our overhearing open-channel chatter about our destination and the case that was awaiting us.

{ii.}

The town of West Briarwood was far more typical of communities in Burgoyne County than was the small, seemingly featureless village of Surrender: grouped around the intersection of Route 7 and yet another randomly numbered county road (for there has never been any system other than whim involved in the ordering of New York county byways) were a Stewart's convenience store; a mini-mall that featured a liquor vendor; a run-down grocery store; and several other shops, each of which was constantly having either a grand opening or a closing sale. Residentially, there were about two dozen run-down but quaint late-nineteenth-century houses (most of them long ago gutted and refashioned into apartments), along with more recent ranch houses that did nothing but provide a reminder that time had brought few enlightened developments to the county. Our business that day, however, lay beyond the town proper: again taking to one of the ubiquitous hollows of the county, this one hopefully named Daybreak Lane (despite the fact that the foothill it was cut into faced west), we rode up about five hundred feet in elevation and two miles in distance, past farmhouses in need of repair and surrounded by old cars and trucks, as well as lawn and farm equipment, nearly all of it for sale.

Finally, we closed in on a seemingly ancient mobile home that stood amid a group of secondary-growth trees at some remove from the lane. It was plainly abandoned, although how long it had stood so was impossible to say. Much of its siding was missing, revealing loose insulation, and several windows had been replaced with thick plastic that had once been relatively clear, but was now dismally murky. A large, plainly visible and badly encrusted sewage hose had served for a septic system, running away from the house and into an obliging field; and small amounts of a brown liquid, driven, in all likelihood, by a rusted, running toilet drawing on the trailer's defective well, still trickled steadily into a patch of discolored grass. Yet all these signs of decay and ignorance would, sadly, have almost certainly been as much in evidence when the trailer had been inhabited as they were now. Realizing this, I glanced back at Mike, and could see that his unadulterated anticipation had grown mitigated by apprehension: if ever a place promised not only a crime but a history of singularly grim details, we had reached it.

Additional unpleasantness, of a more mundane but still troublesome variety, was indicated by a collection of vehicles that had already gathered around this standing testament to desperation: the personal squad car of Sheriff Steve Spinetti was closest to the trailer door, and behind it was parked a battered black Chevy Impala that I recognized as belonging to Dr. Ernest Weaver, medical examiner for not only Burgoyne but several other counties, as well. Finally, jammed in behind Weaver's car, there was a van drawn from the fleet of the New York State Police Forensic Investigation Center in Albany, the central crime lab that served all counties that did not have their own forensics facility (such being most) or that were not near one of the FIC's field stations. The FIC had fared as badly, during the era of forensic scandals, as had most labs in the nation, and neither Mike nor I was pleased to see it represented. Nor, to his credit, was Pete: the deputy's lead foot on the highway had apparently embodied his effort to get us to the scene quickly enough to avoid territorial and philosophical disputes. But such encounters now seemed inevitable. The van had likely brought to the scene one or more of a group of lab techs, almost all of whom were known to both Mike and myself; and, judging from the bored, slightly angry look of the state trooper who had evidently been ordered under duress to ferry the tech and his equipment, he, she, or they must already have been on the scene for a fair amount of time.

Pete pulled in alongside the van, on what had once been the trailer's lawn, and as he released Mike from the back seat of his car, I used my cane to get out and upright, catching the eye of the state trooper just long enough to see him turn away in various forms of disgust, not the least of which was likely the realization that he would not be getting back to Albany any time soon. As for Dr. Weaver and the tech, they were evidently inside, while Steve Spinetti was approaching us, waving one large arm and hand as he smiled in enjoyment.

"You must've drove pretty fast, Pete," he said with a chuckle, his long nose reaching down toward his upper lip as he did. His merriment was characteristically needling: he had obviously known that the ME and the FIC tech were coming even before Pete had left to fetch us. The sheriff was hoping less to make our mission irrelevant than to be sure that it would be carried out in competition with the other crime scene investigators, thereby subjecting all points of view to immediate challenge: such was the man's custom, and it was not without its merits. "Not fast enough, though," Steve went on. "Weaver and the state tech got here in a big damned hurry, especially for them. Almost like somebody gives a shit . . ." The slow, thoughtful way that Steve said these last words seemed to indicate something out of the ordinary; but then he stuck his right hand out and shook my partner's and my own, apparently as upbeat as ever. "Dr. Jones—Mr. Li. You'll be glad to hear that Weaver says we've already got it covered. Straightforward, he says: got to get some details, but according to him it's just another teenage murder, though this time it's pretty nasty."

"'This time'?" I echoed; but before I could pursue it, Pete spoke up, sounding surprised:

"That right, Chief? Well, can't be much objection, then, to these guys looking around a bit, if it's all sewn up already."

Spinetti cast Pete a knowing look, followed by an even wider smile. "Well, hell, Pete, I don't want to discourage initiative, do I? And you fellas did make the trip. Sure, I'd be grateful if our distinguished guests could stick around." His undeniably perspicacious grey eyes plainly showed that he was pleased he would be able to fully hedge his bets. "Just let those two boys make their preliminary assessment official, and we'll see what the ringers from Surrender can do for us."

Steve Spinetti was one of the few high-ranking members of law enforcement in Burgoyne County, to say nothing of the entire Empire State, with whom I had managed to maintain even a guardedly collegial relationship, following Mike's and my own not quite voluntary exile from New York City. He ruled his domain in the style of one of the better class of small bureaucratic tyrants: not with an utterly closed mind, but with one that would use any means at hand to close a case as quickly as possible. He thus avoided extra time spent looking for details that would only complicate his paperwork and threaten his own authority as well as his ability to grab primary credit for a solution. This is not to belittle the man at all: Steve was a tough yet compassionate first responder (unlike many, who never got past the tough side), and his honesty about his motives concerning paperwork and proper acknowledgment simply made him more straightforward and far easier to work with than most men or women who had reached similar levels of authority.

And yet he had a very cagey side, too; and I was about to get a pointed demonstration of it. "Say, uh, Doc," he said; and his voice had suddenly gone down in volume, although he never lost his smile. "While we're waiting, I'd like to mention a couple of things, but I don't want anybody here—and that includes you, Pete—to give that trooper sitting in the van any reason to think we're doing anything but shooting the shit and having a good time. Okay?"

Mike and I had been in dozens of such politically tricky situations before, and we both immediately smiled and affected a chuckle or two for the trooper's benefit as I replied, "Of course, Steve—just so long as our little talk is going to include an explanation of what you meant by 'just another teenage murder.'"

"Oh, it will, it will," Steve said, his own phony grin getting wider. "And one day I'm going to learn to watch every fricking word that comes out of my mouth around you, Doc. But here's the thing: Weaver and the tech, they're real sure about their call on this. And I don't know, maybe they're right. But me and Pete were the first ones here, and we've checked out the girl's background, and the whole thing just feels wrong, to both of us."

I eyed the deputy. "That right, Pete?"

"That's right," Pete said, turning his head away from the van. "I mean, besides the way she died, or maybe because of it—I don't know, I just don't like it."

"Okay," I replied. "So what makes Weaver so sure?"

"We'll get to all that, after you see the body," Spinetti said, looking at the trailer and himself appearing to become, if only for an instant, somewhat melancholy; but remembering the trooper, who was indeed keeping a careful eye on our little conference, he forced out a laugh. "Damndest thing," he said through it. "What these meth heads will get up to. Or when. Or why . . ."

"'Meth heads'?" Mike echoed.

"Yeauh," Steve droned, in his upstate drawl. "The parents were, anyway. Dead girl's name is Shelby Capamagio—they all used to live here, but the folks disappeared about two years ago. Took their younger girl, left the older one with some relatives further up the road. At least we think they're relatives, they don't communicate real well. Or can't. Won't, maybe."

"Hunh," Mike noised, maintaining his smile, but troubled, now. "So—another throwaway kid?"

My partner wasn't just being flippant: the death of Shelby Capamagio had apparently taken place, like many others of its kind, against the backdrop of a nation in which increasing numbers of parents, faced with financial catastrophe of one kind or another, were simply disappearing from the lives of one or more of their offspring and making themselves impossible to trace, by taking on new identities or going off the grid. In the process, they were creating an entirely new variety of young people who did not fit into the state's official classifications for either "orphaned," "abandoned," or "homeless," but rather had formed a new category of their own, one that New York, among other states, had labeled with brutal concision: "throwaway children."

"Yeauh," Steve said again. "Looks like it could be. Not quite sure yet, though . . ." It was something of a nervous tic, the sheriff's insistence on running through every option in a speculative statement; and I had to concede, it was indicative of an investigative mind that, if somewhat undeveloped, was still instinctively keen. "I been up to talk to the people she first stayed with, didn't get much—but from what I did, lemme tell you, it ain't a nice story. She was trouble, I guess—and when whoever those people are had had enough of it, they moved her out of their house to their equipment shed. Fed her meals, when they could catch her, gave her a space heater in the winter. I guess I don't have to tell you she only got worse. Took it for about six months, then disappeared. They figured her for a meth head just like her folks, and thought she went to find them."

"Any idea where they went?" I asked.

"Rumor was," the sheriff replied, tiring of the story in a discouraged way (for it had become a dishearteningly familiar one, in recent years), "they took off to the desert somewheres. Vegas, Phoenix, outside L.A., maybe—"

"Ah," Mike sighed. "The Crystal Triangle. Where meth is king, and hope goes to die . . ." The depressing reality of Mike's statement momentarily overcame even his ability to laugh at almost anything; but he tried hard to recoup, asking with a smile, "And that's where she got into the drugs?"

"So everybody seems to think," Spinetti answered. "But—"

"Sorry, Steve," I said, trying to keep my expression upbeat, "but who's 'everybody'?"

The sheriff laughed once more. "Just be patient, Doc, I won't hold out on you. Anyway, the girl had no involvement with drugs here, that we know of, though we're checking further—but Weaver, the tech, and their bosses seem to buy that she picked up the habit somewhere." Steve glanced at the trailer again, evidently thankful that the ME and the FIC tech hadn't appeared yet. "Which is part of what I wanted to talk to you two about." And then, rather suddenly, he slapped my shoulder and laughed loud. "You guys've been a lot of help to us, on other jobs, and don't think I don't appreciate that. But trust me when I say—this is a-whole-nother animal, this case. There is shit going on in this one that— well, that I'm not even sure *I* really understand. Not yet, anyway. So . . ." He laughed again, straightened my jacket and my tie convivially, then added, "I'm gonna bring up a subject I never have before, and neither has Pete. But—well, we both know all about why you got shit-canned from your last jobs." Mike was on the verge of launching into a reflexive objec- tion and defense, but Steve held up a hand. "I ain't saying that either of us believes any of the bullshit that was passed around by your bosses or the papers down there. What I *am* saying is this—" And suddenly Steve's smile vanished, and he looked me square in the eye. "When you go in there, and you're thinking up your theories and grabbing all your little bits of evidence that nobody else sees—*don't . . . fuck . . . up.* Because when you come back out, I need to know if Weaver's genuinely full of shit, and not just because we all think he's a fuckin' asshole. Right?" Steve did not wait for a reply before saying, "Okay! Now, I'm gonna go find out what's holding those two bastards up. So you three stay here, try to keep looking like abso-fucking-lutely nothing is going on, and I'll be back . . ."

Spinetti vanished through the half-hanging door of the mobile home, leaving Pete to look a little sheepish. "I'm sorry I couldn't tell you more on the way over, guys," the deputy said. "I was actually kinda hoping that Weaver wasn't even going to be here, yet. But you know how Steve likes to do things."

I studied his troubled features. "We do, indeed, Pete. But something more's on your mind, isn't it?"

He hesitated for a moment. "Well—don't quote me, right? But I was on the scene before even Steve was, and I was the first to go talk to those people up the road. And, well—the whole time I been a deputy, I don't think I've ever come across any case that was so *wrong*, in so many ways. Starting with how many of the higher-ups seem to have how much inter- est in the damned business."

"Indeed?" I said, my faith in Pete's instincts as solid as ever. "Well, then, Deputy, I'm glad you came to get us. And don't worry about Weaver being here. I can handle him."

"Yeah," Mike said, with a laugh that was very genuine, this time. "We've all seen how you can *handle* Weaver." He pulled out a cigarette and elbowed the deputy. "But don't sweat how your boss does business, Pete—we do, just as you say, know how he likes to manage things. And he's not wrong. It's actually smart, in a lot of ways. You set people against each other, sometimes, you're going to find out things they wouldn't usually tell you."

"I appreciate that," Pete said, in quiet relief. "And whatever the sheriff may say, he does, too. Because neither of us wants to get this one wrong . . ."

There it was again: the unelaborated implication that, whatever the death we had come to witness in fact was, it was only the latest in a series. "'*This* one'?" I echoed, trying not to hit the point too hard. "Pete? Would you like to explain what your boss was very careful not to?"

"Don't worry," Pete said. "He'll get around to it. But he wants to get your opinions without any, whatever you call it, without any prejudicial statements from us."

And, even given Mike's and my own ability to maintain impartiality, it wouldn't have been hard, I had to concede, for Pete and Steve to have created such prejudicial feelings about the opinions of the two men who, in a few seconds, emerged from the trailer with Steve. Dr. Ernest Weaver was an obese character with a round, fleshy face and a small mustache that appeared ever ready to fall from his upper lip; while the second figure was small, balding, sheathed in a sterile blue jumpsuit, and trying his hardest not to look overwhelmed. Despite his unassuming manner, however, this shuffling little FIC tech was in fact the representative, at this particular crime scene, of nearly everything that had gone wrong with criminal investigation over the last hundred, and especially the last thirty, years, as well as the embodiment of why forensics had never truly earned the rank of "science." Like his colleagues, the tech bore the responsibility of being the first and therefore the most important expert interpreter of physical clues at such sites, and he was viewed by the uninitiated—especially when he appeared in the full field getup that he was wearing now—as the semi-mystical master of an unimpeachable evidentiary machine, an apparatus beyond the power of most mortals to understand and any to question. In truth, however, such characters were scarcely the keepers of secrets so great that they could speedily unlock the mysteries of unnatural death; that was a fiction *of* fiction, one created by novels, movies, and especially television. In fact, CSIs (as they dearly loved to be called) were the fragile human cogs in the engine of detection, the components that nearly always weakened and gave way, or could be made to give way, under the pressures of laziness, incompetence, ambition, and corruption.

And who was the particular mortal that bore the burden of all this potent folklore concerning what men could do regarding crime, on this particular July day in the humid Taconic foothills? By name, he was one Curtis Kolmback, and he had just come, to judge from his face, from a scene of death somehow more disturbing than those with which he was used to being presented, at least of late. Fortunately, he was also a man that both Mike and I knew well enough to cope with fairly easily: like many such techs, Kolmback had come over from another discipline (in his case, again as in many, from anthropology), and gotten his technical certification from the American College of Forensic Examiners Institute—the online equivalent of a school that one might, in an earlier time, have found on a matchbook cover, and an organization that had been hit particularly hard by scandal in recent years. Unlike most of his colleagues, however, and to his personal credit, Curtis was usually in the market for a helping hand, and as he glanced over to see us near Pete's cruiser, a look of relief flooded his features.

"Dr. Jones?" he called, starting our way. "Mr. Li? You here in an official capacity?"

Mike nodded to Kolmback, but murmured to me, "You know, L.T., I'm a damned doctor, too—why is it always 'Dr. Jones and *Mr.* Li'?"

"I don't know, Michael," I answered, lowering my own voice as I took my turn nodding toward Kolmback. "Maybe you need to eat more powdered rhinoceros horn—isn't that what your countrymen usually do to project greater strength?"

"What fucking countrymen?" Mike answered, reverting to the speech pattern of his native Queens. "I'm as American as you, you WASP son of a bitch, and you know it."

"*I* know it," I replied, "but perhaps these gentlemen do not . . ." Moving toward the approaching tech, I held out a hand that was quickly and gratefully taken. "Curtis!" I said, in as friendly a manner as I could muster. "You look a little rattled. Uncertain of your findings?"

"I don't know about uncertain," Curtis answered, wiping his sweating, balding pate with a rag and shaking Mike's hand in turn. "But if you wouldn't mind taking a look, I certainly wouldn't be averse to any input." He glanced back at the trailer, and his face, too, filled with a look that was both bewildered and simply mournful. "Dr. Weaver is satisfied with just murder, maybe sexual assault, too, but I—there's just *something . . .*"

Looking at Pete again, I said, "Well. Seems like just about everybody with a brain in his head thinks there's 'just something.' So why don't we have that look?"

Kolmback nodded, then indicated the ME. "Better talk to Weaver, first. He's the one certifying wrongful death. And I know how much you two'll enjoy catching up." Curtis allowed himself a small grin.

Sighing deeply, I noised, "Hmm, yes. Well, then, no way around it." And so I began the tiresome walk to pay some sort of homage to the ME, who was busy writing notes on a clipboard full of forms that lay on the hood of his car.

Ernest Weaver was not an uncommon sort of man, in the Empire State, although this fact was far more an indictment of the system (if such it could be called) of medical examiners and coroners that prevailed in New York than it was an acknowledgment of his belonging to any superior class of investigator. County by county, the crazy quilt of ways in which non-medical deaths were investigated and officially determined continued to leave room, as it had since the earliest days of the republic, for abuses of every variety. Some counties still clung tightly to the ancient system of coroners: Albany, employing no fewer than four, was at the rather ironic forefront of this category. And under its terms, anyone from doctors to funeral home directors to butchers could get themselves elected to the posts. It was cronyism at its very worst, for coroners almost invariably tended to be favorites of political and law enforcement officials, and they could currently earn hundreds or even thousands of dollars per death certificate and autopsy (if they were qualified to perform the latter), despite most of them being no better at their jobs than their predecessors in centuries past had been. Precisely how many suspicious deaths had been falsely categorized over the generations because of this method of doing business would have been impossible to say; but it was certainly an enormous number. Only in the late twentieth century had various forces in certain counties risen up against the coroner system, and where these fights had been successful, they had most often been led by an unlikely group: the hospitals in which the actual autopsies of the bodies in question were performed. Tired of having their genuine medical knowledge frustrated by the interference of largely untrained political hacks, the pathologists in many hospital morgues simply refused to do business with the coroners, after a certain point, and submitted their own findings separately. This had led to successful calls by groups of forward-thinking legislators in many counties (remarkably enough, Burgoyne among them) to dispense with the coroner system altogether.

But a further complication then presented itself: the hospital pathologists could not very well abandon their posts every time a body turned up in some distant and very non-medical setting. Sweeping new responsibilities and authority, and far higher salaries, were then allotted to what forensic science had decided were the best candidates to carry on the work of investigating such matters: the medical examiners (or, as men like Weaver liked to be called, "medicolegal death investigators"). Persons both qualified for this post and willing to undertake it were, however, in critically short supply; and so, another inadequate solution was applied, this one allowing MEs to work for more than one county at a time. Weaver himself spent the vast majority of his life on various interstates, moving between Burgoyne, Rensselaer, Schenectady, and Washington Counties; and the particular aroma of McDonald's grease, both on his person and in his Impala, told of how he sustained his great girth during all those drives to and from places of death. Whether this lifestyle had made the man rather peculiar and ghoulish, or whether only a peculiarly ghoulish man would have been attracted to such a post in the first place, was impossible to say; all that could be judged with any certainty was that he was a very odd duck.

"Dr. Weaver," I said, hobbling up the slight incline that led to his car.

"Dr. Jones," he said, his annoyance plainly exhibited by the fact that he refused to even look up from the notes he was scribbling. Fixing a small pair of reading glasses tight on his nose and ears, he let out a blow of exasperation. "I understand that the sheriff has agreed to allow you to view the crime scene."

"He has. Any objection? I thought the matter was cut and dried, so far as you're concerned."

"Not so far as *I* am concerned," Weaver answered, with heightened irritation. "It *is* cut and dried. Murder of a teenage runaway, with possible sexual implications, although that's the pathologist's domain. But you'll no doubt observe all this for yourself."

"Any idea why her killer dragged her all the way back home to do it?"

A dismissive laugh escaped him. "No, no, not at all—I leave such things to you *profilers*. No doubt you will be able to provide a motive for that, as well as for the act itself, and even a family history, just by observing a few simple details . . ."

And there it was, in record time: the utter contempt that forensic scientists of all stripes had developed for us criminal psychologists, now that trace analysis and DNA typing had become the supposed bedrock of criminal investigation. Before Weaver could embellish on his condescension, however, the radio in his car suddenly crackled to life, and he moved toward and then into the passenger window awkwardly to grab it, making sure to stay in that position so that I couldn't hear the few seconds of conversation that was exchanged. When he came out again, he announced, "Now, I regret to say, I'll have to be leaving you gentlemen."

"What happened?" I asked. "Drastic shortages at your favorite Golden Arches?"

Weaver's snooty smile vanished. "Droll, as always, Dr. Jones . . ." Slamming his notebook shut, he made for his driver's-side door. "Well, anxious as I shall be to hear your contribution to the case, I've got to get over to the Northway." He was speaking of Interstate Highway 87 above Albany, where it morphed from the New York Thruway into a multi-lane express route to the northernmost parts of the state and then Canada beyond. "Someone took a header from an overpass fence, and there seems to be some question about whether or not he had assistance."

"Oh," I answered simply, relieved that he was going. "Well, for God's sake, don't let *that* stop you from getting a hearty meal on the way, Weaver."

Unprepared to continue with such banter, Weaver said simply, "Someone will be by for the body soon enough." The Impala lurched over to one side as he sat in it, and the door knocked up against the doctor's fat hip several times before it agreed to close. Waving angrily to the state trooper and telling him to move the FIC van so that he might escape, the ME finally departed, and I turned to find myself facing Mike and Sheriff Spinetti, who had come up behind me to watch the interchange in amusement.

"I swear to God," Spinetti laughed, as the black Impala disappeared. "That guy's gonna shoot you one of these days, Dr. Jones."

I could only grunt. "I've been shot at by far better. Besides, how would he ever get one of those fingers inside a trigger guard?"

That amused the sheriff still further, and he nodded. "Okay—but remember, whatever you think of Weaver and the tech, it's still *my* crime scene. So you'll remember what I said, right? After all, this ain't *New—York—City.*" The sheriff emphasized the last three words with the slow, almost satisfying distaste that characterized the speech patterns of many upstaters.

"Indeed we will, Sheriff," I replied. "Just give us about fifteen minutes, and then you can send Mr. Kolmback back in to make sure that we're not creating any problems."

Spinetti didn't have to allow us the time inside on our own; but despite his sparring speech and attitude, making use of our services on several similar occasions over the last few years had saved him from the embarrassment of relying too quickly on Dr. Weaver's opinions, as he'd acknowledged a few minutes earlier. Even so, I knew that fifteen minutes was about all he could safely afford, before someone like the state trooper might take careful note of what was happening and report it to the state lab, which would then back Weaver to the hilt, whether it embarrassed one particular county sheriff or not. Mike and I would need to formulate any thoughts that might best go unshared with Kolmback quickly, for his amiability and fleeting sense of integrity did not take precedence over his desire to please his superiors and rise in the ranks.

Aware of all this, Mike wrangled the trailer door open, holding it as I went about trying to get my legs and cane through. "Just remember our method, Michael," I said, aware of my awkwardness, momentarily ashamed of it, then angered by the shame. "Always remember our method . . ."

"I know our method, damn it," Mike said, quietly and quickly. "Now get your clumsy ass inside, and let's get some work done . . ."

Once I was finally through the door, Mike let it flap noisily closed again, and we entered a quiet chapel of dreary tragedy, centered on a nave of heartbreak.

{iii.}

I f the outside of the trailer had been battered and unpleasant, the inside was something very different—and very much worse. The initial assault was not to the eyes, but to the nose: mold of every variety—black, green, the highly toxic and the more moderately so—had seized complete control of the structure, dominating its ceiling panels, its damp walls, and its damper floors with its clinging, heavy stench. This was augmented by the different but nearly as dangerous fumes that are peculiar to years upon years of accumulated and aerosolized rodent and bird excrement. I immediately regretted not having considered the issue of air quality, and having left proper breathing masks back at Shiloh. But Mike at least had several surgical masks in his trace kit, and we immediately strapped two of them on: for mold, whether fungal or animal-generated, can addle a brain and cause fantastic headaches within an extraordinarily short amount of time, and we would need our wits very much about us during the minutes immediately to come.

The next problem was darkness: there was, naturally, no power in the trailer, and the plastic apertures that had seemed merely clouded over from the outside were in fact, like the few glass panes that remained, almost completely blacked out by untold hours of cigarette smoking, the collected nicotine stains making a mockery of the word *window*. Our way was lit mainly by the distant glow of a pair of small work lamps that Kolmback had evidently set up at the far end of the trailer, and which were being powered by lengthy cords that extended through one of many rotted holes in the sides of the trailer and out to the augmented electrical system of the FIC van.

"It would appear," I whispered (for anything other than a whisper suddenly seemed inappropriate), "that our destination lies that way ..." I pointed to the far-off lights that sat on the floor of the last room in the structure, one of which cast some of its beams, fortunately, down the hallway.

As our eyes adjusted to the various if scant sources of illumination within the trailer, Mike said, with a look of deep apprehension, "Yeah, it fucking *would* appear that way ..." His exuberance at a "real case" had vanished, as it almost always did, when he was faced with the realities of human suffering and death—particularly a child's. "Well," he went on, doing his best to steel himself, "let's—"

A sudden metallic crash sounded, and each of us shook visibly: some kind of ancient, battered cooking pot had fallen from an equally aged stove nearby. We were evidently in the trailer's kitchen, although the pot and the stove were the only real clues, along with a filthy sink so rusted and piled high with rodent nests and droppings that we could have been forgiven for missing it altogether. Just as we were gathering our wits, I heard Spinetti call with a laugh:

"Hey, you two! I said don't screw things up in there!"

"Yeah, yeah," Mike called, trying to buck himself up. "Watch the city boys freak out, the sport of fuckin' kings—"

But then we both started suddenly for a second time, as another loud crash came from an equally close spot. It was the door of the kitchen oven slamming open, a disconcerting enough event without the blurred image that came next: a moderately sized raccoon leapt from the oven, and hissed in a savage way as it blocked our path. The masked features of the animal were nearly insane with some kind of unnatural rage; and as I studied its emaciated body in the half-light, I saw several patches of bare skin, where the creature's heavy fur seemed to have been scorched off. It tried to issue a cry of warning, but evidently could not, and instead sprayed spittle our way with an evil purpose. Its eyes, while not quite red, were utterly lacking in any trace of the comprehension that one expects to find in such ordinarily clever animals.

"Easy, Mike," I said, standing dead still.

"What?" my partner asked in badly shaken reply: Mike had a deep fear of such encounters, for which his upbringing in Queens had done little to prepare him.

There was, however, no time to explain the situation twice. "Hey, Steve?" I called out. "Were you aware that there's a rabid raccoon living in here?"

Mike silently mouthed the words *What the fuck?* as Spinetti answered, very seriously, "What? Kolmback, how the hell did you and Weaver miss a rabid coon, for fuck's sake?" As Curtis tried to mumble an explanation, the sheriff cut him off and called to us: "You got a gun, Doc?"

"Not at the moment!" I replied; but even as I did, the raccoon sprayed a second salvo of spit, and then obligingly hurled itself through another of the undetectable holes in the wall of the trailer. "He's out, and coming to you!" I went on, at which the men near the vehicles shouted urgent orders and acknowledgments. Mike and I made no move until we heard the sudden, sharp report of a large-caliber revolver, which was followed by another, then several more. Finally Spinetti shouted:

"Okay. We got him. Watch yourselves, though!"

As we finally began our progress toward the work lights, keeping to a runner of protective plastic that Kolmback had wisely rolled out along the hall of the trailer to protect the floor of the scene, I paused for just an instant by the open oven. Peering within, I saw several close-set pairs of tiny eyes amid vague, writhing shapes: the raccoon had been no "him" at all, and I closed the damaged oven door as far as it would go (which was not quite completely), knowing that the pathetic occupants of the cavity would soon meet a fate to match their maddened mother's, but wanting no part of that process. Certain that the litter of sickened kits were too small and weak to either reopen the broken door or escape through the narrow gap between the ceramic portal and its frame, I urged Mike quickly past the appliance; and on that rather pointed note, we continued on our way.

An attempt had been made, how many owners or tenants ago it would have been difficult to say, to make the trailer seem what so often passed for homey, under such circumstances: peeling off the walls were various light-colored wallpapers—yellow, baby blue, a sickly pink—each stenciled with a delicate floral design. On the floor was a patterned carpet, more tasteful than the deep-pile shag that ordinarily covered the particle board platforms of such domiciles, but heavily stained and missing large patches in various spots. The several rooms we passed were all empty, save for one in which a double mattress lay on the floor, its covering riddled with gnawed holes that would have been enough to demonstrate, even had we not seen large mice dashing in and out of them, that at least one variety of rodent was in active residence.

An ugly thought set up shop in my head: "Do you suppose the vermin have been at her?"

Mike nodded. "If she's been here long enough? Afraid so."

It was not the kind of thought likely to propel us forward any faster; nor was the fact that we were leaving the front door farther behind, and with it all hope of fresh air. As we crept on, the distinctive smell of the formaldehyde used in the manufacture of various parts of mobile homes rose and mixed with that same, ever-thickening stench of mold, and breathing, even through the surgical masks, became an increasingly difficult and unpleasant task. It was all deeply unsettling, in a way that at least partially explained the unusual expressions of sadness and bewilderment that had flitted across the faces of the seasoned first responders outside; despite this, however, the manner in which the scene was slowing our steps soon began to eat at me.

"Damn it, Michael," I said—yet I continued to speak very quietly. "We've been in worse places, after all. Let's find the girl and do what we came to do."

Mike nodded, trying to join in my effort to assume a more professional demeanor; and our steps did begin to fall a little faster, as we steadily concerned ourselves less with the overall condition of the trailer's interior and fixed instead on that last room, where we would finally find the object of our inquiry:

Her presence was not immediately evident. The room was typically large, for one located at the end of such a structure: three exterior walls stood on either side of and facing the doorway, so that the chamber took up the full breadth and remaining length of the trailer. Ancient, curling pictures—some cut from the pages of magazines and depicting ideally formed young men and women, but some far more interesting digital snapshots of a girl surrounded by various groups of boys, in differing places but always happy poses—still clung bravely to the unpapered surfaces of the walls, while the floor was now covered with the kind of thick, near-colorless carpet that I had expected to find throughout the place. But this was the extent of the room's details; and as we took the space in, Mike shot me a slightly puzzled look. I think that we had both expected to find a body crumpled in a corner, perhaps with some methamphetamine paraphernalia nearby, if local rumors were to be believed; but no such predictable spectacle awaited us. We soon realized, however, that the work lights were not trained on the room proper, but on some nearby, partially obscured remove: a closet, in fact, its frame obstructed by a folding particle board partition that had been covered with a plastic veneer patterned after a dark wood grain.

Mike saw her first; and I am not too proud to admit that this was because I hesitated to look within the closet, at the spot where the two beams of the small work lights met in a fashion more suggestive of an alcove in some hellish place of worship than a mobile-home hiding place. But when Mike groaned, quietly and mournfully, I could avert my eyes no more.

"Jesus, Trajan," Mike said softly. "A 'throwaway child,' all right—she could be their damned poster child . . ."

Shelby Capamagio was not crumpled on the floor after all, but was upright, her two arms secured just below the elbow with duct tape to the wooden bars on either side of the closet so that her toes brushed the floor. She was clothed only in her bra and panties, the latter torn, though not violently; indeed, they seemed more cut than torn. Above all, she displayed the particular delicacy and vulnerability of an adolescent that precociousness can sometimes disguise in life, but that always becomes sadly plain again in death. Her otherwise very pretty face was marked by just a few blemishes that might or might not have been signals of meth use, but the remainder of her body was not, nor had it in fact been violated by the trailer's other occupants. Thus her unspoiled, slightly translucent skin was free to warmly feed some of the illumination of the lights back into the room. Her blond hair, fashionably cut just below her shoulders, had been artificially colored, if the sandier roots near her scalp were any indication; and the open, downcast blue eyes, although beset by heavy bags of exhaustion, along with her mouth, which seemed on the verge of speaking, continued to convey much of the innocence that one should find in the face of any child her age, as well as of the fearful disillusionment that had evidently marked the last minutes—or perhaps days and weeks—of her life.

Indeed, so pitiable yet riveting an impression did her face and body convey that it took both Mike and me an instant to realize the very worst aspect of the image: a length of bright yellow, quarter-inch nylon cord was looped tightly around her neck. The apparently fatal ligature was tied into the infamous double constrictor, or strangler, knot, which bit into the side of her neck, its tightening length leading up to and around her right hand.

"Okay," Mike whispered, swallowing hard and moving closer to her. "Let's see what we've actually got . . ."

I kept alongside him, glancing around at the walls again and then back at Shelby. "Quite the brassy girl, for around here" was my immediate impression.

"Yeah?" Mike said, as he set his kit down and opened it. "What makes you say that?"

"A few things," I answered, wishing for all the world that I could tear off my jacket and cover the dead girl; but I knew that we could best serve her, now, by being analytical rather than emotional. "The coloring and styling of her hair was no cheap job. Almost certainly not local—fairly recent, too: the roots have barely grown out. And the bra and panties— that's not normal teenage gear, that looks like fairly high-end merchandise. Then there are these pictures on the walls: she's always with boys, only boys, and lots of them, going back at least two or three years. Not a female friend in sight. Yet she's plainly no tomboy. By Burgoyne County standards, that's all pretty precocious behavior . . ."

Mike had begun dusting for and lifting fingerprints, and as he did, he moved ever more into his own examinatory mode, beginning to see Shelby's body as a corpse and her death scene as a puzzle to be solved. This, again, was not insensitivity: he simply believed, as much as I did, that a solution to the apparent crime was our only way to honor the girl. "Okay," he began. "So we start at the beginning—with what Weaver and Curtis have said: murder with the possibility of sexual assault. And, if we take what you're saying into account, maybe she just met the wrong guy, while she was being so precocious. Pretty common. Or maybe when she got back from out West, she met up with somebody who wasn't so glad to see her."

"Meaning what?" I asked.

"Meaning that somebody seems to have known where she lived. Because you're not describing a girl who would come back to this shithole, which she apparently hated—very understandably—just because it was an available place to hook up. And remember what Steve said: she stayed up in her relatives' equipment shed, instead of coming back here, after the rest of the family disappeared."

"That," I mused, "could simply have been because the utilities here had been shut off . . ."

I turned to step ever closer to Shelby, and to gaze into that peculiar look that occupied her face and eyes. When people die, facial expressions can come over them for any number of reasons, pain, terror, and the relief that death often brings from such traumas being only a few (if common ones). But this girl, who we had been told was strangled and perhaps violated, bore no such look. Of course I knew that eyes, for their part, are notoriously poor indicators of a person's state at death: once again, popular entertainment has told us that people violently killed die with their eyes wide open, while those who die peacefully die with a more relaxed position of the lids, even to the point of their being fully closed. But Shelby's partially hooded blue eyes were nonetheless eloquent, it seemed to me; indeed, the more I studied her features, the more the innocence that I had at first seen there seemed to me to be augmented only by sadness and resignation. And as I peered into that not yet completely vacant blue gaze, I tried to see if I could divine something even more specific. "She can't have been dead long," I said quietly, losing myself still further as I went on studying Shelby's features. "And there's something in the face . . . something that does not fit . . ."

Just how long I stood in that position before I again heard Mike's voice I couldn't say; but at length his somewhat alarmed repetition of my name did break through: "Trajan . . . ? Trajan! Come on back, dude, you're doing it again, goddamn it."

"Doing what?" I answered, never breaking my gaze.

"Your whole 'Sorcerer of Death' routine," my partner answered. "Seriously, we don't have time for it."

Mike was referring to a ridiculous nickname given to me by a typically sensationalist headline in the *New York Post* about seven years earlier. We had, at the time, just concluded a case in which we'd gone completely against the thinking of the NYPD and its crime lab, and in the process divined the correct solution to a string of upscale robbery-murders. Having embarrassed the powers that were, we had naturally burnished our growing reputations among the tabloid press; little did we suspect, however, that such popularity was only increasing the determination of the mayor and the police commissioner to banish us from the city, and that those same tabloids would follow suit, once the public mood had swung.

"No," I said, finally backing away from the closet again. "Perhaps we don't."

"You fucking freak . . ." From the corner of my eye, I saw Mike shake his head with a chuckle as he moved to grab an extremely high resolution camera from his kit, after which he began to study and photograph the closet around young Shelby, looking for any likely spots that might turn up well-hidden hairs, fibers, or any of the other especially discreet traces that most techs like Curtis Kolmback could be relied on to miss, but that my partner was quite expert at detecting; and when the camera's flash revealed them, he quickly lifted them from their hiding places with strips of wide, clear tape. "How can you *not* know when you're doing it, that's what gets me . . ." He paused, using a pair of magnifying eyeglasses to gently examine a spot on Shelby's right arm. "Hunh," he noised. "Skin doesn't look to me like it's been exposed to a lot of sunshine—like southwestern sunshine, for instance—and that's her hitching arm."

"Her what?"

"Well, if she hitchhiked out West, or even took a bus, that'd be the arm that was most often exposed while she was riding. But—pretty pale . . ." He glanced up at me. "Well? Have you come out of your trance enough to actually contribute something to the conversation, here?"

"Right," I replied, shaking myself a bit and finally looking away from Shelby. "So the obvious answer is just what Weaver said: death by strangulation, with the possibility of sexual assault. But I don't like it, for the reasons we just stated, among others. First of all, they're presuming that at some point she, too, had gotten into meth. Which would open a lot of possibilities for murder, I admit, but—there's nothing about her to suggest it."

"Meaning . . . ?" Mike said, collecting more specimens and sealing them away in bags and tubes.

"Well, besides the fact that Steve says he can't find any link between her and the drug—"

"A purely preliminary estimate," Mike cut in, checking me.

"All right, but look at the physical evidence—her face, and her teeth in particular. Does she *look* like the usual meth head? The destructive physical effects of the drug start pretty quickly—and she's awfully healthy looking." I returned to study Shelby's face. "There are a few adolescent blemishes, all carefully covered by either makeup or medication, and a certain amount of *petechiae*"—the tiny red hemorrhages that appear as faint dots on the face during strangulation—"but otherwise, nothing. And the skin on the rest of her body's in even better shape."

"Well," Mike argued, "I *have* picked up one or two traces of a crystalline powder, here and there."

"But you can't just assume it's crystal meth."

Mike looked slightly irritated. "No. I can't. All I'm saying is—"

"All you're saying is we don't know, but that what physical evidence we are presented with speaks against the drug-abuse aspect to her case."

"Yeah. I guess." Having conceded the point, Mike moved back to his kit, to open the second of its two large compartments. "What about the assault angle, then?"

I shook my head, glancing again at the lower portion of Shelby's body, but looking away quickly, with a kind of reluctance I would never have felt around an adult in her position. "I'm not buying *that* right away, either," I said. "Those panties weren't violently ripped, for my money. The tear is almost . . . gentle. If it wasn't a knife, I'd say—human teeth, carefully applied."

"Okay." Mike returned from his kit with a familiar, boxy piece of equipment and a tripod. "But that could have been a fetish of the murderer's: tormenting her with a slow, careful cut or tear once she'd been restrained."

"It could," I said with a nod. "Or it could not. And I'm betting not, unless you see some sign of sexual activity on the tear that I don't."

"Nope," Mike conceded. "And let's face it, sex, any sex, is always a *little* messy."

"Not a universal truth—the killer may have had a particular fetish about tidiness, and prepared accordingly. Yet if it was rape, as Weaver and Curtis are saying, and if I'm reading this girl right, then she would have put up some kind of a struggle. So what you say is almost certainly the case. All right: so for now, we don't buy the sexual assault—"

"I don't know," Mike cut in. "I'm not sure we have enough to rule it out."

"I said *for now*. Ultimately the pathologist will have to determine that, anyway. What about the m.o. of the supposed murder?"

Mike puffed himself up a bit. "That's why I got this baby out." He pointed to the boxy piece of equipment, which we proceeded to place on the fully extended tripod. Handing me a metallic tray that was about a foot square in size, he said, "Hold the exposure plate, will you? Right behind the profile of her neck . . ."

It was Mike's habit to be ever on the lookout for new technological methods of advancing the cause of physical evidence that would not be apparent to others in the field—perhaps because he was, as he so often reminded me, himself a doctor. And we were now holding the components of one such device, which we'd used many times in the past. A gambler by habit (and perhaps, as I sometimes taunted him, by heritage),

Mike had grown fascinated by just how quickly and precisely the injuries suffered by horses at racetracks could be determined; and he had discovered that veterinary medicine had for quite some time been using and perfecting mobile X-ray units. This only made sense: while it's always been easy to bring one's cat or dog to a veterinary clinic for such exams, large animals present a different problem—the clinic, in effect, must come to them, hence the development of the portable X-ray units. Law enforcement and the military had been known to use such gear to determine, say, the existence and entry angles of bullets in background materials—wooden walls and the like—as well as for the examination of such threats as improvised explosive devices; but when it came to dead bodies, X-rays and other forms of exams were left up to pathologists, once the body had been brought to them. And that, to Mike, was just the problem: the bodies had already been moved, and the story of just how the victim had died perhaps altered in the process. So, borrowing a page from his acquaintances at New York's various racetracks, Mike had purchased a portable X-ray unit—and gained one of the advantages that had created our "magical" reputation.

Mike stated his reason for putting that advantage to use in the Capamagio trailer with a succinctness that belied the thought and research that had gone into determining it: "I just don't like the angle of that neck," he murmured. "And by the time she gets to the pathologist, I'm a little concerned that rigor won't keep it in place, anymore. God knows Weaver's idiots won't be careful to, whenever they bother to get here and move her."

"What's bothering you about it?" I asked, moving closer again with the exposure plate and placing it on the side of Shelby's neck opposite the imager that Mike was positioning.

"Well," Mike began, "that strangler knot is on the *side* of her neck; and that means that somebody was pulling pretty hard on it, to achieve the necessary force. Now, it's been looped around the end of her hand to make it look like it was her, but that's bullshit, because she couldn't have maintained the amount of force required to constrict the throat sufficiently to kill herself in the way that's indicated—especially with her arms restrained in that position."

"No," I said, "but the killer could have, and then bound her in the closet afterwards."

"Why the hell would he have done that?" Mike asked. "He must have known that even an idiot like Kolmback, hell, even Weaver, would be able to see it wasn't suicide."

"All right," I tried again, "what about cerebral ischemia? She tightens the knot to the point where it cuts off the carotids just enough to starve the brain, then dies slowly."

"How about if we just let her neck tell us how she actually died," Mike answered, pleased to be able to lecture me. "Because, even if it was ischemia, I still don't think she could have done it, taped up like that; and besides, her body doesn't indicate much trace of your idea. In those cases, there's usually some involuntary, violent struggling—but her hands and feet, especially the nails, are clear of any sign that she clawed or kicked at anything. So are the walls and carpet. Now, the killer could have done it, but the lack of fighting-back trace goes for skin, too. And besides, the same question comes up all over again, on that: why? Why does the guy slowly deprive her brain of oxygen, when he didn't rape her, or so we think, and then string her up like this?"

"He panicked," I answered. "Or, if he was devious, then he would have known that adding as many contradictory elements as possible would work in his favor by confusing the cops—and anybody else they brought in. Which it did, in Kolmback's case."

"Yeah, but a strangler knot?" Mike said. "If he was that smart, he would have known—and, more importantly, he would have known that any investigator would have known—that she could have held on, maybe, until she passed out, but that's it: the release of her pulling force would have locked the knot in a non-cataclysmic position. She might have been brain-damaged and died hours later, but her neck says it was all at once. It doesn't work."

If it appears that my partner and I had been taking turns ruling out not only the ME's and Curtis' ideas, but each other's, as well, such was actually the heart of our investigative method, of which I had spoken upon entering the trailer. Modern law enforcement agencies—again, contrary to whatever impressions have been created by popular entertainment—had used forensic science to reinforce their traditional habit of most energetically pursuing whatever suspects and theories for a given crime either came most readily to hand or, more importantly, were those that they most favored. Mike and I, on the other hand, had gone farther back in history to find a philosophical framework (simplified

Hegelian dialectical reasoning, with its thesis-antithesis-synthesis frame-work) that would allow us to question *all* conclusions, including and most especially our own, almost as quickly as we came upon them, and to *keep* questioning them until we could find no opposing theory that worked. This seemed to some a complex intellectual system, but it was in fact a relatively simple process (although we kept that fact to ourselves); and using it, we were able to proceed with our analyses at a pace that was perhaps surprising, and to reach agreements that were far more indepen-dent, and therefore more reliable, than law enforcement's reliance on what amounted to confirmation bias.

By now Mike had gotten the X-ray unit into place. "Which brings me," he declared as he worked, "to my central point." Having set the imager, he returned to his kit, inside of which sat the small control console, and flipped a few switches. Then he returned to me and took the imaging plate, attempting to somehow get it set on the side of Shelby's neck op-posite the imager, between her shoulder and the rack on which her arm was bound: an awkward process undertaken so that I wouldn't have to hold the thing myself. And, while I appreciated the effort, I had to laugh a little.

"Really, Mike?" I said. "With all the radiation the doctors are shooting into me these days, you think one X-ray exposure is going to make a dif-ference?"

Mike pondered that, then nodded. "Point taken. Okay, then—you hold it. Steady as you can, L.T., I've only got one plate. Didn't figure on those fuckers overlooking *this* . . ."

With that we changed places again, and in a few seconds Mike had gotten his image. "It's more than just the knot," he said, picking up the conversation right where we'd left off and starting to pack the X-ray gear away.

"Yes," I said, beginning to get it as I focused my eyes more intently on the area around the deadly ligature. "Her neck has been snapped back, suddenly and violently. I don't think this was strangulation at all, Mike—this girl looks like she was hanged."

"Yeah, sure, steal my idea now, motherfucker, when it's obvious what I'm driving at," he replied, a little annoyed, yet a little pleased, too. "*But,*" he continued, "there's one more possibility: the killer originally had the knot in the traditional spot—on the back of her neck—and was able to jerk it with such force that he snapped the spine clean."

"Come on, Mike." I was still studying the apparently fatal break in Shelby's neck. "What are the odds of that? Achieving a hanging-like force with one pull of your arms? You'd have to be pretty monstrously strong."

His cheeks fattened with another smile. "Well, maybe that's a clue for your profile, genius. Anyway, the X-ray is the only thing that will tell us for sure."

"Either way . . ." I stepped back from Shelby's body again, and glanced around at the pictures on the shadowy walls of the room once again. "One thing is clear: somebody has staged all this—I think our method gets us to that point safely. Yes, somebody very badly *wants* us to believe that Shelby was murdered here, in this place, by a violent sex offender. And it would make some sense—one might, under other circumstances, even call it clever. Burgoyne County has always been a safe place to relocate sex offenders. People mostly mind their own business; plus, it's mostly rural, so there are plenty of spots where they can hide the modern-day lepers away."

"Very true," Mike said, going back to tracking down any other items of notice around the body that he could find.

"But what does that leave us with? We've dealt with all elements of the ME's and Curtis' theory—what are we going to tell Pete and Steve to replace it with?"

"Okay," Mike replied, standing. "If drugs are out . . . and we think sexual assault is out . . . and the case for the murder-rape is at least weak—what does that leave us with?"

"You forget one more thing we've eliminated," I said. "The notion that she somehow killed herself from that strung-up position."

"Right," Mike agreed. "But what, then? There's a lot of possibilities: could have been a sexual encounter that went bad—she didn't want to go through with it, the guy got so pissed off he killed her, and then, like you say, staged all this to confuse investigators."

"But that just leads back in a circle," I replied quickly. "Because anyone with that kind of strength could have gotten physical control over her and completed the rape, as we said. And remember, that's a strangler knot—it's not like he just grabbed her by the throat, there's no evidence to back up manual strangulation. And the strangler takes time to prepare."

"He could have had it ready."

"So murder was the main motive, and not rape? Why? What the hell did this poor kid have to make her a target, if not herself?"

"I don't know, Trajan," Mike said in frustration. "Maybe she was dealing, and held out on her supplier. Or maybe she was turning tricks, and did the same to her pimp."

"Mike," I droned skeptically. "You're applying big-city rules, now. Do you know the incidence of white rural prostitution nationwide, much less in this county? Not to mention drug dealing—Steve might not have known if she'd been using, but I can guarantee you, if she'd been hooking and dealing, there would have been rumors. No—whatever happened here . . ." I glanced around the room again. "It's something we haven't seen before. And I say that with a full appreciation of the fact that we've seen just about everything."

"Yes, we have," Mike answered, starting to put the remainder of his equipment back in his kit. "So—what do we have that we can say we're even half-assedly sure of?"

"All right: we believe she was hanged. And yet, if she *was* hanged, she apparently experienced none of the other bodily functions generally associated with the act."

"Yeah, but she may just have had nothing to eat or drink in the hours before she died," Mike commented. "In fact, in the case of a girl like this, I think we can pretty much assume that much."

"Fine—but even if that's true, you're going to have to find me a spot in this trailer where she could have been hanged that would have allowed a sufficient drop to achieve the kind of break in her neck that we both believe the X-ray will reveal."

Mike took a quick glance down the hallway. "I can't do that. Unless it was a tree outside."

"Which would have risked the killer's being seen. No, either her neck was snapped by someone hugely strong, who would have overpowered her and raped her, or the hanging was an effort to cover a different crime by someone who knew where she lived. And if it was done to cover something else, what's the crime that hanging is most often an attempt to disguise?"

"Suicide," Mike said immediately. "Which, we've already said, doesn't seem to make sense. Even if she did it, what did she care about covering it? It's not like she had life insurance."

"Right." I paused, mulling it all over. "None of it makes sense, Mike . . ." Taking one or two steps away from the closet, and pacing on Kolmback's plastic sheeting, I pondered the apparent conclusion: "Suicide makes no sense, rape seems not to have occurred, murder without rape, too, seems to make no sense, and we can't ascertain anything that makes us believe that drugs were even involved. So we know Weaver and Kolmback are wrong, but—"

Suddenly I stood very still, having caught sight of something on the floor that had been hidden in the shadows behind the beam of one of Curtis' work lights. It was such a poignant, yet, in its way, terrible sight that I only half-heard Mike when, as he finished repacking his kit, he mused, "I know this is going to sound crazy, L.T., but—it almost seems like somebody is trying to tell us something, and we're just not—"

I could no longer stifle a soft oath, however: "Good Christ, Mike . . ." Shaking myself, I waved to him. "Come here, and tell me what you think of *this*." Even as I said it, voices became audible outside the trailer: Curtis Kolmback returning. "Fast."

Mike moved to stand by me, also having heard the voices that were coming our way. But then he, too, froze, less with dread than with shock; because what was on the floor before us suddenly and rather resoundingly confirmed the theory that my partner had only begun to voice.

{iv.}

In a very ordered pile, one that was in no way suggestive of a fifteen-year-old girl with a supposedly entrenched meth habit, lay a half-dozen articles of clothing, each folded carefully, one would almost have had to say *lovingly*. They proceeded in order from the floor: jeans, shorts, a delicate shirt and two similar tank tops, then a bra and two pairs of panties that seemed as fashionable as those she had on, and finally shoes. A pair of black leather high-top sneakers studded to look like biker boots, along with (less predictably) an obviously costly brace of gladiator sandals, had been placed on either side of the pile. The supposedly telltale meth paraphernalia was nearby, along with a goodly supply of the drug in a small, clear bag; but these items, too, were arranged, not strewn about in anything like a desperate manner that might have indicated their use.

"Well, fuck *me*," Mike breathed, quickly reopening his kit and grabbing for a few more strips of tape and his camera. "That's *really* something I've never seen . . ." He speedily took photos of, together with samples from, each article of clothing in the pile, being careful not to disturb the collection in any noticeable way. "*This*," he mused, as his hands expertly went about their work, "is goddamned bizarre . . ."

"It's worse than that," I answered. "It's one more thing that makes no damned sense."

"Doesn't seem to," Mike replied.

"First, there is the body," I continued, saying what we both were thinking. "And the obvious attempt to make us think the girl had been abused and violated; yet then there is *this* attempt to be so considerate of her effects? It's a blatant contradiction, one I doubt that she was responsible for. I mean, does it *look* like the work of a rebellious fifteen-year-old?"

"Nope," Mike judged certainly, finishing up his work. "That, it does not."

"Right; so whoever it *was*," I continued, utterly mystified, "had a very seriously fractured approach to whatever he—or she—was doing. Almost as if . . ."

"Almost as if there were two people doing it," Mike said, completing my thought as he returned his samples and his camera to his kit and closed it back up.

"Two people would be easier for us," I said. "Because if it's one, we are dealing with a far more deeply troubled and troubling profile. And yet— I'm afraid the second possibility is exactly what we face." Feeling the chill of certainty run up my back, I looked at my partner; and I hesitate to admit that there was likely a certain gleam in my eye, the gleam of facing some horribly new yet bracing challenge. "I think that we're being drawn into that rarest sort of murder case, Mike," I whispered, less out of fear of being overheard (even though Kolmback had entered the trailer) than in awe of our discovery: "A case in which a perverse dialogue has begun to take shape. Someone is *talking* to us with all this, just as you said, and hoping we will read it well enough to respond in some way."

Mike's face grew a bit puzzled. "But why us? How could whoever it was have known that we'd get pulled in on this thing, that it would go unrecognized by those saps outside?"

"If he knows the county, he knows how inept Weaver and the FIC are," I said quickly. "And it hasn't been any enormous secret that we've helped

Pete and Steve before. Plus, you heard the pair of them before we came in here: both spoke of 'another,' and 'this one.' I think this killer has been at work before, Mike, and we haven't yet been told about it. *Yet*. But we're going to be, I am going to make good and goddamned sure—"

My statement was cut off when Kolmback finally reached the end of the trailer. Steve was now bellowing at us to finish up, and the tech was moving our way at a fast pace. Mike lifted his kit by its handle as he took a quick step away from the clothing, creating the impression that he had not yet performed any significant examination of those items or much of the rest of the scene. I took several steps back, myself, looking around the room but trying not to allow the fascination engendered by the detail that Mike and I had just discovered to register in my gaze.

"Hey, guys," Kolmback said as he came through the doorway, wearing a surgical mask of his own. "Sorry about the raccoon," he went on, a bit sheepishly. "We never saw him."

"Her," I murmured.

"Hunh?"

"There are a litter of kits in the oven—they'll be rabid, too. You might want to leave that job for Steve."

"Yeah," Curtis breathed, looking back toward the kitchen in apprehension. "I might just, at that. So—" He tried to become more self-assured. "You guys have anything to add?" His tone was confident, yet bespoke a willingness to hear either simple agreement or informed dissent; as yet, however, I was inclined to keep our cards very close.

"Doesn't look like it, Curtis," I said. "Did Weaver name a t.o.d.?"

"Eight to fourteen hours ago," Kolmback replied.

"His usual precision," I said with a nod. "Well, there's no apparent sign that she was spending any time here."

"No," Curtis answered, pleased to agree with our conclusion. "Just a small flashlight that we bagged. No evidence of any kind of food, though, not even a candy wrapper. And nothing to sleep in, or on, except that mice-ridden mattress in the other room."

"All of which," I sighed with a nod, "naturally makes our ME even more confident that someone dragged her home to kill her . . ."

"All that," Curtis answered, "along with a couple of other things that rule out suicide. But I'm assuming you've examined those."

"Yeah, we've examined them, Curtis," Mike said. "The big question is, why does a guy who's strong enough to strangle her on the floor, or somewhere else, go to the trouble of trussing her up like this to try to make it even *seem* like suicide?"

Curtis' face suddenly grew very puzzled; and I knew we had our first crack in the official presentation. "What do you mean?" he asked. "She wasn't killed *before* she was put up there—it was *after.*" To Mike's and my own apparently dumbfounded looks, Curtis continued, rather proudly, "Well, maybe you guys missed it for some reason, or maybe you just didn't want to get too close, but—she died up on those bars, all right. Come on, I'll show you."

As we followed Curtis back to Shelby, I looked at Mike, who, like me, seemed to be trying to determine what in the world Kolmback could have been driving at, and if we'd really missed something crucial. Then, after just a few seconds, my partner realized what he believed that thing must be, and he turned to me, mouthing, *Holy fuck,* and rolling his eyes as if to say, *Just wait until you hear this one . . .*

Curtis took up a position within the closet and beside the dead girl, as best he could manage. "Now," he began, getting an enormous kick out of playing instructor to us. "You've already ruled out the idea that she hanged herself in here, or that she could exert enough pressure on the ligature to produce what looks like the break in her neck."

"We have," Mike said. "But that was good work on your part, Curtis, spotting the angle of the cervical spine."

"Thank you, Mike," Curtis said, genuinely grateful for the compliment. "But I'm afraid you've fallen into the killer's trap of trying to make you think he must have inflicted that break somewhere else. But there is a way it could have happened inside the closet, if you'll just bear with me for a second . . ." Curtis moved his latex-gloved hand up to take the pulling end of the nylon cord from Shelby's supposed grasp. "Okay, now," he went on, holding the yellow strand over his head. "You're a strong man. You've raped the girl, then taped her up like this. But you still need to finish her. So what do you do?"

As Curtis fumbled to get himself wedged tighter in the closet and then shimmy up its walls to reach what would have had to have been, according to his theory, the killer's height, I moved closer to Mike and whispered, "What the hell is he *doing*?"

"Don't sweat it," Mike said. "Not that I think you're sweating it. But I know where he's going, and the mistake he's made—fucking hell, it is *painful . . .*"

"All right," Curtis continued, having been able to move himself up a good couple of feet off the floor. "So we'll assume our killer was not only strong, but tall—say, six foot three, at least. Does that line up with your preliminary thoughts, Dr. Jones?"

"Hmm?" I said, by now simply stunned at the image of Curtis, his legs straightened now so that his neck was being pushed downward by the ceiling. "Oh, yes, I'd say that's about right."

"But you still don't know how he achieved the force, even with his height and strength, to bring about such a violent snap in the girl's neck, am I correct?"

"You are correct, Curtis," Mike answered. "But hurry the hell up, man, we don't want to see you fall and break *your* goddamned neck."

"Not a problem," Curtis answered, though it clearly was. "Anyway, from this position, the answer is simple: he took his foot, which was backed up by a leg many times more powerful than his arms, pressed it against the small of her back, here—" With great difficulty, the poor tech removed one of his feet from the closet wall and tried to demonstrate his theory. "Then, still holding the rope, he slammed the foot down—"

And at that point the presentation became too much: Curtis came tumbling back to the closet floor, bumping rather clumsily into Shelby's body, and would have ended up flat on his ass had it not been for Mike, who moved quickly to rescue him from so undignified a fate. "I warned you about that," my partner said, trying not to smile but unable to quite complete the effort. "You all right, Curtis?"

"I'm fine," the tech answered, getting to his feet again quickly and immediately resuming his story: "Anyway—you probably didn't notice it because you didn't examine the posterior surface of her skin. Or maybe because it's obscured by the rather wide filigree tattoo she has at the small of her back—but it's there."

Mike, glancing at me to say that the exercise was wholly perfunctory, moved around to Shelby's back, took a look, and said, "Well. You're right, Curtis, it's there. A bruise."

"Very common, in forced hangings within confined spaces," Curtis went on. "As I'm sure you know."

"Yep," Mike agreed. "Hey, Trajan, come over here and take a look. I guess it probably *was* the tattoo that made me miss it . . ."

Moving around the opposite side of the dead girl as Curtis extricated himself from the closet, I put my head near Mike's, realizing that he wished to communicate something. At the same time, I followed his indication to observe a broad area of discoloration across the small of Shelby's back, beneath a rather commonly designed tattoo of the variety that has come to be called, perhaps unkindly, a "tramp stamp," or, just a bit more cleverly, a "California license plate." The tattoo told me far more about the girl and her death than did the bruise, however, as I quickly told Mike:

"But that's no bruise," I whispered, to his quick nod. "That's—"

"Shut the fuck up, will you?" he whispered back. "I know what it is. And Curtis may be a likable chump, but we both know who he works for, and there's no reason to give them an edge, right?"

Getting the point, I announced loudly, "Well, I don't know how you missed that, Michael. And you're right, Curtis, it pretty much confirms how the girl could have died in this closet." Mike and I came back out to face the tech, who was ear-to-ear with pride at the thought of having bested us. "But I don't understand," I went on. "When we got here you told us that you had a problem with the scene, that something just didn't seem right. Seems to me that, other than tying it up with firm evidence of just who the killer was, you've got what you need."

"Well—it's other things," Curtis said, his uncertainty returning. "For instance, I guess you've seen her clothes, and the drugs? I left them unbagged when Steve said you were coming, so you'd be sure to notice."

"Yeah," Mike answered. "We've seen them."

"Well, then," Curtis concluded, as if our reaction to those items should have been as immediate and conclusive as was our supposed realization of the "bruise" on Shelby's back. "It says just one thing, doesn't it? Especially when you put it in combination with the position of her body?"

"What about the position of her body, exactly?" I asked; and this time it was my turn to glance at Mike and tell him silently to be ready for what he was about to hear from the tech.

"Well, it's really up your street more than mine, Dr. Jones," Curtis explained, "but doesn't her position very strongly resemble something? Say, a crucifixion?"

I could just hear the sound of Mike's hand moving up in a rush to smack his own forehead; but fortunately, he covered the move by letting his hand linger there, as if to indicate, not impatience with Curtis' conclusion, but frustration that we hadn't reached so "obvious" an observation on our own.

"Which means," I said quickly, not wanting to give Curtis any time to question my partner's reaction, "that you suspect some sort of ritualistic killer?"

"Ritualistic *serial* killer—I mean, it's pretty plain, isn't it?" Curtis asked.

And there they were: those two little words that, for techs of Curtis' generation—weaned as they had been on movie and television tales of such people—represented the Holy Grail of investigation. "Indeed," I answered, as collegially as I could manage. "Although first you would need the 'serial,' wouldn't you?"

The tech's eager nod openly stated what Mike and I had already concluded silently: that such a serial—although by no means such a serial *killer*, necessarily—already existed. "Think about it—the religious positioning of the body, combined with the tender care of her personal belongings? He rapes her, kills her, and then, out of what motivation you'd have to tell me, he treats her and her things with an almost worshipful emotion—wouldn't be the first time."

"No, it wouldn't," I said, disheartened less by Curtis' fatal misreading of several key clues than by the fact that the tech had already formed his own solid analysis of what had happened to Shelby Capamagio. At this point, he was only interested in any ideas we might have that would help him pursue it and win the considerable prize of upstaging a man with the kind of inter-county power that Weaver possessed, thus elevating his stock—and perhaps his position—within the FIC. There was nothing unusual in all this. Curtis was simply embodying a problem that had plagued his profession from its beginnings:

That problem, in a nutshell, was the second part of what had made the human link in the chain of forensic investigation so fatal to the field's ascension to a true science. The first was the bullying, incompetent collection and observation of evidence that Dr. Weaver had already demonstrated; but there was also the careerist ambition that led to "tunnel vision," the desire among investigators to see and hear only those facts and theories that will reinforce their initial impressions and suspicions, and thus satisfy their law enforcement superiors all the quicker. This tendency, of course, had been the original sin of most criminal investigators dating back to ancient Rome; but in our own time, tunnel vision had been layered with new euphemisms that criminologists had mined from the social sciences in order to put an intellectual face on a very ancient shortcoming. The habit had been reborn, in recent decades, under such impressive names as "bounded rationality," "focused determinism," and "satisficing" (a shotgun marriage of "satisfying" and "sufficing" that was precisely as dangerous as it is sounds), until finally it had adopted the name of that field to which impatient cognitive scientists of all subdivisions had devoted thousands of pages and dozens of volumes: "heuristics." It was a deliberately arcane word used to describe "cognitive shortcuts": the kind of shortcuts that might make one's initial instincts, prejudices, and simple hunches appear the result of legitimate—or, occasionally, even profound—intellectual processes.

And it was because of his occasional display of this second fault that the otherwise inoffensive and occasionally even perceptive Curtis Kolmback was not to be trusted with all the thoughts and theories that Mike and I had formed inside the trailer, some of which we had spoken of to each other, some of which were of a variety that we had, over the years, learned to read in each other's faces without even acknowledging them aloud.

"But here's what's so strange," Curtis continued, moving closer and speaking quietly. "And when I said all this to Dr. Weaver, he was actually very encouraging."

"Then he agreed with your circumstantial findings?" Mike asked, trying very hard, now, to maintain the patience necessary to take what we were hearing seriously.

"Yes," Curtis said. "He agreed with everything I said, in fact. And when I mentioned the words 'serial killer,' he told me to pursue it, that it would be good for my career."

Suddenly my attention was brought very seriously to bear: "Those were his actual words to you?"

"Word for word," Curtis said with a nod. "*Good for my career*. Pretty unusual, for Weaver, to offer that kind of encouragement."

"Well, then congratulations, Curtis," I said, giving him an indulgent clap on the shoulder. "And you're right: Weaver doesn't like to dish out the compliments." With my grip on his shoulder, I pulled the younger man's head closer to mine conspiratorially. "And for what it's worth, I think your theory has a lot of merit, too."

"You do?" the tech answered, so eagerly that it was close to embarrassing.

"Indeed, Curtis," I said. "In fact, here's what I'd like you to do . . ." I took out one of my cards, and slipped it into the only open pocket I could find on his jumpsuit. "Keep us posted on your findings—not just on this case, but on future ones that look like they might have been the work of the same killer. Can I count on you to do that?"

"Well . . ." The man wasn't quite sold, just yet. "Just as long as it doesn't get me in trouble. It's hard enough to get anywhere, inside this unit—"

"We wouldn't mess with you like that, Curtis," Mike threw in, evidently having caught on to my scheme. "Just let us know as much as you safely can, or need to—that's all. Our involvement here's strictly advisory, anyway—we might as well advise you, too. No harm in it."

"But for now," I said, hoping to wrap things up before he had any more time to hesitate, "I think we'd better get going. I can hear Steve bellowing even louder outside, he must be wound up about something—"

"Oh, shit!" Curtis said, quickly recalling the business that had sent him inside in the first place. "He is—for some reason, we got a lot of brass on the way to this one: the ADA, my boss, somebody from the BCI—" Meaning the State Police's Bureau of Criminal Investigation, New York's own version of the FBI.

"*Albany's* interested?" I said, the fact reinforcing every idea I had been forming in the last few minutes. "Well, well . . ." I looked to Mike: the interest of such luminaries had enormous implications concerning not only the cause and importance of Shelby Capamagio's death, but a larger chain of events into which that death likely fit, and my partner and I now knew as much—although Curtis evidently did not. "We'd better make ourselves scarce indeed, then, Michael," I continued, in a quiet, even tone; then I offered the tech a hand, which he shook gratefully. "Thank you for the time, Curtis," I said, as we all started for the trailer door. "And I'm sorry we couldn't offer any theories to augment your own—but that fact should at least give you some satisfaction, right?"

"It does, believe me," Curtis said; and he was about to further express his relief when he turned to find me lagging a couple of steps behind. "Aren't you coming, Dr. Jones?"

"Hmm?" I noised. "Oh, yeah, don't worry, Curtis—I'll be right along . . ."

"Don't worry about him, Curtis," Mike said, putting his free arm around the tech's shoulder. "Likes to get a last look at the scene, without anybody around. You know—his 'Sorcerer of Death' bullshit."

Curtis laughed along with Mike, glad to be let in on the jibe, as I glanced around that room, Shelby's room, one last time, burning every detail into my brain and then finally re-approaching her body.

"Well, young Shelby," I said, reaching up to carefully close her eyes, which was the least I could do morally, but the most I could do legally, to offer her some measure of dignity. "We will find out what happened here. You have my word on that . . ."

Once I'd joined the others outside, the impatiently waiting Spinetti herded Mike and me quickly to Pete's cruiser, and the deputy just as speedily opened both the front and back doors on the vehicle's passenger side; but neither Mike nor I was about to climb in until we'd straightened a few things out:

"Steve," I said, my voice now dead serious, "I understand your desire to get us out of here before your various superiors arrive. Particularly if they are being accompanied by any members of the media."

"You're good and goddamn right I want you out of here," Spinetti answered, his own voice all business. "So will you please get in and let Pete drive you back to Shiloh—"

"We will return, Sheriff, and very willingly," I countered. "But I think that if you genuinely desire our advice regarding this girl's death, then you at least owe it to us to be candid about what's going on."

Spinetti eyed me carefully. "I don't think I'm hearing you quite right, Dr. Jones—you're saying Pete and I haven't been straight with you?"

I held up a quick hand, wanting to avoid useless arguments. "You've been as straight as you've believed you can be—but you've also revealed more than you know. Despite your seeming ambivalence when we arrived, you plainly wanted and continue to want our advice as to whether or not you should align your own opinions with those of Weaver and Kolmback. And if our answer is that you should not, you will want detailed ammunition to use against both of those men, in what I suspect will rapidly become a high-level debate with the assistant district attorney and the BCI. Fine. But in return for all this, you might at least share with us the full story concerning not only this case, but whatever similar case or cases preceded it, and why there should be so much official concern about them." Then I turned to the deputy. "Pete, when we arrived, you spoke of not wanting to get '*this* one' wrong—and when I remarked on the statement, you deliberately ignored me."

Steve removed his own Stetson and slapped it against his thigh in frustration. "Goddamn it, Pete, I told you—"

"Don't blame your deputy, Steve," I said. "It was the only mistake he made, and it was a small one. Yours was worse."

"*Mine?*" Spinetti asked, his eyes going wide.

"Yours," I answered. "If you had wanted to keep certain things secret, you had no business sending Kolmback in to retrieve us on his own, just now. Past experience should have told you he would let something serious slip, as he did, simply by telling us that an entire wave of senior officials are heading to this scene. Those types wouldn't take much interest in the murder of a teenage meth head, unless it was part of a pattern—you know it, and we know it."

Spinetti needed to consider that statement for a moment; and concession came in the form of his putting his hat back on and nodding in resignation. "Yeah. I suppose." Glancing about, he returned his gaze to me with some little contrition. "But like Pete says, neither one of us would have kept anything back from you guys, if we didn't need to. I hope you know that."

"And I do, Steve. All the same, I do think you might tell us the full story of what's happening here, now that we're apparently playing parts in it. Neither Mike nor I are in any position, much less inclined, to provide you with insights that may come back to bite us on the ass, if the arguments over this and any related crime scenes make scapegoating necessary." I paused, allowing all heads to cool a bit. "We had quite enough of that sort of thing down in"—and I emphasized my next words just as the sheriff was wont to do—"*New York City . . .*"

Slowly nodding a bit, Spinetti finally murmured, "Okay—okay, Doc. But neither of you heard any of it from either Pete or me—fair enough?"

"Fair enough," I said with a nod of my own.

"And I'm gonna let my deputy tell the rest of it to you on your drive back," the sheriff continued. "I don't imagine you got much desire to be here when the hotshots arrive—and I still haven't quite figured how I'm gonna explain *what* you were doing here in the first place. But you can help me with that."

"Can we?" I said, stepping into Pete's cruiser while Mike took his place in the back seat. Pete raced around to get into the driver's seat, and in a few seconds the vehicle's V-8 roared to life. Pressing the button to roll down my window, I looked out at Spinetti. "And what form might that help take?"

"Just give me the short version—Pete can take down the details. That way, they'll be so busy arguing with me, maybe they won't care about you being here." The sheriff leaned down and looked by turns at Mike and then me. "So tell me: Weaver and Kolmback—they're full of shit, right?"

I studied Spinetti's gleaming eyes and growing smile, and realized just how serious the political and turf battle that had plainly begun some time ago must have been, and how much more heated it was about to get. I knew all the players, some better than others; but of all the lot, these two, the sheriff and his deputy, were the only ones I actually respected. In Pete Steinbrecher I had discerned only the faintest traces of political ambition, over the years; while Steve Spinetti had long ago satisfied his ego by being repeatedly elected county sheriff. The rest of them, in contrast, represented a stew of men and women whose eyes were forever on the next rung of the political ladder, and who were therefore willing and able to select, bend, and pervert evidence in criminal cases—even murders—to suit their purposes. In short, if I was going to give weapons to anyone, it would be the pair on either side of me, who at least had the virtue of being men who comprised the front line not only of criminal investigation, but of criminal confrontation, pursuit, and capture.

And so I nodded back at Spinetti, although the lingering image of Shelby Capamagio's searching, dead gaze prevented me from returning his smile; and after a few seconds I said simply, "Well, Steve: Weaver says it's a cut and dried murder of a runaway teen. Then Kolmback says that there's a serial killer loose, which we do *not* believe; but instead of slapping Curtis down, Weaver—privately—encourages him. Says it'll be good for his career. In short, in the opinion of *Doctor* Li and myself, both Weaver and Kolmback are, in fact, full of shit. The girl did *not* die here, and she didn't die in the manner either of them say."

Spinetti nodded once, and his smile spread. "Holy shit," he said. "If even that much is true . . ." Then he slapped the roof of the cruiser twice and Pete put it into reverse, slowly rolling back toward Daybreak Lane with the sheriff walking along beside, looking from me to Mike and seeking out some last words of reassurance. "Just give me one solid fact, though, fellas—something to show them that there's more to it than saying Weaver and Kolmback are wrong, so's I don't have to worry about getting my ass shot off."

"That's easy enough," Mike called, leaning forward—for prisoners were of course prevented from rolling down their own windows. "Tell

Nancy Grimes"—who was the head of the FIC, and Curtis Kolmback's boss—"to take a look at the girl's back. She'll either get it, and back you, or miss it, and then you can act like you've got something to hold over them."

"Nice," Steve said, momentarily pleased; then his face turned puzzled, as we straightened out on the lane. "But what *will* I have to hold over them?"

"Something simple, as usual," Mike answered, holding up a finger as he lit a cigarette. "That 'bruise' that Curtis says was caused by the killer's foot stomping down on Shelby's back, as a way of breaking her neck? Well, it's not a bruise at all. It's lividity. It's the kind of easy mistake that rookies like Kolmback make all the time; and I almost feel sorry for him. But not for Weaver. Anyway, it shows that her blood settled in her lower back when she died—which it couldn't have done in that closet. She had to have died somewhere else, and, given the violence of the break in her neck, probably someplace far away from that trailer."

"Jesus," Steve murmured, smiling wider as the car moved forward. "Okay, boys—I owe you one!"

"You just remember that," I called back to him, "as this thing goes on!"

And then we began rolling faster back down the lane. Far more important, however, a cacophony of sounds had become audible, heading our way from the southwest: sirens, and not just one variety, but several different types, the overall blare seeming, to my jaundiced ears, to reflect perfectly the competing interests of the officials from whose cars the loud, rapid whines were emanating. They were doubtless traveling in a column of vehicles, and one siren would have been more than adequate for their purpose; but ever since the 1980s, when Ronald Reagan idiotically militarized Richard Nixon's absurd "War on Drugs," and especially in the era born on September 11, 2001, it has been the consistent habit of senior law enforcement officials to abjure subtlety in favor of a kind of martial intimidation; indeed, it was quite possible that the approaching column would roll up to the abandoned Capamagio trailer with a military-surplus armored vehicle of some kind, along with officers dressed in the black combat gear that had become so fashionable. All of which would have been merely comical, had it not also reflected a very serious reality: most such officials, in their zeal to treat every criminal event as a chance to display supreme control of social order, had forgotten that lawbreakers most often operate quietly and in the shadows, places where men wearing body armor and military helmets not only were out of place, but made the task of investigating the dark deeds that take place in those shadows all the more difficult. I therefore nodded to Pete, urging haste as he positioned the cruiser to take us back down to the highway below.

The tale that Pete related on our return journey concerned not one but two prior cases of recent murders of teenage children in Burgoyne County; and it might be thought that both Mike and I would have had our imaginations as well as a new verbal interchange fired by this information; yet we, like the far wearier Pete, fell into a temporary disheartenment at the thought of so many young lives wasted, and a strange, silent pall fell over the inside of the car. It was a very uncomfortable silence; and it was not surprising that it was Pete who tried to break it, as we once more entered the village of Surrender and drove around its central point, a faded Civil War monument that was surrounded on all sides by taverns.

" 'Surrender, New York,' " the deputy murmured, trying to get a small chuckle out. "They got *that* much right. Say, Doc, you know that story about old Colonel Jones"—he jerked a thumb at the statue, which was indeed a representation of my most famous forebear—"and the last time he came down to town? Are you ever gonna tell me what he was talking about, with that last thing he said?"

"I can't tell you what I don't know, Pete," I replied wearily; for it was a query and a conversation with which people had often tried to force me to grapple.

"Come on," Pete said, relieved by the distraction. "He was one of your own ancestors, for shit's sake. You're still trying to tell me that in all these years, you've never figured out what he meant?"

I sighed, hoping that the deputy would just drop it. "That's exactly what I'm telling you. For the hundredth time . . ."

"Miss Jones *never* told you?" he pressed.

"Miss Jones does not know," I answered. "Just as everyone else in my family, along with everyone in the town of Surrender, does not know."

"So all these years," Pete declared, "alla them been kicking each other's asses over something they don't even understand?"

"You find that unlikely," I said, turning to him, "given your knowledge of the citizens of our town and county?"

Pete hissed in discouragement. "I guess not. But I do wish I knew . . ."

I looked back out the window as we entered Death's Head Hollow, and its darkening countryside moved by us. "As do I, Deputy. As do I . . ."

We were to pass the rest of our ride in renewed silence, silence of an even more downcast sort: *How did this town and this county ever come to witness such things?*, I think we were all asking ourselves, in our own ways; and such being the case, it seems an appropriate point in my tale to take a moment and explain what lay behind the deputy's relentless curiosity, as well as the enigmatic and slightly sinister designations of both the road we were now ascending and the town we had just left behind.

{v.}

The name "Surrender, New York" has long been a source of amusement for passing voyagers making their way north from "the city," or east from the state thruway to Vermont and other points in northeastern New England. The one-word directional sign on Route 7 that points the way to the town is in fact no more than that: an old rectangular piece of standard highway green sheet metal marking the turn onto a lonely byway and toward the northern Taconics beyond. But the message that the white letters on that sign spell out appears to suggest something else entirely: "SURRENDER," they declare tersely, as if the small arrow next to the word reveals some secret path to a place where one might concede whatever struggles she or he has undertaken in life. Many are the uninitiated who have believed, who yet believe, that there must be some sinister or at least mysterious explanation for both the sign and the spot to which it points the way. But the few who actually make the side trip indicated are generally disappointed to come upon nothing more than a small, tumbledown hamlet at the crossroads of County Road 34 and another, unnumbered byway: a village with little to recommend it other than a seemingly common Civil War monument in the small square at its center.

It would be difficult for me to say how many times, as a boy, I heard friends of my parents issue that same laughter at the small green sign, and then sigh in equally predictable disappointment when we reached Surrender and passed through it, during trips north from our home in New York City to visit my great-aunt's farm above the village. Only when such guests found themselves driving through the unexpected beauty of

Death's Head Hollow would they resume their laughter at such a village's being called "Surrender"—and "Surrender, New York," at that, a phrase that has a different but equally amusing connotation. Had those visitors possessed either the time or the inclination to investigate the town, their dismissive amusement might have turned into something more meaningful: curiosity, for a start. Even a brief stop to view the standing blue and yellow plaque at the edge of the village proper, for example, would have told them that Surrender, New York, claims to be the place where the bulk of the British forces that took part in what the plaque dubs the "*so-called* Battle of Bennington" capitulated to Continental troops on August 16, 1777.

The engagement played a key role in the soon-to-be-joined and decisive Battle of Saratoga: the Royalist soldiers near Bennington had been sent east to raid for badly needed supplies by their commander, General "Gentleman Johnny" Burgoyne, who was invading south from Canada along the Hudson at the head of a considerable army. But the raiding party was first halted, then forced back westward, and finally caught and badly mauled by the Continentals, who killed nearly ten of Burgoyne's men for every one of their own number who fell. The remaining Royalists tried to rejoin their commander's main column to the west, and some succeeded; but many more were captured, although just where has always been the subject of much debate. Several villages near Surrender also claimed the honor, while the community from which the encounter would eventually take its name—Bennington, Vermont—had in fact played relatively little part in the affair, and indeed was not even in the correct colony to warrant title to the victory.

Such, one might simply conclude, are the uncertainties of History: victory, runs the adage, has a thousand fathers, while defeat is an orphan. But in this case, defeat might better have been called a bastard, for the competing claims that were deleted from the larger myth of the Battle of Bennington nonetheless helped establish a pattern of often-ugly resentment and rivalry between towns like Surrender and Bennington itself. It was the bitterness engendered by these disagreements that led a group of well-to-do men in the more prosperous communities adjoining Surrender to decide, in 1791, that they had no wish to be incorporated into the new county of Rensselaer, which the government of the now-state of New York intended should cover the area from Albany to the Massachusetts and Vermont borders. Most of these disgruntled merchants were barely reconstructed Tories who had played no part in the disputed battle; but their considerable financial influence in Albany nonetheless secured agreement to their desire to create their own small county, angering their more ardently revolutionary neighbors, who were further enraged when the men perversely named their creation after the valiant if foolhardy British general whose defeat at Saratoga effectively doomed the British cause in America. And, as if all this were not enough, they next added insult to considerable injury by naming their creation's seat after the most famous British casualty of that battle, General Simon Fraser.

Was either name intended to be ironic? Or were the county's founders really trying to enshrine two heroes of Tory America within the territory of one of the new republic's most important states? The answer, never clear, grew even less so with time; all that *was* apparent was that differing factions and clans soon relocated so as to concentrate in the competing counties (or, in the case of Vermont, competing states), while their feuding just as quickly grew violent, sometimes ending in tavern or barroom stabbings, sometimes in unsolved deaths along lonely roads. Both Burgoyne and Rensselaer Counties were laced with dozens of mysterious hollows, those mountain concavities down which flowed angry little streams that sprang out of the stony crests of the Taconics. Along these waterways ran trails and crude roads leading to beautiful, shielded clearings, spots that, whatever their idyllic charms, were ideal places to dispose of embarrassing bodies, murdered and otherwise.

And, like the town of Surrender at its base, the hollow known as Death's Head would seem even today to also be hiding some criminal or even supernatural secret behind its name. Indeed, the suggestion is all the more pointed, in the hollow's case, because its name is far older than that of the town, stretching back to the days when the latter was no more than a collection of a few shacks. What dark rites might those early settlers have been engaging in along the twisting, steep cart path that they cut up into the unusually lush forest of the hollow? The dirt of the path, always in danger of being reclaimed by the grass, ferns, and wildflowers around it, followed the course of one particularly noisy brook, whose rushing waters and small but endlessly chattering falls made it seem larger than it was, thereby increasing the hollow's forbidding effect to the point that the suggestion of deadly—perhaps even ghostly—doings was inescapable even to the sunniest of personalities. (And along certain of the hollow's stretches, such thoughts remain inescapable still.)

But it is our lot to live in an age when names that we might suspect or even hope connote mystery and dark romance are usually revealed as disguising more banal origins and realities. The case of Surrender was one such example; and that of Death's Head Hollow is another. The path that led, as the road that succeeded it yet leads, through stands of maple, pine, ash, and birch trees interrupted only by lushly carpeted glades (now pastureland) was, in fact, not one of those places where feuding men did each other violence; rather, it was simply a colonial dumping ground, a place where weary laborers from surrounding villages unceremoniously disposed of piles of animal heads, useless feet and limbs, and entrails, in addition to the pathetically struggling bodies of beasts too ill to be of further service to their harsh taskmasters. Obliging buzzards, bears, wolves, and wild dogs would rapidly be drawn in to the smell of such offerings, and would quickly dispose of them; and to indicate the dangers of both rotting flesh and wild scavengers, a crude wooden sign bearing the painted image of a skull above crossed bones was nailed to a tree at the hollow's entrance. In this mundane way, the place's name was born.

In one sense, then, it was true that the hollow had seen much death, along with copious amounts of pain and sorrow, during the time that men had ventured into it. But the suffering and tragedies of animals were not then, as they are not now, the stuff of general human interest, much less human romance. Such sentiments would remain elusive in and around Death's Head Hollow for many generations; but this did not keep those sinister auras that accompany any and all forms of human callousness and cruelty from settling over both the cart path and the land below it like a miasma.

In the latter half of the nineteenth century, the fever bred by this noxious atmosphere spiked. Almost a decade after the Civil War, a canny Missouri merchant and former colonel in the Union army who went by the perplexing name of Caractacus Jones (the same ancestor of mine that Pete Steinbrecher had spoken of when we reached Surrender) moved to northern New York State, bringing with him a fortune made during a particularly successful career in lumber that had followed his military service. Colonel Jones bought up all the offal fields along Death's Head Hollow from the ever-impoverished town of Surrender, for a sum small enough not only to make the town's lack of appreciation for the land apparent to the newcomer, but also to breed in him a pointed contempt for the lack of industry and pride among his new neighbors. Hiring several dozen men from nearby towns—men willing to work long but fairly paid hours, unlike the denizens of Surrender—Jones proceeded to clear the bottomland around the stream in the hollow, to plow under the generations of accumulated animal bones and flesh (which only made the soil richer), and to establish there a fine farm, which he named after the battle he always considered the most harrowing of his military career. At the same time, he erected a profitable charcoal-fuel works on the wooded, rocky mountaintop, and in only a few years was taking in healthy profits from both enterprises.

All this earned the Colonel (as his employees inevitably and invariably called him) the unending envy and hatred of the people of Surrender, who could not or would not interrupt their routines of thieving, poaching game, bartering, and drinking long enough to themselves attempt to enter Jones' employ. But the final insult came when the Colonel took the only truly handsome woman in town, one Jenna Malloy, as his wife: the grumbling in the taverns of Surrender now began to evolve into vague and deadly plans, which had as their object nothing less than the death of Colonel Jones and the destruction of all he had built. The goal was as ambitious as the courage and cleverness of the townsmen were inadequate to its achievement; but malice forever trumps prudence, in the minds of such people, and their hateful scheming continued apace.

The eventual fruit of all this outraged bloodlust was the dispatch into the hollow of two young men, relative newcomers to the town who were petty criminals and fugitives. The youths were liberally dosed with the deadly alcohol that was brewed in sheds behind some of the most pestilential houses in Surrender, and their assessment of their own abilities was further puffed up by the wickedly false praise of the men who had devised the scheme of which the pair were to be the instruments. In June, on the night of a particularly bright Strawberry Moon (as the Algonquin Indians had dubbed the occasion on which the Earth passes closest to its satellite), the two set out, carrying jars of the same ungodly substance that they had been consuming, along with canisters of black powder, several firearms, and an axe handle apiece. Their orders were to make their way to the charcoal storehouse, set it ablaze, and then, in the resulting confusion, dash to Jones' large house and kill the Colonel, firing his home as they departed.

It scarcely needs stating that all this was beyond the young men, whose fear steadily overcame their drunkenness the farther up the hollow they crept. Upon passing Jones' house on their way to the charcoal works, they were set upon by the Colonel's faithful dog Cassius, a mastiff who had survived the full four years of the Civil War at his master's side. The brave yet aging animal could not, however, similarly withstand the trespassers' panicked gunshots, along with numerous blows from their axe handles: he died with a series of mournful cries, and the commotion of this fatal confrontation roused the Colonel and the several men who staffed his house and its grounds. By the time these latter guardians, all bearing torches, found the body of the dog, the guilty assailants were on their way back down the hollow at a run, having left their jars and weapons behind; but when the Colonel joined his men, open, tearful grief overwhelmed him, the kind of grief that, in a true warrior, soon turns to rage. It quickly became clear that Cassius' killers would likely never be able to run far or fast enough, and Jones dispatched one of his most reliable men to Surrender to tell the inhabitants that if the names of those responsible for the act were not revealed to him when he descended from the mountain, he could not and would not be responsible for his actions.

It was then that the people of Surrender committed the act that would stigmatize them down to the present day. The townspeople were already drunk, and now became increasingly wild with terror—for not only was Colonel Jones coming, they quickly heard, but he was coming with every one of the men who worked the night shift of the ever-active charcoal works, and they were all armed with rifles, shotguns, and every sort of bladed weapon and tool. The men of Surrender tried to plan some sort of defense; but several of their women, only marginally less intoxicated than their spouses, pointed out that they had neither the means nor the nerve to put up an organized fight. It would be far better, they asserted, for the villagers themselves to punish the two young men before the Colonel came, and thereby appease him. The idea caught on quickly, for the pair of murderous interlopers had no families to protect them; and they were therefore brought forward as if they were suddenly strangers. But what punishment would be stern enough to anticipate and slake the volatile Colonel's thirst for revenge?

Not long thereafter, Caractacus Jones rode into Surrender, where he and his men were presented with the sight of the two youths hanging from the pulley arm that extended out from under the eve of the barnlike building that housed the town's post office and general store. They were not quite dead, when the Colonel arrived; but by the time his men raced up and cut them down, they were. Yet when a note from the now-vanished townspeople that had been pinned to one of the young men's chests was brought to Jones, explaining that the "good people of Surrender" hoped this offering would satisfy him, it had a singularly peculiar effect on the Colonel. His eyes once more filled with tears, he crumpled the paper in his hand, and then, looking around at the buildings along the crossroads, he murmured:

"You cannot escape it, in this country . . ."

Colonel Jones then turned his horse around and headed back up Death's Head Hollow. He would sire three sons and two daughters in the fifteen years of life remaining to him; but he would never again leave the confines of Shiloh. Nor would he ever explain those enigmatic words spoken so quietly in the square of Surrender—indeed, he would never even hint at what the inescapable "it" he had referred to was. His statement became the town's supreme mystery, as well as a kind of curse. The people of Surrender did not speak of what had happened for a period of time that, given their gossiping nature, was a very long one; and when they finally did dare to ponder the meaning of the words, it was in whispers concerning which families among them had been most actively responsible for the pair of murderous schemes, the one that had failed and, even worse, the one that had succeeded, thus prompting the Colonel's unexplained indictment.

This debate was a shrouded but no less heated one: families spread rumors about the involvement of other families, and inevitably violent encounters erupted, first with fists and knives, then with guns, though injury rather than death was the usual result of these contests. Blood feuds were born, in which stealing and vandalism were the preferred tactics: although they would never have admitted it, most citizens of the town had had their fill of murder. As Surrender staggered on through the end of the nineteenth century, and then the beginning and middle of the twentieth, new residents moved to the village, driven by the ebb and flow of economic fortunes in surrounding towns and cities and, later, as ships and automobiles destroyed the meaning of distance, far-off states and, finally, other parts of the world. The largely German-American valley of the Taconics now became a destination for families from eastern and southern Europe, particularly Italy; but the new arrivals who settled in or near Surrender were eventually drawn into the old feuds by obscure causes, coincidental slights, or simple boredom, choosing sides in a battle of whose real origin they were wholly ignorant. Indeed, so ignorant of it were they that when the descendants of the few families that had once worked for Colonel Jones (descendants who themselves worked for the Colonel's heirs) actually proposed erecting a monument to their benefactor in the modest town square—a bronze statue of the man, resplendent in full-dress Federal uniform, with his slain dog proudly standing at his side—the motion was passed by the town's leaders, and the funds appropriated without argument.

Time and still more generations passed. News of war came several times to Surrender, and some of her sons even served, with varying degrees of valor. The mobile home was invented, creating the greatest environmental and scenic impact on Burgoyne County since the inventions of the axe and the saw; yet in a more fundamental way—that way peculiar to towns that lie at the very frontier of our civilization and law— change continued to avoid the village of Surrender in any form more significant than the laying of vinyl over wooden clapboards and the paving of once-dusty earthen roads (although Death's Head Hollow itself, which remained the property of the Jones family, was never to know asphalt). The instruments with which families warred against each other evolved, and there were occasional and tumultuous shifts in clan alliances; and all the while, the battle to expunge something that few of them could even identify went on. There was universal talk of respect denied, of swindles and lies, and of the extent to which enemies were asking, even begging, for a reckoning; but the crimes committed in Surrender (to say nothing of similar acts perpetrated in Burgoyne County more generally), for all the grandiose, drunken talk of most of their perpetrators, generally remained as petty as were the minds behind them.

Yet, though petty, some of those minds and those crimes could on occasion be cruel enough to rise above mere mischief and achieve genuine outrage; indeed, we had just witnessed one such offense, which now formed the first piece of the mortal puzzle into which Pete Steinbrecher and Steve Spinetti were drawing Mike and myself with such evident urgency.

And in the days to come, we would meet another victim of another kind of local outrage. That same unusual character would bring with him up Death's Head Hollow further confirmation of the theories Mike and I were already forming about Shelby Capamagio's death; but he would bring a great deal more. For we were on a collision course to meet one of Surrender's few sons who had managed to defy both his community's past and his own parents' abusive deviousness to become a young man of exceptional character—although he himself would have been loath to admit it.

CHAPTER TWO

THE DEVIL AND MARCIANNA JONES

{i.}

The most apparent points of interest and alarm concerning the account that Pete Steinbrecher gave us during the drive back to Shiloh concerning cases similar to Shelby Capamagio's were not the numbers involved (two additional children of about Shelby's age, a boy and a girl, found dead in Burgoyne County during the past several weeks), nor even the eerily similar fact that both had also been apparent murders in remote locations. No, eerier still was the fact that Mike and I felt sure, after hearing the details from Pete, that both death scenes had been staged. Still more important than all this, we agreed with the pathology reports from the first two cases, which overruled the FIC tech involved in each and declared that the children had probably not been killed where they were found, thus explaining Steve's elation on hearing our theory that the same held true for Shelby. (Rather ominously, the tech in both cases had once again been Curtis Kolmback, a repetition that defied departmental rules, and, further, suggested that political forces were at work about which we knew next to nothing.) But the two most important and disturbing aspects of the three plainly linked cases, we became increasingly convinced from spending the following two long days and nights studying the case files concerning all three killings (the texts of which Pete very decently and discreetly scanned and e-mailed to us himself), were, first, the sex, or more precisely the *sexes*, of the victims, and second, the fact that a hoped-for similarity—that all three had been "throwaway children," kids abandoned by their families—had been contradicted by a report that the first victim had apparently been a simple runaway. Both of these were fundamental inconsistencies: and true inconsistency in the behavior of murderers is never a welcome feature—although it is nearly always a critically revealing one.

During all those hectic hours of focus in the fuselage of the old Junkers JU-52, however—hours interrupted only by the need to deliver lectures to and referee discussions among our students at SUNY-Albany, as well as by the need to grab what few snatches of sleep and food we could—Mike and I came no closer to understanding just what explanation of the crimes these two inconsistencies regarding the sexes of the victims and the circumstances of their separations from their families might indicate. There was one obvious and inviting candidate concerning the first factor, of course, and we had no doubt that the Bureau of Criminal Investigation's officers were currently dashing about the county investigating it: the possibility that a registered sex offender with a known taste for pubescent boys as well as girls was back at work. It was by no means an outlandish suggestion: *hebephiles*—adults who are sexually attracted to pubescent children—are often and even usually interested in age, rather than sex; and the list of registered offenders with such tastes who were either longtime residents of Burgoyne County or had been relocated to its more sparsely populated regions was long indeed. But the possibility that one such character had not only resumed his behavior, but become murderous, as well, was statistically remote, although Mike and I did not discount it on that basis: for it was part of our method never to include or preclude suspects or scenarios on the basis of the numbers game, given that we were firm believers in the maxim of the nineteenth-century British prime minister Benjamin Disraeli, who had declared that there were three grades of falsehood: "lies, damned lies, and statistics." Rather, we based our resistance on certain behavioral considerations that we had been able to glean from the case files we had been sent, as well as from the preliminary results of the tests that Mike had run on the body of Shelby Capamagio:

"It just doesn't work, Trajan," my partner declared, on the afternoon of the third day of our wrestling with the known facts before us. "I can't find any greater evidence of sexual assault, or even sexual activity, in the reports on the first two kids than I've been able to determine regarding Shelby. At least so far. I mean, sure, the girl was no virgin, the pathology report demonstrates that, but that's no big fucking shock. Besides, neither was the second victim, Kelsey Kozersky, and she lived an entirely different lifestyle, on a horse farm. So that's a dead end. And as for anything else, anything violently telltale . . . Well, it just isn't there."

I nodded as I stood up, my lower body unsteady after too many hours of work and too few of sleep. Taking out a cigarette and sticking it in my mouth without lighting it, I picked up a heavy, retractable dog's leash and said, "Which means that we are almost certainly not dealing with any known sex offender; perhaps not with a sex offender at all." I chuckled once, more out of a desire to find something amusing than because anything was genuinely humorous. "And wouldn't the folks from the BCI just love to be sure of that. They could stop racing around back roads with their hair on fire, rousting unsuspecting schmucks who've already been put through the mill by anyone who's found out about their pasts. A shame nobody in Albany would ever listen to us . . ."

"Yep," Mike agreed glumly.

"As for the thread of throwaways," I went on, "it speaks for itself. If it's not there, it's not there, and if Kelsey ran away, then her being brought home after being killed is simply not consistent in any way that is of fundamental use. Simple diversion. Which this killer—or group of killers— has an increasingly apparent taste for . . ."

"Yep and yep," Mike murmured, already knowing this fact to be plain.

Checking the pocket watch in my vest, I realized with some little concern just how late in the afternoon it was: we had been burning through both possibilities and hours, the former dead ends and the latter seemingly wasted. "Almost four-thirty," I said, taking up my light cotton suit jacket and my cane. "You're up."

"Already?" Mike said, lifting his forehead from one hand and speaking with no little dread. "Oh, Jesus, man—where's the Visine? My eyes must be shot to shit."

"Might be," I answered, getting my jacket on and then shoving a small black book I'd been studying into its pocket. "But I don't know why you're worried about it—nobody can see your damned eyeballs, anyway. Besides, a nice, exhausted squint just makes you look even more inscrutable."

"Fuck off, you ethnically insensitive pig. Where's the fucking Visine?"

"In the top drawer of your desk, where you left it last night."

As Mike found the small plastic bottle and began to drip the liquid into his bloodshot eyes, he made his own rather strained effort to inject at least a little humor into the frustrating moment: "You know, Trajan, we *could* put these students to work for us on this—without giving them specifics, of course. Just the basic, anonymous facts. And who knows, one of them might turn out to be the—ah, you know, that thing about how you put a thousand monkeys in a room with a thousand typewriters and eventually one of them will write *War and Peace*? Well, one might be our monkey, and end up giving us the key to the whole thing by accident."

Mike was, of course, only expressing frustration at being pulled away from a potential triple homicide to perform our academic obligations; but his idea was one that, in the days ahead, would come back to haunt us. For the moment, however, feeling as irritated as my old friend that our difficult role as informal advisors on the case was not yet supplying us with enough information to indicate a path forward, yet still believing that the solution of the murders might somehow depend on our work, I felt the rather desperate need to get out of the plane and the hangar. I wouldn't be able to get any sleep, of course, for it would be my turn before the students in just a couple of hours; but I might at least clear my head. So I began to walk down the aisle between the few remaining leather passenger seats of the JU-52 and toward the forward hatch of the fuselage, replying to my partner's suggestion by saying, "Just try to get through your lecture in something resembling a coherent fashion, Michael."

Eyes cleared, Mike took his copies of the case files we'd gotten from Pete off his desk and slammed them on the floor, in an effort to find the text for his next course. Once he'd located the blue volume, he began the work of preparing both the rear portion of the fuselage and himself for the work ahead: he switched on the bank of flat-screen video monitors that sat in a shallow semicircle in front of the doorway to what had once been the plane's lavatory, then began moving into place a black felt backdrop that we employed to hide the actual nature of our headquarters from our students.

"Ah," I said, as he tugged at the felt with the book under his arm. "The National Academies report. So today you go after the big fish."

"Damn straight," he replied, stepping onto my side of the backdrop once the thing was in place. "Although I'd rather keep going after the local species. But they don't seem to be biting . . ." The book Mike was holding was the Research Council of the National Academies' report on *Strengthening Forensic Science in the United States,* which, despite its title, was as much a scathing indictment of what had gone wrong with forensic science generally (and especially the many forensic laboratories in the country, particularly the famed national lab of the FBI at Quantico, Virginia) as it was a prescription for improvement. Mike's evident focus on it that afternoon, I knew, meant that he intended to work off some of his present frustration concerning our case by showing his students just how the patterns for corruption and incompetence that were so rife at the local levels of laboratory work had also grown entrenched in the hallowed federal evidentiary analysis center. The FBI lab had been one of those places—through its imagined appearance and activities in books-turned-movies dating back to *Silence of the Lambs*—that had doubtless inspired many of our young scholars to pursue a career in forensic investigation in the first place; yet somehow, at that moment, with just our two exhausted selves in the plane, the report seemed as much a reminder of what we were up against, in trying to challenge our effective professional exile and provide answers to three murders from our completely unofficial position and our most unlikely headquarters, as it did any embodiment of defiance.

I let out a long sigh as my partner looked at his reflection in one of the darkened, low windows of the fuselage and buttoned up his short-sleeve white shirt, which was somewhat the worse for wear after two straight days of use. "It isn't the old days, is it, Mike?" I said, bitterly wistful. "Steaks and scotch at Luger's, when we beat the city lab on some headline case . . ."

"No, it sure as shit ain't that," Mike said, his voice admirably free of remorse. "But that's not why we got into this business, L.T., and you know it." Picking up a clip-on tie and fixing it to his collar, he went on: "And we're not done on this one yet—once I get through this class, I'm gonna finish those last tests on Shelby. The trace on her clothes—there's something about that . . . And if I find anything worthwhile, I'll buy you a twelve-pack of Genesee to celebrate. Besides, you just need to get the fuck out of here and spend some time with you-know-who. Once we get a break on this thing, you won't be moaning about steaks in Brooklyn."

"Yeah. Well, get this damned class over with, so you can test whatever you need to test and find whatever you need to find." With that, I finally headed out the hatch of the plane and onto the set of steel steps just outside it. "Always remembering, of course, that we continue to give these kids their money's worth, insofar as we're able. It's them, not the citizens of Burgoyne County, that are keeping us alive, just now."

"Them and Miss Clarissa Jones, of course," Mike answered, straightening his ridiculous but convenient neckwear and pulling on a sports jacket of matching functionality. Then he nodded at the leash in my hand. "Go on and have your quality time—maybe you'll think of something we haven't yet, and start pulling your weight on this case."

"Unh-hunh," I noised. "And you quit flirting with that Chinese exchange student. Some of the others have started to notice, and they're cracking wise on the subject."

"Tell 'em to mind their own business," Mike shot back, disappearing behind the black backdrop and, I could hear, taking his place at the desk before the monitors. "That *is* why they call it a *graduate* education, after all. Now get the fuck out of here, I'll see you in an hour or so."

"Good luck," I answered, starting down the steps. But as I did, I felt a sharp pain in my hip and stumbled rather badly, letting loose a loud "Mother-*fucker*!"

"Trajan?" Mike called, pulling the backdrop away just enough to get a glimpse of me regaining my footing. "You all right?"

"Yeah, just slipped," I said, trying not to give away the true cause of my clumsiness. "But I'm fine, Mike."

"You've been 'slipping' a lot, lately," he said carefully. "And working awfully late. Plus you slept in that enclosure with her again last night. Don't push it *too* hard, L.T.—remember what the doc said last time."

"I am forever remembering 'what the doc said last time,'" I answered, finally gaining the concrete floor of the hangar; and in a few more seconds, I was on my way to the only true comfort I'd ever known, during the lowest moments of our pastoral banishment.

The afternoon light outside the hangar was the kind of late day sunshine that warms and reveals without burning and blinding; and, feeling somewhat enlivened by it, I made the short walk up to Marcianna's gate at what passes, in my case, for a fast pace, knowing that she would be waiting impatiently for me. Her wild excitement upon observing my approach was a unique and almost indescribable tonic, an outpouring of complete trust, a mutual trust that it had taken us years to develop, and which was now so strong that before I had even arrived at the gate, I was mirroring her joyous anticipation as plainly as my exhaustion and my discouragement over the case would allow. Marcianna and I were, as Mike often put it, "like a couple of kids—big, fucking freaky kids" when in each other's company, a phenomenon not difficult to explain. After all, when you care for and then gain the trust of, say, a small white dog such as my great-aunt Clarissa kept almost constantly at her side, it's a thing to be expected; but to be granted the faith of an animal never intended for human companionship—one who, though captured in her infancy and held through her youth for the amusement of human children, was thereafter shut away in cramped, filthy cages and exposed throughout her early adulthood only to disease and abuse by her keepers, without ever losing her essential freedom of spirit—well, that is another matter entirely.

I opened the lock on the tall, thick gate that separated us, perfectly aware that Marcianna could, if she wished, have killed me on the spot and vanished into the mountain wilderness that surrounded her enclosure. Instead, she submitted gladly to the clipping of the leash in my hand to the collar that she had long ago agreed to wear—and I felt any sense of sadness about the past disappear altogether. In welcome contentment we began our walk through the grounds surrounding Shiloh's square-columned farmhouse: grounds that, like the house itself and, indeed, the whole of the farm, had been the vision of peace that Colonel Caractacus Jones had carefully formed and nurtured during his four horrifying years of service in the Civil War.

Our stroll took us first by the hangar and then down to the barns, inside one of which—the milking barn—I could hear my great-aunt Clarissa's little white dust-mop of a dog (Terence, he was improbably called) yapping away as always, the wolf from which he was not so far removed as one might think driving him to try first to herd and then to nip at the heels of the incoming cattle. He was prevented from such mischief by Clarissa's own gravelly, sharp voice, a sound that exuded complete command and authority, whether she was shouting at the farmhands, keeping Terence from running amok, or dealing with local political and law enforcement officials. Marcianna's ears went forward at the sound of Terence's sharp bark with evident interest. But it was just this interest that I had lately been working with her to eradicate: for the only thing that disturbed my otherwise hard-nosed great-aunt about having Marcianna on the farm was the threat that she might pose to the creature who was, somewhat inexplicably, Clarissa's darling.

I was teaching Marcianna not to give in to her ancient instinct regarding Terence in a moderately sized clearing located beside a relatively straight stretch of the noisy stream that flowed down from the mountain-tops through Death's Head Hollow. The flat, recently mowed bit of field (a pasture for goats, in times gone by) lay beyond a screen of trees that ran along the hollow road itself. To reach it, we needed to walk across a wide stretch of lawn on the west side of the farmhouse; and as we did, Marcianna's interest picked up again, the smell of beef and chicken being grilled just outside the kitchen in the back of the house reaching her black, triangular nose. But we had business to attend to, and she knew it; thus she was happy enough to press on, knowing that there would be rewards of a different kind very soon.

Once across the dusty hollow road, we walked through the line of maple, birch, and oak trees along it and toward the twin limestone posts of the pasture's old, rotted gateway. Other than the gate, nothing much prevented access to the bracing waters of the stream, where one could cool off, get a drink, or go trout fishing. And it was fishing that, unbeknownst to Marcianna and myself, was about to bring about a most peculiar encounter: one that would prove a shot in the arm to Mike's and my efforts to solve the deaths of the three local children.

Inside a weathered wooden box that I had placed beside one of the gateposts, I found my tool of instruction on these occasions: a long nylon string tied at one end to an eight-inch piece of broomstick, and at the other to an old white pillowcase, which I had stuffed with sawdust and tied into various sections, making them resemble a torso, legs, and a head. The final touch had been the supergluing of large cotton balls to the puppet's head and extremities and black buttons to serve as eyes. Holding my cane under my arm, I found a suitable spot to place the decoy, behind a low, mostly ruined stone wall that had been part of the original fencing of the pasture. Then I led Marcianna to the opposite side of the clearing, letting the cord out as I went, and together we found a hiding place behind a fallen member of the stands of still more trees that ran along the stream. Finally, I released a long section of Marcianna's leash, and tugged at the nylon string until the decoy began to appear from behind the stones some thirty yards away.

Her eyes locked onto it and her ears went forward, the memory of Terence's yapping at the milking barn fresh in her mind. I immediately began speaking to her, issuing gentle but firm warnings as I ran a hand along the upper portion of her long, gently dipping spine, where her fur had already begun to stand in preparation for a determined stalk. My first efforts along these lines appeared to be in vain, however, and she quickly began to move out from our hiding place, keeping her body low as her ears sank slowly back on her head. I let her go until impatient movements of her hind legs seemed to indicate that she was getting ready to strike out across the clearing, a distance that she could have covered in a mere instant at her top speed. Then I spoke her name sharply, and pulled on the leash in a firm manner to tell her that this was just the sort of behavior she was to suppress, when faced with the image of such prey—at which point something unprecedented, something truly remarkable, happened:

She not only took my meaning instantly, but turned and issued one of her many chirping sounds, this one the most like a quick laugh, which she followed up by returning to the fallen tree at a quick trot. We repeated this process several times, Marcianna seeming to curb her instinct more each time as her amusement at the situation mounted. In return for her cooperation, she received praise spoken in the soft tones she found most pleasing, along with gentle scratching of my fingers behind her ears and along her back, and finally, some soft-cored, beef-flavored dog treats that I kept in my jacket pocket. (Ironically, my great aunt bought the treats in bulk for little Terence; but Marcianna enjoyed them every bit as much as did her nemesis.) She was learning more quickly than she ever had before—or, I wondered, was it that she only *seemed* to be learning something that she already understood perfectly well? Was Marcianna simply toying with me? She had shown signs of playfulness on many occasions, certainly; but she had never exhibited this deliberate pattern of making me believe she might be embodying dangerous, regressive behavior, then releasing the tension with a mischievous laugh, ultimately returning to my side to demand her reward.

Her amusement suddenly stopped, however, when she caught a sound on the light western breeze; and in an instant, she turned her gaze toward the rocks of the stream bed behind our fallen tree, beginning to growl in an alarmed, though not yet threatening, manner. Following the line of her sight, I became aware that there was indeed a foreign element intruding on the scene of our shared triumph: it was a pair of young voices, murmuring excitedly somewhere behind the rocks and in the stream. They were boys; certainly not older than about fifteen, I determined. The exact words of these very intrepid observers—for it was well known in Surrender that trespassers received stern treatment from Clarissa Jones—were difficult to make out, at first, given that I was trying not to turn directly toward them; but as the pair became more excited, individual phrases grew clearer, and as they did, I shifted my head very slightly to see the upper portions of faces that were strange to me.

They were staring at Marcianna and me in wide-eyed fascination—and fear. (In fact, they were so transfixed that they apparently did not notice that a pair of fishing rods they were carrying were by now waving high above their heads, offering a clear indication of their whereabouts.) The boy on the left was the shorter of the two, with sandy hair and a pair of sharp blue-grey eyes that contrasted with the darker hair, skin tone, and black eyes of the boy on the right. The smaller boy soon began to whisper even louder, in order to be heard over the waters of the stream, and I strained hard to make out fully what he was saying without giving myself away. But Marcianna, whose mood was changing quickly, foiled this attempt: her ears went steadily back on her head, and loud chirps of alarm punctuated her growling. Events in the clearing were no longer a piece of theater, for her: very soon, she began to make the scratching, hissing sound that in her case indicated threat. That sent the two boys' heads back behind the rock, a move negated by the increased volume that heightened fear put into their voices:

"I told you to keep down!" said the smaller boy, in words that came quickly, their tone one of accustomed command—in the company he was presently keeping, at any rate.

"I ducked down as fast as *you*!" said the second boy; and, although his voice was deeper, indicating that he might be slightly older (or had simply developed faster) than his companion, he was evidently used to defending himself on such occasions. "He ain't seen us, anyway," he went on, at which he apparently rose up again to have another look.

"Derek!" the first boy ordered. "Get back down here!"

"I wanna see," the second boy insisted; and from the corner of my eye I did indeed observe his head reappearing.

The sounds the pair were making, and especially the bobbing of their heads, were now disturbing Marcianna quite profoundly, and she began to look from their hiding place to me, moaning out questions as to why I was not allowing her to pursue the interlopers immediately. But I continued to stroke her back and to issue soothing but firm instructions that she was not to move from our own hiding place, despite its being fully exposed to the stream. Meanwhile, the next statement that the second boy made indicated that he had ducked down again to report some urgent intelligence:

"Lucas," he said, breathlessly but with a very peculiar and particular sort of confusion and fear. "Lucas, he's talking to his dog!"

"Yeah, so?" said the first boy. "Lots of people talk to their damned dogs, Derek, don't you even know that much!"

"Yeah, but Lucas," the boy called Derek insisted, still in apprehensive amazement, *the dog is talking back to him!*"

"What?" said young Lucas, whose every utterance confirmed him as the leader of their band of two. "What the hell are you talking about now? Aw, stay here, I'm gonna find out for myself. 'The dog is talking back to him,' Jesus, Derek, it's no wonder people think you're so . . ." But his voice trailed off as, I presumed, he took his turn peering around the rock. I kept my own eyes locked on Marcianna's and continued to try to calm her; but the task became steadily more difficult, until finally, she could restrain herself no longer. In a sudden, snarling burst, she leapt out of our hiding place and, landing in an upright, defiant pose, faced the large stone that sheltered the two boys. Then she issued one of the hoarse yet startling bark-like sounds that were her most extreme call of warning and threat. Turning my head, still not fully, I could see that the observer behind the rock was utterly terrified—yet his eyes, instead of being locked on the image of the still-enraged Marcianna, were fixed on the ground just behind her:

There, inside a tight loop of my companion's long leash that I had not noticed curling itself around my left ankle, lay the whole of my left "leg" (and quite a realistic piece of prosthetic work it was), which had been torn loose from its socket on what little remained of my left thigh by Marcianna's sudden leap, then dragged on through my pants and into the grass of the clearing. A painful throb soon reached my brain, and I grabbed at my thigh stump through the fabric of my empty pants leg. Though hardly a shocking sight, for Marcianna or myself, the scene had evidently horrified our young observer, although he quickly disappeared back behind the quartz rock with admirable self-discipline and only a short cry.

I waited for the next exchange from within the stream bed as I retrieved my prosthetic, hopped to a more discreet spot behind our fallen tree, and loosened my pants in order to be able to reseat the leg onto its socket. But what I heard next from the stream was so comical that it made this procedure considerably more difficult than usual.

"I got news for you!" the boy called Lucas declared to his friend. "That thing may be talking, but—it *ain't no dog!*"

"Whatta you mean?" the boy Derek asked, more confused than ever.

"Just what I said," answered his partner in crime. "It ain't a dog—it's a—a whatta you call it—one a those big *cats!*"

"Aw, who's crazy now, Lucas?" came the skeptical reply. "Everybody knows the guy has some weird kinda dog—"

"Yeah? Well, as usual, everybody's full of shit! I seen pictures of those things, it's a—a *cheetah!* And not only that, Derek—" He paused, either for effect or out of disbelief, before declaring fatefully: "The damned thing *just ripped the guy's leg off!*"

"No way," Derek answered. "First of all, Lucas, cheetahs are in *Africa;* and second—aw, shit, I'm taking a look for myself . . ." A few more silent seconds passed, while Derek did indeed sneak up for another glimpse. By now, I had reaffixed my "leg" and reordered my pants, and was standing next to the downed tree, leaning on my cane. The boy Derek went low once more, saying quickly, "You're crazy, Lucas. Batshit crazy. The guy's standing right out there, on both legs—and he's staring *at us!* Or at this rock, anyway."

"Whatta you mean?" Lucas asked. "Like, he *grew it back?*"

"I guess so—but take a look," Derek said. "Maybe he's a mutant, or something, I mean, assuming it was really *off*—"

In the time it took Derek to mutter that brief statement, the top of Lucas' head appeared and disappeared again; and from the way Derek was cut off before his next thought, yelping and gurgling a bit, it was my impression that Lucas had grabbed his friend's shirt, somewhere near the collar. "A mutant—that's it! He can *regrow parts of his body,* like a starfish! But whatever *his* explanation is, the animal took the whole leg right off, it was lying right there in the grass, hell, the fucking shoe was still on it—" There was a brief pause, and then Lucas seized hold of his terror for long enough to grow suddenly suspicious, muttering the words, *"Wait a minute . . ."*

This last statement made me realize that I would not be able to keep from laughing out loud at these two for much longer. Therefore, when Lucas' head reappeared, I took the chance to lock eyes with the boy, after which I put up a hand and beckoned him to come out of the stream bed.

But Lucas just dove behind the rock again, after which even more furious, muted chatter passed between him and his confederate, expressing the urgent need to "get the fuck out of here!"

This, I was not prepared to allow. "Hey, you two!" I finally called aloud; and as I did, I saw the rapidly fluttering fishing poles above the quartz boulder suddenly grow still, their carriers evidently abandoning their planned escape, at least for the moment. "That's right," I continued. "Stand still, and then walk toward me—and if you're carrying anything more serious than those poles, let me see it, right out in front of you."

At that, quickly whispered accusations that ran on into words of defense and mutual recrimination rose up from the stream bed; and I will confess, the ridiculousness of the exchange kept me close to laughter; but I was determined not to allow that until I knew what the pair were up to, which was obviously something more than simple fishing.

"Do you really think you still need to whisper?" I called; at which I could hear what sounded like one of them landing a sharp blow to some solid part of the other's body, likely a shoulder. I presumed the striker to be Lucas, as I heard his voice next:

"*What* did I tell you, Derek?" he said quite audibly. "If he's already seen us, no point in trying to whisper any-fuckin'-more!"

"But you never said that, Lucas," Derek moaned; and when they finally revealed themselves—both dressed in T-shirts of muted earth tones, along with jeans and, as protection against the rocks in the stream bed, canvas sneakers of some inexpensive variety—I could see that the taller boy was indeed rubbing his shoulder, while his face tightened in pain. His nearly black hair was shorter and more neatly cut than Lucas' raggedly shorn mop of light brown; and this confirmed the impression that, despite his size, he was accustomed to following his friend's lead and orders, even when he didn't much like the results.

Derek led the way up and out of the rocks, lumbering along so fearfully that, once they were past the trees and in the open grass, Lucas pulled ahead of him quickly and impatiently, plainly not wanting to give the impression that he was hiding behind his large but timid friend. Then, too, it seemed to me that he was also taking a protective stance, in much the way Marcianna had for me: almost as if there was some weakness in the larger boy of which the smaller wanted to make certain I did not try to take advantage. I knew, of course, what was causing the apprehension in their faces; indeed, I knew only too well what kind of rumors about Marcianna and me circulated in the gossip-ridden town of Surrender: *the freak and his wild beast from across the seas* . . . Whether on a dare or out of simple boyish curiosity, these two were now seeing what they had almost certainly come to see; it was up to me to play my part, next.

Little did I realize how much more complicated things were about to get . . .

{ii.}

"Surely you've seen a prosthetic leg before," I called to the two interlopers, reeling in Marcianna's leash, stroking her back, then feeding her a few more of the dog treats in an attempt to calm her down.

Both boys looked puzzled, but Lucas appeared less utterly overwhelmed by the situation. "What the fu-*uh-uh*—" he started, apparently not wanting to pepper our first conversation with the kind of language I'd already heard him use liberally. "Maybe," he said; and there was an air of game defiance in the way he stood up to me that I found immediately appealing. "But what's the deal with the cheetah?"

"What?" I asked. "You mean my *rare African hunting dog*?"

Derek became very uneasy. "Listen, mister, we ain't lookin' for trouble. We was just fishing in the brook, and kinda wandered up too far—so if you say it's a dog, then—"

He stopped when he caught sight of his shorter friend angrily scowling back at him. But there was an ingenuousness about Derek's manner and voice that was as poignant, in its way, as Lucas' quick, spirited wit was appealing, for it indicated not only a gentleness of manner, but a deliberateness of thinking that went very much beyond the usual plodding mind. He was obviously, as people in Burgoyne County liked to put it, "slow," although there were no physical signs that would have offered an immediate explanation for it.

"You wanna let me handle this? *Derek?*" Lucas spoke firmly, but using what must have been, for him, great restraint. "*Thank* you." He turned to me once more. "Don't pay him any mind, mister. Once he starts talking he'll take your ear clean off—"

"*Me?*" Derek could not help but say. "You're the one who's always runnin' your—"

"I'm *handling* it, Derek!" Lucas called without turning, his eyes rolling toward the heavens in frustration. With his friend silenced once more, he continued: "Anyway—"

But their loud exchange had been enough to renew Marcianna's deepest alarm: she yanked a length of leash loose from its spool as she jumped forward a few feet, raising her hackles again and issuing another of her hissing, barking sounds.

Both of the boys paled. "Whoa!" Lucas noised, although quietly: he'd already learned to mute his outbursts, so that they did not further provoke Marcianna. "Mister, we swear, we ain't gonna tell nobody about the cheetah—"

Eyeing them once again, and deciding they meant what they said, I nodded and pronounced, "All right, then. Let's say it is a cheetah. Just for argument's sake." I offered no elaboration, although they seemed to want such.

"Pretty—pretty weird to find a cheetah in Death's Head Hollow," Lucas went on; and I again had to admire the way he blended nervy curiosity into a harmless comment. "That is . . ." He quickly turned to his left and right, glimpsing what he could of the surrounding grounds and trees. "If you can really call anything 'weird,' up here . . ."

I rewound the leash, and Marcianna came back to my side. "So you've heard stories about 'up here,' have you?"

Derek answered, again without thinking: "Well, sure, who *ain't* heard stories about up here, people tell 'em all the—" Just the sight of Lucas' free hand balling into a fist was enough to make him cut his statement short: "All the time," he finished quickly.

"Do they," I said, with as little trace of interest or sympathy as I could display.

"Oh, not insulting or anything," Lucas rushed to say, with transparent insincerity. "It's just that—you know, people talk."

"Indeed they do," I agreed. "Now—would you mind telling me why I shouldn't have the sheriff's deputy take you down to your parents? You're trespassing, after all."

"But we didn't know we was!" Derek blurted out.

Lucas didn't snap at his friend again, but seemed on the verge of laughing, for some reason. "And if the deputy can find any of our parents, he'll be doing pretty good," he said.

"What is that supposed to mean?" I studied them both carefully, trying my best to look, for just an instant, like the monster they had expected me to be. "Remember, if I should allow my sister, here, to indulge herself by tearing out your throats, I could bury you deep in the hollow, in a spot where no one would ever find you."

Derek's free hand went quickly to his neck, and he looked momentarily terrified. "Aw, *shit*," he blurted out, as if he might burst into tears.

"You don't want to do that!" Lucas said, quickly, urgently, but still quietly. "I didn't mean any disrespect—it's just that we don't live with our parents. Haven't for a while—and we got no idea where they are."

"Indeed?" I replied; and for an instant, I thought of the two children whose murders had preceded Shelby Capamagio's, one of whom, like Shelby, had been abandoned by his family months before his death. "And who do you live with, then?"

"Well, technically, my sister's our guardian," Lucas explained, his mind and mouth still moving with commendable speed. "But that's just technically."

"'Technically'?" I repeated. "You're obviously not brothers."

"No, we ain't," the two said as one, in a manner that might have suggested that they were in fact related, had they not been stamped with such different physical attributes. "No more'n that cheetah, there's, your actual sister," Lucas continued, in that same manner of his: deftly slipping defiance into a plain statement of fact. "But *my* sister, she's our guardian—both of us. See—well, actually, it's kind of a long story."

"I don't doubt it," I said. "Nor do I doubt that it's a terribly interesting one. But you see, I'm fairly busy." I pulled my watch from my vest and popped it open, the archaic nature of the action seeming to further suggest to my two guests that I had indeed walked out of some old horror movie. "So maybe I should just call the deputy, eh? Being as I don't seem to be able to get a straight answer to any of my questions—" But then a thought—an idea, I should say—shot through me, causing a moment of professional encouragement; and I shifted the direction of my inquiries with a speed to match it: "Shouldn't you both be in school?" I asked; for most of the public schools in the area operated year-round, in an effort to meet the needs of their burgeoning student bodies. "I'm taking a wild guess, of course, but I assume you're both in some kind of summer session—we could add truancy to trespassing, I happen to know that it would make the deputy come all the quicker."

Lucas' face screwed up in discomfort; but he wasn't finished with his attempt to talk his own and Derek's way out of their predicament: "Now, see, you just don't have to go there, there's a simple explanation for that, too."

"Is there?" I questioned.

"Yeah, *is* there?" Derek echoed, again without thinking.

Lucas' face winced in irritation once more. "Yes. There is. *Derek.*" He directed his words my way again. "See, we got out early today, and figured we'd get some fishing in before supper. That's all. And then, we just lost track of how far we come up the brook. And that really is the whole story."

"Somehow I doubt that." My earlier thought kept me pressing on. "And what school is it that released you early to go trespassing on other people's property? Especially up a hollow you've heard so many apparently unpleasant stories about."

"Morgan Central," Lucas answered. "The one that's up 34, before you hit Route 7. We're in the tenth grade—you can check."

But his answer was the one I had been looking for, and I let my tone grow suddenly less stern. "Why in God's name would I want to take the time to check?" I said. "Morgan Central, eh? Well—for reasons that I cannot immediately disclose, that may be useful to me."

"Useful?" Lucas said, rightly suspecting that an avenue of escape from their predicament was opening up.

"Yes," I replied. "Did either of you happen to know a boy who went to your school, but was found dead in an abandoned house this past spring? He was about your age."

Both of them nodded quickly, as Lucas answered, "Sure—Kyle Howard. He was in our class."

"Aw, shit," Derek moaned, studying first Marcianna and then me with even deeper dread. "That wasn't you and her, was it? You two didn't kill Kyle?"

"Derek," Lucas said; but his tone was so even, now, that it approached sympathy: for he seemed to know that this discussion might cause his larger, very sensitive, but clearly confused friend to lose control of his emotions. "Nobody knows what happened to Kyle, remember? They found him over past town, in that old cabin, used to belong to Mr. McNair. Kyle used it all the time during hunting season, you *know* that."

Derek faced downward, as if the ground itself might offer him assistance, then at last, his face filled with comprehension. "Oh, yeah," he said. "But people say it was suspicious."

"And *you're* not supposed to listen to people—I told you, they're full of shit! They said *that*"—Lucas pointed at Marcianna—"was a *dog*, for fuck's sake!"

"Kyle had a good life until his parents left him," Derek said, his voice and mind drifting into some kind of escape mode. "It's their fault . . ."

"Yeah, it is," Lucas added calmly; and the next part of his explanation was evidently for my benefit: "Assholes just disappeared—nobody could find 'em, not the law, not nobody. Kid loved school, too, but he had to quit—didn't have any money, couldn't buy supplies nor even new clothes. The bank took the house, so he couldn't stay there—no power, heat, nothing. Had to quit school and make do for himself."

"But he was getting along okay," Derek said, still staring at the ground, his voice and eyes lost in a powerful fantasy, one that was, apparently, important to him.

"You *think* he was getting along okay, Derek," the shorter boy said, still without rancor. "But for all you know, he was living in a hollow tree, eating squirrels and nuts."

"And reading," Derek said, smiling. "Always had his books with him, I know *that* . . ."

The moment sent another quiver of inspiration down my somewhat misshapen spine. Everything the two boys were saying was true, right down to the books: Kyle Howard's body had, indeed, been found next to a satchel full of paperbacks and hardcovers. My sense of encouragement at this wholly random encounter was now easy to explain: the two trespassers before me had known the unfortunate Kyle Howard, perhaps well, and they might therefore represent the first real break in Mike's and my analysis of the three murders. But I wanted to take the exchange one step further, before I launched the plan that was forming in my head:

"Listen, you two," I said. "Forget about the deputy, and all that crap. Just answer me this: did either of you know Shelby Capamagio? The girl who was found dead just a couple of days ago? She didn't go to your school—"

"Didn't matter," Lucas answered, suddenly and rather deviously smiling. "What school she went to couldn'ta mattered less—right, Derek?"

Derek finally came out of his apparent waking dream; and, realizing just where he was and what had been said, he chuckled a bit. "Yeah," he said, his voice at once innocent and slightly conspiratorial. "Didn't matter at all. *Everybody* knew Shelby . . ."

"Did they, Derek?" I said, even more encouraged. "Why did they know her?"

Derek laughed guiltily again and mumbled, "Ah—*you know* . . ."

"Well, it ain't like everybody *knew* her, exactly," Lucas said, stepping in to clarify the two boys' reactions to Shelby's name. "But they sure as shit knew *about* her. Rumors, most of it; almost as many rumors as about—" He caught himself, appearing genuinely contrite for the first time. "Well, almost as many as about *you*—and about what goes on up here."

I was too committed to the idea I'd formed, however, to waste time taking offense. "Okay. Then listen—" Again pulling the anxious Marcianna close to me, I took a few steps toward the boys, and was pleased to see how they held their ground. "Suppose, in return for my not calling the deputy or your sister—what's her name, by the way?"

"My sister?" Lucas said, a bit confused. "Her name's Ambyr. With a *y*."

"*Ambyr?*" I repeated; and my next shot, unkind—even nasty—as it was, would be my last test to see what they were made of, and what their value to our investigation might be: "Ambyr," I said again, glancing knowingly at Lucas. "With a *y*. And how old is she?"

"She's twenty, why?"

"Well, it's just that—she makes enough money to support you two, her name's Ambyr, with a *y*, she's only twenty . . . She doesn't happen to work in the adult entertainment industry, does she?"

The reactions I got were about what I'd hoped for: Derek stepped up beside his friend, with an indignant look on his face and his hands forming fists. Lucas, meanwhile, shot me a bitter glance and spat out: "Hey, fuck you, you one-legged mutant! Don't be talking smack about my sister! She can't help how her name's spelled!"

"Yeah, mister," Derek said in support. "That's a shitty thought, and a shittier thing to say—Ambyr's *blind*, for God's sake!"

This was an utterly unexpected factor. "She's—*blind*?" I murmured, completely nonplussed and genuinely sorry for my supposedly utilitarian crack. "But—I mean to say, your *blind* sister is your guardian? *Both* of you?"

"That's right," Lucas answered. "You got a problem with it?"

I slowly took it all in: but even in the midst of my shock, I was encouraged by the fact that, in addition to having character, these boys must have become quite used to being on their own, much of the time: any absences would likely not arouse suspicion. "I guess it's *legal*," I went on. "But blind? It must have been hard to convince the state."

"There's ways around that," Lucas said. "And trust me, our parents found all of 'em. They wrote her application, and made her think she was signing something else—look, like I told you, it's a long story, and none of it's your business. We're trespassing on your property, fine, call the deputy. But get off the subject of my sister." And then he looked at Marcianna, while pointing at me bravely. "Your friend can be a fuckin' jerk, you know that, cheetah?"

Once again, I had to stifle a laugh; but I also had to put things right: "Listen, that crack about your sister, I apologize. Truly. It was intended to get a reaction, and it did."

"Fuck yeah it did," Lucas said.

"Yeah," Derek repeated. "Fuck yeah it—"

"Okay, okay," I said. "But pay attention—I'm going to tell you something important and confidential, because I get the feeling I can trust you. Am I kidding myself?"

The two boys exchanged suddenly bewildered looks. "Well," Lucas said, "I—I guess you can. As long as you're apologizing. And if you're really not gonna call the cops on us."

"I'm really not—although it wouldn't be hard. You see, I work with the cops in this county, from time to time."

"*You?*" Lucas puzzled with it. "So, what, you, like, cut dead criminals' brains up?"

"What? What the hell are you talking about?"

"Word in town is," the boy went on, "you're some kind of brain doctor, and that's what you do—cut up dead people's brains. And you got run out of *New York City*"—Lucas used the same disdainful enunciation of the name that Steve Spinetti and so many others employed—"because you cut some *live* person's head open. By mistake—or . . ."

I finally had to laugh, at that; and the laughter made me lean more heavily on my cane. "My God . . . Gentlemen, *that* would be murder; manslaughter, at the very least. And you go to a whole different part of 'upstate New York' if you commit it. I certainly wouldn't be standing in front of you two right now, if that story were true."

I could see already that they liked being called "gentlemen," and that it was defusing things: the pair looked to each other again, Derek shrugging in confusion, and Lucas finally nodding once. "Yeah—I guess so," he said. "Just one more piece of bullshit floating around Surrender. Jee-*sus*, those people need to get themselves some lives."

"A statement of rare insight," I agreed. Marcianna was beginning to bump her head and shoulders hard and then harder up against my right (or real) leg, in an expression of her growing restlessness: since these boys evidently presented no threat, she wanted to get back to the business of pretending to go after my little dog decoy and getting her praise and dog treats in return. Looking down at her, I tugged on her leash, trying to keep her from knocking me over. "I am busy, young lady, and you need to wait. Here." I put a couple of the treats into my hand and let her swiftly take them into her mouth. "And that's the last of them, so now you really *have* to wait. All right, then—" Looking up at the pair before me again, I tried to become all business; but Lucas cut me off in the attempt.

"Say, how come you have a cheetah, anyway?" he said. "Ain't that illegal?"

"I have a license," I said impatiently.

"A *license*?" Derek asked. "For a *cheetah*? What's it, on her collar?"

"It's not that kind of license. It's more of a permit. You need one, to legally own an exotic or endangered species, and so I got one."

"How come?" Lucas asked.

"Look, this really isn't what I want to discuss—"

"And I didn't want to discuss my sister—so how come you decided to get a license for a cheetah?"

"It's a long story."

"So's my sister being our guardian—didn't stop you from asking about it."

"Oh, good God," I said, frustrated both by the questions and by Marcianna's refusal to stop bumping up against my leg, which then turned into attempts to stick her face directly into my empty but fragrant jacket pocket. "Marcianna!" I tried to command, as I almost fell over. "I told you, I don't have any more—you're going to have to *wait*."

At the admittedly comical sight of nature's fastest land mammal trying to stuff her big head into my small pocket, the boys relaxed, and even started laughing a bit. "Where the hell did you ever *get* a cheetah, anyway?" Lucas said, taking a gutsy couple of steps closer to Marcianna.

"And how come you call her your *sister*?" Derek added, although he was too scared to follow his friend forward.

"That has to do with her name, and it's a long story, too." Both Derek and Lucas looked at me with expressions that said they had time enough to listen: our roles were reversing, somehow, largely because of Marcianna's suddenly clownish behavior. "I got her when the state troopers and the Humane Society raided that petting zoo off Route 22, over near Hoosick Falls."

"Oh, yeah?" Lucas said. "We used to go there, it was fun. Why'd they shut it down?"

Now very exasperated at the insistent attitudes of both my companion and the two newcomers, as well as the continuing need to keep my balance, I said, "Okay—one more answer, and then we're moving on: they closed it down because when the cute little animals got too big for you kids to pet, they would lock them up in filthy cages and pretty much torture them until they could sell them off, illegally, to private owners, who usually kept them in even worse conditions. So, after I, along with several other people, brought the conditions to the state's attention, they shut them down, and placed the animals in good homes. Refuges, where they would have room to run and get proper care."

Lucas again looked around at the parts of the farm he could see. "Yeah? So, what, you run some kind of animal shelter up here?"

"Seriously," I said, "*one* more answer: no, I don't run some kind of shelter. Nobody would take Marcianna, because she had a disease. A bad one." My inquisitor took a sudden step back. "No, it's nothing you can catch, don't worry."

"What is it, then?"

Sighing at how badly I was losing this information war, I said, "Feline leukemia—only other cats can get it. So she'd been kept by herself, in a particularly nasty little cage, and treated extra badly. Even after we raided them, no sanctuary wanted her, because of the risk. They were going to put her down, but I offered to take her on instead. And no, she's not sick now, and she's not dying, and that's not how I lost my leg, if that's what you're thinking. She has an immune system that manages to keep the virus in remission, so long as she's looked after correctly. Which most people won't do, because it's expensive. That about cover it?"

Both boys nodded quickly, and Lucas pronounced, "Okay, okay. You don't need to get all riled up about it. We were just curious."

"And you've had your explanation. Now—how about you listen to my business proposal?" The pair paused, glancing at each other again; but Derek shook his head quickly.

"I—I don't think so, mister," he said, already pulling away. "I got too much to do."

"You ain't got nothin' to do, Derek," Lucas declared. "But if it freaks you out—"

"It don't freak me out, Luke," the larger boy answered, moving off toward the hollow road. "But I *do* have stuff I gotta do. Plus I don't think Ambyr'd want us getting into anything up here. You can stay, if you want, but—I gotta get back to school."

"What the fuck you gotta do at school?" Lucas said, looking just a little uneasy at the prospect of being left alone with Marcianna and me, but obviously intrigued at the notion of some kind of job in Death's Head Hollow.

"You don't know everything, Lucas," Derek declared. "Besides, we don't even know this guy! He could be a—a—"

"How's he gonna be 'a—a—'?" Lucas mimicked. "He ain't even got two legs!"

But such did not put Derek at ease: "Well, anyway—I say I got things to do. So I'm just gonna head back down to town, and I promise I won't trespass up here again."

I would have rathered they both stay, if only for secrecy's sake; but I also didn't want to push the obviously unnerved and confused kid into a corner. "That's all right, Derek," I said amiably. "But I have to ask that you don't tell anybody about Lucas sticking around."

"Not even Ambyr?" he asked, still backpedaling toward the road.

"*Especially* not Ambyr!" Lucas answered for me. "Don't you snitch, Derek, I swear, I'll—"

"I won't, Luke, I won't!" the older boy said, now very anxious and turning to make his escape at a faster pace. "But I—I gotta go, I got things to do!" And with that final iteration of his desperate excuse, he gained the road and was off down it, moving at a quick pace. "I'll see you at home for supper," he called when he was about to vanish from sight. "And don't be late, you know what Ambyr'll say if you are!"

"She won't say anything, Derek," Lucas shouted to his friend, "if you just tell her I stayed behind to do some more fishing! Right?"

"Okay, okay!" Derek called; and after that, he quickly disappeared. His decision to leave seemed without deeper meaning, then; but I would soon be given sound reason to reassess it.

{iii.}

Lucas turned back toward me, a little uneasily. "Derek's—he's all right. Just gets that way. You probably noticed, he ain't exactly . . ."

"I noticed," I said, accepting the fact that I would only be able to try my luck with the one of them, and pleased that, if it did have to be just one, it would be the more emotionally steady of the two. "And that's fine. I'm not *drafting* anybody. Besides, he's right about one thing—you don't know me, I *could* be a threat." I gave him a second before adding: "One leg and all . . ."

Lucas smiled self-consciously, scratching at his rough-cut hair. "Oh. Yeah, sorry about that. I was just trying to get him to stick around. But you don't seem like the type to be a *threat*. And I seen 'em." I found his reliance on his own correct perception, in addition to his self-confidence, even more of an encouragement. "So—what's this 'business proposal' you got?"

I regained my stability, now that Marcianna had finally given up trying to get more dog treats out of my pocket. "Have you ever heard of another girl named Kelsey Kozersky?"

"Sure," Lucas said. "They told us that story, too, but I didn't know her. She went to West Briarwood, that was Shelby's school. But she wasn't— well, she didn't get around like Shelby. Liked horses. She died the same way, though. 'Suspiciously.' We had a special assembly. I guess after they found Kyle, the whole school system was afraid we were *all* gonna wind up dead."

"Predictable," I replied, pointing with my cane toward the gateway of the little clearing and starting toward it. Lucas made sure to stay on my left side, as Marcianna fell in on my right. "But you see, Lucas, there's some question, as far as the law is concerned, about just what *did* happen to those three kids. The investigations are still officially open, though nobody's supposed to know that. My partner and I have been brought in as—*advisors,* you might say."

"Oh?" the boy noised. "So you're working the case with the sheriff and them?"

"With the sheriff, yes, but not the rest of them. That's confidential, too. And it occurs to me that we could use what you might call an expert advisor of our own."

Lucas grew ever more intrigued, plainly liking the sound of *expert advisor.* But he wasn't yet entirely convinced: "'We'?" he asked. "Who's this partner of yours?"

"An expert in trace analysis—do you know what that is?"

"Sure," Lucas said proudly. "I'm studying forensic science in school."

The statement was enough to stop me dead in my tracks. "You're *what?*"

"Studying forensic science," the kid answered simply. "One of the science teachers, he does a middle school and then a high school course on it. I got in, no problem—see, I've always been into that kinda stuff. I used to watch *CSI,* and alla them shows, before they got canceled, I mean. But I still watch the reruns."

This was bad news on top of a wholly mysterious statement: although I knew that some schools downstate had begun to teach courses in forensics as a way to get young kids interested in science, I had no idea that the practice had spread so far north, much less to a school like Morgan Central, where the student body struggled simply to maintain a steady, rather than precipitous, rate of decline in their annual test scores. Both of Lucas' revelations required deeper discussion; but the second, which he had intended as proof of his competence, was the more dangerous.

"Listen, Lucas," I said, as we made our way through the gateway. "I want to hear more about your course at school—but the first thing you're going to have to do, if you want this job, is forget anything you ever saw on *CSI,* or on *Criminal Minds* and the rest of those shows that are still on. Stop watching reruns, even. They've got nothing to do with real investigations."

"*Whaaat?*" the kid droned, skeptical of this notion. "What're you talking about, I thought they showed what really goes on! They got all that up-to-date equipment, and experts, and—"

"Fantasy-land, Lucas," I said. "As you'll find out soon enough. Just try bringing it up with Mike—that's my partner—and see how he reacts."

"Well—if that's not how it really works . . ." The boy was struggling with the same preconceptions that had been put into the heads of so much of the American public—and worst of all, American jurors—by television producers who didn't care how much damage they did. "Then why does our teacher assign those shows as part of our homework?"

"Because he's probably never observed a real investigation," I replied, not wanting to openly insult the teacher of a course that Lucas plainly liked. "If he had, he'd know better."

"But—it's true that he's just my tenth-grade science teacher, not an ex-cop, or anything. But if that's not how it really works—well, then, how the hell *does* it really work?" He kicked at the ground of Death's Head Hollow as we crossed it, in a way that suggested, at least to my eyes, that he suspected he'd been had by his school as well as by television, and didn't care for it one bit.

"You're about to find out how it really works," I answered. "But remember—you're going to have to keep everything you hear and see to yourself. In return, I'll make sure nobody knows you're coming up here."

"Just make sure my sister doesn't know," Lucas answered. "She'll tear me a whole new one, if she finds out."

"She won't," I said. "There's too much riding on it. And so—what do you say? Are you ready to become a true consulting detective on a real case? I think I can guarantee it'll be far more educational than what you've *been* learning."

"A 'consulting detective'—you mean, like Sherlock Holmes?" The boy's game attitude returned in full: "And don't try to tell me Sherlock *Holmes* was full of it—because he is the *shit*."

"You've read the actual Holmes stories?" I queried, surprised.

"Yeah," he said proudly. "I read 'em all the time."

"Well, then, we can agree on one thing, anyway—he is, indeed, the shit. Although I doubt your teacher thinks to assign *those* as homework."

"Nope. I read 'em on my own," Lucas said. "Gives me a jump on the other kids."

"Indeed—if you are listening to Arthur Conan Doyle, instead of to the TV shows you've been watching, never mind whatever actual books this science teacher assigns, then you would certainly have a jump on most kids here. Most kids anywhere, for that matter."

Lucas puffed himself up again, though not obnoxiously. "You know, those shows, they're entertaining enough; but I always *did* kind of wonder about some things that happen in 'em . . ."

"As well you should," I replied. "Because that kind of 'entertainment'— and that's really all it is, Lucas—has done more damage to real criminal investigation in this country than almost anything in history. As you'll discover. So—what do you say?"

"Well . . ." Lucas' characteristic confidence seemed to waver a bit. "I'm just not sure how much good I can do. On an *actual* case, I mean."

I had been given two more things to admire about the kid: he had sought out a sound fictional model for his detective ambitions in Sherlock Holmes, and his mind was adapting to the realities of his present situation, rather than insisting on the validity of the television-based tripe he'd seen and evidently studied. "Trust me. You're going to do fine—"

At that instant—and I cannot help but think, looking back, that it was a sign, of sorts—the small black book that I had forgotten I was carrying fell to the ground from my left-hand jacket pocket. Lucas saw it immediately and, realizing that I had no free hand, picked it up. "Hey, you dropped your—" Studying the thing, his face grew puzzled. "Book? Or whatever the hell it is."

"It's a journal," I replied, allowing him to leaf through the thing, so long as he was careful with it. "Haven't you ever seen a journal?"

"It ain't *your* journal, though," Lucas said, making the kind of sour face that the young often do, when faced with something very old. "Been around a while."

"Indeed," I answered. "Almost a century."

"Yeah? So whose was it, originally?"

"It belonged to an early psychiatrist," I answered, taking the journal from him. "One who was vital to the history of criminal investigation. Although most people don't know his name."

"Well—he couldn't've been *that* important, then, could he?" Lucas meant the question honestly, not as a challenge, and I treated it as such.

"Yes. He could have. But I'll explain that story to you, as well." I caught the boy eyeing my companion somewhat nervously again as I replaced the volume in my pocket. "Don't get jumpy, Lucas. Marcianna might even like you, once she gets to know you."

"Yeah? O-*kay* . . ." Lucas allowed himself a slight smile, again betraying his actual youth. "You know—she's kinda cute, once you stop thinking she's gonna eat you."

"You don't know the half of it," I answered. "Now let's get up to where we do our work, and you can begin telling us everything you know about those three dead kids."

Lucas' steps started to fall faster and more easily; and I began to feel much better about trusting my instinct that here, at last, was the break in the case that Mike and I needed so badly . . .

Although it plainly wouldn't come without its own form of expense. As he grew more comfortable with the idea of being in Death's Head Hollow, and as he caught sight of the farmhouse ahead, Lucas brightened, already aware that he was going to have an inside track on things that had been topics of discussion in Surrender for longer than he'd been alive:

"Say—" He caught himself in mid-thought, and then asked, "I just thought of something—what am I supposed to *call* you, anyway?"

"For the moment, you can call me what most people do—Dr. Jones." It was my turn to look puzzled. "And, by the way—I don't know your last name, and probably should."

"Kurtz," he said. "And I guess I shoulda *deduced* that you were a Jones." He returned to his original question: "So, Doc—has anybody up here ever figured the story? You know, that one about the guy who built this place, and what he said the last time he came down to town?"

It was all I could do to keep from bursting out with an oath. "No!" I exclaimed, but with a smile. "I do not know what Colonel Jones meant when he rode to Surrender, damn it."

"*Ouch*, geez! I guess you been asked a few times, hunh?" Clearly fascinated, he pressed on: "But come on—*nobody* in your family has *ever* figured it out?"

"Nobody."

"*Seriously?*" he nearly squeaked, as we moved back across the western side of the farmhouse lawn. "All this time, and nobody *ever*—"

"Lucas," I said, trying to hide my impatience. "Have you ever been told you may have problems maintaining your focus?"

"Hey, don't *you* start—I get enough of that from my teachers. *And* my sister."

"I can just imagine," I replied, as evenly as I could.

"I'm serious!" Lucas defended. "If you're gonna start right off riding me about that—"

"I won't. But if you intend to become a detective, even a consulting detective, you will find that a certain ability to maintain your focus on one topic—"

I stopped and, defeating the lesson I was trying to teach just a bit, looked ahead to see Mike outside the JU-52's hangar, waving his arms. "Hmm," I said, controlling my own excitement. "It would appear that there's been a development."

"Who's *that*?" Lucas asked, having caught sight of Mike.

"My partner," I said. "Michael Li, also a doctor."

"*Lee?*" Lucas said. "Like the general, you mean?"

"No," I answered quickly. "I most emphatically do *not* mean like the general. *L-i*: Li."

"Oh—Chinese, hunh?"

"Chinese-American," I replied. "But do yourself a favor and don't bring that up."

"Whatever," Lucas replied blithely. "So what's he going so crazy about?"

"Well, if I had to guess, I'd say he's found something." A thought suddenly came into my head, and I quickly checked my watch. "Either that or—damn! I'm late. I've got a class to teach."

"Aw, shit," Lucas declared. "*Class?* So this *is* gonna be like school . . ."

"Don't worry," I explained. "You might even want to sit in."

"Great," the boy declared. "*School.* Wish you woulda told me that, to begin with . . ." Then Lucas' mind hopped tracks yet again: "Though I still think it's awful strange that nobody in your family's *ever*—"

"Lucas!" I countered. "Focus, kid, *focus!*"

"Hey, don't call me 'kid,'" he shot back. "All's I'm saying is . . ."

Thus did we continue our walk toward the hangar, my new colleague forcing me to wonder several times just what I had wrought by bringing him into the investigation. But in he was; and there was no turning back now. By the time we neared the barns, my great-aunt and Terence were safely back inside the house, and there'd been no unfortunate sighting as we passed its western windows that would have led to difficult questions concerning our guest. Mike, however, was a different story: as soon as he saw that I was not alone, he stopped his frenetic signaling, and simply watched in confusion as the boy and I made our way up the path to the hangar.

"Thought you weren't going to make your class, L.T.," he said, his cool manner doing little to mask his suspicions; then, studying Lucas, he added bluntly, "Who's this guy?"

"Relax, Mike," I said. "He's here to help. Meet Lucas Kurtz—I've just engaged him as a consulting member of our investigative team."

Mike studied Lucas for a brief second, saying only, "Yeah? Hey, kid." Then the rest of my statement reached his brain: "As a *what*?" he asked, stunned.

"A consulting detective," Lucas replied defiantly. "And I already told your friend, I don't answer to 'kid.' You can use my name, Dr. Li, it's what they gave it to me for."

"'*Dr. Li*'?" Mike echoed, smiling in spite of himself. "Well, I beg your pardon, Lucas—I know what it's like when people don't show the proper respect." He took the kid's measure. "So you're a 'consulting detective,' eh? Like Sherlock Holmes?"

"Exactly," Lucas replied, gladly accepting Mike's offer of mutual esteem. "Which means that—whoa, *shit*!" He had suddenly caught sight of the nose of the JU-52 presiding over the scene. "Sick . . . Completely *sick*! What in the fuck *is* it?"

I had forgotten, during a lifetime of familiarity, just how imposing and impressive the image of the plane could be, especially to a boy of Lucas' age; and, heading just inside the hangar to fetch another slab of beef from a refrigerator-freezer that sat on the concrete floor, I said, "That is the Junkers JU-52/3m, Lucas—one of history's great airplanes." I put the beef into a microwave that occupied an old table next to the freezer, then set the machine to run for long enough to defrost the meat and heat the blood in the package. "It was brought here from Germany by my great-grandfather," I went on. "Right after it was built, in 1935: rescued, as it were, from Nazi use. And now it does noble service as our headquarters."

"No shit . . ." Lucas began to move toward the plane with careful steps, full of wonder. "What, he flew it all in one go? I thought planes didn't have that kind of range, back then."

"Some did," I answered. "But not the JU-52. So, from Europe he flew her south to Africa, then crated her up on a freighter, shipped her to Brazil, and flew her up here."

"Oh, I get it!" the kid said with a delighted smile. "So you guys, like, fly around in it, when you're on a case?"

"Afraid not, Lucas," Mike answered, watching the newcomer. "Dr. Jones' ancestor, being a genius like the rest of his family, took the secrets of how to maintain and run it to his grave."

"We could probably get her going, if we needed to," I retorted. "But its real purpose now is to offer secrecy, instead of transport."

"Well—*that* sucks," Lucas said, his steps becoming more certain as he got a small, good-natured chuckle out of Mike. "But I guess it *is* just about the last place anybody'd come looking for you. Nobody around here'd think of it, anyway . . ."

"Michael," I said, pulling the beef from the microwave as the appliance chimed, "why don't you show Lucas around, while I take Marcianna back up and feed her?"

"Uh, yeah, sure thing, L.T.," Mike said casually; then he caught my eye, adding, "First, though, I've got one or two messages from the university to relay—and you really do have to be ready to teach soon. If I gotta do it, so do you." He turned to the newcomer. "Lucas, just hang on a second, and then I'll give you the grand tour."

Still transfixed by the dulled silver of the JU-52's skin, Lucas replied, "Sure thing, Dr. Li."

"Hey, and now that we're speaking the same language," Mike added, "you can drop the 'Dr. Li' garbage. My partner likes that kind of crap—but if you're Lucas, then I'm Mike."

"Yeah?" Lucas turned for a moment, deeply appreciative that the playing field had been at least partially leveled. "Okay, Mike."

"I will remain Dr. Jones, however," I said. "A little democracy goes a long way."

At that Mike and I moved outside; and as we did his expression changed from amusement to alarm. "Have you lost your damned mind, L.T.? A *kid*? In on *this*? What is he, fifteen—?"

"Just hear me out, Mike," I replied; and as quickly as possible I explained Lucas' qualifications, assuring Mike that the kid's involvement did not have to be particularly deep, but could still prove crucial, given both what he knew and his ability to move in worlds that we could at best visit under a cloud of suspicion.

"Well," Mike judged, after listening to this defense. "Maybe. Just as long as you're sure we're not going to put him in any kind of danger. He gets hurt doing what we ask, and I don't have to tell you, it'll be Christmas for everybody who wants us nowhere near this investigation. Not to mention the media, they'll get out the fucking long knives."

"I know, Mike—but talk to the kid. He's sharp, he knows what's going on in this county, and I really don't think we have to worry about him."

Mike shrugged at that, accepting what was already, so far as I was concerned, a *fait accompli*. "You're the boss," he said at length, scratching his head.

"Bullshit I am. But on this, I'm right. Now, then—what were you going so batshit about a few minutes ago?"

"Oh." Mike tried hard to switch gears. "Some things about the girl—Shelby—don't line up, like I figured. I'm still researching it, but—it could be something solid."

"Well, try Lucas on that. Apparently Shelby had quite a reputation in the county, and he knows a few things about her."

"Yeah?" For the first time, Mike began to see the point of my having brought the intrepid young man onto our team. "Well, maybe I *will* ask him . . ." Heading into the hangar, he called, "Okay, Lucas—let's get you aboard and show you around . . ."

I guided Marcianna back up to her enclosure, meanwhile, and performed the evening's chores, filling her dinner with the same soluble tablets I had given her earlier: supplements that, her vet had long ago assured me, could help keep her immune system powerful enough to hold all strains of leukemia at bay, and give her something like a normal life span. Then I watched her eat and lingered in the enclosure a few extra minutes, knowing that she required this attention to keep her calm until I returned later that night. But her full belly soon made her begin to roll and loll about in the enclosure's grass, which was generally the signal that I could depart; and so I locked her gate up tight and went back down the hill to the hangar.

When I got there, I could hear Mike's and Lucas' voices echoing from within the plane, the boy's questions and declarations reflecting his increased excitement at finding what must have been to him a dream world of modern investigative techniques inside an already astonishing, secret space to which he'd been admitted as a privileged member. I wasn't surprised: at his age, when my own cancer had kept me away from the normal activities that a young man should enjoy with his peers, both my great-aunt's farm and the old JU-52 had been wonderlands where, during weekends and vacations, I had retreated from the unkindnesses of both my immediate family and my schoolmates into a universe where I fancied myself not only the equal but the superior of the average, two-legged youth. Knowing at least the rough circumstances of Lucas' own life, I could readily imagine what he must have been feeling at having the run of a machine that, though long since grounded, still emanated power and command. And, sure enough, once inside the plane, I caught sight of the kid's quick form darting back and forth from the equipment that Mike and I had installed for our teaching and investigative work to the intact controls of the JU-52's cockpit: the most exciting feature of the plane, and intact in every detail, from its multi-paned, panoramic wind-shield right down to my great-grandfather's pair of leather and fleece flight jackets and sets of radio headgear. Sympathetic as I was to his excitement, however, I knew that we had to get his wildly firing brain under control; so I immediately took on the air of the teacher that I would momentarily have to become for my actual students.

"All right, Lucas," I called. "Plenty of time for that later. Right now I'd like you to take the"—I checked my watch yet again and frowned—"damn, the five minutes or so we have until my class begins to acquaint yourself with a few basic concepts, so you can follow the talk."

"Already done, L.T.," Mike said, stepping out from behind the black backdrop that separated our working area from the classroom and indicating one of the several desks at his work station, which ran aft from the bulkhead of the cockpit. "I've given Lucas the basic gist of your 'Context' course, and cleared a space for him to take some notes."

"But don't expect me to do much of *that!*" Resplendent in a flight jacket that was much too big for him, with headphones and attached mouthpiece around his neck and goggles on his forehead, Lucas was in the pilot's seat, and he jerked a thumb back at the desk Mike had some-how managed to free of some of his clutter. "I can keep it all locked up right here," the boy went on, tapping on his temple. "Just like Mr. Holmes. And I wanna see how this whole college-by-TV system works, L.T." At a mindful glance from me, the boy corrected himself wearily. "*Dr. Jones.* Hey, how come those initials bug you, anyway?"

"Who says they bug me?" I asked, collecting a group of papers from my own desk, which was beside the open hatch.

"Mike does," Lucas answered simply. "So what's the deal?"

I looked at my partner. "Just couldn't resist, could you, Michael?"

"Hey," Mike said, moving beyond the cloth screen and switching on the video monitors, then making sure the computer that handled them from the instructor's desk was powered up. "You wanted the kid—the young man—to feel at home, bud."

"Unh-hunh . . ." I drew aside the partition and sat at the desk. "It's entirely unnecessary for you to know why I object to those initials, Lucas—"

"But they *are* yours, right?" the kid interjected. "Dr. *Levon Trajan Jones*?"

"That is not the issue at hand!" I called out, waiting for my students to check in on the screens before me. "Suppose you just tell me what my communist associate has taught you about 'The Theory of Context'?"

"'*Communist*'?" Lucas echoed. "Hey, look, even *I* know the Chinese ain't really communists, anymore—"

"And I am not Chinese!" Mike bellowed. "My family came here in—"

"All right, all right, let's just knock it off," I answered. "If we can quit being entirely childish before our paying students log in, we may just be able to preserve the illusion that we know what we're doing. Now, then, Lucas: three minutes, 'The Theory of Context'—go."

Lucas launched into an explanation that was clearly an effort to prove that he was qualified to join our team: "The Theory of Context has to do with making sure that every case and every suspect *in* a case is treated individually, so that you build your conclusions about all the events and all the—the, whatever, all the circumstances—of a crime, and about the suspects, too, in their own particular *context,* and don't just let the kind of statistics that crime scene investigators normally use make you decide which things to pay attention to. Like, for example, just because eighty percent of my school can't pass the standardized tests they give us every year doesn't mean that, if you meet a kid from my school, he *must* be an idiot. You just don't—" His brain was working hard, I was gratified to see, at mastering the concept. "You just don't decide who's the most likely suspect *first,* based on statistics and past cases, then pick your evidence to match that one suspect. You look at *every* suspect, and figure what each one *usually* acts like, then let all the evidence lead you in the right direction. Because somebody might *seem* weird or suspicious, but in the context of his usual life, the way he does things might not be *incriminating* at all. Like that."

I was impressed to hear that the statement, even if abbreviated and slightly jumbled, was only minimally dosed with language that he'd clearly picked up from television. "Very good," I pronounced. "Very good, indeed, Lucas."

"And if you want to know how this 'Context' stuff all got started," he went on proudly, "it was the dude who wrote that weird book that fell outta your pocket before."

"Whose name was—?"

Lucas paused for an instant, then called, "Doctor—Doctor—" He'd clearly forgotten; but then Mike whispered something and he shouted, "Dr. Laszlo Chrysler!"

"*Kreizler*," I replied, calmly and carefully. "Put a *t* before the *z* when you pronounce it. And I heard you, by the way, Michael."

"Give the kid a break, L.T.," Mike answered. "He got the important part. Pretty much."

"Pretty much?" Lucas cried indignantly. "I *nailed* it, you two assho—"

"*Class is in session!*" I declared, silencing further nonsense as the screens in front of me filled with large squares, each containing the face of one of the SUNY-Online students enrolled in my "Theory of Context" course. Michael got Lucas calmed down while I dimmed the lights and greeted the dozen or so participants who had shown up for the session. The space before me darkened and transformed into the rather other-worldly and uniquely intimate arena that from the first had surprised me with its capacity to offer an exciting learning environment. Yet there were greater reasons for the charge I felt as I readied myself for that evening's lesson: for this would be the first time that Mike and I would be part of an active murder investigation while conducting our courses, thus giving their subject matter special immediacy. And I, in particular, had the en-couragement of both a new source of information concerning the case— Lucas—as well as Mike hard at work on what he believed would be his own breakthrough. In short, while I was teaching truly life-and-death concepts inside the JU-52, future lives and deaths would actually be hanging in the balance in the world immediately around us; and so I would have to try hard to focus on my students without letting my con-centration drift too often toward what was transpiring beyond the back-drop just behind me, shielding those same pupils from the terribly nonacademic application of the principles they would be discussing. A great challenge, to be sure—and one that, I quickly found, Lucas had no intention of making any easier.

{iv.}

A good half-dozen students were missing from the class, a fact that demanded quick comment from me: "I will remind you all that the time zone differences which affect some of you won't be considered legitimate excuses for absenteeism." In fact, Mike and I took it as a compliment that we had enrollees from all over the country; but when seated at the desk, the taskmaster in me had to take over—gently, if possible, but always pointedly.

Our video system was so constructed that each of the students could see not only my face but those of their classmates on their computers (albeit in much smaller scale than Mike and I had designed to appear across our three huge screens); and a look of partial but still commendable embarrassment filled the expressions of the members present upon their realization of just how many of their number were absent. Most of the class, in keeping with the current national enrollment in all aspects of the criminal sciences, was made up of women. But it was one of the men present—an often annoying yet somehow appealing twenty-five-year-old, raised on my own home island of Manhattan but now residing, at his wealthy parents' expense, in the dormitory for such people that the borough of Brooklyn had become—to chirp up with:

"Well, it *is* a Friday night, Dr. Jones."

"Thank you for stating the obvious, Andrew," I answered. "But in this classroom, we operate not by Eastern Trust Fund Time, but by Eastern Daylight Time, according to which it is only Friday *evening*. In addition, as you will recall, Dr. Li and I agreed to teach this extra session of courses because of demand, not because our own lives are so impoverished that we needed to spend our summer days and twilights basking in the glow of your eager faces."

"Just shut up, Andrew," murmured one of the better students in the class, a black woman in her early thirties named Linda, behind whose impressive if intense features could be seen a window that displayed a view of a housing project in the Bronx.

Andrew attempted to defend himself: "All I'm saying is—"

"Andrew, just put a lid on it!" declared yet another voice, which belonged to one of the class' younger members, a girl from Tennessee named Amy, whose delicate features belied quite a forceful personality. "You're wasting time."

"Precisely, Amy," I said. "Now—when we left off last time—"

Suddenly I heard Lucas' voice float over the partition: "That Andrew dude is gonna get his ass an *F!*" he laughed, drawing an immediate but amused shushing sound from Mike.

"*Who said that?*" Andrew demanded, glancing quickly about his computer screen.

"Nobody said that," I declared, without, I hoped, missing a beat. "It was your conscience, Andrew, telling you that you truly are wasting time." Cutting off his attempt to protest further, I said quickly, "Now, then—last time we were talking about how much attaching the forensic sciences to law enforcement agencies at the beginning of the twentieth century weakened the ability of early criminal investigators to apply The Theory of Context with real force. Remind us, Andrew, why this was so."

As the rest of the class tried to suppress smiles of satisfaction, Andrew grimaced uneasily and answered, "Because criminal scientists lost their independence, and began to bend their findings in a strictly prosecutorial direction."

"Not right away, Andrew," Linda said. "There was a period of give-and-take."

"Indeed, Linda," I judged. "Although that period was not quite as long as most think. The shift to a prosecutorial bent by criminal scientists in fact occurred fairly quickly, forcing Context, in its formal sense, more and more into the hands of relatively few criminal psychologists. In fact, by the early Nineteen-twenties . . ."

The class proceeded in like manner for the first forty-five minutes, after which we took a five-minute break, one that permitted me to retreat behind the black partition and fix a firm scowl on Lucas, who was already holding up his hands.

"I'm sorry, I'm sorry!" he whispered. "I didn't think they could hear me!"

I tried to maintain my arch attitude; but Lucas now had the flight goggles over his eyes, and was a pretty comical sight. "You somehow figured that this piece of fabric is soundproof?" I whispered back, slapping at the partition. "No more of that, Lucas; we'll get to *you* soon enough. Meanwhile, it's important that you listen to and absorb the discussion in this class. Check?"

"Check, got it," Lucas murmured. Then, as I began to turn away, he lifted the goggles back onto his forehead, and nudged Mike, who was working feverishly at his computer. "Kind of a hard-ass, ain't he?" the kid whispered.

Michael busted up, causing me to spin back around and lift a finger to the both of them. "I'm not kidding, you two—*knock it off*." But I couldn't suppress a slight smile of my own, as I grabbed a bottle of water from a nearby case and went back behind the partition.

"Now then," I said, retaking my seat, opening my water, and suddenly noticing that an additional two faces had appeared on the screens: a tough but handsome and amiable young mestizo man from southern Arizona called Frankie, as well as a classic Californian blonde in her mid-twenties named Vicky, who was in fact one of the smartest students I had. "I see the Southwestern contingent has decided to join us—does that really mean we have to discuss the irrelevance of time zones to attendance once again?"

"*No es mi culpa,* Doctor," Frankie said, although his English was fine. "I got profiled on my way home—bastards searched my whole damned car."

"If true, Frankie," I said, agreeably enough, "then I apologize for the white race. If untrue, points for inventiveness. Vicky?"

"Can't beat that," she replied a bit sheepishly, in a voice roughened by liquor and cigarettes. "Unless you'd like to count being profiled by God for getting drunk last night."

That brought some soft laughter from the others, and I chuckled, myself. "Afraid not," I replied. "But we will let this one go as a warning. All right—we had been discussing the erosion of Context due to the attachment of independent criminal science to law enforcement, and the creation thereafter of *forensic* science. The subsequent dominance of statistical rather than contextual analysis has been covered, as well, a rise that was soon cemented by what evil tool, again?"

"The computer," said an unusually soft-spoken young woman from Boston, Colleen, who was moving straight from her undergraduate work into graduate studies, after having won an internship with the BPD's Crime Lab Unit, during which she witnessed several large-scale scandals involving techs tampering with evidence in order to increase conviction rates. She generally hung back in discussions, although I would have preferred her to speak up more; for she had much to tell, as I had learned during one-on-one sessions concerning her papers and grades.

"Thank you, Colleen," I said. "Anybody else care to add anything to my summary?"

"Well," Vicky said, still a bit embarrassed, "you may have already gone over it, but there's the twisting of profiling itself: an emphasis on those behavioral elements that indicated abnormal or criminal activities, and the interpretation of innocent or even exculpatory behavior as fitting a criminal pattern, because the context of the subject's ordinary behavior was ignored."

"Indeed," I answered, admiring the young woman's ability to jump into a discussion midstream and sound like she'd been there all along, which was why I'd forgiven her being late. "Thus we have the twin evils of the failure of criminal science to remain independent—to retain what Conan Doyle rightly saw as the virtues of a *consulting* position: first, gathering evidence began to be taught and learned as a way to find and emphasize only those physical traces that would serve the cause of establishing a favored or simply an obvious suspect's guilt—"

"Now, hang on, Doctor," Andrew said, at which the other students groaned. Andrew was good-natured enough to smile at the others' objections, yet enough of a pain in the ass to press forward: "Seriously, I think I have a legitimate question—"

"*I* got one," Frankie murmured, in his most entertaining *cholo* accent. "How the fuck did *choo* ever get into *theess* class, *wedo*?" The groans from the rest of the group turned to laughter: a lucky thing, because it covered another round of irrepressible amusement from Lucas and Mike. But Andrew, although he was laughing at being the butt of the joke, was not to be denied:

"Yeah, yeah, thanks, Frankie," he said. "But I *do* wanna know: you keep talking about what a perversion it was for criminal science to become part of law enforcement, and to take on a prosecutorial bent, finding only evidence of guilt, but—I mean, what the hell is forensic science supposed to do *otherwise*?" Yet even as he asked the question, the slow dawn of comprehension crept over his features. "Oh. Yeah, okay, I think I get it."

"And what is it you think you 'get'?" I asked. "Just so that we're all sure."

"I get it, I *get* it," he repeated sheepishly. "They're not supposed to be looking for guilt. They're supposed to be looking for the truth."

" 'The truth'?" I echoed. " '*What is the truth, said jesting Pilate—*' "

" '*—and would not stay for an answer!*' " my class called out in a unified drone, having heard me voice this quote of Francis Bacon's a few too many times. Apparently.

"Indeed," I replied. "And never forget it. Let us leave troublesome, elusive truth be, Andrew, and ask criminal science only for *facts,* eh? Now—where in the hell were we?"

"You had just said," answered Colleen, the scribe of the class, as she checked her notes, "that we'd reached the twin evils caused by criminal science's attachment to law enforcement: first, um, that 'gathering evidence began to be taught and learned as a way to find and emphasize only those physical traces that would serve the cause of establishing a favored or simply an obvious suspect's guilt.' "

"Word for word, as always, Colleen, thank you," I said. "And second, there was the perhaps even more shameful drift of so many criminal psychologists in the same direction, which would eventually give the lie to names like the FBI's vaunted 'Behavioral Science Unit.' "

"Because they don't study *all* behaviors," said Amy, in her light Tennessean drawl.

"Don't now, and didn't ever," I agreed. "And by focusing their attention so strictly on criminal—and let's try to lose the word 'abnormal,' Vicky, because, horrified as it would make many of your psychology professors to hear, it's meaningless—but by focusing so strictly on criminal behaviors, such labs and their staffs have learned to find precisely what they are *trained* to find; and, worse yet, to understand what may well be innocent or even exculpatory behaviors only in their possibly incriminating contexts. Everybody up to speed? Good. And so, let's proceed to specific cases. Who's got one? We're talking about early examples, now."

"How about the Lindbergh kidnapping?" Linda offered.

"Fine," I said. "A good start. The Lindbergh kidnapping: Baby Lindy, Bruno Hauptmann, the New Jersey State Police, and Mr. J. Edgar Hoover—a nice nexus of the various subjects under discussion. Thank you, Linda . . ."

For the remaining forty minutes or so, we all discussed half a dozen early examples of the prostitution of criminal science and psychology to law enforcement, district attorneys' offices, and federal officials. I could only suppose that Mike had somehow managed to duct-tape Lucas' mouth shut, because there were no more whispers or laughs from beyond the screen. It did not occur to me that the boy might actually be engrossed in what was being said; but in this as in so many things, he was set to surprise me.

"Okay," I declared, when the class' time was almost up. "Since even Andrew has managed to grasp the concepts we've gone over today, I think we can count our blessings and end the week on a high note." A few students chuckled, but more sighed in relief beneath the sound of papers and books shuffling. "Just one more thing," I said, drawing the laptop that sat on the desk close. "I am transmitting to all of you, and to our absent members, a PDF file containing several more pages of Dr. Kreizler's final journal—the *last* few pages, actually—and I hardly need say that the same rules apply as have for the other installments: this document was only recently discovered, and it was found privately, by a colleague of mine. Therefore its use in this class should be considered confidential. Its bearing on what we've been discussing should be obvious, but I'll expect at least one written page from each of you explaining just what that relevance is by Monday afternoon." I transmitted the file with a few keypad depressions. "It'll be encrypted in the usual way, and you can use the same password. I'll see you Monday, then."

The screens before me began to go blank, and my mind immediately turned to what was going on behind me: to what I would say if Lucas and Mike were just wasting time—

But when I stepped behind the screen, I actually saw Lucas at the desk Mike had assigned him, busily if unfamiliarly scrawling notes onto a legal pad; and I don't mind saying, I was both gratified and impressed, a feeling that only increased when he looked up at me and declared:

"Hey, Doc, I get it! *CSI, Criminal Minds,* all those shows, they really *are* full of it!"

Under ordinary circumstances, I would have quit while I was ahead, as I had done with Andrew. But in Lucas' case, I felt the need for a little more proof than this one comment, which could have been uttered merely to undo the mischief that he'd caused during the session. "Oh?" I said. "And what exactly makes you say that, Lucas?"

"Well," he replied quickly, "see, on those shows, they always start by saying what the statistics of a certain kind of crime have to do with whatever suspect they've picked out, or picked up, instead of letting whatever evidence they've found give them a whole list of possible suspects, or, even better, letting it build a real profile of a suspect—one that's got to do with the *context* of the *particular* crime, not with freaking statistics. That's practically all they ever talk about, statistics! But every case has to be looked at on its own."

Such was, indeed, a minor triumph, whether of the boy's innate talent or my teaching ability or both did not matter. And, as I say, it should have been cause enough to call the evening's proceedings a complete success. But Lucas' introduction to our work had only begun; and, as he continued on to learn more, it would simultaneously become time for the flow of information to be reversed, and for him to begin telling us what *he* knew about the three deaths under consideration. That, he would do— but only after Mike, who had never stopped laboring at his computer despite all distractions, revealed his stunningly unexpected discoveries.

{v.}

"Okay, here's what I've got." Mike took up a legal pad of his own that was covered in his usual combination of scrawled bullet points and shorthand symbols that only he could read. "The X-ray, as we know, came out as we figured: a hanging, and not in the trailer. But along with that, there were, indeed, traces of a crystalline drug on Shelby's clothes, which at first I figured were probably just the meth that we'd been told she was using, and a bag of which was found next to her clothing."

"Wait," Lucas said, now wandering about the JU-52's fuselage and taking a deeper interest in the known aspects of each of the three deaths that we'd posted at various points, together with photographs of the victims. The pictures had been supplied to Steve Spinetti by the two schools the victims had attended, and were then sent to us by Pete Steinbrecher. "You're saying that the cops think Shelby was a meth head?" the kid continued dubiously.

"Not, apparently, while she lived in West Briarwood," I answered. "But they're presuming she picked up the habit, as Mike says, during the time she went missing."

"*Context*—I call it!" Lucas declared. "If that's what they think, then they didn't know much about her. Meth was *not* Shelby's deal."

"Oh?" I replied. "And what *was* Shelby's deal, then?"

"Sex!" our young expert went on, removing the flight jacket, which was causing him to sweat profusely even as the warm day turned to cooler evening. But the cockpit headgear, which seemed to give him some feeling of authority, remained in place. "That's what Derek and I meant before, when we said that everybody knew about Shelby."

"Oh, yeah?" Mike inquired. "Got around with the boys, did she?"

"Some boys, maybe," Lucas replied, "but that wasn't the big story about her. See, she used to come to games a lot, at our school—just when West Briarwood's teams were playing ours, at first, but then she came to almost any of our games. It was kind of weird, I mean, she had a lot of friends at Morgan, but still, you don't see a lot of girls showing up at other schools' games, unless they've got a boyfriend on one of the teams or something. But she didn't."

"Okay," I said. "Maybe she just liked athletics."

"Come *on*, Doc." Lucas looked more closely at the sheet of known behaviors we'd posted concerning Shelby, seeming to relish his new role of expert. "You're really telling me the sheriff's office doesn't know about it? Because I don't see it up here."

"What the hell are you talking about, junior?" Mike asked.

"And I don't like 'junior' any more than 'kid,' Mike," Lucas shot back. Mike apologized quickly, and the boy went on: "I mean about the scandal. *Everybody* knew about it—it got our asshole phys-ed teacher, Mr. Holloway, fired. Or forced to quit, whatever. Which made Shelby kind of a hero, to a lot of us." Considering the matter for an instant, Lucas then decided, "Although the school *did* try to keep the whole thing pretty hushed up, so maybe it never got to the sheriff. You gotta ask Ambyr, she knows more about the details than I do—"

"Lucas?" I asked, as patiently as possible. "Care to tell us what *you* know?"

"Right," he said, his brain in overdrive. "Well, at first it had to do with Mr. Holloway getting the tires on his car slashed. He's, like, maybe a little younger than you guys, used to be a big deal in college sports—total asshole, though I guess he's good-looking. Technically. Anyway, everybody thought that it was some kids on a team from a school we beat that did it, since he also coached all the boys' teams, when he wasn't making us non-jocks miserable in PE. Then there was a rumor he was having an affair with a girl in our school—one of the cheerleaders—and that *she* did it. The guy's married, and the story went that he'd told the girl he was gonna get a divorce, but went back on his promise. But that turned out to be even *more* bullshit. *Then* it turned out that his *wife* got caught for it— there was a real short shot of her on a security camera in the school parking lot, which they missed, at first. Pretty soon after that, Holloway quit, without any reason. Except that there *was* a reason—turned out he'd been doing Shelby in his office after games. She was fucking fourteen! Which he didn't know, or so he said—she told him she was seventeen, and the dumb-ass bought it. Not that she didn't *look* like she was seventeen, or frickin' twenty, when she got all made up. Anyway, he said he was going to leave his wife and live with her, since her parents were gone."

"How . . . ?" I was dumbfounded. "How can you possibly know all of this to be fact?"

"A girl who worked in the school office," Lucas said simply. "Friend of my sister's, she saw all the records, which they shredded, afterwards. And, like I say, Shelby had a lot of friends at Morgan. It got around. But her parents *were* gone, and the people she was staying with didn't seem to give two shits about it."

"That much certainly fits," Mike judged; and indeed, it did not seem that the family members that Shelby had been left with—and who had kept her in an equipment shed—would have wanted to get mixed up in such business. "But what's all this got to do with whether or not she was a meth user?"

"Because her *parents* were," Lucas answered simply. "And she told all her friends at Morgan about how much she hated having to live with them, with all their meth-head friends around all the time. Man, I cannot be-*lieve* the sheriff didn't know any of this."

"What'd I tell you, Mike?" I said, quickly grabbing a notepad and jotting down the particulars of Lucas' tale. "The kid's a gold mine . . ."

Lucas erupted: "How many times I gotta tell you guys—!"

"Okay, look, Lucas," I said, still scribbling notes. "You have to get over this whole 'kid' thing. See, where we come from, it's not an insult. Hell, Mike and I call each *other* 'kid.'"

"You do?" Lucas began to slowly accept another reality of the secret society he had chosen to join.

"We do," I said. "All the same, I'll put it differently: our *consulting detective* is a gold mine."

"Damned straight!" Lucas declared, pointing triumphantly at the fuselage ceiling.

I shook my head. "'Today's Tom Sawyer,'" I chuckled toward Mike, getting a look from Lucas that, perhaps surprisingly, exuded both recognition and pride.

"Hey, I know that song," he said. "PYX-106 Albany, classic rock, I listen to it all the time. That's Rush, who are *awesome*. So if you were trying to talk shit, it didn't work."

I shook my head with a grin. "There is no end to his wisdom . . . All right, then—" After tacking my sheet of notes onto the fuselage wall below the information about Shelby that we already had from Pete, I turned to my partner. "Now, Michael—suppose you continue relating your discoveries, in light of this new intelligence."

"It fits, all right," he said, growing quietly excited. "Like a damned glove, it fits. You remember, L.T., that we couldn't find any physical evidence on the body that indicated heavy meth use? Or *any* meth use? Well, Pete e-mailed the coroner's report this afternoon, while you were down taking your afternoon stroll with Marcianna—" Mike grabbed at some sheets of paper on top of a large pile on one of his desks, which turned out to be several copies of the report that he'd run off. He handed one to me and kept two, one for our files; but Lucas dashed over, his hand out, to receive what he assumed would be his copy. Mike held the document back, however, looking genuinely concerned. "Easy, Lucas. There's a couple of photos in here. Color ones. You ever looked at an actual autopsy picture? It's not like what you see on TV."

"Really?" Lucas questioned anxiously. "Then hells, yeah, I want to look!" he decided, with the kind of prurient enthusiasm that I had often observed in the uninitiated.

I turned to Mike. "Well? He's going to find out, eventually."

"Your call, boss," Mike answered. "You're the one who brought him on board."

"And *you're* the one who agreed to his being brought on board, Michael," I replied. "We are partners, correct, in this as in all important decisions?"

Mike considered that one for a moment, rubbing a hand through the thick black shock on the top of his head so that it eventually stood up like a brush. Then he nodded, slapped the papers in his one hand with the other, and turned to Lucas. "Okay, Mr. Consulting Detective. Trust me, though, when I tell you that this isn't the Hollywood version. Those people spend as much time dolling up those phony stiffs as they do on the actors. You say you're ready, but remember—this is somebody you used to know, even if only a little. It can be a shock."

"Mike," Lucas said, as if he were talking to an idiot, "I've been on Facebook for *two years,* for shit's sake—last week I watched some Indonesian dude chop his wife's head off! And I seen plenty of other real shit like that, but I ain't been scarred for life. I don't think. So will you two please stop acting like the school nurse—who isn't even a real nurse, for fuck's sake, and never even saw that my sister had a problem, when she got sick!—and lemme see the damned report?"

With one more doubtful glance my way, Mike handed the third copy of the report to Lucas.

It is entirely possible that, in the end, I took the glaring photo that I encountered harder than Lucas did. Not that his face didn't initially sink, both with recognition of the girl and at the way in which she was displayed: in the harsh white light of a typical hospital pathology lab, with none of Hollywood's shadowy, colored effects or wondrous surroundings. Her skin was fully revealed as having gone beyond pale, so that almost every major blood vessel, now turned dark blue, showed in harsh relief, as did the similarly colored lips and drawn cheeks. Then there were the various parts of her skin that had been cut open and roughly sewn back up, almost like a burlap sack, revealing the areas that had been of first standard and then special interest to the pathologist. Yet Lucas recovered from all these sights with a speed that was, to say the least, surprising; whereas I, who thought I had seen such a searching question in Shelby's azure gaze when we first came upon her body, was now faced with the dull resignation of her closed, dead eyes, and felt her for the first time to be truly gone. Such a reaction may seem strange, to some. But it was one that I had experienced many times, regarding the deaths of children: ever since I had been a boy even younger than Lucas, in fact, and had begun to endure the long and ultimately fruitless effort to save my left leg, an effort that had inevitably entailed witnessing the deaths of fellow patients who had often become close friends during our long weeks of treatment.

I gave Lucas a few more minutes to study this last picture that would ever be taken of Shelby Capamagio, perhaps hoping that his reaction to it might deepen; but it didn't. Why this should have shocked or disappointed me, I don't know. I tried to remind myself that Lucas was, at that moment, just another kid who had spent far too much time looking at terrible things on the Internet, things that no boy his age should ever have seen, much less seen over and over again. He had already reminded us, for instance, that, thanks to Facebook, along with other social media culprits like Twitter, it had become possible for children as young as thirteen to watch beheadings and other incredibly graphic acts of violence from around the world; and while such might have seemed a bizarre and terrible new reality for people like Mike and myself, for Lucas, it was simply the world into which he'd tumbled from the womb. Thus there was really no reason at all for me either to be surprised at his quick recovery from the sight of Shelby's autopsy photo, or to be startled by his simple, strangely detached spoken reaction:

"Wow—poor Shelby. Fucked up . . ."

"Yeah," Mike said, himself fairly mystified at Lucas' reaction. "Fucked up, all right. And now that we're clear on that, and since you seem ready to move on, Lucas, you're going to want to pay particular attention to the bruises on her neck, and to the part of the report that explains them."

Lucas did as he was told, and I followed suit. We both found that there were indeed two distinctly separate yet similar markings on Shelby's neck, one on the side and one at the back: one left, I knew, by the knot of the rope Mike and I had seen. But the other had been the one that, consistent with Mike's X-ray, snapped her neck and crushed her hyoid bone. It was centered, just as Mike had thought, at the back of the neck, and had been covered by Shelby's hair when we had examined her: hair that was now pulled to one side and partially shaved to reveal the fatal injury. The report agreed with this conclusion, declaring the cause of death to have been hanging in a manner and by a person or persons unknown.

"But that isn't the interesting part," Mike declared.

"It isn't?" Lucas said, finally surprised. "Well, you'd better tell me the interesting part, then, because *that's* pretty interesting."

"Maybe, but not as interesting as this: you remember that discoloration at the base of Shelby's back, L.T., that Curtis thought was a bruise, but we saw was in fact lividity disguised by her tattoo?"

"You mean her slag tag?" Lucas threw in with a small smile.

Mike paused, shook his head hard, then answered, "Yeah, Lucas. That's just what I mean. Well, that lividity proves that she wasn't left hanging, that in fact she was cut down fairly quickly, then put into a position on her back where the blood could pool there. Only several hours later was she strung back up in the trailer."

"Unh-*hunh*," I noised, nodding and starting to pace the plane, my own brain beginning to fire on all eight cylinders.

"And there's more," Mike went on, flipping to the next page of the document. "The toxicology report. Which matches the traces of the drug I found on Shelby's clothing. There was, in fact, no meth in her system—but there *was* a small amount of cocaine."

"*Whaat?*" Lucas droned, in what I was learning was his characteristic reaction to unexpected information that he doubted. "Shelby didn't have money for no coke."

"Which doesn't mean that someone didn't have the money to buy it *for* her," I mused quietly. "Now shut up, Lucas, and let Mike finish, please."

Lucas was wise enough not to protest at that, and Mike went on: "Not just cocaine, but good cocaine. Very good. What we would once have called Peruvian Flake, although it's now Andean from any number of countries. And startlingly pure—not the kind of thing you would find in Burgoyne County too readily. Which got me thinking about those clothes of hers." He picked up another notepad and pulled up several windows of what looked like various shopping sites. "I enlarged the pictures of her things, enhanced any identifying marks like maker's labels, and tried to match what I saw against stuff that I could find online—and sure enough, those clothes weren't just some average kid's fancy summer duds. No, each piece—especially the lingerie and shoes, which I found exact matches for—was something that cost real bucks. Take the bra and panties: you figure, okay, for a girl like her, Victoria's Secret is going to be hot enough shit. But they're *Bordelle,* the most expensive lingerie in the world. The damned panties alone could have cost seven hundred bucks."

"Fuck you!" Lucas erupted, in a moment of astonished disbelief; then, considering his choice of words, he added, "I mean—that's impossible! Where'd she get that kind of money?"

"You tell me, Lucas," Mike said. "You're supposed to be the expert on what she was up to."

"Not on her *underwear,* for shit's sake." Lucas' tone became more thoughtful. "Although—maybe Ambyr might know . . ."

"Maybe," Mike replied. "And we're going to want to ask her, if that's the case. Then we come to those biker sneakers—Betsey Johnson, more than three hundred bucks. But the capper? The gladiator sandals: *Prada,* almost a *grand.*"

"Get the fuck outta town!" Lucas fired off again. "There is no God damned way!"

"There is a God damned way, Lucas, and it's called facts," Mike said. "And it also fits: designer clothes that she could not find in Fraser, or even in Albany, and certainly not in the shithole parts of the Southwest that she was supposed to have traveled to, if the rumors about where her parents went and her following them are true. Tie in a variety of cocaine that has a very limited clientele, and it all points in one direction."

I sat down in the chair at my desk, not a little stunned and, if my bitter heart be truly known, perversely pleased by the conclusion: "South," I murmured.

Mike nodded. "Our hometown. Rearing the ugliest and wealthiest of its heads."

"What?" Lucas asked. "New York City?"

"Indeed, Consulting Detective Kurtz," I said quietly. "New York City . . ."

"But . . ." Lucas was now having real trouble with it all: a girl he knew principally as the source of a sordid local scandal hanged in an unknown manner, and at that moment dead on a slab, cut apart and stitched back up, yet somehow, before all that, having made her way to New York City and made some very fancy friends in the process. "Damn," the kid pronounced at length. "Fucking Shelby. She did it up, all right."

"And died in the process," I said, still softly, as I rose to pace again.

Several silent moments passed before Lucas gave voice to his continuing struggle with the idea: "But I still don't get it—if she got all the way to New York City, and had money, why would she come back to West Briarwood, the asshole of the state? *Man* . . . If I got that far and had those kinda bucks, I'd *kill myself* before I'd come back here."

I halted in my tracks and glanced at the kid, slightly disbelieving of the statement he'd made, which mirrored my own thoughts precisely. "Yes, Lucas," I murmured, staring away into space blankly. "That might be *just* what you might do . . ."

A few more seconds went by without any words exchanged; then I heard Lucas whisper to Mike, "What—what's the matter with him?"

"The whole 'Sorcerer of Death' thing, like I told you," Mike mumbled in answer. "Don't worry, he'll snap out of it—though not before he creeps the shit out of you."

"Shut up, Mike," I said, again in a near-whisper.

"Well, I'm sorry, Trajan," he answered. "But it *is*—"

"No, just shut up. Lucas is right. These supposed murders—they may very well not be murders at all." I turned to them, my gaze becoming more focused. "They're suicides."

Mike immediately shook his head. "L.T.—we already said that suicide was unlikely, even though it *is* the thing that staged hanging is most often used to cover."

"True," I answered, still perfecting the notion in my head. "That's what we said. But we also said that we couldn't find *any* sensible explanation. Now we can."

"Because of what the kid said?" Mike asked incredulously.

"Because of what he said, and because we now know so much more. Just consider it, Mike: Shelby leaves her hometown, and somehow hooks up with somebody with real money down south. That person buys her serious clothes, and introduces her to serious drugs, although it stays recreational—you said they only found a small amount of the coke in her blood, right? So, then—she gets to enjoy that life for a while; but then that somebody we're talking about, the person—or, who knows, maybe people—with money, get tired of her; or they just get tired of the risk of horsing around with a minor. For whatever reason, they dump her back up here."

"But I don't get it," Lucas said in frustration. "So how the hell does she end up back in her family's trailer, stark naked and stuck in a closet in a fake hanging?"

"She doesn't end up at home, Lucas." I stared at him, and I have to admit, he did look a little unsettled by whatever expression of discovery was on my face. "This is the heart of our method of investigation—Mike's and my own. Question everything as soon as it comes up: every theory, every supposed fact, every assumption. And law enforcement's assumption here has been that she went home to die, picked up a stranger or someone who just wasn't happy to see her, along the way, and was killed in or, given the pathology report, near the trailer. But what if she wasn't? What if she came home and stayed with friends, but, while staying with those friends, became so depressed about losing the high life that she did just what you stated—killed herself?"

"But Shelby wasn't suicidal, for shit's sake!" Lucas protested. "And neither was Kyle."

"No," I agreed, looking at each victim's picture. "Neither was the Kozersky girl. At least, before she ran away from home. But each one had some interest that gave them great ambition: Shelby, the classic gold digger; Kyle, the scholar who kept his books with him even when he couldn't go to school, or even home; and Kelsey, whose great passion was ... horses, if I remember, Mike?" He nodded to me, and I went on. "These are not lost souls, wandering the streets and highways listening to Goth metal or hip-hop or staying in their rooms playing video games. They were motivated, they had ambition—and, I would be willing to bet, each one of them ended up meeting someone in New York City who seemed to offer them a way to fulfill those dreams—then snatched that dream back away, crushing them. Yes, Mike—suicides. And the description of Shelby's lividity, and the condition of her things, matches perfectly: she hanged herself, but was soon cut down and laid someplace where the blood could pool—like a soft bed. Would that be about right?" Mike signaled agreement again. "But then whoever cut her down realized that they might be implicated in her death; so they took her home and created what they thought was a convincing murder scene. And, left to law enforcement, it would have been. But the clothes—what kind of brutal murderer goes to such trouble to carefully arrange her clothes?"

"Could be a serial killer," Mike said. "With a fetish about the clothes."

"Could be," I said with a nod. "But if it's a fetish, wouldn't he *take* the clothes, both as trophies and to make sure his ass was covered?"

Mike had one more line of doubt: "And what about that stuff you said in the trailer? About our being in some kind of 'dialogue' with the killer?"

"I never said with the killer," I answered. "I said with whoever is behind it all. And I still believe it. In very large part because, again, while it's unusual, nothing else makes sense at all."

Mike considered that, finally conceding, "Yeah, it fits, L.T.; and goes good with the fact that the pathologist couldn't find any trace of sexual violation. But what about proof?"

"Aren't all the things you've just listed, along with the pathology report, along with what we now know about these kids, at least the beginnings of proof? Isn't—" I was suddenly interrupted, and we all jumped a bit, when what sounded at that moment like a firehouse alarm went off: but it was only the bell of the old wall-mounted telephone that my great-grandfather had installed on the cockpit bulkhead years ago. The phone had originally been an extension of the line in the main house, put in when it had become clear even to the old man that, after a career of adventure flying in the JU-52 around the States and Canada following the plane's long and perilous journey to reach this country, the old girl would fly no more, without the kind of overhaul that the Second World War had made impossible. But when Mike and I had set up our headquarters, I had convinced my great-aunt that it would be better if she allowed me to have the phone company make the plane's a separate line, so that she would not be disturbed every time our SUNY-Albany employers or students needed to contact us. Of course, the phone also served as a secure way for Mike and me to do business with Steve Spinetti's office; and such was the purpose it was evidently serving now.

Mike immediately leapt to his feet, shot toward the bulkhead, and shouted, "I got it, it's for me!" He grinned with anticipation as he said, "I had Pete send over the FIC's report on some hair fibers found on the second victim, the Kozersky girl, along with any photos they took; and I've asked if we can have a look at some things relating to the Howard case, too . . ." He snatched the old black Bakelite plastic receiver out of its worn silver cradle; but the conversation that followed did not, apparently, convey what he wished: "Yeah, Pete," Mike said, still smiling. "You got that bag for us? Good, what time will you be—" His face suddenly filled with concern as he listened to Pete Steinbrecher's news. "Hunh? . . . Aw, no. . . . When . . . And where . . . Wait, what? What the . . . *Who?* . . . But how the hell did *they* find out . . . And they want us there?" Another long pause, during which both Lucas and I could hear the vague sound of Pete's voice reverberating out of the earpiece of the receiver, and then Mike said simply, "Okay, Pete. Thanks. . . . Yeah, if you bring the bag there, I'll get it when no one's looking. And we owe you one, Deputy . . ." With that, Mike slowly set the receiver back into its cradle and turned to me. "The rest of your theory will have to wait, L.T.—we have an appointment."

" 'An appointment'?" I echoed, not liking the expression on Mike's face. "Since when does anybody phone us to make an appointment? They generally just drop by."

"No, it's more like *we* got an appointment with somebody *else*. Some-*where* else."

These were ominous words, when placed in relation to Mike's brief exchange with Pete on the phone. "Ah—we've been *summoned,* you mean," I judged at length.

"Pete was trying very hard not to put it like that," Mike answered. "But yeah, we have."

"Whaaat?" Lucas said once again, plainly skeptical of the idea that his new partners could be thus commanded. "Whatta you mean, 'summoned'? Where? What for?"

"Over to the north side of Fraser," Michael told him, glancing around the plane and obviously concerned about our various displays. "And if I'm any judge of how devious the fuckers we'll be seeing are, we'd better lock this place up tight, and you'd better scurry your ass home, kid."

"I ain't 'scurrying' nowhere," Lucas replied, "until you tell me why you have to go and who can just order you around the county like that—and why?"

"The last part of your question is fairly obvious, Lucas," I answered. "And I would have hoped you'd be able to figure it out, by now."

"Me? How?"

"Context, Lucas—put all the statements Mike and I have just made concerning the case, including what he discussed with Pete—or the half of that conversation that you and I heard, anyway—in relation to one another, and you've got what?"

I watched his young brain start stoking the fires of cogitation, and was pleased when, after only a few moments, his eyes grew wide and he looked up at Mike. "Ho-lee *shit . . ."* he exclaimed quietly. "They found another kid's body!"

"Well done," I said with a nod; and it really had been a good little piece of extrapolation.

"Yeah, *just* found one," Mike said, busily shoveling away what papers he could from desktops into drawers and then shutting down his computers.

"And they want *you* guys there?" Lucas asked, very puzzled. "I thought you being in on it all was supposed to be on the down-low?"

"It was." I tried not to sound as uneasy as I felt. "But apparently, no longer."

"Hunh!" was all the sense Lucas could make of that; his mind was quickly moving on to what, for him, was the juicier part of the tale: "So— who's dead this time?"

{vi.}

"A boy from some town just outside Fraser—North Briarwood," Mike told Lucas, as he continued to try to conceal, insofar as it was even possible, our work on what would likely have to be considered, now, the *first* three deaths. "Went to the local school," my partner went on. "You know which one that would be, Lucas?"

"Hey, North Briarwood covers a lot of territory—a lot of pretty fucked-up territory," Lucas answered; and again I noted how easily he took news that ought to have been at least as unsettling to him as it was to Mike and me. Yet the revelation that another teen in his own county had died under what were more than likely going to be revealed as suspicious circumstances seemed more to heighten the thrill of the endeavor that he had so recently embarked upon than to frighten him; and this reaction, in turn, intensified my own sense of Lucas' mind being, in its way, as unnerving as it was impressive. "But he probably got bussed down to South Briarwood Combined—they go from elementary all the way through twelfth grade at that school, it's big as fuck-all."

"Well, I could only get a few more details, understandably," Mike replied, nodding to acknowledge Lucas' report. "Pete was calling on the sly. But he said it was a young black kid, maybe fourteen or so. OD'd on smack in an abandoned apartment block on Fraser's north side." Finally slamming down a stack of papers, Mike erupted: "Damn it, Trajan, we can't hide all this! And we certainly can't eat it. Have you still got that monster padlock for the hatch door? We'll just have to close it up and hope one of them hasn't managed to get a search warrant . . ."

"Michael," I said, fishing through my top desk drawer and producing the enormous, shining padlock, which fit into a latch I'd had welded onto the outside of the JU-52's forward hatch. "Calm yourself, on that score— and tell us, if you can manage it, exactly who the 'them' you're referring to is."

"Seriously, dude," Lucas said, snatching the lock out of my hand when I held it up. "Get a grip, Mike. Look at this fucker: even if they have a search warrant, they'll need a blowtorch to get in here. So, like L.T. says— who are 'they'?"

"Oh, you can probably guess," Mike moaned, holding up a batch of papers in one hand and a bag of trace evidence in the other, then dropping them as a gesture of resignation. "Pete and Steve'll be with them—but the others, shit: Cathy Donovan and Nancy Grimes, for starters."

"Jesus," I whispered, absorbing it; for this was unexpected and unsettling news.

"What, what, *what*?" Lucas anxiously questioned. "Who are they?"

"*They* are the assistant district attorney and the head of the State Police's Forensic Investigation Center," I replied, myself looking around, now, at all the various sheets of information to which we were not supposed to be privy: if this was a diversion, and somebody from the county or state busted into the plane while we were gone, we could say goodbye to a lot more than our involvement in the case. Our jobs, for example, would be on the line. "Who else, Mike?"

"Frank Mangold," Mike answered, with even more concern.

"Who's *he*?" Lucas asked, still breathlessly.

"*Damn* ..." I was now amazed, as well as shocked; and, looking to Lucas, I added, "He's a detective from the state Bureau of Criminal Investigation—and a nasty piece of work. Anybody *else*?"

"Mitch McCarron," Mike went on.

"*Major* McCarron?" Lucas said, drawing surprised looks from both Mike and myself. "I know him—I mean I've *met* him. He's the head of Troop G, State Police—my cousin's one of his troopers, works outta the Fraser station. I've run into him a couple of times."

"So have we," I said. "And he, at least, is one we don't have to worry about. Ever since I helped him shut down that damned petting zoo, he's been a friend. But the rest ..."

"And there may be more," Mike continued. "Pete said he's not sure, but it's possible that Grimes may also be bringing one of her own forensic psychologists."

"Jesus Christ," I breathed. "A touch of overkill, isn't it? How much do they know?"

"Nothing definite." Mike had finally given up the idea of hiding the materials we'd compiled on the three cases, although he wasn't at all pleased about it, and had thrown himself into the chair behind his trace examination table, where he thrust his face into his hands and spoke through his splayed fingers. "Apparently they heard a rumor that we were taking an interest in all this, and may be giving some informal advice to the sheriff. They want to warn us off of anything more serious—and warn us hard."

"Does Steve or Pete have any idea how they heard?"

Mike shrugged. "Pete says it could have been someone in their office, although he doubts it—he's been pretty careful about the information he's sent us, about when he sent it and who might've seen him do it. Steve's sure it came from outside their bunch, but from *where*—that's a very fucking interesting question."

"Not right now, it isn't," I said. "The far more interesting question is, why invite us to a murder scene if all they intend to do is warn us off any further participation in precisely such proceedings? It doesn't make any sense."

"Since when does senior law enforcement have to make any sense?" Mike murmured. "Around here or anywhere else . . ."

"True," I told him. "But this is a little extreme. You know . . ." I took a few more steps up and down the aisle of the JU-52. "If I didn't know better—" I began to wag a pensive finger at the floor beneath my feet. "If I didn't know better . . . I'd say that when they found out that Steve and Pete had been consulting us, they got together to go talk to the sheriff and his people, after which they planned to come over here and give us their warning about getting in any deeper. But suddenly this latest case happened. Did you get any idea of the timeline?"

"All Pete said was that they *just* found the kid," Mike answered, lifting his head with the first ray of hope. "It was a security guard working the block of buildings—he found the body, called it in to Steve's office. Some junkie hanging out in the building ID'd the body."

"And so I ask you again," I said, knowing that Mike's thoughts were running along the same lines as my own, "why invite us to a scene like that, just to tell us not to get further involved in this case? Unless they're panicking."

"Yep," Mike said, standing up and pulling on his jacket. "Synchronicity at work."

"Uh—guys?" said Lucas, who had taken to wandering around the plane, himself; but he'd stopped before the section of wall on which hung the information about, and picture of, Shelby Capamagio. "Guys, I think I gotta ask you something . . ."

"Hang on, Lucas," I said, and then I turned back to Mike. "Apply the basic logic. Question the assumption that they want us there at all—they just happen to be there, and—"

"And," Mike went on, wrapping an actual tie around his collar and beginning to knot it, "they've reached *such* a panic point that they feel like they need to talk to us, there or anywhere else, ASAP. They may even *want* outside advice, at this point—but they want to hammer it into our heads that our involvement has to remain informal, and under *their* control."

"That's great, guys," Lucas said, "I'm really impressed, but just for one second, can you tell me one thing?" Lucas pointed at the posted papers concerning Shelby and then indicated his copy of the autopsy report. "It's just that—who found her?"

"What the hell are you talking about?" I said, turning to him. "Who found who?"

"Shelby!" the boy answered. "Who found her body? Who reported it?"

That dull queasy feeling that comes over one when an obvious consideration has been overlooked grabbed my gut, and I glanced at Mike, only to see that he'd had the same reaction:

"Who the fuck *did* find her?" Mike whispered to me.

"And who reported it?" I mumbled quietly. "It *must* be in the report, right? Mike?"

But Mike only began to shake his head slowly; and as our gazes mutually widened, he murmured, "Holy fuck!" and began to retrieve a goodly portion of the files that he had only just finished stuffing away so hurriedly.

"Oh, good Lord," I said, hobbling over to stand behind Lucas and before the display of papers concerning Shelby's case. "It has to be here, somewhere!"

"What?" came Lucas' insistent voice. "Hey, what's going on—you mean you really don't know?"

"Hang on, Lucas," I said, getting to my own station, opening my laptop and then the drawers of my desk. "We'll find it, we'll find it . . ." But Mike was already murmuring:

"It's not here—Jesus Christ, L.T., it's not fucking here!"

"It has to be," I said, giving up on my documents, joining him, and scanning his papers, especially his notes on the initial sheriff's report; and, when they revealed nothing, I began moving to the other displays around the fuselage once again, out of desperation. "The first two are here: the Kozersky girl was found by her family, the Howard boy by some kids. This is basic stuff, damn it, somebody *has* to have made a note of it in Shelby's case—"

"Yeah?" Mike said, quickly moving to the desk that held his computer, then booting it back up and reading his file on Shelby's death. "It's so fucking basic that neither one of *us* thought of it. Took Lucas to catch it. *How the fuck could we possibly have missed it . . . ?*"

"So I *did* figure it out!" Lucas declared. "Well, you guys'll be treating me with a little more respect, I have a feeling."

"I told you to keep quiet for just a damned second, you truant!" I rejoined Mike at his desktop computer. "Is it there? Was it that bunch of morons in her family, up the hollow from the trailer?"

"Nah," Mike said quickly. "No phone, remember? And even if they had found her, did it seem like they would have reported it?"

"Yo!" Lucas said. "Listen, guys, why would you be so shocked? I mean, the sheriff didn't even know she was doing that asshole Mr. Holloway— I'm sure they could have missed a detail like this."

"Which doesn't explain how *we* missed it," I answered without thinking.

Lucas paused before replying: "Oh. Yeah, you're right—there you're on your own."

"Just shut up, will you, for five minutes," I said, moving over to him and retrieving the big silver padlock. "Unless you have something constructive to offer."

"O-*kay*," the kid answered, somehow seeming to grasp the gravity of the moment without taking it entirely seriously.

"It's not here, it's not here," Mike was repeating, scanning every inch of the reports. "And I'll tell you what I think happened—somebody in Steve's office took an anonymous call, a tip, then got on the horn to his squad car and the whole thing snowballed, especially given the panicky mood of the ADA and her crew, before anybody bothered to make an official note of where the call originated—it just got lost in the whole craze over having another teen suicide on their hands."

"Yeah, I'll buy that, if we're speculating," I said.

"*Exactly* what I was going to say," Lucas announced with a grin.

"But the main thing," I continued, "is that we do not know. And what's worse, it didn't occur to us any more than it occurred to them to ask so fundamental a question."

"Okay, okay," I finally conceded to him. "It was a very good catch, and you're a damned genius—that help?"

"Maybe," Lucas said, skeptical of my tone; but I couldn't stop for any more banter.

"Come on, Mike," I said. "We need to get going; and looking at these things over and over isn't going to make it appear. Besides, it suddenly occurs to me that this may be information we can use, however much it reveals how rusty at this sort of thing we are. But for now, what we need is a reason to pull Pete and Steve aside when we get there . . ."

"I've got one," Mike said, grabbing some papers from beside his stereomicroscope. "After I formed my little theory about Shelby, I asked Pete if he could get ahold of the trace tests that should have been run on the Kozersky girl. He did, and, like I say, sent over the report. But I also asked him to bring some of the physical evidence that will confirm my theory—and we'll need to view that in private with Pete, which provides an excuse for pulling him aside. And I think I know what you're driving at . . ."

"All right, then—for the time being we go with that, and get ready. And by 'ready,' I'm being rather pointed." I began to move toward my own desk again. "Let me put it in terms that our young friend might even recognize: 'There may be some little danger, so kindly put your army revolver in your pocket.'"

"Hey, I know that line!" Lucas declared; and when I looked over, I saw that he was hanging and swinging from the plane's hatch. "That's Sherlock Holmes—the one about the guys with red hair."

"Jesus," Mike said to me, leaning down to open a lower drawer of one of his own desks. "You really think it could get that serious?"

"What I think," I answered, as my partner drew a 1.875-inch-barreled Smith & Wesson .38 Special revolver out of his desk, "is that we still have permits to carry, we're headed for a crime scene, and we now know that senior county law enforcement is beginning to take an interest in our activities. We have no reason to trust senior law enforcement *anywhere*, anymore, Mike—you know they all cover each other's asses."

"Hunh?" Lucas continued, still shouting from his monkey-like perch on the hatch. "You're going to get in a gunfight with the cops?"

Sighing, I said, "Not unless we have to. But if you've been paying attention to the news lately, Lucas, you know how trigger-happy they've all become—toward just about *anybody*." And then I finally managed to locate my own handgun, an original Model 1911 Colt .45, a little bit of history that, like most things in the hangar, had been a prized possession of my great-grandfather's.

"Yeah," the boy agreed. "That's true." Then he switched gears once more: "'The Red-Headed League'! *That's* the name of that story. You guys think you're so smart . . ."

"*'Omne ignotum pro magnifico,'*" I shot back at the self-satisfied youth, as I quickly got my jacket off and slipped on a shoulder holster for the .45, while Mike slapped a Velcro-banded neoprene receptacle for his .38 just above his ankle.

"And I know what *that* means, too!" Lucas shouted defiantly; then his voice drooped a little as he added, "Or at least, I used to. It's Latin, from the same story—my sister told me what it meant when I read it, she takes Latin from her tutor."

"I'm overjoyed for her," I said, following Mike through the hatch of the JU-52. "At least there's one scholar in your family. But didn't I tell you to go home already?"

"Fuck *that*," Lucas replied merrily, heading down the steps outside the plane in front of Mike as I made sure the hatch was tightly closed and the padlock firmly fastened in place. "I got it all figured out—I can hide in your car and go with you guys!"

"Lucas," Mike said sternly. "Come on, man, this is serious shit, you're a minor—they catch you in our car and they'll cart you off to a nice little room for a few hours, and believe me, you *will* end up telling them what we've been doing, here—Frank Mangold's got guys who'd make you admit to being Jack the Ripper."

"Bull-*shit!*" Lucas replied, snatching up his fishing pole and standing with it defiantly. "I ain't no snitch—and they ain't *gonna* see me. Besides, how am I ever supposed to really learn anything if I don't get in on the action?"

I didn't engage this question, but went instead to the nearby freezer and drew out another hunk of plastic-wrapped beef, slamming it into the microwave in an attempt to ease my mounting nervousness and irritation. "Be serious, Lucas," I replied, in a voice that I hoped carried an honestly stern tone. "Like Mike says, you are a God damned minor, and if those people catch you with us, and find out what we've been up to, Mike and I will likely lose a lot more than your company—our jobs are on the line, here."

That seemed to crack even the resilient Lucas' determination. "Yeah—I guess," he mumbled in defeat, as the microwave droned away, doing its work on Marcianna's dinner. "But I wanna hear all about it, next time I come up here."

"And we want to hear all about anything you can discover in town, and in your school, particularly. About this Mr. Holloway, for one—"

"Is he a suspect?" Lucas said, with sudden and happy anxiousness. "Oh, *please* tell me he's a suspect!"

"Well," I said, as the chimes of the microwave sounded, "he is certainly a—what's the name of that idiotic TV show that you probably watch—a '*Person of Interest.*'" Taking the meat from the machine, I turned to my partner. "You wanna get the car, Mike?" I said. "While I feed you-know-who again, so she won't make a fuss while we're gone?"

"Yeah, sure," Mike said, checking his jacket pocket for his keys and then heading down toward the barns.

"Come on, Lucas," I said, beginning the climb in the other direction. "We've got a few more minutes, and it'll be good if Marcianna begins to associate you with things other than sneaking around the rocks in the stream bed." Lucas fell in beside me and even took the plastic bag full of Marcianna's gory dinner, as I leaned more heavily on my cane and tried to make my way quickly up the hill. "Now," I said, "your Mr. Holloway is not a person of interest to the law, obviously, as they seem to know nothing of his connection to Shelby. But for us? Well, let's just say that a man nearing middle age who had a long-standing sexual relationship with a fourteen-year-old—and don't kid yourself, the likelihood is that he was perfectly aware of her age—such a man, even if that is the extent of his illegal activities, may have like-minded friends who it would be worth keeping an eye on." Having reached the gate to Marcianna's enclosure, Lucas and I discovered that she was, once again, nowhere to be seen.

"Don't tell me she escaped," Lucas said, a little nervously.

"No," I chuckled, pointing across the grounds of the enclosure toward the entrance to her stone den. "She's in there, sleeping off her last meal. I wouldn't ordinarily feed her again so soon, but because of her time as a cub and a young adult, she has terrible anxiety that she'll be abandoned and then taken back to that God-forsaken zoo. So I tell her not to worry, and leave her something to eat—it seems to do the trick."

"Man," Lucas said, shaking his head. "That fucking petting zoo, who woulda thought—we really did have fun when we went there, in the old days."

"Yes, and that's how those pigsties stay in business—seduce the kids, and the parents will follow." I indicated the bare patch of earth just inside the enclosure's entrance. "Do me a favor, will you—just chuck the meat over the fence and onto that patch of ground." Lucas did as asked, managing to hit the target. Then I issued my approximation of one of Marcianna's chirruping calls, used by cheetah with their kin; and, as Lucas tried to suppress laughter that grew, I could see, out of a kind of shock that I would engage in such behavior, called out to tell her again that I had to go to the store for a little while, but would be back soon.

"You might," Lucas said, as we turned around to head back down the hill, "not want to let anybody in the criminal science business—at least, anybody that you're trying to impress—hear you going through that routine. They'll think you're nuts."

"And they might just be right," I answered, quietly pleased—though I thought better than to mention it—that Lucas had used the term *criminal,* rather than *forensic,* science: he was learning, without question.

Looking ahead, I could see that Mike had brought what I had called *the* car, which was really his car, around and up to the front of the hangar. It had been his fleet vehicle when he'd worked for New York City's crime lab, which was located in a big, mirthless old institutional building that had formerly been a part of York College of the City University system, out in Mike's native Queens. Upon our dissolving all relations with city law enforcement, Mike had demanded that he be allowed to buy the car from the fleet as part of his severance. It wasn't much to look at, just an old Crown Victoria that the fleet keepers, I always thought out of bitterness, had stripped not only of its official crime lab markings but of its halogen searchlights on both the driver's and front passenger sides of the cab before turning it over. Mike had immediately replaced these, out of pride as much as necessity; but what the fleet boys had not been able to strip the car of was the late-Nineties police package that gave both the engine and the suspension a shocking amount of power and stability at high speeds. The car was, in fact, a consummate sleeper, an inauspicious-looking vehicle that could actually keep up with almost anything on the road; and I loved it because of the enormous amount of comfort it offered my left side, on seats well broken in and far more spacious than anything law enforcement officers almost anywhere were currently driving. We had always called her "the Empress" out of respect, a fact that I communicated to Lucas as we reached the car.

"Yeah, well," the kid said, looking over the old girl's big, navy blue silhouette, "every car's gotta have a name. Just one thing I don't get."

"Yeah?" Mike said, as the V-8 in the Empress idled hungrily. "What's that, Lucas?"

"How the hell do you see over the dashboard, Mike?" Lucas began to laugh, immediately anticipating Mike's furtive attempt to chase him by moving around to the back of the car.

"All right, knock it off," I said. "Lucas, do you want us to drop you home, or is that going to raise more questions than you'd like to answer?"

"Yeah, I think it would," he replied, glancing at the sky. "Besides, it'll be light for a while, yet—I don't think I have to worry about seeing the ghost of Colonel Jones on the hollow road before I get out of here."

I looked at him in surprise. "You're kidding, right?"

"No way," he said. "That's always been the story: go up Death's Head Hollow after dark and you're likely to get run down by him and his horse. Ask any kid in town."

I shook my head as I opened the passenger-side door of the Empress. "My God, the things I've learned today," I murmured with a smile. Then, once in, I powered down my window and said, "Stay to this side of the car until we're a little ways down the hollow, Lucas—I don't want my great-aunt seeing you. The ghost of Colonel Jones would be nothing compared to her catching you and wanting to know what the hell you're doing here. Mike, take it slow until the kid's clear."

"You got it," Mike said. "Although, given my limited visibility over the fucking dashboard, I might just swerve and—"

"Fuck off, Mike," Lucas said, more as a plea than an indictment; and as we began to move along, the kid crouching by my window, I continued to exhort him:

"Remember—you've earned your stripes for today, Lucas, but that doesn't mean you can relax your efforts in the field. And don't limit them to going after Mr. Holloway, who I'm sure you have every reason to hate. But in fact, adults in general are probably not your main target."

"No?" the boy asked, surprised. "So who are?"

"Your schoolmates, their friends, anybody who might have access to information about which kids might want connections to the kind of rich people downstate we're talking about. Remember: somebody knew, and knew well enough to be right, that Shelby, Kyle, and Kelsey would go for this arrangement. So it's somebody who knows the general situation, but doesn't have a high profile to make it obvious. A—"

"Wait!" Lucas declared, his finger going up. "I know the word: a fa— a fuh—"

"You're close," I said. "A facilitator."

"Ah, *fuck*! Yeah, that's it." Lucas crouched ever lower. "A facilitator."

"And keep a low profile. You'll be working on your own—keep it that way."

"I can't even tell Derek?" Lucas asked, apparently realizing, now that he was out of the womb-like safety of the JU-52, the magnitude of what he was involved in.

"Derek chose not to be involved," I said. "Let's respect his wishes." I saw no reason to remind the kid that Derek's mental proficiency was not something that I wanted to hang any aspect of our unofficial investigation on. "Nor should you consult your sister, wise though I'm sure she is." We made the turn out of the farmhouse driveway, and Mike, perhaps a little devilishly, picked up some speed, forcing Lucas to jog. "The hardest part of being an undercover man on your own, remember, is *keeping* your cover—but do it." Then the needling side of my own nature kicked in, prompting me to add: "And remember one more thing, on your way home—Colonel Jones wasn't murdered by anybody in town, so you don't have to worry about his ghost, *or* his horse's. His *dog,* however—that huge mastiff that you see in the statue—he *was* murdered. And when my brothers and my sister and I would get caught on this road in the dark when we were kids—that's who *we* used to worry about. So good luck. Okay, Mike—let's move."

And with the trees that lined and overhung Death's Head Hollow closing in to form a canopy that blocked out most of the remaining evening light, Mike put his foot to the gas, and we left Lucas behind in a cloud of clay dust to call a string of half-serious, very nervous curses after us, as we headed toward what we thought would be another examination of another crime scene in the rough neighborhood that was North Fraser. This examination would be accompanied, we knew, by some pointed questions from the several members of senior law enforcement that we knew to already be there; and we quickly began to boost our courage by reminding ourselves that we knew most of the principals involved, and that surely we could, if careful, handle them.

But this conception of our foray was to prove wholly inadequate, in manifold ways; and my partner and especially I would ultimately be glad that we had taken the precaution of arming ourselves before leaving our headquarters.

CHAPTER THREE

SIREN SONGS

{i.}

To reach Burgoyne County's seat, Fraser, as quickly as possible, Mike and I would need to travel in a zigzag pattern along several of the area's major highways. Yet on this particular occasion, all sections of the trip would not hold equal value to our undertaking: indeed, one of them would provide us with at least the suggestion that we had speculated correctly, during our cogitations inside the JU-52. It is, of course, always dangerous for the detective to read too much into the past histories of places: to allow ghosts to take on solid form. But this time, the whisperings along that one stretch of blacktop proved irresistible.

We navigated the necessary stretch of Route 7 without either Mike's or my saying much to each other: we were too full of both foreboding at the thought of facing the collection of senior law enforcement officials who were awaiting our arrival and eagerness at the mere notion of being privy to another murder scene for either of us to comment on much of anything. When we turned onto Route 22, however, and passed through the picturesque nineteenth-century town of Hoosick Falls—once a bustling center of the textile trade, before its mills poisoned the Hoosick River and the industry moved on—and then back onto a stretch of highway that was lined by woodlands interspersed with farms that were mere shadows of their former selves, my thoughts took an ever more morbid turn. The sudden memory of what seemed an ancient precedent to our current case stormed into my head, causing me to speak up with what must have seemed rather desperate urgency:

"Michael!" I cried, causing my partner to bolt upright. "Pull over."

"What?" he answered, glancing over at me. "You all right, kid? Is it your leg?"

"No," I replied, indicating the breakdown lane along a stretch of the road that was especially remote, and thick with woods on either side. "Just pull over, right up there!"

Mike slowed down and switched on his hazard lights as he coasted onto the highway's shoulder, which was unmarked even by rural mailboxes. Then he hit the passenger-side searchlight and, after I had hastily exited the Empress, moved into my seat to manipulate its arm so that the beam shone on the coarsely mown grass in front of the tree line about twenty feet from the road. It would have been difficult for even inebriated drivers not to have seen us, lit up like that, and such was a good thing: we had reached that time of the evening when a lot of desperately unhappy people in the county, having sought refuge somewhere other than home, were starting to make their ways back to their sources of misery; and drunken collisions into vehicles in the breakdown lane were not uncommon. But for the moment, Mike and I were alone, at just the hour when it was impossible to say whether it was dawn or dusk, or whether the little light that separated us from the shadows came from the sun behind the horizon to the west or the moon that was ascendant over the mountains to the southeast.

"Right here," I said, hobbling about the loose asphalt of the highway's shoulder and ignoring the pain that the twenty minutes' drive had already put into my stump and side. "It was right along here . . ."

"Okay, okay," Mike said, his tone sarcastic but his voice betraying a deeper uneasiness. "Don't start the Sorcerer shit again—not out here. If your leg's not bugging you, L.T., just tell me what the fuck *is*, and stop trying to freak me out." Mike looked around at the darkening landscape. "Because it's fucking working . . ."

I smiled, glancing at him. "I don't know why you always get so pissed off about that *Post* business, Mike. They *did* call you 'The Sorcerer's Apprentice,' after all . . ."

"Fuuuck *you*," he answered, spitting on the highway. "Goddamned *Post*, think they're so fucking funny . . . Come on, what the hell are we doing here, L.T.?"

I kept watching the tree line. "How soon they forget," I mused. "One afternoon a few years back, Mike, we drove to Steve's office to deliver some advice about a *genuine* murder case. We were coming back along this stretch of road, when I pointed out the spot where, back in the early Eighties, they found the body of a dead kid—a boy just fourteen, a supposed runaway—"

"Oh, yeah," Mike replied, his voice trembling just a bit as he recalled the incident. "Something about it being connected to those NAMBLA disappearances?"

"Indeed," I answered, moving into the grass off the breakdown lane. "Those disappearances—and *deaths* . . ." I nodded toward the woods. "They found him inside the trees, alongside the start of an old logging road, but only after they'd searched the mountains for miles around. He'd been hitching a ride back from Fraser, or so his friends there said. But right along here, something happened to . . . *interrupt* that journey."

"I remember," Mike said. "They picked up some guy who'd been going around offering young boys rides home, right?"

"Right. He used the same line on all the kids: said their fathers were late, and had sent him to pick them up. They only caught him because one boy finally had the good sense to run, and to tell his folks about it. And when they eventually arrested him, the man claimed to be a member of NAMBLA. Had a membership card that seemed to prove it."

"Yeah, *but*," Mike added skeptically, "he was also found to be mentally deficient."

"So the state said," I replied. "Wasn't too deficient to fool upwards of two dozen young boys, however. None of whom were ever heard from again, and a few of whose bodies actually turned up. And it was true that *this* boy had been hitching the last time anyone he knew saw him alive—but that day was *two months* before his corpse was discovered, which was within twenty-four hours of the time of death. And that happened to match the m.o. in four other cases of pubescent boys who'd been found dead within a good stone's throw of major, but not *too* major, north-south highways . . ." The darkness had advanced, during this exchange, making the line of the woods hit by the searchlight even more impenetrable and ghostly.

"Unh-hunh," Mike noised—and then he got it. "*Wait a minute* . . ." There was such a heightened tone of apprehension in his voice that, even without turning, I knew that his eyes were widening enough to allow the glow of the car's various lights to be reflected in them. "If I remember right, the presenting peculiarity of that crime scene was . . ."

I pointed at what I thought was just about the exact spot where, as a boy, my brothers and sister had told me that the victim was found. "The presenting peculiarity of the scene was that he was found with his clothes neatly folded next to him. Strangled."

"But, L.T., hang on." Mike, as always, was using skepticism—the basis of our method—to get a grip on himself. "That guy, whatever the fuck his name was—"

"Loudon Odell," I said. "A driver for various antiques stores in Manhattan, who were swindling upstate dealers out of merchandise that was worth far more than they were asking. He was originally from Clinton County, up on the border, but at the time of his arrest he was listed as residing in Greenwich Village. Though no one at his address would confirm as much."

"Right," Mike answered. "And he eventually got four consecutive life sentences—which was the *plea deal,* for Christ's sake, because the cops swore they could have saddled him with quite a few more counts. So there's no way *he's* out."

"No way, indeed," I said. "He was killed in prison."

"Fuck. That's right—at Auburn."

"Had his throat cut from ear to ear, about six months after he got there."

"Yeah. Frankly, I'm surprised he lasted *that* long. Guy running young boys from upstate and Canada down to the city, to the waiting clutches of pedophilic men—" Mike stopped himself suddenly. "Don't," he warned. "*Do not.* You know better than to suggest that kind of connection, L.T."

"Michael, I haven't suddenly lost my senses, nor forgotten my own present theory." I finally turned around, to see that the look in Mike's eyes was just as freaked out as I'd imagined it would be. "I'm not talking about any connection to some other killer. Not at all . . ."

"Then what the fuck *are* you talking about?"

"If we are proposing that these kids got to New York—" I lifted my cane toward the highway. "How did they get there?"

Mike sighed impatiently, and looked around at the highway: to find yourself along such isolated stretches of Route 22, especially at that hour, can be frightening; and Mike was rapidly becoming caught up in that sensation: "Yeah, that's *half* of what I was afraid you meant . . ."

"Well?" I parried, pulling out a cigarette, lighting it, and beginning to pace, letting the exercise of the few muscles in my left stump ease some

of the cramping pain in my side. "Consider it: someone could be following an entirely different agenda concerning the dead children—in fact,
we know they are, since the victims are not only boys but girls—and yet
using the same . . . *delivery system*." I jabbed toward the road several
times with my cane. "To wit, Route 22, one of the 'NAMBLA highways,'
as they were called."

"Trajan," Mike said, taking out a cigarette of his own. "I am begging
you—do not bring up the fucking subject of NAMBLA—*any* aspect of it.
Not when we get to this next murder scene, or at any other time during
this investigation."

"I don't intend to. But the fact is that Odell claimed to have been paid
to bring what he said were runaway boys to New York, to members of
NAMBLA, using *this* road."

"So what?" Mike nearly shouted. "The guy was a half-wit!"

"Ah," I replied. "Now, *that* was never actually established. In fact, Dr.
Abrahamsen said that the whole mentally challenged line was an act, just
like Berkowitz's claim that he got his orders to kill from his next-door
neighbor's dog." Dr. David Abrahamsen had been one of the great criminal psychiatrists of our time, the man who had effectively sent David
Berkowitz—the "Son of Sam"—to prison rather than a psychiatric center,
after rightly asserting to the court, over the dissent of half a dozen other
doctors, that Berkowitz's insanity act had been just that. He had also
been a mentor of mine, prior to his death in 2002.

"So *what*?" Mike repeated. "What has any of this got to do with *our*
case? Those supposed 'members of NAMBLA' were never even *named*."

"That's not my point," I replied. "He picked up boys along highways
that we happen to know were associated with NAMBLA, from other
missing-children cases. And he delivered them to *someone* in New York,
that much we do know—"

"Or he just killed them all."

"He confessed to killing four, Mike, and got the max four times over:
they couldn't have done much more to him if he'd confessed to another
dozen. So why didn't he? He was a serial killer, after all, that *would* have
been the usual behavior."

"And you and I don't go by 'usual' anything!" Mike shook his head in
weary frustration. "Trajan, if you bring up that NAMBLA shit with these
people now, I warn you, there will be backlash, from law enforcement,
from the gay community—"

"And quite right that community would be to lash out," I said, nodding. "'The North American Man-Boy Love Association'—has there ever been a more reprehensible euphemism for a gang of child molesters?"

"Which doesn't change the fact that a lot of its members were some very influential and famous people," Mike interjected quietly, as if we might be overheard.

I tried to recall a quote: "'To label pedophilia as criminal is ridiculous.'"

"Who came up with that gem?" Mike asked. "Or is it one of your own?"

"One of their more illustrious members," I said. "A New York poet whose place on the Lower East Side had been rumored for a long time to be one of the last stops for the routes that were used to get kids south: from Canada, upstate, anyplace where their 'liberators'—of whom Odell was only one—found lost boys looking to get to the big city, or susceptible to such persuasion. The adults waiting in New York would then subject them to a period of 'self-discovery,' during which they'd realize that their restlessness was only an expression of their repressed homosexuality."

"And if they weren't repressed homosexuals?" Mike asked.

"No such animal," I replied. "Not in the NAMBLA book. All boys were innately gay, to them—just needed a friendly hand to allow them to come out, to embody the true nature that the narrow communities they'd come from had forced them to keep hidden."

"Which doesn't explain why some of them wound up dead," Mike said, indicating the increasingly black line of the woods somewhat fearfully.

"Sure it does," I said. "If they proved uncooperative—if it seemed like they might blow the lid off the entire operation—then they just disappeared altogether. Without the knowledge of NAMBLA's organizers, of course. No, the supposition in each case was that they tried to make their way home and met with the wrong person or persons along the way." I shrugged. "It does happen. Anyway, the point is, a few that we know of ended up on the sides of highways, or in the woods somewhere, or in abandoned barns, dead—you starting to get the idea?"

"Yeah," Mike answered. "But I'll say it again: you *can't* draw that kind of connection."

"I'm not suggesting *copycat* deaths," I answered. "After all, in this one case—but *only* the one—Odell left the folded clothes behind, just as Shelby's were; although he later admitted that he only did so because a passing driver caught a glimpse of him, and he had to abandon his trophies. No, I am noting a single *circumstantial* similarity, while pointing out— and this is the key—that *that* case was well known. Anybody could have read about it, and seen that it worked as a way to get kids to the city and into the company of welcoming pedophiles. They could then have picked up on the—*logistical technique.* You were the one, after all, who detailed how Shelby Capamagio likely reached New York, and somehow found some pretty well-to-do sponsors."

But Mike was shaking his head determinedly. "Damn it, Trajan, that's just what I mean—that's exactly what will make senior law enforcement around here explode. You remember the rest of the story? Like how long it took for the towns that those kids came from to ditch the stigma of allowing their 'lost boys' to get picked up and victimized? Think about it—how many of those 'NAMBLA Murders' happened in Burgoyne County?"

"Two, that we know of," I replied quietly.

"Okay—you think the people we're on our way to see want anybody in the media to even *suggest* that something similar is happening now, to some of the children involved in the biggest youth scandal of this generation—to *throwaway* children? And can you guess how long it'll take them to accuse *us* of being the source of those suggestions, just as fucking punishment? We'll be skinned, L.T., you *know* all this!"

"Of course I know it," I said. "And no, I don't intend to bring it up—not outside our own investigation. But don't you think it's just a little bit odd that, once again, four child deaths have occurred within shouting distance of one of the main 'NAMBLA highways'?"

Mike sighed his concession: "Yeah. It's weird, all right . . ."

"And you talk about suggestions, Mike—the people around here aren't idiots, and a lot of them are old enough to remember that time very clearly. You think that if enough kids go missing now, no matter what law enforcement or the media says or does, that it's not going to suggest things to them, and they won't go looking for their *own* answers? At which point similarities or precedents won't matter—there'd better be some God damned answers waiting."

"But there's always the chance," Mike said, struggling, "that it's just a—a—"

"Oh, no," I said, holding up a hand. "Not that damned word, Michael, not to *me*."

"Well!" he protested. "Coincidences *do* happen, Trajan. Not as often as they do in movies or on television, but they happen. And at this point, we have no concrete reason to believe that this is anything but one. Particularly since the gay community is now a powerful force in state politics: if we let it slip that we're looking, or causing the sheriff to look, at any kind of connection between Burgoyne County and an old, disgraced gay organization that managed to put a black eye on this county, the shitstorm that will descend on *us*—"

"We're not *going* to let it slip. How could we? We're unofficial advisors to the sheriff and his chief deputy. It's not like we're going to be holding press conferences."

Mike's hands went to the sides of his head hard. "We don't *have* to hold any fucking press conferences—you've brought a *fifteen-year-old kid* into our investigation! What do you think *he's* going to do with this idea—keep it to himself? Is that your experience of boys his age?"

"I think we can trust him—I really do, Mike. And *if* we can, think of it: we will have an unprecedented chance to find another ring of predators by learning who they are targeting *before* they make their next move." I paused and lifted my cigarette toward the woods. "So don't tell me about coincidences—you don't believe in them any more than I do. But, in recognition of your misgivings, I'll agree to keep this theory between us, for the time being. All right?"

"Yeah," he said, opening the driver's-side door of the Empress. "Between *us*. Now get your crippled ass into this car, so we can go see what is actually happening in Fraser."

"Done," I said, opening my own door; but I had to give the edge of those woods one long last look, if only out of respect for that poor kid who had been found in a condition so eerily similar to Shelby Capamagio's, all those years ago, and who now seemed to be guiding us . . .

Soon enough, however, we were back under way, Mike hitting the gas especially hard: he was right to be irritated, of course, just as he was right to warn me against moving too quickly toward the belief that some group had studied the "NAMBLA Murders" and was now using a similar method to move children who had been abandoned by their families down to New York City and into the company of waiting pedophiles. Statistics, as Mike had said, told us that the odds of such a parallel, intentional or not, were slim; but the two of us had spent most of our careers debunking statistics, although Mike was in no mood to be reminded of that fact.

And he was right, too, that if we openly heeded the strange call of that tormented stretch of highway, it would spell ruin for far more than our advisory role with regard to Steve and Pete. Rather than admit that such a parallel existed, county and state officials would surely see us disgraced and deprived of the livelihood we'd established at SUNY-Albany, in just the same way that we'd been run out of New York City for rather brazenly investigating several cases that connected people of means to a particularly salacious series of murders. Yes, Michael was right to warn me of the dangers of raking up the NAMBLA matter, in any connection—

None of which meant that privately betting on the seemingly slim chance that such a connection existed might not be the right way to go. And so the possibility remained irretrievably lodged in my brain, as well as in Mike's, I knew, to become nothing more until we had evidence to support it. Until, that is, we could make it stand up as something other than just one more example of that most seductive, common, and corrosive of all investigatory phenomena: the hunch. Yet somehow, I believed, we might very well do just that, eventually . . .

What I could not have guessed at was just how soon "eventually" would prove to be. The rest of our ride was passed in pointed silence, Mike plainly not wanting to hear another word out of me until we reached our destination. And his desire to keep me quiet kept his foot heavy on the accelerator of the Empress along the highway now, until we hit the eastern outskirts of Fraser and had to slow down to avoid being picked up by either a state trooper, a local Fraser cop, or one of Steve's junior deputies who knew nothing about where we were going or why.

The county seat was very quiet, by the time we found ourselves on its streets and looking for the turnoff to Route 4 North; or rather, the streets of its manufacturing and government districts were quiet. The former was an even greater monument to lost enterprise than were the darkened textile mills that dotted the rolling landscape of Hoosick Falls: Fraser had once been—like most of the old industrial towns that ringed Albany— a center for the production of mammoth machinery, some of it so large that it was hard to imagine its being made in a place that sat so close to enormous stretches of farmland and wilderness. In Schenectady, to the west, the manufacture of train locomotives—most of the locomotives

used in the United States and, indeed, in much of the rest of the world—
had been the source of long-departed wealth; in Fraser, the production of
the boilers that fit many of those same locomotives had been the well-
spring. But the now-ghostly factories that had produced those controlled
infernos had long since had their very guts—their mills and their
furnaces—cut to pieces and sold as cheap scrap to Chinese traders who
shipped them abroad to be melted down and become factories in that
country; and only a few of the hollow brick shells left behind had been
converted to the production or purposes of anything else. Most simply
sat in the growing darkness through which Mike and I moved, staring
back at us in accusation, as if to ask—as such buildings throughout the
Northeast and indeed all of America forever ask—how we as a people
could have let such greatness slip through our fingers, merely to allow
their proprietors to move production abroad to maximize personal profits. *The country that manufactures nothing,* ran the old saying in such
towns, *eventually becomes nothing;* and you could not argue with the
logic, when it was displayed by such buildings as we passed in Fraser that
night.

Nor did the downtown business section of town lift one's spirits very
much more: though the recipient of endless grants from Albany to revive
its storefront enterprises, as well as to sandblast the marble and limestone of the oldest official buildings, the efforts thus funded had never
truly succeeded in removing an aura of decline and decay from the place.
Over the whole of this area, as well as over Fraser's one park, the old
Beaux-arts county court and clerk's offices—long since deserted by such
really active agencies as the Department of Motor Vehicles, which had
been moved to a bunker-like structure on the southern edge of town
during the 1980s—presided with the appropriate air of a madam long
past her prime, in whose rooms were conducted affairs of dubious taste
and questionable legality. It was impossible not to be charmed by the old
girl, even though one was certain that most of the lights that still burned
within were illuminating the work of lawyers whose sole interest was
shoehorning ever more tax dollars out of an overburdened population,
and causing many such citizens—like the families of at least two of our
murder victims—not only to give up the struggle to survive in the county
of their birth, but to abandon at least one of the hungry young mouths
that would only complicate their settlement in other, purportedly more
promising climes.

"Hey, check that out," Mike said as we passed the courthouse, rousing me from my dismal reverie. "Steve and Pete's office—there's almost nobody there."

The sheriff of Burgoyne County's various rooms occupied the northeast corner of the courthouse's grand old mass of stone, and was usually the hub of quite a bit of activity, especially on a warm summer's evening; but looking toward the parking lot that should have contained half a dozen deputies' cars, and then at the windows on the first and second floors of offices, I could see that Mike was right: all the cars were gone, and of the offices, only the receiving desk betrayed any sign of light or human movement.

"What do you think?" Mike asked, with just a trace of dread.

"Don't jump to anything," I answered. "We haven't hit the fun part of town yet—could just be a long night on Broadway . . ."

To find any real nighttime action in Fraser, you had to wait until you'd passed through downtown and hit the low-rent, dilapidated apartment houses of the north side, where the county seat's most thriving businesses—bars—were lined up along each block, at least two to a side, on the two-way street that had long ago been rather ambitiously named Broadway. The thirst brought on by desperation was the bars' common reason for prosperity; the only things that varied among them were the races and nationalities of their patrons. No gentrification, of the kind you invariably found to have transformed such places in New York, had yet complicated matters: old-time whites, the descendants of the county's original settlers, defended their bars, just as the more recent arrivals from different regions of Europe watched over theirs; then, as one moved north, it was blacks who kept vigil over the places they frequented, while Asians went literally underground, and did their drinking amid basement gambling joints.

As Mike and I drove north on Broadway, which eventually merged into Route 4, we began to laugh at the consistent sight of bodies flying out the doors of these bars, all of them faced with white vinyl clapboarding broken only by small windows whose neon signs declared both their names and allegiances. And yet, on this night, no law enforcement could be seen attending to the brawling. Steve's deputies' cars, along with those of Fraser's police force, had evidently been drawn somewhere else: and we would soon find out just where—and why . . .

We hit as little traffic as we expected, once away from central Fraser's traffic lights; and in a few more minutes, we merged onto what was now four-lane Broadway, which ran down the middle of the county seat's black ghetto. A depressing succession of the kind of two-story developments that had been laid out in the 1960s, the neighborhood was a dangerous place for white people after dark, perhaps the only part of the county of which such could be said. Because we were native New Yorkers, this fact generally made Mike and me less nervous than it did local and state law enforcement, although it did not make us any less realistic: experience had taught us that, though North Fraser was not a patch on, say, East New York, we would do well to show it the same careful respect we exhibited in that section of the southern metropolis, making sure not to exhibit the compensating arrogance that Fraser cops tended to do.

When we finally reached the address that Pete had given Mike, we found that we had special reason to heed the native New Yorker's instinctive respect of unfamiliar neighborhoods: instead of being faced with a crime scene investigation around the particular abandoned building where the young boy's body had been found, we encountered a cordon of more than two dozen police cars spaced some two blocks from the site. Local Fraser cops; almost every car in Steve Spinetti's county fleet; several unmarked vehicles that I knew belonged to the officials with whom we had been summoned to conference; a hand-me-down MRAP armored combat vehicle, painted blue-black, one of half a dozen that the Army had given to the various regional units of the state's Special Operations Response Team, most of whom were on hand to support a collection of Mitch McCarron's Troop G State Police interceptors: all these and more were in attendance. It was as much law as I'd ever seen assembled in Burgoyne County; and when you added the fact that all the marked vehicles had their respective roof lights spinning and flashing, it created quite a display. Head- and searchlights, too, were on, all fixed on the building that should have been the quiet scene of activity on the part of Ernest Weaver and one of Nancy Grimes' FIC techs—

And just then I noticed something: "Mike—can you see anybody from the FBI around?"

Mike scanned the area, then noised, "Hunh. No, I can't, now that you mention it."

"But they ought to have been called into this case by now, correct?"

"Yeah," Mike answered. "Abandoned and supposedly murdered kids? Absolutely."

"Odd" was all I could conclude, a bit uneasily; then, when we asked a Fraser cop at a checkpoint, we discovered that our names were on the guest list for the party, a fact that neither Mike nor I much liked:

"Trajan," Mike said slowly, finally lighting the cigarette that had hung on his lip for half our drive. "This smells more and more like a trap . . ."

"Indeed," I said; then I pointed suddenly. "There's Pete, directing traffic. Let's get over to him—we'll have our chance to talk without the others butting in."

Pete caught sight of our car, and indicated a spot to park, into which Mike pulled the car. "Just as long as we don't get our heads blown off, in the process," my partner murmured.

"Well, Michael," I said, opening my door and planting my cane outside, "your mother *did* want you to be a lawyer."

Mike opened his own door, then pulled deeply on his cigarette before flicking it away and murmuring, "Don't fucking remind me . . ."

He might have gone on in this vein had not Pete turned his traffic duties over to a Fraser cop and rushed to meet us. "I'm glad you guys are here," he said. "We have got one screwed-up situation on our hands—nobody spotted him earlier, but there's a black guy in the same building as the kid's body, and he's talking pretty nuts, we can't really make out about what. Looks like he's got a gun—and the only person who even pretends to be some kind of hostage negotiator here is Frank Mangold."

"Oh, Jesus," I groaned; for the hard-nosed Frank Mangold of the state's Bureau of Criminal Investigation was about as unsuited to such a role as could be imagined. Yet even as I considered this unfortunate fact, the full peculiarity of Pete's words hit me. "But what the hell do you need a hostage negotiator for? The kid's dead, Pete, isn't he?"

"It's not the kid, Doc," Pete said. "The guy's got Weaver in there."

Mike and I were both dumbfounded. "But—who the fuck would take *Weaver* as a hostage?" Mike murmured; and then, suddenly, the musical chime that indicated the arrival of a text message on my partner's phone sounded from inside his jacket. "Whoa!" he said eagerly. "Hang on." He snatched the phone out, quickly read the lengthy message, and then looked up at the deputy. "Okay, Pete—it appears we got what we were waiting for." Without bothering to tell me what he was talking about, Mike went on to ask, "Did you bring that sack?"

"Yep," Pete answered. "Come on to my car and check it out there, before the others notice you've gotten here—they see you and we won't have time to go over it."

We followed Pete through the maze of busily chatting officers, keeping our faces as obscured as possible with our hands; but I nonetheless demanded of Mike, "You want to tell me what's going on, or are you in one of your inscrutable moods? This *is* a hostage scene, Mike, it may not be the time for evidentiary analysis."

"Oh, yes it is, *gweilo*," Mike replied earnestly. "And you're going to want to get it straight before we see that collection of saps. Because it *could* be confirmation that your demented ramblings back on the highway weren't so twisted, after all—and that's going to make you think twice about just what you want to say to our hosts . . ."

{ii.}

When we reached Pete's car, I caught sight of a large knapsack lying on the floor behind the driver's seat. It was a worn, olive-drab number, not the kind of thing you saw kids carrying much, anymore, save in wealthier prep schools and colleges, where the style was intended as radical chic; even so, I quickly realized that it looked familiar. And then I remembered the crime scene photos of the first victim, Kyle Howard, who'd been found hanging in an abandoned house on the outskirts of Surrender: a knapsack much like the one Pete was evidently hiding from view had lain below the boy's body. The thing had plainly been carrying books, in the photo; and it was just as plainly carrying them now, though just what use such a collection could be to our work was as yet obscure to me.

Pete opened the rear door of his cruiser very slowly and quietly, although no noise he might have made could possibly have risen above the confused din of the siege that was tightening on the central section of one of the long rows of brickface-and-clapboard structures that ran east of us in a herringbone pattern. Broadway had been closed off and barricaded with patrol cars, first some two blocks to the north, and, since our arrival, at a similar distance to the south: the Fraser cops were evidently expecting quite a show, within their cordon, of the variety that was best kept shielded from the public. Yet their efforts had apparently been in vain. Even from a distance, it was easy to see that curious, boisterous crowds ("aggressive with intent to incite," the Fraser cops would later call them, the kind of meaningless jargon employed by officers unused to dealing with such situations) were gathering and growing, most of their members black, some probably just trying to get home after a long week and a longer Friday. But others, particularly the younger men in the crowds, were pulling off their shirts and waving them as they hollered vague indictments at the various officers on the perimeter.

"All right, you two," I said, moving as quickly as I could into the front passenger seat of Pete's cruiser. "Whatever it is you're up to, make it fast. This thing's set to blow."

"What'd I tell you?" Pete said, as I turned on his radio and listened to several voices that were arguing over whose actual hostage specialist could get to the scene first, the BCI's or the state troopers'. "Hey, Doc, go easy, there," the deputy went on. "It'll be my ass if somebody sees you listening in on confidential police matters."

"Yeah, and it's gonna be *both* your asses if you don't tell me what the fuck you're doing," I said, giving up on getting anything clear from the radio, lowering its volume, and then peering over the seat. "What gives with the books and the messages, Mike?"

"It's very simple, Trajan," Mike mumbled, his eyes once again on his phone, which had sounded again, bringing in a new message that was accompanied, this time, by several photos. After enlarging them, Mike handed me the phone and said, "What's that look like?" Then he opened the knapsack and began pulling volumes out of it.

I studied the photos, enlarging details of them, but gaining no insight that would have allowed me to improve on my initial, rather dim answer: "Hair. Animal hair, if I had to guess. Two samples, side by side."

"Which makes you smarter than most so-called trace experts," Mike said, "who can't tell the difference between animal and human samples. They're from two horses' manes, actually. A colleague in Louisville sent them along as examples. One is taken from a horse very much like the ones bred by Kelsey Kozersky's family; the second from a pure thorough-bred. Our concern, however, isn't with their looks, but with their DNA."

Mike had suddenly switched gears, and was now talking about the second victim in the case. Kelsey Kozersky had been fifteen at the time of her death, and for most of her life had lived on a hardscrabble horse farm not all that far from Death's Head Hollow. Two parents and a like number of younger brothers had rounded out the family, which had been thrown into a prolonged crisis when Kelsey—a tall, very pretty girl whose affection for horses Lucas had understated on our first meeting—had reached adolescence and begun to violently question her father's treatment of his stock. This indicated more than just a classic example of a young girl's passing infatuation with horses: Kelsey had proved willing to sustain domestic discord in the name of decent treatment of the Kozersky horses, which were undistinguished beasts, in terms of bloodlines, but were hardworking, easily ridden, and quite strong; and the girl's principled commitment to them had been unusual for anyone her age.

The crisis had come when Kelsey's favorite horse—a mongrel born of a sire who'd had a smattering of thoroughbred blood, and happened to produce a colt who was unusually beautiful and quick, leading Kelsey to claim it for her own—had come down with equine protozoal myeloencephalitis, or EPM, an infection of the central nervous system. The disease is wasting and heartbreaking, often leaving afflicted animals unable to use their legs and, eventually, dead. The treatment for EPM is fairly lengthy and expensive, and for Kelsey's father, who was barely eking out a living, there had been a far easier solution: a bullet from a .30-30 Winchester. The death of the horse that had been her great love had caused Kelsey's behavior to become increasingly unmanageable: not only deliberately disruptive but dangerous, involving all-night drinking binges and other self-destructive patterns.

Mike and I had learned all this from Kelsey's file, which contained statements from the girl's parents as well as from an independent pathologist, whom Steve had brought in when Ernest Weaver had delivered another superficial verdict. Kelsey had apparently run away from home, and several months later been found by her father hanging in the family's barn, from a beam above the empty stall that had once been her horse's home; and for Weaver, that had been that. The pathologist's report, however, had shown that Kelsey's fate had been similar to Kyle Howard's and then to Shelby Capamagio's: the girl had been dead for far longer than the barn incident indicated. Her blood lividity said that she'd been cut down after the original event, laid out somewhere for a number of hours, and then rehanged. In addition, several hairs from a horse's mane had been found on the girl's clothes. These were thought to belong to one of the animals staying in the barn at the time Kelsey's lifeless body was discovered there, and no one had thought to examine them any further; that is, until Mike made his determination about the drugs on Shelby's clothes, and went looking for an element common to the two girls' deaths.

"I was about to tell you about it, along with the Kyle Howard evidence," Mike said, as he continued to scan the books in the knapsack, one by one, "when Pete called. Then you got into your insanity on the highway, so I figured I'd just wait until I knew for sure. See, earlier today, while you were—" He was about to say "meeting Lucas," but thankfully did not. "—walking Marcianna, I did a quick DNA sequence on the sample that Pete sent over—"

"You can do that?" Pete asked in some astonishment. "With your operation in the *plane*?"

Mike shook his head with a smile. "Listen, Pete—I'm betting ADA Donovan has told you county guys that her boss plans to update as many local law cruisers as possible with portable DNA sequencers, right? So they can keep up with Albany's plans for the Staties?"

"Yeah," Pete said, wiping his brow. "But to tell you the truth, I thought she was full of it."

"Nope," Mike answered. "They're already doing it in other places. Pretty soon, when you pull somebody over, you won't have to check their record against their license—you'll just swab their mouths, or take a secondary source out of their car, if they're being difficult, and then run it through your own fucking sequencer, and boom!—instant DNA matching. I'm sure it'll be challenged on constitutional grounds—since it would give cops permission to assemble a database of anyone behaving even 'suspiciously'—so it's not as close as people like Donovan would like to think. But it gives her a great way to argue for increased federal funding. Anyway, my rig's better than those gadgets, if I say so myself, and I used it to do the sequence on the sample you sent over, the hairs on Kelsey's clothes, which the FIC techs had been more than happy to say were her father's horses'. It was the simplest explanation, after all, and that's what everybody wanted. But after I was finished, I sent my analysis on to my colleague in Louisville, who dug into it deeper. Ever heard, L.T., of the Equine Genetic Diversity Consortium?"

Shaking my head impatiently, I said, "You know damned well that I haven't, Michael."

Mike smiled in satisfaction. "And yet you're the one they always call 'Doctor' . . . Well, the EGDC, of which my colleague is a member, has been working to establish a genome database for horse populations, to increase the ability of scientists, breeders, and buyers to establish the origins of animals—particularly thoroughbreds, of course—from around the world, going back to their original, ancient herds. And what the message you're looking at says, basically, is that the hairs on Kelsey's clothing do not match the kind of horses that her father raises. Instead, they are samples from some very purebred, expensive lines—thoroughbreds."

I began to nod, getting it. "So—she had not been cavorting with her father's horses before her death, but had instead—"

"Had instead been riding," Mike went on, "not long before her death, some very pricey animals. The kind most likely bred, if she stayed in our general neck of the woods during the months she ran away, in stables down in horse country. Meaning—"

"Meaning Westchester County," I finished for him. "The nicest parts, that is. Maybe a few farms farther upstate, but most likely Westchester. And that places her . . ."

"That places her," Mike said, again picking up the theme, "in close proximity to two things: Route 22, which cuts right through horse country, and New York City. Because most of the people who own those really nice thoroughbred farms don't live on them. Not most of the time. And so—the indicators are the same as they were for Shelby: she likely never went any great distance; not in terms of miles."

"But in terms of worlds," I mused, staring at the photos of the magnified horsehairs, "very far from the life and the world she had known." I handed Mike his phone. "On a farm owned, in all likelihood, by someone whose base was in the city—someone with whom she had probably been living."

"Of course, we don't know what conditions were put on her to *get* that lifestyle," Mike said. "Remember—Kelsey diverges from the others in one crucial aspect: she was a runaway. Not an abandoned kid. But if you place the cause of death and the lifestyle immediately before it in relation to what we've also posited about Shelby's last days . . ."

"Then both girls made their way to the city," Pete reasoned, somewhat sadly, "and took up with people who were pretty well off."

" 'Pretty well off' might be a big understatement, Pete," I added. "And as to whether both girls 'made their way to the city,' or if they were *taken* there by someone who had made certain extravagant guarantees about the lives they would find there—well, that's the crux of it."

Pete just stared out the window of his cruiser blankly. "And you mention Route 22 for a reason," he soon murmured. "Don't think I don't know it. You're talking about something like the damned NAMBLA killings all over again."

Mike quickly looked at me, then at Pete, and back at me. "I never said a thing," I stated.

"Yeah, well," Mike answered, returning to the books, "we have to make sure *nobody* says a thing. You'll have to tell Steve, of course, Pete, but—that's it. I've already explained to the Sorcerer that if you even mention the NAMBLA Murders to the senior people here—"

"You don't have to tell me," Pete answered. "They'll lose it; and life'll get a whole lot less pleasant, not to mention a whole lot less private, on this case. My God . . ."

Pete's grim reverie was interrupted by a quiet cry of discovery from Mike: "Ha! Got one. Exactly what I was looking for . . ." Pulling a hard-cover book from among Kyle Howard's collection, Mike held it up to the lit roof dome of the cruiser. "Yep." He handed the book to me and then shoved his searching hands back into the knapsack. "Notice anything, Trajan?"

I examined the book's fine leather binding quickly, along with the faded gold lettering on its spine. *"Oliver Twist,"* I said; and then, moving to the inside of the front cover, I noticed an elegantly lettered bookmark stuck inside. "'The Odyssey Bookstore,' eh?" Then I went directly to the title page: "First American edition, signed by the author . . ." My understanding of what Mike was up to had finally grown complete. "Hell's bloody bells, Michael—so you've got it . . ."

"And I'm about to get more," Mike declared, having yanked one more volume from the sack. *"Catcher in the Rye*—signed by J. D. Salinger. Also from the Odyssey, also a first edition—a first *American* edition, if you can believe it."

"Yeah," I murmured rather grimly, putting down the copy of *Oliver Twist*. "I can believe it. The Dickens is enough, but the Salinger? Given the market—especially in New York, where nine out of ten trust-fund babies are walking around trying to be Holden Caulfield—that has got to be major bucks."

"Okay, boys," Pete said, picking up the Dickens. "You mind explaining it to *me*?"

"Well, it's good, and it's bad, Pete," I said. "The Odyssey Bookstore is a very upscale joint selling rare editions on the Upper East Side of Manhattan. Both these books were bought there, for enormous amounts of money. The Dickens is rare enough, even though it's not a first British edition. But a signed first edition of *Catcher in the Rye*? God only knows what that must've gone for. Yet a boy who we know loved books shows up dead in Surrender with that kind of merchandise?" I shook my head. "Put it, again, in the context of what we've found out about the two girls, and I'm afraid we have a definite pattern. Three kids, all separated from their families in Burgoyne County, end up having gone to or near New York City, and return with evidence of having spent time with people of impressive means who were plying them with the specific kinds of things we know they were most attracted to . . . This is no God damned coincidence."

"Well, L.T.," my partner said at length, genuinely conceding the issue. "Looks like you were right, too. Congrats—even if I *did* have to supply the pesky evidence. As fucking usual . . ."

"Yeah," I said gloomily, sitting against Pete's dashboard and taking another look at the scene around us. "Well, we certainly can't tell *them* any of this. No matter how true it may be."

"You mean," Pete added, no great joy in his voice, either, "that the notion of something like the NAMBLA killings is actually *proved* by all this?"

"Not the particulars, Pete," Mike answered. "We've got a different group of target kids, in this case: girls *and* boys. So it's something more generalized, and more shielded. But the method? When you add the remarkable proximity of one of the main routes of—*supply* . . ."

"Meaning Route 22?" Pete asked.

"Meaning 22," Mike said with a nod. "So, given all that . . . Then yeah, it's looking like somebody, either coincidentally—which is awfully unlikely—or intentionally, is repeating the damned method." He finally let go of the knapsack. "There's a couple more books in here that fit for the Howard boy, not that it makes much difference . . ." He pulled a cigarette out of his shirt pocket and lit it. "It definitely does appear that we've got some new person or group following the general NAMBLA pattern."

"But with one more twist," I explained to Pete. "They're not just picking up kids around here who have no future, and then taking them downstate—they're offering promises beforehand of whatever appeals to each kid's wildest dreams. He, she, or they *know* these kids. Personally.

Know what they want out of life. And the parallel goes even further—because some of them have ended up back up here, probably for the same reasons some of the NAMBLA kids did: they didn't like the price they were being asked to pay for their very fancy lifestyle, in the end. So they had to be gotten rid of, to protect the rest of the operation." Both Mike and I were dancing, now, to avoid the subject of possible suicides: we didn't want, in light of our last important experience with law enforcement in New York, to give away too much too soon.

Pete was, understandably, very apprehensive. "And the county and state people—I mean, I know they're not gonna want to hear it, but . . . you're saying we *can't* tell them?"

"That's what we're saying, Pete," Mike answered.

"So what *do* we do?" Pete protested. "We have to tell them *something*."

"Not yet, we don't," I said. "We have to do just the opposite: keep it to ourselves. Let Steve know, of course, like Mike says, and see what he can do with it. But the rest of them? For all the reasons we've mentioned, we say nothing. This is going to have to be *our* theory, for now. Because we have to put it through a much more serious set of tests—it's too radical not to." I gripped my cane tighter, struggling to get out of the cruiser. "Our immediate concern, however, is to make sure that Mangold and his boys don't slaughter that guy in the house. Because there's a good chance that, far from being crazy, he's the first living person we've encountered who may be able to shed some light on exactly what is happening—the hows and the whys. So, come on, both of you—let's get out there . . ."

Pete led the way through the increasingly anxious ranks of the various officers who were watching the building on which were trained the lights of the fleet of official vehicles around us, along with a couple of high-powered searchlights that had by now been brought in. It was the kind of scene that, again, had become dreadfully familiar, in the years since 9/11: cops strapping on black Kevlar and donning military-style helmets of a matching shade, all looking forward to executing some sort of paramilitary maneuver in order to—what? To pursue one evidently terrified man who, even assuming he was in fact armed, had not fired a single shot, nor done anything else much, save be seen in the same building as a dead boy and heard uttering phrases of which no one had been able to make any sense? That he had then snatched, upon the arrival of a steady stream of aggressive law enforcement officers, the first person he came upon—Weaver—either as a hostage (which was clearly what the officers all thought) or simply in an effort to explain himself to someone who wasn't holding a gun to his head, was eminently understandable. However, such distinctions were of no concern to the growing assault force around us: a special buzzword had gone out among the ranks, and whatever those men and women knew about actual police work was fast giving way to the new vision that most law enforcement officers had of themselves, of something between an occupational force and an absolute guarantee against any and all that was contained within that one electric word that had taken on such terrible connotations in daily American life since 2001: *threat*.

Grouped around the open rear end of a black, unmarked van (clearly belonging to the Bureau of Criminal Investigation) and behind the girding troops was the group of people we had been summoned to see. At their center, her diminutive size and smart black pants suit belying her toughness, was Cathy Donovan, the assistant district attorney for Burgoyne County. One always got the feeling that Donovan must have been something of a hot ticket, at whatever high school she had attended, but that the demands of achievement during law school, along with those of the family that was so necessary to the political career that had filled the years thereafter, had turned her good looks hard, and caused her to constantly exude the air of someone who was not to be trifled with. And I did not: because for all that she may have been an ambitious political *apparatchik* in county and state affairs, Donovan was also smart and discerning, and not at all predictable.

No such assessment, however, could be offered of the woman who was standing next to her. Nancy Grimes, head of the Forensic Investigation Center, was garbed, as ever, in a white lab coat large enough to fit her hefty frame, beneath which she wore some sort of bland clothes that were of no account: the only article that concerned her was that eternally crisp white coat, which she sported like a field marshal's uniform—an analogy that applied perfectly to the manner in which she ran her laboratory. Although it had been beset, before and during her tenure, by scandals (most of which centered, like almost all forensic lab troubles, on techs falsifying results, either out of simple incompetence or to suit the needs of prosecutors), she nonetheless carried her impressive bulk with an attitude that dared any who came close to try to impugn either herself or her staff. That she almost always kept close to Donovan, in every way, on such occasions was only a further reminder of how very much criminal science, when it became forensic science, had prostituted itself to the requirements of prosecutory officials. But Grimes never seemed to mind in the least that she was projecting such an impression; and certainly Mike and I, two exiles from the official world that she still very much inhabited, were always meant to be particularly impressed by her lack of concern on this score.

Facing these two women was Frank Mangold, the detective from the state BCI, along with Nancy Grimes' criminal psychologist, someone whom I was disappointed and not a little disheartened to see and whom I had once known well: Dr. Grace (Gracie, to more-than-official acquaintances) Chang. But the real danger in this last appearance lay with Mike: Gracie had been something of an apprentice among the NYPD crime lab's group of criminal psychologists, when Mike and I were still in the city, and Mike always had a bit of a thing for her. And so, observing that my partner still hadn't spied his old heartthrob, I said:

"Uh-oh. Get hold of your hormones, Mike."

"What, what, what?" he shot back, nervously but eagerly.

"Standing next to Grimes," I answered with a nod.

"Where, who—?" he asked, in the same rapid, uneasy tone; and then he caught sight of her. "Well—fuck *me . . .*"

"I will do no such thing," I replied quietly. "*She* might, if we handle this correctly."

"Oh, eat shit, Trajan," Mike murmured. "How long have you known that she's been working in Albany, anyway?"

"Hey, I don't get appointment reports from these people," I defended. "I can only assume that she got tired of being a small fish in a big pond, and decided to enhance her stature by decreasing the size of her swimming hole. It would have been a sound move, for a girl as smart as Gracie."

"Yeah," Mike answered uneasily. "Fantastic. Now what the fuck am *I* supposed to do?"

"You're supposed to be your normal charming self," I answered, dead serious. "And remember, above all, that she may be here simply because she told Nancy Grimes about your jones for her."

"Gracie?" Mike's face went wide with disbelief. "No. She'd never be that ruthless, or that manipulative. Unlike certain of *your* girlfriends."

"Oh, really?" I answered. "Mike, she's a criminal psychologist, and was a good one, if a relative beginner, when we knew her; and she's doubtless only gotten better, with time and experience. In addition, like everybody else in the state system, she's ambitious. I don't like to think it, either, but—it's an awfully strange coincidence, isn't it?"

Mike began to nod, his cognitive functions steadily melting away in the face of Gracie Chang's animated and charming face and figure. "And we don't believe in coincidences . . ." he finally mumbled, as if in a trance.

"I don't get it," said Pete, who, up to this point, had been maintaining a bewildered silence. "You're saying that Mike and Dr. Chang were once involved?"

"No!" Mike shot back; then he softened: "Sorry, Pete. But no. I've just always thought she was pretty hot."

"Well," Pete judged with a nod, studying Gracie, "I guess she is. But are you saying that's going to be a problem, Dr. Jones?"

"I'm saying the rest of them likely *intend* her to be one, Pete," I answered. "But I'm sure Dr. Li knows how to be professional, now that he is aware of the score."

Mike turned to me, the pace of his words picking up: "So I assume you have a way to use this to our advantage—and give me a straight answer, Trajan, because I've been stuck on that farm with you and your fucking cheetah for an awfully long time . . ."

Glancing back at Gracie, I decided I couldn't really blame Mike for his attitude. Like my partner's, Gracie's family had originally been from southern China, and she had the classic look of the region, with eyes that somehow hid hints of night-sky blue amid the brown and black, high but gentle cheekbones that formed a heart-shaped line with her small, soft chin, a diminutive nose, and a lovely smile that hid just one or two charmingly crooked front teeth. She was one of those girls that you saw all over New York, growing up and in college: always carefully turned out (though since she'd become a criminal psychologist, she'd learned, with a few hints from me, to understate it), and now able, it seemed, to move among even the ethnically parochial officials of Burgoyne County with a kind of mature, genteel, yet self-possessed polish: something you perhaps wouldn't have expected, if you'd seen such girls as teenagers and then students at design or pre-med programs in the city, and watched them laughing and giggling uncontrollably on the subway, always three or four at a time, their hair often changing color from month to month or even week to week. Almost inevitably, they'd be swaying along on one of the three or four routes back to Long Island City or Queensboro Plaza, from whence they'd catch the 7 Train up to Flushing, which has the highest concentration of Chinese businesses and residents in the borough.

None of which, of course, mattered to Mike, at just that moment; and, sympathy aside, I knew I had to get his mind back on business quickly. "How it may work to our advantage," I said, "will, I think, become obvious—because if I know Gracie, she did not, in fact, come here just to play somebody's puppet. Not for the likes of these people—or haven't you noticed who's standing on the other side of her?"

"Yeah," Mike said, shifting his gaze with not a little dread. "*That* asshole . . ."

Senior Investigator Frank Mangold of the BCI was, in appearance, a throwback to another era, a man on whom the absurdly tight-fitting men's fashions of our own times always looked like they were hand-me-downs from the early 1960s—especially when matched against his buzz-cut grey flattop and rather sallow face. But despite his appearance and his unimposing height of five foot nine or so, one would have committed a terrible error by considering him less than the physically powerful man that he was: he'd gotten his earliest edification as a Marine, then his academy and detective's training in New York City during the era of Mayor Rudy Giuliani and Giuliani's right-hand police commissioner, Bernie Kerik, influences that Mangold enjoyed demonstrating by personally pursuing and wrestling to the ground suspects who elected to take flight rather than submit to arrest. That such suspects usually returned to the other officers on the case badly beaten and sometimes wounded was never questioned by anyone in a position to do anything about it; for the Bureau, perhaps even more than the New York State Police below it, had become a shoot-first, investigate-later crowd, in recent years.

But for the moment, it was the curious presence of Gracie Chang, and Mike's reaction to it, that continued to concern me. "Yes," I said, turning to Mike. "*That* asshole. And we're going to have to deal, at the same time, with Gracie's apparent commitment to the politics of prosecution. You going to be okay if I have to get rough?"

Mike, probably through the prolonged study of Frank Mangold's face, had come out of his sex-starved daze, and shot me an annoyed look. "Hey, quit worrying about me, L.T.; it's not like we ever had a thing. I just thought she was good-looking, that's all."

"Good," I replied. "Because we don't need any complications, at this point."

Finally I glanced over to discover who completed the circle of law enforcers we were facing; and I was more than happy to see that the two remaining figures were men that Mike and I actually liked and trusted. One was Steve Spinetti; and the other was Major Mitch McCarron, a tall, reticent man who had seen much of the considerable dark side of life in Burgoyne and its surrounding counties during his career. McCarron had risen from the ranks of patrolling officers, like most troop leaders in the State Police; but, unlike many of the gun-happy younger troopers that he commanded, McCarron had developed a true mastery of all elements of first response, from talking criminals out of unwise decisions to tracking and capturing alive some of the worst offenders in the area over the last twenty-five years. His voice was tinged with the same slow, ambiguous dialect that marked Pete and Steve's conversation, which had once been so common to upstate New York, and which I could still detect in the older farmhands on Shiloh, among others. Whether I warmed to this style of speech because of my childhood memories of life on my great-aunt's farm—the only unequivocally happy recollections I had of my youth—or whether all people found it equally pleasant, I could not say. But my adult years had borne out my trust of those who spoke in a similar manner.

There was only one topic under discussion, as we approached, and since all involved had to speak over the din of the action around them, it was easy enough for us to tell what that subject was long before we had been spotted (although we certainly could have guessed it): how best to approach the man inside the building without further endangering the life of the unfortunate Dr. Weaver. Or rather, the question at hand was *who* was best fitted to this task: it seemed that neither the BCI nor the State Police could get an official hostage negotiator to the scene anything like immediately (for they had few such people, to start with), and somebody had to try to save Weaver before the momentum of the assault force—which was slowly but steadily closing in on the abandoned apartment house, without anyone ordering it to—caused a manifold tragedy.

"Okay," Pete said as we approached, "let me handle taking you in. The distraction'll give me a chance to tell Steve about what's up. From there, though—you're on your own."

"We'll be all right, Pete," I said, trying to evoke more confidence than I felt.

Mike was clearly even more anxious than I was; but we had, after all, been brought before such tribunals to explain our actions before, and had faced far more powerful and impressive inquisitors. Even so, as we pressed forward, Mike murmured, with evident trepidation: "I really hope you know how the fuck we're going to handle this, L.T. . . ."

{iii.}

As we reached the van, Pete called out to the others, interrupting their debate: "Okay," he said amiably. "You said find 'em and bring 'em, so I did. I think everybody here knows each other. So I'll leave you to it—Steve, I had a call from the office, couple of questions for you. Nothing too important, but I'll need your okay on some things . . ." And with that, Pete pulled Steve aside to explain how matters secretly stood, leaving Mike and me to face the others.

I slapped as sincere a smile as was possible on my face, placed my latest cigarette in the fingers that gripped my cane, and stepped forward with my right hand outstretched. "Assistant District Attorney," I said, gently shaking Donovan's small hand.

"Dr. Jones," Donovan answered, returning my smile in a manner that was not at all reassuring. "Nice of you to come on such—short notice . . ."

I moved on. "Inspector," I continued, taking Grimes' meatier paw. "A pleasure."

"Spare me, Doctor," Grimes answered, although she chuckled when she said it. "And you can stick to 'Director,' in my case. I've got no law enforcement rank."

"Well, for God's sake, don't tell any TV viewers that," I jibed. "It'll ruin their fantasy lives. I think you two know my partner, Dr. Li?"

"Indeed," Donovan replied ambivalently, maintaining the smile as she shook Mike's hand. "Nice to see you, Doctor. And I'm sure you both know Investigator Mangold?"

"We do," I replied; although when the sour-faced Mangold made no move to press the flesh, Mike and I returned the favor.

"Doctors," he said, in a tone to match the look on his face, "I think you've also crossed paths with Dr. Grace Chang, here."

Gracie stepped forward with a grin. "Good to see you, Dr. Jones," she said, shaking my hand warmly. "And Mike!" she continued, even more brightly, turning to embrace him and give him a lingering kiss on the cheek. "It's so good to see you both," she added, pulling away from my slightly disarmed partner. "A nice reminder of our New York days, isn't it?"

"That kind of depends on which days you're talking about, Gracie," Mike said, with a charm that was as defensive as he could make it—which wasn't much at all.

"True, you got me there," Gracie laughed very coyly; and as I glanced at Donovan, Grimes, and Mangold, I saw that this had indeed been their opening gambit in a ridiculously heavy-handed effort to try to divide and conquer Mike and me. Quickly turning back to Gracie, however, I soon grew doubly reassured that she was not in on the scheme. "Some pretty up and down times, back then," she went on; and her smile continued to seem, unlike those of most of the team around her, quite genuine. "But just now, I have to say, I'm really anxious to hear how you've applied your famous method to this case."

Despite the genuine respect in Gracie's voice, a dismissive snicker got out of Mangold's mouth, one that Cathy Donovan tried to smooth over quickly: "And Major McCarron is here, too," she said, indicating the chief of Troop G, who stepped forward.

"Boys," he said, removing his Stetson as we exchanged more handshakes, which were very hearty, in his case. "You've talked to Pete and Steve, I hear, about what's been going on."

"We've offered a few thoughts, Mitch. Just the little we've been able to suggest from a distance."

"'Distance'?" Grimes echoed, getting down to business quickly. "We were told that you were actually *at* one of the crime scenes. One that we *know* of, that is . . ."

"It was just the one, Director," Mike replied. "We only heard about the other two."

"But Pete must have told you that there's been one more," Donovan said, carefully gauging our responses.

"Well, yes," I said simply. "When he told us that you wanted us to get over here, he couldn't really avoid telling us what was happening." With that much said, it was necessary to cover Pete's ass a bit: "But if I may ask, who *is* this latest victim?"

"Young black kid from North Briarwood," Mangold answered flatly.

"Fourteen or so. Can't find his family, but he OD'd on smack in that apartment house." And one of Mangold's nicotine-stained fingers pointed at the object of all the lights and attention.

"He have any help?" Mike asked. "I only ask because, contrary to the opinions of the ME, it seems like the other three did."

" 'Seems like'?" Grimes echoed. "You have some reason to doubt the pathologists' reports on the other deaths?"

"We might," Mike replied coolly. "Except that we haven't *seen* those reports. We're just going by what Steve and Pete have told us, as Dr. Jones has said."

"Well . . ." Donovan looked at Steve and Pete, who were still huddled a short distance away. "I'm relieved to hear that the sheriff has not, at least, been sharing official documents."

Trying to keep her from pursuing that line, I asked, "What, exactly, can Dr. Li and I do for you all, this evening? Looks like you've already got your hands full—although it's a lot of heavy equipment, if I may say so, if all you're faced with is one dead boy."

"Come on, Doctor," Donovan replied. "No need to be evasive. Pete has at least told you that there's a man in the building, too. What his relationship to the boy was, we don't know—but he's presumed armed, and he's holding Dr. Weaver hostage."

" '*Presumed* armed'?" Mike asked. "Meaning you don't know?"

"Oh, like you do?" Mangold erupted angrily. "You guys are so fucking smart—well, then, prove it: tell us how to handle this situation, I'm sure you know *that*, too."

"Frank" came Mitch McCarron's calm, stern voice. "That's out of line, and you know it. We didn't bring the doctors here to participate in this."

"And I didn't mean any disrespect," Mike lied coolly. "Just not exactly sure what we *are* doing in the middle of this situation."

"Well, Dr. Li, our original purpose was simple." Cathy Donovan quickly regained control of the situation. "We wanted to be sure that, whatever role you and Dr. Jones have played in Steve's investigation, it's actually an informal one."

"What else could it be?" I replied. "We have no legal standing in this county."

"Exactly what *I* said, Doc," Steve added, as he and Pete rejoined the group; and there was more than a pinch of resentment in his tone. "But it seems the word of a simple county sheriff isn't good enough, anymore, for state law enforcement."

"Easy, Steve," Nancy Grimes said, attempting to match Donovan's tone of authority but failing badly. "We've already told you, that's not the case."

"Yeah, you have," Steve replied. "But the two docs're here just the same, aren't they?"

"*All right,*" Donovan pronounced. "We're trying to keep this collegial." Then she threw a stern glance at Grimes. "I don't want to hear anything else. I'm sure you can understand, Doctors, that when we're faced with a series of child murders, my boss' office has to be sure that we don't open ourselves up to charges that we've allowed investigators who have—just as you've said, Dr. Jones—no legal standing in Burgoyne County to play an active part in the proceedings."

"Especially two who don't have the cleanest reputations," Frank Mangold added.

"Hang on, now," Gracie Chang said. "The doctors' reputations are absolutely solid, Frank." I was a bit taken aback by how much more mature she'd become since we'd known her in the city; and I very much admired the tough tone she took with Mangold. "Their leaving New York was never shown to have anything to do with any questionable behavior."

"Thank you, Dr. Chang," I replied; then I turned on Mangold. "You see, there's a difference between disagreements on procedure and actual illegal activities, Frank. As I'm sure you learned from Bernie Kerik. By the way, have you been in touch with him since he was released from federal custody?"

"I'm not kidding, *gentlemen,*" Donovan said, this time scowling at Mangold. "This is not going to be anything other than cordial. But, Dr. Jones, local emotions concerning this business are already running very high—something you may not have noticed, up in Death's Head Hollow." Glancing around to make sure that the others were behaving, she went on: "At any rate, we've got more immediate problems. So, if you'll just wait, we've got to determine what we're going to do about Dr. Weaver's predicament."

"I thought we *had* figured out what we're doing," Mangold said. "I'll distract the crazy bastard who's got him, and then we go in, fast and strong."

"'Overwhelming force,' eh, Frank?" Mike and I had followed Pete a few steps away, but the words jumped out of my mouth before I could contain them.

"You're goddamned right, Doctor," Mangold answered testily. "And you were told to wait—unless, of course, you've got some brilliant *profiler's* idea of what to do."

Sighing once at the usual contempt for my profession, I answered, "I do, although I'll wager you've already discussed it." I looked to Mitch and nodded once. "Allow Major McCarron to handle things—alone. He may not be an actual hostage negotiator, but he's your best bet, from among the"—I lifted a hand toward the mass of impatient police forces— "*resources* available. Mitch, I'm happy to be of any use to you that I can."

The idea wasn't quite as off-the-wall as it sounded: when McCarron's troopers and I had raided the illegal zoo outside Hoosick Falls where we'd found Marcianna, it had been my job to handle the owner of the place, who was a stew of neuroses, most of them very unpleasant, and all of which worked themselves out behind the scenes on his animals. It had been a dicey assignment, because the guy's home was a veritable armory, while all I had was my .45 to give me the courage to explore his tortured mind and convince him to give himself up.

"You must be fucking joking," Mangold erupted at my suggestion. "You've never shown any respect for Weaver, Jones; now you want us to put his *life* in your hands?"

"Hang on, Frank," Mitch said, intrigued. "First, whatever Dr. Jones' professional disagreements with Weaver, I have every confidence that he would never put a life in danger, especially a colleague's. And isn't that the whole point, Cathy? To get Ernest out alive? I've been in other tight spots with Dr. Jones, and I'm sure we could handle it without any bloodshed."

But Cathy Donovan just shook her head. "Again, Mitch, Dr. Jones has no legal standing in this county; you're asking me to invite exactly the kind of criticism I've been trying to avoid."

"All right, then," Mitch countered, indicating the sheriff. "Let Steve deputize him. Just for tonight. That'd be legal, wouldn't it, Steve?"

"Sure, I can do that," Steve said. "If you think it's your best shot, Mitch."

Recognizing the dangers inherent in this turn of events, Mike whispered to me urgently, "Trajan, what the fuck are you up to? They let you do this, it's only because they want you to screw up—it'll give them more ammunition to shut us out completely, you know that!"

"Yeah, I know, Mike," I murmured in reply. "But remember what I said: getting to this guy is our only chance so far of actually talking to somebody who may know what the hell is happening to these kids. You brought the theory closer to home with evidence; now it's my turn to do whatever I can."

But when I looked to Cathy Donovan, she was still shaking her head. "It's just too dangerous, Mitch. I admire your thinking outside the box— but I can't take the risk."

"Excuse me, Madam ADA," I said, stepping closer to her. "But I think you have to look at the bigger picture, here. Although Mitch is right to say that I would give Dr. Weaver's safety first priority, we may also have a chance to fill in some holes in your official investigation."

It was a fairly startling challenge, and the others took it as such: Mangold, for once, was too stunned to speak, while Donovan was too smart to even acknowledge what I had said; but Grimes said angrily, "'Holes,' Dr. Jones? Just what the hell kind of *holes* are you talking about?"

The time had come to play the one card we had: "Perhaps 'holes' is too strong a word, Director," I said, as humbly as I could. "But I have noticed that connecting certain events to their agents of commission has not been fully explored, yet."

"Speak fucking English, Jones," Mangold growled. "Give us a for instance."

"All right, Frank. For instance, there's the matter of who reported Shelby Capamagio's death: not only that she *was* dead, but the location of her body, as well. So far as we can tell, that key point has gone undeveloped—and the man in that building may very well be able to shed some light on the problem. He may, in fact, have been the person who phoned in the report, which we understand that Steve informed you was an 'anonymous communication.' And yet, to this point, he's gotten no help from the BCI in determining a possible origin of the message, by using all state, and, if necessary, NSA resources regarding phone records."

I was concerned that Steve might take umbrage at the unexpected presumption of this statement; but when I glanced at him, I saw the light of full comprehension in his face. "Exactly," he said. "That's a detail that *you* people may not care about, but, as sheriff of this county, I have to. I'm the one who's gotta answer for it, and before I can do that, I need an answer *to* give." He nodded once to me, then went on: "So, yeah, I'm willing to deputize the doc for just this evening. Maybe then we'll get some *real* answers."

We had put Donovan in an embarrassing spot, and she knew it; and I silently thanked Lucas Kurtz for having given us a way to move further into the official investigation, a gift that only further proved that Mike and I had been right to allow the boy to play a part in our work. Yet even as I enjoyed this moment of self-congratulation, I saw that a look, not of capitulation, but of satisfaction was filling the ADA's features: her agile mind had clearly detected a way to make our ploy work to her own and her allies' benefit.

"All right," Donovan decided at length. "If you're willing to take the responsibility, Steve, and if Mitch is willing to take the risk—let's see what you two can do, Dr. Jones."

"Are you *all* nuts?" Mangold squawked. "Suppose he goes in there and gets his ass shot off? How are you going to explain *that* to the DA, let alone the governor's office?"

"I'm not," Donovan replied, playing her part with all the guile that I knew her to possess. "Steve and Major McCarron will have to take care of that. The rest of us will be on record as saying that this was the least bad choice we were offered, when presented with the immediate and overwhelming threat to Dr. Weaver's life, and that we only accepted it with the gravest reservations, and only at the insistence of the sheriff and the major."

So there it was. The rest of their asses would be officially covered, while my own and Mitch McCarron's would be placed in harm's way, physically and politically; and Steve's would be officially on the line, as well. It was an extreme gamble—but we had to take it.

"Well, then," Mitch stated, moving over to me. His look said that he, too, understood the predicament full well. "I assume you're armed, Dr. Jones?"

" 'There may be some little danger,' " I murmured with a nod, repeating the line from the Sherlock Holmes tale with which I had attempted to stump Lucas earlier. The words confounded Mitch a bit; but he grew re-assured when I patted the .45 inside my jacket. I turned to Mike, who could only shrug in acceptance, and then to Steve. "Care to swear me in, Sheriff? The O.K. Corral awaits . . ."

Just how much legal standing Steve's perfunctory deputizing would actually prove to possess, if the plan Mitch and I had proposed went wrong, or whether in fact I had any right to carry the badge that Pete lent me, I did not know; but in minutes, we were making our way through and then past the assault force and its vehicles. Only at that juncture did the full weight of the peril in which we were placing ourselves overtake the bravado that I had exhibited when standing *behind* all that physical power; and I was very relieved when the ever-courageous Mitch took the lead, turning to the men and women in their combat gear and shouting:

"Let's have those lights off—all of them, *now!*" Very quickly, the order was obeyed, and as the blinding glare of the various beams was replaced by the comparatively slight glow of the few working streetlights above us, a hush came over the formerly vociferous officers. "And get this, all of you," Mitch went on. "I don't care who you usually take your orders from—you keep your weapons at the ready, and nothing more, unless you hear *me* telling you to do otherwise! We've got one of our own in harm's way, in there, and I don't want any overeager son of a bitch screwing things up. Understood?"

Without waiting for a response, Mitch turned to me, offering a smile that was clearly meant to bolster the uncertainty that must have been all over my face. "Well, Dr. Jones?" He indicated the path forward. "*You* got us here, Trajan," he added, as we moved at what seemed to me an almost surreally quick pace up a slight incline toward the abandoned apartment house. "I just hope you've got some idea of what our next move is."

I took a deep breath as we reached the front door of the building, which was covered in graffiti tags and knife carvings. "I think our tactic the last time around will work, Mitch," I said, as he put his hand on the door's broken knob. "If they're together, you do your best to get your hands on Weaver, and I'll do my best to talk this guy down."

"Yeah, that's what I figured," Mitch said, drawing his Glock 37 side-arm, for which his belt-bandolier carried a full complement of .45 GAP cartridges—which I was glad to see, as I had brought no extra ammunition, and though his high-powered rounds would be mighty hard on my old Colt, it would fire at least a few of them before jamming, if such proved necessary. Cracking the door open just a bit, Mitch chambered a round quietly, asking in a hushed voice, "And if they're not together? If he's got Weaver restrained somewhere?"

"Same answer—you try to find him, and I'll try to engage the guy. Somehow . . ."

Pulling the front door fully open and seeing no one in the entryway,

Mitch nodded once, giving me another quick, reassuring smile, then indicating that I should follow him in. "You're awful ballsy," he whispered with a small laugh, "for a God damned criminal psychologist. Anybody ever tell you that?"

"Not with a similarly polite intent, Mitch," I answered, also very quietly. And then I closed the door gently behind us, and we stood in the darkness of the building's front hall.

{iv.}

It was easy to see why the latest victim in the case had been found in that particular location: the warren-like series of apartments had clearly been uninhabited for a long time, and the place bore all the sights and smells of a shooting gallery and crack house. There had been a time, during my earliest professional years in New York City, when my job had made similar visits to such places common; but the administrations of Rudy Giuliani and his successor, Michael Bloomberg, had driven all such establishments, as well as far more benign houses of ill repute, first to the outlying areas of the city, and then very nearly out of existence (or at least far underground), all to facilitate the most extreme gentrification. And the heavy-handed police policies of profiling, stop-and-frisk, and "overwhelming force" that had underlain all this social cleansing had been the metropolis' main and most pernicious export to other American cities.

These tactics were in evidence even in a town like Fraser, particularly on the county seat's north side; but the expected gentrification was not. Thus the building in which we were standing, redolent as it was of human urine and excrement, of sweat and suffering, and littered everywhere with well-used, blood- and drug-encrusted needles and pipes, was something of a return to my own past; and not, although it may sound strange, an altogether unpleasant one. For it reminded me of a time when my native city had made room for not only all races but all classes and aspirations, and was truly cosmopolitan. This sense of something like nostalgia eased my nerves considerably, as I walked behind Mitch; and even when he told me to wait in the hall so that he could check the first of four ground-floor apartments, the doors of which had been removed completely, I waited, not with dread, but considering what life in my home city might yet be like, if its citizens had not bought so thoroughly into the politics of fear peddled by Giuliani and Bloomberg, particularly in the aftermath of the 9/11 attacks.

"You're awfully chipper," Mitch said quietly, returning from his run-through of the first apartment. "For a guy who's just put himself seriously on the line, in a lot more ways than one."

"Just recalling old times, Mitch," I whispered, following him to the next apartment.

"Oh, yeah?" he murmured, as we reached the second entrance. "The glory days, eh?"

"Something like that," I replied. "But—"

I was cut off, and Mitch's progress was halted, when we both poked our heads into the second apartment, and an unmistakable stench hit us hard: the smell of human decomposition.

"That tears it," Mitch said, keeping the Glock at the ready but pulling out a handkerchief with his left hand, which he placed over his mouth and nose. I had no such aid, but it didn't really matter: this was a stink with which I was very familiar, and I adjusted to it quickly.

"Better get that Colt out," Mitch told me before moving further into the apartment. When I signaled that I already had, he nodded approval. "Looks like this may be the place."

I decided to follow him in without chambering a round in my gun, despite (or perhaps because of) the fact that I did not share his opinion about the apartment. "Maybe" was all I would concede. "But it doesn't really fit, does it, Mitch? Our guy hasn't made any violent moves, yet; and even if he has done something to Weaver, not even that fat bastard's body could start to smell this bad so soon."

McCarron could not help chuckling into his handkerchief. "Yeah, I don't guess it could. Plus the smell's pretty confined—didn't hit us until we reached the apartment door. Any idea what *that* means?"

"Latter stages of decay," I answered. "Confined to one room in the apartment, I'd say, which must reek to high hell—but only enough of it gets out, under or around some door, to make its way as far as the apartment entrance. How big is this place?"

"They're all laid out the same," Mitch replied. "Kind of four-square around the stairs. The last one had two bedrooms, one bath. But all the doors were either gone or left open with the knobs removed, probably by the owner, who was trying to avoid exactly this kind of thing."

"But, Mitch—" I pointed all around us. "The doorways in here are open, too."

"Yeah," he said grimly. "All but one . . ." And then he nodded toward the far end of what I took to be the living room, in which I saw, beyond the sort of old, stained pieces of furniture typical of such joints, a short hallway, with one doorway at its start; and that one door was indeed closed. "It's the bathroom," he said, girding himself. "Okay—you wanna stay here?"

"No," I answered. "I am, as you pointed out, the one who got us into this. If the kid has actually been dead for a while, well—that means a certain amount to the timeline of the case. And I *am* a doctor, Mitch. It's not as though dead bodies hold some sort of dark power over me."

"Some might," he replied, walking toward the door. "Doctor or not . . ."

When we reached the bathroom door, the darkness caused Mitch to get a small Streamlight Stinger flashlight out, and, gripping it in his right hand as he continued to cover his nose and mouth, he prepared to open the door. "Just stand down the hall a little, will you, Doc?" he said; and when I made the move, he took a deep breath, put his handkerchief away, then used the fist that held the light to support his pistol hand. With his heavy boot, he knocked at the door; but no answer came, so he reached down to try the knob, which was locked. "State Police!" he called out, without drawing a breath. "Open up!" Still no answer; and so, resuming his cross-fisted posture, he raised a leg, kicked the light door in fairly easily, and entered.

After a few seconds, I heard him say, "Hunh. Nobody here," in a muffled tone that indicated he had replaced his handkerchief over his face. His light was still flashing about the room, however, so I started to move toward it—

But I had only gotten about a step and a half before I heard the sound of plastic on porcelain, and then Mitch recoiled from the bathroom in a burst. He slammed against the far side of the hall, dropping his flashlight in the process; yet it was clear that no blow had struck him, that only his own legs had been responsible for the violent retreat. Moving forward and picking up his light with my cane hand, I held it to his face. Mitch's thin brown eyes had grown very large and slightly bloodshot, and his mouth gaped in a way that made a mockery of his usual thin-lipped stoicism. But he had not lost all sense of himself. His eyeballs soon rotated and focused on me, without his body moving, and he murmured, in genuine dread yet with all due command, "Do *not* go in there . . ."

"Take it easy, Mitch," I said, turning toward the bathroom; for the insatiable and dangerous curiosity of cats is only one characteristic that has always made me feel something more than akin to their species. "After all," I went on, stepping toward the door, "as I told you, I'm a doctor, what in hell can be so bad . . . ?"

I had entered the bathroom with the flashlight before he could get the words "Trajan—*no!*" out of his mouth; and yet there seemed little reason for his alarm. The small chamber—which contained a sink, toilet, and small tub with shower—was bare of any embellishment, and bare, too, of any blood; there was no reason for it to be giving off such a stench. And yet it was. It did not take long to realize that the reek was coming from the toilet; and as I turned toward it, moving to pick up its closed lid, I said to McCarron, "Oh, I get it, Mitch—we've got somebody's severed limb blocking up the toilet, right? Maybe an organ of some kind? Well, it's not anything I haven't—" At which point, I opened the lid.

It had sometimes been my lot, in New York City, to do double duty at crime scenes by determining causes of death, times of death, things of that variety, when a medical examiner simply could not get there fast enough; and I fancied that I had, during my years in what had once been, after all, the greatest and most roiling metropolis in the world, seen a good deal of just how foul human beings can be to each other. I had inspected the body of a Mafia informant who had been killed by securing him to a wall in a tenement and coating his body with a highly sulfurous cheese, after which rats gnawed off his face, ears, genitals, and toes before he finally died; I had seen a member of a Mexican drug gang whose head had been systematically sectioned in a butcher's meat slicer; and I had seen women violated before and after death in so many ways that they defied counting or description. In addition, I had been present at the death scene of many a child, both before and during my professional life; though never an infant. Never an infant . . . And, although it took several seconds, I did eventually grasp that such was precisely what lay in the bowl of the toilet before me. What made the scene especially confusing was that the child was half in and half out of the water: he had been shoved in headfirst, his soft pate stopping up the toilet's exit almost completely; and down to about the chest, he was protected (if such is the right word) by that same liquid. But from chest to toes, he was out of the water;

and that half of his body had suffered far more severe deterioration and verminous violation. The look of terror and confusion that had been on the baby's face as it drowned, however . . . that, unfortunately, was still very evident, despite all the devastation: and this was plainly what Mitch had reacted to so violently.

All of these details entered my brain before any thought to be horrified arrived; when the latter came, however, it didn't take the form that Mitch's had. I simply closed the lid of the toilet and stepped back into the hallway, pulling the door—its latch bolt and lip obliterated by Mitch's kick—as far closed as I could. I returned to the head of Troop G, who was gathering himself by turning his Stetson uneasily in his hands.

"You, uh—" he began quietly, trying hard to form a sentence as he neatened the hat's brim. "You seemed to—to take it pretty easily."

"No—I didn't, Mitch," I said. "Just a different form of the same reaction. That's all."

He nodded, still without looking up at me. "Any idea what might have happened?"

"If you're asking if there's some connection to our case," I said, wishing that—for his sake, if not my own—I could be more demonstrative in my behavior, "then no. Certainly not to our present business, at any rate. As for what actually *happened*—plainly, the child was an unwanted complication. It doesn't take babies very long to drown; whoever was responsible likely slipped him in and closed the lid, then sat on it for the few necessary seconds."

"God damn it, Trajan," Mitch said, putting his hat back on his head as his voice gathered renewed force. "We're talking about a baby, not one of your exotic animals! Could you at least *sound* like you give a shit?"

"I could," I said, "but it would be obvious to you that I was forcing it. It's just different . . . *life experiences*, Mitch. I've seen a lot of ugliness, one way or another. And I've seen a lot of very young people die."

He nodded, almost apologetically. "You mean—with your cancer, and all."

"And *all*—that's right, Mitch," I said. "Try not to take it the wrong way. I'm just as outraged by it as you are, and I'll have some of the same horrible thoughts. Just not right now. We've got other things we've got to deal with." He nodded again, as if to tell me he was sorry for his outburst. "You about ready?" I asked.

He grunted out a mirthless laugh, and we started back through the apartment. "Isn't that supposed to be *my* line?"

"When we were back at that zoo, Mitch," I replied, as we passed through the front doorframe, "it *was*." I sighed once, as we pulled up by the building's stairway. "Don't ask me to explain it. I claim to understand only some few parts of the *criminal* mind—not why the hell anybody else does anything."

We both chuckled a little bit, at that; but our relief was short-lived. From somewhere in the darkness of the building—above us, I soon realized—a voice sounded:

"I ain't no goddamn *criminal*," it said: quietly, but with an enormous amount of anxiety. Handing Mitch back his Streamlight, I got behind him as he resumed his defensive posture. He pointed the Glock and the light up the stairs, at the top of which was the thin figure of a black male, his eyes glaring: obviously athletic, he seemed ready to leap down upon us.

"State Police!" Mitch called out. "Are you the one who's holding Dr. Weaver?"

"*I—ain't—armed,*" the voice from the shadowy figure said, as steadily as he could. He sounded younger than I'd expected: certainly no older than eighteen or so, I guessed. "And if you mean the fat guy, I ain't *holdin'* his ass." He glanced about, his voice a bit frantic. "Aw, man, it was all supposed to be *easy* . . . But then—" He seemed to come back to the point: "Look, when the cops came, I just wanted to try to explain to *somebody* what was really happenin', here—and then, shit, outta nowhere more cops than I ever *seen* show up, and they start yellin' about how I gotta come out with my hands up, and that fat fuck just ran away into the apartment, I couldn't *get* him to leave!" Even in the shadows of the upper floor, I could see his hands go to his head, and rub the sides of it hard. "It was all supposed to be easy; mother-*fucker—easy!*"

"What was?" I said, stepping in front of the flashlight so that he could see me, and prompting Mitch to try to hold me back, unsuccessfully. "What was supposed to be easy?"

"Who the fuck're *you*?" came the nervous reply.

"I'm a doctor," I told him evenly. "Trying to make sure everyone's all right—and I think there's a dead boy around here, somewhere. Am I right?"

It took several seconds, but he finally answered, sniffing back tears: "Yeah—he's up here. You wanna see him, I guess."

"I do," I answered. "And I'd like to talk to you about him, if that's possible."

"Not much I can tell you," he answered. "I just brung him here—supposed to be *easy* . . ."

"All right, then." I took the first step up, making my cane very obvious, so that he might feel less threatened. "We'll talk about *you*. But how about sending the fat guy down to my friend, here—then they'll leave, and we'll work something out. That sound all right?"

His head began to nod, and more tears were sniffed back. "I just hope he'll come *out* . . ." Then he signaled into the darkness beyond, at which point what seemed the utterly tremendous silhouette of Ernest Weaver appeared: and my impression that the figure with whom I'd been speaking could not have been much more than a youth himself was confirmed.

As I started up and Weaver started down, Mitch warned, "*Trajan* . . ."

"It's all right, Mitch," I said, pausing to turn back toward the beam of the flashlight. "We're just going to talk. You take care of Weaver, just as you heard."

"I'm gonna get him out to the others," Mitch replied, "then get right back here."

"Fine, Mitch. Good." I turned and started up once again; and it wasn't long before I passed the disheveled, descending figure of Weaver, who was covered in the malodorous sweat of fear. Half of his oily hair was on end, and his shirttails were out; but he passed me by with what I imagined he thought great dignity, saying only, "Doctor," with a nod and no eye contact.

"Doctor," I answered, amused and amazed by his appearance and manner; and then I added, with a small smile, "There's a pair of golden arches right down the street . . ."

"Indeed? Thank you!" he replied in a daze, marching on and then out of the building with Mitch; after which, I turned and stared up into the void at the top of the stairs.

"Come on up," the voice said, its speaker now utterly indistinguishable from the darkness. "I got a candle . . . in *there*. Where the kid is. But it's still pretty dark . . ."

{v.}

His name, by a peculiarly fortunate turn of fate, was Latrell, a fact that he offered as I reached the top of the stairs and my eyes began adjusting to the darkness. Upon further learning that he had just turned eighteen, I did some quick math, and asked if he had been named after the basketball player Latrell Sprewell, whose career would have been just at its height when the young man was born. His long, panicked, but nonetheless handsome features eased their tension a bit, at that, and he told me that indeed he had: his mother had evidently had quite a crush on the volatile Sprewell, and since there had been no father in the picture to argue her choice, she had been free to bestow the name.

"You seen him play, ever?" Latrell asked, sweat still dripping from his face; for it was much hotter on the second floor, and, though the change in subject had calmed him a bit, he knew that Dr. Weaver's departure had not diminished the police presence outside.

"I did," I replied genially. "For the Knicks, during the '99 finals."

"My moms always said that was his best season," Latrell revealed, starting to smile.

"She was right—first eight-seed team ever to make it that far."

"Yeah," he said, rather proudly, as if Sprewell had actually been his father. "I play ball myself," he went on; but then he wiped his face with one shoulder strap of the plain black jersey, piped in green, that he was wearing, and, staring down farther at his long, baggy black shorts and his black Nike Air Jordan Retros, he stamped one foot in annoyance. "But I guess you kinda figured that out," he added, plainly feeling that he'd made himself look stupid.

"Not necessarily," I told him. "I've known a lot of kids in my life who dressed like they could play, but could barely dribble a ball down the court."

"Ain't *that* the damned truth," he said, allowing himself a single laugh. "Did you play, Doctor—uh—say, I didn't get your name . . ."

"Don't bother with the 'Doctor' thing—most people call me L.T., why don't you?"

"Yeah?" Latrell answered, now flashing a smile full of very healthy, very white teeth, one of which was framed in gold. "You mean 'L.T.,' like Lawrence Taylor was L.T.?"

"I do, exactly," I said, taking out my pack of cigarettes and offering him one, which he took. "Although I try to keep people from making that connection anymore, out of respect. You see, I wasn't named after him or anything. Just a coincidence of the initials that I liked, when I was a kid. He was kind of a hero of mine, but we can keep that between you and me."

"Hey, man, who the fuck'm *I* gonna tell?" Latrell let out another short laugh, as he lit his cigarette off my lighter. By the glow of its flame, I could see his handsome features in more detail, along with the deep, plum-tinted brown of his skin. "So—you ever play ball, L.T.?" he asked, blowing out a large cloud of smoke. "Basketball, football, anything?"

"Only in my dreams, Latrell," I answered; and to his puzzled look I added, "You need two legs for ball." Then I tapped at my artificial left limb with my cane.

"Aw, shit, man," he said, embarrassed and moving from one foot to the other quickly. "I—I'm fuckin' sorry, man, I didn't know—"

"Of course not," I said. "Don't worry about it."

"What, uh—what happened? If you don't mind me asking."

"No, I don't mind. It was cancer. The leg was never right, but the doctors didn't diagnose it correctly until I was twelve." I failed to say that those doctors hadn't had the chance to so diagnose it, because my father wouldn't believe that, after producing three star athletes, his genes had handed down such a defect; and in his deliberate blindness he prevented any proper scans for over two years, during which time much more than more bone was eaten away . . .

"Shit, man, doctors," Latrell said, wiping his nose and snorting some snot back hard. "I hate them motherfuckers. Growing up, I got hurt, I'd always let my moms take care of it."

"Your mother sounds like she was a good woman," I said carefully.

He looked off into the apartment to his left, where I could now see the small butt of a candle burning. In the absence of any other illumination, it seemed quite bright: bright enough, at least, to light the look of melancholy that came into Latrell's face. "She was," he said quietly; and then, turning to see my quizzical expression, he added, "Died. Three years ago last March. She had cancer, too—breast cancer. Fucking doctors didn't get it in time."

Pausing briefly, I replied, "I'm truly sorry, Latrell. I lost my own mother. A car accident." He didn't need to hear that whole ugly story of her drunkenly plowing into a tree after a fight with my father. "Long time ago, though—not that that helps. You don't really get over it."

"Truth, man. But ain't that kinda what you people are supposed to do? Get people over shit?" To another puzzled look from me, he said, "You told that state cop that you study the criminal mind—so you're a shrink, right? Like them criminal psychologists on TV?"

"I'm a shrink, and a doctor, too. But—not like the ones on TV."

"But you're here to figure out if I'm, like, fucked in the head, right? And if it was maybe me who killed Donnie, insteada him doin' himself?"

I sidestepped the larger issue: "That was his name—Donnie?"

"Yeah," Latrell said somberly. "I didn't know him, much—didn't even know his last name. He come from over in North Briarwood, went to school down at South Briarwood Combined. Played ball for them, point guard; was fuckin' good, too. But that was before . . ."

"That was before his family disappeared on him?"

Latrell looked up at me from his cigarette in wonder. "Now, how the fuck you know that?" he said; but before I could answer, he agitated again: "Aw, man, you ain't supposed to know that, *nobody's* supposed to know, you can't tell the cops I told you that! He's just some junkie kid OD'd, that's all. Shit, where those motherfuckers *at*, anyway . . ." And with a sudden move, he pulled up his jersey and reached toward an object that was somehow secured beneath the band of his shorts: perhaps the gun that Weaver and the cops had thought him to have, although the possibility remained remote, to me. Still, his mental state was highly volatile, and it was necessary to get him back onto a safe subject quickly:

"Latrell?" I said; but he continued to fret about where *they* were. "Latrell," I repeated. "Listen to me." That seemed to break through: he let his jersey fall suddenly, and looked me in the eye. "I have to ask you, Latrell—you must know that we saw the dead baby downstairs."

"Oh—yeah," he said. "That's why they wanted Donnie here, in the first place—they figured somebody's going to find the baby, stinkin' like it does. Nothing brings the law like dead babies. Then they'd find Donnie."

"Do you know what happened? To the infant, I mean?"

Latrell shrugged. "Junkie hooker fucked up, maybe; maybe just some kid thought she could handle it, and couldn't. Most can't. It don't matter, does it? Whoever it was just dumped the little guy in that fuckin' toilet, man. But that ain't got nothin' to do with this."

"Except that *they* were using the baby to make sure that Donnie would be found?"

"Yeah, like I said. See, after Donnie's family cut out, he heard in school that there was people who could get him a new home, and he found 'em. They sent him off pretty quick, I don't know where. But he came back, after a couple-few months. Didn't like it, much, I guess. And they were gonna try to find him somewheres else, but—well, he got tired of the whole thing. OD'd over in their place, but they couldn't let anybody find him there. So I got a call; it's a shit thing to say, but I needed the dough, and somebody told 'em I knew Donnie . . ."

This statement was full of intriguing details, but I couldn't press him on them; not in his current state. He seemed willing to relate the tale at his own pace, anyway, and so I merely replied, "All right, then. Why don't we go into the apartment, so that I can confirm that Donnie did, in fact, kill himself. Then we can get you out of all this—how's that sound?"

"Sound like you don't know what the *police* get up to, when they come into North Fraser," he answered. "That's what it *sound* like. But okay, L.T.—let's go . . ."

We passed through the front doorway of the apartment, Latrell leading the way and my cane seeming to make a very loud sound in the silent building. The boy Donnie was in the large room at the end of the small entryway, alone in a corner, propped up against some cushions that appeared to have been scavenged from other apartments. But a light blanket of deep blue wool had been draped over them and around the boy, I assumed by Latrell himself.

"Must seem stupid, putting him in a blanket in this kinda heat," Latrell said quickly. "But it just didn't seem right, leaving him around here, like just another piece of shit. I swear to you, I had nothin' to do with him dying, I was just supposed to get him over here from their place in their big-ass capped truck, that's all. But I just couldn't leave him like that. I had the blanket at home; it's soft, anyway, and . . . well. You'll want to take a look at him, I guess."

I had more questions about nearly every part of this statement; but it wasn't going to do any good to start asking them too quickly. And so I walked over to the boy, near whom the small piece of thick candle burned on something that might, once, have been a brass candle base, before a great many people had used it for a drug cookstove and an ashtray. Leaning down, I pulled open one of the boy's eyelids, and held the candle close to his face; after that, I moved down to various parts of his chest, back, arms, legs, and feet, getting a sense of his lividity, and trying to determine if this had been the position in which he'd died, or if, like the other three victims, he had been in some significant way posed after death.

Soon enough I found the telltale mark. Less visible than the others, due to his skin tone, but there: encircling his thin neck and causing a large bruise at the back was the telltale sign of a narrow cord that had been used to hang him. Yet, so far as it was possible to tell from so cursory an examination, it seemed that little Donnie had also been quickly cut down and then spent a significant amount of time in a position not unlike that in which he now lay. His blood had pooled in his lower back and buttocks, and there were no signs of bruising that might have indicated he'd been restrained. In addition, the 28-gauge needle that still protruded from a spot very close to the cross branch of the median cubital vein of his left arm, and was attached to a good, clean hospital syringe (the packaging for which lay on the floor), had apparently entered the vessel neatly, giving no indication that it had been forced in. To all appearances, then, Donnie had died by hanging, and then someone had cut him down and used a needle and syringe—a brand-name medical model—to try to stage an overdose; and the toxicology report might show, I suspected, that they'd done it so soon after his death that the heroin could actually have entered his bloodstream.

Yet I knew that I could not trust the FIC techs that would gather the trace evidence to confirm this theory; and so, looking around to see that Latrell was not yet hovering over me, I picked up the syringe packaging from the floor and tucked it into my pocket. Such amounted to removing evidence from a crime scene, true; but I believed that Mike would be able to read the syringe's significance far more ably than Nancy Grimes' crew. Indeed, if I had thought I could take the needle from the boy's arm without upsetting Latrell, I likely would have done so.

Pulling away a bit, I held the candle a little higher, and seemed to see the boy *as* a boy for the first time: a cute kid, he must have been in life, but one no less desperate to leave this world. And not necessarily a junkie, either: for there were no track marks on his body, save in the arm with the needle in it. All these details fit the pattern we had established for the other dead children, the key difference being that the person who had been ordered to create the illusion that Donnie had died in that drug den was not long gone, but rather was readily at hand: he was the amiable, very sensitive young man with whom I had been speaking—and it was time to test whether he could answer some more pointed questions than I had yet dared put to him.

"Latrell," I said, returning the candle to the floor, "I need to ask you—is this the first time you've done this kind of thing?"

"What kind of thing?" he responded uneasily.

"Moved a body—for *them*," I said.

"Fuck, yeah, man!" At that he was back to shifting from foot to foot nervously—and then he looked down at the object that was held in the band of his shorts. "Shit, you think I could do this *twice*? Where the fuck are they, why the fuck don't they hit me *back*?"

It then became obvious what was around his waist: not a gun at all, but a cell phone on a nylon belt. And *in* that phone was likely all the information we would need to track the people who had given Latrell his orders. He would plainly not name them; indeed, such questions might so frighten him that he would bolt, taking the invaluable phone with him. I needed to persuade him instead to come outside with me, and to place himself in Mitch's custody, before Frank Mangold got ahold of him, locked him into a BCI interrogation room, and subjected him to treatment that might, in his nervous state, cause a breakdown. Mitch and I had the right to ask for such: we had taken the risk, and we could legitimately demand that this young man be made our charge. There would be an argument, of course; but I believed that we would win it.

"I don't know why they don't, Latrell," I finally replied, praying that his phone would remain silent. "But it doesn't look like they're going to— and that means you're on your own." He groaned tearfully, but I pressed on: "So you have to start thinking about yourself. You've done nothing terribly wrong—you can still walk away from this. But only if you give yourself up to the right group of cops. The man who was with me, Major McCarron, he's the head of the State Police's Troop G—he's an honorable man, and if he and I can keep you away from the Fraser cops and the Bureau of Criminal Investigation, I think you'll be okay."

Latrell tried to get a grip on himself, sniffing back more tears and mumbling, "Yeah—yeah, I gotta get outta this. And the state cops are better than the Fraser assholes. But I ain't no snitch, man, I ain't giving anybody but myself up! You gotta know that."

I nodded to reassure him. "I do, Latrell. But we need to get you somewhere safe."

He paused for a moment, studying my face. "You ain't bullshittin' me, right, L.T.?" he finally said, not so much suspiciously as desperately. "I gotta trust somebody, here, man, they fuckin' left me hangin' on this—but I can trust *you*, right?"

"You can trust me," I answered. "But let's get down to Major McCarron. He'll back up what I've said, I promise you that. We can leave Donnie here, they'll take good care of him."

"Okay," Latrell said at length. "Okay, it's my only play. I gotta trust you."

"Good," I said. "You're doing the right thing, Latrell. So let's go, now . . ."

We left Donnie behind, and left him the candle, too, because Latrell believed that he owed it to the kid to keep him, not only wrapped in his blanket, but with some kind of shield against the lonely darkness, as well. This seemed further proof that Latrell's denial of having kept Weaver a hostage was genuine: I had little trouble believing that the ME had become so disoriented by fear, not only of the young man, but also and likely even more of what he knew to be the various police forces' capacity to shoot the wrong person, especially amid such general confusion, that he'd gladly surrendered himself without Latrell demanding it, until he could be rescued from his own terrors—when all his "captor" was really requesting was understanding.

But there are, of course, two sides to every story, truthful or false though they may be; and the false side of this one was about to cause an unexpected crisis. I was surprised, when we reached the top of the stairs, to see that Mitch was not waiting below; but I was not overly concerned, as I had only a vague recollection of his last instructions, and determined that he would be just outside the house, not wanting to scare Latrell off with his Glock. So, in the renewed darkness, I did my best to sound encouraging, and urged the young man on below.

"Let's just get outside," I said, "and then Major McCarron can get us over to the State Police cruisers before anybody knows what's up."

Latrell nodded, silently and nervously, and we descended into the open night air. The few working streetlights outside were almost blinding, in comparison to what I'd grown accustomed to within; and I could see that Latrell was similarly affected. Yet as I held up my right hand to shield my eyes, I gradually determined that it was not the streetlights that were causing the problem: the lights of the fleet of squad cars and cruisers, along with the searchlights, were back on. And Mitch was still nowhere to be seen.

"Hang out here a second, Latrell," I said, when we got a few yards from the building's front door. The young man's anxiety was mounting fast; but he'd come to genuinely trust me, and he held his ground. I took a few steps farther down toward the cars: the first real mistake I'd made. With my hand still above my eyes, I called out, "Mitch? What the hell's going on with those lights?" But no answer came. "Mitch, where are you, he's coming out freely, there's no problem!" Still nothing; so I turned back to Latrell, with my hand still up, and shrugged: my second error. I hadn't realized that, in such a position, my jacket would be pulled up just enough to reveal my shoulder holster, onto which I'd pinned Pete's badge: and the sight of that gleaming object, along with the butt of my Colt, pushed poor Latrell right over the edge.

"Aw, fuck!" He made a move to bolt. "You a fucking *cop*, man, you fucking *lied* to me!" Stepping back toward the building, he also grabbed his cell phone from his waist. I was sure he simply meant to see if the people who had hired him had finally called; whatever his intent, it was a fatal mistake. "This was supposed to be *easy!*" he declared one last time—

And, knowing what would happen next, I called out, "Latrell! No!" just before one of the cops shouted those words that have become too familiar to so many Americans:

"Suspect has a gun!"

I was going to declare the truth to the officers when the wind was knocked out of me by Mitch, who flew out of nowhere and into my chest, knocking me to the ground. "Get down, Trajan!" he shouted as he did— and then the rest of them opened up.

I would learn only later just how many shots had been fired. Some two dozen bullets slammed into Latrell's head and body, at various points, and at least three hit the hand that held the fatal cell phone, causing it to whip backward. But these were all gratuitous injuries: the first was the only one that mattered. It caught Latrell right in the center of the forehead, paralyzing his nerve reflexes and freezing his movements—all save his fall backward, that is. A Savage 10FP scoped rifle had fired the mortal .308 Winchester round, I would soon learn: the work of one of Mangold's snipers. Latrell struck the pavement just as he'd been standing, despite the impact of his other wounds. I saw all this, even though Mitch was preventing me from getting back up until the cease-fire had been called.

"God damn it!" I then shouted, grabbing my cane and struggling to my feet. "What the fuck is the matter with you, Mitch, the kid was un-armed!"

"*What?*" Mitch said, already horrified. Also rising, he explained: "But Weaver told us he had a weapon—he said the boy had held him forcibly with it!"

"And you *believed* that fat fuck?" I bellowed, rushing over to Latrell's body. I already knew he was dead, or at least I knew it cognitively; emo-tionally, I was praying that he'd only been wounded—and, if the shame-ful truth be known, I was also praying that none of the bullets fired had managed to strike his cell phone. But I was to be bitterly disappointed on both counts. Latrell lay on the ground, his perforated corpse still looking for all the world as if it intended to make a call. As soon as I'd fully ac-cepted the simple fact, if not the full emotional implications, of his death, I immediately grabbed at his right hand; but it had been mostly shot away, and its mangled remainder held only a smashed few bits of tiny, useless cellular technology.

Everything that either Latrell or his phone could have told us was gone: when I at least came to terms with this one aspect of the innocent young man's death, I turned angrily back toward the squad cars, drew my own pistol, and brushed off Mitch's attempts to restrain me. I started toward the cops, holding the .45 high.

"You idiots!" I called, letting off a couple of rounds into the air. "Go ahead, shoot me, too—I'm more dangerous to you than that boy ever was! Go on, shoot! Because if I ever get to your lying ass, Weaver, or to you, Mangold, you're going to find out—"

But then Mitch seized me again, getting one of his powerful arms up under both of mine and grabbing the Colt away from me with his other hand. "Try to understand, Trajan!" he said. "You were in there a long time, we thought he was holding you like he'd held Weaver."

"And how was that, Mitch?" I shouted. "At the point of a *phone*? Go look in his hand—all the poor kid had was a *cell phone!*"

Once he was sure I'd regained some semblance of self-control, Mitch released me, and went to Latrell's body. Kneeling down to confirm what I'd said, he sighed heavily, stood back up, and then signaled to the assault force. "All right!" he called. "It's all over—shut those damned lights back off!" The street went relatively dark once more; and when it had, I saw a figure dash out from behind the cars—Mike. He ran over to me just as Mitch came back down to join us, shaking his head and returning my Colt to me.

"Trajan!" Mike called. "You all right, kid? What the *hell* just happened?"

"I'll tell you what happened," I said, still seething, if more quietly. "And you, Mitch—we just lost what will probably be our only chance to get a firsthand account of who's behind these deaths, and how they're working."

Shaking his head, Mitch said, "I'm sorry, Trajan; we truly thought you were in trouble."

"This *case* is in trouble now, Mitch!" I struck the pavement hard with the tip of my cane. "And you can tell Donovan and that crew that I'm in no mood to explain myself—in fact, they'll be lucky if *they're* not the ones doing the explaining, when it's all over. Come on, Mike—there's no reason for us to be here, anymore. God damn it all . . ."

McCarron made no move to stop Mike and me as we moved back through the cars, stared at by almost every one of the various officers present. Some of them looked almost contrite, and Gracie Chang actually did apologize quickly to Mike; the others, however, were defiant; for they had done no more than embody the new definition of "police work" that they had been taught by a terribly changed society. Asked to pound a street beat, where the true value of the policeman has lain for centuries—asked, that is, to get to know the places and people in their jurisdiction on a daily basis, and thereby to recognize the small vibrations of ominous change that can grow into crimes both minor and major, and where they might even have learned what both Donnie and Latrell had been going through—nearly every one of them would have been helpless. But on this night, the new version of "cop" had been on display, and the rapid response of paramilitary force to even the suggestion of threat had been completed.

Somewhat miraculously, I was able to control my sorrowful anger over all this as we left: that is, until Frank Mangold came forward to intercept me. "Hope you appreciated that, Dr. Jones," he said. "Looks like my shooter did a fine damned job."

Later, when I'd regained my full analytical skills, I would realize that there had been a strange lack of true gloating in the BCI Senior Investigator's tone; but at the moment, I became enraged again, and spun on him, grabbing my .45 and fully intending to pistol-whip him with it. "You stupid fool," I said angrily; but then yet another pair of arms grabbed me: Mike's.

"No, Trajan!" he said quietly. "Not like that—and not here . . ."

I turned back to Mangold, shaking off Mike's grip. "One question, Frank," I said. "Just which one of your fools was it that did that 'fine damned job'?"

"Which one?" Mangold said, in that same tone that I would later find so odd. "I think it was—yeah, Dennis Shea. Got a hell of an eye—why, you want to thank him? Hey, Shea, get your ass out here—*now*, the profiler wants to thank you!"

At that a thin, slightly red-faced young man with bright blue eyes moved out in front of the pack of cops, his rifle butt held triumphantly at his hip. He was smiling a bit, although the smile vanished when he heard my next words: "Thank him?" I said. "You congenital idiot, Mangold, I don't even want to *speak* to him. But when *you* do . . ." I began to get better control over myself, and replaced my Colt in its holster. "I want you to tell him that he may just have blown any chance of solving this case. They won't make a mistake like that again."

"Come on, Trajan," Mike said quietly, urging me toward our car.

"'They'?" Mangold called after us. "Did the boy *know* who the murderers are?"

"Yes," I said, turning around one last time. "The 'boy,' who had a name, knew who is responsible—for these *deaths*." I was perilously close to giving away too much, and Mike indicated as much by touching my shoulder. "But it doesn't matter. Your 'ace' just eliminated our one hope. That young man wanted to *help*, and he trusted me when I said that we would keep him *safe* while he helped. Now—he's gone, and the opportunity is gone with him. You don't get two, in a case like this. So you tell Officer Dennis Shea—"

"Sergeant, actually," Mangold announced, attempting some kind of pride.

"Even better," I shot back. "You tell *Sergeant* Shea that *we're* the ones who've been crippled by his 'fine damned job.' That poor, desperate bastard is dead, but at least his troubles are over." I turned to keep walking with Mike. "Ours are just beginning," I added, as much to the night as to Mangold.

But the BCI man couldn't let it go. "'Ours'?" he called after me, almost laughing. "Aren't you forgetting something, Cinderella? Your official involvement in this case ends tonight! As of tomorrow, you're just another interested bystander."

The cold truth of this fact was just salt in the wound of what had taken place; still, I could not let it be the final word or gesture. As Mike and I pushed on toward the Empress, I took Pete's badge from my holster and flung it over my shoulder at Mangold—a ridiculous action, but one that I knew would enrage him, even if it only made me feel more idiotic and wretched.

PART TWO

TUNNEL VISION

Tunnel vision is insidious. It can affect an officer, or, indeed, anyone involved in the administration of justice with sometimes tragic results. It results in the officer becoming so focused upon an individual or incident that no other person or incident registers in the officer's thoughts. Thus, tunnel vision can result in the elimination of other suspects who should be investigated. . . . *Anyone, police, counsel, or judge, can become infected by this virus.*

—JUSTICE PETER CORY (CANADA)
COMMISSION OF INQUIRY REGARDING THOMAS SOPHONOW,
2001

What we see depends mainly on what we look for.

—SIR JOHN LUBBOCK
*THE BEAUTIES OF NATURE AND THE WONDERS OF THE
WORLD WE LIVE IN, 1892*

CHAPTER ONE

MICROBURSTS AND MACROBURSTS

{i.}

That weekend was an uneasy one . . .

Late Friday night, a sudden and violent storm cell, of the kind that had been appearing all too frequently in both winter and summer, cracked open above Death's Head Hollow, bringing rain and howling winds and particularly sharp pains in the remnants of my left thigh. I could usually find a way to endure such periods (caused by drastic shifts in barometric pressure) while maintaining a fairly normal schedule; but the rage and guilt I felt over the killing of Latrell made social niceties impossible, this time. And so, on Friday evening, I used the convenient truth that Marcianna was frightened by such thunderous, lightning-streaked weather to absent myself from my great-aunt's house for the weekend. I gathered what notes on the case I considered necessary from the hangar, along with a blanket and a half-bottle of Talisker twelve-year-old scotch, and passed the next two days inside the stone den that I had had designed for Marcianna. Cheetah do not ordinarily favor such homes, preferring to hide in the open, where their greatest defense—speed—can be used to full effect; only in times of great danger and need do they resort to such enclosed places. And it was an indication of the trauma that Marcianna had endured that, almost always, she chose the den as her safest retreat. Thus our reasons for being there together, on this occasion even more than most, were strikingly similar.

I spoke my thoughts on all that was happening—the case, the thunder and lightning—aloud to my companion, who was always comforted by my ramblings: too frightened by the storm to be playful, she simply curled up on my blanket next to a small fire that I kept going and tried to sleep. When I grew so tired that I had to hammer my own mind into unconsciousness, I turned to the Talisker; but most of the time I paced the den, puzzling over the case and mumbling about what had happened, trying to come up with new connections, new answers, anything that might both help our investigation and somehow lend meaning to La-trell's death, as well as determine exactly what he had been so persistently talking about when he spoke of "them."

By Saturday evening, the violence of the storm had let up some, which helped both Marcianna's nerves and my leg; and my general outlook was also assisted by small acts of human decency. That night, and then again on Sunday at lunchtime, my great-aunt's housekeeper and cook, the del-icately built yet indefatigable and eternally kind Annabel, appeared at the gate of the enclosure, bearing trays covered in plastic wrap that conveyed some sort of typically delectable nourishment. She left the trays atop the cooler in which I kept Marcianna's thawed beef and medicinal supple-ments at the ready; and only when it was time to fetch those supplies did I check Annabel's compassionate offerings, which Mike augmented with, on Saturday, a couple of packs of cigarettes, and then, on Sunday, a note generated from his printer that said simply:

```
We are having what may be an important guest
this evening; care to be present?
```

As I studied this intriguing message, I picked out and discarded those portions of Annabel's midday effort that had been nibbled on by mice, then retreated to the den, eating as much as I could of the remaining fare and enjoying the decreased pain levels that came with the rapidly im-proving weather. By late afternoon, both Marcianna's and my moods had improved enormously, as the storm cell finally dissipated altogether.

With the renewed sunshine came the sound of Mike's voice, just outside the den: "Yo!" he called. "Knock, knock. Please don't kill me, Marcianna."

In truth, Marcianna was very fond of Mike; and she rushed outside (for Mike, like most people, dreaded coming inside the den), jumped up, and placed her front paws on his shoulders in an effort to win his trust and affection. This was an ongoing task, being as Mike, apart from his typically urban aversion to wild creatures, believed he had good cause to yet be wary of her.

"Whoa! Okay, there," he said, stroking Marcianna's head uneasily and steadying himself. "Jesus . . . It's no wonder you've got the people in town so convinced that there's some rare dog up here, L.T.—she acts more and more like one all the time."

"As all cheetah will do." I emerged from the den with the bottle of Talisker, and saw the depth of Mike's uneasiness clearly. "Oh, get over it," I said, although part of me was, as ever, perversely amused that he never had. "She's fine, now. Mostly."

"Yeah—*mostly*," Mike replied, as Marcianna jumped back off of him. "But I'm the one who had to take you to the hospital, remember, and cook up some story to feed them. A *bear attack*—I still can't believe they bought it. Not to mention the fact that you bled all the fuck over my passenger seat . . ."

"A lifetime ago," I pronounced. "When I still didn't know just how to handle her. Not to mention that I *paid* for the God damned seat to be replaced." I handed him the whiskey. "Here. Calm your nerves. I took it with me, by the way. Forgot to tell you."

"Yeah, so I noticed," Mike answered, taking a pull off the bottle. "Leaving me with the Johnnie Black. Nice." He paused, studying my face. "Have *you* been drinking today?"

"Nope, not today," I answered. "Why?"

He indicated the hangar. "The kid is here again. Lucas. Says he needs to talk to you."

I offered Mike one of his own cigarettes. "That what your note was about?"

"Oh, good," Mike mused, taking a smoke. "My favorite brand. No, that was about something else, actually."

"Well, you want to tell me, or do I have to guess—" And then something occurred to me: "Say, how'd you get through the gate, anyway? It's a combination lock."

"You used your bank PIN for the combination," Mike answered. "Fucking troglodyte."

"How the hell do you know my bank PIN?"

"Trajan . . . How many databases have we hacked into, over the years? And your *bank PIN* is supposed to be a problem? Besides, I can't draw from the petty cash fund without it."

"We don't have a petty cash fund," I said, as Marcianna bumped into my good leg.

"Oh, yeah, we do," Mike said with a nod. "It's called your bank account."

"Okay, okay," I conceded. "So what *was* the note about? And what's Lucas want?"

"I'd say he heard about Friday night. As for the note—we may just have a defector heading our way." Before I could start fuming about letting anyone from the state near our headquarters, Mike waved me off. "Take it easy—it's only Gracie."

"Gracie Chang?" I said, a little taken aback. "What the hell does she want?"

"I'm not sure. But she says it's important, that it's information we need to hear. I figured, I know Gracie, she wouldn't stab us in the back. So I told her to come on over."

"Mike," I sighed. "*None* of those people can be trusted. You know that. Or you ought to."

"The rest, maybe," Mike answered. "But Gracie? Not for nothing, L.T.—and I didn't mention this on our way back here Friday, because I didn't want you to hit *me* upside my head with that antique firearm of yours—but I heard Gracie arguing with the others while you were inside that building. Saying that maybe they were going about it the wrong way, that maybe Weaver was just covering his ass when he said Latrell had a gun. So just see what she has to say when she gets here. Could be useful. Meanwhile—should I tell Lucas to come up?"

I considered the matter for a smoky moment. "Yeah. I guess you'd better."

Mike nodded, then started back down toward the gate. He paused, however, just a few steps from the den. "How'd it go during the storm? With the leg, I mean?"

I shook my head. "Not good. Better now, but—not near where it's supposed to be."

Mike looked momentarily concerned. "Well, it's only been, what? Six months since the last radiation? The doc said it might take a while."

"Doesn't six months qualify as 'a while'?"

Mike nodded judiciously, sticking his cigarette in his mouth. "So what you're saying is, you *don't* want to hit that topless bar in Albany?"

I shook my head, laughing grimly at Mike's fatuous attempt to cheer me up, while he continued on his way. When he'd gotten about halfway to the gate, I called, "Hey! Dr. Li!" He turned again, blowing out smoke that faded into the moisture that was evaporating from the ground and the grass under the resurgent sun. "You've still been working the case, then?"

"Why the fuck not?" Mike answered, continuing on his way. "You don't think those shitheads we dealt with the other night are going to solve it, do you?"

"No," I answered, reassured. "And I've been going over some ideas of my own, too."

Mike held up a hand to signal acknowledgment, while I turned back to the waiting Marcianna, who, with Mike's departure, had begun to run back and forth in the grass, glad to be outside and trying to engage me in roughhousing. "No, no, you," I said, stepping her way with the intention of getting her under control for Lucas' visit; but in an instant, she had knocked me to my knees (or knee), and was keeping me from getting back up. It wasn't her weight that gave her the edge—even the largest cheetah are not heavy, and Marcianna came in at only 75 pounds or so— but rather her speed and agility, and my lack of the same. Soon she had her forelegs on my shoulders, while I locked one arm around her neck and struggled to get back up with my cane—

Then I heard Lucas: "Uh—do you two need a minute? Should I maybe come back later?"

"No, no, Lucas," I said, as Marcianna turned her attention to him and I finally got to my feet. "Easy, young lady," I told her. "You remember Lucas." With perfect comprehension, she looked up at him with nothing more than curiosity, recalling his face and even more his voice:

"Hey, there, Marcianna—you *do* remember me, right? One of the *good* guys . . ."

As Marcianna went to inspect the kid, I pulled myself together and said, "That's a wise idea, Lucas. Stay friendly but careful, for now. She's never actually *killed* anybody, but you want to remember, at least until she really knows you, that she could."

"Whatta you mean?" Lucas said, surprised and pulling back the hand that he had gingerly extended to touch Marcianna's head and neck as she took to smelling his pants and shoes. "You said she acts like a dog, that she's safe!"

"I never said she was safe. Though ninety-nine percent of the time, it's true. But there's still a bit of wildness in her, and it can shock you . . ." And then I lifted the tail of my shirt, revealing four parallel, nice-sized scars in my side.

"Holy fuck," Lucas gasped. "*She* did that—to *you*?"

"It was early in our relationship, and it was my fault," I explained, tucking my shirt back in. "I had just fed her, and was leaving the enclosure. She began getting agitated, and I thought she was being playful— but something else, or something more, was happening. Maybe she'd been spooked, or maybe she'd had a flashback to her time in that shithole petting zoo. Maybe she'd just never played with a human before. But when I reached the gate, wham!—She let me have it." Marcianna turned to me, a genuinely apologetic look on her face. "Didn't you, beast?"

"But—" Lucas was at a loss; Marcianna was beginning to show him playful affection, and he wasn't sure what to do. "But me and Derek looked it up online, after we were here the other day—cheetahs make good pets, a lot of people say."

"First of all, there's no such word as 'cheetahs.' The plural is the same as the singular: 'cheetah.' Second—a lot of people say a lot of things. Especially online, and most of it's bullshit. Just don't get *too* cute with her, yet, if I'm not around."

"Yeah—don't sweat that. Geez." He looked down to speak to Marcianna. "A lot more complicated than you seem, hunh, cat?"

"That she is—and I don't want to ever stamp that part of her out. Not completely—in case someone or something that's genuinely dangerous ever comes around. She needs a little of the savage in her. Now—you didn't come here just to discuss *her*, I hope."

"Hunh?" Lucas noised. "Oh, yeah, my assignment. Well, I ain't got much for you—it's the weekend, remember? No school. But I got feelers out, don't worry, there *will* be results. No, it's my sister I came to talk to you about." He was beginning to get steadily more friendly with Marcianna, despite my warning; in addition, she had smelled something on Lucas that interested her. "Hey," he said bravely. "Hey, Doc, does she actually like me, or am I about to die?"

"Do you have a cat at home?" I asked.

"What?" he said, making a few spirited attempts to shove back when Marcianna bumped up against him. "Oh, yeah—Ambyr, it's her cat. I do play with him a lot, though."

"There you go," I said. "She likes people with cats; likes the scent."

"Uh—yeah, I *guess* she does," Lucas cracked, as Marcianna got between his legs and, with a strong heave, lifted him a few inches off the ground and sent him tumbling. "Hey!" he called with a laugh. "Ow, shit, that hurt, Marcianna—" In another instant she was on top of him, happy to have so small a human, smaller than any she had ever touched in her adulthood, to make into her own plaything. Pulling at the windbreaker he was wearing, she maneuvered him about the grass as a housecat would a victim mouse.

"Okay, okay," I decided at length. "Come on, miss . . ." I pulled Marcianna off of her victim by her collar. "Let Lucas up, he's not quite ready for the full treatment."

The kid stood, wiping at his back with his sleeve. "Man—*that* was an experience nobody will ever believe. Except Ambyr, she will—and speaking of Ambyr, Doc . . ."

"Yes, I'd like to hear what's on your sister's mind. Although I'll bet I can guess." Having spotted a group of three crows that had foolishly thought to land in and strut about the middle of the enclosure, I looked down at Marcianna. "Go on," I said. "Go chase a crow, you malingerer." I gave her a little whistle, and she ran like an utter exhibitionist after the birds. I called after her to say that I was leaving, but would return soon; and then Lucas and I started toward the gate.

The kid took on a more serious tone: "So I heard—about what happened Friday night."

I didn't really want to return to the subject, having escaped it so effectively for a time; but the discussion was unavoidable. "Did you?" I replied. "And what did you hear?"

"Hey, Doc, it's all over the local news!" Lucas grinned. "Some kid got shot after you got him to give up a hostage? You're a hero, they say—you and Major McCarron."

I grunted. "Yeah, that *would* be the official version. Perfect for the local news. Except that there *was* no God damned hostage, Lucas. Just the lousy ME covering his own cowardice. They *murdered* that kid, after I told him he'd be all right. But they'll never admit as much."

"Really? Shit . . ." Lucas was, once more, mildly angered. "Fuckin' television. *Again . . .*"

"Indeed. And now that we've reviewed that point, suppose I take a guess at what's up with your sister: she's isn't sure she should let you spend time up here with Mike and me."

The kid glanced my way. "Didn't take Sherlock Holmes to figure that one, hunh? Though I still wouldn't mind hearing *how* you knew it. Never having met her, and all."

"All right. Those old superstitions you repeated about Death's Head Hollow when we first met, for a start, along with that insanity about my chopping up brains. And . . ." I tried, now, to tread carefully. "Your friend Derek no doubt told your sister *his* impressions about what I said that day." Lucas began to look indignant, so I rushed to explain: "It's not that I'm accusing him of snitching, or anything, but—you and I both know how he is, don't we? And he was scared and confused, that day. So he let his concerns slip to someone he trusts. Finally, your sister almost certainly *heard* what you *saw* on television. So—she's worried."

"Well, can you blame her?" Lucas protested; and that same quality of quick defense of his sister that I admired shone through again. "They had a damned riot in North Fraser, after you left. Busted through cop barricades, burned all kindsa shit—"

That halted my steps. "Really?" I said, feeling a peculiar sense of satisfaction.

"Fuck yeah, they did," Lucas answered. "And the funny thing *now* is, people in town who'd usually be screaming the N-word all over the place are shouting about the *cops*, instead."

I thought of Latrell, and how fitting it was that there had been some kind of demonstration, if not in his honor, then at least in protest of his death; and one aimed at the right target, too. "Well," I mused. "That's something, anyway . . ."

"And to top it all off," Lucas continued, a bit puzzled, "I don't know what the hell you thought you were doing, but they got a picture of you on TV letting off a couple of rounds into the air with what looked like an old .45—that *was* you, right?"

"Ah." I remembered the moment of my outburst that night. "Yes, I fear it was."

Lucas' face screwed up in puzzlement. "What kind of psychologist packs a damned .45, anyway?" He caught himself. "Right, right, a *criminal* psychologist."

"*Any* criminal psychologist, who's got some sense in his head," I replied, as we passed through the enclosure gate. "So, returning to the original question, add all of that to what you've told us about your sister, who would only need to be *sane* to be worried about you getting too close to this investigation, in the first place—but she's more than sane, isn't she? She's smart, she's been through hell, and she doesn't want the same for you and Derek. So, no, I can't blame her for being worried. In fact, it's a miracle that she's even *considering* letting you go on."

"Yep," Lucas said. "That's about it. And she says that if I *do* want to go on, you and Mike have gotta come down to the house. She says it'll be just to meet her, but I'd guess my cousin will be there, too. Remember I told you I got a cousin, Caitlin, who's a state trooper? She keeps tabs on us, since our folks ran away—"

"*'Since our folks ran away,'*" I repeated slowly. "It still sounds so strange . . ."

"Hey, you're telling *me*," Lucas replied quickly. "Anyway, Caitlin. She kinda showed Ambyr about keeping track of the house and the bills and shit, in the beginning, and she busts my ass if I ditch school too much or my grades go down too low; that kind of thing. So she'll swing by in her cruiser, if she's assigned to this area for a day or two. *Anyway . . .*" Lucas had to pause to catch his breath after repeating the word, because he was rattling off personal facts fairly quickly, which made him very self-conscious, especially because of his genuine desire to make his participation in the investigation work out; and that was good to see. "Ambyr's worried about me blowing off school to come up here, which I told her I ain't gonna do, and I ain't, since school's the place where you want me to find stuff out. But yeah, she's also worried about it being dangerous because of what happened Friday night. And then there's one last thing, about when the summer term lets out in a couple of weeks."

"Why, what happens then?" I asked, watching the hollow carefully for signs of Gracie Chang's approach.

"Well, see, the end of July and August," Lucas went on, still quickly and nervously, "that's when most guys my age can get jobs with one, maybe two farmers, getting hay and corn and anything else in. And we make some good money during that time, which Ambyr's worried about losing. *So,* well, I kinda told her that I would talk to you. About, uh—about getting paid."

"*'Paid'?*" I repeated, turning to the boy in mostly mock indignation. "You expect to not only learn the ropes of true criminal investigation, but to get *paid* for the privilege?"

"Hey, it's not me!" Lucas quickly defended. "But it's what's got Ambyr worried."

"Right," I droned. "So I assume, then, that you couldn't work for us *and* get the crops in?"

"Oh, no way," Lucas said smoothly, having plainly anticipated the question. "See, I'll have to make the investigative work I do, learning it *and* doing it, pretty full-time."

"Unh-hunh . . ." But in fact I felt for Lucas, who was truly sweating these considerations. "Okay, kid," I finally determined. "Take it up with Mike. He's in charge of my finances—apparently. Tell him what you would usually make for honest labor, and we'll try to match it."

"Yeah?" Lucas said, enormously relieved.

"Sure, why not?" I answered. "The way this investigation's going, we may all be in jail, soon, anyway, so let's be sure your family won't suffer while you're doing time."

"And you'll come down and meet Ambyr?"

"I will. And so will Mike. And we'll behave. Let's say Tuesday afternoon, we need to work through tomorrow."

"Awesome!" I thought the kid was going to do a little jig right there on the dirt path to the hangar. "And you know what else you could do, Doc—bring Marcianna with you."

"To *Surrender*?" I was astounded and unnerved by just the thought.

"Yeah! We could smuggle her into our house, nobody'll know. Derek's already blabbed about seeing her, and Ambyr, she would *love* to meet her. She loves *all* kinds of cats. It would ice the deal—unless you think Marcianna might go crazy."

"No, it isn't that," I answered slowly. "She'll behave, if she's on the leash and nobody messes with her. But I'll have to think about it—" I stopped short, having caught sight of what could only have been Gracie Chang's car: a zippy new Ford Focus ST, metallic blue, headed up the hollow and then turning in toward the barns below. "Uh-oh," I said. "Company."

Lucas followed my gaze. "Whoa—somebody big? Should I make myself scarce?"

"No," I answered slowly. "No, in fact, stick around, Lucas. This may be just the chance to take the next step in your education." I thought the matter over quickly. "Just get up in the plane and lay low, until I tell you otherwise."

"But if they're from the state," he protested. "I mean, I can't get into any trouble like that, Ambyr'll frickin' *butcher* my ass."

"Don't worry," I said. "It's nobody with that kind of power. Just another psychologist—she was there Friday. But what she wants to talk about now, I don't know. Mike thinks she's not happy with how the state people are doing things. So just stay calm and keep your trap shut."

"Well—" Lucas got that game tone back into his voice, and headed up the steel steps into the JU-52. "Okay, Doc. If you think it's important."

"Oh, I think it might be more than important," I said, starting to smile. "I think it might actually be fun . . ."

{ii.}

It of course occurred to me to wonder, at several points during our meeting with Gracie Chang, if maybe I shouldn't send Lucas racing home, being as I knew fairly early on that the fun of the meeting might involve "some little danger," or at least trouble; and given his sister's stated concerns, it seemed we might be passing some boundary that, if things went badly, would be impossible even for a boy of his quick wits to find his way back across. Still, there were probably going to be very real principles—both investigative and psychological—involved in the meeting, all of them necessary for Lucas to begin to understand. And so at each moment of doubt, my mind turned back to the riskier option, in the hope that it would not become the most reckless.

After Gracie had parked her Ford and joined Mike and me at the hangar, we exchanged very pleasant greetings as we prepared to gather around an old Formica-topped kitchen table that sat under the nose of the JU-52. It took some time to get seated, however, as Gracie proved to have a youthful and entirely charming enthusiasm for the plane itself. She peppered me with an almost endless stream of questions about not only the aircraft, but the man who had brought her to the Americas and then barnstormed with her around the New World.

"Was he always a pilot?" Gracie asked, her face filling with a wonder to match Lucas' expression when he'd first come upon the plane.

"From his youth," I said with a nod. "A smaller hangar originally stood on this site, and he filled it with a succession of biplanes, before he joined the Lafayette Escadrille and flew in World War I." That set off a long burst of inquiries about my great-grandfather's wartime service, one that displayed a rather surprising breadth of knowledge; and I did my best to answer them, but quickly, given Mike's and my rather urgent desire to get down to business.

"Well, Gracie," I asked at length, attempting an easy air that did not match my mood, "what do you say we discuss your actual reasons for coming?"

"Oh!" she noised, her lissome frame straightening. "I'm sorry, it's just—" She gazed at the plane a final time as she approached the table. "You don't usually see things like this, just sitting on somebody's farm. And so you run your investigations from inside it?"

"Along with our teaching," Mike replied. "Maybe you'd like a tour, Gracie, once we get done with this other stuff—"

"*Although,* we've really got to start getting tomorrow's classes ready," I cut in, remembering the hidden Lucas as I tried to remind Mike that we didn't yet know enough about Gracie's true purposes to allow her to see what was on display inside the JU-52.

"Hmm, true," Mike said, realizing his mistake.

"Oh, hey, don't worry about it," Gracie said cheerfully. "If we don't have time today, we'll do it some other time, when you're less busy. So— to *our* business, then . . ." She shook her head a few times as if to clear it; and by the time she sat down with her narrow back to the plane, her countenance indicated that she'd fully resumed the persona of mature psychologist. Those usually genial features quickly filled with anxiety as she leaned over the table and began to speak in grave tones about how sorry she was for how things had turned out on Friday night:

"I suppose Mike's told you that I argued pretty strenuously against their taking the course that they did, Dr. Jones." She had slung her simple black Bottega Veneta hobo bag on the back of her chair, and draped her similarly reserved but costly Alexander McQueen linen jacket over it (Gracie was prepared to sacrifice much to living upstate, but not being the clotheshorse daughter of a well-to-do Queens merchant); and it was easy to see very light perspiration forming through her sheer Anne Fontaine white shirt. This was not due to the evening heat, however, for if the microburst had done one good thing, it had cooled the temperature off considerably. "And frankly," she went on, folding her hands tightly, "I've been extremely concerned about their approach to this case from the beginning. There's been a lot more talk about political and bureaucratic agendas up and down the line than there has been about working out a sensible theory that fits the deaths of these kids." To her credit, it was evident that this fact, predictable though it was, did indeed disturb our guest in a deep way. "I mean, I'm no babe in the woods, here, I've seen prosecutorial bureaucracies in action—hell, I worked in New York, just like you guys did. Well, maybe not *just* like you guys, I was still learning the ropes, then, but I saw the kind of pressures that can sometimes be brought to bear on a case. And I'm telling you, I never saw anything as egregious during my time in the big city as I've seen in this county, on this case."

"So," Mike asked carefully, "you've been in on their investigation from the start?"

"Not from the *very* start," Gracie answered, folding her hands tightly. "No one at the senior county or state levels was. After all, they only had one apparently runaway girl, then, who seemed to have come home to kill herself, although the pathologists later judged—"

"Hold on, Gracie," I cut in uneasily. "'One *apparently* runaway girl'? Meaning what?"

Gracie nodded. "That's right—you haven't been told about Frank Mangold's latest discovery. In fact, I don't even think that Sheriff Spinetti's been told about it yet."

"Suppose you tell us, then," Mike pried with amiable charm. "Sounds like it's important."

"It is," Gracie said. "See, nobody really thought that Kelsey Kozersky was just a runaway. Not after they got the path report on the Howard boy's death—that's when I came in, by the way—and especially not after the pathologists said the Capamagio girl fit the same pattern that Kyle and Kelsey did: choreographed scenes of death. All of which made it, well . . ."

"Obvious enough even for Frank Mangold," I said, still more apprehensively.

"Exactly. So, Frank and a couple of his BCI boys revisited the Kozersky farm just a few days ago—and sure enough, they got the parents to admit that Kelsey *hadn't* actually run away at all. They'd thrown her out, when her behavior got out of hand."

"But—she was only fifteen," Mike murmured. "They could be prosecuted for that."

"Yes," I almost whispered, my sense of uneasiness now turning to outright dread. "But more importantly, it also placed her within the official ranks of throwaway children . . ."

"Correct." Gracie sat back, pleased by the exchange of ideas that was taking place, and by her own ability to stoke it with new information as an equal. "You guys are up on the whole subject, I see—which, I have to tell you, is fairly impressive. Most people don't know or care about the subject of throwaways, much less who fits the criteria—"

But I interrupted her rather abruptly, unable to contain my anxiety and standing suddenly. "You're right, Gracie," I said grimly. "But what, then, returning to the matter at hand, is *your* theory of the case?"

Gracie was a little mystified by my behavior; but Mike tried to cover it up, flirtatiously making spooky hand motions and mouthing *The Sorcerer*. "Well," Gracie began, smiling and a bit reassured, "I don't really *have* a theory. And I thought that you, using your method, might."

"Did you?" I began working my cane as fast as I could, making my way to the corner of the open hangar closest to Death's Head Hollow, which offered the best view of those parts of the road, as well as the pastures and trees around it, that could be seen from our vantage point—and from which, just as importantly, *we* could *be* seen.

"Well, I *thought* so," Gracie said. "Though your confusion makes me wonder, I'll admit. I expected the easy answer from the others, but I assumed that you guys . . ."

"Sorry, Gracie—the 'easy answer'?" Mike asked, now a little perturbed, himself, by my behavior.

"Well, yeah," Gracie stated simply. "That we have a serial killer on our hands."

Mike's hand involuntarily shot to his forehead; but greater cause for concern came when I heard a sudden thumping sound resonate from inside the JU-52, which I assumed was Lucas falling from whatever hiding spot he'd chosen and hitting the floor in excitement at the sound of the words *serial killer*. To cover his reaction, and since I hadn't yet seen any of the signs of trouble on the hollow that Gracie's presence and thoughts had led me to believe might be coming, I turned and took several steps back toward the table. "Why do you dismiss the idea so readily, Gracie?"

"It's too convenient!" she declared simply, still surprised. "And too useful, politically, to everybody involved. I mean, in most situations, you'd want to avoid creating the impression that a serial killer was at work—but here, as we've just discussed, we've got a bigger scandal going on, one that worries officials at every level even more."

"The throwaways," I said, nodding and returning to the corner of the hangar door to study the hollow once again.

"Right," Gracie answered. "In comparison to that, everybody from the Burgoyne DA's office all the way up to—well . . ." Gracie held back for the first time, perhaps uncertain as to whether or not *she* was revealing too much. "Well, *all* the way up. They'd all take a serial killer case over any revelations about the throwaways."

"Okay, I'm lost," Mike said, eyeing my nervous movements with ever more confusion. "Why would anyone be willing to *take* a serial killer case before they have to?"

"Use your imagination, Michael," I answered from my lookout spot. "The throwaways are a huge political embarrassment with no apparent solution. A serial killer case, on the other hand, is sexy. It could get them all sorts of publicity, some good, because the public is so fascinated by them—especially serials who hunt kids—and some maybe bad, if they don't handle it smoothly. But even if it's bad, it's better than the throwaway scandal. Nobody wants to be the first state in the Union to acknowledge a terrible problem that they're not addressing."

"Exactly," Gracie said, throwing her hands in the air. "And everybody official is toeing just that line—so I figured that if I was going to try to talk alternate theories, I had to come to you guys. I was genuinely sincere the other night when I said I'd love to know how you're applying your method to the case. I didn't get much chance to observe or study it in New York, but I can tell you, it gained you quite a reputation in the community."

"Did it?" I murmured, growing very apprehensive once more and searching those areas around the hollow road that I could see. "Good to know . . ."

"Trajan, what the *fuck* is wrong with you?" Mike finally demanded.

"Nothing that wouldn't be wrong with *you*," I said. "If you'd think about everything that Gracie's just told us."

"But I haven't really told you much of *anything*," Gracie protested, utterly flummoxed by what was taking place.

"Oh, you've told us plenty," I answered, already working out the details of how the hell we were going to handle the very delicate and perhaps dangerous situation into which her visit had thrown us. "Think about it: you've said that a few days ago, Frank Mangold and some of his BCI boys went to the Kozersky farm, where, I'm sure, Frank and Mr. Kozersky had a nice private 'talk,' during which the old man revealed the truth about kicking his daughter out."

"So what?" Mike said. "You think Mangold's all of a sudden worried that we're going to discover he uses abusive methods? Jesus, Trajan, every law enforcement officer in the state knows—*ow,* damn it, fuck you!"

As Mike had been chattering away, I'd walked over and, with an open hand, whacked the back of his head; then I demanded, "What the hell is wrong with *you,* Mike?"

"Um—Doctors?" Gracie said, concern in her voice; for she had certainly never seen *this* side of our method. "What, ah—what's going on here?"

"I'm sorry, Gracie," I said. "But despite my partner's temporary idiocy, there is every chance that you were followed by the BCI to Shiloh. Not that they'll show themselves, but—" I went to the corner of the hangar again. "That doesn't mean the fuckers aren't out there . . ."

"Oh, come on, Dr. Jones," Gracie chuckled amiably. "Don't you think you might be having an extreme reaction to recent events—understandable, but extreme."

"A fucking *paranoid* reaction, you crazy son of a bitch," Mike threw in, rubbing the back of his head.

"Oh, really?" I replied, returning to them. "Okay, let me run it down for you all the way, this time: a few days ago Mangold gets Papa Kozersky to admit that he kicked his underage daughter out of her home. So she's officially a throwaway, just like the rest of these dead kids."

"Wait," Gracie said, holding up one delicately manicured finger. "We don't know about the boy who overdosed in North Fraser yet."

"Well, see, Gracie, that's the cause of my impatience with my partner." I faced our guest, trying to remain calm. "Because *we do* know about him. His name was Donnie, by the way. And if you check the records and get his last name, I think you'll also be able to confirm that he was abandoned by his parents. The other boy, Latrell, the one that Mangold ensured never made it out of that building alive, knew such to be true, and told me. Certainly, the BCI has found out as much, by this point. So you've got a straight run, now, four-for-four, all throwaway children. Which means that everybody involved in this thing is losing their shit more than ever, trying to figure out how to keep a lid on it, and prevent the media *or anyone else* from drawing the connection. But *you,* Gracie—

you've been having steadily more profound doubts about how the case is being conducted. You may not have openly doubted their serial killer preference, but trust me when I say that Mangold is watching everybody involved in the investigation and waiting, because he figures that at least one person on the inside is going to get tired of the political handling of the case. And that person, he knows, will eventually act on their discontent—although just what outside source they'll go to when they decide to break ranks he doesn't know. What he *does* know, and I mean no offense when I say this, Gracie, is that you're the most likely to do it. You already voiced open disagreement with a crisis decision on Friday night, and you've never been very good at hiding your doubts. So I'm betting he's watching you twice as closely as anybody else, and reading your reaction to events perfectly."

"Ahhh, *shit,*" Mike said suddenly, getting to his feet. "I really, *really* hate to say this, Gracie, but—I think my demented friend may just be right."

I glanced at my partner. "Took the local getting there, didn't you?"

"So . . ." Gracie said. "You're honestly suggesting that Mangold's had me *followed*?"

"He's acting to steer this thing in *one* direction," I answered. "And to cover the politically costly dimension. With orders from somewhere higher up, as you've already intimated. And so are *you* honestly suggesting, Gracie, knowing him as you do, and considering how alarmed you've made them all, that he'd do anything *less* than have you followed? But let's not leave it to supposition—" I looked up at the JU-52 and called out: "Lucas!"

The boy's head soon popped out of the plane's hatchway. "Yeah, boss?" he said.

"Who's *that*?" Gracie asked, shocked by the presence of the kid.

"Our expert advisor," I said, in all seriousness; then, to Lucas, I continued, "In the bottom right-hand drawer of my desk you'll find a pair of old binoculars—bring them down, along with you-know-which items belonging to Mike and me. We need to talk about a couple of things!"

"You got it!" Lucas answered, disappearing again.

As the sounds of his rummaging around above reached us, Gracie turned from me to Mike, searching for signs of sanity. " 'Expert advisor'?" she said. "He's just a *kid,* guys . . ."

"Yeah, he's a kid," Mike answered, as I maintained my vigil. "But he's got particular knowledge of what's going on in this case—as I suspect you're about to find out, Gracie . . ."

Lucas reappeared, bouncing onto the steel steps, placing his feet on their pipe banisters, then sliding down and landing on the hard floor without missing a step. He gave Gracie a quick smile and nod, handed Mike his .38, then brought me my leather-encased .45 and binoculars.

"What are you thinking, Trajan?" my partner said, bracing himself for whatever we had to do before remembering his manners: "Oh. Dr. Gracie Chang, Lucas Kurtz. And vice versa."

The pair shook hands, Lucas very excited about once more being included in the discussion of the case as an equal, and Gracie, I could see with just a quick glance, still bewildered, but increasingly intrigued: both by the kid's presence and by our faith in him.

"I'm thinking that we have to make a show of getting Gracie out of here," I said, pacing the front of the hangar. "Then, after we've managed that, we can bring her back up on the sly, and finish our conversation. But not in this spot. Not in this spot . . ."

"Now, come on, fellas," Gracie protested. "This is crazy! I mean, I'll admit there's a chance that Mangold may be watching the members of the investigation, to see if anybody will go rogue. And maybe I *am* the most logical choice for that. But really, if I come up here to have a collegial exchange with members of my profession, what can he possibly say or do about it?"

"He can take your *derrière* into custody, Gracie," Mike answered quickly. "Officially, for sharing privileged information. And he wouldn't need to actually arrest you, he'd just get you out of here before we had time to decide if our investigative interests coincide. Then he'd spend a few hours scaring the living shit out of you, maybe in an interrogation room, maybe in your own damned office, doesn't matter. Try to remember where this guy got his training: not up here, but down in the city, at a time when that kind of behavior was really being perfected. If you're in Death's Head Hollow, you're no longer an ally, to him: you're a *threat,* and he'll deal with you as just that."

"But we still don't know that they're even around!" This time, however, Gracie's protest held little trace of incredulity: she'd begun to realize that Mike might just be right.

"Yeah, well—we're going to see if we can't change your mind on that,"

I said as I put the pair of Lemaire field glasses that my great-grandfather had carried during his days in the Escadrille to my eyes, and at the same time got my shoulder holster on. I heard Mike tearing the Velcro on his holster open and then slapping it into place on his ankle, after which a thought occurred to me: "How about you, Gracie?" I asked. "Are you still carrying, since you left the big city?"

"Are you kidding?" Gracie answered, grabbing her black leather bag. From it, she drew a Heckler & Koch USP Tactical 9mm semi-automatic with a blued steel finish. Lucas gasped in appreciation when he saw it, and I couldn't help but laugh a bit.

"What?" Mike said defensively, already suspecting what the kid and I were thinking.

"Nothing," I chuckled, going back to searching the hollow. "Just kind of funny that Gracie has a manlier gun than you do."

"Oh, suh-*nap!*" Lucas chuckled; then he added, "Tight piece, Dr. Chang."

Gracie laughed a bit, herself. "Thank you, Lucas. If I may call you Lucas." The kid blushed just a bit. "And Mike—oh, *Mike . . .*" Gracie had watched my partner putting on his holster, and feigned pity. "I wasn't going to say it, but—the snub-nosed .38? *Really?*"

"Hey, I like the ankle holster!" Mike said, covering his embarrassment. "Try strapping that cannon of *yours* to your leg, Gracie—anyway, may I remind you that we have more important things to deal with?"

"You may." Gracie smiled, putting her HK back in her bag. "But we'll see through it . . ."

"Actually, I fear he has a point, Gracie," I said, in a far more serious tone. "Join me, will you?" She moved over to the corner of the hangar where I stood, accepting the field glasses as I took them from my neck. "Have a look for yourself—down there, among those apple trees just off the road, where it begins to wind out of sight . . ."

Still fairly incredulous, Gracie looked through the binoculars, following my indication. For a few seconds she maintained that look of uneasy disbelief, until finally she spotted what I wanted her to see: crouching amid the trees that I'd indicated were two dark-suited men, who were holding their own pairs of more modern binoculars. Fortunately they were not, just then, looking back at us, probably because we'd disappeared into the hangar for as long as we had; but their mere presence was enough to make Gracie's face droop visibly.

"Oh, my God," she whispered in real dread. "You were right . . ."

"Unfortunately so," I replied. "I suspect they've left their car some-where out of sight, farther down the hollow. And that will help us, pro-vided you still want to discuss this case in full: your own misgivings, as well as what it is you think we can do to help you."

"This—this is insane," Gracie said, having only half-heard me.

"Maybe," I answered. "But just give me back those glasses, if you would, before they have the chance to see us watching them. Then we'll decide just how to proceed."

"How to proceed?" Gracie said indignantly. "Well, I'm just going to go down there and tell them this is none of their goddamned business—"

"Gracie," Mike interrupted firmly. "I wasn't kidding—you even try something like that, and you'll only confirm what they're thinking. You'll be buying yourself one world of trouble, and when you come out the other side, you'll find yourself off this case, and maybe off any case in the future around here. At least, any case that matters."

"They can't do that," Gracie insisted.

"Can and will," I said. "Don't doubt it. These boys and girls play rough, Dr. Chang."

Reality began to sink in fully on our guest, and after a long pause she murmured, "Well, then—what do we do?"

"Again, we get you out of here. *Now*. Create a new notion for them to deal with. Maybe you came here to repeat their warning that we stay off the case in anything but an unofficial role—something that would take you no longer than the time you've already been here to deliver."

"And how do we do that?"

"Okay," I said, turning the whole thing over in my head. "First thing, you get in your car and go. Head to town. Around the square you'll see three bars—taverns, as they once were."

"*Three bars?*" Gracie echoed. "Why has one little town got three bars?"

"Because the fourth one closed down," Lucas replied, dryly but accu-rately.

"Pull in at the first one on your right," I continued. "Let the BCI boys see you having a drink there: a plausible thing to do, after a confronta-tion. They'll probably sit outside in their car, you'll know it when you see it. And then you stay inside for a bit, just to be sure they buy the act. In about five minutes Mike will follow you into town in his car and park across the square. The manager of the bar you'll be in is named

Francisco—he's Salvadoran. Once you're sure they're convinced, slip him twenty bucks and tell him you need to use the back door. He won't be surprised, it happens all the time. Then use the cover of the statue in the middle of the square to get over to Mike's car. Get in the back seat, and stay down. He'll bring you back up here."

"And then what?" Gracie asked, the scheme having done little to ease her nerves.

"Then, Dr. Chang, we hide. I'll stay with Lucas and appear to be tending to my—my dog, on the chance that they stay behind."

"So where do we go when we get back?" Mike asked.

"I'm figuring that out," I replied. "The important thing is that you get under way—*now*."

"I don't know . . ." Gracie looked from me to Mike. "I still think this is kind of nuts."

"It is," Mike said, trying to reassure her. "It's what has to happen, though, if we're going to go on with this meeting. But listen, Gracie, it's *you* who's gotta decide: is the discussion you came for worthwhile, or should we just bag it right now?"

Allowing herself a steady pause, Gracie at length answered, "No. No, I think it's worthwhile. I don't want to see any more throwaways turning up dead, and their cases going uninvestigated, just because of politics."

"Well said, Doctor," I told her. "Okay, then—we'll be ready." I tried to assist Mike's attempt to gently buck up Gracie's courage. "Try not to worry too much—we'll be okay. You have no idea of the number of hiding places that Shiloh offers. But you do need to get out of here."

"All right," Gracie said, still a little fearfully, as she seized hold of Mike's arm and they started down toward their cars. "But don't you dare lose sight of me, Michael Li . . ."

Mike turned just long enough to give me a determined nod as they went—whether in reference to their chances of a safe return or to his personal chances with Gracie, I couldn't tell. All I knew was that I had to come up with the most secure place I could imagine to continue our discussion; and with that in mind, I went to an ancient nail that protruded from one of the wall beams of the hangar, and retrieved a large collection of keys that hung on it. Picking out two fairly new ones, I informed Lucas, much to his delight, that in a lean-to shed behind the barn where the cars had been parked there were two side-by-side Arctic Cat Prowler ATVs; and I told him to get them started, as their engines could sometimes take a while to warm up if they hadn't been used in a bit, which was the case just then. Overjoyed at his luck at being given the assignment of getting such big gas-powered beasts running and ready, Lucas shot off, and I went up to call Marcianna away from a crow she'd managed to kill and put her onto her leash. I had to laugh when she finally appeared, the last bits of small black feathers still stuck to her muzzle.

"You slob," I said, brushing the mess away. "Come on, I need you to do your favorite thing—parade for the public . . ."

And parade she did. I saw no further sign of the Bureau boys, so whatever their shock at having glimpsed Marcianna, they were obviously keeping to their first assignment closely. Having tasted wild blood once that day, Marcianna kept her wide eyes on special lookout for little Terence, during our quick walk; but even thoughts of that quarry vanished from my companion's thoughts when we returned after a half an hour or so to find that Lucas had pulled the Prowlers out of the shed and into the open, where he was busily making sure that first one and then the other got fully warmed up. Marcianna knew exactly what this sight indicated: she and I frequently took trips up the mountain in one of the rigs, trips that delighted her to no end, and it would have been difficult to say whose excitement was the greater at that moment, hers or Lucas'.

"Damn, Doc!" the boy exclaimed, ready for anything. "Six hundred ninety-five cc's and four-stroke engines—not bad, for utility rigs! They'll get you up that mountain, all right. Suh-*weet*. So—what's the plan?"

"The plan is, you get as comfortable as you can in the bed of the one I'll be driving. Marcianna goes in our passenger seat."

"*Passenger seat?*" Lucas echoed. "She's going to be all right, riding up there?"

"Always has been," I said. "*You're* the one I'm worried about—the ride's going to be a little rough, especially toward the top of the mountain. When we get where we're going, you stay outside and keep watch—but listen, too, Lucas, I want you to keep hearing what's discussed. And at the first sign of any real trouble, you bolt, got it? I take your very sensible sister's worries very seriously, and I don't want anything unfortunate happening."

"Hey, don't worry about me," Lucas said, jumping into the small bed of the first of the Prowlers. "I done crazier shit in ATVs, and I know my way around these mountains pretty good."

"I have no doubt, you God damned little trespasser," I said, turning the binoculars on the hollow road once more, this time a little more worriedly: for it was about time for Mike's car to be getting back.

"What *I* want to know," Lucas asked, getting himself as braced as he could in the Prowler, "is what you think Dr. Chang is really up to. She doesn't seem to know what the BCI's next move will be—and you can call me crazy, but I don't think she came here just to hear about your *method*."

"A shrewd analysis, Consulting Detective," I said without turning.

"Plus," he pressed, pleased with himself, "when she told you about Kelsey getting the boot out of her house, didn't she just *give* you what you were looking for?"

"She gave us a lot," I said, leading Marcianna—or rather being led by her—to the passenger seat of the ATV, after which I secured a sheet of nylon netting over the opening from the roof of the open cab to the floor, just to make sure she didn't go tumbling out: though such was always unlikely, given her ability to grip the seat with her ever-extended claws.

"So," the kid went on, still proudly, "why are we taking her someplace you obviously think'll scare the shit out of her if you know she's already told you everything she has to say?"

"I never said she'd told us *everything*—there's more about the official investigation that Gracie *hasn't* told us. Besides her not buying into the serial killer idea, I mean."

"Damn," Lucas said in quiet disappointment. "And that woulda been so cool . . ."

"Oh, yeah. That would be just *awesome*—you'd shit yourself, Lucas, if a serial was loose, grabbing kids in this county. But, returning to the realm of the sane, what we're doing, other than trying to find out what more she knows, is trying to get Gracie to start acting as a conduit of information between the senior county and state levels and our own investigation."

"So you figure this whole escaping the Bureau guys and then going someplace super-secret to have a conference is what's going to ice the deal? Take her up the mountain with Marcianna, generally freak her out so much that you guys'll be the only people she really trusts?"

"Something like that—" I said, stopping suddenly as I caught sight of dust rising from about halfway down Death's Head Hollow. I couldn't see the actual car yet, but from the cloud that was rising into the trees along the road, it could only have been lead-footed Mike driving. "Okay, here we go," I announced.

"And you're *sure* Marcianna's going to be okay with a stranger?" Lucas questioned.

"I'm only sure of one thing," I told him, as we got under way. "You, me, Mike, Gracie—we're *all* about to learn a lot. Provided there's no shooting."

"About that," Lucas said without missing a beat. "I don't suppose there's any chance—"

"No!" I told him. "You don't get a gun, for God's sake."

"Aw, *man*," Lucas said, kicking at the wall of the ATV's bed. "Not even one lousy gun for self-defense? This really *is* getting to be like school . . ."

{iii.}

The Empress pulled into Shiloh's driveway and up to the barn as speedily as it had approached, roaring to a halt before us. Mike bounced out, his mood dramatically improved, and Gracie followed, at a much slower pace that indicated her amazement at what she was seeing.

"The Prowlers, hunh?" Mike said with a grin. "Excellent—let's hit it."

"Hang on," I said, looking from him to Gracie, who continued to approach the ATVs very cautiously. "What, exactly, happened?"

"Went like clockwork," Mike said, as if he'd just carried out the most routine maneuver imaginable. "The Bureau boys didn't stay around very long, just did a pass-by—right, Gracie?"

But Gracie had her eyes fixed on Marcianna, who was staring back at her with wide golden eyes as she tried to determine who our guest might be.

"That—" Gracie began nervously, holding up a finger. "That is no *dog*!"

"No," Mike said, a little apologetically. "It's not . . ."

"But—everybody's always saying that you have some strange kind of *dog* up here," Gracie protested, before repeating, "And *that* is no *dog*!"

"I think we've pretty much established that, Gracie," Mike said, taking out two cigarettes, lighting them both, and then handing her one. "But there *is* an explanation." Then he gently lowered Gracie's arm. "Don't point, she doesn't really like it."

This was nonsense, but I was glad to see Mike playing along with the idea of keeping her off-balance until she'd told all she had to tell. "*'Don't point'?*" Gracie echoed in disbelief, still too shocked by all she'd been through to accept the sight of Marcianna. "That is a damned *cheetah*, Michael, how do you explain *that*? I mean—" She once again gripped Mike's arm hard. "I know a damned cheetah when I see one!"

"Yes, you do," Mike said, getting Gracie seated in the second Prowler. "But try to keep your voice down, too—their ears are really sensitive."

Gracie was about to launch into another round of sarcastic invective, which she finally abandoned in favor of asking, with some resignation, "So—is she safe?"

"As long as Trajan has hold of her," Mike said, "then yeah, she's safe. Basically."

"All right," I said. "Mike, have you got Gracie strapped in?"

"Ready to roll, L.T.," Mike answered, dashing around to the driver's seat of his ATV. "Where are we headed, anyway?"

"Up the mountain!" I called over the revving of the two engines. "It's getting dark fast, so keep up."

"But *where* up the mountain?" Gracie called, her fear of Marcianna having given way to a new sort of bewilderment. "I mean, exactly?"

"Oh, I think you'll know when you see it," I answered. "All set? Then let's move . . ."

And with a hard motion I threw my Prowler into gear and stepped on the gas, steering away toward the first of the trails that would take us to our high destination. Yet even as I pulled out, I heard Gracie continuing to protest to Mike: "I mean—I'm being followed by damned Bureau men, okay, I get that. But what the hell is your partner doing with a damned *cheetah*?"

I didn't stick around to hear more. The farming trail we were initially on took us to Shiloh's highest crop field, where tall, soft alfalfa was just maturing; and when we'd completed the trip around half of this expanse, we came to a spot where an old road into the woods became visible. Without pausing, we turned and burst through a border of huge maples, oaks, and ash trees, plunging on into the wilderness.

Suddenly we found ourselves in a world where the rust color of years of dead leaves on the earthy floor and the light green of the undergrowth that grew up through that base formed a shadowy contrast to the brilliance of the sunset that we were literally chasing up the mountain. Its light was splintered into emerald flakes by the countless leaves of high summer in front of us, as the shadow of night crept up in a line just behind the racing Prowlers. Marcianna, unable to contain herself, let out a sharp chirrup of pure joy: for the woods were teeming with life, and she could see, smell, and sense far more of it than the rest of us could. But, while she was anxious to get to the ground and pursue some of the creatures that scattered before our approach, she nonetheless loved the speed of the Prowler and the quick, endless panorama of new sights and sounds that it offered; and she ultimately decided, as she always did on these trips, that the ground could wait. Sitting back on her haunches, she clung expertly to her seat with her claws, and reveled in the ascent to ever higher ground.

Lucas, however, was a little less happy: at one point, when we hit the third or fourth in a series of strong bumps in the agèd road, he let out a particularly sharp cry of pain, one that was followed by his similarly passionate voice: "I can't believe this—*she* gets to enjoy the ride, while I'm back here getting my ass kicked by every rock and hole that, I'm beginning to think, you're hitting on purpose? That shit is *wrong*, Doc . . ."

As we began to move up the steepest trails and roads, many of which predated even Caractacus Jones' purchase of the land, a white-tailed doe burst out of nowhere at one point, coming close to being struck by the Prowler. I had to lean over and put my arm around Marcianna for a moment, for fear that her predatory desires would get the best of her, and cause her to try to leap from the racing vehicle. But she continued to understand that there might be even more alluring visions ahead, especially when we finally stopped; and so she kept her seat with admirable discipline.

On we climbed, from one mountain level to another: from beautiful, unexpected glades full of ferns and mountain flowers to high rock escarpments, where the Prowler sometimes skidded a bit on the moss that grew atop the stone. And although such motions drew small cries of theatrical terror from Lucas, we were never in any danger throughout the full fifteen or twenty minutes that it took us to pass first two thousand feet, then twenty-five hundred, and finally to the three-thousand-foot mark, where the Taconics reach their interconnected and surprisingly pastoral summits. Once we gained this mark, new trails became visible before us, more clearly worn than any we had thus far used. Some showed signs of small, nearly buried railroad ties: the most clearly preserved remnants of the routes used by the carts and, later, the steam trolleys of Colonel Jones' charcoal business. We were nearing our destination, and with a powerful new snarl, the Prowler engine answered as I called for greater speed along the ridgetop, so much so that we were soon doing an improbable forty miles an hour through the high forest—in darkness, for the night had finally overtaken us. At that pace, our goal quickly became visible: an impressive group of semi-ruined, seemingly ancient structures in the middle distance, lit, now, almost exclusively by the Prowler's headlights.

"Whoa," Lucas said in wonder. "What the fuck are *they*?"

"The old charcoal kilns that the Colonel built," I said.

And at last I slowed down just a bit, Marcianna chirruping again in anticipation of our coming to a halt. In moments Mike and Gracie were right up on us, and I indicated the ruins ahead with motions of my left hand. Mike nodded, and together we sped down the last stretch of old road until the great brick structures—five in total, each the size of a small, round, domed house, and all but one collapsed to greater or lesser extents—stood before us. I pulled up to the most intact structure, shut the Prowler down, and got a firm hold of Marcianna's leash, locking the handle of her retractable lead. She did not, after all, know Gracie yet, and I wanted to make sure that she didn't consider our guest either an enemy or yet another creature of the wilderness to be hunted—particularly if Gracie's fear and confusion, which would only excite my companion, completely got the better of her. For there was, as I had told Lucas, still a bit of the savage in Marcianna; and although I had no more interest in removing it from her soul than I had in purifying my own spirit of the lifelong rage that had almost cost Frank Mangold a cracked skull a mere forty-eight hours earlier, I certainly did not want to see it unleashed on Gracie.

Mike, I soon discovered, had finally given in and explained to Gracie just who and what Marcianna was, on their trip up the mountain; and, given that we had now reached our remote destination, I, too, decided that our guest had been through enough. I carefully guided my young colleague over to my companion, telling Gracie to put her hand before Marcianna's nose so that she could get her scent and grow used to the fact that she was simply one more human that was not to be either feared or attacked. Gracie, to her considerable credit, braved this introduction well: she had indeed grown into quite a brave and intrepid woman, since the time I had known her as a young apprentice in New York City. In-deed, by the time Marcianna turned away from her, fixing her predatory attention on the forest that had long since encroached on what had once been a bustling little industry on the ridgetop, Gracie had in turn shifted *her* focus from the improbable presence of a cheetah in the Taconics to the origin and purpose of the ruined kilns. What, she wanted to know, could possibly have warranted the building of such ambitious structures in so remote a location?

"Charcoal fuel," I said simply, as I wrapped and tied the now-unlocked handle end of Marcianna's twenty-five-foot lead around a slender young maple tree outside the most intact of the kilns.

"*Charcoal?* Come on, they didn't exactly have barbecue grills in those days," Gracie observed, quite accurately. "So what else would you need charcoal for?"

"Well," I answered, indicating the narrow entrance to the kiln, "to heat homes, early on; but when the steel industry first arrived in the North-east, charcoal was used to fire the furnaces."

"They didn't just use coal?" Gracie asked. "And are you positive that it's safe inside there—it won't collapse?"

"The roof's already collapsed about as much as it's going to, in our generation," Mike explained. "And the walls on this one are surprisingly secure."

"And to answer your first question," I added, "charcoal has always been a much better fuel than coal for furnaces, whether the old pot-bellied jobs you still find in a lot of local basements, or the big beasts that pow-ered the steel mills in Fraser, Troy, Schenectady, all those cities and towns. But when really cheap coal, backed by big money, arrived, the charcoal industry died off."

"Hunh!" Gracie determined, staring at the kilns again. "But—to build these things, I mean, how did they get all the bricks up here?"

"Well, Gracie," I said, indicating one of the stretches of ground where the faint outlines of small railroad ties could be seen. "The first thing the Colonel constructed was a very narrow-gauge railway, one that ran from the kilns all the way down the mountain."

"A *railway*?" Gracie echoed with a laugh. "With little steam engines and everything?"

"Absolutely," Mike answered, moving into the kiln and preparing a seat for first Gracie and then himself on the ground beneath the conical roof of the structure.

"The steel rails were stolen for scrap by locals, when the industry died," I continued. "But you can still see some of the ties." I waited for Gracie to follow Mike in, which she did very slowly, then called out to Lucas, who had begun lightly playing with Marcianna. "Okay, kid—like I said, you keep an eye out, and your ears open. Got it?"

"No doubt!" Lucas called, moving back toward the kiln. "I'm ready, L.T."

Once the rest of us were inside the cavernous kiln—still deeply redolent of charred wood and brick dust, with the rising moon shining through the partially fallen roof—Gracie looked around at the blackened, molding, and decaying bricks of the walls and said, "I suppose that it's an appropriately morbid place to discuss murder, isn't it?"

"Morbid?" Mike said brightly. "Come on, Gracie . . ." And he swatted the ground beside him, urging her to sit down. "These places are fun, admit it. They're ghostly, maybe, but not *morbid*."

"Okay," I pronounced, not wanting to get sidetracked by Mike's ongoing flirtations. "Now that we've disposed of the BCI and gotten you here, Gracie—shall we get about the rest of the business of the evening?"

Gracie had to consider that proposition for a moment, swiping a suddenly loose shower of her shoulder-length black hair behind her ear with a practiced move of one delicate hand as she sat beside my partner. "Well—I suppose so," she said at length. "As long as we're really safe in here . . ."

"Well," Mike teased, " 'safe' means a lot of things to a lot of people, Gracie."

Which only netted him a sound punch in his shoulder. "Don't you screw around with me, Michael Li," Gracie said, as Mike moaned in real pain. "You knew all along we were coming up here."

"Gracie," he defended quickly, "I didn't! Not until we got back from town, anyway."

"Maybe," she answered coolly, poking a finger at his nose. "But you've certainly seen that cheetah before, don't deny that, and you didn't give me *any* warning. So just cut all the coy hooey."

"What's *hooey*?" Lucas called in bewilderment from his post just outside.

"Bullshit," Mike explained. "Gracie's being polite because she thinks you're an innocent kid."

To Lucas' sharp laugh in return, Gracie said, "Oh, no I don't. I might have earlier, but not anymore. Anybody who would be involved with you two . . ." Then, trying to gather her dignity, she snatched a plain elastic hair tie out of her bag and skillfully pulled her hair back into a short, bouncy ponytail, one that I thought might make Mike expire. "All right. You want to get down to business, so let's do it. One thing confuses me, right off—shouldn't *I* be the one asking about who knows what? Because, like I said, my main interest is in how you've applied *your* method to these murders. For instance, even if I agree with you, how did you rule out the idea of a serial killer so quickly?"

"I didn't say we'd ruled it out," I replied carefully. "Ruling out is not what Mike and I do. But it's not the principal avenue we're pursuing, for a variety of reasons. All of which I'll be happy to share with you—once I know what it is you really want to tell us."

"What I . . . ?" Gracie answered hesitantly. "But I already told you, down in the hangar. You two are pretty unique, in this county, in your understanding of the throwaway-children problem—or at least, in your willingness to talk about it. There's a lot of awareness of it in the county seats, and in Albany, too: in fact, 'throwaways' has become one hell of a buzzword—but a very quiet one. The truth is, everybody knows there's a political storm brewing over the whole subject, and so it's produced, naturally, a pretty dark little effort to keep it contained, because it's currently viewed as a problem without a solution. I mean, it's hard enough to find runaway kids—but to find runaway *parents,* who've really figured out how to hide out and reinvent themselves, usually out of state? That's next to impossible. And then there's the fact that our current governor has staked a lot on what he's doing for the children of New York—"

"All very true," I interrupted, as evenly as I could. "But true in only a general sense. So—suppose you get specific. I don't want to appear falsely modest, Gracie, but Mike's and my method, which you claim got us such a reputation in New York, isn't so tough to grasp that someone as bright as you couldn't have figured it out. The fact that we don't do what most of law enforcement does—that we won't give in to tunnel vision, or to any of the more complicated names that the social sciences have given the same old habit of hunches, whether it's 'bounded rationality,' 'focused determination,' 'heuristics,' or whatever—doesn't make us rocket scientists, after all. You know that; and you didn't come here for some class in dialectics, in how to immediately put counterproposals to any and all investigative assumptions. You came here because something specific is on your mind."

Gracie looked from me to Mike, a little helplessly. "Well," Mike said, shrugging. "He didn't get his nickname for nothing, Gracie. So—is he right?"

Gracie paused to gather a deep breath. "Yeah. He's right."

"It's not a tribunal, Gracie," I said, trying to make it easier for her to get the rest of her story out. "And listen—my friend out there? The cheetah who's got you so worried? Let me give you a quick summary of how she came to live on Shiloh, because it's not what you're thinking . . ."

The tale of Marcianna's captivity and release, featuring as it did Mitch McCarron's role, proved enough to charm the naturally compassionate Gracie out of her fears. By the time it was over, she had moved to the kiln entrance, where she studied the romping if tethered Marcianna with true fondness; indeed, there was growing affection and empathy in her gaze.

"So," Gracie said at length. "*Nothing* around here is really what it seems, hunh?"

"Well," Mike said, making an attempt to stick up for the closeness that he and Gracie had, until they'd entered the kiln, been sharing, "*some* things are. Have been . . ."

Gracie laughed a little, and moved back to sit by him. "Michael Li," she said, indulgently scolding him. "You change girlfriends like you change socks."

Mike's expression turned to umbrage. "How can you possibly say that, Gracie? Where am I going to find so many girlfriends in this town, living with this miserable *gweilo* and his 'pet'?"

"Oh, come on," Gracie answered. "I'm sure there are some online students who find you just irresistible. After all . . ." She put her hand very coyly to his gun-bearing ankle, at which point I thought he really would lose it. ". . . any man who is secure enough to pack a snub-nosed .38 must be *very* confident with the ladies." Mike was about to gasp out a response, when Gracie touched his mouth with a finger and said, in the same sexy tone, "Tell me—are we going to go bust a speakeasy, after this? Maybe look for remaining members of the Capone mob?"

Mike fell back into disappointment. "Nice," he said quietly. "I told you, I like the ankle—"

"The ankle holster, yeah," Gracie replied. "You're an idiot in more ways than you're aware of, you know that, Mike?" That crack brought another laugh from Lucas; and then, without any prodding, Gracie's manner became much more serious, and she looked up at me. "Okay, Trajan," she said, dropping all formalities along with all pretense. "You want to know what specifically is bothering me about the way this case is being handled. So I guess I'd better tell you, since you've gone to all the trouble to create this"—she wafted a hand around the kiln—"effect. To start with, I'm sure you know that just about every law enforcement official in this part of the state, with the exception of Steve Spinetti and his people, has been given a long list of native and relocated sex offenders, and is trying to find a likely suspect that they can pin these throwaway killings on. And while they haven't come up with the name of a particular sucker, yet, what they *have* come up with is a method to make the rap stick."

I glanced quickly at Mike, and found him shooting a similarly shocked look my way—because we had both taken Gracie's meaning perfectly: "You're talking about a deliberate attempt to frame somebody," I said, slowly and quietly.

"And not just the idea," Mike added, in a similar tone, "but a method— evidence. A plan to plant evidence."

Lucas whistled, low and quietly, from outside, and it was not hard to understand why. The deliberate planting of evidence in a serial murder case was something that was not altogether uncommon, in big-city cases involving, say, victims who were prostitutes; but to find law enforcement in someplace like Burgoyne County contemplating it in a child murder case was unusual, to say the least, and I took heart from the fact that Gracie had specifically excluded Steve Spinetti's department from any such plot.

But our guest had not yet exhausted her cache of surprises; not by a long shot. "Yes, I'm talking about exactly that," she said, "but I'm also talking about something significantly more. The word is that evidence alone isn't going to cut it, this time. Apparently somebody in the BCI, acting on orders from higher-ups—maybe *very* higher-ups—has gotten hold of a body. A dead child, one who matches the background profiles of the other three—or, I guess you're now telling me, the other four. And as soon as they pick their target offender, they're going to plant the body in the dumb schmuck's home, or some other place only he has access to.

Then Mangold will bring the guy in, interrogate him for as long as it takes, and bang, that ties it up with a bow."

Once again, I had begun pacing, this time to try to order my racing thoughts. "But—for this scheme to work—it would be necessary that no more throwaway kids suddenly turn up dead."

"Correct," Gracie answered. "And I guess you can understand the level of my concern, now."

"Holy shit," Mike murmured. "That would mean—Trajan, that would mean that whoever gave the order to go out and find somebody to frame, along with a body, *that* person has to somehow be able to guarantee that the deaths will stop. Which means—"

"Don't say it," I warned, taking out a cigarette and pointing it at Mike. "You know how I feel about that word."

"What word?" Gracie asked.

"Sounds like you're talking about a *conspiracy,* is what it sounds like!" Lucas called, causing me to grab a small piece of old brick from the floor of the kiln, rush outside, and hurl it at him. It caught his right thigh and he yelped loudly.

"Damn it, Lucas!" I told him. "Do *not* use that word! First of all, it's fucking dangerous, and second, though I'm sure you've learned to love conspiracy theories from your TV shows, in the real world we understand that for every thousand of them proposed, maybe one turns out to be true."

"So maybe this is the one," Lucas moaned in defense, rubbing his leg. "And didn't you have to take some oath about 'first doing no harm' when you got to be a doctor, you psycho?"

Mike brought me a light for my cigarette as I reentered, a very grave expression on his face. "Kid's got a point, L.T.," he said. "I mean, about the first thing. We all *know* you're a psycho."

"Ha!" Lucas declared. "Yeah, L.T., kid's got a point, and we all—"

"Um—boys?" Gracie said, as Mike went back to her side. "If you're finished with recess, can I get back to what I was trying to say? I'm afraid that Mike and Lucas *do* have a point, Trajan, insofar as a possible conspiracy is concerned. I don't like it any more than you do, but for all that I'm hearing to make sense—and I'm hearing it, not just through denials, but through confirmations from people I trust, in the BCI, the FIC, even the DA's office—then yes, whoever is behind this idea has got to be able to guarantee that no more kids will turn up dead. And how else do you do that without a conspiracy of some kind? Maybe even a high-reaching one? I mean, from the beginning, I thought it was very strange that the FBI Field Office in Albany—you know, the one on McCarty Avenue—"

Mike chuckled. "Oh, yeah. We know it."

Gracie gave him an indulgent smile. "Yeah. I'll just bet you do. Anyway, I wondered why they hadn't been brought in, or hadn't *forced* their way in. After all, one of the FBI's mandates is to investigate crimes against children, especially if those crimes present any evidence of being the work of a serial killer."

"True, Gracie," I answered. "But remember, those are their *stated* mandates. Like most FBI franchises in the country, the Albany office spends less time doing their local jobs—less time doing them with real dedication, anyway—than they do sitting around trying to get ready for the next terrorist attack. Or at least trying to uncover a good terrorist *conspiracy*, which is one of the reasons I don't want to hear us throwing that word around."

"I know," Gracie said, waving off my cynicism. "But that wasn't what really worried me. See, I straight up asked both Cathy Donovan and the DA just why the FBI wasn't stepping in, because it seemed to me that we could use their resources. And sure enough, the field office *had* tried to horn in on things, at first—but then both they and the DA's office got a message—"

I had begun to grasp it: "From somebody on South Swan Street," I said, referring to the location of the Alfred E. Smith State Office Building, which was across a park from the capitol building in Albany but connected to it by a tunnel; and both were just a quick drive from the Governor's Mansion.

"Yes," Gracie said. "And all of them, along with Frank Mangold's boss, were all being told that the FBI would stay out of this case, at the urging of the governor and with the blessing of, it was pretty obvious, the state attorney general and even the AG in Washington. But what possible interest could the Justice Department have in interfering with a crime in a little county in upstate New York?"

I hadn't expected this from Gracie: it was an unusual and dangerous bit of business, for someone in her position to first have such doubts and then to voice them, along with fairly dramatic speculations, to people on the outside of an investigation. It was, indeed, genuinely brave; and she wasn't done yet: "I mean, I don't want to get too ambitious about it, but the governor *has* spent a lot of political capital on his handling of child welfare; and the subject of throwaways, if it busts loose, is going to be a major black eye, to him, maybe to the entire party and to his closest political ally, who just happens to be the guy sitting in the White House—"

Lucas, awed and excited by what he was hearing, let out a low, "Whoa, *shit!*"

"Jesus," Mike agreed. "Could we actually have stumbled onto something that big, L.T.?"

The tone in their voices, on top of everything else, was enough to make me immediately hold up my hands. "Okay, okay, okay. Everybody just get a damned grip—and that means *everybody*," I called, making sure Lucas heard me. Then I tried to calm myself: "Now—I'll entertain the idea of the FBI giving our governor a hand: he's taken stupider risks in the last six years. But no *president* lets himself get involved in this kind of thing—"

"Hey, Nixon told those five morons to rob the Democratic national headquarters," Mike parried, earning points with our guest. But I had to check him again, and fast:

"Nobody knows that, Mike. Not for sure. Obstruction of the investigation, yes, that's what got him. But initiation of the original crime? That's only supported by a whole lot of speculation."

"But isn't *this* just obstruction of an investigation?" Gracie asked.

"You guys aren't getting it—that was national politics, this is a state scandal, at best, so far as we know. So don't get sidetracked, let's just proceed with only those aspects that we're *certain* have relevance to the case."

Gracie nodded. "All right—I take it you mean the subject of a serial killer. But, having told you what I have, I think you really should let me know why you think one can't be responsible."

"Fine—Mike?" I turned to my partner, suddenly feeling a sharp pain in my hip. "You want to take this one?"

"Okay, Gracie," Mike said a little indulgently, which got him a frown from our guest. "Let's start with the simplest facts. First of all, like Trajan said, we don't rule things out—not in the usual way. We just analyze the facts, the evidence, and the profiles, even if they're preliminary, then look at the prevailing assumptions, and propose counter-suggestions, and keep doing that until we get to something that we can be fairly sure of.

That's what we've done, in this case, on the subject of serials. Let's start with the basics: most serials work alone—you know that. And even before Latrell, the kid who got shot Friday night, talked about 'them' to Trajan, we'd pretty much determined that the staging of Shelby Capamagio's death—and probably the others, except maybe for Donnie—would have required more than one person, logistically. It just would've been too hard to get the body into that fairly dramatic position, for starters; and then to keep an eye out for anybody who might have been passing by? We're talking at least two, maybe three people. That's very unusual, in serial cases."

"I thought of that," Gracie answered, "when I heard about what Latrell said to Trajan. But even if serial teams are unusual, they're not unprecedented, especially in cases involving child victims. There was Ian Brady and Myra Hindley in England, the Gallego couple here—"

"True, the list can be made long, Gracie," Mike cut in. "But only if it's also made international in scope. So, given the circumstances you've heard us mention, why do you insist that it has to be true?"

"Besides the consistent m.o.?" Gracie said, still offering a peculiar sort of resistance, one that now seemed less like genuine advocacy than some kind of test of either our views or our loyalties. "Well, just look at the victims: in every case of past serial teams who preyed on children that I know of, the victims were described as somehow 'subhuman,' as not worthy of continued existence. It's not too hard to see how such people might view kids already *officially* labeled by the state to be 'throwaways' as similarly *disposable*—it's why I think it's a terrible classification for them."

"You'll get no argument there, Gracie," I said. "But remember, in almost every example of serial couples you're referring to, sexual assault was also a feature—and none of the throwaway deaths have exhibited any such aspect."

"Yes, but you just said it," Gracie protested. "In *almost* every case—some teams got their gratification simply from the murders."

"Correct again," Mike replied, all seriousness, now, his flirtation for the time suspended. "So let's go on to say, for the sake of argument, that we have a serial team on our hands: two people—or probably, like I said, more than two—for whom sexual assault is not part of the goal. They get off on the killings alone. But how do you explain the staging of the death scenes? When has a serial team, or *any* serial killer, for that matter, exhibited that kind of careful, tidy cover-up? Serials take trophies, and even, in most cases, *want* their victims found, usually in horrifying shape. Look at Ted Bundy, supposedly the king brain of the serials—he used to take victims' heads home and use them as centerpieces on his table, for Christ's sake. Plus serials, again almost always, claim the credit for the kills, in some way—if not before then after they're caught. Some even boast about the details—as Bundy eventually did—in terms that're deliberately provocative."

"Right," I agreed. "And think about the notification to Steve Spinetti's office, in that light: it contained none of the attempts to taunt law enforcement or, conversely, of the furtiveness of usual serials. It was a simple, straightforward statement, one that seemed to say, 'Go there quickly, and find her body before it is further and publicly desecrated.' It was so nondescript that nobody even made note of it, at first. None of that suggests your usual stranger murder, does it?"

Gracie shook her head at last, and let out a long breath. "No . . ."

"But even then," I added, "the official investigators didn't get the main point: the *intimacy* of parts of the scene—the arrangement of Shelby's personal things, along with the actual lividity in the body, which showed that not only was someone with her right after she died, but that she'd likely *known* the person who was with her, quite possibly well. Contrast that with the supposed brutality of the 'murder scene,' and the profile simply doesn't work. To say nothing of the fact that those carefully tended possessions would have been prime trophies, for a serial."

"Yeah." Gracie nodded, less reluctantly than as though she had some difficult facts to add. But she had one last ounce of fight left in her: rallying, she shook her head, as if to clear it of all we'd said, then protested, "But, see, there's still one thing I don't get. I've read your book on Laszlo Kreizler, Trajan. And I've heard both of you, in other places, voice your objections to the limits of forensic science—but you used forensic science yourselves, in reaching your conclusions about Shelby Capamagio!"

"You apparently didn't read my book very closely, Gracie," I countered. "We object, as Dr. Kreizler did, to the manner in which *criminal* science has consistently been coerced into becoming *forensic* science—not only because it so heavily serves the aims of law enforcement and prosecutory officials, but because it supports their tendency toward pursuing their initial theory of a case."

"And so, Gracie, we limit ourselves to criminal science," Mike added quickly, speaking once again with what I suppose he thought was great

216 | CALEB CARR

charm, but which was coming off more like indulgence, and as such didn't appear (to my rusty eyes, at least) to be having much effect on her. "Which means we pay careful attention to the differences between the way evidence is collected by experts and teams who are independent, and the idiots—not you, of course—who are the paid employees of the state, meaning the prosecution, ninety-nine-point-nine percent of the time. The Capamagio scene was a good example of that. Weaver and Kolmback collected what they needed to support their own as well as law enforcement's initial theories—theories they *wanted* to be true, or were told *would* be true, to serve both their investigative purposes and their own as well as their bosses' political ambitions. But once *we* were in, we collected anything that we could, in the time we had, regardless of where it might lead. On the scene and later, we sorted through all that information, guided by only one thing."

Gracie nodded a bit. "The context of Shelby's life," she said, looking from Mike to me. "As Dr. Kreizler would have put it."

"Correct," I replied. "*The context of Shelby's life.* Those theories that only made sense given who she was, what she'd been through, who her friends and boyfriends were, what she wanted out of life—things that the DA's office, and the governor's people above them, really couldn't care less about. To that crowd, Shelby was and remains just one thing: another throwaway child, and therefore part of a growing and embarrassing problem. But she was, let me tell you, a whole lot more. That girl was a house afire—indeed, in some particular way, *all* of the dead throwaways seem to have had one thing in common: they were not pathetic, lost souls, they were kids fighting back against the situation into which they'd been thrown, and they were kids with ambitions of their own. Shelby, bound and determined to enjoy the good life, rather than slide into the tweaker hell of her parents; Kyle Howard, who wanted to be a literary scholar; Kelsey Kozersky, who had a passionate desire to defend abused horses, and to work with the best of those animals, too—in all of these, and I suspect in the boy Donnie's life, there isn't the suggestion of passive victims, willing to accept what life had thrown at them. That, I believe, is the most important connection, concerning how and even more *why* they died; a connection that we will need to examine more closely—when we get the chance . . ."

And I hoped that chance was coming, now: for Gracie had finally hung her head in resignation, as she began to toy with her little Jimmy

Choo black flats. "I see that—I do," she murmured. "And I also see that your way of looking at the case does effectively rule the serial aspect out. But—I'm afraid there's another reason I've been asking all these questions. I'm about to tell you guys something that, and I'm serious, will mean the end of my career, if it's revealed that I was the one who leaked it. I'm not like you two—I can't just go off and teach some course at SUNY. I've got to keep my public career going, at least to the point where I can publish—maybe not publish anything as fundamental as your book on Dr. Kreizler, Trajan, but *something*. On the other hand—you ought to know. You've been straight with me, and I owe you that much. But I warn you, guys—it doesn't get any more reassuring, or smell any better, the closer you get to it. Because you think you're one step ahead of them, but—I'm not so sure. And when you hear exactly what they're doing, you might understand why it's taking them so long to set their scheme up . . ."

{iv.}

Mike and I glanced at each other, somewhat surprised at the depth of Gracie's passion. She'd already told us an awful lot, without thinking that she was putting her career in jeopardy; but there was plainly another dimension to be explored, one that frightened even her, and it was all I could do to override the growing pain in my stump and continue to sound measured.

"All right, Gracie," I said. "I think we can manage that pledge."

"And you'll vouch for your—" She jerked her thumb in the direction of the entryway. "Your apprentice out there?"

"Hey, who'm *I* gonna tell?" Lucas called.

"Lucas!" I said sternly. "This is important—get serious or I'll hit you with an *entire* brick!"

"Nice," Lucas mumbled. "Nice way for a doctor to talk . . ."

"Don't worry about him, Gracie," Mike said. "Go ahead."

Our guest turned from one of us to the other a last time, trepidation all over her face; but then, at last, she began: "Okay—so, when I say that they might be more than a step behind you guys, I'm not making it up. And I'm afraid you only have yourself to blame, Trajan. When you delivered your lecture to Frank Mangold and his sniper buddy the other night, the pair of them may not have taken you seriously, but everybody else who was listening certainly did. See, I think you guys have let yourselves get a little overwhelmed by being run out of New York—"

"We weren't run out—" Mike started, but I cut him off:

"Shut up, Michael, and let Gracie finish."

Mike shrugged the point off, and Gracie went on: "My point being, whatever it was that caused you guys to leave New York, I think you underestimate how much of a worry you can still be to law enforcement upstate. Hell, even in the city, now that that nasty little Irishman's left the police commissioner's office, there are already rumors—which you did *not* hear from me—that his replacement and the new mayor regret what happened, and might be open to you two coming back in your . . . *informal* capacity. *If* you'll agree to check with them in the future, that is, before going public with your conclusions, and if you won't keep making the NYPD and the lab look stupid."

"We promise nothing," Mike said imperiously, once again trying to be coy with Gracie; but this really wasn't the time for it:

"Mike, I thought I told you to shut up," I said, very seriously, before Gracie continued:

"Anyway, up here, the effect is even more pronounced. Just look at how the mere thought of your getting actively involved in this case has made law enforcement in this whole area—not just Burgoyne County— have kittens."

"All right," I said, perhaps a bit impatiently. "So we still have our mojo. Or something vaguely resembling it. What's that got to do with the case?"

"Well, like I said," Gracie answered, "everybody was listening very closely when you declared that Latrell had told you about who was behind at least the positioning of the boy Donnie's body, using the word 'them.' There were reporters around, by that point, and they heard it, too; so the higher-ups knew they weren't going to get away with pinning this on a lone killer—which made their job about a hundred times harder. I mean, think about it, if they'd just wanted to haul in one repeat offender and frame him, don't you think they would have done it by now? Of course! But too many people are aware that you've said pretty definitively that this is not a one-man job—that's part of the reason I wanted you to give me your argument. I wanted to know that I could be sure, myself." She paused, glancing at Mike and smiling just a bit. "It certainly wasn't for the pleasure of listening to Dr. Smooth, over here . . ."

"Hey," Mike replied instantly, moving a few inches away from her.

"I've just been trying to protect you from the thoughtlessness of my severely desocialized partner over there, Dr. Chang. But if you consider it such a huge imposition—"

"Oh, I'm sorry, Michael," Gracie laughed quickly, pulling him back. *"Wo oi ni."* (Which I knew meant "I love you," from hearing, I'm sorry to say, Mike call it out to Chinese strippers, on nights when he was particularly plastered.) "You know that."

Mike was pleased by their renewed proximity and her words, but he still managed to groan, "You know, I really do not remember you being this cold in New York, Gracie . . ."

"Stop digging your hole deeper, idiot," I told my partner, at which our guest laughed again, this time in sympathy, and touched Mike's chin, pulling his head up. "Come on, Gracie," I said, sensing we were nearing the point of this meeting, and not wanting to dilute it with any more nonsense. "Let's have the whole thing, if you please."

Taking one more big breath, Gracie lit one of her own cigarettes and began to tell the tale I'd been afraid we were going to hear: "The reason it's taking them so long to pick their sucker, Trajan, is because, like I say, it can't be *a* sucker, anymore—it's got to be at least a pair of them. And finding one chump you can sweat into confessing to any part of child serial murder is enough, but finding two? That's not easy. Oh, there's candidates available, but so far, none of them have been half-witted enough to fill the bill. But today . . . Today I heard that they've actually got a couple who look like they'll do. A man and a woman, married, who've been brought up on molestation and child pornography charges before. And they're getting it all in place, the couple, the body, the evidence—they're right on the verge of making it happen."

I said nothing, just kept trying to pace the pain in my thigh away; but Mike managed to murmur "Jesus," almost breathlessly, having once again halted his attempts at flirtation dead in their tracks. It wasn't hard to see why, either: the moment of confrontation seemed to be dead ahead, and what that might mean for the two of us was hard to judge—but it wasn't likely to be pleasant. Everything from our exclusion from all future cases in the area to threats against our jobs at SUNY certainly seemed in the offing.

"What about names?" I asked, forcing myself to move on to more concrete matters. "Have you found out who this couple are, where they live, anything we might actually use?"

"I'm getting there," Gracie answered quickly. "See, one of Cathy Donovan's minions has got a huge crush on me—"

Mike stared at her in disbelief. "Oh. That's *great*. I take endless shit, while you're off playing around with some Irish *gweilo* in Fraser who's got an Asian fetish."

My partner was, in truth, generally a fairly suave character with the ladies—but he really didn't know which foot to put in his mouth next, in Gracie's case: she once again frowned and whaled on his arm with her fist, a sight that gave me some small satisfaction. "Damn it, Michael, I just told you—*he* has a crush on *me*. And I'm using it, that's all."

As Mike moaned I studied Gracie more carefully, finally asking, "And us? Are we being used, as well, Gracie?" She looked suitably taken aback, which had been the point of my question; and before she had time to express her resentment, I continued: "Forgive me. An unworthy remark, but one designed to produce the response it did. I believe you have come here with only the best intentions, which include beating the tar out of my colleague."

Gracie smiled, though Mike did not, and I half-expected to hear Lucas laugh from outside; yet—strangely, it seemed—he did not.

"But do tell me one thing," I continued. "How, exactly, have you come to work so closely with all these people, including, apparently, Frank Mangold and the BCI?"

Gracie nodded. "Very good, Dr. Jones. See, a while back, I came to the realization that I'm sure you did long ago—that the job description 'criminal profiler' just doesn't mean what it used to."

"No," I said, trying not to let my own emotions on the subject show. "It certainly does not."

"Oh, I get it, Gracie," Mike needled, sensing an opportunity to return fire. "You've changed your business card."

But she only balled another fist at him, making him cover his arm and shy away. "Don't start with me again, you. I did what I had to, when I got up here. Just like you guys did. And in my case, yes, that meant a slight change in how I defined myself, professionally."

"And just which title did you pull out of your hat, Gracie?" I asked.

She turned my way, figuring that I wasn't going to like what I heard. "I'm now known as an expert in 'Criminal Threat Assessment.' Fairly clever, if I say so myself—and it's opened a lot of doors."

I nodded. "It's actually quite brilliant," I said, surprising her. "Exploiting all the current fears in one name—seriously, Gracie, well done. But can we ask what the job actually consists *of*?"

"Yes," she replied, "although I'm sure you've already guessed. For the most part, I've been dealing in geographic profiling. Not quite the same thing as psychological profiling, but it covers a lot of the same ground— mapping out kill patterns, trying to determine stalking grounds, anticipate where murderers may strike next, all of it. Not a tough leap."

"No," I answered. "You'll get no argument from me."

"Yeah?" Mike said skeptically. "Well, you will from me. I mean, come on, Gracie—in the old days, *wǒ de ài*"—which I was also aware, from the same unfortunate experiences with Mike and strippers, translated to "my love"—"the main elements of geographic profiling—and Trajan will check me if I'm wrong here—were *part* of psychological profiling. All that mapping of crimes, connecting the sites through the idea of the killer as a predator with a defined hunting ground—there's nothing new, there. Even Dr. Kreizler practiced a form of it, and that was over a century ago."

"Hang on, Mike," I interrupted, knowing his last point to be accurate, but now certain that Gracie had come to us with no mixed motives and wanting to help her out. "I've met Kim Rossmo," I went on, speaking of the Canadian police criminologist–turned–Texas State University professor who had devised geographic profiling, "and he's a dedicated, clever man. Coming up with his system was, at least in part, a way to keep some of the most controversial principles of psychological profiling alive, in a professional world that's grown increasingly hostile to them."

"Correct," Gracie answered proudly. "And, like I say, it's opened a lot of doors. Particularly on this case. After all, the murders *did* all occur in Burgoyne County, and it *is* therefore logical to assume that the killer or, rather, the killers have some kind of passionate feeling toward or about the county itself. Which is a valuable thought to consider. Even Frank Mangold's been able to see that much, and that's how I've been of some use to him; and, in turn, how I've ingratiated myself with some of his people. Now, I'm sure I don't need to show you the map I made up for them—it's nothing that you haven't already done yourselves, I'm betting."

"Probably a safe bet," I said, smiling just a bit.

"Right—but the main point is that, using it, the BCI were led to focus on Burgoyne County, and over here in the eastern part, in particular." Steeling herself, Gracie retrieved another cigarette from her bag, lit it off her last, and continued: "I don't know, though—I'm afraid I created a bit of a monster . . . See, Cathy Donovan's boss basically does whatever Frank tells him to do when it comes to this kind of stuff. And so, using my map, Frank convinced the DA to go after a pair of suspects in this area. They're on the offender rolls, but they're not murderers, for God's sake, and that's what makes me feel so bad."

"Don't beat yourself up," Mike told her, being as genuine as his hormones would allow. "It's not your fault—it's just plain old confirmation bias."

"Yes, Gracie," I added. "They almost certainly had the couple on their list, already—your work just gave them a hook to hang them on."

"I'm afraid that particular term doesn't make me feel much better," Gracie said quietly. "But—anyway . . ." She tried to rally. "What it *did* do that was helpful was to convince this guy in Donovan's office that I was already so on the inside that he could speak freely about the names of the selected targets. They're Jimmy and Jeanette Patrick, both in their early forties, both with deep Burgoyne County roots. They did a short stint for molestation and child porn, like I say, but now they just lie around their latest house—they've had to relocate at least a couple of times because of neighbor trouble—getting high and watching a lot of free kiddie porn on the Net. And when I checked some of the free sites, just to get an idea of what was keeping them so busy, Jesus, there is a *lot* of that kind of thing *to* watch. 'Mature couple seduces teen girl,' 'Older couple with young boy'—that kind of thing. Really just . . . dreadful stuff."

"Yeah, you can find just about anything on the Internet," Mike mused quietly; then, when he found Gracie staring at him in seeming disbelief, he quickly defended, "Hey, don't give *me* the hairy eyeball, Dr. Chang, *you're* the one who's been looking at it."

"Unh-hunh," Gracie said, continuing to appear dubious in a way that momentarily made Mike very worried about his chances with her; but then she offered a quick smile that said her concern had been an act, and finally continued: "Some of it gets pretty aggressive, bondage and whatnot, which is what these two had been up to, before they were finally arrested about four years ago. After they got out, they were relocated, then moved to another, and then *another,* supposedly safe spot away from any schools and families, outside of Heinsdale"—which was a town about fifteen miles south of Surrender, just on the Rensselaer County line— "and there hadn't been any official complaints. But now—well, you know the drill. Offenders like that who have acted out and been caught once aren't likely to be rehabilitated, says accepted law enforcement wisdom, and when they're released, the further assumption is that the crimes will continue and probably escalate in violence. Although empirical evidence does not back such conclusions up, any more than it does the recidivism rate generally."

"Contrary to popular belief," I added.

"Contrary to popular belief," Gracie agreed with a nod. "Anyway, when the Patricks moved from their previous relocation spot to some hovel on one of those endless Heinsdale roads into the woods, they didn't even report that they'd gone, to their parole officer, but after a while they started getting some more death threats from their neighbors, who'd found out their records. So they showed up on police rolls again, at which point whoever's running this show realized they had their perfect dupes. I can give you their exact address before I leave, but here's the important thing: the DA got the legal wheels rolling right away, and the BCI will be picking them up *tomorrow*. They're getting warrants to make all the usual moves: seize any computers for evidence of trolling kids on Facebook, Twitter, in chat rooms, e-mail, anywhere else on the Net, along with proof of continued visits to those same porn sites, which they're not supposed to be doing. In general, they'll rip their place apart for signs they've not only been looking at materials, but contacting kids and maybe acting out again—specifically, with the throwaways from this case. After that, well—you've already told me, although I didn't really need telling, what Mangold will do, once he's put them into interrogation rooms. And I . . . I just can't help but feel awfully responsible. Even if I shouldn't."

Mike said nothing, but offered a comforting hand to Gracie's shoulder, which she was grateful to have. I, in contrast, had begun to pace the earthen patches of the kiln floor even faster—because I was starting to get angry.

"It doesn't fit," I murmured, thinking of every detail of my encounter with Latrell. "It just doesn't God damned well *fit*, Gracie. When Latrell spoke to me about 'them,' he wasn't talking about some penniless, middle-aged couple who like to diddle kids. He had the real 'them' *in his phone,* their names and number; and if you ask me, they were, they *are,* people he usually trusted—which was why he was so upset and confused, that night, when he couldn't get ahold of them. And everything about the crimes—all of the trace and research work we've done, things we haven't even told you about yet—*none* of it points in a direction like this. There's money, real money, involved in every one of these deaths, along with a common direction from which that money is flowing—and it isn't from some hovel in Burgoyne County. It's south, damn it, the answer lies *south*—in the big damned city . . ."

Gracie looked both confused and stunned. "Wait—you're saying these kids had somehow made it to *New York*?"

"That's exactly what I'm saying," I answered, my mood very dark, now. My face in the moonlight that crept through the broken roof of the kiln must have reflected as much, for both Mike and Gracie were recoiling in a kind of horror. "And I'm saying it because it's exactly what all the *profiles* tell me—not geographical profiles, but *psychological* profiles, *real* profiles. I'll say it again, these kids were ambitious, they were determined, and *none* of their profiles work, in connection with a couple of perpetrators like the ones you're describing—not that anybody hounding this couple will give a shit!"

Gracie nodded certainly. "I do get that much, Trajan. I realized it as soon as you started to talk about the victims. It's why I wanted to know about how you'd figured it all out, even if I was a little nervous about telling you what I knew I *had* to tell you. And I'm sorry—"

Suddenly, Gracie was cut off by an entirely incongruous yet strangely appropriate series of sounds coming from outside the kiln: ugly animal snarls of at least two kinds, and full of genuinely ominous intent. The first were issued by Marcianna, who was letting loose the kind of sharp barking growls and powerful hisses that she only made when real danger was evident. The others, however, were deeper, true growls, and were clearly being made by larger animals with no good on their minds.

Gracie was first to her panicked feet: "What the hell was *that*?"

"I'm right there with you, Gracie," Mike said, standing by her, then offering her a hand to hold, whereupon she threw her arms around his, her face paling. "What the hell *was* that, Trajan?" my partner demanded.

But I was already on my way out the door, drawing my .45 and worried to death about Marcianna. "Stay here," I said. "And get your damned guns out!"

{v.}

Once outside the kiln, I turned to my left, expecting to see Marcianna; and my heart sank when I found that she wasn't there. Her lead was wrapped around several trees, and wound away to the southern side of the structure, which was out of my view.

"Marcianna!" I bellowed, repeating the name two or three times as I untied the handle of her lead and hurried as best I could to follow the flat blue nylon trail. With great relief I discovered, once I'd gotten about halfway to the neighboring kiln, that she'd hung the lead up on the low branches of a short pine, and was being held back to a spot relatively close to and between the two structures. The easing of my anxiety, however, was short-lived: for although she had assumed her bravest defensive posture—her head and forelegs low, her hind quarters ready to spring—about thirty yards in front of her in the woods, their jaws snapping and their lips snarling in that particularly repulsive ursine way, were three black bears, one a very good-sized sow, the other two her fairly mature male cubs. There was no sign of a boar anywhere, which meant that the two cubs were still learning from their mother: together the three were on a family hunt, the most dangerous configuration in which one could encounter such beasts. The female, if she reared, would have measured a good seven feet, and the young males not much less: big enough, in other words, that our pistols—man-stoppers though they all were—might only have pissed the three off, if we shot them in less than vital spots. Even with multiple wounding rounds in them, they were perfectly capable of mauling us badly out of sheer rage before they died.

"Don't look as cute as they do on *Animal Planet*, hunh, Doc?" came an urgent, whispering voice: Lucas'.

I spun around to find him on top of the first kiln, as close to the jagged hole in the roof as he could manage without collapsing the structure. "Lucas!" I whispered. "What the fuck are you doing up there?"

"Uh—what the fuck are *you* doing down *there*, would seem like the more logical question," he hissed. "Don't worry, I heard everything you guys said. It was all very interesting. Now *what the fuck is going on?*"

"You tell me," I said, still quietly, keeping my face toward the bears, holstering my gun and inching forward, first to free Marcianna's lead and then to back away with it, retracting it slowly until she gave enough ground to return to our position near the first kiln, where I could grab her collar, if I needed to. "You're the one who's been out here all this time—what the hell are they after?"

"You don't know?" Lucas asked. "I thought it was part of your brilliant plan. I didn't hear anything till about five minutes ago, and that was just a rustling sound coming from that next kiln, the one with the roof all caved in and the door that faces south. I looked over and noticed a huge trail of blood leading into it. That got the scent in the air, all right. These three fuckers showed up just a few minutes later."

"You didn't see what left the blood trail?" I asked. "Maybe they wounded something, but it got away and ran here for shelter."

"Nah, I didn't see nothin'," Lucas answered. "But I woulda heard a fight like that."

I thought the matter over quickly. "All right—here's what we're going to do . . ." I took out my .45 again and let off a few shots. The sound seemed to give the mother bear and her cubs a moment to consider whether the prize they had either wounded or were smelling was worth it; but I knew they wouldn't consider such things for too long—not given how hungry they looked, and how much blood, I could now see, was on the ground, and must therefore be, as Lucas had said, in the air.

"Trajan!" came Mike's voice from within the kiln. "You all right?"

"Yeah, fine," I answered. "There's three bears out here—I was just keeping them honest till I get Marcianna's lead clear."

"Is Lucas okay?" Gracie called.

"Yeah, he's fine," I answered. "I'll be inside in a minute, don't worry." I looked back up at Lucas. "You get down here," I said, "and take hold of Marcianna's lead." When he'd followed these orders, I gave him more: "Keep her close as you can, and let me get Mike and Dr. Chang out of here. Then I'll be right back. Can you handle that?"

"Do I have a fucking *choice*? And will you leave me your piece?"

Under the circumstances, I could only agree. I handed him the gun, but said nothing to Marcianna—in her present enraged state of mind, she wouldn't have been able to make much sense of my words, and I might only have confused her badly. She was obeying the restriction of the lead, that was all I could hope for; and so I quickly hobbled back through the entrance to the first kiln, to explain the situation to Gracie and Mike, who still had a firm arm around our guest: although I don't think he was getting the enjoyment he'd anticipated out of it.

"*Bears?*" Gracie said, growing even more fearful. "But—why? Are they after *us?*"

"No, it looks like there's a wounded animal nearby," I said. "Maybe they got it, or maybe it was brought down by coyotes, who the bears ran off."

"And where are the other two?" Mike asked.

"Standing watch," I said. "And I've got to get back to them. You have time, though—get to your Prowler, Mike, and get Gracie down to safety, then into town and to her car." I turned to her. "Gracie—Mike will get the address you promised on your way, and explain any remaining details of our work. And I hope we'll have shown, over the course of this evening, that you will be able to trust us with your safety, whatever the situation."

Gracie did no more than nod a few times, and then the two of them started off to the waiting ATV. Mike got it going, and they vanished speedily into the near-darkness of the ridgeline trail, the machine's powerful headlights showing the way, after which I returned to Lucas. He handed me back my .45 rather reluctantly, and the handle to Marcianna's lead far more eagerly.

"Oh, man, there ain't *nobody* going to believe this," he said aloud. "Not even Ambyr! Bear hunting with a 1911 Colt .45 and a cheetah—*who the fuck does that?*"

"Quiet down, will you?" I scolded, softly but urgently. "You're only going to get those damned bears even more pissed off. We've got one chance, here—make sure of that carcass, whatever it is, let them get busy with it, and make for the other Prowler."

"The *carcass?*" Lucas asked. "What makes you think the damned thing's dead?"

"Call it a hunch, much as I despise the word," I replied. "But I want to get a look at it, either way."

"O-*kay,*" Lucas conceded. "But you did say 'hunch,' I won't forget that . . ."

"Yeah, yeah, smart-ass," I said, handing him my cane, which I wouldn't be able to manage with all I had to do. "Here—use this, if they start coming at us."

"Oh, thanks," Lucas cracked. "There isn't a *barrel* in this thing, by any chance, is there?"

"No," I answered, preparing to reveal a secret that I didn't like most people to know. "But pull on the handle, hard."

He was a bit mystified, but did as he was told—and he grew instantly delighted when the gleaming blade of a razor-sharp, two-and-a-half-foot rapier appeared from within the wood of the cane. *"Oooh, yeah!"* he declared. "That's what *I'm* talkin' about!" He held the blade out. "This is one *sick* damned cane, dude. Come on, you bear fuckers, I'm ready!"

"Shut the hell up and put the blade back!" I said. "I'm just telling you it's there—but don't do anything to get them any more aggravated than they already are." Disappointed, Lucas sheathed the cane's business component. "Now," I went on, "let's get going to that other kiln—and remember: we move slow, we don't turn our backs on them, and you maintain eye contact as much as you can."

"Oh, sure," Lucas answered. "Eye contact with three nasty fucking bears. I do it all the time . . ."

I gave him a shove to our left, then reeled Marcianna in just a little bit more. I had to pray that, if I used the right words, she'd understand that I fully appreciated her efforts to protect us, but that shifting our position was a necessary part of that process. I therefore began to shadow Lucas' movements, keeping my eyes locked on the bears as I sidestepped to the left and began my little monologue, using words and phrases that were key to her—*"Okay,* Marcianna, I get it, you're doing good, *good job, girl,* now let's just move and try to *go home—home, girl . . ."*—all of which was made the more difficult by the fact that I had to keep my artificial leg moving fairly nimbly without the aid of my cane, if I wanted to manage both Marcianna and my .45.

The short trip to the more collapsed kiln took us about three minutes, with the bears constantly snarling and occasionally moving forward, and Marcianna, in response, yanking her lead right out of its supposedly locked position a couple of feet in order to challenge them with vicious, hissing barks and the defiant lowering of her head and forelegs. It was hard to bring her back to me, at those moments, but I did manage it; and finally we reached the entrance to the second kiln, the roof of which, as Lucas had said, was almost completely collapsed, along with much of its upper walls.

As the kid had also reported, there was quite a blood trail leading inside; although, in truth, blood was not the gleaming path's only component. There were bits of internal organs evident, as well; and just inside the kiln's doorway, the large, pillow-like stomach of a white-tailed deer lay on some of the bricks that seemed to be pouring out of the old place.

"Well—it's dead, all right," Lucas pronounced. "A deer."

"Indeed. Okay, kid—" I held out my Colt. "I'll trade you again."

"Yeah?" Lucas said, happily handing me my cane and taking the .45. "How come?"

"I need you to stand watch for two minutes. I want to get a look at that deer . . ."

"What the hell for?" Lucas said, his face screwing up. "Doc, if either the bears or dogs got to it, it ain't going to be a very pleasant sight."

"True," I said. "But then, I don't think that's what happened."

"*Another* hunch—you're really slipping, L.T.," Lucas jabbed; and I had to admit, it really was admirable, the way he could hang on to his humor in the face of a dangerous situation.

"No," I countered. "I think we can call this a confirmed thesis," I said, "based on what you've said. After all, Lucas, don't you think that, if coyotes brought the deer down, you would have heard them signaling the meal to the rest of their pack, even if they had somehow managed the kill silently?"

Lucas considered the matter for as long as our perilous situation would allow. "Okay," he said. "But what about the bears? Still coulda been them."

"I give you the same argument," I replied. "Even if the bears had wounded the deer so badly that its insides were already falling out six feet in front of the kiln, don't you think you would have heard the victim let out that eerie cry they do? And why would the bears have backed off of it?"

Lucas mulled that one, too, for about a second and a half. "Okay, okay, you got me. So what happened?"

"Well, that's what I'm about to try to find out," I said, urging Marcianna—who had become somewhat intrigued by the trail of blood and organs leading into the kiln—to move with me. "But if I had to bet, I'd say the deer was shot, not long ago, and gutted with a sharp knife . . ."

And then Marcianna and I moved inside the rubble-strewn structure.

The second kiln was far more open to the light of the rising moon, and by now my eyes were quite adjusted enough to take in the contents of the place quickly. With both satisfaction and deep disturbance, I observed the extent to which my hypothesis had been correct—and I quickly reported as much back to Lucas: "Unfortunately, kid, eliminating the impossible has once again left the only possibility." I was attempting to sound detached and perhaps a bit amusing, in an attempt to overcome the deeply mournful scene of violation that lay on a pile of bricks in front of me: "It's a doe—maybe the one we saw on the way up. She's been split up the middle by a very sharp blade, wielded by someone who knew just what arteries and organs to nick in order to create the greatest blood flow. The carcass is secured to a brick pile with rope, in order to keep the gash open." I noticed a small detail: "*Nylon* rope, although that could of course mean nothing. Or, on the other hand, something . . ." I moved forward toward the doe—but strangely, Marcianna held back, almost as if the carcass was an evil omen of some sort. "It's all right, girl," I said— but then I saw what was bothering her:

Amid the gore on the bricks lay the almost perfectly developed fetus of an unborn fawn. It was so awful and arresting a sight that it literally snatched the breath out of me for a moment; and when air did return, all I could do was let out some of Marcianna's lead. "Okay, girl," I whispered, thinking it best to keep this latest detail from Lucas. "Go back and stand guard with the boy . . ." This Marcianna did, obviously preferring to take on a live enemy rather than explore a butchered mother; for who knew how the latter reminded her of all the horrors of her youth, and of the bizarrely cruel man who had run the zoo where I'd found her.

I continued my examination more quickly, the sight of the fawn spur- ring my actions and thoughts. "The carcass is still quite warm," I called, having touched the doe where I did not feel it would add to her insults. "She has not, in point of fact, been dead long. Probably placed here while you were distracted by our conversation, by someone adept at such things. There is a clean bullet wound through the skull—" And as I ex- amined this, I tried not to look into the dead animal's eyes: for the golden light of a deer's life can take many minutes to finally be eclipsed by its dilating pupils, and it is one of the sadder sights imaginable, even with- out the devastation that had gone on in this case. "Large caliber, heavy load," I concluded. But I did not tell Lucas that this was perfectly consis- tent with a .308 Winchester shot, fired from a Savage 10FP rifle.

"Uh—that's all great, Doc," Lucas called. "Now can we get the fuck outta here? Those bears are getting a little less nervous every second . . ."

With the same respect I would have shown any murdered thing, I un- tied the deer and let her carcass slip to the kiln floor—even though I knew she would be a feast for bears in a matter of minutes. And as she fell, she offered me that sight I had not wished to see: the last bit of gleam in her eyes, fading to black. Fighting against the urge to run with which this sight filled me, I leaned down and, again uselessly, lifted the appallingly warm form of the fawn and placed it back within the mother's body; then, finally, having done all that human decency could do in the face of the onslaught to come, I hobbled quickly outside.

"Okay, Lucas," I said breathlessly. "Give me the Colt, and get your ass over to the Prowler. Drive it here, and put the lights on high beam—with any luck, the bears will be blinded for a minute and Marcianna will be just confused enough to break off and get in with us. Go, go, go!"

Another minute or so, and Lucas had achieved his next task: the lights of the Prowler came flooding onto the scene, temporarily freezing the bears in place. I holstered the Colt and pulled Marcianna's lead enough to get her to turn her head around and look at the machine—and, as I'd hoped, she knew what the sight meant: I was again dragged into the Prowler as she bolted for the passenger seat of the rig, while Lucas leapt into the back. I shifted into reverse, handing my cane to Lucas; and when we moved off, the bears charged forward. By the time they reached the kiln and tore into the doe carcass, however, we were on our way back down the old charcoal trail, moving even faster than we had on approach.

Once it was clear that we were safe from the bears, as well as from any of their relatives who might be hanging around the neighborhood, Lucas, who was crouching in the back on his haunches and clinging to the metal struts of the Prowler's cab, seemed to calm down some, as did Marcianna. Both were helped by our speed, and Marcianna had the additional aid of my continuing words of reassurance, which were too soft for Lucas to have heard; but they did serve the additional purpose of getting my own heated blood back to something like normal temperature. We were halfway back down the mountain, however, before I got real confirmation of just how far back Marcianna had come from those moments of fiery-eyed confrontation with the bears outside the kilns: we hit a log that I hadn't seen, being as it lay beneath the tunnel-like illumination of the Prowler's bright headlamps; and when we were all tossed a good four or five inches from our seats and came slamming back down again, Lucas and I cursing in discomfort, Marcianna let out a moan of anguish and worry, sounding very young and very tired of all the evening's entertainments. Then, inexplicably, she laid her head in my lap for a few moments; but, finding that position too cramped, she flopped her whole upper body into the spot, twisting it over so that her paws reached up and onto my left shoulder and the top of her head ground, not altogether comfortably for me, into my left thigh. I groaned predictably, but the whole thing only seemed to amuse the hell out of Lucas.

"Well, I guess she's a cat, after all!" he called out, sticking his head between the metal struts he was grasping. "That's just what Ambyr's big tom does, when he wants attention for some reason. Damndest thing," he concluded, staring at Marcianna; and then, almost helplessly, he reached forward, as if he meant to stroke her belly.

"Whoa, there," I warned, staying his hand. "We don't know her exact mood, yet, kid. Just because she may *look* like a big pussycat doesn't make her one. Those weren't mice, or even dogs, she was just squaring off against. Let's give her a few minutes' peace before we go getting all cute— she'll let us know if she feels shortchanged on affection, trust me."

Lucas pulled his hand back, saying, "Just trying to be friendly, Doc . . ."

"I know. But if this thing makes very little sense to *us,* imagine how she feels." Then I checked the .45, making sure that, even with Marcianna all over me, I could get to it freely. For I was nothing like certain that we were yet in the clear from the unseen *human* antagonist who had meddled with our activities that evening.

His thoughts perhaps running along similar lines, Lucas picked up my cane and allowed himself another chance to pull the rapier free of its wooden casing, an action that gave him some measure of reassurance. "God damn, L.T.," he said. "You are one weird kinda doctor. You know, back in the 1880s, you would've made a good suspect in the Jack the Ripper case, from what I read."

"Very funny," I answered, although I was in fact impressed by his correct dating and detailing of the Ripper crimes and their investigation. "Now sheathe that thing, will you, before we hit a rock and you end up impaled on it?"

Recognizing this very real possibility, Lucas reassembled the cane and laid it aside, then stuck his face back through the struts. "I still don't get one thing," he said, as we hit the steeper portion of the mountainside and I glanced down at Marcianna, who seemed, improbably, to have fallen asleep in her bizarre position. "You said the deer was shot clean through the head, and probably with a decent-sized rifle, right?"

"That's right," I said, having expected this line of questioning.

"But it'd only been dead a little while, so . . . Why didn't any of us hear the shot? We'd been there for a long time, listening to all your bullshi— I mean, to your fascinating conversation with Dr. Chang. There's no way we could've missed it, even if it was a ways off. So what happened?"

"What happened, Lucas," I said, trying to minimize any alarm my statement might cause, "is why we're moving so fast right now. You can figure it out yourself, I'm guessing. You probably have, already."

I glanced back for just an instant to see him shrug his shoulders. "Only thing I can come up with would be a silencer." He waited for me to contradict him, and when I didn't, that same tone I'd come to know well— half thrill, half fear—entered his voice: "No—fucking—way . . ." he said with a little grin. "That is awesome!" But then the reality of our situation set in: "Hang on a second. If that deer was shot by a—a—"

"You can say it, kid," I told him.

"By a fucking *sniper*?" he queried, now full only of apprehension. "And the guy dragged the carcass into that kiln while I was *right there*? Then—" I glanced back once more to see his head on a swivel, as his voice lowered: "Then where the hell is the motherfucker *now*?"

"*That* is why we're moving so fast. I don't know; and I don't intend to find out."

"Holy shit. Ho-lee *shit* . . ." He stuck his head farther in toward me. "Fucking move it, then, Doc, what the hell! Are you driving with your phony leg, or what?"

I ignored this remark, in the somewhat vain hope that it would be the last I'd hear from my passenger before our return to the base of the mountain. But not thirty seconds had gone by before he piped up with:

"But—*whose* sniper?" Lucas was still apprehensive, but that quality of his—that readiness in the face of the unknown or of danger, which I was coming to realize was rooted in far more than mere adventurousness— had reasserted itself. "I mean—it's not the *military*, right, there's not, like, *Special Forces* guys involved in this shit. Right?"

"Right," I said. "That, at least, I think we can safely rule out."

"So—who, then?"

"Well," I answered, deciding that the kid deserved a frank appraisal, "the BCI has got plenty of snipers, Lucas—remember, they're basically the state arm of the FBI, although the chain of command gets a little complicated. But they pride themselves on their snipers. It was a BCI sniper who made sure that Latrell didn't tell his story to anybody other than me the other night."

"Yeah, but they wouldn't shoot *us*—would they?" His voice took on an estimable, if somewhat naïve, indignation. "They'd never get away with it!"

I had to laugh, a reaction made easier by the fact that the lights of Shiloh were coming into view through the trees off and below the mountain trail. "No, kid, I don't think they'd actually shoot us—but even the faintest possibility is reason enough to get ourselves home. Especially since they *might*, as a warning, take a potshot at Marcianna."

"Fuck *that* shit," Lucas replied, indignation still high. "They try it and they'll find out how easy it is for a throwaway kid to get his butt on the local news and tell his story. Assholes . . ."

And it was at that moment—that quick second or two that it took Lucas to refer to himself as a throwaway child—that the fuller explanation for his behavior at these dangerous moments struck me: I'd never really seen or conceived of my young ally in that way, not with all his bluster, his angry indictments of his parents and defenses of his sister, or what I have more generally called his game attitude toward life. But now I saw more fully where that gameness came from; and it was not an altogether happy realization. Lucas had, after all, endured more than even most throwaways: his parents had not simply vanished—had not merely been there one night and gone the next morning—nor had they exiled him from their house; rather, they had carefully constructed a legally complex plan to disappear, over what could only have been weeks and perhaps months. It had been a plan that, once they were gone, had bound both of their offspring, as well as Lucas' friend Derek (whose own parents had vanished at the same time), to each other particularly tightly, by deceitfully making Lucas' blind sister, Ambyr, the guardian for the boys and creating what was, effectively, a new family. And while I was certain that the elder Kurtzes' behavior throughout Lucas' childhood had implanted a rebellious streak in their son, I was now also sure that his reckless attitude toward his own safety—everything from joining our investigation in the first place to insisting that he should go on every even potentially perilous mission during that undertaking—was the product of that very particular, that very calculated form of abandonment, as well. Such amounted, after all, not to the "usual" splitting or breaking up of a family, but to its deliberate and cunning *erasure*: what danger could he face with Mike and me that would begin to rival that experience?

This realization forced me to do a quick check of my own responsibilities and plans as we blasted our way through tree branches and onto the lower, safer reaches of the mountain road. It was too late to cast Lucas out of the investigation, of course: even had I wished to do so, he would never have gone. But his safety had, at a stroke, become more important than before; indeed, I realized, as I glanced down at the still (and still remarkably) slumbering Marcianna, and thought for an instant of that other game person who seemed now to have joined our cause, Gracie Chang, a great many things had changed, during our trip to the top of the mountain. The stakes of our endeavor had plainly been raised by one silenced bullet and three black bears on the Taconic ridgeline above Shiloh. Indeed, the dangers suddenly seemed more than merely evident: they seemed *close.*

And that, of course, was precisely the effect that our adversary (or adversaries) had tried so hard to achieve, that night; although none of us suspected that they had not yet completed their work . . .

{vi.}

O nce we had safely reached the yard of the barn, Marcianna suddenly woke and sat up, looking about as if we had never left the place; but when I pulled to a halt and stepped out of the Prowler, the manner in which she shot from the machine and nearly knocked me over bespoke a great happiness to be home. I told Lucas to return the ATV to its place in the shed behind the barn while I fetched a slab of beef for my companion and walked her up to her enclosure. Once he had performed his task, the kid raced to catch up to us, glancing about as if he expected sniper fire to start raining in at any minute. He soon lost this apprehension, although Marcianna, as soon as we got her safely through her gate, quickly picked up her dinner and trotted off to her den—an action that told me that she, too, was feeling none too secure.

Whatever Lucas' attitude, however, it was finally time for him to go home, and he knew it. At first he was fully prepared, in keeping with his character, to march off alone down Death's Head Hollow, encouraged by the fact that the bright moon was by now illuminating the entire landscape; but when I reminded him that the same moon glow that he found so reassuring would only allow our latest adversary to draw a nice bead on him as he strode defiantly along, he decided, with great condescension, that he would be willing to wait for Mike to return and give him a ride down to town. He did continue to protest that it could take hours for my partner to reappear, given that he might have pulled off the hollow so he could finally "gnaw on Gracie Chang's face for a while"; but in fact he knew better, seeming certain of Mike's quick return and, paradoxically, disappointed that my partner would be spending the night on his own.

I then felt the need to remind Lucas of something that he had requested when he first arrived that afternoon, something that had seemed to me little more than a social obligation, at the time, but that I now found a pressing concern: the question of Mike's and my visit to his home, to meet his sister, Ambyr. I told him that, in light of all that had happened, even a minimal sense of responsibility required that I keep her informed at least of the basics of his role in the investigation; and that when Mike and I came to his house I would therefore be as honest as professional discretion would allow in explaining to his guardian, not only who Mike and I were, but just what had happened during the case thus far. This, of course, did not make Lucas particularly happy; but I think that even he, after the evening we had just endured, understood that secrecy and deception were not the ways to go, anymore—not *completely,* at any rate. We agreed that the visit should take place as soon as possible: and given that the BCI would be making their arrest the next day, and probably planting their evidence soon thereafter, Mike and I needed to be on call until at least Tuesday. I was sure that Frank Mangold intended for Steve Spinetti and Pete Steinbrecher to discover the frame, thereby giving it independent credibility, and that my partner and I would get a phone call from the sheriff or his deputy soon thereafter. By Tuesday afternoon, however, when both Mike's and my classes finished conveniently early, we'd be able to make the time to come to Surrender. I agreed to bring Marcianna along—secretly, as we had discussed—and with that subject settled, the headlights of Mike's car appeared as if on cue, snaking their way up the hollow road.

Mike himself was in far too jolly a mood to even question the notion of driving Lucas home, or something close to home, which made me wonder what *had,* indeed, happened during his drive back down the mountain and then out the hollow with Gracie; however, I had no doubt that, once our young apprentice was home, my partner would be full of a detailed description for me. And so I directed Lucas into the passenger seat of the Empress, where he shrank down behind the dashboard and declared (much to Mike's mystification) that he didn't want any sniper taking a shot at him under the mistaken impression that they would be "popping" me. To Mike's look of concern I held up a calming hand, saying that Lucas would doubtless explain the meaning of his demented remark on the way to town; and on that typically dysfunctional note, the car roared off again, and I turned to make my way slowly into the hangar. It had, all things considered, been an exhausting evening; and when I'd finally climbed into the JU-52 and tucked my .45 and field glasses back into the bottom drawer of my desk, I took a pull off the Talisker bottle, drew out a cigarette, and lit it, returning to the hatchway and hoping for a moment of peace during which to smoke. But then something caught my eye down below, something that I had missed on my weary entry:

A piece of plain, letter-sized white paper was push-pinned to one of the upright beams of the hangar just above the microwave. I began to descend the steel steps toward the hangar floor, although I didn't need to get more than halfway down before I was able to discern that the handwriting on the paper belonged to my great-aunt Clarissa. In all likelihood she'd brought the message up from the house while we were all on the mountain; and I very much feared that the sound of the two Prowlers dashing about had been the thing that had prompted her to write. However, I was wrong, and unhappily so; Clarissa had a great deal more on her mind than just our escapades with the ATVs, as I found when I pulled the note from the beam and read it:

> *Doctors both: Don't think for a minute that your various activities of late, as well as the presence of certain unusual guests, have gone unnoticed; however, I haven't thought to bring the matter up, supposing that you had either been experimenting with the idea of starting some sort of reform school, or had been caught selling prescription medications to local youths. But I've now heard enough peculiar rumors from my acquaintances in local and county government to make me suspect that something even more disconcerting may be going on. Therefore, I am ordering the both of you to appear for dinner at my earliest convenience and explain yourselves. I have a political meeting to attend tomorrow eve-*

ning, which means I will expect you on Tuesday—
whatever the weather, Trajan! Don't bother RSVP-ing
or trying any other evasive tactics—just be here at
8:30.

—Clarissa

It was plain that, beneath her characteristically caustic humor, Clarissa was less angry than genuinely worried, for she really was not so stern as the note might make her sound. Her demand that we explain what was behind all the comings and goings, both of anyone connected to local law enforcement and of young Lucas, along with her revelation that her contacts in local government (which were quite extensive, given her position as a major landowner and one of the last independent dairy farmers in Burgoyne County) had relayed to her enough chatter about our involvement in the throwaway-children case to prompt her direct intervention, was genuinely alarming; yet she meant all these references to be first and foremost expressions of concern.

In all, it was something of the perfect conclusion to the evening we'd had; and as I limped over to lean against the side of the hangar door and let the unusually cool midsummer breeze toss my hair and cool my face, I looked down at the dimly lit porch of the farmhouse, knowing that Clarissa would not be in any of the rocking chairs on it, but would be firmly ensconced in her study, watching public television. There, fired by a crystal tumbler full of good scotch and cooled by an ancient metal table fan, she would be either arguing endlessly with those shows that she found biased and idiotic, or basking in the glow of those that she thought fair or simply entertaining. She was one of the loneliest people I knew, my great-aunt; lonely, that is, on an intimate level. It was a quality we shared, just as we shared the fact that our lonelinesses had both been caused by tragedy. Indeed, for as far back as I could recall, Clarissa and I had shared many traits, which was, of course, no accident: for she had been the only member of my family who—tough and caustic as her utterances might often be—had ever really given an honest damn about the quality of my life, not only during and after my cancer, but before, when I had been a sickly boy amongst robust siblings sired by equally robust parents, who had had no time and no kind words for a son who limped behind. It had therefore been only logical that I would model much of my behavior, not on my distant, vigorous father or on my drunken, co-dependent mother or even on my blameless brothers and sister, but rather on the small, iron-tough woman who had endured adversity of her own particular and intimate kind throughout the whole of her life, yet who had always opened Shiloh to me as a refuge and a kind of paradise—a paradise that was an education unto itself . . .

I was brought out of this relatively melancholy reverie by the sounds of Mike's car pulling up to the barn below and his triumphal return march up the dirt path to the hangar:

"Oh-ho, *yeah,* baby!" he called out. "Don't ever let it be said that Dr. Michael Li doesn't know women!"

I pulled out my cigarettes as he arrived and offered him one. "I don't know anyone who would dare make such a claim," I said, taking another smoke for myself and lighting first his and then my own. "I take it things went well?"

"Brother," Mike said, "we have not only got an absolutely locked mole inside the county and state investigation, but, based on the very long and deeply meaningful kiss good-night I got after I completed the explanation of why we think the whole thing points toward New York, and involves suicides instead of a serial killer, I would say that I have a very definite shot at finally scoring a relationship with Gracie—how's *that* for a lesson in patience?"

"You're sure she wasn't just grateful for your protection and your confidences?" I queried, knowing that it would irk him a bit.

And it did: "Now, why do you have to say something like that, L.T.? I am trying to tell you that we shared a moment, motherfucker, a completely golden moment; sure, maybe it won't pan out, but I'm betting it will—and who's the gambler here, you or me?"

"I surrender superiority in that pastime to you," I said, offering a smile, putting my cigarette in my cane hand, and extending my right to him. "Congratulations," I said. "So long as you're *sure* she's on board with us?"

"Dude, I understand these things as you do not," he answered, gladly taking my hand. "And I'm telling you, Trajan, we are solid, on that score. Tough evening—but things are starting to look up! When that first drink hit her, and she started to really relax—"

"You stopped for a drink in town?" I said, momentarily concerned.

"Yes, and don't freak the fuck out—we cruised around a bit and made sure the BCI boys were long gone. And over that first drink, I'm telling you, she looked at me in a way she has never looked at me before. Oh, yeah, this is gonna be good . . ." He paused for a moment to glance around, then asked, "So what's the deal up here? Everything okay?"

"A complication concerning Tuesday's activities, but I'll explain that to you later," I answered. "Right now, I fear we really do have to start getting our classes ready . . ."

As we indeed did; or tried to do. On Monday I was scheduled to return to my Theory of Context course, to check on just which of my students had actually read and digested the pages from Dr. Kreizler's lost journal that I had assigned to them, and which had decided that our class talks about the man would allow them to skate through this latest discussion. Mike, for his part, would continue his assault upon the sloppy trace-collection practices of nearly all forensic labs in the country, continuing to offer a special place to the supposedly hallowed halls of the FBI lab in Quantico, Virginia; and he expounded long and loudly on how our current case—if I would only allow him to present it to his students, clothed in a web of fictionalized circumstances—would provide a particularly good example of all that was wrong with those incompetent procedures and institutions. After all, he declared, there had been nothing so exotic about the trace evidence he'd either collected or reinterpreted; it was in fact his independence that had allowed him to correctly follow and decipher the leads concerning the physical clues found on three of the victims, and their relation to each of their personal interests. But while I knew that, despite his protests, he had never allowed his talent to run ahead of his discretion, no such assurances could be given regarding his students. This was, after all, a real case involving real throwaway children: to make its details known, in whatever form, to a bunch of undergrads or even graduate students was to take a risk regarding security that I remained completely unwilling to accept. Mike continued to mumble protests about the need to train a new generation of evidence collectors, as well as about the ability of our students to add some welcome perspective on and insights into the matter; especially since the two of us had become, now, personally involved in the undertaking, no longer able to offer completely objective opinions. This I took issue with, reminding him that I was not the one who was allowing his emotional life to bleed over into his professional work; and we kept at this exchange, fully aware that our class preparations would suffer, but feeling just confident enough about what we'd achieved in recent days to allow ourselves some amusement—until the Klaxon-like cry of the old telephone in the JU-52 began to sound about an hour later.

"I'll get it, I'll get it!" Mike shouted, bolting upright from his chair and speeding to the cockpit bulkhead. "That's gonna be Gracie: when she got home, she probably realized that she can't stand another night without having the great one at her side . . ."

I could only laugh quietly and continue to make notes for the next day's classes, letting my partner run with his delusions. He quickly snatched the old Bakelite receiver out of its cradle and cooed into it: "Hell-oooo?" One or two seconds went by; enough time for me to look over to Mike. "Oh—Major McCarron . . . *What?* No, you don't understand, this is—wait, *what?*" Mike's face had suddenly lost its grin, along with most of its color; then he insisted, "No, Major, this isn't—but—but that's impossible. . . . Wait—*wait!*" Letting the phone slip from his grasp and to the deck of the plane, Mike remained in stunned silence as his limp body followed the course of the receiver; then he finally spoke, very softly: "It's . . . for you, Trajan. Major McCarron, he thought that— Jesus . . ." He stared straight at me, although I'm not at all sure that mine was the face he was seeing. "Jesus *Christ,* Trajan . . ." he went on, whispering, now, but desperately enough that I ran over, seized the quarter-full bottle of Talisker, and placed it in his grasp as I picked up the receiver and put my hand over the mouthpiece.

"Drink," I ordered, and Mike did so, if very slowly. Then, hearing Mitch McCarron's voice continuing to shout through the receiver as he tried to reestablish contact with us, I put the phone to my own face. "Mitch?" I said.

"Trajan? Is that you?" he replied urgently. "My God, Trajan, I screwed that up—I just assumed *you'd* be answering. I didn't want Mike to hear it from me, I know that he—well, I didn't want him to have to hear it from me, I screwed it up—"

"Whoa, whoa, Mitch," I said, to the man whom I had rarely seen exhibit panic; at that moment, however, his voice had something of the quality it had assumed when he'd found the dead baby in the toilet back in Fraser. "What the hell's going on?"

"An accident," Mitch said this time; and I noticed, as he spoke, the sound of sirens and commotion in the background. "I'm at the site, now, we've got the Jaws of Life working—"

"'Working'?" I repeated. "Working on what?"

"I can only talk for a second," he answered, his ordinary confidence returning. "It's Dr. Chang—her car was clipped on Route 7. Witnesses saw a pickup with a cap on the bed. She lost control, and went off the road. Sideswiped a tree at high speed, and wrapped her little rig right around it."

I glanced down at Mike in horror, as he continued to slowly try to take in some of the Talisker. "What the fuck?" I murmured, moving swiftly into the cockpit and pilot's seat of the plane, to try to spare Mike any more shocks. "Is she . . . ?"

"She's alive," Mitch said quickly. "But unconscious—and the paramedics can't revive her. It's a concussion, at least, and a bad one—or maybe . . ."

"Got it." Trying to harness my own emotions, I added: "Do you need us there?"

"No—I do *not* think that's a good idea, Trajan," Mitch replied firmly. "Unless Mike absolutely needs to be. Her family is on the way, and I'll keep you posted. Besides, Frank Mangold's here, and someone told him that she was driving back from your place."

"Yeah?" I queried sharply. "Did he also happen to tell you that his people trailed her here?"

Mitch took a few seconds before he quietly but angrily replied, "Son of a bitch . . . No, he did not. Okay, Trajan—I'm gonna go and deal with *that* little issue. Right now."

"You sure you should, Mitch?" I said. "If it was his people that—"

"Don't go there, Trajan," McCarron told me, in no uncertain terms. "I know Frank can be an asshole, and I'm mad as hell that he didn't tell me about the tail, but—I don't think he'd try anything like this, or let any of his people try it. He seems genuinely shook up—which is maybe why he didn't let me know the full story. Anyway, we're treating this fully as one of our own—it's got priority. We've shut the highway down, and we've got a medevac chopper on its way from Albany Medical. Everything that can be done is being done—but if you guys show up, it might cause more problems than it'll solve. So, like I say, unless Mike needs to be here—but it won't do him any damned good to see it, Trajan, trust me. I'll keep you posted." He suddenly covered his own mouthpiece, in order to shout a command to someone that was muffled and unintelligible to me. Then he was back: "Shit, I've really got to go. But I'll call you again from the hospital."

And then, with awful finality, he terminated the connection. I sat in the pilot's seat of the JU-52 for several seconds, absorbing this excruciating news, before remembering what was what: I then leapt up (or what passes for leaping up, in my case) and went back into the cabin of the plane, returning the phone to its cradle. I bent my right knee to get down as close to my wretched partner as I could, and said what little I could to console him:

"She's alive, Mike—unconscious, but alive. Mitch thinks it's nothing more than a concussion, but they're bringing in a medevac helicopter, just in case. They're treating it as one of their own, and he says even Frank Mangold's upset about it—"

Mike turned to me suddenly, a kind of ghastly detachment in his eyes and voice: "And you buy that shit, L.T.? You *really* think Mangold wasn't involved, somehow?"

"McCarron says that we shouldn't jump to that conclusion," I answered, trying to bring Mike around. "And I think he's right—not even Mangold would be that outrageous, or that stupid. But just in case, I told Mitch about the tail, which Mangold hadn't. Mitch'll put him to the wall about it; but no, in short, I don't think that Mangold—"

"Oh, come on, L.T.!" Mike shouted, although he didn't move from where he sat. "You're the one who doesn't believe in coincidences—fucking Lucas *told* me that there was a *sniper* up there with us, tonight! You think he was just some *guy,* some guy that happened to have it in for us?"

"I don't know for sure, Mike," I answered, still trying to talk him down. "Nor do I know who the truck driver was. But I can't believe that it was one of Mangold's people. It's just too extreme. As to who it was . . . We can't know, not yet—we don't have enough facts."

Mike was about to protest further, but then I saw that glassiness lift from his eyes, and he nodded comprehendingly. "No," he murmured. "No, I guess we don't . . ." And then some tears welled up, although they did not escape his eyes as he moaned pitiably, "Oh, shit, L.T.—*Gracie.* Whoever it was, why the fuck did they have to go after *her*?"

"You know the answer to that," I replied. "They were trying to send us a warning. *Another* warning. Now come on." I stood, leaning heavily on my cane as I offered him a hand up. "We've done enough to be ready for classes."

Mike nodded, reaching for my hand. "*Fuck* classes, I've got to get over there . . ."

As he pulled himself to his feet, I answered, "Mitch says that's a bad idea all the way around—and I agree with him, Mike."

"Oh, really?" he asked bitterly.

"Really," I answered flatly. "Mike, they're going to be a while getting her out of the wreck; she's unconscious, and will likely be headed for some kind of surgery. Her family's coming, and you don't want to be the one they find waiting around—they'll blame you, to your face or otherwise. Believe me, it's all going to be a lot of sights and situations that will jolt you, and upset you even more—and it'll be shocking and upsetting enough when you see her in the hospital *after* she wakes up. Save your strength for then."

"Yeah?" Mike said in frustration. "So what do I do *now*? I can't just sit around here."

"Nor do I suggest that you do so," I replied, my voice (once again, and as it always tends to be at such moments) perhaps too detached. "Instead, I'd recommend that we use the balance of tonight to try to figure out what is happening, and what we can do about it. Remember what a great man used to say: 'Don't *fight* the problem—*decide* it.'" Mike, somewhat encouraged by the notion of doing something, anything, to help Gracie (even though we both were aware, I think, that she might not live to appreciate it), considered the matter as, leaning on my right shoulder in a way that caused my left hip no little distress, he moved with me to his desk. "And, to apply that thought here, whoever is dogging our participation in this investigation, I don't think we have the vaguest idea of who they *actually* are, or why they're coming at us so hard. Most importantly, I don't think we understand just how the hell they're getting their information . . ."

"What do you mean?" Mike answered. "You said that Mangold's people followed Gracie here. Hell, we *saw* them, Trajan."

"Which covers one part of the story," I answered, tapping my cane lightly against the various case files that were posted on the JU-52's fuselage. "But what about the rest of their behavior? Gracie said that even our possible involvement in the case was making local law enforcement panic—"

"Causing them to 'have kittens,'" Mike recalled quietly, staring at the papers on his desk.

"Yes, exactly," I replied. "So was that the moment they began to do things that were professionally risky: when Steve and Pete first began to talk to us? I mean, consider the whole thing: Donovan brought us to Fraser so that the bunch of them could lecture us during an ongoing crisis in an *active* case, knowing full well we'd only get further involved; then they made sure that the witness I brought out never spoke. After that, they tailed one of their own. Isn't that enough? Would they really try to scare us so recklessly on the mountaintop? And when Gracie *didn't* scare, would they take a step on their own that they must have known might be fatal, just to give us—if we were in any way sane—pause? More things that don't fit, Mike—it's far too risky. On the other hand, somebody higher up wants this thing quashed, and quashed now—that's clear."

Glancing up at me almost reluctantly, my partner murmured, "I know what you're saying, L.T: it's the governor. Or somebody in his office."

"Well, you heard Gracie talk about what's happening with those people in reaction to the throwaway scandal," I answered. "And just follow your own lead for one second: if this thing does point to New York, and to people with dough down there—who better to defend them, if it all comes apart, than their chosen lackey in Albany?"

Mike grunted out a humorless laugh. "And I thought it might all be about getting the funding to put remote DNA sequencers in police cruisers . . ."

"And that might be part of it," I told him quickly, not wanting his enthusiasm to wane. "That might've been the payoff for the DA and the State Police commanders. But we've got a bigger tiger by the tail here, kid. Hell, we're already riding the damned thing, whether we want to or not. And you know what your people say about riding tigers."

"Goddamn it, L.T., they are *not* my people," Mike declared, some of his real fight finally returning. "And yeah, I know the deal, you either keep riding the fucker or jump off and get eaten." Mike stared at the papers on his desk once again. "And they've provided us with some pretty nice examples of what 'getting eaten' looks like . . ."

I thought about manufacturing some sort of rousing speech; but Mike would have seen right through it. So instead, I began to roam the JU-52 restlessly, staring afresh at our notes and records and charts concerning the case on my own. And eventually, this had the desired effect: Mike stood and began to do likewise, silently moving away from the emotional ledge he'd been on. "I will tell you this, Michael," I said. "Whoever they are, we've got to try to figure out *exactly* when and why this madness started. Because one thing is for sure—" I stared at the image of Shelby Capamagio lying on a slab, somehow even more dead, it seemed to me, than the doe that I'd left to the bears atop the mountain. "They aren't going to stop. So it's up to us to find the connection—before somebody like Gracie actually ends up in the morgue, alongside these poor kids . . ."

{vii.}

Mike bore careful watching as we worked through most of that night, not because he and Gracie had been close for very long—indeed, they had been little more than objects to each other, over the years, the one of amusement, the other of fantasy (although on this fateful night, I will confess, it had sometimes been hard to tell who had been which to whom)—but because he had been caught by her tragedy at just that moment when infatuation with the exotic becomes preoccupation with the real: that shatteringly perfect instant when illusion and clear-headed vision unite, whether in a touch, a kiss, or even a look—and Mike, I knew, had received all three. I was able to surmise that it had not gone any farther (had not taken the course that, say, Lucas had imagined), but its romantic effect had been all the more potent for this physical limitation; and I therefore had to be understanding when he occasionally withdrew from the JU-52 and the hangar on the pretext of needing a cigarette or to clear his head or both, and did not return for occasionally long intervals.

Having made doubly sure that we were in fact ready for the following day's classes—and having called Pete Steinbrecher to warn him that he was going to get a phony alert concerning Jimmy and Jeanette Patrick of Heinsdale sometime in the next twenty-four hours, and that as soon as he could get us quietly into their house we'd be there—my partner and I divided the work we could immediately do along familiar lines: I would prepare something of an auxiliary profile of just who might have been responsible for orchestrating the sudden breaking off of our conference on the mountaintop, as well as Gracie's "accident," while Mike would use whatever bits of harder information he could assemble to form a sort of timeline or flow sheet to determine just when Gracie's trip to see us had taken its irreversible turn toward the deadly. It remained possible that it had been doomed from the moment she had set out for Death's Head Hollow with the BCI boys on her tail; but even Mike came to think this improbable. Frank Mangold simply did not possess the necessary rogue streak for such a plan: he was fine at intimidating suspects in interrogation rooms and running down fugitives with particular viciousness, but ordering his men to force a fellow state employee into a car accident that might well have resulted in her death was simply not an act that fit his career or his character, much as we would have liked it to.

Then there was the vehicle itself, the one that had clipped Gracie's Ford Focus and sent it spinning into a tree. Once Gracie had been freed from the wreck, a couple of hours after Mike and I began our work, Mitch McCarron called again on his way to the hospital, to say that his witnesses had refined their identification to describe a rusted-out red Dodge Ram 1500 pickup: with a white cap on its bed dating from the late 1990s. Assuming Nancy Grimes' people could be relied on to do their jobs in this particular regard, either red or white paint chips would stand out against the blue metallic finish of Gracie's Focus, and thereby confirm what the witnesses had said. It would take quite a while (far longer than television makes most people think) to definitively match those chips to any model of truck, but one thing was certain: BCI men, unless they were doing some fairly serious undercover work, did not drive around in such hulks as had now been fairly reliably identified.

Who, then? My own preliminary profile became informed by the work that Mike and I had already done, the details of which Mike had revealed to Gracie during their interlude in one of the taverns in Surrender—a fact that at first had seemed insignificant, but that now, given the identification of the truck, seemed to open any other patron of the tavern to suspicion. This early profile, in essence, grew out of the far more definite profiles we'd been able to draw of the victims themselves, based on their belongings and actions, and, most importantly, the fact that none of the children we'd studied so far (although a clear picture of the boy Donnie in Fraser remained to be drawn) would have been the type to simply accept a ride in a truck like the one described. Each of them seemed far too worldly and discriminating; in addition to which, such a vehicle would have stuck out like a sore thumb, in the world of wealth and insulation into which we'd posited the victims as having been either drawn or delivered. Our theory was that Shelby had been taken to her family's trailer by someone she knew and trusted: and a rusted-out old Ram was the world she was running *from,* not toward, while the same could likely be said of Kyle Howard and Kelsey Kozersky. Finally, there was the fact that Latrell had made mention of "their truck"; had the *already*-dead bodies, then, simply been delivered *to* their places of discovery in the Dodge, a vehicle that would have drawn very little attention in Burgoyne County? And was that only one part of the operation?

Everything about the truck, placed within the context of the profiles of the victims we'd been able to draw, Latrell's behavior and statements, our theory that the nexus of the several deaths was located in New York City, and finally the past twenty-four hours of our own activities, confirmed as much: pointed, that is, toward the truck being a vehicle of expedience for someone who was not him- or herself the author of the larger scheme of exploiting the throwaway children of the county, but was rather a hireling: someone given a specific assignment who was aware only of that job, someone who, given the incomplete nature of the work he had done that night regarding Gracie, stood a very good chance of being eliminated by his employers—indeed, it was possible he had already met that fate.

"Okay, genius," Mike said, once he'd filled up a marker board that was mounted to the right side of the cockpit bulkhead with his mad scribblings, all of which I could read, but only just. "You explain to me what it means. Because to my eyes, right now, it's a fucking convoluted mess."

My next words did not exactly comfort him: "Al Qaeda," I murmured.

Mike glanced my way, with an expression that said I'd finally lost it. "*Al Qaeda?* You're telling me this is the work of terrorists? Some fucking sorcerer you are, that's what I'd expect from the law . . ."

"No, Mike," I answered with a frown. "Of course that's not what I'm saying. I'm just giving you an organizational precedent. And that's the key word, here: 'organization.' There's a *cellular* nature to this whole thing. Especially when you consider Latrell's words—" I pointed to Latrell's name on the board and to the point at which, on the timeline of Mike's chart, the dead youth appeared in the case. "—along with his confusion about what to do after the FIC people appeared. Then take it through all the events of tonight—which we've proposed involve a sniper, but could just as easily, and maybe even more effectively, have been carried out by a very good hunter with a decent rifle, scope, and suppressor. That would be more in line with the knife and the truck. *Or,* go the other direction, Mike: the first two deaths, Kyle and Kelsey. Nothing much was heard about them, in the press, except that they were a couple of isolated hangings. Cathy Donovan and Mangold had the case firmly in hand, then: nothing to see, folks, a couple of sad stories, move along . . . And then Shelby happens. And even more to the point, Steve Spinetti calls *us*. No one group or agent on the other side seems to be aware of what the others are doing. And then Pete shows up here, and all of a sudden things start bleeding over. That's what freaked Latrell out. It freaked Gracie out. Who knows who's next?"

"Yeah, I get it," Mike said softly, nodding. "And there's another thing, L.T.—" He circled a large space he'd left blank between our entrance into the case and the disaster at Fraser. "One that would confirm a cellular aspect to it. I don't think that anybody we've described as being involved in the deaths—whether tangential people like Latrell, who knew and cared about the victims they positioned in phony spots, or people like this driver, who was probably hired just for the trouble on the mountaintop and then to go after Gracie—I don't think any of those people, much less the people in the central, controlling cell, ever foresaw one factor. And it is that factor, not our entrance into the case, much as this may be a blow to our egos, that really started to make everybody on what you call the other side lose their shit. Although you're not going to like it."

"It's just that, like I said, you're not going to like it." And with that, he penned the words *Lucas joins up* inside the empty space; and he was quite right, I didn't much like it, especially in view of the heightened sense of responsibility for the boy that I had begun to feel after our trip up the mountain. Rationally, of course, I already knew that he might well be right; but I was going to make him prove it. "Let me get this straight: you're saying that nobody behind this thing got particularly freaked out when *we* appeared—making Gracie's analysis wrong—but rather when they found out we had *Lucas* working for us?"

"That's how it reads," Mike answered, setting his marker down. "Somebody realized that we had just what you said we had—an inside track on the victims and what's going on with the kids in this county generally. And it scared them. Bad."

"But—" I stumbled. "But—we've kept it a damned secret . . ."

Mike shrugged. "Maybe we have, maybe we haven't. We're not always as smart as we think we are, you know. And *then,* there's always the other possibility, though I'm reluctant to bring it up: we could have been as careful as we liked about the kid. But as for Lucas himself—maybe not."

"No way," I snapped back at him. "You're saying he blew his cover in school?"

"Or hanging out with friends outside of it," Mike answered. "We have to entertain the possibility."

"No," I insisted again. "I know it's only been a little while, Mike, but— I *know* this kid, and so do you. That's not his profile at all—the braggart in the schoolyard? No way."

"Come on, Trajan," Mike shot back carefully. "Even given your power to read people—and I'm not being sarcastic, strangely, when I say that— you've known him, what, a week? But you've accepted his story completely at face value. The vanished parents, the blind sister, the half-wit they've taken in—he could have created all of that."

"Not this kid," I retorted. "He's careful, yeah, and he's sharp—but with me, he's been straight. You're just going to have to accept that."

"Up to now I have," Mike said, in a much more conciliatory tone. "Because I've been given no reason to question it. But you have to admit, there now exists the distinct if small possibility—"

And with my partner's last words, I experienced a rather sharp shudder. "Ah, *fuck!*"

"What?" Mike asked eagerly. "Somebody else come to mind?"

I nodded slowly, making a move for Mike's marker, and then drawing another circle next to the one he'd designated for Lucas. "God damn it . . ." I said. "Somebody you haven't met, yet. But you're going to. We have an appointment to visit their house Tuesday evening . . ." And with that, I scrawled the name *Derek* onto the board, with a pronounced question mark after it.

"The retarded kid?" Mike asked.

"*Mike* . . ." I said, my warning inspired by my own childhood memories of words like *crip* and *gimp*. "I think Surrender is starting to rub off on you. But yeah . . ." I stared at the name, very unhappy with myself for having overlooked something so obvious. "*Derek*. They're like brothers, the two of them. Hell, legally, I guess they *are* brothers. And I doubt there's much Lucas wouldn't trust him with. Even though I warned him about it."

"You actually think that a—whatever, a *mentally challenged* kid is *in* on this whole operation?"

"Maybe—maybe not," I said, shaking my head. "You just said it yourself: all he has to be is careless about what he says to whom." And then the full stupidity of it hit me: "Aw, fuck, Mike—it's even worse than that! God*damn* it." I hurled the marker down on a nearby desk. "It all fits together exactly: Lucas hasn't had to tell Derek much of anything—because he was *here*. He knew what Lucas was staying for—*I told them both,* or at least, I told them enough so that even a kid with his brains could work it out." Moving away from the board, I recalled that first encounter with the two boys: "I thought Derek was too dim to be a problem—but I *did* mention the first three victims. I asked if they knew the kids, and even asked if they could help us—I didn't give them specifics, but they had a general idea of what I do for a living. He *must* have put it together, because he got very scared, very suddenly: the kind of scared you get, maybe, when you've been found out. And after that day, with Lucas spending all his spare time up here, Derek would have felt resentful, even abandoned. So Lucas didn't have to tell him any details: Derek could've started talking to the right, meaning the wrong, people, if only out of bitterness. Either way, innocent or involved, there's no counting on Derek's discretion, no matter what Lucas says. I'm not even sure that he really knows what discretion *is*." I slammed my cane into the deck of the cabin. "I am such a fucking idiot . . ."

"Yeah, well, you're the 'idiot' who got us *this* far," Mike said decently. "And relax, we're going there Tuesday, you said—so we can grill the kid then, and find out if he's been talking, and to who."

I looked at my partner dubiously. "You going to bring your .38 and pistol-whip him if he doesn't cooperate? No, Mike. We've got to find another way."

"Wait a minute—you said *Tuesday*?" Mike's face screwed up in momentary puzzlement. "Didn't you tell me we're supposed to be having our explanatory dinner with Miss Clarissa on Tuesday? So that *she* can grill *us*?"

I nodded, looking at the board again. "Yeah. And our dance card is going to be very full, for that evening, because Pete may call about the Patricks' house, too, and the planting of the body." Then an idea hit me: "*Although*—you know, you may have hit on it, Mike. *We* don't grill Derek at all." I waved my cane at the board, suddenly feeling like maybe there was a way out of the blunder. "No, we do not do it at all . . . We leave that to an expert."

"Like who? Frank Mangold?"

"Nope. Somebody closer to home." I began to move toward the plane's hatchway. "And while you figure *that* out, I'm going to feed Marcianna. Oh, holy shit, what an evening this is going to be . . ."

I was halfway down the steel steps outside the hatch before I heard Mike suddenly realize, with a horror that was only partially affected: "Wait—no way. No way, Trajan! You can't subject a mentally-whatever kid to *that!*"

But I had reached the freezer, by then, and pulled out a package of beef that I placed in the microwave; and the loud hum of its mechanism drowned out Mike's further protests.

CHAPTER TWO

PRESENT AND UNACCOUNTED FOR

{i.}

Tuesday could not come fast enough for me, although Mike's enthusiasm was far more muted. He had had little enough experience of
serious illness and injury, in his life, to altogether trust my assurance that
it was just as well that Gracie Chang was in a coma, one that her doctors,
according to both Mitch McCarron and Pete Steinbrecher, did not consider life- or brain-threatening, but rather curative. I told my partner
again and again that he would not want her conscious, in pain, and alert
to all that was taking place around her: for, excellent facility that the Albany Medical Center was and is, it could not protect her from the vying
interests of the various official investigative agencies, to say nothing of
the local press, which had gotten wind of the accident and of the air of
suspicion that surrounded it. And so, to Mike's continued expressions
of his desire to visit Gracie, I continued to offer only discouragement,
reminding him that he would only further confuse and endanger our
position within the investigation, while at the same time (and just as importantly) upsetting and bewildering Gracie's family. When she attained
consciousness, I told him, there would be plenty of time for visits; for
now, we needed to develop, insofar as we could, our theory of the direction in which the profiles and the evidence we had assembled concerning
the case thus far pointed.

After Sunday night's work, we grew only more reassured as to the validity of that theory's two key elements: first, that the deaths—which we
continued to believe were suicides staged to look like murders—of the
throwaway children were not the work of the two or three people neces-

sary for the mere staging of the bodies, but at their root were somehow tied to an organization; and second, that this organization was headed by people capable of pulling strings long enough to reach even into such remote areas as Burgoyne County. That the power base for these people was the now-supreme bastion of the international economic elite, New York City, we had already demonstrated with hard evidence. The main question now turned upon how the second theory related to the first: just who were the initiators in the city who were using locals to steal away children for whom New York State, along with their families, had made no provision—had "thrown away"—and to what purposes were they bending these children that they had driven at least four of them to suicide?

I would be lying if I did not say that there was a personal edge to all this formulation, during those first days after we survived our ordeal on the mountaintop; for I began to believe (and I sincerely thought that Mike did, too) that we now had a chance for one last slap in the face of the metropolitan leviathan that had puked us out five years ago. Now, at last, we had enough dead (or in Gracie's case, nearly dead) bodies, and a strong enough indication of who had put them in that condition, to rip the lid off a huge drum of moral toxic waste and send it spewing through the streets of the city, something I had longed for since our involuntary exile had begun. As for Mike, the mere thought of Gracie lying comatose in a hospital bed was enough to work him into an intensely active rage, a kind of anger that I was certain indicated that he had gotten fully on board with my plans for swooping down like a righteous scythe on our hometown. My partner and I had always fancied ourselves two servants of justice; with the throwaways case, the always exquisite and rare opportunity to combine justice with revenge had opened up before us. Oh, yes: in my fantasy, we were going to make the big city pay for the kind of moral outrages we had observed, the kind of callous and degenerate crimes that generally accompany wealth unregulated by ethical or physical restraints; and we were, at the same time, going to punish it for having used us so badly . . .

I don't mean to say that this attitude compromised either my partner or myself on the operational level: our work thus far had been solid, and it would continue to be. During the time spared us by our teaching obligations between Sunday night and Tuesday afternoon, we began to construct a more detailed picture of the people by whom these dead children might have been taken in: and they were, we found, a group that was unusually *discriminating*, if such is not too vile a word to use in this context. For, again, the throwaway victims were not simply good-looking kids plucked at random from off the streets or along the highways: they were sharp, ambitious, even brave young souls who had had the most basic elements of childhood stolen from them, and yet were still trying to realize their various goals. *The kind of kids anybody would want*: that phrase suddenly took on an entirely new and terrible connotation, for somewhere there existed a group of people who had wanted them, were hunting for them, though in precisely what way, and for precisely what purposes, we had yet to accurately define. Yet wanted them they had, and *wanted them in the worst possible way*: another seemingly benign term that now assumed sinister dimensions. Mike was always made visibly uncomfortable when I started using such mundane expressions in this manner when constructing profiles; yet during our years of working together he'd learned that adults who target children, for whatever reasons, hide behind just such socially acceptable masks. And so, while he may have groaned occasionally, he never openly objected.

The general notion that we were dealing with children who had been selected for more than merely their looks (although they had all been attractive, of course, each in his or her own way) was momentarily challenged when we finally received personal details concerning the boy Donnie, victim of a seeming heroin overdose in Fraser. Pete Steinbrecher brought us the report himself, after he had clocked out at the sheriff's office on Monday evening. I had been teaching my Theory of Context course for over an hour already, while Mike had been busy dragging out the symbol of his ultimate commitment to any case or line of investigation: his White Monster, the largest dry-erase board he possessed, a four-by-seven-foot beast that had to be set up on a stand that Mike himself had long ago built out of two-by-fours. Fortunately, on this particular occasion, the noise of his so positioning it had been covered by a particularly lively and—I was happy to find—informed discussion of the pages of Laszlo Kreizler's final journal that I had distributed to my class. But when Pete entered the JU-52 (he was the only law enforcement officer that we allowed to do so, and always on his oath that he would reveal nothing that he saw inside), the heavy tromp of his boots on the deck of the plane came cutting through the debate, followed by his voice loudly announcing:

"Uh-oh—the White Monster's out!"

This drew some fast shushing from Mike, but not before my ever-troublesome student from Manhattan, Andrew—who had been engaged in something approximating an online brawl with the far wiser Californian Vicky over the meaning of Dr. Kreizler's pages—had once again detected sounds emanating from behind what was apparently, to him, the endlessly fascinating black fabric backdrop of our virtual classroom, and demanded to know who had made them. Assured by the ever-steady student from the Bronx, Linda, that it was once more his imagination at work, as well as by the petite, no-bullshit Tennessean Amy that it was none of his damned business anyway, Andrew finally stilled his inquiries. It had been a close call, however, especially as some sort of truncated account of the doings in Fraser on Friday night had apparently made its way to local television news and the inside pages of the tabloids in New York, where Andrew had seen it; and it would have been just like the kid to pursue the issue and try to find out if my supposedly "heroic actions" in Fraser actually meant that I was actively involved in some sort of a murder investigation upstate. At length, however, the class ended without further incident. The big screens all went black, and I banged the laptop on the instructor's desk closed as I raced around to find out what news Pete had brought us.

He removed his Stetson with one hand and waved a folder in the warm air with the other slowly. "Got the file on that kid in Fraser—the one who supposedly OD'd. I made you a copy. And the BCI picked up the Patrick couple in Heinsdale, right on schedule."

"Right on schedule," I murmured, as I leaned back on the closest of Mike's desks, which he had shifted (somewhat irritatingly) to make room for his board, and began leafing through the file, while glancing up at our guest. "I would offer you a seat, Deputy, but as you can see . . ."

"No problem," Pete said. "I been through the Monster before, I know the drill."

"I appreciate that," I answered, studying the rather complex combination of conviviality and nervousness that filled the deputy's face at that moment. "The thing is annoying as hell, but I'm afraid it does get results. How about the Patricks? They lawyered up?" I kept my gaze on the increasingly uneasy Pete as he shook his head.

"Too dumb. They buy the old line about only guilty people getting lawyers, don't seem to know that cops made up that argument."

"We'll have to attend to that, then," I answered, looking over to Mike, who was also studying Pete's manner.

"Deputy?" Mike asked. "You got something on your mind besides this file and the Patricks?"

"Well, yeah-ah," Pete droned, giving his head a wipe with his kerchief. "Although the file's a puzzle, for sure, on its own. I don't mean to go above my pay grade, here—"

"But you think maybe it contradicts some of the things we've explained to you," I said, scanning the file's pages, which were mostly composed of clerical paperwork.

The deputy offered no immediate answer, prompting Mike to say, "Is that so, Pete?" My partner was now standing before the White Monster and sketching out ideas, indicating how he meant to incorporate all elements of not only our own theories, but the victims' backgrounds, the locations of their bodies, anything that was pertinent to the case into the great, complex flow chart that would eventually fill the board. "Have you lost faith in our reasoning?"

"Well, there's a couple things I noticed, to be honest," Pete said, clearly hoping that whatever he had to say wasn't going to get shot down immediately. "First off, seems that, although the pathologist confirmed that *he* was hanged, too, the kid did have heroin in his system—recently injected. I don't know if that helps your theory of how the rest of them died or not, since you still haven't told me exactly what your theory *is*."

"Can't do that, Pete," I answered grimly, now studying the file. "Not until we're sure." I glanced at the pathology report. "But that heroin is a particularly cunning touch . . ."

"Hunh," Pete noised, dissatisfied. "Well, then, second: when we were in Fraser, you talked about how these kids were interested in better lives, and the things that come with better lives."

"We did," Mike said, still madly writing, now with a lit cigarette hanging from his mouth.

"Well, the file's pretty straightforward," Pete said, cautiously now. "He was an orphan—"

"Or so we are led to believe," I said, checking the beginning of the file. "The deaths of the parents were never certified, before or after the infant turned up at Van Ruyter Hall, the oldest and *only* home for such children—and yes, that *is* a criticism—in Burgoyne County. From there—"

"From there," Pete said, anxious to offer a contribution, "he went through the foster home system, but didn't luck out until the third try, where it seems like he was happy enough. Mr. and Mrs. Archibald Butler, of North Briarwood. Spent—what was it, seven years with them?"

"Correct," I said, eyes still on the file. "Until he was fourteen." I began to nod in a by-now familiar but no less mournful way when I caught sight of one infuriatingly small form that reported the next important event: "And then Archie and Mrs. Butler disappeared on him . . ."

"Yeah," Pete said. "About a year and a half ago. He tried to stay in South Briarwood Combined, where I guess he was kind of a star basketball player. Made varsity at fourteen."

"So Latrell told me," I murmured, flipping report pages. "Point guard, if memory serves." Which, of course, it did; and all too vividly.

"Yeah," Pete agreed, still more uncomfortably. "Anyway, you have to have a valid home and address to keep attending public school, which he didn't, anymore; and I guess none of his teammates' families were willing to take him in—"

"Are you shocked, Pete?" I asked, holding up a copy of a team photo that had been placed in the report. "Here are the South Briarwood Bobcats, in all their regional championship glory."

"Don't tell me," Mike said without turning. " *'One of these things is not like the others—'* "

" *'One of these things does not belong,'* " I said, slowly enunciating the end of the old *Sesame Street* verse. "An all-white team with one black player. Even if he was liked by his teammates—"

"Which he was," Pete said. "The guys were fine with him—I been down there, and it seems like he was a likable kid, generally. But the coach and the parents . . ."

"The younger generation is more tolerant, my dear Pete," I sighed, pulling my watch from the light cotton vest I'd donned before my class. "But they do not yet determine who lives where. And we'll see how many of them are still tolerant when they grow up and things get tougher—"

"Anyway," Mike said, impatient with my observations and wanting to hear the rest of Donnie Butler's tale.

"Right," Pete hurriedly continued. "Anyway, after that, the kid dropped off the grid and right out of the system. Kind of just—didn't exist, anymore. Couple of social workers tried to find him—"

"Not very hard," I said, scanning still another section of the file.

"There's no mention in their reports of having checked the building in which his body was eventually found, for instance."

"I thought you said that Latrell *brought* his body to that building," Mike called out, again without turning toward us.

"I did—but don't you think it's a fairly safe bet that the building was known as someplace you could at least crash, if you had nowhere to go? And that, ultimately, his body would have been positioned, like those of the others, in a place he had been known to frequent before he died?"

Mike nodded judiciously. "True . . ."

"True is right." I checked my watch again. "And shouldn't you be getting ready for something?"

That brought my partner around. "What? Aw, L.T., you're not saying I have to teach? Not with all this shit going on, and the White Monster to fill?"

"That's exactly what I'm saying. *I* had to. Bring home the bacon, son, it's what pays our bills."

Mike dropped his marker in frustration, then stomped over to a coat hanger that held his short-sleeved white dress shirt and clip-on tie, mumbling obscenities. But as he began to change into his garb, he suddenly caught himself. "Wait a minute: Okay, the kid dropped out of sight, and didn't turn up again until he was dead. So what makes you think he doesn't fit with the others, Pete?"

"Just that," Pete answered matter-of-factly. "There's no further information, not in the file, not anywhere, so far as we can tell, that says Donnie Butler—who was a star on the high school team, nobody's questioning that—ever really thought seriously about going to the big time, or about anything but being a playground junkie. He didn't have any way that we can find of getting to the kind of people you're talking about, rich New Yorkers, anywhere on his person. No applications to schools, no college brochures or rejections from high school or college scouts, nothing like that. *And,* the FIC techs haven't found any evidence at all that he was dealing along with using the heroin, which might at least've been a sign of *some* ambition. All he owned was a bunch of basketball jerseys stuffed in an old gym bag, along with the clothes on his back. So *you* guys tell *me* how he fits."

I wanted to tell him that we already had at least one strong indication that Donnie more than likely fit the pattern of the deaths: that Mike had done his homework on the syringe, and found it to be an unusually expensive brand used, in New York State, only in a few hospitals—in New York City. But we needed still more concrete evidence of what we were thinking before we could tell either Pete or Steve our suicide theory in full, on the off chance that they would find it simply too outlandish, and might therefore casually let its details slip to the wrong person: after all, even so much as a receptionist in their office could prove a conduit to the BCI. So, as Mike continued to grouse about his being forced to teach on that evening in particular, I kept at the file, although I didn't have to go much farther before it began to give up its secrets:

"Pete," I said slowly, reading one enticing page that plucked at youthful chords in my own heart—and which, more importantly, sent a tremor of sorts concerning the case up through my cranium. "You're not much of a basketball *fan,* are you?"

"Me?" Pete said, surprised. "Nope. Played some football, when I was a kid. But frankly, even in high school, I knew I wanted to be a cop, and I knew that jocks who got straight D's or hung out with the wrong crowds—and half the JDs we pick up are football players—stood way less of a chance of getting into law enforcement than the ones who went to at least junior college. So, I—"

"Yes, yes," I said, holding a hand up to him with my eyes still on the file. "An admirable policy, and one that I'd encourage you to share with the New York City Police Department. But I ask that seemingly random question because you apparently haven't realized just what Donnie Butler was carrying around in that old gym bag of his." I craned my head around as far as I could without losing sight of the papers before me. "Hey, Mike."

"*What?*" Mike barked back, as he began to do up his shirt and tie.

"I need you to listen to something: 'Magic Johnson, Los Angeles Lakers jersey, signed, dated 1985; Larry Bird, Boston Celtics jersey, signed, dated 1986; Michael Jordan, Chicago Bulls jersey, signed, dated 1992; Shaquille O'Neal, Los Angeles Lakers jersey, signed, dated 2002.' "

"Hunh," Mike grunted. "Nice collection, assuming they're real. Which I'm not assuming for a minute—well, all right, I'll give it a minute. Assuming they're real, what's Donnie doing with them stuffed in a gym bag?"

"What do you mean?" I asked, slightly irritated by his skepticism. "Doesn't it further prove your hypothesis that these kids all got hooked up, at some point, with people who had serious money and gave them the kinds of things they'd always dreamt of having?"

"It only further proves that theory," Mike answered, "if you assume that the jerseys and the autographs are real—and I'm not, like I say, ready to do that, because, if they *are* real, as I'm sure you picked up on, L.T., every one of them's from a championship season. Which is incredible on its own, I mean—that kid must've been dragging around, depending on how many he had, a minimum of . . . ten or fifteen grand, anyway, in that gym bag. *If* he had verification of them all, that is. And *if* he did, why didn't he cash them in? Couldn't he have used the money?"

"Mike, you've answered your own question: if they were real, and if he tried to sell them, the buyer would want verification of the provenance, which he'd check with the company that certified that provenance. At which point the law would pick Donnie up for grand larceny. *Unless* they'd been signed over to him. And I think I can help, on that count. In the bottom of the bag were found a group of documents, which the FIC tech who examined them—"

Mike sighed heavily. "Who was it?" he droned.

"Umm . . ." I flipped the page to look at the signature on the report. "Uh oh. You're gonna love this. Anne Meyers."

Mike let out another loud groan, as he continued to struggle with his clip-on tie: an unlikely difficulty, yet one that always plagued him, because of his continual refusal to believe that knotting an actual cravat would require less work. "*That* moron?" he said. "She wouldn't know genuine evidence if it bit her on the ass and said hello. All right, let me have it, what does she say?"

"She refers to the documents as '*seeming* papers of identification.'"

"Yeah, and there you go," Mike concluded in disgust.

"Whoa, now," Pete interrupted. "*Where* do we go? Other than saying that another one of Nancy Grimes' techs doesn't know her job, I'm not sure I understand what you're telling me."

"Well, Pete," I said, looking for any further clues I could find in the work of the unfortunate woman who signed her name "CSI Anne Meyers" as if that had any real meaning outside of a television show, "the strong likelihood is that those documents are not papers of *identification* at all. That's a fairly idiotic idea, in fact, because anyone can see that they're that much. What they are is *seeming* papers of *authentication*. Yet if they're real, meaning a reputable firm prepared them, then Donnie was carrying a small fortune around in that bag. Now, we only have the first page of each paper, here—see the fold-over at the corners?—and we need all of them. Because *that'll* tell us . . ."

"Still doesn't make any sense!" Mike warned, as he began to assemble the materials for his class on the desk beyond the black partition. "Before you go sinking back into sorcerer mode."

"What doesn't make sense?" I demanded, again annoyed by Mike's skepticism. "It puts him right in line with the other three. There's no way he could have laid hands on that kind of memorabilia legitimately—not without the change of ownership being recorded, anyway."

"I don't deny that," Mike said, switching on the bank of large and as yet silent video monitors. "But there's just one thing—Donnie was, what, fifteen, when he died? So let's say he found himself some sugar daddy—"

"Or mommy, or daddy *and* mommy," I reminded my partner. Then I turned to Pete. "Around here, Pete, we are equal-opportunity skeptics. We're willing to believe the absolute worst of *anyone*."

"Yeah, don't I know it," Pete replied, not quite so amused as was I. "Go ahead, Mike."

"Well, those are all players from other eras," Mike said. "Having Shaq's jersey I can maybe understand, because he's a TV star, now, and Donnie probably watched him, at least when he could. But the others? Even Jordan's is a little weird: I mean, a legend, true, but if somebody offers a boy who's a basketball freak whatever he wants along those lines, wouldn't the kid go for the heroes he watches every night, and probably pretends to *be* in the playground?"

I had to pause. "It sometimes disgusts me when you have a point," I said, rustling through more pages of the report, trying to find some basis for battling back.

Mike, meanwhile, chuckled in triumph. "But you know I'm right. I mean, where's the LeBron James jersey? The Kevin Durant, the Chris Paul, hell, even the Kobe-fucking-Bryant—"

"Ha!" I suddenly retorted, slapping a finger down onto the report. By now I had turned around to spread the thing out on the desk upon which I'd been leaning. "I'll tell you where they were—they were right *on* him!"

"What the fuck are you talking about, L.T.?" Mike asked, uneasy at the notion that I might be onto something.

"The 'clothes on his back,' that Pete was speaking of—they included a Carmelo Anthony Knicks jersey—*signed* by Melo in 2013, the year they made the playoffs with him. In addition, the jersey appears to bear the signatures of at least three of the four people you just named—not Kobe, but everyone else, along with one or two others. And you know what that means, don't you?"

Mike took just a few seconds with it. "I've got a pretty good idea, yeah."

"Come on, fellas," Pete said. "Just assume I'm lost again and explain it to *me*, please."

"It becomes clear if you assemble the parts, Pete," I said, ever wishing to avoid insult or condescension with the man, but nonetheless excited. "The stuff Donnie was carrying in the bag, those things bespeak an older person—almost certainly a man, but maybe not—who's been a fan for a long time and is also a collector, just as Mike says. The jersey the kid was wearing, however, tells us that Donnie got up close and personal with the players who signed it, almost certainly at Madison Square Garden. Which means that the person who owned the first set of jerseys was likely a figure of some note, around the court—maybe a celebrity, but probably someone who just had a lot of dough. The kind of dough that gets you not only the attention of athletes and the media, but *political* access, as well. A broker, or maybe a lawyer . . ." I crushed out my cigarette in an ashtray on a nearby desktop. "Yes, young Donnie Butler was working his situation, all right . . ."

"But what about that first batch of jerseys?" Pete asked, not unreasonably. "If they're real—and we still don't know that they are—how in the world does he end up in an abandoned building in North Fraser with them?"

"Mike?" I said.

"The jerseys?" Mike answered carefully. "The most likely scenario there, Pete, is that something happened to piss off young Donnie with his patron. Or patrons. Tough to say just what—"

"Like hell it is," I murmured, a bit more angrily than I had intended.

"No, given the information, L.T., it *is* still tough to say," Mike continued. "He may never have gotten over the Butlers abandoning him, and so was angry with all adults. Whatever the case, before Donnie left his latest home, he almost certainly did a little smash-and-grab on the collection. Because I'll guarantee you, those jerseys were framed carefully, at some point. You don't leave assets like that lying around casually—unlike most things, their value will only hold or increase, over time."

"So the whole business," I said, eagerly anticipating the conclusion we were reaching, "really comes down to those certificates of authentication. *Were* they signed over to Donnie? And far more importantly, *can* they be traced—because, if they can, we'll get a name, and with a name—"

"With a name, we get an address, even if the theft—assuming it was a theft—went unreported," Mike called out. "Which it probably did: the owner or owners would not have wanted the cops to know that Donnie'd been living with him, or her, or them."

"But *we* can find out if he was," I finished, closing the file, thinking that we had wrung just about all we were going to get from it. "We can determine what no police department or social services department has apparently been able to about Donnie Butler, and in so doing we can drive the first real wedge into this case—not here, but where its secrets truly lie . . ."

"In New York City," Pete said, following closely.

"Exactly," I replied, gently patting the stack of papers, exhilarated as I reached the crucial question to which all our reasoning led: "So—" I pronounced, grabbing my suit jacket and starting to pull it on, assuming Pete's and my departure was imminent. "Whose car shall we take? Yours is the more official, of course, but ours might be more discreet."

"You guys aren't going anywhere without me!" Mike moved to leave the instructor's desk.

"No—we ain't," Pete said, his voice betraying disappointment.

"We *ain't*?" I parroted. "What do you mean, Deputy? Donnie's clothes, and especially the complete papers of authenticity—hasn't Steve got it all back at your office?"

Pete went from disappointed to dog faced. "Afraid not. That's an FIC report I gave you, Doc. Meaning Frank Mangold's got control over that evidence."

I stood up, leaning on my cane and navigating around the crowded desks as a substitute for pacing. "I see . . ."

"Well," Mike tossed in, reseating himself in disappointment and feeling (like me) a little outmaneuvered. "*That* sucks ass . . ."

"It does, indeed," I murmured, in no way ready, however, to so easily surrender what represented the first steps to putting actual names to the theory of the throwaway deaths that Mike and I had developed. And in that defiant mood, I spun on Pete again. "And there's really only one way to make it *un*-suck: can *you* get us access, Pete? Firsthand access?"

Pete sighed. "I figured you were going to ask me that, though at the time I didn't know what you'd want the access for. And you're asking me because you figure there's no way Mangold's going to just *offer* you guys a chance to look that stuff over—"

"Yeah, I'd say that's a fairly safe assumption," Mike pronounced. But that was to be the last we'd hear from him concerning the case, for a bit, being as his next words were, "Ah, here comes the first and the brightest of my students—good evening, Mei-lien . . ."

A very soft-spoken young Asian woman answered: the Chinese exchange student with whom I'd often warned Mike not to flirt too overtly, who had come to SUNY-Albany's School of Criminal Justice from one of the oldest and largest of the Chinese schools of forensic medicine, at Kunming Medical University in Yunnan Province. "Good evening, Professor Doctor Li," she said rather skittishly: a skittishness that was reflected not only in her name (*Mei-lien* meaning "beautiful lotus," or thereabouts) but also in the striking delicacy of her face and frame, which reflected her province and city's close proximity to the southern border of the People's Republic. All of these delicate aspects, however, were belied by her skill and courage when working through trace evidentiary lab and field exercises.

"I've told you before, Mei-lien," Mike said indulgently, "either 'Professor' or 'Doctor.' It's not the way, to use both in this country."

"Yes, of course, my apologies," Mei-lien answered, embarrassed; and as Mike assured her that there was no need to be apologetic, more students' faces began to flash up onto the monitors. At that point I urged Pete to follow me quietly out the hatch of the plane and into the warm, humid night.

"Well!" Pete said, once we were safely down the steps. "Mike is certainly the operator, among ladies of his own kind."

It wasn't really a racist crack; or at least, it wasn't intended to be. Pete would never have intentionally slighted anyone in that way; but if you grew up in Burgoyne County, you developed certain . . . tendencies, which could be either malicious or benign in intent. So I thought it a good idea for both of us if I said simply, "Pete, you spend more time with that guy, and you'll find he's an operator with women of *all* kinds. Keep him away from your very pretty wife, for starters."

"Really?" the deputy said, realizing that I was (mostly) kidding with my last line, but still more impressed by Mike. "Ain't that something," he judged at length. "Well, more power to the guy."

"Indeed," I said impatiently. "Now—you said that you'd been considering how to get us in to see Donnie Butler's personal effects."

"I said I'd been considering a way for *Frank Mangold* to even consider letting you see them," Pete corrected carefully. "And trust me, I know that it doesn't look good, on the surface. But there might be a way around the problem: Frank knows his people screwed up the other night—hell, *everybody's* people screwed up the other night, and there's going to have to be a bitch of an investigation. That boy Latrell was shot *forty-six* different times, by *four* different law enforcement agencies—and was never found to have been in possession of a weapon."

"Facts known only too well to me," I said quietly, considering again the mess that so many bullets had made of Latrell's body.

"And at any investigation, you guys're gonna be called to testify— Frank knows that as well as I do," Pete went on. "So you've got a chip— question is, do you want to play it here, on this?"

I began to smile. "Oh, I think you might find that this is one of those chips that can be played over and over," I murmured, genuinely surprised and pleased by Pete's metaphor and by his understanding of the machinations of the departmental politics that were swirling around us.

"Maybe—and maybe not. You don't know what it's like over there right now, Doc. They're getting things set to arrest this Patrick couple, like you figured, down in their own HQ at the Harriman Office Park in Albany, where the State Police's academy is. But there's something weird about it. Neither me nor Steve can figure out just what, and they sure aren't telling us."

"So they haven't made the arrest yet—that means they're still getting the pieces in place."

"So you've said," Pete answered, "but you haven't bothered to tell me what those 'pieces' are."

"Oh, trust me, Deputy—you'll know them when you see them. The main thing now is whether you think there's really a way to get us a look at those verification documents."

Pete considered it. "I do think there *may* be. But you've got to give me a day or so, Doc."

"A day or so, I think we have," I replied, rejoining him. "Maybe not much more, though. In the meantime, we're going to work a couple of things from our end."

"Yeah?" Pete said. "What kind of things?"

I half-smiled at him. "I could tell you, but then Steve would have to kill me. Or you. Or both of us—"

But Pete already had his hands up. "Okay, okay. I don't want to know."

"No," I said, grabbing Marcianna's evening meal. "You don't. Now— how about coming along to feed my 'dog' with me?" I laughed lightly. "Face your fears, Deputy!"

"No, thank *you*," Pete replied firmly. Putting his hat back on, he backed away from the hangar toward the path to his car. "I have to face Frank Mangold, that's about all I'm ready for."

In some strange way, I found his fear reassuring. "Oh, come on, Pete," I called with another laugh, this one more openly tormenting. "You'll *have* to get to know her, eventually."

"Yeah, so *you* say!" Pete called, turning to walk faster. "But I *got* a dog at home—and not my dog nor any dog anywhere sounds like that thing you got up there, I know that much!"

I turned to start the walk up the hill, already beginning to silently mull over the events that we'd scheduled for Tuesday. "No, Pete," I murmured with some satisfaction. "No dog you've ever heard of sounds like that— and let's just hope she can continue to work her magic tomorrow . . ."

{ii.}

By the time Mike and I had finished our respective classes the follow- ing day, I was feeling more than a little braced and even optimistic about the challenges that faced us that evening. What had seemed like difficult hurdles just a day before—first, convincing Lucas' sister, Ambyr, of the importance of our investigation (and, even more, of Lucas' own importance to it), and then the ordinarily intimidating prospect of simi- larly trying to secure my great-aunt Clarissa's blessing for our undertaking—now seemed more like opportunities, so convinced was I of the righteousness of our cause.

I received my first wake-up call along these lines from Mike; and I received it as soon as we embarked. Having gotten Marcianna onto her leash and then down to the hangar during the waning minutes of my partner's last class, I waited with her while Mike got his books and notes stored away; and it would have been tough to say who passed the time in a more heightened state of anxiousness, Marcianna or myself. She began her usual games—bumping up against my good leg with ever-increasing force, searching for Terence's dog treats in my pockets (I'd filled them with the things for use during our coming excursion), and finally sending loud chirrups up toward the JU-52's hatch, whence she knew Mike must soon emerge—while I tried without much success to keep her amused. I pointed her attention to the Empress, which sat in the usual barnyard parking area for cars and equipment below us. But Marcianna, despite the fact that she loved a ride in the car almost as much as she did an expedition in the Prowlers, was taking one thing at a time; and when Mike finally did come out of the plane, he and not I became the focus of her head-butting and mock games of trip-bite-kill, amusements that my partner found of limited charm. I tried to calm his irritation, first by inquiring after Gracie—who had emerged from her coma in the wee hours of that morning, and on whom Mike had been keeping careful tabs throughout the day—and soon thereafter with rousing thoughts of what I saw as the clear path that lay ahead of us.

"Gracie's improving at about the rate you'd expect a girl like her to recover, which is pretty quick," Mike answered to the first of my questions. "The doctors are optimistic that the concussion will have no lasting effects, especially if it's not compounded by another in anything like the near future. Which I assured Pete and Steve that it won't be—we're not putting her in a spot like that again, L.T."

"We don't need to," I said, hoping that it would sound reassuring rather than self-serving. "Her role as a conduit will be an entirely nonoperational one. All we need are regular reports—there's no reason she has to come back here to deliver them."

"Are you shitting me, L.T.?" Mike said, astonished, yet still keeping an eye on the playfully stalking Marcianna. "I'm not going to let her play *any* goddamned future role in this investigation, passive or otherwise." Suddenly, Marcianna made a move forward (not as quickly as she could have, of course), and Mike, displaying fast reflexes of his own, dashed around to walk on my left instead of my right side, leaving the disappointed Marcianna feeling cheated and wronged.

"Don't listen to him, girl," I said. "He's just being a pain in the ass."

"I fucking well am not," Mike replied. "I'm just getting you prepared. We are not putting Gracie in anything close to harm's way again."

I considered the matter. "Gracie won't agree to being ordered out—you know that."

"Yeah, well, we'll *make* her agree," Mike declared. "No bullshit, L.T.: she does not get anywhere near our work, from here on out."

Considering the matter for a moment, I then nodded. "You're right, Mike. I'm sorry."

"Fucking well better be sorry, asshole."

I eyed him critically. "What obscure reptile made its way up *your* rectum and laid its eggs before dying?"

Mike sighed, lighting a cigarette. "None. Let's just drop it."

Hoping to dispense with this argument, I asked, "You clear on our present objectives?"

"Probably not," he answered, in the same tone. "We're going down to meet Lucas' sister. Then we fetch the two boys up to get examined by Clarissa; but first, while we're down there, you give this Ambyr chick the real story about our investigation—or as close as you ever get to telling anybody the real story."

I ignored his little dig. "Just remember how important it is to get the sister's blessing for Lucas' involvement in what we're doing. During the next phase he will be particularly important."

"You mean, if we go down to the city?"

"I mean *when* we go down to the city. The people these kids end up with, like most wealthy degenerates, probably like to have degenerate-club parties—after all, they've got nobody else to enjoy their lifestyle with. And, whether those gatherings take place in town or at the nearby horse farm we've posited as an alternate site, we won't be able to either get any answers or infiltrate such an occasion without a young man or girl—a *ward*, if you will—of our own to bring."

Mike exhaled smoke in a disgusted fashion. "You'll be putting that kid in one lousy situation, Trajan, one that may mess with his head—and mess with it for years to come. You sure it's worth it?"

"*He's* sure it's worth it, Mike," I answered, perhaps a little sharply. "You going to do *everybody's* thinking for them?"

"No," he said, matching my tone. "Just one more person's—yours. You need, between now and whenever we leave for the city, to cover some basic possibilities that we haven't yet, about this group of 'degenerates' that we're supposedly going to take down."

"What the fuck is *that* supposed to mean?"

"It means that we haven't got all the pieces to state with absolute certainty that such a group exists—but you're talking about it in certain terms, anyway, to anyone who will listen."

"Hey, look, pal," I defended, as we reached the car and I got Marcianna into the back seat, "*you're* the one who came up with all the physical evidence that points south."

"Yeah," Mike replied, not at all fazed. "I did." Just before getting behind the wheel, he interrupted his lecture to warn: "If Marcianna tears up that seat, you're paying for it."

"When the fuck has she ever torn up that seat? What the hell's the matter with you, anyway?"

"*Nothing's* the matter with *me*," Mike said, starting the Empress up and letting the V-8 idle for a bit. "But *you*, on the other hand—you have been making one big assumption ever since that night over in Fraser. And the things that happened up on the mountain on Sunday, along with Gracie's crash, have only accelerated the process."

These were words that Mike knew would cut me to the quick. "Is this still your concern for Gracie talking?" I asked carefully. "Because, if it is, I have to tell you, Mike, it's not me that's letting my judgment become clouded—"

"No, it's not my concern for Gracie talking!" Mike pretty well shouted, at which Marcianna issued a long, sad chirrup that tailed off into a kind of whining groan: a sound she made whenever Mike and I raised our voices to each other. Mike, to his credit, turned to her, and, as she laid her head on the inner edge of each of our seats atop the gap between them, he said, with as much affection as he could muster, "I'm sorry, Marcianna . . ." Then, to prove his point, he gently stroked the top of her head a few times. "We wouldn't *have* to shout, if your boyfriend over there would be straight with me."

"And again I must ask—what the hell is bugging you?" I lifted my own hand to continue calming Marcianna as Mike turned back to the dashboard. "Because we've got to settle it before we get to the Kurtzes': we need to come off like an expert investigatory team that has gotten its most basic shit together on this case."

Mike sighed and put his forehead to the steering wheel. He seemed to be puzzling with some deep quandary, but when he lifted his head once more, his face had taken on an expression of quiet determination. "Okay," he breathed, taking a last drag of his cigarette and then powering his window down to throw the butt out. "Listen to me, Trajan—I know you think you've covered all the angles on what could be happening, in terms of these kids and the adults they interacted with before their deaths. And instinctively, I agree with you. But we do have a method; and that method should tell you that there are still unknowns that stand in the way of en- dorsing it *absolutely*."

I was somewhat taken aback: as I had told Mike, it had been his trace work that in large part had allowed me to assemble my profiles both of the throwaway kids and of the proposed group of wealthy pedophiles or hebephiles in New York City that were behind the deaths of those kids, if not directly, then through agents of procurement and disposal. And he had seemed to accept—and more, to agree with—that theory completely; yet now he was questioning some basic aspect of it, to an extent that was at least troubling, and perhaps something a good deal more than that. "All right, Mike," I said at length. "Suppose you just tell me what factors should prevent us from endorsing the theory that I put together—and would not have been able to put together without your own work."

Putting the car into gear, Mike adjusted the front and rear windows to the heights that we usually employed when Marcianna was aboard, which would allow her to enjoy the especially strong wind created by Mike's greed for speed, while preventing her from jumping out of the moving vehicle. In response, Marcianna plopped her big head down on my right shoulder, so that she would receive the full force of the wind from my window in particular. In doing so, she completed the necessary illusion of actually looking like some breed of enthusiastic but well- behaved hunting dog.

"Look," Mike said, as he, very uncharacteristically, backed slowly out of the barn lot and then started down the hollow at a similarly deliberate speed, to underscore what he was trying to say. "I get it. I get what you're after, and I get why. I saw the way your brain lit up out on 22 at the mere thought that there might be some new NAMBLA-type organization at work, tied to some of the people in the city who you see—and okay, maybe I do, too—as representative of everything that's gone wrong with the place, *our home,* including the fact that we don't live there anymore."

"And you're saying that you don't accept that theory, all of a sudden?"

"Trajan," Mike replied, attempting supreme patience, "of course I accept the theory—as just that: a *possible* explanation, maybe even a probable one. But I'm asking you to remember that there are still too many questions we haven't answered about these disappearances, reappearances, and suicides for us to draw *absolute* conclusions. I mean, yes, the theory is possible—"

"But look at the reactions, Mike—don't they make it more than possible? You heard Gracie: in the space of—what, about a week?—our theory has put real fear into politicians and law enforcement, and, it looks like, the people actually responsible, as well."

"But it could still be *wrong*," Mike replied, with rising volume to match mine, which brought another little growling whimper from Marcianna, who stuck her face a little closer to my window. "Suppose," Mike continued, "that the attempt to provide those kids with new lives, lives with futures, was actually benign, in many or even most cases?"

"'*Benign*'? How the hell do you figure it could be benign?"

Mike was ready to shout again, but he got the urge under control. "By using our system, damn it. By positing an opposing idea that works. And what are its central elements? Well, we can't say, for instance, just how many children went down to the city, shepherded by this organization. And we therefore can't say how many landed in the homes of adults who had perfectly understandable, even laudable reasons for taking them on in the way they did: maybe they were just couples who failed New York State's adoption regulations—which are fucking arcane and arbitrary, at times, and you know it. Or maybe some of these throwaways have taken the place of kids who went missing without explanation sometime in the past, and whose parents, because of that fact, live under a cloud of endless suspicion, one that prevents them from ever adopting anyone legally—because the city and state of New York view most such parents with just such suspicion, and you know *that*, too. But the suspicion doesn't stop the parents from continuing to want a kid to raise—one to take the place of the lost child. These are real possibilities, possibilities that contradict our theory, and our method demands that we fucking factor them into the process before we leap to the conclusion—a leap the moron state investigators have, I remind you, already made—that sexual exploitation was the sole motive behind both the disappearances and the strangulations. Remember what the goddamned state has apparently put out of its mind: *no signs of sexual assault or even recent activity on any of the victims' bodies. That* is what I'm saying: you've been cutting corners, and it's gotta stop. For the moment, we've got a theory—a good theory, but it is not definitive. Not yet."

I sat back, a bit stunned. Everything Mike had said about our method was accurate, and he had provided not one but two credible antitheses to my theory of a cabal of ultra-wealthy child abusers. Was I, then, filling in blank spaces with assumptions, in order to make the theory fit the mold I wanted it to, and thus employing confirmation bias? Was I, in fact, guilty of one of the things I most indicted law enforcement agencies for—tunnel vision?

"Hang on, now, Mike," I eventually said. "If what you're saying is true, then how do you explain the stagings themselves? Why make the suicides look like murders? And how about what happened on the mountain the other night?"

"Could you go to court with any of that?" Mike replied. "No, you couldn't—because it's not definitive, not conclusive enough. You *know* that, L.T.—it's fucking *Jurassic Park* logic!"

Now he was really swinging hard. "*Jurassic Park* logic" was a uniformly derisive phrase that Mike and I often used, especially in relation to forensic science television shows, to describe a habit displayed by both real and fictional law enforcement officials of filling in blank spaces in their theories of a crime with the most desirable or necessary possible elements and circumstances, despite the implausible or even fantastic nature of those elements. The phrase arose out of the mutual enthusiasm that Mike and I still shared for Michael Crichton's novel, an enthusiasm we had developed when we were each about Lucas' age, and the book had first appeared; and when we met later in life, we spent long hours affectionately dissecting the logical and scientific improbabilities whose resolution had to be achieved in order for the tale to work: the kind of improbabilities that, according to my partner, I was exhibiting, by filling in gaps in our theory not with what I was actually seeing, but with whatever facts would make that theory work.

"Gracie *could* simply have had an accident, Trajan," Mike explained further. "We need to get a look at the truck that clipped her, but we have no idea about how close they are to even finding it, because you've been so fixated on getting a look at those authentication documents—which Pete could perfectly easily photograph on the sly, and then transmit to us electronically, if he doesn't want to risk a confrontation with Mangold. Above all, the throwaways still *could* have been unconnected deaths, all of them: proving that they spent some time in moneyed company down south says nothing about why they killed themselves—maybe they were just a few out of many who didn't like the experience. Throw in what Latrell said about 'them,' about how 'they' had engaged him to place Donnie Butler's body in that abandoned building, and you have every reason to think that the suicides happened locally; we're almost certain that Shelby's did. And didn't you say that Donnie OD'd at '*their*' place, wherever that might be?" I only nodded a few times in response. "Well, there you go—do you really think that Latrell got called in to the luxury apartment or fancy horse farm of some ultra-wealthy person so many miles away from Fraser? Did he really seem like the type? And did he really expect to hear from such people when he ran into trouble like he did?"

"No," I murmured, so softly that I doubt Mike even heard me over the wind rushing through the windows; but he would have seen my steadily shaking head. It took a few more silent moments, but I finally managed an answer, one that made me not a little embarrassed: "Okay, Mike. Your points are taken. And you're right. I've moved a little too fast on a theory that . . . I happen to like."

"I get no fun out of saying it, kid," Mike answered, in a decently sympathetic tone. "Because I know, like I told you, what's making you do it. You're pissed. You're pissed because, on that last case in the city, we won the battle, but lost the war. We figured it out—and then they shit-canned us. We didn't deserve that. Yeah, sure, we'd become a little arrogant, a little full of ourselves—but we'd maintained the record to back it up."

I grunted once. "*Is* there a record that ever really backs up arrogance, Michael?"

"Yeah," he said, with reassuring definitiveness. "There is—and we assembled it. Name me any one team in the New York law enforcement system that had a higher solve rate than we did—even though we were technically 'advisors.' You can't. But . . ." Mike sighed once; a big, sad sigh of a kind I hadn't yet heard from him, and one that made Marcianna pick her head up and look his way, as if to make sure that he was all right. "In the end, it didn't matter. The new citizens of New York want to believe that their police department is both strong and infallible. That's what

9/11 did to them. They don't care if the wrong people go to jail, or if rough justice is handed out to suspects out of the public view, or if people on the outskirts are still having their rights violated fairly constantly. Just so long as the town becomes something that it was never intended to be."

I glanced at him. "And what's that?"

Mike let out another sigh, this one shorter and angrier. "Los Angeles," he soon said. To my bemused expression, he explained further: "That's what New York is playing by, now—L.A. rules. As long as the town is a safe playground for the rich and famous, let the cops do what they have to. Or hire private cops, which, I don't know if you've noticed, more and more neighborhoods in New York are doing. I'm telling you, it's fucking perverse. New York's supposed to be the rough-and-tumble melting pot, where the rules for the rest of the country are hammered out. Now . . . every place is going to become Los Angeles. A desert-town-turned-city that wouldn't even exist, if Nature had anything to do with it. Fucking *perverse . . .*"

I did not hide my confusion: "What the hell happened to me needing to get over our exile, to 'you wouldn't want to live there now, anyway'?"

"You wouldn't. Not the way it's become. Face it, L.T.: the city we grew up in is gone, dead, wiped out. Drowned in dough. So you do need to get over it. Our life up here is pretty damned good, for a couple of guys who could be doing a lot worse. That's why I want you to be really fucking careful on this case—do not let the same thing that happened in New York happen here. Don't blow our deal on an answer that's right, but makes it necessary for the powers that be to get rid of us. Because, assuming you're not holding out on me, we're fresh out of places to be exiled to. Unless you want to go to Yunnan with Mei-lien and teach at the Kunming Medical University–slash–forensic science training center. I'm sure they'd be happy to have us, although I think we'd have to change our curriculum just a bit—like, the whole fucking thing."

I couldn't help but chuckle. "And what happened to you not being Chinese?"

"I'm not! That's the whole point. Two *American* experts in trace evidence and criminal psychology? They'd let us in so fast—"

"Nah," I finally decided. "China doesn't seem like a good fit."

"No," Mike replied. "It doesn't. Okay—now, where the fuck does that little freak live again?"

"Just go around the square in town and head out 34," I answered. "He said it's a little white house with peeling paint not too far along—wait, I've got the number here, somewhere . . ."

As I began checking my pockets, finally finding Lucas' address tucked in behind my watch in the right pocket of my vest, I caught sight of the statue of Colonel Jones in the square: and, despite the green and white streaks of tarnish caused by countless rain- and snowstorms, he continued to look ready to head into battle, as did the noble mastiff Cassius at his side.

"Wish us luck, Colonel," I called weakly, lifting the head of my cane in his direction. "We now enter the world that you turned your back on forever—and God knows if we'll ever get out . . ."

{iii.}

The Kurtz house turned out to be a surprise: not because of its generally run-down condition, but because of what it had originally been. It was, indeed, a little white house with peeling paint by the side of the road; but it was not a modern modular home, which I had been expecting. Rather, it was a house of about the vintage of Shiloh, and in a similarly Italianate style, but something of a Potemkin-village version of that breed. The front of the building had a shallow porch, with narrow square columns and the requisite filigree at the top of each; but, once you moved around to the sides of the rectangular structure, the porch vanished, and you could see that the roof was simply sloped toward the back, rather than being composed of the four triangular sections that gave the more genuinely Italianate houses their feel of solidity and scale. The rooms on the second floor must have been quite cramped, little more than attic quarters with hard-angled ceilings and half-windows at the base of their walls; and yet it could not be denied that the place, for all its design shortcuts and peeling paint and collapsing black shutters, had far more charm than most of the intact modular units that dotted County Route 34, and then dominated Route 7 beyond.

Houses like the Kurtzes' were not entirely uncommon in Burgoyne County; but more and more of them were being abandoned to foreclosure and collapse, and it was always heartening to see one still up and inhabited. When we arrived, Lucas and Derek (Derek Franco, I had learned his full name to be) were out on the small, steep bit of shaggy front lawn that rolled right down to County Route 34. They had probably been waiting to welcome us, originally; but that dull chore had descended into a bout of no-holds-barred roughhousing, or, as they would later label it, "mixed martial arts combat." Such appeared to involve (in their case) not only that so-called sport's punching, clenching, and kicking, but biting, gouging, and blows to any and all parts of the anatomy. It seemed playful enough, as they were both laughing in fits, although it was hard to see how Lucas would not take the worst of it, so much larger and stronger was Derek. Yet as we pulled over and into the driveway (Mike murmuring, "Those idiots are going to kill each other"), I was reminded of the essential gentleness of Derek's character, and of the deference he usually displayed toward his smaller friend: it was clear that he was not fighting at full strength, although the same could not be said of Lucas, who was battling away like a dervish on amphetamines.

It was an ordinary boyhood scene; and it troubled me for just that reason. I had become so used to seeing Lucas as the precocious member of our investigative team that I think I had, to some extent, lost sight of how young he actually was; and this reminder—much like the jolt of hearing him refer to himself as a throwaway child on the way down the mountain on Sunday night—was not entirely welcome. But, whatever my misgivings, at the sound of the Empress' throaty twin tailpipes pulling into his driveway, Lucas popped his head out from amid the mass of his own and Derek's tangled arms and legs, and then convinced (or, based on his gesticulations, it would be more accurate to say ordered) his friend to get off of him. He grinned and moved toward the car, trying to do what he could with his grass-strewn mop of hair while straightening his usual uniform, a neutral-colored T-shirt and jeans. Derek, for his part, hung back, making a small effort to tidy his own appearance but never smiling, and clearly apprehensive about our visit. Lucas ran to a dilapidated, barn-red garage at the end of the short driveway and pulled open its two doors, revealing an empty bay: evidently the elder Kurtzes had taken whatever the family's vehicle had been with them. Mike followed our young partner's directive to pull into the garage, and Lucas immediately closed the door behind us. This would almost certainly guarantee that no one in the area would be aware of our visit, provided they had not been watching during the few seconds it had taken to get us hidden away: thus far, then, Lucas seemed to have planned the meeting well.

The kid moved to switch on a lone light bulb that hung from one of the garage's crossbeams; but during the few seconds before light shone down and Mike and I opened our car doors, my partner reached for the Empress' glove compartment and pulled out his neoprene-encased .38. Moving swiftly, he fixed the gun's holster to his right leg by its Velcro straps. I watched as he completed this ominous task, a little dumbfounded; and finally, when he'd rolled his pant leg back down and Lucas had got the light in the garage on, I asked, "What the hell are you doing, Mike?"

"What the hell's it *look* like I'm doing, L.T.?" he said calmly. "Aren't you strapped?"

"No, I most certainly am not '*strapped,*'" I said, opening my door and then leaning to my left as Marcianna leapt over the seat back and then poured her lithe form out the door. "What the hell are you thinking is going to happen here, Li?"

"Trajan," Mike breathed wearily as he opened his own door, "I no longer have any idea of what is going to happen anywhere, on this case . . ."

It was a somewhat less than rousing thought; but I could not deny its essential truth. And with it in mind, we stepped into the world of the Kurtz family, a small group as representative of the evils that have grown to plague contemporary working-class America as anyone could hope to encounter. Lucas led us from the car into the backyard, which was shielded on all sides, by the back of the house itself, as well as by two steep earthen embankments covered with trees, and finally by the garage. Within this little area, the only adornments were an old swing set, rusted away, and a picnic table, benches, and chairs that, like a low platform-patio that stood outside the back door of the house, were made of pressure-treated wooden boards that had long ago faded to that depressing shade of moldy grey-brown. But the hidden siting of the yard meant that the ever-curious citizens of Surrender would not observe Marcianna's presence; and as I grew calmer on this score, so did she, allowing me to give her a little more lead on her leash.

Turning to the larger of the youths, who continued to hang back a few steps from the very gregarious Lucas, I said, "Hey, Derek. Good to see you again."

"Hunh?" he noised, as if I had just roused him from some deep reverie. "Oh, uh—yeah. Hi." Lucas rolled his eyes in that same comical way he had during my first encounter with the pair, then balled a fist and lightly punched his friend in the upper arm, nodding to him to continue. "Hunh?" Derek noised again; and when I glanced briefly at Mike, I could see that he had already taken the measure of our second host. "Oh," Derek went on, "yeah, sorry, it's, uh, nice to see you again, too."

"Hello, Derek," Mike said, stepping forward and offering his hand, before the kid was put through any further torment. "I'm Dr. Li—Dr. Jones' partner. And no, not gay partner, before you start wondering. His professional partner."

In his inimitable way, Mike had gambled correctly: what could have been a politically incorrect, inane, or even insulting remark (suggesting that Derek was too dim-witted to grasp the situation) instead brought a good-natured chuckle from the slow, deliberate young man, whose deep brown cheeks flushed a bit. "I *know,*" he answered, shuffling his feet in a way that would have seemed affectedly *aw, shucks* had one not known him. "Luke told me who you are," he went on. "Said you weren't Chinese, but . . ." Derek's face grew puzzled. ". . . you sure *look* Chinese."

At which Lucas spun on his friend and gave him another slug in the shoulder, this one much harder, as he said, quickly, quietly, and involuntarily, "God-fucking-dammit, Derek. I told you about watching what you say today, didn't I?"

"But, Luke—" Derek began to protest.

His friend cut him off: "And I told you *that,* too! I ain't *Luke*—at least, not in *professional* situations." At which Mike stepped in again:

"Don't worry about it, Lucas—and don't you worry about it, either, Derek. I get comments like that all the time. Can't think why." As Derek grew even more confused, Mike indicated Marcianna. "So—Dr. Jones tells me you've already met his favorite sister."

Derek's expression quickly changed, and became one of knowing amusement. "Nah, that ain't his sister. We been through that. He just says it is because of the name." The young man looked past Mike to me. "We Googled it, Dr. Jones—we know why you named her that, and why you say she's your sister, and all."

"Really?" Mike said. "You Googled 'shape-shifters' and got a reasonable answer?"

This comment of course confused Derek again, so I hurried to say, "Don't pay any attention to him, Derek—when he was a baby his mother hit him in the head with a mallet. I'm glad you were able to find out what you did—but has it made you any easier about approaching her? It's the best way to put her at her ease."

Derek looked at Marcianna, whose head was bobbing about with curiosity, and then to Lucas quickly; and Lucas gave him another disappointed scowl. "And we talked about *this,* too, Derek," he said. "You need to make her feel comfortable, else she's liable to tear your throat out." .

"*Lucas . . .*" I warned.

"All right, maybe not tear your throat out," Lucas conceded, "but come on, Derek, just do it—and don't be nervous, because she'll know it and it might make her freak out."

"That much is true, Derek," I said. "Do you think you can approach her in a calm way?"

Derek took a very deep breath, and none of the rest of us said a word as he began to move toward Marcianna. "Well . . . I been practicing in my head, so maybe I can . . ."

"Good man," I replied; then I leaned down to Marcianna's ear. "Marcianna, this is a friend. A *friend,* okay?" *Friend* was one of the keywords that Marcianna understood instantly—at least she usually did. But as Derek approached, her manner became odd: not aggressive or defensive, but something beyond ease or curiosity. She stared at the oncoming boy, then began to purr rather loudly; and as Derek got very close, she approached him—causing him to freeze on the spot—and began to grind her head and neck into and past his left leg. I stayed with her, keeping her on a short leash as I worked my cane quickly and she circled around to his front side again; and then, inexplicably, she raised up to put her paws on his shoulders, though not playfully or in some sort of mock aggression. Rather, it was a tender movement; but one that nonetheless caused Derek to stiffen further. Marcianna was not deterred by this reaction, however, instead continuing to purr and then beginning to lick Derek's face, one would have had to say affectionately, even lovingly.

Both Mike and Lucas were looking to me silently for an explanation, which I had, but did not want to share with them in front of Derek: for it has long been known—and had been my own vivid experience, as well—that cats are extraordinarily alive to the illnesses of people. It is a reaction that is quite distinct from that which they embody toward weakness; rather, sensing that a person is in some way ill or simply "different" (as many put it, today) tends to make them very protective. Often during my cancer, for example, a small buff beauty that I called Suri never left my bedroom, during my diagnosis period and then my convalescence; and she was even allowed to spend brief periods with me in the hospital, a practice that Sloan Kettering has, I understand, discontinued, more's the pity. And certainly, such had been a marked feature of Marcianna's behavior for almost as long as I had known her—with the exception of that one early moment of confusion and bloodshed, of course . . .

As for Derek, it had been my suspicion since meeting him that he was mildly to moderately autistic, although he had never been diagnosed (not surprisingly, in Burgoyne County, where "slow" generally served as a folk analysis). Marcianna was simply demonstrating the feline protective instinct in its most profound and vivid form; but to say so, I would also have had to share my thoughts about the young man she was exploring, and so I remained silent. At length, having made her intentions known, Marcianna released Derek; yet the entire time we were at the Kurtzes' that afternoon she seemed always to know where he was and what he was doing: ready, should the need arise, to come to his aid. You would have had a tough time convincing Derek of that fact, of course: once she was back off of him, he wiped his face quickly, let out a long breath that he'd been holding, and glanced in some fear from me to Lucas and back.

"Doctor—Dr. Jones," he finally blurted out. "What in the hell was *that*?"

"Hey!" Lucas called to him. "*Mouth*, dumb-ass, especially when you're talking about the cheetah. And she just showed she likes you, shit-for-brains." Lucas' tone was not mean, but a routine form of address; and he demonstrated his point by approaching Marcianna and stroking her head, which kept her purring. "What's so weird about that? First time I really spent any time with her, she dragged me around like a deer carcass—I told you that, too, remember?"

Mike and I exchanged a quick look: this was our first hint that Lucas had been sharing details of his experiences at Shiloh with Derek—and we would need to talk to him about it. Yet Marcianna's reaction to the bigger boy had also convinced me that there was no danger to be feared from him, no angry tempestuous fits such as one often finds even in the mildly autistic; and so I was not overly concerned.

"Yeah, I know you told me that, Luke," Derek replied, at which Lucas rolled his eyes in frustration, one of his fists balling up; but he did not move from Marcianna's side. "But you never told me I might get jumped on and licked all over my face!"

"Don't sweat it, Derek," Mike said, wisely moving to block Derek's ability to see Marcianna, which calmed the young man. "It's better than the alternative, I can tell you that."

Just then, a voice drifted out of whatever room lay beyond a screen door in the back wall of the house above the low wooden patio: "Hey! What's all this about getting your face licked by the cheetah—is she here? Don't you two morons go getting her all tired out, I'm going to want *my* face licked, too!"

There was nothing remotely girlish about the timbre of the voice itself—it clearly indicated a woman—but at the same time, some of the inflections were very youthful, making it equally plain that the speaker was a *young* woman: which meant, almost certainly, Ambyr Kurtz.

"That's my sister," Lucas confirmed, his voice low. "She's been making tea and some weird little cakes for you guys. She thinks that because you come from New York City that's what you do every afternoon. I told her that was bullshit, but she wanted to do it."

"You mean she's in there working at a stove—alone?" I said, somewhat concerned and glancing up from Marcianna to the kid. "I mean, can she—well, does she need any help?"

I still had my back to the house when I heard the old steel spring of the screen door creak as it stretched; and as soon as it did, I felt a sharp slapping at my cane arm. It was an alert signal that I knew Mike to use only in certain situations: if someone was holding a gun on us, if he'd discovered a body in an unlikely place, or . . .

"Dude," Mike whispered. "Trajan—*dude*. You're, uh—you're gonna want to turn the fuck around. Right the fuck *now* . . ."

I did as I was instructed; and it is no great exaggeration to say that from that moment forward, neither my own life nor the path of the investigation we had undertaken would ever be the same.

{iv.}

"Don't worry, Dr. Jones," the same voice said pleasantly, as its speaker let the screen door close behind her. "I can handle myself in the kitchen. It *was* Dr. Jones who asked that question, wasn't it? I told Lucas to explain the differences in the sounds of your voices, so that I wouldn't get them wrong—although, if you screwed me around on that, Lucas, you are going to *pay.*"

Her manner and speech were so self-possessed that at first I didn't notice the very light white cane that she held between the fingers and thumb of her right hand. Nor did I immediately notice the very slight glaze that covered her violet eyes—and they *were* violet, although I'd always doubted the existence of such coloring. But now I observed that it was real—and, along with my partner, I observed a great deal more. Surprisingly, she was tall; I don't know why I should have *been* surprised, except that I had only ever extrapolated from Lucas, forgetting his age, and somehow thought of her as about his size. But she stood a slender yet still shapely five foot eight or more, and her hair—the same sandy color as Lucas', but falling in long, natural waves to the middle of her back—accentuated this stature. As for her face—that was where one found the subtlety that prevented the kind of outright lasciviousness that I knew Mike was just dying to embody with a knowing look or crass aside to me. Beneath that unseeing yet strangely knowing gaze sat a mischievous, diminutive nose, whereas the full-lipped, expressive mouth, like the eyes, bespoke experience and wisdom beyond her years. She was the kind of woman who, at any age, one found both very attractive but a little too perspicacious to approach forwardly. Even Mike, after his initial swatting at my arm, appeared to straighten up—almost as if Ambyr could see what he was doing.

"Yes, that was me, Miss Kurtz," I said, stepping onto the patio and moving closer to her, after the initial shock of her appearance had taken its few seconds' toll. "I hope you didn't think it was intended as an insult."

"Ha!" Lucas laughed, bounding along at my side. "'Miss Kurtz,' I like *that!*"

And then came the first display of how finely tuned Ambyr's other senses had become after she'd lost her sight: with a quick movement made easier by the fact that her light cotton summer dress had little above the waist to restrict her arms, she located Lucas by sound and caught him on the upper arm with her cane—a precise shot that, while not serious, must have smarted.

"And what's wrong with 'Miss Kurtz,' you?" she said, not harshly, but with sisterly purpose. "Even though—" She switched her cane to her left hand and held out her right toward me. "—you *can* go ahead and call me Ambyr, Doctor. Please."

"All right," I said, taking her hand briefly. "Ambyr, my name's Trajan, and let me introduce my colleague, Dr. Michael Li, who, I assure you, will be happy if you call him anything at all."

"Funny stuff, *gweilo*," Mike mumbled, stepping up onto the patio. "Just call me Mike, Ambyr, everybody else does. I doubt anybody in this town even *knows* I'm a doctor."

"Okay, Mike," Ambyr answered, smiling a little wider; and then she turned toward Lucas again. "And you, my smart-ass brother, can go inside and get the tray—which does *not* have any hot tea or 'weird little cakes' on it. Not in weather like this, because I'm not that dumb. Iced tea, lemonade, and fresh ginger cookies are what we've got. I hope that's okay with you both?" Mike and I mumbled assent quickly. "I don't keep any beer or alcohol in the house, because Dumb and Dumber would drink it all as soon as I bought it."

"Oh, right!" Lucas said, stomping toward the screen door. "And I suppose keeping the house alcohol-free *wasn't* one of the rules for you being our guardian, Ambyr." But the mere indication that she was moving the cane back to her right hand made Lucas quickly open the screen door, get inside, and pull the thing closed again. *"Baaah!"* he called. "Too slow on that one, sis!"

"If I ever seem too slow to catch your gawky butt," Ambyr laughed, once more revealing the same taste for good-natured banter that Lucas possessed, "you can bet I'm not really trying."

"Yeah, right," Lucas scoffed. "Come on, Derek, help me carry this shit out to the table, or do I have to send you an engraved invitation?"

As Derek complied with Lucas' order, Ambyr moved closer to me, by small, deliberate steps. I wasn't sure what was going on, and glanced quickly over to Mike, who shrugged even as he let a sly grin come into his face: he knew that I was growing increasingly uncomfortable because of a very pretty young woman being close. Finally, when Ambyr was just about half an arm's reach from me, she held up her hands.

"Do you mind, Dr. Jones?" She moved the hands closer to my face. "I'd kind of like to know what the face of the man who lives with a cheetah actually looks like."

"Oh," I said, rather simply; and as I realized that she intended to get the feel of my features, I finally added: "I mean, of course. But I thought that was an old wives' tale about blind people."

"Not *this* blind person." Ambyr moved a little closer, and then, hearing a small animal grunt come from below her, asked, "Will Marcianna mind? Lucas says she's tame, but I'm with you, on that subject—I think there's a part of wild animals that can never really *be* tamed."

Which was yet another indication that Lucas was doing a lot of talking at home about what went on up at Shiloh; I really would have to read him the riot act.

"She appears to be fine," I said, glancing down at Marcianna, who in fact seemed somewhat agitated, rarely having seen any stranger—and certainly not any female, save my great-aunt—in such close proximity to me. "But maybe you want to meet her, before me. Put her at her ease."

There would be many moments in the days to come when I simply could not believe that Ambyr Kurtz was actually blind, so knowing were the glances that those dead violet eyes turned on me. This time, they seemed to say that she knew exactly what I was up to, just how uneasy I was with her physical scrutiny; and as she smiled coyly, she said, "Okay. If that's what you think's the best way to go."

"Oh, he does, Ambyr," Mike threw in. "Believe me."

Ambyr smiled in a different way at this crack: still knowingly, but with affectionate familiarity. "Yeah, I can see why Lucas likes *you* so much, Mike," she said, without turning to him. "You guys have exactly the same sense of humor."

"Well," Mike said defensively, "I like to think mine's a *little* more developed."

Ambyr only shook her head as she started to bend down to where she heard Marcianna panting. "You can think it," she said, softly and simply. I turned to see Mike looking rather shocked, then leaned down to join our hostess.

"If you'll just put one hand under her muzzle, Ambyr, and let her get your scent, then she can start to get used to you." Without my giving her any more direction, Ambyr located just the right spot to place her left hand. Then she began to murmur softly:

"Well, hey, Marcianna . . . My name's Ambyr, and I've been waiting a long while to meet somebody like you. Did you know that?" As Marcianna registered no complaint, Ambyr inclined her head up to me. "She seems okay—do you think I can go ahead and pet her head?"

"Try her neck and chest, first," I said. "Just so she's sure you don't intend any mischief. If that's okay, then sure, move to her shoulders and her head. I've got a pretty good grip on her."

Repeating various soothing phrases softly, Ambyr completed this ritual, her sense of wonder undiminished. Marcianna bore it very well,
which I was glad to see; because frankly, I really hadn't been quite certain
of how she would react. The pheromones of a young woman were still
new to her; yet having seen her accept Gracie only forty-eight hours earlier, I believed I was on fairly safe ground with Ambyr. The combination
of a new location and a new type of person did confuse Marcianna a little; but she had seen an awful lot of the bad in people, early in her life,
and then the other side during the last five years at Shiloh, and she
seemed to be able to tell that this was not a situation she needed to fear.
Ambyr, for her part, displayed little variation in either her words or her
expression—until, as she was stroking my companion's head and left
shoulder, Marcianna turned suddenly to allow her access to the rich,
deep fur of her back and flank. Into this, Ambyr's delicate hand disappeared almost completely—and she gasped, in a way that was utterly
awed, very affectionate, and completely charming.

"So amazing . . ." Ambyr said quietly. "I've never . . ." Then, daring perhaps more than she should, she put her cheek to Marcianna's shoulder;
but, realizing she hadn't cleared it with me, she pulled back for a moment
and asked, "Is that okay?"

"Hey, you seem to be doing just fine," I said. "Better than I did, when I
first met her."

"Yes, but . . ." Ambyr waited to complete her statement until she had
first satisfied her desire to feel Marcianna's warm fur on her face, and
then withdrew her head again to say, "But you first met her when she was
in that horrible damned place, that 'petting zoo'—which I hated, by the
way. Lucas used to make our folks take us there, but it was obvious that it
was just a moneymaking nightmare, that the guy and his people didn't
give a damn about the animals. I was really glad when Lucas said you
were the one who got it shut down."

Her awareness of things that I had shared with her brother was now
not only obvious but expansive; and it probably should have concerned
me even more than it did, just then. But this one fact was so harmless,
and I was so flattered and thankful to meet someone who actually appreciated why Mitch McCarron and I had put an end to the petting zoo,
that I paid it no mind. "It wasn't just me," I said. "But I guess I was pretty
much the one who pushed it hardest." The words sounded dumb enough
to me when I said them; but it wasn't until I looked at Mike and saw him

curl his finger, stick it inside his cheek, and yank hard, imitating a hooked fish, that I realized I was being a little obvious, myself. "Anyway," I concluded, ignoring my partner, "we did get it shut down, and that's the important thing."

"Yes, you did," Ambyr said, stroking the top of Marcianna's head once or twice, and then standing to turn to me again. "So—do I get to see what *you* look like now, or not?"

"Oh," I replied, once again uneasily—for I thought that maybe I'd dodged this part of the meeting. "Sure, of course. I guess."

The boyish silliness of my words made Mike put his hands on his knees and bend down to breathe in, deeply and quickly, in order to keep from laughing out loud; but he hadn't counted on that extraordinary hearing of Ambyr Kurtz's, and when her hands were about to touch my face, she said, "Careful, Dr. Li—*Mike*. I might ask to see what *you* look like, next . . ."

At which Mike suddenly straightened up, looking almost as apprehensive as I felt. "Oh," he mumbled. "I don't look very interesting, really."

"Well, then—let's see about Trajan, here . . ."

The first touch of those thin-wristed, elegant hands was not coy or flirtatious, but rather directly probing: softly, but with the genuine purpose of discovering what my features resembled. Their intent, however, could not halt my reaction. It had been a very, very long time since I'd come into contact with a human female (excluding my great-aunt) in so close, even intimate, a way. And it wasn't simply the contact. As I say, the light blue dress she was wearing—standard summer issue from any Walmart or Target store—covered very little of her upper body, coming up in a simple sweep from a mid-thigh-length skirt to conceal her chest and then turning into two negligible, crossing spaghetti straps that were the sole covering of her back and shoulders: and from all her exposed areas of skin came the mixed aromas of light perspiration and a gently scented soap. The cumulative effect of touch and scent meant that for the first time since the radiation treatment six months before, which I had thought might have killed off my ability to experience such things forever, I felt a stirring: not blatantly sexual, it was rather a simple suggestion that the physical side of my life might not, in fact, have been shut down forever. As her fingers moved from my forehead and eyes slowly down to my nose, delicately seeking out each detail, then circled both ears on their way to and along the jawline, I found that I could not look for long into that violet gaze, blind though it might be: pure self-consciousness and insecurity wouldn't allow it. There was no way in which I could turn, however, without catching sight of Mike, who I knew must be reveling in the situation once again; and so, as Ambyr's fingers reached along my cheeks to my mouth, I simply closed my eyes—

But when her fingertips found my mouth, I cannot deny, a sudden shudder went down my spine. It was thrilling, yes; but it was also, in some way that is difficult to describe, a little frightening, and as I felt it my eyes suddenly popped back open and my head snapped instinctively back, a movement that made Ambyr chuckle.

"Don't worry, Trajan," she said. "I'm done. And Lucas was right—you've got a nice face."

"When the hell did I ever say *that,* sis?" Lucas said, coming out of the house through the screen door. Derek followed behind, doing the work, predictably, of carrying a heavy tray that bore a pitcher each of iced tea and lemonade. "Alls I said was, he ain't ugly enough to turn you to stone."

"Stop it," Ambyr scolded gently. "That's not what you said, Lucas—don't worry so much about acting like a human being, every now and then."

"O-*kay,*" Lucas replied airily. "But you might regret saying that, some-day. Where do you want the stuff?"

"Bring it this way, Derek," Ambyr answered, knowing full well which one of the boys was pulling the laboring oar, and finding the edge of the patio easily with her cane. Then she stepped down onto the lawn and pointed with the slender white stick. "Let's put it on the table, but let's make sure the table's in the shade, first. The chairs, too." She glanced back toward me as she led Derek away, a peculiar move: she couldn't actually see my reaction, after all. Was it for *my* benefit, then? Nothing else seemed possible. "I hear you get uncomfortable very fast, with your leg and all, Trajan," she said, smiling. "So we'll get you one of the big chairs, and keep it out from the table, in case you want to get up and pace around . . ."

That was it. Before Lucas could follow the other members of his un-usual little family, I horse-collared him by his T-shirt and yanked him back to where Mike and I were standing. "All right, you," I murmured, trying to regain my full composure. "Is there anything about life up the hollow that you *haven't* told your sister-mother and your friend-brother, you little worm? I warned you about security, Lucas, damn it."

"Hey, I didn't let on about the *case,* don't worry," Lucas answered, fully in control, as he shook free of my grip. "But I had to give them some kind of information, or they would have gotten suspicious. So I told them details that don't matter." Straightening out his shirt, he added, "Jesus H. Christ, what the fuck has got into *you*, Doc?"

"Something that's long overdue, kid," Mike answered with a smile. "So don't give him too hard a time about it."

Glancing from Mike back to me, Lucas finally declared: "Fuck you, Mike. No way. L.T.'s got a thing for *my sister*?"

Mike tilted his head judiciously. "Well—let's just say that the last time I saw him act like such a sap in front of a good-looking woman, he ended up going out with her for three years." He paused for an instant, almost not sure how mischievous to be; but then he just blurted it out: "And she ended up in a mental hospital."

"The last part of which had nothing to do with me, Michael," I seethed quietly. "As well you know. And I am not being a sap."

But neither of them, of course, was going to listen to a thing I said.

"So—the doc's got a thing for Ambyr . . ." Lucas mused; and it occurred to me again that he was neither as surprised nor as outraged as I would have expected him to be, given how protective of her good name he'd always been. "Well, Doc," he decided at length, "she ain't got no boyfriend—and she *is* blind, which at least gives you a shot."

He tried to bound away, with that crack, but I snagged him again with my cane hand, making him groan for the fate of his T-shirt. "Really, Lucas?" I said, trying to affect a severity that I did not feel. "Blind jokes about your sister—from *you*?"

"Hey," he answered, flailing his arms. "*I* can make 'em, *you* can't. Now let me go, damn it, this is my last clean T-shirt!"

"I don't doubt that," I finally said, releasing him to take off across the lawn. Marcianna strained to join him, wanting to play; but I held her back, stepping off the patio. Mike moved with me, his smile becoming a shit-eating grin. "Come on, Mike," I preempted. "I'm almost twice her age."

"So what?" Mike said. "She's twenty, not fourteen. You've been waiting a long time for something like this, L.T.; I say go for it."

"Of course you say go for it, Li," I answered, still tightly controlling my volume and speaking toward the house. "You've never met a good-looking woman that you *didn't* say that about."

"Only because, generally speaking, it's true," Mike chuckled, as we started to walk toward the big, heavy picnic table, which Derek was maneuvering into the shade as if it weighed very little.

The first part of that late afternoon passed pleasantly enough, Ambyr presiding with extraordinary competence and, when it came to lifting the fat pitchers of lemonade and iced tea, surprising strength and ease. But when the refreshments had all been consumed, Derek and Lucas became increasingly restless, starting something out on the grass that looked to develop into another round of MMA fighting. Ambyr had heard this coming, however, and suggested that, if they couldn't control themselves while the adults talked, they should at least turn their energies toward something that might not get them both injured. There was on old basketball on the ground, and an equally old hoop hanging from the side of the garage above a bare patch of dirt, and she swung her light white can to indicate it.

"Now you're speaking my language," Mike announced, clearly sensing that I wanted time to draw Ambyr out minus the presence of the two boys. "Come on, you pair of losers—think you're up to taking on one old criminologist?"

Derek and Lucas responded in a shot, dashing over, seizing the basketball, and showing quickly that they were both adept at using it. "Trash, trash, trash, Mike," Lucas said. "You can talk it, all right—let's see how you walk it. We'll even spot you some points."

Mike grinned, though part of him clearly took the kid's words to heart. "Yeah," he said, "We'll see, Mr. Mouth."

I took a couple of steps after him, enough to be able to say, without being overheard, "Good idea. I'm going to take Marcianna on a walk someplace with Ambyr. See what she's got for us."

Knowing he was safe, he leered at me. "Oh, I think we *know* what she's got—at least for *you*," he chuckled. "The question is, can she help on this *case*?"

"Fuck off, Li," I said, trying not to sound too self-conscious. "I just want to calm Marcianna down and—"

"Yeah," Mike said, moving off again with another laugh. "*And.* You are so dead, L.T. So. Fucking. *Dead . . .*"

With that Mike moved to the little basketball court, and I walked back to the table.

"You sure you don't want to join them?" Ambyr asked. "They can get a little out of hand, two-on-one, and I used to be a pretty good JV player before I got sick. I can still dribble and shoot, too, just by feel and sound. Together we ought to make one decent player."

There was nothing like mocking or teasing in her tone; far from it, had I not known better I would have taken it for flirtation. "No, not me," I said. "Not anymore. Once upon a time, but these days . . ." I tried to shake off the sad thought. "Anyway, Ambyr, I need to take Marcianna somewhere fairly discreet, give her a chance to poke around, or she's liable to go crazy trying to join the game. Do you have a spot?"

"Yeah, sure," she answered, quickly getting to her feet and pointing off to her right, toward the earthen embankment at the rear of the yard, where a small path led up through some trees. "One of Morgan Central's practice fields is up there. Nobody will see us."

"Ideal," I said. "Shall we go, then?"

Ambyr nodded happily, and then, as I let Marcianna have a little more lead, locked her left arm with somewhat startling suddenness around my right. Thus did we begin the climb to the most remote of the school's playing fields, which seemed to grow in number every year, in direct proportion to the collapse of the students' basic competency levels.

It was on this hidden field, onto which I had a great deal of trouble not loosing Marcianna, that I would learn Ambyr Kurtz's full, terrible story. And by the time it was all over, I very much feared that Mike had been right: in a variety of ways, I was indeed a dead man.

CHAPTER THREE

SOMETHING INGENIOUS, SOMETHING INGENUOUS

{i.}

She had been a voracious reader and an avid student from as far back as she could remember, she said, and this, combined with having a pair of verbally abusive parents—the kind that had made Lucas such a smart-ass, and that will either silence children or make them learn linguistic sparring as a means of defense and psychological survival—had apparently been responsible for her possessing, like her brother, such sharp conversational skills. But because of her also being a protective older sibling, she had what Lucas did not: that eerie sense of awareness, of understanding not only language but the motives of the people who spoke it.

She had also been heavy, in early adolescence; and by the time she was thirteen, her heaviness had joined her bookishness to make Ambyr the object of great derision. Such kids do not tend to become athletes, ordinarily, but Ambyr had been unable to withstand the pressure, and used her sprouting height in tandem with her weight to become an effective center for the girls' JV basketball team. In an earlier era, the mockery might have stopped there, for Burgoyne County had once been full of heavy, even obese adolescent girls. But Ambyr had had the terrible misfortune of growing up in the age of the Internet. And under the influence of this "leveling" technology, American girls in villages far removed from anything that could reasonably be called a cosmopolitan atmosphere had nonetheless begun to model their bodies on what they saw, not only in the occasional magazine or television show, but on the nearly constant input that they received on their computers and phones, both at home and at school.

"I'm not sure any guy can ever really understand the difference," Ambyr said to me, as we made our way around the rough border of the practice field, both of our canes seeking out safe spots in the close-clipped lawn of the soccer pitch.

"No," I answered quietly. "I'm not sure any of us can."

"I mean, the Internet, it's *everywhere*," she went on, trying to maintain her good-humored detachment, but not quite able to do so; not on this subject. "We were all supposed to have our learning rates sped up by having computers in our classrooms, but half the time the kids were just online. And even when they tried to take access away a few times, the phones were there. So, one way or the other, we always had access. And the bad stuff got to be pretty constant: we didn't even need the God damned stuff in print and on TV—computers at home, computers at school, phones all over . . . We just got lost in it all. Some girls were figuring out ways to get skinnier and hotter, and some girls were giving up and just getting heavier and vanishing into fantasy lands where they could become some made-up creature or create a superhot avatar—and they took endless shit for *that,* on top of being overweight, and took it *on* the damned Web, because half the hot girls and boys started blogging and chatting about looks, weight, sex, who was in and who was—*out* . . ." She paused. "Sorry, Doctor. I know my language isn't exactly polite, sometimes."

"Then you'd be right at home among our merry band," I said, already prepared to include her, if only informally, in the group. Indeed, I was instinctively certain that her participation would prove, in one way or another, vital to the solution of the case; for even more than Lucas, she had her hand on the pulse of Surrender. That—and more . . .

Ambyr quickly turned the violet eyes—partially shaded, as ever, behind a slight opacity—up and toward my own gaze. "Really?" she said, with an alluring sort of anxiousness that was surprising, to say nothing of arresting. "I was hoping you were going to say something like that. I mean, I don't want you to be mad at Lucas, but—you know how excited he's been, to be part of what you're doing, and he and Derek and I have always been really close, so it's been hard for him to keep all of it to himself. And I have to tell you, if what you're doing really will help make sure that those dead kids get justice, then I'll do whatever I can to help, too. If you'll let me, I mean."

"Well," I answered after taking a moment with it, "I'll talk it over with

Mike, and we'll tell you if and how you might fit in. Which I believe you will."

"Good," she answered happily. "Although I really could understand, with what happened in Fraser, and to Dr. Chang and all—not to mention with how things work, or *don't* work, in this town and this county—why you wouldn't be too anxious to include anybody else in on what you're doing. But—well, I don't guess it would do any good for me to tell you that you can trust me not to reveal anything. See"—and again the eyes seemed to meet mine, while her voice became scarcely more than a breathy whisper—"I've learned an awful lot about the damage that people can do with just careless talk. So I know. Oh, I know . . ."

"Indeed?" I answered. "Well, suppose you start by telling me *about* all those big, careless mouths around here. If you're okay with it."

"Sure. Just so long as you believe that I really *do* understand what you're trying to do—I mean, the importance of it. You're the only hope those kids have *got* for justice, you know that, right? Jesus Christ, so many people have gotten away with murder in this county—people I've even *known*—because of lost evidence, evidence that wasn't collected the right way, juries that didn't believe eyewitnesses because the prosecutors didn't have the kind of scientific evidence that they see on *CSI* and those shows . . . unbelievable."

"It's not, Ambyr," I answered. "There have been so many cases where juries have done exactly the same thing, all over the country . . . It's outrageous, but not shocking."

"Hmm," she noised, taking in that fact. "Can you really get to a point where you're not shocked by stuff like that? I wonder. Of course—" And then she smiled in that very coy way, again halting our progress to turn up to me. "If you're the famous Sorcerer of Death, maybe you can."

Sighing and blushing, I said softly, "I am really going to skewer that brother of yours . . ."

That made her laugh quietly, and place her cane hand on mine. "Oh, no, don't, please, Trajan—I *love* that story, I love the whole idea of it—and Lucas is really so impressed by it, you'd crush him if you said anything. And who can blame him? There's a lot of—*romance* in it."

"Romance?" I scoffed lightly. "That's about the last thing you'd expect to hear, in connection with the New York tabloids."

"Maybe. But it's true." She turned so that we could continue on our way around the field. "*Anyway,*" she said, again using the word in just the manner that Lucas did, "there's just been too many times that people have gotten away with murder in Burgoyne County, all because nobody really gives a shit what happens in towns like Surrender. And I don't want to see that happen with this case. It's so important that it doesn't; so if there's any chance that you guys can finally shine some kind of a light on this throwaway-children business—" Her grip on my arm became tighter. "I don't know if you can really understand how important that would be. What you'd be doing for so many kids who've had to live through it. See, I've been looking after Derek and Lucas for a long time, now, really since way before our parents disappeared, and I think about what would've happened to them if I hadn't been here—or if I suddenly wasn't around. Who knows but that they wouldn't have gone in exactly the same direction as Shelby and the others did. So I get mad, and scared, too, and just plain sad—sad for those kids. So this time, I want the people who are responsible to get caught. That's all."

"That's all?" I said, my conviction that she was necessary to keep close to our effort again drifting, as it so often would, dangerously close to something else. "That's quite a bit. I mean, from what I understand, taking care of Lucas and Derek wasn't your idea."

She shook her head hard. "No, it was *not*. Not that I don't love them both, pains in the ass that they are. No, if it had been up to me . . . But it wasn't. Things were just the way they were."

The use of the past tense, I remember thinking; *has she simply grown used to the burden, or . . .* "Yes," I answered, as I gave Marcianna—who had made the walk quietly, thus far, but was now checking the playing field for woodchuck and mole holes—a little more lead. "But suppose you tell me how your situation came to be. It might help, you know."

She laughed again, without the sad edge, this time. "Are you offering to be my shrink, Trajan?"

"No," I chuckled. "But, even though I've gotten a rough idea from Lucas about what happened with your parents, it would help to know more about the—*mechanics* of one throwaway case. Also, I don't want you to think that Lucas has talked about the actual *cause* of your illness— about that, your brother is very careful."

That brought an affectionate smile to Ambyr's face, as she looked to the ground: *Out of habit?* I wondered. "Yeah, even my brother knows where to draw the line, I guess. And it's not a really new or interesting story. People just think it is, because I went blind." She took a deep, ambiguous breath, then glanced about the soccer pitch as if she could still see it all. "Yeah, when I went blind, look out . . . All these people suddenly thought I was so interesting, so perceptive about life. But the whole thing really isn't that fascinating—people just need to believe it is, because of what happened. Isn't there a name for that, in your part of the world?"

"It has a lot of names, in psychology and philosophy," I answered. "But basically, yes, it's the principle that says people need to believe that momentous events have momentous causes. It's a logical fallacy, one of the very biggest."

"That's all I'm saying," Ambyr concluded, very satisfied. "But you see for yourself if I'm wrong: you want to know what happened, and I'll tell you—and you can decide if it was really such a strange or unique story. Deal?"

I murmured some vague sort of assent, and she began; and before long, as she proceeded to tick off the bare facts of her tragedy in a very captivating if somewhat weary way, I had to admit that she was right: it wasn't a terribly new story, although it was indeed awful in its degree and consequences. The torment of her schoolmates, which had been merely heartbreaking in junior high school, had become unendurable in senior high. It wasn't hard to see why: as she had already intimated, the drastically increased array of weapons—cell phones, instant messaging, e-mail, YouTube, Photoshop, Facebook, Twitter, and all the other marvelous weapons that information technology has put at the disposal of the young and vicious—had so revolutionized the kind of cruel jokes that were once merely verbal and slow-spreading that they could now be given vivid form, phrasing, and even animation, in a matter of minutes or hours. In my own youth, I had discovered that not even the magic word *cancer* could stop the cruelty of many such excuses for children; what they could and would have done to my spirit had they possessed such diabolical tools, I cannot say.

But for Ambyr, the solution had been horribly simple: she had stopped eating. Or, on those rare occasions when she could not get out of stuffing food down her throat, she had become expert at immediately excusing herself, finding the nearest bathroom, and vomiting it all back up. The weight that had been, in her young mind, the source of all her unhappiness began to come quickly off, given this combined program of anorexia and bulimia; but before she had a chance to enjoy her different appearance, she discovered that what had seemed a reasonable reaction to her lifelong predicament was in fact a compulsion—or, to use an applicable term that I have already employed in other contexts, she found that she had developed a *cognitive bias* that no longer allowed her to see her image in a mirror in anything like accurate terms. She could never be thin enough; and she simply could not stop starving herself.

It had been Lucas who had first realized what was happening, and who was the first to tell both the school nurse and his parents that Ambyr was sick; but not even her collapse on the floor of the school gymnasium one day had made them believe him. The physical education instructor, Mr. Holloway—whose name I vividly recalled because of his willingness to sexually exploit fourteen-year-old Shelby Capamagio—had of course attributed the collapse to overexertion. And this kind of stupidity had also meant that, after she awoke from that first episode, neither Holloway nor any of the crack health team at Morgan Central had realized that if the girl fainted in like manner a second time she might never wake up.

As, in the event, she very nearly had not. Her blood sugar had crashed through the floor as she sweated listlessly through a subsequent basketball practice, experiencing typical forms of auditory and visual hallucinations that had made her teammates, along with Mr. Holloway, believe that she might be possessed; and she had quickly entered a nondiabetic hypoglycemic coma that the doctors at Fraser's small medical center had been almost powerless to counteract. Yet Ambyr had clung to life with what she had been able to identify, even in her deep state of unconsciousness, as determination: determination, above all, not to allow the younger brother who came to see her on every one of the five days that her coma lasted (and one can only imagine the contrivances through which Lucas had managed that feat), and whose was the only voice to which her body showed any sort of even minimal response during that time, to be abandoned to their parents' and their school's tender mercies. When she finally did awake, it was to the crushing news that she had lost her sight (her optic neurotransmitters had apparently been degraded past recovery, an infrequent but very established reaction to anorexic collapse); and once again Lucas had been the only person who had seemed able to offer her any consolation, during those first few weeks, when things like learning to walk with a cane and read Braille had become unavoidable.

The conclusion of Ambyr's tale saw her brought home to begin life anew with a private tutor, paid for, as were all her subsequent special needs, by the state, which doubtless thought itself lucky to get off without a lawsuit, being as Ambyr had collapsed in a public school that had had ample reason to think that she might be in real danger. But the epilogue to her saga was perhaps the most horrifying part: for it was the story of just how the Kurtz and the Franco parents had not only made their escape to sunnier climes, but had managed to ensure that Ambyr assumed complete legal responsibility for everything they left behind: the house, the boys, and all that went with them.

"They were clever," Ambyr told me, in a voice that indicated that she'd had time to absorb the experience pretty fully and gain some, if not complete, perspective. "They managed to keep me out of all the court proceedings, by getting their shitbag lawyer to plead that it was too soon after my 'ordeal' for me to be there—and when the judge asked if someone who'd been through an ordeal like that really wanted to assume legal responsibility for two boys, the lawyer told him that it was just a financial thing; just a way for my folks to avoid being any more liable than they already were for the debts they'd run up, so they could be sure to be able to take care of me. But what sealed it was that they all told the judge that I was perfectly happy to go along with the whole thing, and then gave him a signed affidavit of mine that said so—the only problem being that, at the time when I signed it, I thought I was finishing an application for a program for the visually impaired over at the Disability Center in Fraser."

"Yes, I know the place," I said. "And I have to say, that was particularly cruel of them—it would have been a good place for you to begin to adjust."

"It *has* been," Ambyr said. "After our folks disappeared, my cousin Caitlin and her dad kind of strong-armed the state into getting me in, on a non-boarding basis, and even into paying for a driver to take me there and back every day. But it was the stipend that *really* helped—they offered a pretty fair amount of money per month for me to use to take care of the boys, and at that point, Caitlin, her dad—that's my uncle Bass—and me just said the hell with it. Best to get on with the rest of life, whatever it's going to be."

I studied her apparently placid countenance carefully. "That's a pretty philosophical attitude to take, for someone in your position, and at your age."

"I guess," she answered evenly. "But I'd been taking care of the boys, even when our folks were around, for so long that it all seemed to fall into place pretty naturally, once we knew we wouldn't have to worry about money too much. Though you paying Lucas to make up for the farm work he usually does this time of the year is really going to help, and I wanted to thank you for that, Trajan."

"It's—only fair," I said, suddenly and strangely self-conscious. "I only wish I could offer more. But I fear that we are teachers, now, not paid police or legal consultants—"

"Hey, don't sell it short," Ambyr rushed in to say. "It's a huge help. And the state people have been really good about everything, about making sure we get what we're supposed to get on time. And then there's Caitlin, and Bass, and even some family people that I never knew about—they've helped out a lot. Yeah, everybody's been really nice to the blind girl . . ." Her voice trailed off for a moment, until she seemed to shake herself, after which she turned her head up toward mine and smiled in a mischievous way. "At least nobody's made any nasty cracks about me making ends meet by working in something like *porn*. That is, nobody *had* mentioned it—*before* . . ."

I stopped dead in my tracks, causing Marcianna to glance my way. "Aw, Jesus," I said. "They didn't tell you *that* part of the story."

"Of course!" Ambyr answered. "They were under orders to tell me every part of the story, once they got back."

It was a striking statement. "Hang on," I said. " 'Once they got back'?" My forward steps resumed, but more slowly. "You said, 'They were under orders to tell me every part of the story, *once they got back*.' "

She actually seemed pleased by this. "Yep. I did."

"But that means—that means that you *knew* they were coming up the hollow . . ."

"*Knew?*" she said, letting her head fall backward and laughing very freely, now. "Come on, Trajan—are you really trying to say that the Sorcerer of Death hasn't figured it out by now? That would be very disappointing. I mean, it's pretty obvious: I *sent* them up the hollow, that day . . ."

I was surprised, though not stunned; for it was, to me, only further confirmation that we needed to keep Ambyr involved. "Not that they hadn't been itching to go for a long time," she continued, "but I'd always told them in no uncertain terms to respect your privacy. Those stories, though! About the freak with the bizarre kind of dog, they just kept building up in their brains; and finally, when there was a good reason for them to go, I agreed to it. I did tell them to argue and beg if you threatened to get in touch with me, just to make it look good. But see, I'd heard that you'd worked for the sheriff's office on a couple of murder cases, and I knew that nobody around *here* was going to solve these latest ones on their own. So I told Lucas to keep an eye out, and let me know if he happened to see Pete Steinbrecher's car go up the hollow—which, of course, it did, after Shelby's body was found, and Lucas just *happened* to see it go. Lights flashing, but no siren: that meant one thing—it was headed for Shiloh. And, like I say, *this* case, these cases, they matter to me. So I told the boys to go on up the hollow, not that they needed much encouragement. They were dying to do it—at least they *were*, until they saw your lady friend, there." She cast an indicative hand toward Marcianna. "But even then, they kept at it—they stuck to the job of trying to find out if you were working on the case. And it's all turned out better than I ever thought it could . . ."

Obviously, the entire Kurtz family had a genius for deception: honestly come by, of course, but nonetheless honed. I took a moment to go back over Lucas' various protests about not wanting his sister to know he'd been caught trespassing in Death's Head Hollow, about keeping her from knowing that he was working on the case with Mike and me, and about the need to explain his presence on the case to her: it had all been revealed as a performance, and that initial fact caused me to murmur reflexively, "Why, that little shithead—I am going to take this right out of his hide . . ."

"No, you're not," Ambyr answered, indulgently and calmly, as though she had expected some such statement. "In fact, you're not even going to tell him I told you. Come on, Trajan, what's it matter? Now I'll be a part of the investigation, too, so everything'll be on the level. That is . . ." She stopped my forward progress, moved around in front of me, and turned those obscured violet eyes up to my face again, her voice becoming an odd mixture of pleading and something I cannot call anything but alluring. "That is, if you've decided that you *can* let me be a part of it, Trajan."

It was a peculiar moment, dominated by a sudden thought—a question, really: here was a girl who had known herself as both over- and underweight, but probably had never had any true idea of how she looked when she was neither one nor the other, but was something in between, something like the very healthy, very pretty young woman before me. Her eating disorders would have prevented her ability to so perceive herself, constantly telling her that she was still too heavy: that was how she'd been dragged into the dangers of emaciation. And yet she now seemed to handle herself with extraordinary confidence, and, more, with a full appreciation of the effect that her present looks had on the opposite sex, even though she had never, herself, observed those looks.

I wasn't going to resolve this dichotomy right there, and so it didn't occupy my mind for very long. Rather, I again became preoccupied by the almost-forgotten feeling that I was not yet entirely dead to something vital: call it infatuation, call it romance, call it what you like. Such sensations, as I have indicated, had been dormant in me pretty much since Mike and I had moved upstate and I had been forced to once again endure occasional radiation treatments. My oncologist had warned that a recurrence of my sarcoma was likely on its way and we would want to treat it early, but that there might be a—*price* to pay, which indeed there had been. But I did not feel any signs of such sickness just then, as I gazed into Ambyr's face, and saw the look of both happiness and flirtation that occupied it. No, in that frame of mind I merely replied:

"Yeah, I can't see any reason why you shouldn't be. I was going to invite both you and Derek, along with your little beast-brother, to dinner at my great-aunt's tonight, anyway—I guess you could get an idea of what we're doing then, if you can make it."

Ambyr's look of happiness bled over into excited joy: "Dinner with Miss Clarissa Jones?" And with that she pulled me forward, realizing (apparently) that we had made the third turn in our route and were now moving along toward the path that led back down to the backyard of their house. "You bet your ass I'm coming! Trajan—this is all going to be a really good thing. But you have to remember—" And she stopped me one more time. "The rest is going to be our secret, yours and mine. You can't let the boys know—especially Lucas, it would kill him. Because he really has come to look up to you so much, and he'd hate it if he knew I let on that your original meeting with him was, well . . . *designed*. And you guys have worked well together, from all I hear—so let's make sure we keep it to ourselves, okay?"

I'd been played, or so Ambyr and Lucas obviously thought. And this manipulation might have proved a dangerous one, if things had gone differently. But as Ambyr had said, and I now calculated in my head, things had not gone differently, and no harm had been done; quite the opposite, or so it seemed. Thus I accepted her logic, and simply reveled in the return, albeit brief, of that feeling that somehow, in some way, I might hope to be restored to at least the three-quarters of a human being that I'd once been. Would I do so with this young woman in particular as a romantic object? On the most superficial level, the difference in our ages, as well as her blindness, might seem to have argued against such a possibility; and yet, beneath this common sort of reaction, I knew that neither her age nor her condition had precluded *her* from trying to play *me* like a harp— why, then, should I regard her as an innocent who could only experience manipulation and misuse at my hands?

With these thoughts running through my head, I pulled Marcianna along, making sure to give her some of the dog treats in my pocket. She had shown no hostility toward Ambyr; but neither had she indulged her as she had Derek. She simply bore Ambyr's presence with good grace, and began to chirrup quietly for more of the treats. Ambyr read these noises almost correctly, and stopped, stepping around me and reaching down until she felt the fur of Marcianna's back. "Hey, you don't have anything to worry about, beautiful girl," she said, stroking the top of Marcianna's head. "I'm not looking to invade your territory. At least—" She reached up and took some of the dog treats from my pocket, feeding them to Marcianna, then returning to my left arm. "Not *all* of it, I'm not . . ."

{ii.}

Once down in the Kurtzes' backyard again, I found Mike very concerned that we get back to Shiloh so that he could change into appropriately clean clothes for dinner with my great-aunt Clarissa: as usual, his fear of offending her in any way was very real. And, as cocktail hour was in fact fast approaching (and you did *not* mess with Clarissa's cocktail hour), I asked Ambyr to pull the boys into shape so that we could get under way. This she did, quickly morphing from the secretive, wise, and flirtatious young woman I had just observed to the full-on matron of the house, barking at Lucas and Derek, using her cane at once to navigate, herd, and threaten, and telling them she didn't want to hear about their coming back out of the house in clean T-shirts and jeans. The two youths apparently knew that this was Ambyr's no-bullshit voice, and moved quickly to wash up and change. Eventually they reemerged, scrubbed, combed, and wearing collared shirts and khaki pants that, during their first few minutes in them, might just as well have been medieval plate armor. Ambyr herself came out a few minutes later, having changed into a more elegantly styled summer dress than the one in which she'd greeted us; and apparently my reaction was a little too obvious, because Mike began laughing quietly again, passing me by on the way to the garage, twirling his keys and muttering those same words: "So fucking dead . . . *so* fucking dead . . ."

But, whatever our respective conditions, we all piled into the car, Marcianna in the front seat, now, by the window, and me sitting between her and Mike. I told Lucas and Derek to let Ambyr have the rear window behind Mike, an order they didn't question, I can only think because they immediately recognized its purpose: if she could not actually see Death's Head Hollow and Shiloh, she could at least enjoy its scents and sounds.

This she did, and quite a bit. Lucas played guide, sitting in the middle of the seat and pointing out the sources of the various sensations that Ambyr experienced. I confess that I had long since taken many of these for granted: not just the obvious ones, the songs of birds whose young were just fledging, the ancient fruit trees that grew in discrete clusters at various spots, even the smell of the cow dung that filled the pastures with the arrival of the rich, midsummer grass that the animals mowed down as if they were precision machinery. I was a bit ashamed for not having more often appreciated all these and more of the riches that the hollow offered up without fee; and at one point, when I turned to Mike as Lucas kept up his commentary, I saw in my partner's face a very deep sort of contentment and even happiness, one that matched the statement he had made to me before we departed for the Kurtzes' house: that our life in this place, brushes with law enforcement aside, was a good one—and not simply because we were fresh out of other options for our exile.

Feeling better about things in general, I began to scratch behind Marcianna's ears as she pushed the front half of her head out the partially open window; and then, as the Kurtz siblings continued to enjoy the trip, I saw Derek out of the corner of my eye, sitting way back in his seat and looking very uncomfortable, even frightened.

"You okay, Derek?" I asked, knowing full well that he wasn't.

"Me?" the young man replied, shaking himself. "Yeah, I'm, uh, fine—I just don't wanna make Marcianna nervous, that's all. So I'm giving her all the room I can."

The lie was a smooth one, but I let it go with a smile and a nod: soon enough he would be in a spot, if all went well, where such fabrications would not be so easy to hand out . . .

Once the Empress was parked, it was each to their immediate and respective duties: we still had about twenty minutes to kill before we needed to be at the house, and so I dispatched Lucas, who could not have been more delighted with the task, to the hangar, to give his sister and Derek a guided tour of the structure and the JU-52 while Mike changed his clothes and I got Marcianna back to her enclosure. Before our guests got fully under way, however, I yanked our apprentice back toward Mike and myself, the collar of his new shirt making the familiar task an easier one . . .

"Hey!" he cried; but he was clever enough to suppress the sound somewhat. "Come on, L.T., this is my good shirt, don't get it all wrinkled before I even meet your great-aunt, for shit's sake—"

"Shut up, kid, and listen," I ordered firmly. "You can take them wherever you want, and describe whatever you want to Ambyr—she doesn't seem the squeamish type."

"Believe me, she ain't," the boy answered, shaking his head and raising his eyebrows. "Sometimes she catches me on Facebook, and makes me describe the stuff that I'm watching, the crazy violent shit from whatever country, and man, it gets kind of hard for me to do it."

"Ever think that might be the point, genius?" Mike asked with a grin.

"Hunh." Lucas scratched at his increasingly (and more characteristically) disheveled head quickly. "Nope. Never did."

"The point is this," I said. "You don't let Derek see *any* of the raw stuff, and you don't describe it to your sister while he's close by—he'll only get freaked out, and that's not what he's here for. So if you spot any of the autopsy pictures within easy sight, anything like that, take them down and slip them into my desk. Got it?"

Lucas squinted with raw condescension. "Is that all? You think I hadn't figured that much out already? I haven't even *told* him about that kinda stuff at home—it's not good for him. Man, you guys must think I'm a fuckin' idiot."

"That'd be one way to put it," Mike said.

Lucas nodded calmly; then, with lightning speed, he balled a fist, slammed it into Mike's shoulder, and trotted off with a mad laugh, toward the waiting Ambyr and Derek. "And that'd be another, Dr. Li!"

For his part, Mike couldn't help an indignant, instinctive move to pursue Lucas; and their movements, in turn, got Marcianna excited. She made a move to follow her young friend, a move that she would have successfully executed, probably scaring the living daylights out of Derek in the process, had I not quickly locked her lead down with my right thumb, even as I lifted my cane and held it out in front of Mike, doing my best to remind him of the need to maintain decorum, or something resembling it.

And then Lucas' brain kicked in: he realized something suddenly, stopped running, and turned back toward us, carefully retracing a few of his steps. "Hey," he said slowly. "Hang on . . . Doc—you said, about Derek, 'That's not what he's here for.' Right?"

"Yeah?" I said, affecting an utter lack of concern.

"Well, then," Lucas said. "What the hell *is* he here for?"

I was deeply grateful that Mike stepped in at that moment, because I was at a bit of a loss, and Lucas caught it: "To have dinner, you dumb-ass," he seethed at the boy. "Now get the fuck out of here before I murder you . . ."

Lucas shrugged, turning once more. "O-kay—but lying'll make you old before your time, Doc. Not that you ain't already. It might even age you, Mike, though I don't know, the way you lie to women, you oughtta be about a hundred and five, by now."

"Get!" Mike barked, and finally Lucas rejoined his little family, Ambyr putting a reassuring arm around Derek's shoulders as they made their way toward the hangar.

"I got about a thousand reasons why that's a really stupid idea, L.T.," Mike said, nodding after them. "Thank God I hid most of the really tasty stuff when you came up with it."

I glanced at him. "The White Monster?"

"Turned toward the fuselage, and duct-taped there for good measure," Mike answered. "I know how that little fucker's mind works . . . I don't suppose anything I could say would make you shitcan the whole thing, and just take them down to meet Clarissa?"

"We're halfway across the desert," I replied. "It's too late for that." Pulling Marcianna toward me, I straddled her dipping spine by lifting my real leg over it, then gave her a good scratch from collar to tail for all she'd done that day. "And Ambyr would only suspect something."

"Well, don't go saying I didn't warn you." Pausing as Marcianna began to pant and purr, Mike couldn't help but smile. "I guess you're gonna go feed her, hunh? In which case, I'll go get cleaned up and changed, and then it's off to face Miss Clarissa. Your plan for her is still in place, I take it, from the way you were talking to Lucas."

"It is," I answered. "And thanks for bailing me out on that one, by the way. I blanked there for a second."

"I saw," said Mike. "And so did the kid. He'll ask you about it."

"By the time he does, it'll all be over." Then I started up the hill to Marcianna's enclosure, as she lifted her forelegs into the air like a rearing horse. When they hit the ground again, she chirruped and shot off, as I'd given her enough lead to run some toward home. She slowed up as the lead became taut again, not wanting to pull me over, and as I worked my cane quickly to follow her, Mike said, just loud enough for me to hear:

"You're gambling on a lot of things, right now, L.T.—you know that, right?"

I didn't bother to answer him. Once again, Marcianna's mood infected mine, and I didn't want to hear predictions of doom and gloom. My blood was up; and it was time to see Clarissa.

By the time I came back from the enclosure, Ambyr, Lucas, and Derek had long since made short work of the hangar's attractions, and they were busily moving about the inside of the JU-52, two pairs of their footsteps loud and rather boisterous within the nose of the plane: Derek and Lucas in the cockpit seats, I surmised, and as I listened further, I heard them loudly calling out in something that I could only imagine was their best approximation of German, issuing wild orders to each other. Hollering up through the hatch, I was eventually answered by Ambyr, who appeared in the entryway looking lovelier than I had recalled. Telling her that I needed an extra pair of hands to help with shucking some corn, I asked that she send Derek down, which would allow Lucas to continue her tour about the plane. Ambyr protested that she herself would be only too happy to help, but I pointed out that the boys needed constant supervision, and from the way she agreed with this statement, I gathered that if Lucas had at least not revealed the worst that our investigation had to offer (for Mike had indeed hidden most such items when I'd announced my plan for the evening), she knew that there was always the risk that, if

Lucas and Derek were left on their own, their antics might turn unintentionally dangerous. Thus she went back inside and, in her usual take-charge tone, called for Derek, bringing on cries of disappointment from both boys; but by the time she returned to the hatchway with her "adopted son" in tow, she was speaking in an entirely different voice.

All questions of my romantic admiration aside, her treatment of the young man was thoughtful and poignant; and in a few more minutes, Derek and I were making our way down the dirt path toward the barns and then the house, myself more convinced than ever that including Ambyr in the investigation had been the right move. Among many other things, her contributions would be made from Surrender and Fraser, where her school and training program were, and where, Latrell had indicated, the "they" who were orchestrating the connections between the throwaway kids and the people downstate who were offering those kids new and often perilous lives were located. For the moment, however, it was Derek who needed to be further handled—or so I thought.

"Well, Derek," I said, as we neared the barns, "what did you think of the JU-52?"

"The plane?" Derek asked, to which I nodded, lighting a cigarette. "You mean the machine 'the plane' or the headquarters 'the plane'?"

It was a question of promising discernment. "Whichever one impressed you more."

"I like the machine-plane, frankly," he replied; then, when I offered him one of my cigarettes conspiratorially, he studied me in that strikingly ingenuous way that so many autistic children can—which often tells you they know just what you're doing—and simply said:

"I don't smoke—Ambyr doesn't like us to."

"I'm sorry, I should have known. She's a very smart young woman, your sister." I caught myself: "Okay if I call her your sister? Is there something else you prefer?"

He smiled and began scratching his dark hair in reply, the latter a movement he'd clearly picked up from Lucas, but which looked undeniably appealing when he did it, as well. "I, uh—I don't really know *what* to tell people she is. I mean, she's not my *mom*. But she's not my sister, either—not really. So, I mean—what is she?"

"Well," I answered, keeping our pace slow, "she's your guardian. And, of course, your friend."

"Right, I remember that word—'*guardian*.'" He began bouncing one fist in an open hand uneasily. "But—I just can't remember what that's supposed to make *me*." He had raised his voice, not so much in desperation as in frustration; and I tried quickly to explain the situation further:

"Technically, that makes you her *ward*—did anyone ever use that term, after your parents and Lucas' disappeared?"

He nodded. "Right, yeah, ward. But—I don't know, I never really understood what it meant, even after they told me."

"Well—you remember Bruce Wayne?" I asked, calculating that the *Batman* reference might be one that he'd understand.

And he did: "Yeah, that's right." Then, finally, he let himself laugh, if only a bit. "Bruce Wayne, he had Dick Grayson for a ward. But me and Ambyr, that ain't the same thing at *all*!"

"Well, actually it is," I answered, chuckling along with his laughter. "Money isn't the thing that defines us, Derek."

"Simple for you to say!" he answered, still laughing quietly. "Look where you live, look what you've done—solved crimes, been on the covers of newspapers—"

"Don't tell me Lucas actually *showed* you that stupid newspaper cover?"

"Sure, it's right on your Google page!" Derek said. "'The Sorcerer of Death,' with a picture of you coming out of some old building that looks like it was *built* for *Batman*—"

"The Criminal Courts Building," I explained. "In New York City."

"That's right, I remember." Derek began to nod certainly again, an action that clearly gave him a sense of reassurance and calm. Then he laughed once more. "And there was this little picture of Mike—of Dr. Li—in the corner, and it said 'And His Apprentice.'"

"Do yourself a favor," I said. "Don't bring that detail up to Mike."

"Don't worry," Derek laughed, in his disarming way. "I wouldn't."

"You know, Derek—I'm starting to understand that you're a lot smarter than almost anybody gives you credit for being . . ." I grasped my cane in my right hand and put my left forearm on Derek's shoulder, seemingly for greater support, but in fact to build on the at least momentary camaraderie that appeared to have been established between us. "Come on," I said. "There's somebody I want you to meet—"

And then I caught sight of something: just as we were passing by the shed behind the equipment barn where the twin Arctic Cat Prowlers were tucked away, what seemed a crack of some kind in the raised center portion of the roof of the machine I'd been driving the night we took Gracie up the mountain became visible.

"What the . . . ?" I murmured, lifting my arm from Derek's shoulder and moving toward the shed. I initially thought that the damage must have been done by a tree branch that we had passed at high speed. Still, it was something that, if I could catch it from that distance, I could count on hearing about at dinner that night; so I figured I'd better have a quick look. "Shit, that's all I need," I mumbled. "Come on—I've got to check something out before we go to the house . . ." Seeing that I was headed toward the fairly secluded back of the barn, Derek seemed to grow edgy once again, even frightened. "What's the matter?" I asked, moving back toward him.

"This ain't about shucking corn, is it?" he said, haltingly and tremulously.

"Of course it is, Derek—I just noticed that I may have busted the roof on one of the ATVs we took up the mountain the other night. And trust me, if my aunt has already seen it, then I'm going to get my ass handed to me—you know the feeling, right?"

Derek paused a moment, his gaze shifting from side to side but his head remaining very still. "That's really it?"

"Yeah, that's really it," I said, waving him over, and then continuing on my way again. "What'd you think I was going to do, take you out back and rough you up?" I asked, chuckling a bit.

He stepped quickly to pull up almost even with me. "I—didn't really know," he said, scratching at his head in that same way again and trying to laugh along with me; but he'd been rattled.

"What possible reason could I have for doing *that*?"

I studied his reaction as we neared the shed; and a wave of darkness, of gloomy experience, passed over his features. "People don't always need reasons for what they do," he said quietly.

It was a sad summary of all he'd known at home or in school, I thought; but I also knew that if he'd wanted to talk about it, he would have. And so I simply added quietly, "No. No, they do not . . ."

Once at the shed, I made straight for the damaged roof of the one Prowler. The side of the raised center of the roof had been damaged, all right, but only after being pierced by a bullet, one whose report neither Lucas, Marcianna, nor I had heard during our descent from the mountain. I knew that there was little to no chance that my great-aunt was unaware of the matter: it was likely one of the reasons that she had insisted on our coming to dinner that evening. More important, it meant that someone had come perilously close, not simply to frightening us, but to harming or perhaps even killing at least one of us: someone who was a good enough shot to hit a fast-moving vehicle, and who possessed a high-quality suppressor. The bullet hole had pierced the roof just above the back of the driver's seat at an almost forty-five-degree angle, a trajectory that, when I traced it, meant that it had passed out the open side of the Prowler's cab, just behind Marcianna and in front of Lucas, which would make retrieving the slug an impossibility. Marcianna, Lucas, and I had only narrowly escaped injury; and I immediately started seething.

"Those mother-*fuckers*," I murmured slowly, in near-disbelief. "Those absolute pieces of shit . . ."

Derek, meanwhile—probably as a way to either avoid or try to defuse my anger—had stepped up onto the machine to fix his attention on the spot where the bullet had pierced the roof. "I don't know who did this, but I don't think it was, like, a *mistake* or anything," he announced. "The fiberglass up here is good and thick. Wasn't any varmint gun, either, even one with a heavy load—say a .22-250 or some such. Nope. Bigger lead, more powder—probably a hollow-point .308." He glanced my way once, quickly and furtively. "Somebody was trying to tell you guys *something*."

"You know about guns, do you, Derek?" I asked, hoping to learn more.

"Me? Oh. Sure . . ." He stepped back down off the Prowler. "That was about the only thing my dad and me had to talk about, being as I didn't drink beer. But when we'd go hunting every year, chances were good that it would be me bringing a buck home. And it drove him crazy, most times. He'd tell me, 'Derek, you're stupider than a box of rocks, but you can shoot, all right.' Later, since he figured that was *all* I could manage to do right, he started yelling about me joining the military and becoming a sniper. He was just being an even bigger jerk, of course, because he knew the military wasn't going to take me . . ."

"Sounds as if our fathers might have known each other," I said, still probing, and getting a small but welcome laugh out of him. "You're sure about that round?"

"Hunh?" I'd caught him trying to puzzle with the idea that his life might have in any way borne a resemblance to my own. "Oh. Yeah, like I say, a pretty hard-core .308 shell, with a hollow-point slug, would be my guess. Probably."

"And what kind of gun would shoot it?" I pursued; and slowly but surely, I could see Derek's uneasiness and confusion turning to pride at being consulted on this matter.

"Plenty," he answered with a shrug. "In fact, pretty much everybody has some kinda one that does. Remington, Marlin, SIG Sauer . . ."

"How about a Savage 10FP?" I suggested innocently.

"Well, yeah, sure," he said. "And if you guys didn't hear the shot, that means a silencer or a suppressor—about the same thing, really—and you can buy a 10FP that's suppressor-ready pretty easy; don't even have to go to a gun show, though if you go to the show, you could pick up the rifle and the suppressor at the same time. But, see, the Savage, that's like the SIG Sauer, I mean, it's more of a *tactical* than a real *hunting* rifle. It's what the state's snipers use, mostly. You got any reason to think it might be them that were trying to—" He stopped suddenly, either frightened by the thought he'd just given voice to or realizing that he'd said too much, I couldn't say which; but I didn't want him going back into his defensive mode.

"No," I said quickly, "nothing *that* serious. I hope anyway."

His brows arched and his eyes went wide. "Well—either way, somebody was sure out to at least scare you guys, and really bad . . ."

"Maybe," I said, as casually as I could. "But we don't scare so easy." That didn't seem to reassure Derek much; as for me, I now had a whole new range of things to consider about the unusual young man before me: was his talk intended as mere expert advice? Or was it what he understood to be (probably because he'd been told by someone that I would take it as) a coded warning? Was he less the facilitator that I'd thought must exist, and had told Lucas to scout for, than he was a dupe—a willing dupe, yes, but a dupe, nevertheless?

"Well," I said, turning away from the shed. "It happened, nothing we can do about it, now. I'll just have to go take my punishment. Come on, Derek." I headed once more for the house, much more quickly than I'd been moving before. "That corn isn't going to shuck itself . . ."

I didn't feel any too proud of myself, as we walked on: learning the things I had from Derek, important as they were, was one of the simply shitty parts of the job of criminal profiling. When someone of whom you are suspicious also turns out to be someone for whom you feel enormous sympathy, and when you must go on playing a role that will allow and encourage him to draw himself further into a psychological snare that you have devised using his own unsuspecting statements . . . Well, there is a cheap, ugly feeling that accompanies the process, and I'm not sure I've ever felt it quite so intensely as I did just then.

My qualms about Derek aside, however, I had to push on; for whether the young man was or wasn't hiding something vital was now a matter for Clarissa to determine. It was from my great-aunt that I had learned to give voice to whatever ability to read people I possessed as a boy and still retain; besides, testing Derek would help keep the old girl off *my* back . . .

{iii.}

To make everything at least appear on the up-and-up, I led Derek around to the back of the house and the kitchen, where all preparation of food and cooking would be done. The modern kitchen had been built into the old winter kitchen, while the former summer kitchen—that space in which, long ago, meals had been prepared when the weather became too oppressive to stand over a hot wood stove inside—now formed a large pantry and preparation area, with a table where the household staff could eat indoors.

Of course, "the staff," these days, meant only Annabel, whose duties included those of what would once have been three people: cook, housekeeper, and all-around attendant to my great-aunt. When we reached the open kitchen door, out of which were just beginning to float the smells of a full steak dinner such as we were usually granted when company was present, Derek and I discovered, as I had hoped, that Annabel was in on what was taking place, at least enough to have asked two of the hands if they would stay on, for a few extra bucks, and do the shucking of the corn that I had told Derek was to be our job, as well as prep the other vegetables for dinner. Those two, Happy Dearborn and Chick Thorne, were solid men that I knew, both in their late thirties with families of their own in towns other than Surrender; and I knew that Annabel had likely had no trouble talking them into the extra work. Plus there were perks for doing such jobs as they were now laboring over, the main one being that Clarissa allowed them, along with several other hands, to hunt the mountain during deer season, so long as each gave a portion of the meat from their kills to my great-aunt, allowing us to enjoy venison year-round.

After greeting Happy and Chick, I led the way into the kitchen, where piles of garden-grown carrots, broccoli, and lettuce sat on one butcher-block table. Pots of potatoes were boiling on the gas stove; but the grilling of the steaks would take place just shortly before we ate, on a large brick-and-grate structure outside, one used for that purpose during all months of the year save the very coldest.

Annabel—a deceptively delicate-looking woman, with carefully styled white hair and remarkably youthful skin—stood stirring the potatoes, wearing one of several nearly identical dresses that might have dated back decades, or might just as well have been made yesterday: for she did all her own sewing, as well as all the mending for my great-aunt. As Derek hung back, I rushed up behind her, but my cane gave me away: before I could grab a fork and stick it into one of the nearly cooked potatoes, Annabel said with a gentle smile:

"If I were you, Trajan, I would get myself cleaned up and ready for cocktails, instead of trying to steal potatoes." Then she began drying her hands on her grey apron, which was bordered in lace, and turned her marvelously perceptive blue eyes on me. "You have some explaining to do, unless I'm mistaken."

I released the fork with a frown. "And you are never mistaken, Annabel. How bad is it?"

"Well," Annabel answered, heading for the vegetables, which I helped her load into an ancient ceramic trough sink, "she seems to have gotten it into her head that you put your life in danger Sunday night. Yours, Marcianna's, and the young boy's, the one who's been working with you." She turned to Derek inquisitively, but never let go of the charming smile. "Speaking of which . . ."

"Oh, right," I said. "Come on in, Derek," I told the kid, who was almost clinging to the doorway.

"But—" he mumbled. "But I thought *we* were going to shuck the corn."

"Well, if you'd like to help the men," Annabel said, "I'm sure you can."

"Oh, come on, Derek, just say hello and be thankful that Annabel saved you from all that." I introduced them, and watched Derek very shyly give Annabel his full name, after which he tried to identify himself within the Kurtz family structure: no mean feat. But Annabel cut him off, gently saying that she was fully aware of his background. The kid eased up some, to which I clapped him on the shoulder and pronounced, "Well, then, come on—let's see if we can roust Mike. He in his room getting cleaned up, Annabel?"

"He's in his room," she answered, starting in on washing the vegetables. "Just what he's doing there, I couldn't tell you. It involved a telephone, a computer, and a printer, that's all I can say for sure." She gave me another enigmatic smile. "And he's been none too careful about watching his volume, if you know what I mean . . ."

I frowned momentarily. "I know what you mean, all right. Jesus-fucking-H—" Annabel slapped the rim of the sink with a wooden spoon: for she was, like Pete Steinbrecher, one of the very few people, in Surrender or anywhere else, that I would have called a genuine Christian, and I'd transgressed. "I'm sorry!" I rushed in to say. "I'm sorry, Annabel. But that means Clarissa is aware of whatever he's been babbling about, right?" She nodded certainly. "Well—all right, then, Derek. Let's see what Mike's so worked up about, and how much damage he may have done . . ."

I led the way through the swinging door that connected the kitchen to a long hallway that terminated at the dining room, and off of which branched several bedrooms originally designed for the staff. The wide, original wooden floors of the hall were covered (here as in most of the house) by Oriental rugs that my great-grandfather had begun to collect on his flights around Europe during the 1930s in the JU-52, a passion that his daughter Clarissa had carried on during her own wanderings around North Africa and the Middle East throughout the Sixties. On the hallway walls were dozens of pictures of people Clarissa had met during these travels, some of them already famous, some of them soon to be famous (or infamous), and some simple Tuareg or Arab tribesmen: black-and-white shots of the type considered highly romantic, at the time, but which looked, in the post-9/11 world, as if they had been taken in a parallel universe.

As I moved toward Mike's room, which was situated below and slightly to the side of the house's back staircase (built so that the staff could get to the family rooms above from the kitchen and outside without being seen by their employers unless summoned), Derek paused to study what was, for him, the strangest and most exotic element common to each image, which he pointed out to me:

"So, the blond lady who's in all these pictures," he said. "That's your great-aunt? She's beautiful . . ."

I moved over to glance at the photo he was studying, which had been taken in Wadi Rum, near the Gulf of Aqaba in Jordan, which was a fairly famous tourist destination despite its being in the middle of very little save relentless, and relentlessly contested, desert. The picture showed two people with their arms around each other, standing amid a fairly fearsome group of al-Huwaytat Bedouin tribesmen. The first Western figure was dressed in khaki gear, the other in much darker clothing, and both wore Bedouin *kaffiyeh*—the traditional headdress that today can get you instantly detained at almost any American airport—wrapped around their necks. The young woman Derek was pointing to was dressed in the khaki, and she was indeed quite beautiful, with somewhat frizzy golden hair and Gaelic features, as well as loads of native jewelry bedecking her wrists and ears; the figure beside her was shorter, and carrying her trademark leather jacket over one shoulder.

The problem being that Derek was pointing at the wrong person. "No," I told him. "That's Diana Forbes. She used to live here, too, but she died. *That*"—I pointed at the second figure—"is Clarissa." A boyishly styled but still pretty woman in her twenties: such had been my great-aunt at the time. She wore her dark hair slicked back, a striking look known by many names, Clarissa preferring *DA* for "duck's ass"; and there was not a bangle, bracelet, or earring to be seen on her.

Derek's eyes went wide as he stared at the picture. "*Whaaat . . . ?*" he noised, at which I realized that, because of my immersion in matters pertaining only to the case, I had forgotten to prepare him for this; indeed, I had forgotten to prepare any of the members of the Kurtz household for the full realities of life at Shiloh.

"I'm sorry, Derek," I said. "I ought to've told you. My great-aunt is a lesbian. The woman you see her with, Diana, was her 'longtime partner,' as the phrase goes. They backpacked over much of the world together, and then, when my great-grandfather died—you remember, the lunatic who brought the JU-52 over from Germany—Clarissa decided that she had to take over the farm and keep it going, which was tough, because my great-grandfather had let a lot of things get pretty run-down. But even with all that work to be done, and even knowing what kind of reception they could expect in Surrender, Diana came along to live here with Clarissa, and they were together until the end. Diana actually died upstairs—breast cancer."

"She's dead?" Derek murmured. "*Geez,* that's sad . . ." He continued to stare at the photo. "She really was pretty . . ." It was hard to determine whether he was attracted to the image of Diana because his mind was spinning some romantic or even sexual fantasy around it—and Diana really had been quite a stunning woman, especially at the time that that photo in particular had been taken—or if it was a kind of a maternal call that he was answering: for Diana—with whom I'd grown up, during the weekends, vacations, and summers I spent at Shiloh, and most especially during my periods of recuperation after my surgeries and treatments—had been a wonderfully tender and caring human being, qualities that tended to radiate out even from her photos.

"Yes, she was," I answered, continuing to observe the young man's reactions. "Mind you, Clarissa was quite pretty, herself. It's just that—"

"It's just that she looks like a *guy* in these pictures," Derek answered, innocently enough. "I mean, they teach us about tolerance and all in school, what we're supposed to say and think about gays and lesbians, but we don't really *have* many."

"You may have more than you think," I said, aware, through my work, of the rough official estimates of actual teen and young adult homosexuality—and the various responses to it by parents—in Burgoyne County.

"Could be," Derek answered with a nod, going back to the entrance into the hall and studying the other photographs anew. "But we sure ain't got any that are this—what do you call it?"

"You call it *butch,* is what you call it." Derek and I turned to see Mike standing shirtless in his doorway, with a pair of charcoal suit pants covering his lower half. He was speaking in little more than a whisper, for all his desire to shock Derek: he knew that Clarissa could be almost anywhere, and that a crack like that, if overheard, would earn him a serious dressing-down, if not a smack from the rattan stick (actually a camel crop, a memento of her traveling days) that she usually carried. "So you found out the big secret about Miss Clarissa Jones, eh, Derek?" The kid nodded silently. "Yeah, well, trust me, things only get weirder, the longer you stay up here."

"What's so weird about being a lesbian?" Derek asked, with that same artlessness.

"Nothing," Mike said. "In New York City, that is. In Surrender—you have to admit, it's a little bit strange."

"Oh," Derek noised. "You mean 'weird' like *unusual,* then? Not like it's a sick thing, like they used to say in the Baptist church that my mom sometimes dragged me to." He turned back to the photos, still enraptured, even as the beginnings of rage came into his voice: "Dragged me when she wasn't too hungover, that is. Right up until she broke just about every rule in the Bible and left her own kid on his own . . ."

Mike and I exchanged a look of both shock and grim satisfaction at our continued success: we had taken the young man out of his familiar environment, and his usual defenses were crumbling. Yet he kept staring at the photos, seemingly unaware of what he had said.

"But, Derek," Mike said, quietly and engagingly, "you've got Lucas and Ambyr, right? They're taking care of you."

The young man's voice at that moment became so deliberate, so *peculiarly* ingenuous, that it was chilling: *"Not . . . the same . . . thing . . ."* he murmured.

"But they don't ever hold your living with them over you, do they?" I asked carefully.

"Don't have to," the boy answered. "It's *already* over me. And it ain't like they can *move* it. But I'll get out from under it, one day. One day—it'll be *my* turn to go . . ."

It was a moment with the young man that I could only have hoped for when I suggested that he come to the house; and best of all, I had Mike there as a witness—

But we were interrupted at just that instant: the swinging door into the kitchen suddenly opened, revealing Annabel. Each of us jumped a little at her arrival, prompting her to say, "Oh! I'm sorry, I didn't know you were all standing right there—excuse me. But, Trajan, dinner will be ready in about half an hour, and you know how your aunt is about cocktails, so you may want to gather your guests up."

"Thanks, Annabel," I said, smiling but knowing that the moment with Derek was now irretrievably dispelled. And, as if to seal the deal, Annabel went over and stood by the kid, looking at the photograph with him as she wiped her hands on her apron.

"Isn't it a lovely picture?" she said to Derek.

"Yeah, it is," he replied with a nod, once again and completely returned to his usual "slow," innocent state—not through calculation, but simply because he had returned from whatever strange and more forthcoming place his mind had been visiting.

"We were just discussing how many gay and lesbian citizens Surrender actually has, Annabel," Mike said, quickly pulling on a blue polo shirt. "Care to make a wager?"

Annabel blushed deeply, but she did not shy from the question—mostly because she did not shy from much, which was why she had lasted forty years at Shiloh, arriving when my great-grandfather died, running things throughout my own and then Diana's cancer, enduring my great-aunt's terrible period of adjustment, and finally lasting through Mike's and my entrance and a return to something like peace on the farm. "Well," she said, "I know that it's unusual; but I also know that there're more than most know of. Yes, indeed . . ." And then she went back through the kitchen door, having stated her point and needing to stick to my great-aunt's unalterable timetable.

"See?" Derek said, although to whom he was trying to prove his point was unclear. "Just 'strange' as in unusual, maybe—and maybe even not *that* unusual."

"Isn't that what I said?" Mike asked collegially. "It's certainly what I *meant*. Trust me, Derek, there is *nothing* weird or sick about lesbians. Why, some of my best friends are lesbians."

"Like who?" I droned.

"Well," Mike defended, "let me put it this way: I *wish* some of my best friends were lesbians—"

"Just knock it off, will you?" I said, lowering my own voice as I increased its urgency. "We don't have time for your rich fantasy life, right now. Annabel said when we came in that you'd been going on about something in your room, and that Clarissa could hear your voice through the door and the walls, though I hope not what you were actually *saying*. So what's that all about?"

"Oh, shit, I almost forgot! Given the, uh, *moment*, here," he said, inclining his head toward Derek, who had returned to being enraptured by the initial photo that he had seen on the wall. "Will you excuse us for just a second, Derek? I gotta bring my ignorant partner, the esteemed doctor, up to speed on a couple of points."

That got a smile out of Derek, whose eyes stayed on the photo. "Sure, Mike. I'll be right here."

Then Mike grabbed my arm and pulled me into his train wreck of a room, closing the door. An iMac was sitting on a small desk under the window, and a printer alongside it was busily churning out an e-mail that filled the screen of the computer. "I don't know about you, L.T.," he whispered, "but that kid is starting to give me the distinct creeps. Not in a bad way, necessarily, but—we have tapped into something that I hope we don't end up wishing we'd left alone."

"Yeah, I know the feeling," I answered, just as quietly. "But it's forward motion, you have to admit that. And I assume you've made some of the same on your own?"

"*Some?* Ha! I got you a frickin' *gift*, kid." He snatched the page out of the printer and handed it to me. "Direct from the detection gods to the Sorcerer of Death."

I was too confounded by his excitement to argue the stupid nickname one more time. "What the hell is it?" I asked, although I had already perceived the letterhead of some kind of "memorabilia emporium" in New York, which made my heart begin to race. "I hope it's good enough for you risking being overheard by Clarissa—"

"Go on, look more closely," Mike said, still smiling. Unable to wait for me to figure it out, he quickly divulged: "*That* is our target, or at least the initial one. It's the name and address of the guy that Latrell stole those jerseys from."

I kept staring at the paper, seeing that it was indeed a reply to a request Mike had made concerning information about a collection of basketball jerseys that Mike had told the company he had reason to believe were missing and might have been stolen. It culminated with a name, telephone number, and address in Manhattan: an expensive if garish address. "No fucking way," I murmured, feeling the beginnings of a sense of excitement. "But how . . . ?"

"Like I told you, I called Pete, and asked him to use his phone to get as many pictures as he could of *both* sides of the authentication documents that the BCI has—and he did it, then texted the pictures to me. Apparently it wasn't even that hard, Mangold's bunch're busy grilling the hell out of those two freaks from down in Heinsdale—"

"Jimmy and Jeanette Patrick," I said.

"Yep—and there's more. Pete *just* called me, which is the conversation Clarissa must have heard, though it wouldn't have made any sense to her."

"Don't be so sure."

"Whatever, motherfucker—the point is, even *I* couldn't help getting excited—seems like the pair were picked up last night, on schedule; Steve and Pete were called in on the bust, and watched the BCI tear just about everything that might have information on it or in it out of their house. Pete, knowing what we'd told him, went over the whole place, after that; didn't find anything weird, then left with Steve. But later, Steve decided to post Pete on the scene, which'd been all taped up, just in case. So there was a period of about maybe three or four hours where nobody was there—supposedly. Then I get a call just a little while ago—Pete's still down there, and he's shitting bricks, but he won't say about what, even though he's on his personal cell and not calling over official communications. So I figure, *What the fuck?,* but all he says is that he needs us to get down there tonight, and the sooner the better, because he doesn't know who's going to show up when."

"Or," I said, considering the matter, "who exactly may be watching the scene from where. Which means . . ." I tried to arrange all that I'd just been given and all that already lay before us for that evening in my head. "Which means that we do indeed have to get down there *tonight.*"

"What about dinner?" Mike asked, trepidation bleeding through his words. "We bug out on this, and Clarissa will have our asses. Plus we've got them all here, already."

"Dinner, we do," I stated certainly. "We're just going to have to give her the edited version, and hope she can still find out something on her own." I studied the piece of paper before me for a few more seconds. "You're sure this is genuine?"

"Yeah, I'm sure," Mike answered, pulling on a dark grey jacket that matched his pants. "Told them I was a PI; hell, one of the guys had even heard of me—*me,* dickhead, not you. 'Apprentice' my ass. Come on, let's get them all rounded up and get a drink—*I,* at least, have fucking earned it."

"Yes, you have," I answered. "But listen to this, first: I just found a bullet hole in the roof of the Prowler that Lucas, Marcianna, and I were riding in the other night." Mike's hand, which had been on his doorknob, came off it, as his face went straight with sudden alarm. "Yeah," I went on. "On top of that, it turns out our friend Derek is something of a firearms savant—and he figures it was the same caliber bullet that the State Police snipers use."

Mike's expression of concern blended, at that point, with bewilderment. "What the fuck?" he whispered. "You think the *state cops* would actually get involved in trying to hit one of you?"

"No, not really," I answered. "But somebody could've been trying awfully hard to make it look like they were."

"Jesus . . ." Mike stood staring out the window over the desk for a moment. I knew he was thinking that whoever had been shooting at us was likely tied up in Gracie Chang's "accident," as well; and I was therefore reassured when he suddenly said, "Well, if we didn't hit 'pause' for Gracie almost getting killed, we certainly can't hit it for this kind of bullshit. Not with a lead like this. Fuck 'em, you go deal with Clarissa, and I'll entertain Derek while you check her mood. And get my drink."

"Right," I answered, turning to leave the room, but then remembering that I still had the printed e-mail in my hand. I started to hand it back to Mike, who moved to take it; then I held it up, gave him a small smile, and said, "This was nice work, Dr. Li."

"Damn right it was," he declared.

"Just watch how *much* you drink," I said. "We're going to need our wits about us, later . . ."

Mike got Derek to continue hanging out in the hallway and to go on studying and discussing some more of the photographs on the walls, and then in the rooms beyond. Not that Derek needed much urging to hang back: whatever he'd heard about *me* before he'd first wandered up Death's Head Hollow with Lucas, he'd apparently heard some distressing things about my great-aunt, as well (although not, at that point, about her sexuality), and he preferred to wait until he had the backup of his guardian and foster-brother before he made her acquaintance. Unfortunately, I couldn't permit that: moving quickly to prepare Clarissa to encounter Derek alone, I made my way through the dining room, with its high, grey-green wainscoting and series of extremely valuable antique sideboards interrupted by Aubrey Beardsley prints (which would have been merely hackneyed, had they not been real), then crossed through the living room to the narrow French doors that led out onto the porch, going past Diana's old Steinway grand piano, which was crowded with more pictures taken during the couple's journeys. I paused, finally, taking a moment to straighten my attire a bit, until I heard Clarissa's voice, which was deep and resonant, despite how many unfiltered Camel cigarettes and belts of scotch she had gone through in her life without managing to kill herself:

"All right, Trajan—get out here and try to explain why I shouldn't shut down this operation, since it's already come close to getting you, along with a valued state employee, killed . . ."

{iv.}

I gave up the battle to make myself any tidier than I already had or could; instead, I grabbed a shot of scotch from a nearby sideboard, downed it, then pulled out my watch as I stepped onto the porch. "Really, Aunt?" I said. "I'm here a full fifteen minutes early, and I don't get at least a little credit?"

Clarissa was seated in one of a group of old, barn-green Adirondack chairs that lined the west side of the porch, her face to the setting sun. I rarely studied any of the various collections of photographs of her that were around the house before these little meetings of the minds of ours: such could sometimes cloud debate with emotion. But on this evening, perhaps because she was awash in the sunset, or perhaps because she was wearing a light, black leather jacket much like the one that she had had slung over her shoulder in the photo from Wadi Rum, it occurred to me how little she had changed over the years—and most of that little had taken place during the ten years since Diana had finally succumbed to her cancer. That tragedy had caused stern, grey-white streaks to appear in the hair that she continued to wear short and combed straight back, and had wizened the skin around her brows, eyes, and mouth rather suddenly, or what had seemed to me at the time to be suddenly; but her green eyes were still penetrating, and her small frame was still remarkably agile. A checked shirt, black jeans, and a pair of old deck shoes completed her appearance, each a tiny variation on what she could be found wearing almost every evening; and at her feet was the (if pressed I will concede) undeniably amiable little ball of white fur, Terence, who—less out of habit than because my jacket pocket was giving off a distinct aroma—rushed over and began panting and pawing at my knees.

"I take it you've been feeding his treats to that cat of yours," Clarissa said, watching Terence do his mad little dance, but telling him to be quiet as soon as he began yapping: an instruction he obeyed, returning to her feet as I took the chair next to hers.

"Nothing of the kind," I quickly lied. Then I leaned over to lightly kiss her cheek, which had been made rough less by age than by years in exotic climates. "How are you, old girl?"

That brought me a quick smack across the head with a rolled-up copy of *The Wall Street Journal,* one of three newspapers—the others being *The New York Times* and the Albany *Times Union*—that she had delivered to her post office box and read thoroughly every day. "That's about enough of that kind of wise-assery," she said, taking up the pack of Camels on the arm of her chair. Sticking one of the nails in her mouth, she took out an old pipeline lighter and lit it, offering the flame first to me. "I take it you'd like a light? Although I wish you'd knock it the hell off. Isn't one leg enough?"

"Apparently not," I said, pulling out one of my own cigarettes and accepting her light, then watching as she took a deep drag of her own, which was held between nicotine-stained fingers. "Besides, may I remind you that osteosarcoma is overwhelmingly a *congenital* cancer?" She let out an avoiding, dismissive blast of smoke from her mouth and nostrils, then pressed her point:

"So—are you going to tell me why there's a rather large bullet hole in one of those machines you made me buy? Or are we going to pretend that it didn't happen?"

"Well, I could tell you what I know, Clarissa," I answered, "but it isn't much, and I think you'd get more information by talking to the kid who explained it to me. The one I told you about last night, Derek Franco. I'd like you to talk to him, anyway, see what you think. Some form of autism, would be my guess. Whatever the case, I need to know if the things he says can be relied on."

"Franco . . ." Clarissa mused, glancing up from her paper. "I've been trying to place the name ever since you mentioned it. I had some contact with his parents, can't remember what. A town meeting, maybe. He's better off without them, though, I *can* tell you that."

"Well, he *is* without them," I answered. "I'm not even sure his legal name is Franco, anymore—not since all this disappearing and adopting business."

That made her slap the *Journal* down in her lap in tightly controlled anger. "How does that happen? How is it *happening*? What is wrong with this society, that people 'throw away' their own children?" She lifted her paper again. "This country has changed, in the last fifteen years . . ."

"There was a time when you desperately *wanted* it to change," I pointed out.

"Yes, when it *needed* changing!" she declared. "When that fool Nixon was in the White House talking about kikes and niggers and fags!" Sighing, she added, "And who knows? That day may be approaching, again." She got her outburst under control. "Oh, hell. So what do you want me to try to get out of this boy? Since you aren't yet ready to tell me the truth about what happened Sunday night."

"I *can't* tell you all of it, Clarissa, until you talk to Derek," I insisted. "Because I simply don't know the truth, and I think he may—but he isn't telling *me*."

"And what makes you think he'll tell me?"

"Well," I gambled, "we were walking through the back hall, just now, and he became quite impressed by the pictures of you and Diana. I think he developed a kind of a crush on her."

Clarissa paused, glanced at me quickly, then sniffed away any sentimentality and stated, "That's very discerning of him."

"And I think he was quite fascinated by you, too—in a different way, of course."

"Naturally."

"So—maybe you could start there, build on that, construct something of an intimate relationship, move on to the gunshot, and then—who knows what?"

Clarissa put her paper down slowly and turned to me. "Do you ever stop using that psychological training of yours to manipulate people? Or has it become like breathing, at this point?"

"*You've* got some right to complain," I mumbled, preparing for another assault. "Where do you think I got my start?"

That netted me a long stare, as she deliberately blew smoke in my face. "I beg your pardon?"

I decided to ignore the question, and said: "Will you try?"

Sighing, she lifted her paper again. "I swear, if you hadn't inherited my eye color, I would believe you had been left here by Gypsies . . ."

"Well, you never know—I suppose *some* Gypsies must have green eyes." I lifted myself with my arms and leaned over to give her another kiss. "Thanks, Clarissa. This will help immensely."

"Stop doing that," she said, feigning annoyance and rubbing her cheek. "And I take it that what this will 'help' with is the little *démarche* on New York that you're apparently planning in the next few days?"

This time, I was the one taken aback. "Now, how the hell . . . ?"

"Your partner," she replied with a smug smile. "He evidently thinks that the walls of this house are made of concrete—and he's been chattering away with someone in the city about a missing collection of antiques of some kind, and mumbling to himself about how it will give you a place to start when you go there. Given the nature of the case, I assumed you'd be moving on the tip soon."

"Hmm," I noised. "Yes, Michael often forgets that he doesn't live in a housing bunker in Queens anymore. The nitwit. But I can explain all that to you later."

"And you will—that and much more." Clarissa snapped her paper fully open with both hands and didn't turn as she said, "Because I'll tell you something, Trajan—that 'political meeting' I went to last night? It wasn't a political meeting at all. It was several of my more trusted friends in the county government, and one from the Governor's Mansion, explaining to me just exactly how much you and Michael have been pissing certain people in law enforcement and the county and state governments off. They urged me to talk you out of carrying on with what you're doing. And, depending on what I hear from you all this evening, I may have to try to do that. Shiloh is supposed to be yours, one day, Trajan—and I'd hate to see it go to those preppy siblings of yours because you screwed up and got your head blown off. Clear?"

I let out a deep, heavy breath. "Clear," I said.

"All right, then. Go and get the boy, now," Clarissa continued. "Leave us alone while you gather the rest of your band in the living room for drinks. Well? Go on!"

Grinning, I got to my feet and started back through the doorway to the living room.

Michael and Derek had by now made it to the photos on the piano, most of which had been taken in places other than those in the hallway, since they dated to the period after 1967, when the Six-Day War had turned much of the "romantic" Middle East into a perpetual battleground. Indeed, I think the fact that there had ever been a time when such places had been considered exotic or alluring was even more foreign and fascinating to Derek—a child and victim of the post-9/11 era—

than it was to me. And so I understood the look of wide-eyed wonder with which he beheld the images of two women whose lifestyle marked them, after all, as technically damned in most of the locales they had visited, moving as freely as if they had experienced no censure at all: which, in the main, they had not, a fact that spoke as much to their charm and force of character as it did to anything else.

"I hate to break this little party up, fellas," I said to Mike and Derek, as they leaned on the piano with their backs to me. "But we've got to round up the other two and gather in here for drinks."

"I can go get them!" Derek made a move toward the back hallway; and once again, I had that peculiar feeling that he was seeing through my little charade.

"That's all right, Derek," I said. "Mike and I have got to lock the JU-52 up for the night, anyway."

"Well, then," the kid maneuvered quickly, "I can at least come with you, can't I?"

"You could, but you could also do me a favor, if you would."

"A favor?" Derek asked, reverting to his default attitude of suspicion.

"Yeah," I replied. "A favor. See, my great-aunt is kind of a big shot in local politics, but she doesn't know, as most of them don't seem to know, very much about the whole 'throwaway children' thing. And she wants to. Plus, she doesn't want to say anything impolite by mistake, once Ambyr and Lucas get here. So—do you think you could take a few minutes while we do what we need to and tell her about what happened with your folks and Lucas', and with Ambyr—all that stuff? It would mean we don't have to cover it during dinner, when it might be slightly more embarrassing."

"Oh." Derek was clearly relieved, having likely thought the favor I was going to ask would involve something more onerous; that, and he enjoyed being treated as an adult. "Yeah, I guess I could do that much, anyway."

Leaning on Derek's shoulder with my free arm once again, I turned him to the doorway to the porch. "Okay, then, let me just introduce you, and then we'll see how it goes."

As I let the kid walk ahead of me toward the brightly lit French doors, the sunset blurring the lines of his silhouette, it seemed to me that he might be passing into another world; which, when Clarissa greeted him with a firm handshake and a smile, I realized that he was, given the town he'd grown up in. I might have been a strange character to Derek; but Clarissa represented, for all practical purposes, another race of beings, although the careful work Mike and I had done to exploit his attraction to the photos inside and particularly to the captivating image of Diana made certain that this was a species—unlike, say, Marcianna—that Derek now felt no uneasiness about; one that, on the contrary, he would immediately trust.

"Nice work, L.T.," Mike said. "And me, too, of course. Not to mention Clarissa. The kid'll be putty in her hands."

He gave me a pat on the back, one that I found disturbing rather than satisfying. "Was it such nice work, Michael?" I asked.

"Well," he answered, moving to the defensive, "we proved our point, didn't we?"

"Exactly," I said. "We proved our point, all right—the point that those throwaway kids probably walked into their final situations with their eyes open and smiles on their faces."

"But—this isn't the same, L.T.," Mike protested, "Derek *has* a family, he's got Lucas and Ambyr."

"He's got a family," I answered, still angry, mostly with myself. "But they're not *his* family—not even those two, no matter how much they want to be. No, Mike. That boy bears watching; because whatever the four victims fell for, he might just fall for it, too. Anyway . . . Let's get the others, before I start feeling any shittier . . ."

Which I soon ceased to do, harsh as that may sound. But Mike, I soon remembered, had supplied us with the concrete first step we needed for our attack on those members of the world's "new" wealthy who embody the same approach to impoverished and lost children that old money has always displayed; a desire to make use of them, in this case in very intimate if as yet still (to us) unproven ways. Our trip to New York would, I had no doubt, clarify just what those ways were, but first we would require a sponsor, which was a large part of the reason for my wanting Lucas and Derek present for dinner: we were going to have to get not only Clarissa's blessing, but her financial backing, so that we could move among the people we were targeting with complete credibility.

Thus Mike and I, after making sure all was well within the JU-52, hurried Lucas and Ambyr along toward dinner, Ambyr once again locking her arm onto my free one, and Lucas once again describing everything to his sister, as we approached and then reentered the house. It was a task made all the easier for the kid to perform with real excitement because he was himself so amazed by all the things he came across. I will admit that I had never truly appreciated just what a beautiful home Diana and Clarissa had created out of an already stately, if idiosyncratic, one until I heard Lucas describing every detail of it: the colors of walls, moldings, curtains, floors, rugs, the textures of them all, the antiques that remained from the Colonel's time and the artifacts brought home from all over the world by my great-grandfather and then by Diana and Clarissa. There were a few hiccups—"She's a *dyke*?" Lucas exclaimed in a voice that was close to being too loud, after he'd seen the first of the photos of Diana and Clarissa and had them explained to him—but all in all, things went well; Ambyr's excitement was just as great as Lucas', and was expressed by her holding my arm tighter with hers, or at times even wrapping both her two around my one, so that her body pressed against mine, further heightening reactions that had seemed to have gone from my life forever.

Once we were all in the living room, exploration having come to an end, we found that Annabel had set out a tray with Clarissa's usual ice bucket and bottle of Talisker, along with smooth crystal glasses and a smaller container of crushed ice in which sat two bottles of Genesee beer: Clarissa's standing rule was that kids of fifteen should be allowed one or two beers on social occasions, while young ladies of twenty could be given the good stuff. Lucas, ecstatic at this enlightened approach, quickly informed his sister that she couldn't do anything about it, because it wasn't her house and she didn't make the rules, here; to which Ambyr replied that one beer was fine, so long as he drank it slowly, rather than getting so suddenly hammered that he acted like an idiot all through dinner. This agreement struck, we sat on the matching olive suede couches that faced each other in front of Colonel Jones' massive fireplace, the mantel pillars of which had been fabricated from two 12-pounder Napoleon Model 1857 cannon, the principal field pieces of the American Civil War. Pyramids of shot for each stood at their bases; and upon these items Lucas waxed especially rhapsodic to his sister, especially after he'd had a couple of deep pulls off his bottle of Genesee. As for Ambyr, one Talisker and I felt her head resting on my shoulder, as if she had finally reached the sort of place she had long dreamt of calling home. Only Marcianna's absence disturbed her, to which I said that she would soon meet Terence and understand all.

For Mike and me, however, there was always the proverbial and disturbing ticking clock: whatever else we needed to do during this dinner, we also needed to stay relatively sober and get down to Heinsdale as soon as we could . . .

Eventually Derek appeared from the front porch, looking quite happy and even rather pleased with himself: whatever Clarissa might say about my abilities to manipulate people psychologically, she truly was the past master, and she had evidently done quite a job on him. As he immediately snatched up his own beer and joined Lucas at the fireplace, I excused myself from Ambyr's side and rose to intercept Clarissa, who followed Derek into the room in a few minutes, ambling at an uncharacteristically slow pace toward the scotch bottle. I knew this was because she had some message she wanted to give me, so I lit a cigarette and stood close as she pulled out one of her Camels, took the light I offered her, and then murmured to me, in a very urgent tone:

"I don't know exactly what that kid is hiding, Trajan—but it's important, and it's weighing him down. It wouldn't surprise me a bit if he experiences some kind of nervous breakdown within the *next few days* . . ."

We would talk more of this later, I knew; but for now, I simply turned to Mike, who had been watching us both, and nodded very certainly. Clarissa, meanwhile, went to fill a crystal tumbler full of ice and Talisker. This she downed fairly quickly, before spending some time talking with Lucas and Ambyr and then saying that it was time to get to the table. Right after she'd made this announcement, however, she asked Lucas if he would guide his sister to the dining room, as she needed to discuss some family business with me while we went in. I knew this to be an absurdity, because Clarissa and I never had any family business to discuss. My great-aunt disliked the rest of my family even more than I did: her antipathy toward my father had been rooted in his doing nothing at prep school and then his Ivy League college save go out for sports and drink, but it had reached critical mass when he had failed to get me to a qualified oncologist in time to not only save more (or perhaps all) of my leg, but also avoid the kind of nightmarish experiences that I had been enduring that summer. For this, Clarissa had never forgiven him; and after my final boyhood surgery, she'd made it known that the rest of my family—including my brothers and sister, who were, in the end, quite similar in tastes and personalities to my father—were no longer welcome at Shiloh, allowing me my first experience of self-esteem.

None of which explained what she might want to discuss with me that evening before dinner, unless it was more about Derek; but her look told me that this was not so. We moved more slowly than the others across the living room and toward the candlelit dining room, one side of which opened onto the porch. Clarissa said nothing in the time it took us to reach the arched partition between the two rooms, while I, in my vanity, began to think that perhaps she had simply wanted to walk in with me, and reached out with my arm to take hers, only to be slapped away as if I were a mad dog.

"Don't *do* that," she said. "You know how it pisses me off." As I let my free arm drift back to my side, Clarissa whispered on: "Although I understand why your brains are so scrambled that you're acting like an idiot. I'm just glad I was here to impartially confirm how much trouble Derek is in." Pausing to watch as Lucas described our dining setting to Ambyr, my great-aunt at length concluded, "She's quite a beautiful girl, isn't she? And smart. Very smart."

"Yes, she is," I answered without thinking; then, catching myself, I jibed, "Why, do you want me to put in a good word?"

That got me not a slap but a closed fist in my arm, and a painful one, at that. "No, you little changeling," Clarissa said. "Don't be crass. Besides, I wouldn't dream of interfering with destiny."

"Destiny?"

"Indeed." Clarissa extinguished her Camel on one of the cannon and threw the butt in the fireplace. "You two've known each other, what, a few hours? Yet you're already acting like star-crossed lovers. It's rather adorable, in that horribly sickening way."

"Hang on a second," I said, as we entered the dining room. "We're just—just making sure that we're on the same page, for the sake of the boys and the case, it's not what—"

"'Making sure you're on the same page'? Is that what you call it?" Clarissa put a finger to my chest. "Trajan, you get on much more of the same page and you'll find yourselves hitched. And I wouldn't mind, I have to tell you. She's all right, that one—a lot better than those unbearable New York doctors and therapists you used to bring up here."

"But, Clarissa," I said urgently, since we'd only be able to get in a few more words before we sat down. "I'm about twice her age."

"And you'll need to be, to keep up with her. Count your blessings, nephew, and enjoy it . . ." She raised her voice suddenly to address the others at the table. "Now, then—have you all found spots? Good. Oh, but, Mike, you can't be between Ambyr and me—get over here and sit between the boys." Mike looked at her in confusion. "Do it, Dr. Li," Clarissa insisted.

From no one else would Mike have accepted this order; but move he did, and then Clarissa took me firmly by the shoulders and deposited me in the seat he'd been occupying. When I was tucked in and Annabel had started to appear with plates piled high with freshly grilled steaks, mashed potatoes, and summer vegetables, Ambyr took my hand under the table and leaned in to murmur in my ear, her lips so close that they occasionally brushed against my flesh:

"You and Clarissa might want to learn that, when people lose their sight and start to rely on their hearing, whispering is one of the quickest things they learn to overhear. I couldn't quite make out what you were saying in the living room, but your last conversation was pretty simple."

I turned to stare into those veiled violet eyes, and found that Ambyr was smiling wide. "I'm so sorry," I said, my voice as quiet as hers had been. "She—she's not always the most tactful—"

"No, no, don't be silly," Ambyr said, her mouth near my ear again. "I think it's flattering. And who knows? Maybe it'll happen. Although you'll have to get over this thing about your age, Trajan—I mean, don't you think that what we've each been through kind of puts us on the same level?"

I could do no more than nod vacantly; and then, remembering that she couldn't see the movement, I said, "I do. Absolutely."

"Good," she concluded, feeling for her silverware. "Now, if you can just turn out to actually *not* be a jerk, underneath it all . . ."

"All right, all right!" Clarissa interrupted, banging the meeting to order by tapping her fork on her glass. "Let's get to it . . ." By now, wine brought over by my great-grandfather from France was on the table, in addition to the Talisker, which pleased Ambyr; and after it'd been poured, Clarissa tore into her steak with knife and fork. "Some people still say it's wrong to discuss business over food, and usually I agree. But tonight, we have no choice. It is now time for you all to give me as quick a summary as you can, of this case, and we'll go from there."

I sighed, pulling my watch from my vest and opening it: Mike and I didn't have much time to explain ourselves, even with support from the others. Whatever was looming down in Heinsdale, whatever it was that was so serious that Pete felt he couldn't even speak of it over a cell phone, we really would need clear heads. So, reluctantly, I reached for my water glass . . .

{v.}

During the summary that followed, any shreds of conviviality at the table were replaced by an air of rather grim purpose. After that, the first new business to be addressed and incorporated was just what Clarissa had been able to learn Monday evening about the lengths to which the agents of state law enforcement were willing to go to keep us out of the investigation:

"So far as I can tell," Clarissa said, "this whole matter of throwaway children, along with the murders of four of them, just gains in pressure as you ascend the heights of power, as it were. The possibility for scandal has gone from limited and obscure, back when it was just a child welfare issue, to full-on orange alert, when it grew into a series of deaths that might reflect on the governor. And a lot of people are blaming you, Trajan, along with you, Mike, for that fact. Given the presidential ties and aspirations of our state's chief executive, well . . . The way I heard it, he'll do just about anything to keep it quiet. That effort started with simply trying to discourage you from advising Steve Spinetti and Pete Steinbrecher. It escalated when you were present at that shooting in Fraser— and when you managed to get yourself caught on television. The need to convince you to give up your involvement became almost a panic, because everyone, at every level of law enforcement and government, saw their ambitions and their promotions threatened by this case's being laid open to the public. And so, I don't know who took that shot at you. But the truth is—it could have been almost anybody."

A long pause ensued; and then Mike, emboldened by a bellyful of beef and another, ill-advised tumbler of Talisker, replied, "I'm not so sure, Clarissa. Because you see, while it *might* have been anybody, the simple fact is that it *was* somebody."

There was another hush as Clarissa eyed Mike, in a way that said he'd better demonstrate his point, if he didn't want trouble. In the meantime,

I gave my partner some backup by standing (it was high time for me to do so, anyway, as my left thigh and hip were throbbing even through the whiskey) and pacing around the table, listing our most apparent and definite possibilities for who had, in fact, shot at us. There was, of course, the idea of an actual state trooper acting under orders from his superiors; but I felt very confident in eliminating this notion, as I believed that Mitch McCarron would have gotten wind of any such thing going on. Mitch, in turn, would have warned me, unless he'd received very specific orders from no one less than the governor; and, fool that I knew our governor to be, I didn't believe he'd reached the point where he'd make those kind of Nixonian errors. Next up was the possibility of a rogue cop, acting out of uniform but using his service weapon; but here the last question repeated itself (who would have been telling him to make such a bold move?) and was joined by a second: what kind of personal reason could he have for doing something that might not only finish his career, but net him a lengthy prison sentence, as well?

This left the idea of someone using a weapon that would make us *think* that a trooper was behind the shooting, in order to give the impression that the state meant to get us by whatever means possible. That, in turn, pointed to someone directly involved in the deaths, someone creating both a red herring and a warning with a single act. Mike, his courage bolstered, said that we favored this theory; but Lucas, trying admirably to demonstrate that he had been paying attention during all previous explanations of our method, arrived at still another option: that whoever had shot at us had simply been someone who owned a .308 rifle and, perhaps at an earlier date—or perhaps just for this job— had fitted it with a suppressor. This person could have been trying to settle a score that had nothing to do with the throwaways case: an old enemy out of the past, come to finally use the advantage of people's attention being fixed elsewhere to take vengeance. It was the wild-card theory, the notion of a free radical splitting off inside the organism of the case; and while I made sure to give Lucas points for thinking outside the box, I also explained to him that there was simply no way to account for these types of possibilities—and that, with all we had inside the box already, we'd be plenty busy enough. But the notion was worth remembering.

Thus did we narrow the field of suspects in the shooting (and by extension, of course, so much more) from the "almost anybody" that Clarissa had mentioned to one very good option and several unlikely ones, all of which we would have to debate at greater length as the case progressed. Still, the talk that we *did* have—which covered just about the amount of time that I thought we could afford—impressed Clarissa deeply, I could see that; and I could see, too, that during our discussion she slowly but steadily came around to the notion that we might indeed have some idea of what we were doing. I also sensed that the implications of the case—not merely political implications, but moral ones, as well—were indeed weighing as heavily on her as I had hoped they would.

Alone among our group, there *were* two who remained reluctant to speak: Ambyr and Derek. Ambyr, of course, was still learning things as fast as she could pick them up, and so her reluctance was understandable. But Derek, whenever I deliberately asked him to throw in an opinion on one point or another—even on firearms—simply fidgeted uncomfortably and reverted to his usual halting failure to grasp facts as quickly as they were given to him. None of the others saw anything remarkable in this; yet none of the others had been present when Derek had delivered his insightful analysis of the bullet hole in the roof of the Prowler. True, it was possible that he, like many other autistic young savants, simply felt more comfortable displaying such behavior in one-on-one situations; but that explanation felt inadequate to me. Whatever was behind the complexity of his behavior, that evening the young man seemed to me as much furtive as mentally challenged, and I became steadily more convinced that he might well be the facilitator between (if not the ultimate organizer of) any children in the county who were seeking new lives and the New York City residents ready to provide those outwardly dreamlike existences.

All of which made it more important to talk to Clarissa about Derek privately, to get a sense of what she thought she had divined about him; but even more urgent was the necessity to get her backing for what she had called our *démarche* on the city. And, somewhat to my surprise, it was my great-aunt herself who broached that topic. Once our discussion of potential suspects in the shooting had been completed, I returned to my seat, and all became quiet at the table, until Clarissa finally said:

"All right, Trajan. I'll do it."

"You'll—do it, Aunt?"

"You heard me." To Mike's and Lucas' smiles and my own sigh of relief, she looked past me and explained, "You see, Ambyr, I've realized ever since mumblings started going around this house about a trip to New York, and as people I knew within and connected to local and state government began to warn me about what Trajan and Mike were up to, that I was going to be asked to play an additional role in this affair." She looked up at me. "To become, in essence, your sponsor, Trajan. I also took it, from the expanded guest list for this evening, that everyone present would be playing a role in the undertaking. Lucas' part is—characteristically, I suspect—painfully obvious. He's the bait."

"Uh-oh," Lucas piped up. "Couldn't we just say 'lure'?"

"As you will, Lucas, it's your neck. But I wonder if you know—I wonder if you've informed him, nephew—just how unforgiving the NYPD can be."

"I'm not sure *I* know," Ambyr said quietly.

"Yes, I realize that," Clarissa answered, with a rare smile of genuine indulgence. "I knew it earlier. Because you're smart, Ambyr. And from where I sit, you—and perhaps you, Derek—seem to be the only ones taking this as gravely as is warranted. You other three, you just want to get to New York, to rush into this group of wealthy child-seekers that you believe exists and eventually uncover the prime backers who are financing its operation in this county, as well as other counties and locations in this state, and perhaps in the nation, thinking that the NYPD will let you do it. You're proceeding from the assumption that your effort will be a lesser priority. Just as it has now become easier, with the attention of our politically correct media investigators focused on abused foreign children, to exploit young American children who increasingly are being left to fend for themselves by their own parents. And Ambyr, Lucas, Derek—I hope you know I say this with full sympathy for, and full outrage over, your personal situation."

"Thanks, Clarissa," Ambyr said. "We all appreciate that."

Clarissa passed a smoky hand before her. "No need. Apologies are owed you. Not only the apologies of your families, but the apologies of this state, which, instead of trying to find new ways to accommodate young people in your kind of predicaments, has tried to cover up the problem. A problem that they can't even be bothered to come up with a better name for than 'throwaway children.' Well, you are *not* throwaway children. My nephew and his partner are trying to prove that, and I actually applaud them for it. The exposure of the systematic abuse behind these deaths, whether it's sexual or emotional, will force a completely new look at the problem; and the fact that it may just get our idiotic governor tossed out is just a bonus. Yes, it *will* be dangerous. However . . ."

Stubbing out one cigarette, Clarissa refilled her scotch tumbler, lit another Camel, and prepared to go on. I think at this point that her words, combined with her capacity for both nicotine and alcohol, were greatly impressing our guests, as they—even Derek, for whatever reasons of his own—had adopted postures of genuine fascination. And I suspect that they were all learning why my great-aunt enjoyed the respect that she did in the township and the county.

"I'll find a way to do it," Clarissa said at length. "Because you don't think you can solve this thing from here in Surrender. I agree. Whoever the agents of this game are locally, they're not the ultimate planners of it. You think this New York trip is essential. I agree, again; but you know you can't fund it, because when you get there you're going to have to move in fairly top-level circles to find your quarry. So I'll back it. Because, known as you are to the city police, you are not well known among your target . . . 'demographic,' shall we say. And you're not well known in the kind of places you want me to foot the bill for. Have I got it, nephew?"

"In a nutshell, Aunt," I answered.

"Then you'll stay in some five-star hotel, one that's in close proximity to the target you've already obtained, so you can blackmail that target into getting you past certain doors. The doors where this whole scheme is planned and paid for. It will be a financial strain, Trajan, there's no question. And I can't promise to keep it up, prices being what they are in the city, for more than, say, a week."

"More than enough time," Mike threw in, "if things go right."

"Then make them go right," Clarissa said. "And clear the mess up, in this county—because I want to tell you something . . ." As she took another deep drag of her Camel and another belt of Talisker, I knew that we were getting closer to her personal, inward thoughts on what we were doing. "You are too young, Trajan, to have had a full understanding of what the last crisis like this one in this county was like."

I nodded: as always, Clarissa's thoughts and mine had been running in some kind of tandem. "The NAMBLA murders," I said.

"Correct."

Lucas offered no comment on this, nor did I expect him to, being as I'd told him all about the long-ago killings. And from the manner in which neither Ambyr nor Derek said anything, I took it that our young partner had, once again, brought our business home.

"The NAMBLA killings," Clarissa repeated. "It wasn't long after Diana and I had moved back to take control of the farm that they happened—and I want to tell you something: in the wake of those few murders, it was not a good time to be living an 'alternative lifestyle,' in this county. I don't want to see anything like that happen again. If the responsibility for these latest child deaths can be laid at the door of New York City, no one in Burgoyne County will be surprised, or likely even care much. But if they pin it on someone local—and as you know, that's just what they're trying to do—well, let's just say that I don't want to see it happen again. So go, place the blame at the feet of that city, a place I don't even *pretend* to understand, anymore. If it will keep things around here peaceful—then do what you have to . . ."

We all absorbed the weight of what we'd just heard, even the boys seeming to understand that it meant a great deal; and, after Mike and I had tried to thank Clarissa—difficult to do, precisely, because we wouldn't know just how indebted our endeavor had become to her until we'd made our final travel arrangements—we all said our good-nights and (with Ambyr's help, in the boys' cases) our thank-yous. Then, filing our way out of the house that neither Ambyr nor Lucas wanted to leave, but that Derek seemed awfully anxious to depart, we walked up to the car, the mood in our little crew generally very good. I half-lied to Ambyr, who had again grabbed tight onto my arm, telling her that I needed to stay behind and both go over details with Clarissa and feed Marcianna, and that Mike would drive them all home. There was disappointment, playful but real, in her voice as she said that she understood both these needs; but the unexpectedly tender kiss that she planted on my cheek as she got into the front seat of the Empress was a potential blow to my clarity of thought, making it all the more urgent that I attend to my alter ego and then get back to the house.

Having taken care of the first task, I moved quickly downhill to find Clarissa back in her chair on the porch (which was surprising, because ordinarily she would have been in her study, with public television blaring) and simply staring off at the western sky, where the faintest halo of soft, orange-purple light remained just above the mountains in the distance.

"Well, Aunt?" I said, as I slowed my approach to match her obvious mood.

She nodded a few times thoughtfully, no decisiveness or call to arms such as she'd uttered at the table in her manner or in the words that followed: "It's a hard thing, Trajan . . . To think that a boy with such obvious difficulties, who has been used so despicably by his own family, might be caught up in such a shitty business as the one you're suggesting . . ."

I studied her face for a moment, leaning on one of the square columns of the porch with my right side to give my left hip a break. At length I said, with a quiet regret to match her own, "But you think he is."

She blew out a strong gust of smoke and nodded, tapping her ash in a tray on the wide arm of her chair. "You saw his reactions during the various parts of our conversation, I'm sure." I nodded. "That would be enough to confirm that he's mixed up in it somehow. He could barely stay in the room when we were discussing the structure of this supposed ring of child users, child abusers, whatever it in fact is."

"I did, as you say, observe as much."

"Yes, but what you *didn't* observe was my earlier conversation with him."

I took out a cigarette of my own and lit it. "I may not have needed to." She gave me a short glance, arching an eyebrow. "Before you were alone with him, when we were in the kitchen hallway and he was studying the photos of you and Diana—something odd happened. He revealed—and I'm still not sure if he's aware that he did it, because he seemed to go into a severely detached state—but he revealed how very separate he feels from Lucas and Ambyr, for all that they are good friends and live together as a family. And then he hinted at something particularly strange: he said, 'One day, it'll be *my* turn to go.' I'm sure, now, that there's only one thing that could have meant: that it will be his turn to find a wealthy new family, someday, just as the others did—but *he* will make his new situation work out. That belief is an unshakable rock on which his entire mental stability rests. And who knows, Mike may be right—maybe others *have* made it work, somehow. But if a girl as smart as Shelby Capamagio couldn't do it . . ."

Clarissa studied my face again, more steadily and critically this time. "You're certain that's what he said? Because he used language very close to that with me, when talking about getting out of Surrender and never caring if he saw it again."

"Oh, it was what he said," I replied. "And the thing is, it reminded me of the time I first met him: he tried very hard, when discussing the matter with Lucas, to believe that the first victim who was found, Kyle Howard, had had a good life after his family disappeared. Derek *needed* to believe it, even when presented with a series of facts that proved that it wasn't so; and I think what made him nervous—so nervous that he had to haul ass out of the hollow—was that, not only was *I* contradicting his narrative about Kyle, but so was Lucas. He didn't go because he believed all the stories about Death's Head, or because he was afraid of life here on Shiloh—hell, he was fine with it, earlier this evening. It was that same terrible idea that maybe things hadn't gone for Kyle the way he believed they had. So, before dinner, he unintentionally revealed that he might be intending to find out for himself—and the only way to do that would be to follow in Kyle's footsteps. Escape, using the same path. So, yes, while we were at dinner, every mention of the case reignited that very scared and scary conflict of his—because he seems to want and need to follow that unknown path, a path that he *must know the way down*."

"Yes," Clarissa said, nodding again, her gaze still on me. Then she smiled, just for an instant. "You know, Trajan, it's a good thing that you had me around as a role model—you've developed quite a head for these things . . ." But as she turned back to the horizon, her momentary satisfaction seemed to fade quickly. "At any rate . . . I don't think, as you say, that he's going to really believe your version of facts until he's gone through that other experience himself. Yet somewhere within him he's aware that taking that path could be very dangerous. That's what I meant about a nervous break. He clearly needs—not so much wants, but *needs*—something to happen, and soon, or the conflict will cause some kind of crisis."

"Indeed," I said. "All the more so because, as is typical in such cases, I don't think his fear of any danger will ultimately make him disobey the imperative to find out."

Clarissa took a final drag off her cigarette, stubbed it out, and, rising to go inside, said, "Any more than anything any of us might say will stop him. It's just a lousy, lousy situation, nephew . . ."

She started into the house, hands thrust deep into the pockets of her pants; and then the sound of tires spinning into the driveway became audible. Mike halted at the base of the lawn below the house and got out, calling, "Okay, Trajan—Pete just called again, and he wants us there *but now*."

"No reason to get the cattle riled up, Dr. Li," Clarissa said, quietly but firmly. "You two go about your business—but at a civilized pace, please. And *you*—" She poked a finger in my chest. "You give that girl a chance. She's something special, nephew . . ." Then, at last, Clarissa turned to the house again and I said good night to her as she went, a statement she acknowledged by raising a hand. It was a movement that seemed, at that moment, to require a great effort; and I knew that the entire dinner, to say nothing of what had underlain it (not least Derek's predicament), had brought up difficult memories for my great-aunt, as well as reminded her that these were the kind of trials that she had best been able to manage when Diana was still alive; and I felt a moment of guilt about the need to involve her at all. Yet there was no other way to do what we needed to do.

So I stepped off the porch and moved quickly toward and into the Empress. Mike backed a little more easily out of the drive, then turned the car's V-8 loose once we were out of sight of the house, hurtling us into something for which, we would find, even we were wholly unprepared . . .

{vi.}

As Mike and I drove first along a high, roughly north-south, and unnumbered roadway that paralleled Route 22 in the Taconic foothills, eventually leaving even patches of blacktop behind, and then started to snake our way up often-hidden hollows ever higher into the mountains—sometimes jumping onto roadways that, far from having no numbers, had not even names—we both realized without needing to say it that we were approaching no "ordinary" scene of bloodshed and sorrow. No, what we began to sense, as even the scant light of the night sky was obscured by the thickening woods, was an act or acts so outrageous that they would make one truly feel, yet again, that society as we understand it in this country is unraveling at its edges: is, indeed, beginning to fray so badly that if the process is not stopped, we as a people shall soon be utterly unrecognizable to ourselves.

As this knowledge of where we were going sank ever further in, the only sounds in the car were my occasional instructions on what turn should be taken—provided the next road was even marked on Mike's GPS system, as several were not. Yet Fate would not tolerate our becoming lost, that night; and when the Empress' headlights finally began to reflect off something white and metallic, we rightly suspected that it must be the back of Pete's cruiser. Before long we had pulled up with an angry skid beside it, Mike having raised a great cloud of dry dust into what was becoming, that night, a steadily stronger east wind.

The house that stood before our cars, gloomily illuminated by the Empress' headlights, was one of those hideous old A-frame chalets, built in the 1970s out of dark wood stained even darker, so that over time it had become almost black. It featured, of course, a deck with a hot tub out front: a wooden-sided monstrosity of the type euphemistically called "Swedish," which, like most of its vintage, had come to resemble some sort of soiled cauldron in which were boiled things about which it would be wise not to know too many particulars.

In the years since its construction, the house had evidently changed hands many times, and fallen in value with each new owner's failure to maintain it, so that it was now nothing short of a hovel. The wooden walls, their protective treatment left unrenewed for too many decades, had begun to warp and crack in many spots, while the shingled roof had sprouted greenery. The wooden railings on the decks outside each of the two upper levels of the dwelling had rotted and fallen away and, where replaced at all—presumably outside the bedrooms, so that some sleepy drunk inside did not go wandering off the edge—had been traded out for pre-EPA-code pressure-treated wood, which had taken on that forbidding grey-green tint that copper and arsenic produce as they age. The shutters on the windows, once undoubtedly thought picturesque, with their orange paint and heart-shaped cutouts, were now wind-whipped and falling away, to the point that a few were simply missing, while others had been screw-gunned back onto the walls for appearances' sake, never to swing on hinges again.

We found Pete standing amid what had once been the hillside lawn of the place, which was rapidly being reclaimed by the forest around it. Woodland undergrowth had already performed the advance work, and now there were saplings of the same kinds of trees that had slapped at the Empress during our drive up joining the invasion. But young pine trees were also present, whose parents surrounded the house, quite probably having been planted by the builders to increase the effect of being in some European hideaway, but in the end only cutting off nearly all direct light, even the little available that night. Pete himself was bare-headed, always an odd informality, when he was working, and was wiping his brow with a bit of shammy cloth that looked to have come from his cruiser—this, despite the fact that there was nothing in that strange breeze that seemed like cause for perspiration.

As we approached him, we caught sight of the house's final peculiarity: a pestilential-looking little equipment shed, built entirely of more carcinogenic pressure-treated wood. I could see from Mike's expression that his mind was racing in the same direction that mine was: whatever we had been called to see, it was inside that shed. But when we turned, we found Pete just shaking his head.

"Yeah, that's what we thought, at first, too," he said. "But that ain't it. Just an outhouse, must've been dug after the builders sold out. And the pump's for water—guess the septic went a long time ago, and since the building inspector, assuming Heinsdale even has one, never comes up here, they figured they were safe. Anybody else—say, the tax assessor—likely did a real fast drive-by. Not the kind of place you'd like to go into."

"No, it is not . . ." I said, my voice barely audible over the wind.

"So, okay, then," Mike announced, his trace kit in his hand and his voice all business. "Where do you want to start?"

"The basement, Mike," Pete replied nervously. "Start and finish, right down there . . ."

The interior of the house, lit by work lights identical to those Curtis Kolmback had set up in the Capamagio trailer, displayed the same level of decrepitude as did the outer shell, while at the same time exhibiting many of the bizarre priorities that dominate modern American life. The sunken floor of the very large room that we stepped into was still covered by the same vile brown shag carpet that was likely original to the house. Its color hid a multitude of sins—all save the occasional burn from a cigarette or joint, as well as the rising and permanent stench of beer and wine. The once bright yellow walls, too, had probably not been painted in forty years, based on the extent to which their fading and peeling had advanced; while the very Seventies fire pit in the center of the open space badly needed cleaning, and was clearly the main source of heat for the entire house, augmented only by a few small electric space heaters: a suspicion confirmed by enormous piles of cut and split logs—some green and covered, curing for next year, some dry and ready to be burned anytime—that were stacked in the backyard and just visible through a large window in the kitchen. That same kitchen was an adventure in itself, strewn with dirty dishes and aging takeout boxes.

And yet, hanging on one brick-faced wall of the living room, above a DVD player, was a wide-screen television: the only thing in the whole place that seemed to have received any investment, care, or cleaning. Such was not unusual, we'd found, in such places, both urban and rural; the only thing that *was* unusual was that anything else that wasn't nailed down had been dragged away by the BCI, in that way that such agencies can sweep through a habitation and leave it looking like a dust bowl. Yet the house did not feel one iota more sanitized for their actions.

"Okay," Mike said to Pete. "So it's a shithole. No big surprise. And your colleagues have taken away everything that might be of any use—no surprises there, either. It also appears, from the dusting and the chalk marks, that some FIC tech has had a little party."

"Yeah-uh," Pete droned. "I called you as soon as Kolmback left. And, like you say, it is, being a genuinely disgusting mess, just about what we had expected to find."

"Curtis worked *this* scene, too?" I asked; and when Pete nodded knowingly, I could only frown in disappointment: I had thought better of Kolmback than to get mixed up in something like this. "Well," I continued, "based on the television, I'd say that the Patricks had at least one computer."

"Yeah," Pete answered. "Nice one, too. Driving around a piece-of-crap old Ford that was a danger to them and everybody else on the road, but they had one nice computer."

"Which is now in Frank Mangold's hands, along with the Ford?" I asked, to which Pete nodded again. "That computer likely had some interesting things on it. Things they valued. Password-protected, or actually encrypted?"

"I don't know," Pete said. "The BCI computer geeks are working on it now."

"Oh, well then," Mike laughed. "We ought to have an answer in a month or so."

"And when we do," I added, "it will be—guess what?—exactly what Frank and Cathy Donovan were looking for. Even if they have to pull the pictures off of kiddie porn sites themselves, it'll still be going to the Patricks' IP address. Ah, the conveniences that the Web has brought to law enforcement . . ."

"Well, that's kind of the way that Steve and I were looking at it," Pete replied, his face becoming quite grave. "That is, the *first* time we went through the place, after the BCI boys were done. Top to bottom, there wasn't a trace of anything you could've found objectionable. Couple of sex toys and a bottle of knock-off Viagra from Pakistan, but that was about it—and we pretty much figured the BCI left those behind, after they examined them, just for us to find. Make us feel like we were doing something."

"Sounds about right," Mike judged. "How's it feel to be the dog getting thrown a bone, Pete?"

"Lousy," Pete said emphatically. "Especially when all this other crap happened . . ." To Mike's and my questioning looks, Pete nodded toward a doorway off to the side of the kitchen. "Come on . . ." And with that, Pete switched on a large Maglite he'd taken from his belt, then led the way down into a basement that had been formed of poured concrete, much of which was now crumbling.

We had experienced, upstairs, the better portion of a house that— quite beyond being old and decrepit to the point of unhealthiness—was devoid of the most basic amenities, which had been moved, for reasons of cost or of laziness or both, to a hole in the ground within the equipment shed outside: an environment, in short, that was in every way a testament to filth. That much, however, we could prepare ourselves for, and had; but when filth turns first to degradation and then to sickness, well . . . Those are the types of situations where, whether you're in New York City or a town like Heinsdale, there's simply no way to fully brace yourself for what you are going to see.

A solitary work light sat pointed at the ceiling atop an old zebra-skinned barstool (an obviously forgotten piece of the original furnishings of the house) in order to diffuse as much light as possible through the bunker-like basement. Because the high windows in the concrete walls had long since been coated in dirt and overgrown by brush and vines—to say nothing of the fact that it was so unusually dark outside— this was the only source of illumination in the chamber. Due to the clinical yet insufficient halogen glow the lamp gave off, Mike and I reached the bottom of the stairs before our eyes had really adjusted to what was around us. But when they did, we could not help but be further appalled, because all that the basement had evidently been used for, since the demise of the furnace, was the disposal of large plastic bags full of household waste. It must have been the Patricks themselves who had started this practice, because the bags were still not numerous enough to do more than fill the farthest reaches of what we came to see was a fairly expansive basement, one fully as large as the footprint of the chalet wonderland above. Perhaps the original owners had intended to use this space as the kind of basement den that was so popular in the 1970s; whatever the case, it was now the part of the house that was, quite literally, a dump.

But I was at a loss to understand why Pete should have been so unnerved by this, for reasons other than the basic; until Mike, who could turn and take in every corner of a room faster than I could, began slapping and grabbing at my sleeve (much as he had when we'd first met Ambyr at the Kurtz house, although for diametrically opposed reasons) and said, "Trajan—L.T., turn the fuck around—*now*."

In a slight recess among the garbage bags—one that looked, even on first examination, suspiciously like it had been created, not by the random placement of bags, but by their careful and recent rearrangement—sat a simple, medium-backed chair, old but completely out of keeping with the rest of the house: the first sign of a manipulative hand at work. And on this chair sat the body of a child. That might have seemed shocking enough, but the greater cause for both horror and consternation was the state of the body itself: although dressed in what seemed boys' clothing, it would have been impossible to say upon first look whether the remains were male or female, because the skin was drawn so very tightly over the skeletal structure. The eyes were open, and, remarkably, the eyeballs were hauntingly intact, although shrunken by dehydration. The nose was drawn back toward the face, the cartilage severely desiccated, and the lips had been similarly dried and recessed to reveal the grimacing teeth and the dried gums in which they were rooted. As Mike and I moved toward the sight, borrowing Pete's flashlight to get a better look at details, we saw that the hands had been none-too-tightly bound with a very soft braided drapery cord behind the back of the chair and to several of its slats, while the ankles had been tied, in a similarly loose, careful manner, to each of the front legs of the seat. Simple jeans covered the barefoot frame, along with a plaid shirt; and the only sign of life was the hair, which had continued to grow after death, albeit in a slow, uneven manner, until it formed a jagged frame around the head.

It was, all questions of taste and horror aside, a remarkable discovery: "*Mummified*," Mike declared at length, scarcely able to whisper the word. And yet there was something of a sense of, one hesitates to say challenge, but at least of a forthcoming test of his own skills, in the tone of his hushed voice.

"Yes," I said, finding no other explanation imaginable.

"*'Mummified'*?" Pete echoed; and already, he sounded thankful that he'd gotten us to come to the house. "I don't get it, there's no wrapping on it, any of those bandages."

"Those are Egyptian mummies," Mike answered quickly, continuing to examine the body. "And the bandages aren't what mummified them. They held the body together over the centuries, and added a little extra protection from moisture. They may also have had some religious meaning, but opinions differ on that. But what actually mummified them was that priests and their family members would take them into the open desert and let them dry out, being careful to make sure that no scavengers got to them."

"You can mummify a body in lots of places," I continued, as Mike grew more absorbed in the details of the body. "So long as it's sealed tight and there's next to no moisture in the air. An old attic would work, or . . ." And now I went around testing the windows of the room. "A basement, where the windows have been unintentionally sealed, and where nobody comes, anymore, not even to service the furnace." I grabbed the work light and moved it about, poking the ceiling with my cane and getting a look, not at floor planks, but at subflooring made of particle board, and sealed around its edges and along the seams with the kind of noxious polyurethane spray foam used in the Seventies that has also become illegal in recent years. "Like right here. Or so the BCI boys would have us believe . . ."

"That's what I want to know about, and so does Steve," Pete said. "See, when we went through this place the first time, we came down here, and we looked all around these bags of crap, to make sure that nothing was hidden behind them. And nothing was. Then we get the call to come and spell the BCI guards tonight—we had no idea why, they've got plenty of other people to do that kind of grunt work—and what do we find? A body that was *not* here yesterday. And I would swear to that."

"Unh-hunh," I noised, paying as close attention to him as I could, which wasn't easy: for the face of a body that has been mummified (especially recently) is a particularly horrifying yet transfixing sight, whatever the specific cause of its desiccation. The mouth is almost invariably pulled back, as in this case, into a perpetual grimace or even scream, a desperate plea, if not for help, at the very least for justice; while the eyes, on which the lids have been drawn not quite fully up, bear an expression of dull if enormous agony. The body tends to arch with the tightening of the skin over the torso, giving the appearance of a forever-frozen attempt to break free, both of the bonds of the immediate cause of torment and then, more permanently, of the sentence of premature death.

And in this case, that death had been premature, indeed. Mummification can often make the age of a body as difficult to identify, on first look, as its true features; yet in this case, the simple proportions of the person we were studying dictated a child of no more than fourteen. The excellent condition of the teeth, indicating a life spent drinking fluoridated water, reinforced this notion, as did the dimensions of the skull more generally, especially in relation to the size of the eyes. The height could only be guessed at, but it could not have been much more than five feet, if that. All in all, a child, a child who had died, perhaps, as a result of some accident that had left him or her helpless in the place where mummification had taken place, or perhaps after being deliberately locked away in a space much like the one in which we were now standing.

But of *that* specific space, it was already possible to say one thing with absolute certainty: it was not, in fact, the site of death, and when I was again able to speak, I went on to tell Pete as much.

"But—what makes you say that?" he replied. "I mean, I want to agree with you, I'd like to think we're not incompetent or crazy, but how can you be so sure?"

"Think about it, Pete," Mike said, knowing my thoughts and never pausing in his examination of the body. "What's all around you? Garbage. What's outside? No garbage. So it seems pretty likely that, whatever the Patricks were up to, they had only recently begun to throw their bags down here."

"It's my guess," I added, "although you'll want to determine this after you demand a chance to question them yourselves, Pete, that they started throwing their garbage down here when the throwaway deaths became public knowledge, and they began getting death threats again. They were likely terrified, and weren't going outside for any reason if they didn't have to."

"But we don't know that they started getting death threats," Pete said, a bit confused. "I mean, not at this location."

"Yeah, but has anybody *asked* them?" I queried, my eyes still locked on the mummified child.

Pete had to mull that one over. "Well—no, not that I'm aware of. Nobody had any reason to."

"Yeah, well," Mike said from behind the body. "Now they do. So suppose you and Steve try it."

"I'd be happy to," Pete answered. "If Steve or I could get a foot in the door. I was lucky to get away with photographing those documents."

"Maybe," I said. "And maybe there's another way to do it. But we need to get to the root of this whole stinking business—and we need to do it fast. This is pretty much an open declaration from the state: they're going to do whatever's necessary to pin this thing on Jimmy and Jeanette Patrick. But before they can bang the gavel down on that case and move on, making people think these deaths are over and done with, we've got to get some alternate answers, and bring them out into the public eye."

"Okay," Mike announced at that moment, finally standing from behind the dead child's chair. "Here's what I can tell you: this is one hamfisted attempt at a frame, Pete. First of all, like L.T. says, the boy—and it's a boy, maybe thirteen to fifteen—didn't die here. The reasoning behind that is simple: the Patricks have been tossing and stacking garbage down here for at least a fair period of time. That means opening the basement door. That means allowing whatever's upstairs down here. Now, it's not that the BCI were completely irrational when they cooked this one up—I mean, somebody told them, probably Nancy Grimes, that mummified bodies have been found in caves. So they look at this basement and think, 'Hey, it looks like a cave.' And if they'd been smart and removed the garbage first, it might've worked." At that point Mike produced his digital camera, a piece of equipment that (whatever the hawkers of mobile phone cameras would like us to think) was capable of taking far higher resolution images, and in far more detail, than his phone. Blasting away with the rather blinding flash, he began a panoramic series of photos, not simply of the body, but of the basement as a whole.

"You figure they still might try to remove it?" I asked.

"Hey, they tried *this* stunt," Mike answered disdainfully. "If I were them, and Pete repeated what we're about to tell him, I'd just put the original guards back on and ditch the bags in a truck."

"And what are you about to tell me?" Pete said, very disappointed to be placed back in the role of student, but anxious to hear what was coming.

"Well, look around you, Pete," I said, holding up my cane and pulling out my cigarettes. "What do you see?"

"Come on," Pete declared, a little indignantly. "Don't put me through the whole routine, just tell me, will you?"

"You're looking at bags of garbage . . ." I lit two cigarettes and walked over to hand one to Mike. "It's now midsummer." I picked up the work light, and walked to a pile of bags that was near the deputy. "In spring and summer, what do you get with garbage?"

Pete watched as the answer began to materialize around the light of the lantern. "Of course!" he said, clapping a hand to his forehead. "Flies! And flies means maggots, right?"

"Right," Mike said, still taking pictures. "So between this place not being as low in oxygen or as cold as a deep cave or cavern, and the relatively pristine shape of the body, we can determine that he died somewhere else, and was brought here for this purpose."

"But how?" Pete said, wrestling with it. "Wouldn't the body have basically fallen apart when they tried to move it?"

"Not necessarily," I said. "Not if he died recently enough. In the early stages of mummification, there is still some flexibility in the body, which is probably how they got him into the chair and tied him. And here's where you can pull off a real coup, Pete: all of that means that we're looking for a death that occurred—what's it take, Mike, for mummification to really happen, and to be able to move the body without serious deterioration? Two months, three?"

"Depends on the location," Mike replied judiciously. "The drier the faster, but yeah, at least seventy to eighty days, give or take. No more than ninety, in this case."

"Okay," I continued. "Now, it's obvious the BCI didn't just have this kid mummifying, getting him ready for this purpose. And it's also obvious that, unless they did a little grave robbing—"

"Thought of that already," Mike threw in. "But the condition's too good. And there's no evidence of burial, no specks of earth that would have been incidental to digging him up."

"Good," I replied. "That means he was unidentified. I think we can assume, from the sound condition of the clothes, that they put them on him for this farce—"

"Right again," Mike said. "Found a tag from the Goodwill shop in Fraser, they definitely left it there on purpose: redressed him, to make it look local."

"Which means it wasn't," I explained further. "So that's where you and

Steve begin: you want to start looking around the state—I don't think they would have dared to go outside it—for reports of an unidentified boy's body going unclaimed. Recently. Start with the counties farthest from Burgoyne—Clinton, St. Lawrence, Oswego, Erie—and move in from there. They're going to want to have covered their tracks by keeping it all very far apart."

"Try the ones that are also major Adirondack counties, Pete," Mike said. "Including Hamilton, Essex, Franklin—that's high country, there'd be a lot of seasonal homes with attics where this could happen, all secluded enough that people might not have noticed." Mike began to put his camera away, and withdrew some envelopes and vials, to take whatever DNA samples he could easily get—hair, skin, fibers—from the body. Before doing so, however, he paused for a long moment, staring at the agonized face of the young boy and shaking his head. "Poor little guy. Probably wandered into some abandoned house, or maybe somebody's vacation home, then went up to the attic and barred himself in. Or something fell and barred him in. I didn't pull the pant legs up to see if there's a break or sprain of some kind, I don't want to take the chance—hang on."

Mike had caught sight of something, and as he cut the boy's hands free he lifted one, then used one of his implements to begin scraping under the fingernails. "Jesus . . ." he eventually breathed.

"What is it?" Pete asked.

"Well . . ." Mike went on, in the same mournful tone. "I'd have to put it under the scope to be absolutely sure, but—look at those fingers. You can see it with the naked eye." We did as instructed, as Mike grabbed a magnifying glass from his kit.

"Stone," I concluded. "Stone and . . . ?"

"And moss," Mike answered, putting the magnifying glass to work. He moved over to pick up the other hand, and hissed out a pained reaction. "Man—two of the nails on this hand are *gone* completely . . ."

I picked up on his thinking. "A cave?"

"More than likely," Mike replied, still observing and taking samples. "Or an obstruction. But I'd definitely start in the high counties first, Pete."

"But—what are you guys talking about, what happened to him?"

"It looks," I answered quietly, "as though the boy either fell or jumped into some hole."

"But—I mean, what're you talking about, 'jumped'? Why would he jump? And why would he bar himself into an attic?" Pete's voice was wandering between sadness and horror, although he still had not guessed at just what we were thinking.

And it was time to tell him. So, as quickly as I could, I revealed to him our belief that, as unlikely as it might sound on first hearing, the so-called throwaway murders were in fact all suicides, which had then been staged as murders, by some person or group who couldn't afford to have so many suicides linked to him, her, or them. Pete resisted, of course, as any decent man not steeped in exposure to such machinations would; but when I explained our theory that the throwaways were being effectively sold, literally down the river, for profit to rich residents of New York City, he began to accept the notion. Only when I was finished did he bring up the kind of commonsensical point that I had come to expect from him:

"But what about this kid?" he said. "He doesn't exactly look like he was a suicide, if he was trying to claw his way out."

"His death *may* have been just an accident," Mike answered. "Remember, his importance to whoever's behind this frame—and we think it's the BCI—is only that he's dead and fits the profile. That's why it's so important to find out who he was."

"And think about the rest of the poor kid's life," I said, too clinically, I think, for the deputy's liking. "If he fits the profile, he was on his own; or suppose he was in the foster program, and landed in some foster farm where they were only interested in him for the monthly check."

"That'd be my guess," Mike said. "Even in this condition, you can tell there wasn't much to him. Malnourished, I mean. You find that, with a lot of fosters from those farms."

"Okay," I went on. "So he finds a high cave, enters it, starts exploring some hole, and gets stuck. Then, when the terror of his situation really sets in, he tries to claw his way out. An accident—but one that the BCI can use."

"I can't believe it," the deputy murmured; although it was clear from his face that he did.

"Well, one thing's for sure." Mike sighed out the obvious but terrible conclusion as he exhaled a large cloud of smoke: "This does not tell a happy story. And then to get used by the cops like this . . ."

There was little to add to Mike's final indictment; at least, not down in that wretched basement. I needed to begin to tie up loose ends by making a couple of phone calls, and so climbed the stairs back into the sea of filth that was the house. I was almost certain, now, that at least some if not most of the Patricks' recent slovenliness had been caused by their genuine fear that their lives were in danger: a fear prompted not by paranoid fantasies but by death threats made by their current neighbors, who, like Lucas, got too much of what they thought was criminal psychology from television, and held to the belief that child molesters, once punished and freed, will always slip back into their sly and sinister ways.

It is true, of course, that it is nearly impossible to erase the urges that motivate such offenders: for they are almost always rooted in childhood abuse that they themselves have suffered, and in the confusion of these early, perverse notions of intimacy with later romantic and sexual urges. *Well, so what?* comes the all-too-common answer from people who want child abusers disemboweled, or at the very least lethally injected. *Plenty of people suffer abuse as children, without abusing children as adults.* And this is not only true, it makes for what is known on the idiot box as "compelling television." Yet what is also true—what many in my field first began to suspect in the late 1890s and early twentieth century, when Dr. Laszlo Kreizler, in New York City, and his colleague Dr. Adolf Meyer, more nationally, began to seriously work with and classify abused children—is that nearly all sexual offenders, and especially child abusers, can and do learn to control the actions that grow *out* of such urges. Thus the infamous recidivism rate among them is actually fairly low—vastly lower, for example, than among thieves, burglars, and illegal weapons traffickers, and only slightly higher than the tiny number of murderers who kill again after incarceration.

It has never been very hard to understand all this, even if one has not done (as most of us who choose to enter criminal psychiatry and psychology as a profession are required to do) a residency of some kind at a state mental facility, where all save the most violent and lethal child abusers usually end up. "We make of such men and women," Dr. Kreizler wrote, in the same final journal that I had slowly been sharing with my criminal psychology students during that summer, "living reminders and repositories of all the hidden evils that we commit when we close ranks to live among each other as a society. And having made them such, we feel that we can expunge the fact of their crimes and the manners in which they resonate within so many of our own lives by killing them—an easy enough act, because, what with our failure to find a way to reach and converse with them, they cannot defend themselves in any coherent way.

But the day is coming, and it is not far off, when we will find the keys that allow them to participate in conversations about their abysmal acts, candidly and without fear, and tell us what planted such unnatural desires in what must have been their young souls."

He was right, of course: those conversations now go on every day with imprisoned child abusers, most to good effect. But again, how can one expect the average television writer to turn such statements into "compelling television"? Statistics, after all, serve not public education, but the least common denominator; and so long as *any* child abusers are repeat offenders, it is far easier to sell the public on the notion of a race of child-stalking pseudo-vampires, who, the minute that they are unchained, will *all* thirst once again for the souls of our most defenseless citizens. Such myths, propagated throughout the media, go on to inform the attitudes of most prospective jury members, which is to say most Americans. Indeed, as I stood in the Patricks' living room, I found myself staring at that one item of expense in the room: ironically, their television, the very instrument through which the myths and misconceptions that the Bureau of Criminal Investigation was hoping to exploit in order to lock the couple away forever were propagated; *their television,* hooked up to a small grey satellite dish outside, for which the Patricks, choosing not to maintain even their indoor plumbing, had nonetheless found some way to pay.

Shaking myself hard, I remembered the two calls that it was necessary for me to make at that juncture. Both were crucial to the plot that had already hatched in my head, that I knew Mike was quickly anticipating, and that Pete would have to sign off on, if he didn't want the sheriff's office, which meant Steve Spinetti and himself personally, to get a rather serious black eye for failing to find the mummified boy's body, and if he wanted further to take some revenge on the BCI for even attempting to place them in such a spot. It was a risky plan, certainly; but by this point, such amounted only to a slightly twisted sign that we were on the right track.

{vii.}

The first call went to Clarissa: waking her was like baiting a tiger, but she needed to know what had happened, in order to get her, in turn, to call her lawyer, the indomitable Paul O'Brien, Esq., and tell him to get over to BCI headquarters in Albany as soon as he could and start screaming about the rights of even penniless sex offenders to counsel. The national disease of allowing impoverished suspects, in almost any kind of case, to go without their constitutional right to such representation had become a pandemic, in New York, particularly under our current governor, a man who knew as little about what it meant to be poor and/or truly vulnerable as almost anyone alive; and I was convinced that O'Brien, an old-school, capital-P Progressive, would charge right into the Patrick case, fee be damned, and begin to put matters right immediately.

The next call was somewhat more delicate: after telling Pete to come upstairs while Mike continued his work, I suggested that we both call, on speakerphone, a pathologist that we knew and trusted at St. Elizabeth's Hospital in the city of Troy, the seat of Rensselaer County. Despite all that we had learned and decided about the mummified boy, I pointed out to Pete, we had yet to address our chief problem: in order to prevent the framing of the Patricks (and by extension the sheriff's office), we had to get the unknown deceased's body out of the arrested couple's house. Once it was gone, the BCI could hardly claim to know that it had ever been there (especially if Steve and Pete said that they had never seen it) without admitting their culpability in the affair. But that left the ticklish problem of who might be willing to take the body off our hands, and how. Mike, listening from the basement, shouted up to point out that we could take the remains and bury them high on the mountain behind Shiloh—"since you're always fucking bragging about how you could kill somebody and bury them on the mountain and nobody would ever find them, L.T.!"—but I replied that, while I still believed this theory to be true, I did not want to run the risk of implicating Clarissa in that kind of skullduggery unless we absolutely had to; and I didn't think we had to, yet.

Not, that is, if we could bring on board Dr. William "Indian Bill" Johnson, so nicknamed because he was directly descended from the original Sir William Johnson, Baronet, Godfather of Montgomery County in the pre-Revolutionary era, and the first truly great ambassador of the British crown to the Mohawk tribe and the Iroquois nation more generally, Sir William had founded a virtual kingdom west of the Hudson, which he was able to maintain peacefully because of the enormous (and validated) trust that the Iroquois placed in him. This trust grew not only out of his honoring commercial and alliance obligations, but also out of such personal details as his taking a Mohawk woman (some say a princess) to be his consort after the death of his first wife, and then fathering a series of children with her. From one of these, it was rumored, Dr. Bill Johnson's branch of the family was descended. Like many of the most brilliant and important figures in all categories of "British" history, Sir William Johnson had actually been an Irishman, by birth; and his descendant, Dr. Bill Johnson, shared his ancestor's love of making the system work whatever way it had to in order to see justice done. I therefore felt that there was at least an even chance that we could tell him honestly what was happening, and that he would devise some way to see our scheme through.

I was not disappointed. My iPhone gave out its characteristically loud cry, over the speaker, and after four or five rings, Bill answered:

"Yeah, what do you want?" he asked, with well-practiced but theatrical irascibility.

"Bill? Trajan Jones, up in Burgoyne County."

"I know who the hell it is, I saw your name, for God's sake—now what the hell do you want?"

I couldn't help but smile: I could readily imagine him toiling away, even and especially at that late hour, in the basement morgue's examination room (Indian Bill's own version of his ancestor and namesake's private kingdom), his six-foot, agile frame surmounted by fair features and coal-black hair that hung down to the midway point of his neck in sheets. "Nice to hear your voice, too, Bill," I said. "Listen, I've got Pete Steinbrecher, here—"

"Hey, Dr. Johnson," Pete said.

"Pete!" Bill called back, more amiably this time. "Good to hear your voice—haven't seen you in a bit."

"And also nearby," I went on, "but busy at this second, is—"

"*Indian Bill!*" Mike cut in, shouting up from the basement at a volume that was more than loud enough to be heard.

"Mike Li, you conniving Chinaman!" Johnson answered, matching Mike's volume. "You still owe me a hundred bucks from that poker game in the morgue last month—you were dealing seconds and you know it! God damn it, I think you people must come out of the *womb* knowing how to cheat at cards. What the hell's going on, Li, you sound like you're trapped in the Forbidden City."

"I am not Chinese, you scalp-hunting savage!" Mike hollered back.

Bill laughed, heartily and genuinely. "Funny you should mention that! I am at this moment peeling back the scalp of an unfortunate—well, let's just say *dead*—man from Latham, whose wife apparently got tired of being kicked around by a drunk and hit him in the head with a Louisville Slugger. Or so our pal Dr. Weaver believes. Looks to me more like the idiot did what the woman claims, stumbled and hit his head on a steam pipe while he was trying to get hold of her. Tell me, Trajan, why the *hell* did you have to save Weaver's life, anyway?"

"Ah," I replied. "Saw that little item, did you?"

"Uh—*yeah*. Me, the rest of the state, and half the country. Made it all the way to CNN. So how come you didn't just let the kid put a few slugs in him?"

"Unfortunately, it turned out the kid never actually had a gun," I explained ruefully. "Weaver was imagining a cell phone to be a .38, though *that* part of the story didn't reach the media, I gather."

"Ha! That's Weaver, all right, the fat bastard. Well, then, couldn't you have shot him yourself? Maybe claimed that he came at you in some kind of a disoriented rush?"

"Listen, Johnson—" I was trying hard, and failing, to keep us on point. "We've got kind of an exceptional situation over here in Heinsdale. Are you alone in the exam room, right now?"

"I am. As usual. Now, I trust you know that I haven't got a racist bone in my body—"

"Of course not, you're an Indian!" Mike tossed in.

"Shut up, Li, I'm trying to make a serious point, here!" Bill took a steadying breath, and I could hear the distinctively wet yet adhesive sound of scalp lifting from skull. "Which is, that I'm no racist, I just think it's a little weird that the only native-born American in this hospital—"

"Only *Native American* in that hospital!" Mike blurted again.

"God damn it, Li, I'll scalp *your* damned ass if you don't shut up! Anyway—" Bill's voice sped up to avoid further interruption: "I'm the only native-born American in this hospital, but I get stuck working alone in the basement all the time. There. I said it. Hmm, yeah . . ." He returned to his work momentarily. "This skull depression was *not* made by any damned baseball bat—not even close. That fucking Weaver . . ."

I picked up my phone. "Okay, Bill, if you're alone, I'm going to call you back on this FaceTime thing. That all right? I've got something I think you need to see."

"Like what?" came Johnson's immediate and anxious query.

"Well—I guess you've heard about the arrest of Jimmy and Jeanette Patrick over here, for the deaths of those four kids?"

"Of course. BCI's working pretty hard to get it played up all over the local news."

"Yeah, well—" I paused before diving in. "There's just one problem: it's a frame. Let me get you on the visual and show you something that I think even you may never have seen before; then listen to the details, and to a little proposition we've got for you . . ."

After calling him back on FaceTime, and seeing that he was in exactly the spot I'd pictured, down in St. Elizabeth's mortuary lab, hands gloved in latex and covered in blood, lab coat liberally splattered with the same, and his black hair hanging loose around his pale features—a violation of hospital policy that the higher-ups tolerated simply because Johnson was one of the best pathologists in the state, and a small hospital like St. Elizabeth's, they knew, was very lucky to have him—I began to sketch in the situation as quickly as I could, making my way to the basement stairs again. Bill was clearly intrigued; but it wasn't until I got down into the basement—"Where the hell are we going? Do you actually have to keep that cheating bastard locked in the cellar, these days?"—and turned the phone around so that he could see Mike at work on the dead boy that the hook really went in.

"Holy Christ," Bill whispered, the sound still quite loud within the silent basement. "A goddamned *mummified corpse* . . ." His sense of professional thrill was immediately mitigated, however, as both Mike's and mine had been, when he saw the size of the body. "Aw, man—he's just a kid . . ."

"Indeed," I answered. "And thereby—wait a minute. How'd you know it was a 'he'?"

"Who the hell's the God damned pathologist here, you or me, Jones?"

"Point taken. Anyway, upon the fact of his being a kid, boy *or* girl, hangs our tale . . ."

The final portions of the story of how we believed the nameless boy had come to be placed in the cellar, while it was all still fascinating to Johnson, did not elicit the kind of professional thrill that his first glimpse of the body had: nothing could, if you were staring that mummified corpse in the eye, which I made sure my phone camera was doing. But rage proved as good a motivation as curiosity, and the two together sealed the deal: before I even got to what role we wanted him to play, he was proposing it himself:

"So—here's what we do . . ." And as I turned the camera phone away from the body and back toward the steps, a sense of professional challenge began to return to Johnson's voice; more muted, to be sure, but the man really was a true descendant of some of the greatest adventurers and schemers in the history of the Empire State, as he soon demonstrated: "I get over there in one of our DOA wagons—not an ambulance, just the meat haulers we use to transport known fatalities back to the lab. And on the way, we all cook up some bullshit story about what actually happened to the kid. Only our bullshit, to put it simply, has got to be better than their bullshit. You still there, Pete?"

"Right here, Dr. Johnson."

"Please, Pete," Bill answered. "We've known each other how long? That 'Doctor' shit may fly with your downstate friends, over there, but some of us don't need it. Anyway, you'll be waiting to help me with the body, while the other two go off and do whatever it is they've got to do?"

"Yep," Pete said. "Won't be any problem, for the two of us. It seems to be awful . . . light."

"Okay, then." I half-expected to see smoke rising from my phone, Johnson's brain was cranking so hard. "Go through your county in your head, and I'll go through Rensselaer. See if you can come up with an abandoned building—something high, a barn, maybe a silo, but something really shut down, locked up, something the kid would have had to try hard to break into, and where, if he got into trouble, he wouldn't have been able to signal for any help from."

"Well, I did think of one place," Pete said tentatively, much to my own and Bill's surprise. "You know the big abandoned school in Hoosick Falls? The one on 22, as you go up the hill in the direction of North Hoosick and then Cambridge?"

"Oh, yeah!" Bill's exclamation was quiet, but no less confirmational: the idea was solid. "Old St. Mary's, it's perfect—right in the middle of town, almost, on High Street. Made of brick and *stone*. But it's been locked up so long that it's a fortress, now—they tried renovating it, make it into apartments, but the asbestos is just out of hand. Yeah, an adventurous kid could climb in there; it'd be tough, but he could get to one of the upper floors by climbing the stonework on the ground floor. Then he'd want to get into the tower section—plenty high enough, dry enough, nobody would ever have smelled a thing if he got trapped."

"What about vermin, Bill?" I asked. "Wouldn't they have gotten to the body?"

"Not necessarily, Mr. Sorcerer of Death—"

"Oh, my God," I said, cradling my head in my free hand.

"Yeah, they mentioned *that* the other night, too, when you were popping your .45 off—dangerously close, I might add, to what looked like certain state and county officials. Funny stuff! Anyway, Trajan, rodents get asbestosis and mesothelioma, too—they just get it slower than we do. But if they've been getting it for a long time in that building—and it's been shut up for years—I bet they've abandoned ship, and gone on to more friendly structures. Look, the explanation's not perfect, but it's close enough that I can make it stick. Now the question becomes law enforcement—Pete, you know anybody in the Hoosick Falls PD that can help us with this?"

"Yeah," Pete said with a smile, realizing that the whole scheme just might come off. "I got a couple friends—"

"Don't worry about that," I cut in. "Bringing in more people who can be squeezed is too great a risk. Plus, we've got an in with a trooper—I'm betting she'll do it, if the right people ask her."

"You talking about Cousin Caitlin?" Mike shouted up the basement stairway.

"I am, Mike," I replied, annoyed. "Although I was trying to keep names and relationships—"

"You mean like how she's your new heartthrob's cousin?" Mike needled.

I held my breath for an instant, to avoid a string of expletives. "Yes, Mike. That's exactly what I meant. And if we keep that kind of thing out of the whole matter, the safer everybody will be."

"Well," Mike answered, "I guess I kind of fucked *that* up."

"Don't worry, Mike," Pete said. "I know who you're talking about—and Bill will meet her at the scene, anyway."

"So that's the last piece of the puzzle," Bill said. "Except for—hey, Mike, has the kid got any major broken bones? Preferably a leg?"

"I haven't tried looking yet," Mike shouted. "Why, need him to?"

"I was just spitballing," Indian Bill replied. "But now that I think of it, he wouldn't exactly jump and bust his leg if he'd already been mummified. Skip that."

"Yeah, let's just skip that." Mike took a deep breath and closed his trace kit. "Desecrating children's corpses is just about where I draw the line . . ."

"Me too," Pete said quietly.

When Mike got back up to the ground floor, we sketched out the earlier part of the plan for Johnson, about searching outlying counties, including those in the high Adirondacks, for reports of boys' bodies being found and going unclaimed; this, however, elicited a long groan from Indian Bill, who said, "Oh, for crying out—Pete? Do me a favor, and don't listen to those two idiots. You don't want to look for reports of bodies *found,* because that means that too many people know about it, already. Look for items about boys who have gone missing and *never* been found. Frank's no fool, and he will have jumped in and snatched the body and told whoever did find it to keep quiet or else. Jesus, have you guys been fucking up like this all the way through the case?"

"Absolutely not," I answered, more indignantly than certainly.

"But Bill's right about this, Pete," Mike added. "Look for unsolved missing-child cases—not bodies found. Anybody finds a mummified kid, I don't care if it's claimed or not, the local media will have been all over it."

I considered this point. "Hmm . . . True. So do it that way, Pete. It's now going on about—what, eleven-thirty p.m.? Let's just say we'll try to bring this whole thing together within the hour, before the BCI gets ideas about coming back. The weather's working in our favor: it's starting to look like the end of the world, out there. As for Mike and me, we'll lurk around on High Street in the a.m., but if it looks like the BCI is already there and involved, maybe we'll hang back, try not to make things appear any more suspicious than they already will."

"Or screw them up in some other way," Bill said, tearing off his gloves.

"Bill?" I said, hoping to sound at least a little in earnest. "Can we please eighty-six the bullshit for just a couple of hours, and get this done?"

"You bet, Sorcerer," he said, as he began scrubbing his hands in a steel sink; then, with one soapy finger, he reached over toward his phone. "I'll see you in Hoosick Falls!" And with a touch, he was gone.

Pete took off his Stetson to wipe at his head once more. "I hope we're doing the right thing, on this one."

"We are," Mike said, not wanting to go any further down the moral road. For he knew, as did I, that the entire experience had been and was going to be a tough one, on that score, for Pete as for us all; and he was anxious that we just get on with it. To that end, he started toward the front door. "Come on, L.T. We need to go, I think we've had just about enough of the BCI's hijinks, for tonight."

I nodded, and did no more than step toward him before I felt a piercing pain in my hip, one that caused my left side to begin to buckle—indeed, the sudden movement was enough for Pete to rush over and stand by to make sure that I didn't give way. Once I was back upright and had taken a few steps with my cane, the pain began to ease enough for me to indicate that it had been no major thing; but in truth, it was a discomfort and a weakness that I hadn't felt in a very long time.

"You sure you're all right, Doc?" Pete asked gravely.

I tried my best to give him a smile. "Sure, Pete. Lack of sleep, mostly. Plus, I'm still clinical shrink enough to know that we all hold tension in our bodies. And it's been a hell of a few days, even without this night. But we do need to get moving—you going to be okay on your own?"

"Yeah, absolutely," the deputy said. "Once Bill Johnson gets here, we'll handle it fine, don't you worry. Just give that hip some rest."

I nodded once to him in appreciation, then Mike and I headed out to the Empress. He pulled the passenger door open for me, got a pillow out of the back seat and shoved it up against the center console, knowing where it would offer the most support. Then he went around to the driver's side, opened his own door, and sat waiting to prevent any serious calamity if my attempt to lower myself into the car turned into a tumble. He also knew, however, that although I was still in some discomfort, I wouldn't want any help unless it was necessary; which, thankfully, it turned out not to be. Once we were both in and he had started the car up, however, he looked at me sternly.

"You're not fooling me," he said. "That had nothing to do with sleep deprivation. What the hell happened, L.T.?"

I tried with only moderate success to laugh a little, saying, "I'm not sure, Michael—although I think a visit to the old oncologist will be in order, when this case is over."

"When the case is *over*?" Mike echoed, with some astonishment. "You want to go to his hospital right now? I'm ready, and there's nothing else that can't wait."

"*No*," I answered, as firmly as I could without being rude. "When this case is over, Mike—and not a minute before. Now let's get home. Marcianna must be going nuts."

"Hunh," Mike noised, throwing the car into reverse and backing away from Pete's cruiser. "That'll be a short trip. For the pair of you."

"Very funny," I grunted, adjusting the pillow on my hip and then leaning my face up against my partly opened window. "Just get us home, Mike. I'm begging you . . ."

{viii.}

U pon reaching Shiloh, I had a few stiff drinks to dull the strange pain that had struck my leg, then made my way up to Marcianna's enclosure, where I found her in the state of agitation I had expected, having been gone so late into the night. I got her calmed down before I opened the gate—it was always wise to make sure that she wasn't having some severe flashback to her youth that might make her fail to recognize me—and then, when her nervousness turned to relief and finally happiness, I went in, and we horsed around for a bit, as much as I could tolerate, before heading to her den. It wound up being one of those rare nights when I spent the night in that far remove, and I was only woken by the sound of my cell phone, and Mike telling me to get down to the hangar. This I did, after feeding the now-placated Marcianna and leaving her content to find amusement on her own until the afternoon.

The gathering wind and clouds of the night before had not yet turned to rain, telling me that it must be early; and when I checked my watch, I saw that it had yet to reach ten. I now understood, or thought I understood, Mike's urgency: we ought to have heard from Bill Johnson and Pete by then, and I worried that our plan had been interrupted and perhaps discovered by Frank Mangold and the BCI. The tardiness of our co-conspirators' message, however, turned out to be only part of the reason for Mike's alarm: Lucas had shown up early—which was no surprise, his eagerness and impatience to work and learn having grown day by day—but he'd also brought Ambyr with him, after she'd explained to him that she was now fully part of our little team. I was thereby put on even further notice than I had been the day before to expect the unexpected from this remarkable young woman; but we quickly assimilated her presence into our work, and spent the rest of the morning and early afternoon teaching her the rudiments of our method and what had transpired during the case, information that she was (I now knew) going to get anyway, so she might as well have it firsthand. Lucas, of course, was fascinated and even excited by the tale of the as-yet-unnamed mummified boy, although Ambyr seemed more realistically horrified and appalled, both by the prostitution of the unfortunate boy's corpse to the BCI's purposes, and, of course, by his fate.

By one o'clock, Mike had grown nervous, and sent off a text message to Pete asking what was going on; in reply, he received a rather cryptic statement saying that there'd been a delay, but we could expect a green light to head to Hoosick Falls soon. As always, the deputy was true to his word, and by two, we got the go-ahead, and made ready to head over and spy on what transpired when the as-yet-unnamed dead boy was discovered somewhere far from the spot where he'd been planted. I guided Ambyr out of the JU-52 and down to the hangar floor, while Mike pried Lucas—"I can stay! I can mind the store, I know where the guns are!"—from his post. We made it to the car without further incident, and then to the Kurtz house, where I once again got out to escort Ambyr to the kitchen door.

"Such a gentleman," she laughed lightly. "But seriously, Trajan, you don't need to get in and out—I know where my own door is, by now."

"No trouble," I lied.

"You sure?" she said, turning to me at the doorway. "I mean, are you sure you're all right?"

I was as much curious as surprised. "I'm fine, Ambyr. Why do you ask?"

"Your steps," she said. "When you were pacing in the plane, then walking just now, they were different—as if you were limping a little."

I tried to laugh. "It's nothing. Just a bit of overexertion last night, that's all."

She smiled and turned her face up to mine, in that eerie way that said that, for all her blindness, she saw right through me. "You sure you're just not getting the wrong kind of exertion?"

"Meaning?"

She took my arm, then reached up to give me another very tender kiss, this one just brushing the corner of my mouth. "Figure it out," she whispered.

And then Lucas rushed by us and into the house: "Ahhh! My eyes, I can't watch this, for fuck's sake, *whatever* it is!"

But Ambyr, without ever letting go of my arm or turning around, just swatted the doorframe with her cane hard, creating a cracking sound loud enough to still Lucas' outburst, although he kept mumbling to himself. "Like I said," Ambyr continued, putting her other hand to my cheek. "Think about it. And get home safe."

"I'll—try" was all I could mumble in assent; and then I instantly switched roles, and took a small step away from her. "Okay, listen, you two—there's a chance that you may get a call from Major McCarron, while we're gone, looking for us." I turned to her again. "I have a call in to him, and if we're out of cell range between here and Hoosick Falls, which happens, and he does think to try you when we don't answer at Shiloh, tell him that I know what he's calling about, and that we need him to send your cousin Caitlin to the scene. Nobody else, unless he wants to go himself."

"Got it," Ambyr replied, that devious curl coming into the corner of her mouth. "But it's all just a *tiny* bit mysterious, don't you think?"

"No time to explain more," I said. "But I promise to when I get back." And then, God alone knows why, I moved back toward the doorway, paused an instant, and finally turned to ever-so-briefly kiss Ambyr's cheek. This brought another firm squeeze of my cane arm from her and another low but insistent groan from Lucas, which I could still hear as she closed the door and I turned around to find Mike waiting about ten feet down toward the short driveway, grinning from ear to ear. "How's the hip?" he asked me as we headed toward the Crown Vic, seeing that I had begun to once more lean more heavily on my cane.

"Fine—better, anyway," I said, hoping to change the subject.

Which was, of course, a vain hope indeed: Mike laughed out loud, then said, "Well, ordinarily I'd say that spending the night up in that fucking cave was about the worst thing you could have done for it. But it looks like you found a cure, all right. And you'll need it. Because, between what we're doing now, the fact that that girl in there has obviously got almost as much of an instant thing for you as you do for her, and teaching, I've got a feeling you're going to need all the strength you can find. We have a hell of a time ahead of us—or *you* do, anyway . . ."

Sighing, I tried to sound sterner than I felt as we reached the Crown Vic: "Shut up and drive, will you, Mike? Like I told Bill, let's try to keep the banter to a minimum."

But he only laughed again as we got in the car. "Whoa, yeah. Let's just *try*. You are so *dead*, L.T. . . ."

Mike was right: we *were* faced with a hell of a time. Our first move was to hit Hoosick Falls and gauge the progress of our plan, which, we discovered upon arriving, could not have been going better. We crossed the railroad tracks in the center of town and slowly crept through streets made slick and deserted by the now-rainy and still very windy weather, then turned onto High Street and made our way up toward the massive brick and limestone structure known as Old St. Mary's Academy (as opposed to the far more modest new St. Mary's, a Catholic elementary school just steps away), eventually pulling the Empress up past the public library on Classic Street, down a hill on which sat the school. It was a spot that afforded us an excellent view—aided by a small pair of binoculars with antireflective coating on their lenses that Mike had remembered to bring—of what was happening up above.

Indian Bill had, as I'd supposed he would, made it as obvious a case as he could: the body now lay just to the side of the main entrance to the school, a spot to which it could easily have slid without much damage, after being blown out of the enormous, open bell tower above and falling along a gentle eave. One can only imagine what uses that tower had once had, besides ringing the call to students; certainly, it had bell space enough for a giant bourdon from Notre Dame. However, it now stood empty, and a good thing, too, for it made it all the more believable that the boy, in his last moments—probably brought on by massive asbestos poisoning—had climbed to the spot, and there expired, becoming mummified by the strong winds that howled through the unprotected space.

Indian Bill's pathology team had erected a tarp pavilion to protect the scene from the rain, and at present there was only one state trooper car in attendance (Pete having made himself scarce once they'd deposited the body, since Rensselaer County was outside his jurisdiction). The imposing woman wearing a trooper's uniform I took to be Ambyr's cousin Caitlin: though her Academy training was obvious, she was nicely proportioned, and her general good looks made a genetic link to Ambyr clear, even if she was a little broader and tougher.

"Shame you couldn't have fallen for *her*," Mike said, peering through the glasses. "We'd have eyes and ears inside the Staties. Of course, she can *see*, which kinda rules you out right there; and then, from the look of her, she'd break you in half if you ever managed to talk her into—"

"Hey, hey, hey," I said, slapping his shoulder. "I thought this car was going to be a banter-free zone today."

"*I* didn't agree to that," Mike replied, still studying the scene up the hill. "In fact, I think my opposition to that proposal was pretty—hang on. The party has new guests . . ." Mike focused the glasses on two vehicles that were making their way up the hill: an unmarked cruiser and an FIC van. "Looks like . . . well, I don't know the two guys in the cruiser, but I'd say they were Bureau guys. And in the van? Fuck, missed him, we'll have to wait till he gets out."

Which we did, watching the two vehicles pull up onto the sidewalk by the old school. The car released a pair of men who did, indeed, look like BCI types, but when I took the glasses from Mike, I found that I had no better idea than he did as to their identities. The driver of the FIC van was similarly unknown to me; but I wasn't at all reassured by the very professional demeanor he gave off. With crime scene techs, what you see is usually what you get, and most, in one way or another, have the air of either clowns, people in over their heads, or, at most, geeks. But this guy didn't, and I handed the glasses back to Mike for confirmation.

"Oh-ho," he said, a little amused and a little impressed. "Yeah. Looks like word got back to our friends that somebody found a mummified boy's body in Hoosick Falls. That's the big gun, Johnny Cheong. Senior FIC tech, and maybe the only guy over there who knows what he's doing. Man, we've never seen him before, on *any* case that we've worked up here."

"So how come you know him?" I said; and then the irresistible, "Because he's Chinese, and all Chinese people know each other?"

For which I received the back of Mike's hand across my forehead, without his ever taking his eyes from the glasses. "Weren't you the one," he mumbled, "who just said no more banter?"

"Hey. Fire with fire, asshole."

Mike considered that one for a moment, then battled back: "Anyway, no, shithead, not because he's fucking Chinese, which I am not either. He's Korean. And I know about him from seeing his picture and by his reputation. Yeah, they're good and mad, I'll bet, about our spoiling their little operation—they want to make absolutely sure they're talking about the same kid, by matching the basic information they already have to whatever Johnny Boy finds. Oh, yeah, this is getting fun . . ."

"All right," I said, straightening up in my seat. "Enough with the peeping-tom stuff. Let's get up there and ask Indian Bill how it's going."

"What the hell . . . ?" Mike answered, putting the binoculars down and starting the car. "We're going to show ourselves, and fuck it all up?"

"Just drive, and I'll explain," I said. "Take a left on Abbott, up there, then another left on Parsons, and another back onto High Street. Then make a quick entry into the school driveway, which is actually on the far side of the building. And no, we're not going to show ourselves, because in the first place nobody up there's ever met us, except for Bill, so they wouldn't know us, anyway; but second, and more importantly, if we sneak around the back of the building nobody will see us. Just look at them: in this rain, they're not focused on anything but what's under that tarp."

"Well," Mike sighed. "Okay, L.T., you're the fucking genius . . ."

My hastily concocted plan went shockingly smoothly, and we were indeed able to get the Empress behind the far side of the school unnoticed, after which, huddling under two umbrellas Mike kept in the car, we moved around to the back of the place. I pulled out my phone, dialed Bill Johnson's number, and replied to his "Where the fuck are *you*?" by urging him to keep his voice down, and to come around to our position. I heard him mumble some quick tale about it being a private call, and before long his tall, lanky form appeared, a soaked COUNTY PATHOL-OGIST windbreaker the only thing protecting both his upper body and his head, with the hood of the garment now doing a particularly bad job, in the ever more unrelenting rain. I raised my umbrella high enough for him to stand under, and when he requested a cigarette, Mike gave him one and lit it.

"I thought you quit," I said, as Bill took a deep, relieving drag.

"I did—and I've got you two bastards to thank for getting me re-started." He flicked his thumb in the direction of the action around the corner. "This is some heavy shit, guys."

"Yeah, I kind of figured when I saw Johnny Cheong," Mike answered with a nod.

"And we saw the BCI guys," I said, "which means that Mangold and Donovan—"

"No, no, no," Bill answered with a short, humorless, and rather fateful chuckle. "This is not some regular county jockeying shit. You have stirred up a serious shitstorm. Those two suits? One's BCI, all right, but one's *FBI*, my friends. He claims he's just observing, but I heard him saying something like 'Nobody wants to see a case like this break nationally, *especially this year*.'"

"I don't get it," Mike said, smoking, himself, now. "What does this year matter?"

I considered it, then clapped my cane hand to my forehead so fast that its handle knocked into my skull. "Shit!" I went for my own cigarettes. "I didn't even think of that."

"What, what, what?" Mike asked, his words punctuated by bursts of smoke. "Come on, fellas."

"Holy crap," Bill said, looking at him and frowning. "Mike—it's an *election* year."

"Hence the FBI man," I elaborated, making sure Mike got the point. "Even though the FBI has been told they're not needed on this case. But if it keeps going on, well—you know how much trouble the whole issue's been for our sainted governor already. And the powers that be need him reelected."

"Whoa." Then, in a sudden movement, Mike ducked inside a nearby doorway, huddling up against the brick casement of the locked back entrance.

"What the hell are you doing now?" Bill asked.

"I'm *hiding*, fuckstick," Mike answered. "From the Predator drone that's about to launch a Hellfire missile at us, that's what I'm *doing*!"

"Get out here," Bill said, his powerful arm easily pulling my partner out of the doorway. "Of all the stupid things I've ever heard you come up with . . . What, you think because the FBI is here that the *president* has some kind of interest in what you're doing?"

"Well," Mike defended, "you just said it was an election year!"

"A *gubernatorial* election year," Bill answered, swiping some of his soaking black hair behind one ear with his cigarette hand. "You think because some Fed flunkies from Albany are playing cover-up that you're suddenly a priority in the White House? No, I'm just telling you that there's more than the usual BCI guys you're used to dealing with at work, here. I mean, Jesus, fellas, couldn't you have let this one go? Maybe have caught the next train?"

"Listen, Bill," I replied, "if you could've seen the first scene we did, and the way *that* girl had been artificially posed in a place somewhere other than where she died . . . you wouldn't have been able to back off, either. This whole thing is just rotten and royally fucked. And we're the only ones that have a shot at solving it, you know that."

Considering the matter further, Bill let out a long, smoky blast of air. "Yeah—I guess so," he conceded, dropping his cigarette butt and grinding it out with his boot. "Because that's what's going on around the corner, I'll tell you that: rotten, royally fucked bullshit. Speaking of which, I'd better get back—we still on track? Did you come here with some new information, or just to shoot the shit?"

"Just wanted to see what's up," Mike said. "Which it sounds like we needed to know. What was the delay about, anyway?"

"The weather," Bill replied, whipping some of the moisture off of his windbreaker's hood. "I wanted to wait for the rain, it'll make the body that much harder to examine. Okay, boys . . ." Bill shook my hand and then Mike's; but Mike's he did not release immediately from his very strong grip. "But I am not shitting you, Li—I want that hundred bucks. Maybe you're not aware of how much pathologists up here make, but—"

"Yeah, yeah, I know, Bill—ow, fuck, let go of my hand!" Mike quietly cried, finally slipping loose of his tormentor. "While I do not admit to dealing seconds or any other nefarious practices, I will attempt to pay you your hundred bucks as a token of goodwill."

"Yeah," Bill said dubiously. "Goodwill my ass. Okay, lemme get back to it. And listen—" His voice became suddenly and quite genuinely concerned. "You two watch your backs. If this thing reaches even as high as the governor, a couple of dead county advisors won't be much of a price to pay for keeping it quiet. I mean, didn't we already see that with Gracie Chang?" Mike and I could only murmur assent. "Okay, then. You stay low and shoot first, right?" He nodded and started off, then seemed to remember something and turned, speaking in a very hushed voice. "Hey, did you see that trooper? She's a tough girl, man, but she's kinda hot!"

"Go for it, Bill," Mike whispered. "Never hurts to have another friend among the Staties."

As Bill disappeared back around the corner, I turned to Mike. "Let's get moving."

"And where are we moving to?" he asked as we reentered the car. "Back home, I hope."

"Nope," I said, lowering myself into my seat and finding that the pain in my hip had at last subsided. "We've got one more stop to make. The Harriman Office Park in Albany."

I was ready for what I got: "*What?*" Mike whined loudly. "L.T.—you heard what Bill said, why would we go right into enemy territory, just when things are working?"

"Because I want to make sure Paul O'Brien gets this news fast and reliably," I answered. Then I looked at him pointedly. "Or would you rather let two innocent people get grilled by Mangold for longer than they have to?"

"They're not exactly 'innocent people,'" Mike answered sullenly, as he started the car. "And I just don't see why *we* have to go there."

"Because *we're* the ones who can get them released—*now.*"

"Ah, shit, Trajan . . ." Mike turned as he backed quietly out of the school driveway, then faced forward again to slowly pull away from the scene. "You're getting that *tone* again."

"What tone?"

"The one that got us run out of New York," Mike answered. "Remember what I said, L.T.—we're fresh out of places to get exiled to . . ."

{ix.}

Heading west on Route 7 from Hoosick Falls, we eventually emerged from the wilds of the eastern corridor of New York and approached the shell of bright light that, even though the sun had not set yet, marked the location of the old Dutch wilderness fortress that had developed, over the centuries, to become Albany. The bosses and consortiums that had long ago run New York State had not wanted to see political as well as economic power concentrated in the massive port at the mouth of the Hudson; and, when the Erie Canal had still been the nation's most vital commercial route to the West, Albany, as the canal's eastern terminus, had possessed the leverage to make the leaders of the southern metropolis pay homage, despite Albany's being only a fraction the size of its southern rival. By now, however, hard times had fallen on the proud old capital, so that even the late Governor Nelson Rockefeller's vainglorious tribute to himself and his clan, the Empire State Plaza, with its marble and steel office towers, imposing government buildings arranged around reflective pools, and bizarre, saucer-shaped performing arts theater (officially known as The Egg, but referred to by almost everyone in the area as some sort of giant flying saucer that had collided with the Earth at a sharp angle), could no longer quite prevent the city from once again projecting the overall impression that it had in the beginning: that of an outpost in the wilderness working hard to survive.

Nevertheless, when one moved in on the city and crossed the Hudson on I-90, it was hard to deny that Albany was enduring its fall from preeminence with a certain defiance, if not hope: tax incentives and breaks given to companies, especially tech companies, that would move their headquarters or significant outposts to the city's environs had changed many of the former uses of office buildings both public and private. And among the places still struggling to redefine itself was the Harriman Office Park, or, officially, the W. Averell Harriman State Office Campus. Perhaps because it was just across the road from the main group of SUNY-Albany buildings, the ovular park had borrowed that seemingly benign title, "campus"; but there was no confusing it with a place of learning. The architecture was an inconsistent patchwork, none of it very attractive; and while the State Police and Bureau of Criminal Investigation Building just west of the park proper represented that ugly form of official architecture prevalent during the mid-1960s, it at least had some sense of symmetry and vertical thrust (for a three-story building) in its dark windows interrupted by lengths of light stone. But the more recently constructed home of the Forensic Investigation Center next door, with its scattered windows and horizontal lines of tan and beige stone, was an indisputable eyesore that seemed to reflect every scandal in which the FIC lab and its techs had been involved: most recently, accusations that as many as a dozen techs had cheated on the qualification test to operate the new TrueAllele-3 DNA-sequencing equipment. This was a particular irritant to Mike, who had been teaching for years that, while DNA did and does indeed represent the greatest hope for getting at the facts of cases (especially those involving wrongly convicted prisoners who are also poor minority defendants), it is still largely that: a hope, relying as it yet does on techs whose collection and analytical skills range from good to flat-out incompetent or corrupt. The best DNA analysts, on the other hand, tend to be independently minded, and therefore of little use to the state, their careers instead being sustained either by the occasional wealthy client or by crusading academic institutions or both.

After finding the Washington Avenue exit on 90, we made our way to Campus Access Road and then hung a right into the State Police's territory. This little enclave was not marked by the rest of the campus' air of question about the future use of its buildings: one knew that all three of its structures—headquarters, the FIC Lab, and the State Police Academy—having been at last gathered together in one spot, were there to stay. We pulled up at the old HQ building, right in front of which sat Paul O'Brien's unmistakable 1979 black Pontiac Firebird Trans Am, complete with

T-top and massive golden eagle emblazoned across the hood, which couldn't have looked more out of place amid the cruisers, SUVs, unmarked interceptors, and late-model private vehicles of the troopers and detectives. Seeing the thing and pulling into the empty space beside it, both Mike and I began inevitably to laugh: in part out of genuine amusement, in part out of envy, for the Firebird had been meticulously maintained by O'Brien over the years, and was every bit the street-legal monster that it had been on the day of its manufacture.

Such, however, would prove the end of any real amusement during that visit. Asking a trooper at the front desk for O'Brien's whereabouts, we found that he was just where we had feared: in a small observation closet adjoining two discreet, lower-level interrogation rooms, watching the proceedings in each of the latter chambers through one-way mirrors. The silver-haired, black-browed O'Brien, who stood a couple of inches taller than me but was likely twice my weight, shook hands with Mike and me roughly, making it clear from the first that we'd better not be wasting his time.

"Have you got it or haven't you, Trajan?" he demanded. "Because, take a look—" He held a hand out toward the one-way mirrors. "Those poor old perverts aren't going to last much longer. They're almost ready to confess to whatever Mangold wants . . ."

Jimmy Patrick was in the first of the seemingly sterile yet somehow grimy interrogation rooms, while Jeanette was seated in the second. They both appeared to be genial, aging hippies, overweight but not obese, with that peculiarly trustworthy cast to their features that so many child molesters possess. This appearance had not, however, prevented them from getting the full treatment at the hands of Mangold's boys: they were both bathed in their own sweat, the air-conditioning having doubtless been shut off without a drop of drinking water or other beverage being provided. Each of their broad faces had grown haggard with exhaustion, along with dehydration and hunger. Two BCI men stood guard, one per doorway, while Frank Mangold shuttled between the two, taking turns berating his collars. Two additional BCI detectives sat at each of the stainless steel tables, waiting for Mangold to leave so that they could play the good cops, and quietly coo to the Patricks that their best chance really was to forget about lawyering up and make a full confession, after which the BCI would recommend to their judges lenient sentences (an impossibility, for such politically unconnected people). But Jimmy and

Jeanette just sat there, silently shaking their heads, from which I took it that O'Brien had already been in to talk to each of them.

"So how come you're out *here,* Paul?" I asked, to which he held up a styrofoam cup containing something that looked suspiciously like sewage, though its smell did not match.

"I've been in there most of the night and all day, smart-ass," he replied. "Mind if I take a break for a cup of this damned foul BCI coffee while I wait for the two crack investigators who got me into this nightmare to show up with *some*thing concrete that I can use to spring this pair? And you'd better have it: Mangold found a hell of a lot of damning information on their computer, along with pretty terrible DVDs. So if he's also got trace evidence linking them to a body—"

"He doesn't, Counselor," Mike said bravely, netting himself O'Brien's fierce scowl in return.

"That so, Dr. Li?" Paul replied quietly. He was still quietly fuming, but he now showed a glimmer of hope, as well: because he really did respect Mike's work. "And how can I prove it?"

"Habeas corpus," I answered. "The body that they planted in the Patricks' house turned up at the foot of the bell tower at Old St. Mary's in Hoosick Falls instead. Somehow . . ."

O'Brien held up a hand to silence me quickly. "*Don't* tell me any more," he said. "If I ever have to defend *you* guys, I don't want to know *how* that body got there. Just that it did." Taking a deep breath, he threw his half-empty coffee cup into a nearby steel trash can, then hitched his belted suit pants up around his wide, thick midsection in anticipation. "Okay," he said with a nod. "Let's just see how Frank tries to worm his way out of *this* one."

The microphones in the interrogation rooms had not been switched on—a "technical problem," one BCI man informed us—but Mike and I didn't really need sound to determine what was happening. O'Brien chased Mangold out of the first room, demanding to know what actual proof of the Patricks' involvement in any deaths or other crimes the BCI actually had; but it wasn't until they entered the second room, where Jeanette Patrick sat, that Mangold spun on O'Brien with a look of shock, one which said that either he hadn't heard yet that the mummified boy had turned up in the wrong place, or he didn't believe it. O'Brien pointed at the mirror, causing both Mike and me to recoil a bit, and then Frank went out into the hallway. O'Brien signaled to us to join them.

"*Fuck!*" Mike declared in a low voice. "I knew it—China, here we come . . ."

Once in the hall, we looked immediately to Paul O'Brien for guidance, but he only nodded at Mangold. "Well, boys?" he said. "Tell the senior investigator what you've seen."

"We got a call," I replied, trying not to sound as unnerved as I felt, "from Indian—from Bill Johnson, down at St. Elizabeth's in Troy. He thought maybe a body they'd found was one more that fit the pattern we've established."

"That *you've* established?" Mangold scoffed. "Maybe you don't re-member, profiler, but you're off the case."

"As far as *you're* concerned," I answered, locking eyes with him. "But I contacted both Steve Spinetti and Mitch McCarron, and they asked me, along with my partner, to take a look."

That one made Mangold pause for a moment: his gaze shifted from me to Mike and back again. "And you're sure this 'mummified' kid was found in the spot where he died?"

"Bill Johnson is," Mike half-lied coolly. "And that's good enough for us. His body seems to have fallen from the bell tower to one lower roof eave, and finally to the ground. Bill will do the postmortem, but I think it's safe to speculate that the cause of death was exposure, not murder."

Mangold nodded silently—an odd thing, it occurred to me, given the situation—then turned his gaze my way. "And how about the kid's name? Circumstances? Do we know, if he was one of these 'throwaways,' yet?"

The question caught me off-guard: if Mangold was lying, he was doing a damned good job of it. "Nothing, on that front," I said. "We won't know until he's identified, and his identity is matched against the record of missing kids. Obviously, given the state of the body, there's no way to just publish his picture on a milk carton, but Bill will figure out something. There's DNA, of course, and maybe—I don't know, precisely, do finger-prints survive mummification, Mike?"

"If it happened recently, as seems the case here, maybe," Mike replied. "There's at least a good chance of it."

Mangold considered this, then suddenly kicked at the wall violently. Then he slowly moved on Mike and me. "You fuckers are playing straight with me, right? Because if you're not, I'll—"

"Okay, Frank," Paul O'Brien cut in. "Threats against civilians who were good enough to do the Burgoyne Sheriff's Department and a senior

State Police officer a favor are both uncalled for and illegal—you know that. Besides, we've got more immediate business. You've got nothing, now, against my clients, in there, except their interest in certain kinds of pornography. You want to charge them with that, and then admit to the world that that's all you had? Or you want to let them go with a warning, hold their materials, and just save yourself the embarrassment?"

Mangold turned around. "I have to confess, Paul—I knew you were a bleeding heart, but I never thought I'd see the day that you'd be working for child molesters."

"I'm not working for them," O'Brien said sternly. "Because they're not paying me. I'm working for the U.S. Constitution and the laws of the State of New York, which this governor has made a practice of violating by not providing impoverished people like the Patricks, however objectionable their private interests, with adequate legal counsel. Now—what do you say?"

And then the most shocking event in the entire episode occurred: Frank Mangold considered the matter for a moment more, then suddenly and decisively threw the doors to the interrogation rooms open. "All right, fellas," he said ruefully but firmly. "Let 'em go . . ."

There were various protestations of disbelief from the other BCI men, but Mangold angrily overruled them. The Patricks found each other in the hallway like what they were, two unjustly hunted if grotesque animals, and then Mangold delivered his little lecture about how he was keeping their computer and their videos, so that in future they'd better watch their step. After that, however, they were released to Paul O'Brien, who shepherded them toward the stairway that would take them up and into freedom. He paused at its base, asking them to wait, then returned to Mike and me, who were standing, utterly dumbstruck, just where he'd left us in the hall.

"Okay, you maniacs," Paul said quietly. "I've just gone out on a major limb, here. Be good and goddamned sure I was right to. And above all—get this case solved . . ." He nodded with a look that was far more sympathetic than his words had been, then returned to the Patricks and got them going upstairs before Mangold changed his mind.

Mike and I, however, just stood where we were for a few more seconds, unable to quite believe what had transpired—or rather, *how* it had transpired: by the book, not Frank Mangold's preferred method. In addition, we were trying to absorb the fact that what had supposedly been

Mangold's master plan had been kiboshed without his raising much of a holler. But holler he soon did, from behind us:

"Well? What the fuck are you two waiting for, a medal or a monument? Get outta here, will you?" Then he spun around again, walking down the hall shouting, "Somebody get me Dennis Shea, either on the phone or in person! I want to know what the hell this was all about!"

Mike and I wasted no time following Mangold's order: after all, there was every chance that *we* might be the next to occupy those rather scary little interrogation rooms. Even when we were back in our own car and under way east, we were too dumbfounded to speak until we were outside Albany, at which point, speculation began to creep in.

"Dude," Mike said. "Trajan—accepting the fact that that whole thing was seriously bizarre, what the hell else did we learn? Because to me it seems like . . ."

"Like some seriously high-placed strings must have been pulled?" I replied. "In order to get Frank to agree so quickly? Well, you're right, Mike. The only question being, who was the conduit for that message: the message that said, 'If you don't have it, let them go. We don't need more of a mess on our hands than we've already got.'"

"Correct," Mike said with a nod of relief.

"Good questions, all of them," I said, lighting a cigarette. "Frank did mention that utter piece of shit Dennis Shea, the guy who administered the *coup de grâce* to Latrell, but he's just a sergeant in the sniper unit. I doubt there's anything much there."

"Although he could have been relaying messages."

"True," I said. "But why pick him? More probably, Shea had simply been the first one to hear the story that there was a body in the Patricks' house. Although he could, I suppose, have been one of the BCI men that Pete talked about being there—the ones that planted the body. But a sergeant? In the snipers? Unlikely that he was even there, much less a planner. Too much of a career risk. It's something else . . . But we'll have to file it away. And other than *that*? We've learned very little. Except that, if Frank Mangold was bullshitting about being surprised, he did a very good job."

"Yeah; though we know that he *is*, in fact, a very good bullshitter." Mike lit a cigarette nervously. "I don't like it, L.T.—somehow, I have the distinct feeling he's setting us up for something, but I can't say what it is. One thing's for sure—he's still pissed that we're around. And whoever the big shots that Indian Bill mentioned actually are, it's for sure that *they're* pissed, too."

"No doubt. But like I say, we can't go guessing at what unknown people are doing where or how. We've got enough to deal with." I checked my watch. "Shit—you've already missed your class."

"Aw, you don't say," Mike answered with a knowing smile: the first time he'd looked even slightly at ease since we'd entered headquarters.

"Yeah, I know, you're all busted up about it. But get me back in time to at least fulfill my duties—which include taking Marcianna for a stroll before my class. We've got to act as if nothing's going on, even if we know that something is—and we've got to keep quiet to Ambyr and Lucas about how high that something may reach. Won't do them any good. They're in it, now, with us, and there's no way to change that. But there's no sense in freaking them out, either."

"And the last of that tribe?" Mike asked. "Derek?"

"Derek is another riddle to be solved. In fact, at this point, I'd say that we have a rough idea of what the two ends—the high and the low—of the scheme to get these kids down south look like: Derek finds the kids, and the people with money pay for them. The only problem being, who are the middlemen? How many of them are there—how many steps, I mean, from Derek to the money?"

"That's an awful lot of questions, L.T.," Mike said ominously.

"It is. But we've done this before, Mike—worked without a net. We can manage it." It struck me even then that this statement was a pretty blatant display of hubris; but there was no time to dwell on it. "Now punch it, and get us back to Shiloh . . ."

{x.}

During the next few days, Mike, Ambyr, Lucas, and I made sure that we knew exactly who our initial quarry in New York City was to be, Mike and I having tapped several of our still-friendly contacts in the NYPD and among New York newspapers for whatever information they could offer about the man whose name appeared on Donnie Butler's documents of authentication: one Roger Augustine, a senior officer at Goldman Sachs, the financial giant. Along with his equally high-powered wife, Augustine fit the profile of someone who might be looking for a throwaway child to take in illegally, for a variety of reasons we would flesh out in the coming days. Simultaneously with this line of investigation, we began planning the initial stages of our descent upon the city, in between classes. Ambyr became a valued auditor of both Mike's and my courses, or at least as many as she could fit around her schedule of rehab and studies at the Disability Center in Fraser without raising suspicion. Mike graciously offered to ferry her up from Surrender each afternoon, since we didn't really want her state-appointed driver getting an idea of what was going on at Shiloh; and her very serious and attentive presence only inspired her already enthusiastic brother to dive into his studies even deeper, to the extent that he began taking his proposed role as our cover during the trip to New York very seriously, and even offered some genuine insights that helped us sharpen the plan.

After we'd all decided to knock off work that Friday night, we all went down to the hangar floor to enjoy a few beers, along with a small breeze that was kicking up through the hollow after a very still week. Making her way to the hangar opening, Ambyr seemed to be drawn to something; and when I joined her, I realized it was the sound of Marcianna chirruping in a peculiar way that I'd never heard before within her enclosure.

"What's she saying now?" Ambyr asked, hearing my footsteps behind her but continuing to keep her attention on the hill. "She sounds—so strange . . ."

"Yeah," I agreed. "And I honestly don't know the answer. I thought I knew all her voices, but—this one is new."

At that, Ambyr tugged me by the hand toward the enclosure. "Come on, let's go hang out with her."

But I pulled back wearily. "You hung out with her once today," I said, referring to my usual afternoon stroll with Marcianna, on which Ambyr had joined us that day without sparking (somewhat to my surprise) any objection to the additional company. "Besides, I'm so beat that the next time I go up that hill, I probably won't end up coming back down till tomorrow morning."

"Aw," Ambyr noised, taunting me with undeniable charm, as had become her custom. "Is our poor one-legged sorcerer feeling sorry for himself?" Then, in a remarkably agile and swift move, she released my hand, took her cane, whipped it back in a flash to her left side, and delivered a sharp, even slightly unsteadying backhand across my prosthesis. The sound resonated, catching Mike's and Lucas' attention. Lucas started our way cackling, anticipating more; but Ambyr, rightly figuring that I wasn't used to that kind of behavior, simply laughed again and turned to make her escape by quickly feeling her way with her cane to the path up to Marcianna's gate.

I moved after her, once I'd gathered my wits and my full balance; but before clearing the area around the hangar, I glanced back when I heard the sounds of Lucas trying to follow, and Mike restraining him with no little difficulty. When the kid asked why Mike was being "such a God damned pain in the balls," Mike told him that one day he'd reach puberty, and then he'd understand. That set off a genuine donnybrook that echoed through the night, making me pause to check my watch in the hope that Clarissa would still be in her study in front of the television: there'd be no chance of her being alarmed by our racket. Reassured, I finally caught up to Ambyr at the gate to Marcianna's enclosure, where she was laughing harder than ever as she caught her breath. She tried to get her mischief under control, however, when she heard the sound of Marcianna speeding through the high grass of the enclosure and finally leaping up to put her front paws on the gate.

As had been the case that afternoon, Marcianna seemed not at all shocked or angered to find Ambyr on the other side of the several layers of wire; indeed, she was even more welcoming toward the newcomer than she had been earlier. Ambyr, for her part, moved over to and crouched down by the fencing to the side of the gate, which was lighter than that of the entry panels and afforded her space to get her hands and forearms through so that she could pet Marcianna. This was by no means a wise or safe move (Marcianna was sometimes alarmed by grasping, groping hands that came through the fence, an experience, I'd always thought, that was far too reminiscent of what she'd endured as a cub in the petting zoo), and I was about to call out to Ambyr in alarm. Yet Marcianna simply strode over, gave Ambyr's hand a short smell, and then began accepting the scratching and petting that our guest offered; none of which diminished the momentary alarm sparked in me by Ambyr's very rash crossing of a boundary that I'd thought she understood.

I went and crouched by her. "You know that was stupid, right?"

"What?" Ambyr said, with another of her soft, carefree laughs, her attention far more focused on Marcianna than it was on me.

"Sticking your hand through the fence like that!" Only when my outburst had made my point plain did Ambyr lose her smile, retract her arms, and turn to me slowly. "She could have taken off your hands at the wrist, Ambyr—never, ever forget how abused she was in that zoo. Or that the savage in her is still alive, under the big pussycat side. And I want it to stay that way."

Ambyr paused for a long half-minute or so, becoming very still and seeming to develop something of a lump in her throat. "Lucas . . ." she finally said, her voice somewhat obscured; then she cleared her throat and continued: "Lucas told me what she did to you."

"Of course—he's told you everything *else,*" I answered, a little annoyed. "Which makes what you just did that much more foolish. Remember, if she attacks you, she gets put down, almost certainly. Let alone what happens to *you.*"

Ambyr nodded a few times, the hazy violet eyes tearing up a bit. "Yeah—Lucas also told me how afraid you are of something like that happening. But, Trajan, please—" She put a hand on my knee, then swiftly moved in and pressed a tender yet slightly tentative kiss on my lips. It was a disarming enough moment; but after she let the kiss linger for a charged moment, her mouth moved to my left ear, where she murmured, "*Don't ever shout at me like that again.* It's not something I respond to very well. Anymore . . ."

There was such a mix of emotions behind the words that for an instant I didn't know whether to let myself remain in the state of mystified intoxication caused by her kiss, or to raise all my inner defenses because of the very cool, even icy, threat contained in the warning she'd issued.

Having made her point for the moment, Ambyr rose up, turning her face toward the hangar. "Wow," she said, with what seemed affected carelessness. "We let it get pretty late, me and Lucas. Didn't we?" Monitoring the arguing voices and the crashing sounds of small flying objects that echoed up our way, Ambyr smiled. "Will you listen to those two?" she said. "Come on, Trajan, we'd better stop them before they burn the whole place down . . ."

She waited for me to rise and approach her, then took my arm. I told Marcianna not to worry, that I'd be right back, and then we started toward the hangar; although it wasn't until we were about halfway there that Ambyr broke the rather awkward silence, leaning her head on my shoulder and saying, "You shouldn't let it bother you, Trajan."

"Shouldn't let what bother me?"

"*Me*," she replied. "When I get like that." She smiled once again. "I have—*moods*. Apparently. Never used to . . ."

Considering this statement, and wanting very badly to believe it, I said, "Well—things being what they have been, I guess you're more entitled than most people."

"Yeah, but . . ." She was struggling hard with it. "I screwed up that kiss, damn it."

This time, I was the one who laughed quietly. "Believe me—you didn't."

"Yeah, I did," she insisted as we closed in on the two idiots inside the hangar. "But don't worry—I'll do better next time . . ."

Within just a few minutes, she was in the Empress with her brother, who, in the full froth of adolescent combat, was still laughing and trying to get another shot in at Mike, whether with fists or words. Finally, I ordered him to stop, if only for the sake of his sister's safety, and the car took off. My soul was by then a mass of confusion, one eager for the simplicity of a night spent in Marcianna's company; yet Ambyr's very meaningful kiss lingered, to put it mildly. Still, I hung my jacket and vest on an obliging peg in one of the hangar's vertical beams, and headed uphill.

I had not actually intended to spend another night in the enclosure; yet I'd been away a lot, that week, and Marcianna needed reassurance. We got to knocking each other around, and at some point I suppose we must have drifted off in the high grass; or perhaps only I did, for when I awoke with a start, Marcianna was as awake and alert as she'd been when I'd fallen asleep. How long I'd been out was also a mystery: the moon had disappeared, and there was a glow above the mountain behind the den, making it early morning. But I was without either my phone or my watch, making an exact determination of the time impossible. The biggest question of all, however, was what could have woken me so suddenly and sharply; and with a start I remembered that it had been the signature alarm call of the old telephone in the JU-52. Or had I simply dreamt it?

Then I heard Mike, calling from the gate of the enclosure: "Trajan!" he hollered—yet his tone not one of dire emergency, such as one would have expected at that hour. "Get your ass up, the kid's on the phone . . ."

Mike began to undo the lock on the gate: a sound that brought an angry little growl from Marcianna. "It's okay, girl," I said, stroking her neck. "You know who that—" But another growl, this one louder, still angrier, and accompanied by a tightening of her muscles and the slow rise of the fur along her spine, quickly followed. "Stay down there, Mike!" I called. "I don't think Her Highness is in the mood for visitors!"

"You don't have to tell *me* twice," he answered; and I could see his silhouette against the brightly lit hangar, moving back down the hill. "You want me to tell Lucas to call back at a decent hour?" he added. "Or are you coming down?"

"What the hell's he doing calling so early?" I asked.

"How the fuck would *I* know? The little prick woke me up, too. Maybe he's got a lead. His hair's on fire about something, that much is pretty obvious."

"All right," I said, standing as quickly as I could. "I'm on my way . . ."

Marcianna accompanied me to the gate, clearly worried by my imminent departure. As I pulled the chain in the gate around so that the lock was on my side, I said, "Don't worry, you. I'll be right back." The lock opened, and I leaned down to take her head in my hands. "*Right back,* got it?"

Yet her concern now seemed less to abate than to transform, as she gave out with that same peculiar chirrup. Then, very uncharacteristically, she darted away from me, moving along the fence of the enclosure and into her den, still chirruping in that urgent, unintelligible way.

By the time I reached the hangar, I was awake enough to realize that it was odd that Mike was there so early. I said as much, adding, "You been here all night?"

"Couldn't sleep," Mike said. "Too fucking humid, I guess. Something. Anyway, figured I'd try to see if I couldn't do something constructive."

"And have you?" I asked, following him up into the plane.

"Abso-fucking-lutely not," he replied wearily. "Best thing I could come up with was getting Monday's lecture notes together, and that's pretty damned sad."

"Well," I replied with a yawn, "it's better than nothing . . ." Then I took up the waiting receiver of the phone, pulled the winding cord around the bulkhead and into the cockpit, and slumped into the pilot's seat. Finally, I stuck the thing to my ear. "Lucas?"

He gave me no greeting, just shouted into my ear, sounding more than a little crazed: "Finally! L.T.—Derek's gone!"

I used the control wheel to yank myself upright. "What do you mean, 'gone'?"

"He's *gone*, L.T., ran off, he ain't here!"

"Okay, okay, calm down," I said. "I'm sure there's some simple explanation."

"No, there fucking is not!" the boy cried; and at that, I heard Ambyr in the background, urging him to try to control himself and stick to the facts. "He left a note. He *said* he's leaving."

"Did he say where he was going?" I asked dimly, as Mike moved to the cockpit doorway.

"No!" Lucas shouted. "Do you think I would have called you if I knew that?"

"Okay, okay," I answered. "Sorry. So what *does* the note say?"

"Ambyr wants to know if you guys can come down and read it," the kid replied. "It's not that long, but—it just doesn't sound like him, and *I* don't think he actually wrote it! Though Ambyr does."

"Okay, sit tight. We'll be there in five minutes." I heard Lucas shouting at his sister as he hung up the phone, and I tried to get back up as quickly as I could, a task which required a little assistance from Mike. "Derek's taken off," I said to him. "Left a note, apparently, that's got them both freaked out—like maybe he didn't go willingly. Whichever way, he didn't leave any forwarding address, if you know what I mean. We've got to go."

"Yeah," Mike said, rushing to his desk and strapping on his .38. The sight made me retrieve my Colt: because if Lucas was right, and Derek had been taken by force—probably because he'd been seen going up to Shiloh earlier in the week, and questions about his trustworthiness had been raised among his immediate superiors—then they might still be lurking around the Kurtz house, to tidy things up should it prove necessary.

As I was pulling on my holster, Mike located his keys; then we made for the hatch. "We locking up?"

"You're damned right," I said, seizing the big padlock, letting Mike pass me, then banging the hatch closed and securing it. A thought suddenly came to me: "I wonder if I should wake Clarissa up."

"*Clarissa?*" Mike said. "Why?"

"She had a feeling something like this was coming—she had it timed almost exactly right, too . . ." I hobbled down the steps, shaking my head.

"No, forget it. We get her up now, she'll be in no state to do much more than bite our heads off. Besides, she hates going into Surrender."

"Who doesn't?" Mike said, snapping the lights in the hangar off as we passed out its mouth.

"True," I replied, starting down the hill. "But we *are* going. This is it, Michael."

"This is what?"

"You know exactly what I mean," I answered, working my cane hard. "The dam has burst. Whatever happens now sweeps us *all* toward the solution . . ."

He didn't reply, choosing to absorb that statement instead. Mike knew, of course, what I was talking about; but the climax of any case—so easy to view with longing during the hard days of assembling evidence and ideas—is always far more intimidating than one had supposed during those early stages. And so we walked on silently toward the car, the sounds of morning continuing to rise; and above them, that same peculiar chirrup of Marcianna's—part warning, part apprehension, part something I did not yet understand—rose up and into the dawn with ever more insistence.

"What's with her?" Mike finally asked, when we'd reached the Empress.

"I don't know," I said, going around to my door and opening it. "But I don't like it. Let's go . . ."

PART THREE

THE FAUST DIALECTIC

Faust enters into a pact with Mephistopheles . . . who empowers Faust to obtain the pleasure he seeks. Faust then seduces Gretchen. But, in doing so, he indirectly causes the deaths of Gretchen's mother, her brother and ultimately Gretchen herself. . . . Faust realizes that he, like Gretchen, her mother, and her brother, has become a victim—of Mephistopheles. . . . Gretchen has been seduced by Faust; Faust has been seduced by the devil. The *Faust* tale generates several microdialectics. In the first, the thesis is the predator (Faust), the antithesis is the prey or "victim" (Gretchen), and the synthesis is predator = victim (Faust). Predator and victim are united in Faust, who is both. He is the synthesis.

—LEONARD F. WHEAT, *HEGEL'S UNDISCOVERED THESIS-ANTITHESIS-SYNTHESIS DIALECTICS*

Who holds the Devil, let him hold him well; He hardly will be caught a second time.

—GOETHE, *FAUST, PART ONE*

CHAPTER ONE

THE DREAM STEALERS

{i.}

Upon arrival at the Kurtzes', we found things roughly as Lucas' phone call had indicated they would be: the kid was charging around shouting and tugging at great clumps of his hair, as if to cause some physical discomfort that would both balance his shock and keep him from tears, while Ambyr was sitting frozen at a small table in the kitchen, on which sat a single dim light that made it impossible to see into the corners of the space. The more illuminated living room gave a fairly clear picture of how gloomy home life had been for Ambyr and Lucas even before their parents had run out on them: it fairly screamed beer drunks, with furnishings not quite so broken down as those in the dwellings of completely dysfunctional alcoholics, but nonetheless old and worn, reflecting a desire to keep costs down and make sure that the requisite case was in the refrigerator every night. Efforts had been made to clean and cheer things up in a few spots, but these only served to remind one that Ambyr, for all her remarkable discernment, was blind, and could ultimately do no more than supervise two teenaged boys in the effort: boys who likely put as little value on making their home more cheerful as had the Kurtzes' parents, if for very different reasons.

Once one's eyes adjusted to the light in the kitchen, a sad duality became apparent. This was the room that, in most country homes, was both the light, active center of family activities and the receiving area for company: virtually no country house that I had ever seen, including Shiloh, used any other room as its primary entrance. The Kurtz house was no different, save that recent, blatant attempts to achieve greater hominess had been made: a small dinette set was plainly new, along with a set of still-sparkling steel appliances, all of which had doubtless been paid for by a state government desperate to hush up how badly Morgan Central School had bungled Ambyr's physical crisis. But beyond these, wallpaper that had likely hung in the room since the early twentieth century stood fading and peeling. Amid this rather dispiriting contrast, the Kurtz siblings had lived their lives since Ambyr's illness and their parents' departure, somehow managing to become, in a testament to the defiance of the youthful spirit, two fully formed people who would have been exceptional whatever their circumstances.

Ambyr was dressed, I noticed as I drew closer to her chair, in a becoming but arrestingly out-of-place midnight blue Chinese silk robe. In one hand she held what I assumed was Derek's departure note; in the other she cradled her head, keeping her eyes fixed on the table lamp as though she could see it. She must have heard our entrance, although she could not seem to gather the strength to quiet Lucas' repeated protestations: "The whole thing's *wrong*! It's not his writing! I'm telling you, somebody must have forced him to go!"

I went to crouch by Ambyr's chair. "Hey. Are you all right to talk?"

When I spoke to her, she sniffed away what seemed only the latest round of weeping, and nodded, shifting in her chair toward the sound of my voice. "I guess you'll want to see this first," she said, her voice still trembling just a bit as she held the note out.

I took the piece of paper from her hand, but before I had even a chance to glance at it, Lucas declared, "I don't know why you wanna see it, it's obviously a fake!"

"All right, Lucas," Mike said. "We've gotten a good idea of your opinion. So get a grip on yourself and we'll all get to work. Right?"

"Damn straight," Lucas declared. "Get to fucking work is right: finding clues is what you guys should be doing! Get trace evidence, fingerprints, whatever it's going to take. The only one who's done anything so far is Kevin, over there, and he's got no training—"

"Lucas, enough!" Ambyr finally said, warning him with a weary slap of her cane on the floor.

The mention of some unknown "Kevin" was momentarily baffling; but then and for the first time, I noticed that a young man, perhaps a little older than Ambyr, had been standing in the shadows near the kitchen door of the house the entire time. At the mention of his name, he came forward, and stood close enough to Ambyr that I found the proximity at first irritating, and then somewhat disheartening: I knew that Lucas had said that Ambyr had no boyfriend, but whatever her feelings for this presentable young man—who had the handsome looks and wiry frame of local youths who were a cut above their peers—he clearly felt very protective and even proprietary over her.

"This is Kevin Meisner, Trajan," Ambyr said. "He drives me to and from the Disability Center, and he also lives right nearby. I was worried that we might have to get a ride up to your place, if you kept not answering your phones." She turned to face the lamp again, pointing wearily toward the general area where Mike and I stood. "Kevin, this is Dr. Jones, and that's Dr. Li."

I stood to shake the stranger's hand, finding that he possessed a good, confident grip; then Mike did the same. Kevin was very straight and deferential in his greetings—"How do you do, sir? Doctor?"—and he locked eyes with both of us in an admirable way that let us know that he had been called to help Ambyr and her brother, and would do all they required of him to achieve that end. That aside, however, for someone we had not yet heard anything about, he appeared very familiar with and at ease in the Kurtz house.

"Kevin goes hunting with Derek," Ambyr said, "so he knows him pretty well, and I wanted him to see if there was any sign that anyone had been around the place while we were asleep." Then she added, very pointedly, "We've told him *what's in the note.*"

I got the message: Kevin knew about Derek, but that was all he knew. Ambyr and Lucas had kept him in the dark about our wider investigation. I made a noise of assent, then looked to our unaware interloper. "Well, Kevin, it's good that you were able to get here—and *did* you find anything? Or maybe I should ask what you looked for, in the first place."

"Kevin's a very good tracker," Ambyr rushed in to explain, "and—"

But she stopped when Kevin touched her shoulder, very softly and even tenderly, to indicate that he could speak for himself. It was an action that, in my foolishness, I found especially irritating. "I parked my truck up by the Francos' old garage," he explained steadily. "Their house is the next one to the north, and it ain't been sold yet, so the driveway's empty. I wanted to get a look and see if there were any fresh tire tracks in the driveway here that I couldn't explain, but assuming that your Crown Vic's got seventeen-inch Cooper radials—"

"Which it does," Mike said. "Well spotted, Kevin."

Kevin nodded appreciatively. "Then that was the last thing in and out of here. Course somebody likely just pulled off to the side of 34. None of the windows or doors in the house've been forced, although most of the windows were already open. But all in all, I'd say that if Derek went, he went on his own steam, and by his own choice."

"Which only shows what *you* know, *Kev*," Lucas said bitterly. Then the kid turned to me. "Look, L.T., Kevin may be an okay tracker, whatever, but he doesn't *really* know Derek, they just hunt together, which means they sit in different spots in the woods for hours. Other than that, he's just the guy that was assigned to drive Ambyr back and forth to the Disability Center, end of story."

I looked at Kevin again. "Is that the case?"

"Well," the young man said, showing great patience with Lucas' little outburst, "originally, yeah, that was the truth. That's my job, giving people lifts who are out of bus range for the Center."

"But he's been a good friend for a long time," Ambyr said reassuringly. "And you, Lucas, can stop being insulting to people just because you're worried. You know perfectly well that Kevin knows Derek and that he's an excellent tracker—even Derek said so, whenever they went hunting together. Besides, we needed to find *some* way to get Trajan and Mike down here before—"

And then she stopped, rather awkwardly, especially for her, clearly showing regret that she might have made some kind of error. And, in the face of this, I turned quickly from her to Lucas. "Guys? Is there something else that Mike and I should know about? Have you called *other* people?"

Those questions quieted even Lucas, at long last, although his silence was less ambiguous than his sister's. His gaze fell to the floor, as if he'd been caught at something more serious than the many transgressions I'd known him to commit during our acquaintance. Then he started talking fast: "Well—you guys still weren't answering your cell phones at, whatever, four o'clock. I know you sleep up in that frickin' enclosure sometimes, Doc, and I figured Mike was probably passed out in the house from the beat-down I gave him. We hadn't thought of getting a ride from Kevin, yet, and then we didn't know if *he* would even answer his phone. Plus, it was just a kind of an automatic thing, I guess you could say. I mean, she *is* our cousin . . ."

I nodded, glancing at Mike: it was understandable that they would have done it, of course, but it was not good news for us: "You called your cousin Caitlin?"

"I'm sorry, Trajan," Ambyr said, quite genuinely. "But we were pretty out of our minds, and like Lucas says, she's our cousin, and she promised to keep it quiet—"

"An impossibility," I murmured, considering the matter. "I fear . . ."

"What's he mean?" Lucas said to Mike, growing more bewildered and a little scared. "She *said* she would keep it quiet."

"Lucas," Mike explained quietly, "your cousin may be your cousin, but she's also an officer of the law. There is almost no way she didn't report this to her superior."

"Yeah," Lucas readily agreed. "To Major McCarron. She said she was going to, but that it wouldn't go any farther than that."

I sighed out the full measure of my foreboding. "That's what I was afraid you'd say," I told the kid. "Major McCarron is a very good man, Lucas, but he cannot treat the sudden disappearance of a minor as a private matter: particularly a minor who he knows to be—" I tried to find the gentlest wording I could: "Who he has legitimate reason to believe will have trouble safely navigating the world outside his established home and habits."

"So any communication between your cousin and the major was almost definitely *not* private," Mike continued. "McCarron *had* to report the matter. And once it was reported, everybody in law enforcement heard about it, and now they're all gearing up to horn in on whatever happens next."

"Which means we don't have long," I said, sitting in the chair to Ambyr's right. "But before we begin—will you please tell me that you didn't call anyone *else*? Like maybe the National Guard?"

Ambyr smiled and found my wrist with her hand—a gesture that Kevin noted with a quick movement of his eyes, although he betrayed no emotion about it. "No, Trajan," Ambyr said, her voice quite intimate. "Just Kevin and Caitlin. And I'm sorry if Caitlin was a risk, but—can we just move on to whatever we're supposed to do now?"

"All right," I announced, pulling a small notepad and pen out of my jacket's inner pocket and starting to scribble something on it. "Lucas," I went on as I wrote, "you guys have, I presume, a computer with some kind of printer?"

"Sure," Lucas said. "An iMac with a laser printer, upstairs—more goods from the state. Why? Don't you want to read the note that's supposedly from Derek?"

"In a minute," I replied, still scribbling. "Ambyr, we're going to produce a little note of our own for you to sign, if you don't mind, to try to forestall what I'm certain is going to be the interference of the Bureau of Criminal Investigation in what we have to do . . ." Finishing with the pen, I looked up at Ambyr's would-be protector. "Kevin, I trust that your being here means that you understand that Ambyr and Lucas would like Dr. Li and myself to take the lead in finding out what's happened to Derek? And, further, that your being here means that Ambyr trusts you enough to witness this document, and treat whatever takes place in the next few minutes in confidence?"

"Definitely," Kevin answered.

"Good—then Lucas, take this." I handed him my scribbled note. "Kevin, Mike will go with you two, and help you set up the formatting so that it looks like a semi-official document that you can sign right away."

"Hey!" Ambyr said. "Can I at least hear what it says? I've gotten a little tired of signing things without knowing what they are."

"Of course, Ambyr," I said. "I was going to read it to you when it was printed up, so that you'd be sure everything was done right, but if you'd rather—" I leaned back to the others. "Michael?"

Mike snatched the note out of Lucas' hand. "You'll never be able to read it, anyway, kid, trust me." Eyes on the paper, Mike deciphered: " 'I, Ambyr Kurtz, being the legal guardian of Derek Franco, a minor fifteen years of age, residing at,' gives your address, 'hereby authorize Doctors L. Trajan Jones and Michael Li,' yada-yada, our address, 'to act as private investigators in the matter of said Derek Franco's disappearance on,' yada-yada, then comes, 'Said Doctors Jones and Li, having experience and expertise in these matters, as well as being personally acquainted with Derek, are hereby authorized to speak as my legal agents in all matters pertaining to this investigation, and are to be considered as acting with my full authority. Signed, Ambyr Kurtz.' Then our signatures, and Kevin's, 'Legal Witness.' You're over eighteen, I assume, Kevin?"

"Yes, sir," the young man answered dutifully.

"Okay then," I said. "No need for a notary. I left it ambiguous, as we have no idea right now just what we'll need to do. And I didn't go so far as power of attorney, because that *would* have to be notarized, and I suspect that Ambyr's had enough of monkeying with her legal rights, anyway."

"Thanks, Trajan," Ambyr said quietly. "So exactly what *does* this do, then?"

"Well, among other things, it entitles us to be present at any interrogation of either you or your brother, and to do whatever else you or we say is necessary to find Derek. The BCI won't fight it—they're not going to risk that kind of press."

"Yep," Mike said. "It'll cover all that, at least for a while—and L.T.'s right, the BCI do not need any more bad publicity, right now. They're still dealing with having to let the Patricks go."

"Sound okay to you, Ambyr?" I asked.

She nodded quickly. "Of course. I'm sorry if I sounded suspicious for a second—"

"No need for apologies," Mike interrupted. "We get it. But L.T.'s right, we need to get this puppy printed, signed, and witnessed before anybody else gets here." He turned to Kevin, and then to Lucas. "Okay, junior, where's the computer?"

Lucas took out some of his boiling frustration on Mike's shoulder. "Hey! I told you about that 'junior' shit—the 'kid' crap is bad enough."

"The computer, Lucas," Mike answered wearily. "Let's go . . ."

As the three of them started upstairs, the kitchen fairly filled with awkwardness, which Ambyr soon tried to dispel: "I'm so sorry, Trajan," she said, but I cut her off, attempting to force a good-natured chuckle:

"Why? He seems like a very decent guy, certainly nothing to apologize for—"

"Will you stop?" Ambyr more ordered than asked. She grabbed my hand tight. "He's just—he's been doing favors for us for a long time, and I thought we were just friends. Then Lucas started warning me that *he* thought Kevin was going somewhere else with it—I guess I'd been trying to deny it, because there's basically been no one else in Surrender that I've really felt we could trust. And then, when we asked him to come over tonight, in case we needed to get up the hollow fast—well, maybe I guess I couldn't deny anymore that he thought I was giving him some kind of signal . . ."

"Ambyr." I put my right hand atop the one of hers that held my left. "You don't have to explain anything. Your life is your own, to do whatever you want with—you've earned that, God knows. And you certainly don't want to go messing around with a sick old man like me."

She paused for a long moment, and we both sat listening to the sounds of Lucas and Mike, somewhere upstairs, going through one of their arguments. When I dared glance up again, I saw that Ambyr's eyes had teared up, and that her mouth was slightly agape. "What kind of person do you think I am, exactly?" she murmured.

"Oh," I sighed, running for my life inside my head and feigning a smile that I forgot she could not see. "To tell you the truth—my judgments in this area, at least so far as they relate to my own life, have generally been so stunningly bad that . . . that I had to admit, long ago, that I just don't know why most people who enter my orbit do the things they do. Not deep down, I don't."

"So . . ." Ambyr pulled her hand away and folded her arms, becoming the very tough matron of the house once more; but just then Kevin came back downstairs, entering the kitchen with a smile.

"I don't know what those guys are fighting about," he said, "but they're going at it, all right. Anyway, I signed the paper."

The awkwardness of being alone with Ambyr was only heightened by Kevin's reappearance; and I needed to come up with some reason for him to leave, in part because I needed to be able to talk freely with Ambyr about Derek's disappearance, in part because I didn't feel like getting caught up in some struggle of wills with the young man, a struggle that, for all I knew, could simply have been a product of my imagination.

"Okay, then—practicalities," I said. "Kevin, I realize it may sound rude, but you do *not* want to be around when the law gets here. Suspicion will fall on anybody present, if the BCI has its way."

"He's right, Kev," Ambyr said. "Please don't get into trouble."

"You'll be okay if I go?" he asked her.

"Sure, of course—but I won't be if they suspect *you* of anything."

"Take some back road out of here," I advised. "The law will use the most direct route. What do you drive?"

"Got an old Dodge truck I fixed up," he said. "All-terrain tires, can go just about anywhere."

"Good. Then get yourself home quickly, staying off the highway."

"Or do you have to be at work soon?" Ambyr asked.

Checking an old, yellowing plastic clock on the wall, Kevin said, "Yeah, I guess I will have to start heading over to the Center in an hour or so."

"Better still," I told him. "They're not going to mess with someone who works there. So head home, then to Fraser, but keep an eye out, in case somebody's watching and sees you leave."

Ambyr had read my subtext quite accurately. "You'll do that, right, Kev? I'll feel a lot better."

Nodding once, Kevin replaced a blaze orange cap with the Remington Arms logo and a camouflage pattern splashed across its visor on his head. Then he said, again very dutifully, "Sure—it was good to meet you, sir."

"Absolutely," I replied. "And thanks for the help. Get there safe."

Ambyr accompanied him to the door, mumbling a few things that I couldn't hear: intimacies, my mind decided, and I became further irritated—and injured.

Once he was gone, Ambyr returned to the table and sat beside me, though the chill was palpable. "That's what you really think?"

"What's what I really think?" I asked, ready to go on; but at that instant I heard the short squeal of a tire on hardtop, and an ugly thought flashed across my mind: I mumbled some vague apology, ran to the door, heedless of Ambyr's asking why, then dashed outside and down to the county road. I knew what had made the sound, of course: it was Kevin's truck. But what I didn't know, and couldn't tell from the quickly vanishing sight of his running lights, was what color that truck was, and whether or not it bore a white cap . . .

Convincing myself that this was one more manifestation of my jealousy, I hurried back to the kitchen, explaining to Ambyr that I'd thought it might be a cop tailing Kevin. That seemed to wash, and then I sat next to her again, finding that she was ready to pick right up where she'd left off: "You think I'd go ahead and kiss you while I was keeping some kind of *secret boyfriend* down here in my 'normal life'? You really think I'd do that?"

"I think," I said, retreating once again, "that your friend Derek, a minor for whom you are legally responsible, whether you like it or not, has gone missing. And I think we'd better concentrate on figuring out what happened to him . . ."

Thankfully, Mike came downstairs and swiftly into the room at just that moment, bearing the prepared document. "Well, I don't know what I had to go up there with the kid for: his computer skills are fine, though getting him to let go of the thing was—" He stopped talking abruptly, as he observed the scowl that still dominated Ambyr's features. "Of course," he said quietly, "I could always go back up and make sure that he doesn't, you know, start running off extra copies . . ."

"No, Mike," Ambyr said coolly, even icily, as she stood suddenly and grabbed her cane. "You two are the experts, you go over Derek's note, and I'll go up and make sure Lucas is behaving. Besides, I've listened to what Derek said a dozen times, I know it by heart—but maybe Lucas and I will go through his room again, see if we missed anything there." She headed for the doorway. "It seems like I've been off about a lot of things, this week, though I really didn't think so."

As she moved toward the stairs—which were located between the living room and what I would later learn was her own room beyond—Mike watched her go, and I began to spread Derek's note out carefully on the table beneath the small lamp.

Letting out a low, quiet whistle, Mike shook his head as he sat down. "Nice work, L.T.; usually it takes a woman a year of being in an actual relationship with you to get that pissed. What'd you do, tell her the one about the three blind guys who walk into a bar?"

"Michael," I moaned, "can we please go over this note? We've got a complicated situation on our hands, and—"

"No, we don't. *You* do, apparently. As far as the note goes, whatever it says—and Lucas told me some of it—Derek was a kid who was troubled on a whole lot of levels, and something like this was bound to happen. You knew it. Even Clarissa knew it. No reason to suspect that somebody magically snuck into the house and snatched him." Then, seeing that I was almost writhing in discomfort, Mike pulled his chair closer, saying, "All right. Let's go over it, word by fucking word . . ."

We began to dissect the sheet of paper that sat atop a pile of disheartening household bills, credit card charges inevitably on top. Written in pen on lined notebook paper in a simple block writing style, the lone page represented Derek's attempt to explain exactly why he was making his mad run toward an irresistible but perhaps deadly beacon of what he believed was hope . . .

{ii.}

Even a detached analyst could have seen that the message betrayed an emotional struggle: the words had first been drafted in pencil to make corrections less conspicuous, and the paper was stained by a number of tears that had fallen as the work was done. The most immediate and conspicuous fact about the message, however, was that it had been written to Lucas alone. Seeing this, I glanced up at Mike quickly, understanding why Ambyr's look of devastation had been so complete when we came in. "Jesus, Mike," I said. "I mean, she may not have asked to be his legal guardian, but she never shied away from the job, either. And he doesn't even address his goodbye to her?" I stared down at the wood grain of the kitchen table, not yet prepared to move on.

"Feeling kind of like a heel, hunh?" Mike said. "Well, don't worry—based on the way you two have been behaving, I'm sure she'll forgive you."

I just shook my head dubiously at that, then started reading the note from the top once more:

Dear Luke,

I know you never believed me, but I did always tell you that one day it was gonna be my turn to go. And now it is. I can't tell you anything about it, except that you don't have to worry, I'm going to someplace really nice. I mean, REALLY nice, you probably wouldn't believe me if I told you, anyway. But alls I wanted to say was that it's just no good for me here, anymore. You know that. You're moving on, and that's good, but I've been stuck waiting my turn. Well, no more waiting. I won't have to be in this lousy town my folks left me in anymore. And I know how much trouble I been for you and Ambyr, so at least that'll be over. It just sucks that it has to happen this way, all secret, but that's the only way to do it, they say. And it ain't such a secret, anyway, you and Ambyr both know why I'm going. Anyway, as soon as I'm there and settled in and it's safe, I'll let you know where I'm at. Until then, I hope everything keeps going good for you guys, and sorry again for leaving like this. But it won't be for that long. Soon we can get together, and you won't believe where. So, anyway,

See you later, Luke,

Derek

p.s. took some stuff from the refrigerator—tell Ambyr not to be mad. Now she's only got you to feed, after all. Ha, Ha!

"Whoa," Mike breathed, sitting back once I'd finished. Neither of us spoke for a moment, and then he added, "Do you suppose they all sounded that way? Shelby—Kyle, Kelsey, Donnie?" He seemed to be absorbing the possibility that we might soon be adding Derek's name to that grim list. "Do you think they all sounded so—*happy*, once they knew they were on their way?"

"More than likely," I murmured, finally pulling myself away from the table. "At any rate, several things are immediately and plainly apparent—first, he makes mention, just as Latrell did, of 'they'—not one person, but at least two and probably a group. That's strong reason to believe the note's genuine—it's consistent. And, just as vitally, we now know whoever's on the next rung up the ladder, whoever's the point person for the 'they' in question, and is delivering these kids to the *organization*, so to speak—he or she's got serious Pied Piper credentials."

"Like a child molester?" Mike asked. "By which I mean, the kind of person that really knows how to ingratiate himself with kids. Like that teacher in Brooklyn, the one who handed out cigarettes and got high with his kids, and groomed new ones every year for sex—remember the case?"

"I'm not likely to forget it. Oh, the hipness of Brooklyn . . ." But I waved Mike off, still considering the note. "No, no. This guy or woman—and we have to keep the option that it might be a woman open, based on Derek's reaction to those photos of Diana—is on a whole nother level than your average child molester. This person's got something else. Nothing material, that's almost certain, whether we're talking about bags of drugs or dough. Consider what each dead kid had, after all, Mike—the things they were either found with, or that we know they spent time around during the time they went missing, like Kelsey and the thoroughbreds. What do they all have in common, what do they all represent?"

Mike's brow tightened. "Well, each one was pricey, we know that."

"But money wasn't the key," I countered. "Sure, the books, the horses, the clothes, they were expensive, but what about Donnie? We've known since we found out the details about those jerseys that he didn't really care about them for their monetary value, or as collector's items. I mean, he seemed to treasure the one he was wearing most, but for status. And the others? He kept them in that bag with his other stuff and slept on it all, as if he stole them to punish the people he was staying with, as we've already talked about. But it's more: based on my talk with Latrell, I'd say any value the boy himself found in the jerseys was simply what they *represented*: not money; punishment, yes, but he could have thrown them away and achieved that; no, it was the *experience* of being at the games, of meeting the players and hanging out with the biggest names in basketball as if he were on some fantasy playground. And I'm betting that, to greater or lesser extents, it was the same for the other kids: despite the cost of the objects they were found to either possess or to have been in contact with when their bodies were found, possession itself—at least in terms of re-sale value or whatever—wasn't the point. They were symbols of what the kids had always fantasized about, and had finally been offered, as a way of enticing them into their new lives; and symbols, after the arrange-ments had failed, of what they'd enjoyed *in* those lives. All those diverse objects and memories, they were . . ."

Mike gave me a minute, then demanded: "They were *what*, damn it?"

I looked at him a bit self-consciously—for my next words were not my own: " *'The, uh—stuff that dreams are made of . . .'* "

Mike's brow wrinkled even more. " *The Maltese Falcon*? Bogart's last line?"

I nodded slowly. "The last line of the movie itself, actually."

Mike nodded a little blankly. "Hunh—Dashiell Hammett, right? I could check on the list of what Kyle had, see if there was an early edition."

"The only problem being that that line's not *in* the book. John Huston wrote the script, along with directing the picture, and he lifted the line from Shakespeare. Has to be the only time that one line has been the signature of two otherwise unconnected hits written three hundred years apart . . ."

Mike's forehead finally relaxed as he considered what I'd said. "The black bird," he murmured. "Yep. Whoever this piece of shit is, he—*or* she—snatches the dreams right out of their heads, uses them to get the kids on board and compliant, so that when they meet our mysterious 'them,' who do the actual placement downstate—not to mention those people that they eventually get placed *with*—no questions will be asked, and they won't be scared. Hell, that'd work *better* than drugs."

"Indeed."

"So—" Mike had one more issue he needed to wrangle to the ground: "Was *Derek* the dream stealer, then? Because whatever else I'd say about the kid, I wouldn't have called him a piece of shit."

I could only shake my head. "No. Derek certainly was an enigma—we saw that much. I think he *would* have done it, because he genuinely would have thought that he was helping the kids he approached. But at heart, he was a moderately autistic kid who had moments of real intelli-gence: indeed, when he talked about rifles, he displayed all the qualities of a savant. Did he have another area of particular brilliance—interpersonal brilliance—that he employed when approaching the other kids? Possibly. And did that talent not only allow him to pick out the ones that would fall for some very powerful lure, but determine what that lure was, and to proceed to dangle it so effectively that they would bite?" I shook my head. "It's sounds like an awful lot, doesn't it, for him? True, the note tells us that he was operating on levels that not even Lucas knew about—and Lucas was supposed to be not only his best friend, but the sharper of the two, but that's not conclusive. One thing *is* clear, however: if we look at the way Derek addressed this note, along with the way he was behaving at Clarissa's before dinner, we get a clear idea of what dream he himself was pursuing, along with at least a hint of who the 'dream stealer,' as you say, might have been, if it *wasn't* him."

"If I'm following you correctly, L.T.," Mike offered, "you're headed back to the idea of a teacher. But one way more sophisticated than that schmuck in Brooklyn."

"I'm not thinking as much of a teacher," I answered. "Although a teacher is certainly the most obvious type. But there is something that takes even more primary importance than a teacher, based on what we observed with Derek."

Mike began to nod. "A woman," he said uneasily, knowing the minefield of political correctness onto which we were setting foot.

"Not just a woman, but a maternal figure. She doesn't need to be a teacher; indeed, I'd favor someone with even more intimate knowledge, who can blur the lines even more readily. A school counselor, maybe, above all, an idealized maternal figure. Derek's farewell note is the last piece that tells us that."

"Because," Mike ventured, "despite the way that Ambyr took him on and looked after him, he didn't address the note to her, and there's no message, not even a thank-you, to her. So she never filled that role . . ." With that we both fell silent for an instant, absorbing the sorrowful weight of what had been said.

Not surprisingly, as Mike and I had studied the note and engaged in our ensuing conversation, we had been facing the table with our backs to the doorway that led from the kitchen into the living room and then to the front door of the house; and neither of us had heard anything that indicated that Ambyr and Lucas had returned from upstairs. It was therefore all the more disturbing when we were both struck, at almost the same instant, by the distinct feeling that we were being watched. We looked at each other and nodded slowly—the kind of nod we had learned to trust in dangerous situations, over the years—and then started to turn our heads still further toward the doorway. When we'd gotten far enough to see that there were human shapes there, but not to make out who they were, I shouted, "Go!" And before we had time for the action to become more than reflexive, Michael was in a kneeling position with his .38, while I was standing with my .45. Both guns were trained on the kitchen door—right at Ambyr's and Lucas' heads.

"*Jesus-H.-fucking-Christ, don't shoot!*" Lucas screamed, stepping in front of his sister in an act of utter selflessness, yet at the same time shielding his own face comically with his hands.

"What the hell?" Mike managed to say, as he holstered his .38 and I did the same with my Colt. "You guys were supposed to be upstairs! What's with sneaking up on us like that?"

But Lucas just turned to Ambyr and took hold of her arm. "You okay, sis?"

Ambyr nodded quickly. "Yeah. Yeah, I'm fine, Lucas, don't worry. I'm assuming we almost got our heads blown off, just now?" She took a deep breath and steadied herself by letting it out. "Great. Well, there's no point in lying, guys—we did sneak down. We wanted to hear what you thought of the note. We only heard the tail end of it, but from that—"

"From *that*," Lucas interrupted, "before you went all Butch and Sundance on our asses, you guys made it pretty clear that you think that bullshit note was actually written by Derek."

"I'm afraid that's right, Lucas," I said. "You might as well know."

"Really? Well, here, geniuses—" He was holding another piece of lined paper, which he now shoved in our faces. "This is from one of Derek's notebooks. I was using it for comparison before you got here. You try it. There are *obvious* differences."

"Lucas," Mike said. "Come on—even you should know that handwriting analysis is about two steps above voodoo, especially when one sample, like Derek's note, has been drafted over and over to make sure of the wording. Remember, whatever you see people doing or saying on television—"

"I ain't talkin' about television!" Lucas cut in, dashing back into the living room and returning with a large yellow paperback book. "There's a whole chapter on it, in here: and right on the first page, it says, 'Handwriting analysis can be used in forensic science to establish whether or not forgery has been committed.' And forgery is a fucking *crime*, Mike, in case you forgot!"

"What the hell have you got there, Lucas?" I said, moving over to him. Closing the book, I read out its title: "*Crime Scene Investigations: Real-Life Science Labs for Grades 6–12*. Hmm. This looks more up your alley, Mike. It even has cartoon illustrations."

I tossed him the book, and Mike studied the cover. "Ho-lee shit," he said. "And they give you a science credit for this stuff? Despite the fact that they're openly saying that the level of the material is the same, whether you're an eleven-year-old or a seventeen-year-old?" He flipped to the section on handwriting analysis that Lucas had quoted while he waited for the kid to answer.

"Well, yeah," Lucas conceded, in a much more uncertain voice.

"Unh-hunh," Mike answered, skimming the first few pages of the chapter. "Okay . . . Well." He glanced around the kitchen, looking for and finding a trash can. "We'll just put this where it belongs . . ." And with a little more force than was required, Mike did not so much lob as hurl the book into the trash, bringing a brief exclamation of objection from Lucas—who did not, however, attempt to retrieve the book. "And then I'll tell you the *single* guiding scientific truth about handwriting analysis, at this point in history: it's only considered, even by saps like the FBI, to have anything close to a shot at accuracy or value when it's been determined that the sample in question, the one being matched against an original like that random notebook page you've got there, was written without any attempt to forge or deceive."

"*Whaaat?*" Lucas droned. "But that would mean—"

"Right. It means only when the crime being investigated is *not* forgery. You can maybe use it as an adjunct to some other investigation, in other words, although I wouldn't recommend it, but forgery cannot be the primary target."

"But that—" Lucas was struggling. "But that would mean it's basically useless."

"Basically," Mike said. "Although most of the time it's used by law enforcement as a tool *in* forgery cases, because juries buy it. And why do they buy it? Because prosecutors, like the authors of your textbook, there, tell them it's 'forensic science,' just like they see on *CSI*. Which, to the average modern jury, means it's God's revealed word. Still—it's nice to

know that your science textbook, if you want to call it that, is just as useless as everything else in that so-called school of yours." Mike started
running his hands through his hair in frustration, creating the brushlike
effect. "Aw, hell, Lucas, look—we don't even know how damned reliable
fingerprints are, anymore. I mean . . ." At this point, having ignored both
Ambyr and me during his tirade, Mike glanced at each of us in turn, and,
finding that we were both listening rather uncomfortably, rose and
grabbed Lucas by the collar of his T-shirt. "Come on, kid—I'll explain it
to you upstairs, and you can show me what other bullshit books you have
while I try to answer your pissed-off questions about the note . . ."

They departed, the sound of Lucas' vain protests soon fading as Michael told him to keep his voice down. That left Ambyr steadying herself
on the doorway and me standing by the kitchen table, neither of us saying much for a minute or so until she asked quietly:

"You *do* think it's real, don't you?"

"I'm afraid so, Ambyr," I answered. "I don't know how much you
heard, but—"

"We heard—almost all of it." The violet eyes moistened, and she began
to mumble, "I already knew it, though. I knew it was real. It's just that . . ."
Her lips began to tremble and her arms lifted in a manner that I couldn't
read precisely; all I could do was approach, not yet certain whether she
felt helpless or intended to take a swing at me.

But swing she did not. Sensing I was within arm's reach, or perhaps
judging the distance from the sound of my footsteps, she rushed forward
and wrapped her arms around me, sobbing. It was another very delicate
and confusing moment; and all I could do was put my arms lightly about
her and let her sob her pain out into my chest. Soon enough, however,
she began to blurt the same things that Mike and I had been discussing—
primarily Derek's complete failure to address her in the note—and then
went on to wonder if in fact she had done as well by him as she could
have, interspersing such talk with declarations of how little she had
wanted to take charge of the boys in the first place. I knew what I was
hearing: the adult she had only recently succeeded in becoming was
straining against the confines of the arrangement they had all been left in
by the disappearance of their respective parents, and she was decrying
the injustice—heaped upon the other injustices of her younger life—of
losing years during which she should have been allowed to enjoy that
same new womanhood. Holding her slightly tighter, I tried to tell her

that I knew only too well about stolen years of youth, and the irreparable hole they could leave in one's soul; and as I spoke, her sobbing subsided, and she began to nestle into our embrace more out of comfort than desperation.

"You *do* know, you *do* know," she repeated several times over; and before long, after drying her eyes on her sleeve, she moved her arms up, encircled my neck with them, and gave me another long, very passionate kiss, one that had none of the tentative quality that she had exhibited the night before. And such being the case, I could find no strength to restrain myself: I returned the kiss, wondering as I did where this eternally perplexing girl might be leading my confused and ungovernable heart.

"I'm sorry, Trajan," she said, after a few long moments. "About before—I don't mean to be a bitch, I never do, I know you were confused by Kevin being here, and that I should have told you first thing that he was. I didn't mean to put you in the position I did—"

"Don't worry," I answered, leaning down to her face, which was made somehow lovelier by her sorrow and regret. "We're here, now." And then another a kiss, as I grew more certain of what I was doing. It's one thing to receive the affections of such a young woman when one is confused; but to return them, when one thinks one has achieved clarity—then you are, just as Michael had said, truly dead.

And it was Mike who found us in that same position, and more quickly than I had expected. He burst through the kitchen doorway—without, fortunately, Lucas in tow—and, immediately upon seeing us, shielded his eyes. "Oh, whoa!" he quietly reacted, smiling beneath the visor formed by his left hand. "I'm sorry, guys—could not *be* more embarrassed. I should have announced myself. Although I have to say, Ambyr, that I also could not be more delighted." Finally he looked up, observing that we had disentangled ourselves from our embrace. "But I'm afraid I have to ruin the moment even more. There's what looks like cop lights out on Route 7."

In short order I hustled to get Ambyr back to her seat, pen in hand. All that was required was for the three of us to sign the authorization, and my partner and I would, at long last, be given a legal and official standing in the case, by way of Derek's disappearance.

"Lucas!" I called, bringing the kid at a run. "During your little festival of phone calls earlier this morning, did you happen to call any other family members, along with your cousin?"

"No!" he declared. "Of course not! *Although* . . . when I called Caitlin, she did happen to mention that maybe *she* was gonna call one or two of them. Why, am I in ultra-deep shit for it? I mean, come on, Ambyr woulda called somebody, anyway—"

"Lucas!" Ambyr scolded, turning, lifting her cane, and making the kid jump back; but she soon relented. "Oh, hell, Trajan, he's probably right. I would've had to."

"That's okay," I said. "This is one situation where I want you to have as much adult backup as you can—assuming, that is, that everyone your cousin called will understand the arrangement in that document."

"Oh, they will," Ambyr said. "Just let me handle them."

"Okay," I said, taking the printed sheet; and as I did, Ambyr very swiftly and deftly brought my hand to her mouth and let her lips linger on the back of my own wrist for an instant. But the spell of this startling feeling was broken by the wail of sirens outside, which very quickly grew louder, indicating that the column—and I had no doubt that it would, once again, be a column—of vehicles had turned onto County Route 34. I took Ambyr by her hands and began to give her something of a pep talk about the shitstorm that was headed our way, and my belief that she and Lucas could handle it; but in the time it took me to deliver it, the cruisers had screamed into the Kurtzes' driveway and up onto the lawn, flooding the house with their halogen high beams, while still more cars crowded Route 34, making it necessary for some of the state uniforms to set up one-lane traffic with flares.

As the cars before me disgorged their passengers and I saw just who they were, I could not help but smile wide. This moment was going to be, I suddenly realized, even more satisfying than I had hoped.

{iii.}

At the front of the phalanx coming my way were two people I had expected to see—Frank Mangold and Mitch McCarron—along with a few that I had not thought to run into quite so soon: Cathy Donovan, Nancy Grimes, and, more sadly, Curtis Kolmback, whose presence, now, at all five deaths and/or disappearances, fully confirmed that he was in on the effort to obscure any true solution to the case. The why of this was plain, as plain as when we had stated it to Gracie: better to allow a serial killer case to erupt than to permit a child-neglect scandal to break out, in the minds of official higher-ups, perhaps *much* higher-ups, as our encounter in Hoosick Falls had indicated. Nonetheless, I was sorry to see that Curtis' personal ambition was so much more mercenary than I had previously believed. The group came at me in something of a wedge, Mangold in front, but I simply held up one hand, trying to see clearly in the glare of the rapidly pulsing lights.

"I thought I was clear with you in Albany." Mangold tried to wave me off. "You've got no standing in this case, profiler, and we've got a warrant. So move, and let the professionals take over."

I ignored him, for the moment, and turned to Mitch McCarron. "Major," I said, ribbing him. "Glad to see you brought the full three-ring circus, although one really would have been enough."

"Yeah, I'm sorry about that, Trajan," Mitch replied, moving his Stetson back on his head. "Just couldn't convince anybody that this would be better handled quietly."

"Can't say that surprises me too much, Mitch," I said, "given the company you're running with." I looked Mangold's way again. "Where's your MRAP, Frank? Forget to bring it?" Seeing that Mangold was simply too steamed to speak, I turned toward the two women, who were approaching quickly. "Ms. Donovan. Director Grimes." As they each nodded acknowledgment, the first with a knowing smile, the second rather sourly, I looked past them to the ever-harried, ever-shuffling "CSI" Kolmback. "And Curtis. I can't say I'm happy to see you in this company."

Curtis lowered his eyes, and was about to speak; but a look from Grimes shut him up.

"As Frank says, Doctor," Donovan announced coolly, "you have no authority, here, and this is the scene of a child's disappearance. So I have to wonder why you're risking a charge of obstruction."

I held up my hand again. "Yes, I know you're dying to toss the house and start your . . . *investigation*. But, Mitch, if you'll take a look at this"—I produced Ambyr's agreement from my inner pocket—"I think you'll find that it entitles Dr. Li and myself to be present during all the proceedings, and at just about anything involving the Kurtzes *and* the search for the Franco boy that we damn well choose to be involved in . . ."

Glancing over the document, Mitch began first to nod and then to smile. "Well—I'm afraid he's got you, Frank. You too, Cathy. They've got full authority from the family, and it's been witnessed. If I were you, I'd swallow my pride and just let them be . . ."

This caused a heated council among the officials present, while their foot soldiers stood behind them, pressing forward to hear what was being said. But the end result was fairly predictable, though no less satisfying: Mangold ranted, Nancy Grimes complained about infringement upon her authority, and Cathy Donovan just stared inscrutably at me. Finally, I stepped out of the doorway and allowed the flood tide in, reminding the officers as they passed that they had an obligation to be especially careful during their search, since the sole occupants of the house were a teenage boy and a young woman who had been literally blinded by the state's incompetence. Then I turned the management of the search over to Lucas, urging him to instruct the officers rather than respond to them, and to be brief and forthright, but nothing more, in answering questions. Delighted with this authority, Lucas took to it like the young terror that he was, handling the sometimes-rude troopers with impressive aplomb and dispatch. Then I advised Ambyr to lock herself in her bedroom until her relatives arrived; and this several of them soon did, led by Cousin Caitlin and her father, Bass Hagen, a towering man who was almost a dead ringer for Otto von Bismarck, so Germanic were his features. He pushed through the cops—"*Get* your God damned asses outta my way, I was in Desert Storm, and you little shits don't stack up to *nothing* against the ragheads!"—until he locked eyes with Mike and me; and then, Lucas in tow, we withdrew into the kitchen to straighten things out.

"The way the kids tell it, Doctors," Bass said, with what looked like one of Caitlin's brothers, along with that impressively uniformed trooper herself, flanking him, "you been a real help to them. So thanks for that. But now I'm wondering if maybe you're not the cause of *this* whole mess."

"Not the cause, Mr. Hagen," I answered. "But, if I can suggest something, we may be the solution, or as close as Ambyr and Lucas can come to one, for now."

"And what the hell's that supposed to mean?" By now Lucas had fetched Ambyr, and Bass put a huge arm around her, which she plainly found immensely comforting.

"This situation is only going to get worse," I told him. "There'll be more cops, soon, but that's not the worst of it. If I know the media, and

Dr. Li and I know them well, they're going to descend on this place at any minute. You don't want your niece and nephew exposed to that, trust me."

"Hmm," Bass grunted. "You're right, there. Maybe I should just take 'em to our place."

"I don't think so," I replied. "That'll be the first place they'll look. These crime reporters—and a lot of them will be national media—are first-class shits, but they know their shitty business. No, I was thinking that maybe Ambyr and Lucas could come and stay at Shiloh for a while."

Ambyr's expression eased with sudden relief, though I could feel Mike's eyes boring a look of shock into the back of my skull; but Lucas, to my relief, immediately declared, "Oh, hells-to-the-yeah, we can! I'm packing, Uncle Bass." Then he started out the kitchen doorway.

"Hold on, hold on," Bass said, grabbing the writhing kid with his free arm. "That's a generous offer, Doc—maybe a little *too* generous. What's in it for you guys, if you don't mind my asking?"

"Does something have to be in it for us?" I asked stupidly.

"Yeah—it does," he answered. "I know your great-aunt some, from farm business. She's a good woman, so I'm not worried about anything shady. But she'd be the first to ask the same question: what's in it for you?"

"Okay," I conceded. "The fact is that Ambyr and especially Lucas have been great helps to our own investigation. I don't want to see these idiot cops screw that up. Plain and simple."

Bass Hagen considered that for a minute or two, scrutinizing first Mike and then me with eyes the color of the slate that made up so much of the Taconic Mountains. "Plain and simple," he said at length. "And right, I guess."

"Yes!" Lucas declared, unwisely choosing that moment to offer his middle finger to several passing state troopers, who, mercifully, failed to notice him. "Come on, sis—let's get ready!"

"Hang the hell *on*, Lucas," Bass said, keeping ahold of the kid. "When would you figure to go?"

"We've got work to do here, yet," I said. "I'd like to handle the first wave of reporters, who should be here any minute, and try to take the spotlight off your niece and nephew. Then we need to talk to one or two of these people about just what is going on; after that, we'll sneak away. Mitch

McCarron will tape off the house, and we'll head up the hollow to let it all settle down. Right, Mike?"

Mike had yet to speak, and I hoped the tone of my question would indicate to him the importance of his backing me up. This, it evidently did: "Absolutely right," my partner said, with none of the hesitation I'd feared. "It's the wise move to make, Mr. Hagen—if they stay here, the state agencies will try to keep them under absolute control. But we can avoid that, and get them out of here smoothly. It's something we've, uh"— and he coughed once at my head— "prepared for."

Bass smiled, ever so slightly and knowingly. "You're taking a lot of chances, for a couple of guys who've got just about everybody in law enforcement pissed off at them. Been through that before?"

"You . . . might say so," Mike answered, thankfully failing to elaborate.

"Okay, then." Bass finally released the struggling Lucas. "Now you can go pack, squirt. You too, Ambyr. God only knows how long this circus is gonna go on . . ." Looking at me once again, this lone rock of familial stability in Ambyr and Lucas' life nodded. "And I'm grateful. Doctors . . ."

With Lucas' withdrawal upstairs to get his things together, Bass took over the job of preventing the investigating officers from doing any real harm to the house; and that gave me a chance to withdraw into the kitchen with Mike and Ambyr.

"Trajan, are you sure about this?" Ambyr asked. "It's a lot to ask, and you did *not* plan on it."

"No, we didn't," Mike said, giving me a shake of his head. "But—much as I hate to admit it, Ambyr, L.T.'s right: it's the smart thing to do. I just hope Miss Clarissa sees it that way."

"She will, trust me," I said. "So for now—you get your stuff together, too, Ambyr, while Mike and I see if we can't take the heat off of you and Lucas out front. Plus—I want to talk to Curtis, Mike. He knows more than he's telling, and we need to make him spill."

"Check," Mike said, moving ahead through the troopers toward the front door, knowing that Ambyr and I would need a minute. I was grateful for his tact, though it left me uncertain about what to do next; but that decision was quickly taken from me. Ambyr began to pull me, at a careful rate that would cause no notice, into a small pantry that I had not noticed was just off the kitchen, behind the big new steel refrigerator. There she threw her arms around my neck in a rush and once again kissed me, causing still another new (or *re*newed) reaction within my spirit. Then, after offering some final words of encouragement and brushing a few of her foremost strands of long hair behind her ears, I tried to leave her there in that little room and follow Mike out the kitchen door.

But she would not be left; not quite so soon. She pulled me back once again, kissed me more deeply than before, and whispered, "Just tell me this is all going to work . . ."

I wasn't certain just what she was referring to, the immediate situation or our own; so I decided to answer the practical question first: "I can square it with Clarissa, trust me. But you've got to let me handle the first wave of the media. When it goes out that this is the fifth case in what certain sources think is a string of disappearances and serial murders, it's going to go national—and you haven't known hell until you've known that. So let's get you two out of here before it happens. Hell, Lucas practically lives at Shiloh already, and Clarissa really will not allow reporters anywhere near the place—and as for the cops, they're afraid of *her*. And you'll have your own room, don't worry about that, so will Lucas, there's nothing *but* room—"

She pulled close again. "And if I don't want my own room?" she murmured into my ear.

It was all going way too fast, now, for my rusty inner self. "Oh, Ambyr," I sighed, trepidation in every syllable. "Let's take it one step at a time, okay? First, we move you up there."

She kissed me again, quite suddenly and firmly, as if to seal the deal. "You got it. But do square it with Clarissa—she'll probably want to make sure for herself that it's all legit."

"Oh, you don't have to worry about that," I said, starting to pull away again. "Clarissa is very fond of you both. So now"—we finally released our holds on each other—"let me do what I've got to do. We'll be back in a little bit, and right outside if there's an emergency."

"You're the boss," Ambyr said; but just when I had actually come close to leaving the pantry, she called to me in a murmur one last time: "Oh— and Trajan? As soon as we get there, we go feed Marcianna, right? She must be going a little crazy."

"Absolutely," I said, taking a step back into the shadows—far enough for her to grab me and let me have another very deep kiss. By the time I was finally able to force myself from the little space, my head was absolutely spinning; but I had to try to pull it together before I joined Mike outside the front door, even if my heart was thundering with very confused delight.

"Took you long enough," Mike said, eyeing me with a grin. "And you might want to tuck your fucking shirt in, you crippled old dog, you . . ."

"Shaddap" was all I could say, as I straightened my clothes out.

"Come on, it's perfect!" Mike's grin grew wider. "You two will be in the same place, away from everything . . . Just do me one favor, will you? When the big night comes, lemme know." He tried to contain a sharp laugh. "Remember, my room's right under yours, and I don't much like the idea of getting buried alive in century-and-a-half-old beams and plaster when you finally—"

"*That's enough,*" I declared, in a voice that convinced him to silence his stream of torment. "You're a pig, Li, do you know that?"

"Oh, no I'm not," Mike said, still grinning merrily. "You know what I am."

"*Shaddap,*" I repeated, trying not to laugh; but my expression straightened when a new group of vehicles appeared on County Route 34. "Oh, holy fucking hell . . ."

Mike's gaze followed mine, and then he braced himself. "*Shit.* There they are. And unless I miss my guess . . ." He gave the vehicles a few minutes to get closer, and then said, quietly but firmly, "But I don't. That's an MSNBC truck. Leading the way."

"And you know what that means," I said.

"Fuck yes, I do," Mike answered, getting his own attire straightened out as another grin inevitably crept across his face. "It means we're bad, dude—and we're nationwide . . ."

And with Mike humming and singing that ZZ Top tune quietly, we awaited the next round of confrontation.

{iv.}

Almost as soon as the media cars and vans pulled up, Mike's humming turned to laughter, as an obvious model/actress who had decided, like many before her, to give the news a shot was disgorged from the lead vehicle. "Will you look at that?" he said. "These mooks that they send out from Albany to cover local news, I will never get over it . . ."

"Pull yourself together, Chuckles," I answered. "The national CBS truck, *and* the NBC, the ABC, the cable networks—especially MSNBC: they're the ones we need to be worried about."

Sure enough, when the reporters pooled, it was one of the nitwits who was then covering lurid crime stories all over the country for ABC who spotted us at the front door. "Hey," he called out. "Hey, wait a minute, aren't you those guys from New York? You know—*those* guys," he said dimly, as if we might have forgotten who the hell we were. We didn't answer, but then still another dope, a CBS reporter who covered crimes with "national appeal"—school shootings, serial killings, celebrity violence—made us right away:

"Oh, yeah," she said, "those guys who got fired after the hotel prostitution scandal! Jones and Li—excuse me, Doctors, but what are you doing up here? And why are you at this scene, in particular?" Mike and I still did not reply, prompting the woman to take it up a notch: "Is it true that this is the latest in a series of child murders extending beyond this region? And that the governor is personally overseeing the investigation?"

"Shit," Mike breathed. "Doesn't take them long, does it?"

I shook my head, took one or two steps forward, and raised my voice: "Ladies and gentlemen, we have a brief statement to make, after which we will not be taking questions, and you will not be allowed access to this house. Dr. Li and I are acting as the authorized representatives of the Kurtz family in this investigation. Nothing concrete is known about the disappearance of Derek Franco, legal ward of Ambyr Kurtz, at this time. And that's it." I turned around to see Mike staring at me.

"You really think that it's going to end just like that?" he asked.

"No," I answered. "In fact, I'm counting on it *not* ending just like that . . ."

And in just a few seconds, I heard an expected voice: "Dr. Jones, do you really feel fit, or even qualified, to represent this family, or to investigate this case for them, given your record?"

I knew just who was speaking, having suspected she'd be in the MSNBC truck. "Ah," I said, staring at the peeling grey paint of the porch floor. "Melissa Ward . . ."

"That's right," she replied; and I finally turned, raised my eyes, and cast a cold stare on her as she stood on the rear bumper of her network's van. "What I meant was," she went on, arranging something that resembled a smile on her overpainted face, "given the fact that you and your partner,

Dr. Li, were repudiated by both the New York City Police Department and its crime lab—"

"Largely thanks to you," I said, stepping down and moving slowly through the mob toward her. "And your propagation of what you knew to be blatant falsehoods."

"Hey," she said, trying to laugh my statement off, "I don't think you can say—"

"You know something, Melissa?" The sea of reporters kept parting for me, like kids anticipating a schoolyard fight. "There are easier ways to get in good with cops and politicians in this country than by blindly repeating what they tell you. Maybe you've tried those methods already, though. But to answer your question, yes, Dr. Li and I both feel fit to handle this case. And the fact that we were only 'released' from our positions in New York, and never brought up on any charges of, oh, say, contriving evidence, as you told the world we would be, I think speaks for itself. As does the fact that three of the five officials we implicated in covering up those crimes *were* eventually prosecuted, although you didn't waste a lot of time covering *that*. Anything else?"

Ward looked at the faces around her for support and, receiving none, mumbled, "Not—not at this time."

I moved back through the press pool, returning to the porch. "Well," Mike said, as we walked back through the front door and closed it behind us, "you handled that suavely, L.T."

"*But*," I answered, trying not to let anyone see me smile, "I took the spotlight off our guests, didn't I? Now let's find Curtis. I've got a few things I want to ask him, away from the others . . ."

Heading inside, we found Lucas on the living room couch, a large, overstuffed knapsack at his feet. The delight of bossing cops around had clearly begun to lose its luster: he had the television on, keeping one eye glued to a rerun of *That Metal Show* on VH1 Classic and the other on the milling officers, whom he occasionally barked at, although Bass Hagen was now doing most of that work. Most of the men and women from law enforcement had by now plainly realized that they were serving no purpose by being where they were: the scene had rendered unto Curtis Kolmback all that it was going to, in terms of trace evidence, and nobody, not even Frank Mangold, was going to take on the task of interrogating a fifteen-year-old boy and his blind sister/guardian right there in their house.

"Hey, kid," Mike said. "You seen that guy in the blue CSI suit wandering around?"

"In the kitchen," Lucas replied. "He's dusting Derek's note for prints—or some such shit."

"You ready to go, when we give the word?" I asked.

He kicked his knapsack. "Ready as fuck all. We gotta move, Derek's been missing for hours."

Nodding, I made my way with Mike through the cops and into the kitchen, where we found Curtis alone and leaning over Derek's note, trying to raise a latent print with various types of dust.

"Oh—hey, guys," he said as we entered. "Nothing much to see in the house, no trace samples or jimmying signs on the windows, so I'm trying this. But I think the Franco boy must have been wearing gloves, *if* he wrote it—and that would be pretty unusual, right? Why does a runaway—"

"Curtis," I said. "Forget that, for now. We need a word—in the garage out back."

The tech began to sweat just at the request; and the stern tone of my voice was only making things worse. "A word with *me*? Well, what about, I mean, I don't know anything—"

"Easy, Curtis," Mike said, playing the good (or at least the better) cop without knowing what, specifically, I had in mind. "We already know all about it—but we'd like to get your side, that's all."

"My side of what?" Curtis said, as Mike and I took hold of each of his elbows and pretty much picked him up out of his chair, although he didn't really resist.

"You *know* what, Curtis," I said, moving him toward the kitchen door. "You don't really want to go on with this charade, do you? No, I didn't think so . . ."

The poor guy whimpered a few more halfhearted protests as we crossed the backyard and entered the little red garage. "You're not a bad guy, Curtis," Mike said. "We know that."

"The only problem being," I added, switching on the place's bare bulb, "we've now established that you were the only tech at all five crime scenes—and that's not exactly regular practice, is it?"

"No," Curtis finally whined submissively. "But, guys, you have to understand, it wasn't my idea!"

"We know that, Curtis," Mike said soothingly. "We just want to know whose idea it *was*. Who's been giving you your orders, and how high up does all this actually go?"

"Oh, come on, not *you* guys, too!" Kolmback looked from one to the other of us in terror. "Look, I can't tell you that, fellas—I'd like to, really I would. But that'd be the end of my career, and maybe even my damned *life*." He took in a deep breath. "You still don't know exactly who you're messing with, here, do you? I mean, when you moved that kid's body—at least, I'm assuming it was you who moved it—"

"Body?" Mike asked. "We didn't move any body."

"And you're ducking the question—if there's some kind of conspiracy to cover this thing up, how the hell high does it go? And who else has been asking you about it?" I finally abandoned my halfhearted attempt to strong-arm the guy: "Curtis, at some point you have to think about yourself, here, and not just about whoever's been threatening you: this gets to the licensing board, and it *will* end your career. Whatever they're promising you, they've made you break the rules, already: you've been the only tech on five scenes. You're supposed to have—"

"But I did!" he defended, still turning from Mike to me desperately, somehow thinking that perhaps we might be able to get him out of the jam into which his natural vulnerability, combined with that evil streak of ambition that ran through nearly all crime scene techs, had gotten him. "I wasn't the only one there from our department: Nancy—Director Grimes—she was there, too, you should be taking this up with her!"

"We will, but right now we're talking to you," I said. "I'm trying to *help* you, here, Curtis!"

"We both are," Mike added. "But we've got to know who's involved."

"I—I—" Curtis' fear was becoming panic, which I initially thought might be good for our cause; but I had underestimated how much the tension and pressure had gotten to him. "Listen, maybe you guys could get my license revoked, but *they* might kill me—I'm serious!"

"Well, then—" I laid hold of one of his shoulders. "Abandon ship, Curtis: come back down to the house, we'll take you aside with Major McCarron and he'll guarantee your safety."

"McCarron?" Curtis said, with tears plainly in his eyes. "And what's McCarron going to do when the governor calls? Or worse, what's he going to do when the—shit, you guys, I cannot talk about this! I'm getting out of here, I can't do it anymore!"

And with a short, muffled wail, Curtis suddenly tore his no-longer-sterile blue suit from his body and, dressed only in his pants and a white T-shirt, ran through the back door of the garage and up the hill onto the Morgan Central athletic field where I'd strolled with Ambyr. Mike and I followed as quickly as we could, just in time to see the deranged tech vanish into the tree line on the far side of the field.

"What in the *hell* . . . ?" Mike murmured in somber amazement.

"God damn it," I said, glancing around quickly. "God damn it *all*." I indicated the hills beyond the field with my hand. "I truly hate to say it, Mike—but there's at least an even chance that Curtis will never come out of those woods alive. *Fuck* . . ."

Mike got my point: "The sniper on the mountain—you figure he's around here now?"

"Yeah, that's what I figure," I said. "And if he saw Curtis with us, or anybody else did . . ." A guilty wave crashed over me; but it passed as I realized one key fact: "Well . . . we may have triggered his crack-up, but we certainly didn't start the whole thing. One thing's for sure, though,— now, we've *really* got to get the fuck out of here." I spun round on my cane, and began walking as fast as my hip would allow back down to the Kurtzes' house.

"You're just freaking out, L.T.," Mike said, trying very hard to believe it. "It's been a fuck of a morning, and it's understandable, but I think you're imagining things." He glanced around at the sky. "Doesn't help that a storm's blowing in, I'll admit, but—it can't be as serious as all *that*."

"No? Remember what he said, Mike." I tried to recall it precisely as we reached the backyard of the house. " 'What's McCarron going to do when the governor calls? Or worse, what's he going to do when the . . .' Fill in the blank."

"Jesus," Mike said, looking over his shoulder. "Curtis, you poor, dumb schmuck . . . Still—I hope he'll come out of it okay."

"So do I—but, much as we might both like to make it our problem, right now it isn't. We need to get Ambyr and Lucas and make a break. So get to the car, and tell Mitch we're leaving. Ask him to clear a path to the far side of 34. I'll get the other two set, and we'll meet you there."

"Got it." Mike branched off toward the Empress as I stepped onto the deck behind the kitchen door. But before I could open it, Mitch McCarron came walking out. "Trajan!" he said, looking up at the storm clouds. "Say, you haven't seen Kolmback, have you? Frank wants a word with him—he's pretty pissed off about something, though he won't tell me what it is."

I couldn't blatantly lie (not to Mitch), but neither could I be entirely forthcoming—if only because he'd effectively just told me that the other person trying to shoehorn information out of Curtis was Frank Mangold. I therefore had no choice, for the moment, but to bend the truth a bit: "Yeah, actually. We were coming out to find you and get our car in gear—Bass Hagen's agreed to let us take Ambyr and Lucas up to Shiloh for a while, get them out of this business, and then you can tape the house off and have at it. Anyway, we ran straight into Curtis, who was coming out of the garage and headed like a bat out of hell up that hill."

"Really?" And it was a testament to Mitch's decency and trust that he accepted my story at face value. "Well, I wonder what the hell those two are up to . . ." He shrugged, then turned toward the Crown Vic. "You're going to need some help getting out of here, I guess."

"You read my mind," I answered. "Mike's getting the car started, and I'll get the Kurtzes. Mind giving him a hand?"

"No, no, not at all," Mitch said with a nod, holding the screen door for me. "But listen—on your way inside, maybe steer clear of Mangold. I don't know what his deal is, but he's on a tear, sure enough. You might just do as a target, if he can't find the one he wants."

"Thanks, Mitch," I said, feeling even more guilty about not having told him all.

He paused before heading off Mike's way. "Say—you don't suppose that's what made Curtis take off, do you? Knowing that Frank has a bone to pick with him?"

"It'd be enough to make *me* start running," I answered. "If I could run, that is."

"Yeah." Mitch considered it for another moment. "Well, I'm gonna have a couple of my boys take a look up there. Maybe he's just hiding, but it isn't smart. Only gonna piss Frank off even more."

It had been one of the oddest sequences of events during the investigation thus far; and, though I didn't yet know as much, it was also the beginning of another warning to Mike and myself to lay off probing into the conspiracy we had detected . . .

Once inside, I returned to the living room couch and put our junior member on notice: "Take your bag and get out to the far side of 34, Lucas. Mike'll be coming around in the car—we're getting out. Very quietly, kid: keep clear of the vehicles, and don't let anybody in the media see you."

"Aw, come on, L.T.," the kid whined. "I wanna be on *Dateline NBC,* dude, I'll be famous!"

"You want Derek to be famous, too?" I asked: perhaps a little harshly, I realized, when I saw Lucas' expression droop. "Just don't screw around, right now. And where's Ambyr?"

"Over in her room." Lucas signaled toward the chamber beyond the stairs with a nod. "Getting the cat in his carrier."

"Damn . . . I forgot we'd have to tell Clarissa about a cat. Ah, screw it, she's taking *your* rodent ass in, she can take a cat, too. It can stay in Ambyr's room; or, if Clarissa goes batshit, in the plane."

"Sounds like a plan," Lucas said, lifting his knapsack onto his shoulder with a groan. "Okay—I'll make sure nobody sees me, and meet you at the car." And with that, the kid was off.

As I approached the bottom of the staircase and the front door opposite it, I could see that the latter was open, and that the glare of portable camera lights was streaming through it. Moving quickly toward Ambyr's room, I also saw that Cathy Donovan and Nancy Grimes were holding court before a mix of both local and national reporters, and trying to emphasize that the suspected "ringleaders" of a child-exploitation "gang" had already been questioned and were still under surveillance, and that they were sure that Derek Franco, while he had likely been lured from his home by one of the known "associates" of these ringleaders, would soon be found: which was all I needed to hear. I tried to push on, but my path was quickly blocked by Frank Mangold.

"You and me have got things to discuss, profiler," he said. I sighed wearily, but before I could protest, he went on: "Who're you actually working for here, Jones?"

"What gives you the impression I'm not actually working for this family, Frank?"

"I'm not sure, yet." Mangold turned to glance at Donovan and Grimes. "But I'm not getting the whole story—and I just want to know if you're one of the reasons why."

"Frank, if someone's keeping things from you, trust me, it isn't Dr. Li or me. Our interest is in solving this case and getting this family back together—that is absolutely it. Anybody who has a larger agenda than that"—and at these words, Mangold's buzz-cut head snapped around again, so that he was staring daggers through me—"is not somebody I'm either doing business with now, or have any interest in doing business with in the future."

"Maybe," Mangold said in his unsettling manner. "But I'm not so sure I buy it."

"Buy whatever you like, Frank—but buy it somewhere else, and get out of my way."

He grabbed hold of my arm. "Say—you haven't seen that little shit Kolmback, have you?"

"Not lately," I answered. "And I'll give you about two more seconds to move that hand."

Yet—surprisingly—Mangold did not rise to this blatant challenge, instead releasing his grip. "That fucker knows more than he's telling. And I'm gonna find him . . ."

He moved off toward the kitchen without further communication, his points having been made; yet for the life of me, I mused as I approached Ambyr's closed door, I still had no idea just what those points were. My first suspicion, and the one that made the most sense, was that they'd been a series of traps, designed to catch me in a lie; but I simply didn't have time to consider the matter any further. Instead, I knocked on Ambyr's door several times, letting her know it was safe by quietly calling her name into the jamb of the thing as I did.

{v.}

At first I got no answer, which didn't bode well: if Ambyr was going to have trouble leaving her home, and had only realized as much when she started packing, it was likely going to take more time than we had to talk her around. So I tried a few more knocks and calls, then felt as much as heard a click vibrating through the door. Trying the knob, I found the thing unlocked.

"Hope you're decent," I said softly, as I cracked the door open, "because I'm coming in . . ."

The room was almost completely dark, the scarce light provided by whatever could get through the slightly open door and through lace panels backed by opaque blinds that covered the two windows: and that wasn't enough for my eyes to adjust to quickly. I stood there helplessly, then turned with a bit of a start when someone shut the door firmly—from within the room.

"Ambyr?" I whispered, in what was now near-blackness. "Come on, now, no games . . ."

"Oh, it's no game," she replied, in a tone that was hard to define: one would not have called it sinister so much as ghostly. Then, without my hearing a sound, she got close enough from behind me to murmur in my ear, "Now you know what it's like to live in *my* world . . ." The chilling quality in her voice was worsened when the next thing I heard was her laughing lightly from the other side of the room. My eyes had begun to adjust, and I could at last make out some of what was before me, in the eerie dimness:

On each side of the window frames heavy curtains of burgundy velvet hung from iron rods, the ends of which were molded in lattice lines around glass balls of, yes, an amber color. The dark blinds obscured all view of what was taking place amid the rising storm outside; while on a tasteful antique wooden bed frame and queen mattress lay a white lace spread of an equally traditional and pleasing design. A large, rolling black travel case sat on the floor, the handle of which was extended, as if prepared for departure. The fact that Ambyr's cat sat in his large carrier next to the case, rubbing his face up against the thin black bars of the door the minute he saw me, further indicated that Ambyr had in fact gotten herself ready for departure. The only incongruous facts about the little scene were that she herself was still nowhere to be seen, while a small, portable iPod dock on an old chest of drawers was playing Puccini's "E lucevan le stelle" from *Tosca,* heightening the sad, romantic, yet still-unnerving atmosphere of the room. All this, despite what was happening outside.

The sound and comparatively bright light of a match striking caught me completely unawares; and, startled, I made a move for my Colt. Yet even as I did, I saw Ambyr's hands feel their way to light a thick candle on the opposite side of the bed; then she disappeared into the shadows once more. Seconds later, however, I felt a delicate warmth on my eyes and the parts of my face around them, and was reassured.

"*Ah-ah-ah* . . ." came a whispered warning in my ear. "You don't really want to shoot the girl of your dreams, do you?"

I half-raised my hands to indicate surrender (even though she couldn't see it, I realized), then smiled and turned around slowly. "I don't know," I said. "Have I ever *met* the girl of my dreams?"

"You bet your ass you have, Mister Doctor Jones, MD, PhD, who ought to know better," Ambyr answered with a laugh, pushing me back toward the bed. She was wearing yet another summer dress, this one the color almost of flame. It suited her coloring, as did all her clothes, and by the time I felt the back of my knees touch the edge of the bed, I also felt the need to protest:

"We really have to get up the hollow, Ambyr. And this place is crawling with cops, as the saying goes; I'm not sure it's just the right moment for—"

But then another sharp push sent me helplessly onto the bed, and before I could say any more, Ambyr had gotten on top of me, her own movements as lithe as a cat's. "Oh, I'm *totally* sure that it's the right time for *dot, dot, dot,*" she answered, again breathing the words into my ear in a way that was so electric that any aches and pains caused by my brief night of outdoor sleep simply vanished. I quickly discovered that the particular dress she was wearing was quite sheer, revealing—what had to be deliberately—equally thin, delicate undergarments beneath it. But what shocked me most, even as her hair fell over my face in a tumble and her mouth moved to meet mine, was her strength: she took my wrists and held them down so powerfully that it would have been something of a struggle, with only one leg, for me to get back upright. Her thighs, meanwhile, slid out from beneath the skirt of her dress and closed in on my hips hard enough to pin me; yet not so hard, on my left side, that I needed to cry out in pain. Eventually she let my arms and hands loose, and they moved, as if in a thoroughly practiced motion, around her back, my fingers feeling the heat of it for several moments and then beginning to toy, helplessly, with the straps of her dress.

"So," she whispered in reaction, her lips still on mine. "They didn't *quite* kill you with all that radiation, now, did they?"

"I—" It was enormously difficult to find the words: "I honestly thought that they had . . ." Feeling the need to regain some control of the moment, I said, "Why the opera, by the way? You didn't tell me you liked it."

"I don't, really," she answered, pulling her hair back into a murderously sexy ponytail. "But I figured *you* did, and it would get you in the mood."

"What made you figure that?"

"Okay—" A look of deliberately theatrical yet nonetheless enormous pride filled her face. "After I listened to your class the first time, I went online at the Center in Fraser and found out that, guess what? There's a Braille edition of your book about your hero."

I pulled myself up on my elbows. "*You're* reading about Dr. Kreizler?"

"Well, it took a while to come through the library lending system," she answered, leaning down on her arms and again pressing her lips to mine. "So I haven't gotten far. But you do talk about him being a big opera buff, so I figured it would work . . . Why, isn't it?"

"Yeah. Although I'd rather hear the music *you* would want to listen to, right now."

"Oh!" She brightened and popped off the bed and onto her feet. "In *that* case . . ." I heard a few sharp clicking sounds come from the iPod, as the Puccini was silenced and then replaced by Roxy Music's "More Than This." Then she leapt back atop me, her every movement in the near-darkness unhesitating and precise. For a moment, her face hovered over mine, waiting for a response.

"My God," I laughed quietly. "It's a *household* of classic rock fans . . ."

"Hey." She laid a playful little slap across my cheek. "Lucas got it from me, and never forget that. Besides . . ." She leaned down again to kiss me, my arms went around her, and her legs tightened once more as she spoke into my lips. "It's the sexiest, most romantic fucking song in the world . . ."

"Yes," I whispered, taking her warm face in my right hand. "Actually, it may just be . . ."

I wasn't at all sure what we'd been up to, Ambyr and I, in the afternoons and nights leading to that stormy day. But as we lay there on her bed and listened to that song which has wrought decades of ecstatic havoc on so many people's emotions (and which Ambyr had contrived to have her iPod play over and over again), all the while learning whether or not each facet of our respective bodies conformed to the other's in the manner that is so essential, especially for two people who have sound reasons to doubt hasty decisions about becoming intimate with *any*one, much less persons known for so comparatively short a time; and when we went on to find that our bodies did indeed so fit . . . suffice to say that our desires and, more importantly, our hearts raged increasingly toward that hungry compassion that is the only thing I have ever known to constitute human love. The fact that we were surrounded on all sides both by our antagonists from the state and by media hacks who would have loved nothing more than to catch a glimpse, through some narrow slit in the window blinds, into that room, while it gave me some little pause, only delighted Ambyr; and more and more, I found that I was allowing her to set the pace of what was apparently becoming our romance . . .

When we eventually sat up and began reassembling ourselves (one of us literally), I suggested to Ambyr that something rather more conservative than the dress she was wearing might be more appropriate for running the gauntlet of media jackals that were outside the house.

"Way ahead of you," she replied, moving to a closet next to the bathroom door and pulling out a long coat of medium heaviness, one that might have looked quite sexy if left open, but that could also be made to look quite prim, if buttoned all the way up. Then she slid her bare feet into a pair of cork-soled sandals and spun toward me. "Well? Do I look okay?"

"Perfect," I said, although the rather carefree note in her voice was beginning to have the same effect on me that Lucas' similar tone had; and so I carefully asked, "Ambyr—when Mike and I got here this morning, you and Lucas were both understandably devastated about Derek. But now you seem so—so—"

"So . . . ?" she said coyly.

"So—*upbeat,* I suppose I would say. What happened?"

"Think back," she said more seriously, "to our little moment in the pantry." She came over and put her arms around my neck. "Because that's when I figured it out."

" 'It'?" I asked, putting my own head atop hers. "Which *it*?"

She let out a long, somewhat sad sigh. "Faith," she whispered simply.

Which was unexpected. "Hmm," I noised, considering it. "Neither of you has ever struck me as particularly religious. Although," I hurried to add, "if you are, it makes no difference to—"

She thumped an open hand on my chest. "No, you idiot." Turning her face up to mine, with her eyes searching for just the right spot to fix on, she soon smiled and said, "How in the world did you ever get all those fancy-assed degrees? Did you *bribe* somebody?"

I had to pause. "I'm afraid I'm not getting you."

"No," she answered, putting her head back on my chest. "But *I* get *you.* That's what I realized, and what I told Luke—oh, Jesus, don't let him know I said 'Luke' to you, please, he'll have a fit. He's so serious about you guys. And that's why he believed me when I told him that we should have faith in *you*. Well, you and Mike. If anybody can find Derek before anything bad happens to him, you guys can. And no, I'm not trying to say that it's totally guaranteed. Derek is, you already know, not—*like* other people. And it can make him really stubborn, really determined, sometimes. So it's possible that he's gotten into a situation that could go bad, and *nobody* can stop it. But if anybody can, you and Mike are the ones."

"Oh," I said, swallowing hard once. "So—no pressure, or anything."

"Yeah," she answered, quite frankly. "You *have* got a lot of pressure on you, right now. And that's one reason we're going with you. I talked to Mike about all this, and he says you've had nobody but Marcianna for female companionship for way too long. Now, I love Marcianna, I totally get it; but you, Mister Doctor Jones, need something else. So as of right now—"

I didn't let her finish, but leaned down to kiss the rest of the explanation away.

Once we'd gotten back out to the front porch, Ambyr rolling her bag and me carrying Tommy the cat in his carrier, we pulled Mitch McCarron, who'd already guided Mike out, and Steve Spinetti over and worked out a plan: I would make a statement, backed up by Steve, to the press, and as that crowd of information-crazed souls collected around me, Mitch would quietly get Ambyr out to the Empress, which was sitting on Route 34 pointed toward home. I would join them there, after which Steve and Mitch would seal the house as a crime scene.

And it went off without a hitch: by the time I made it to the microphones at the front door, Mitch was already obscuring Ambyr as they moved to the highway; and by this point, even Nancy Grimes and Cathy Donovan had run out of things with which to satisfy the reporters, so they gladly let me step to the fore. There, I elaborated my position as representative of the Kurtz family, and stated calmly that Mike and I would be working in full cooperation with the county and state, along with "any other interested agencies." After that, I moved toward the county road, managing to ignore Melissa Ward, this time; in fact, the only voice I really heard was Steve's: "That looked like it took real effort, Doc—good for you. And keep us posted, right?"

I nodded and mumbled assent and thanks to him as Mitch McCarron took over guiding me, from the edge of the blacktop and across it, whence he rushed me around to the far side of the Empress. The door was already open, and Mitch gave me a firm pat on the back as I lowered myself in. "We'll be in touch," he said, closing the door and slapping its roof.

Mike pulled out with a little squeal onto the wet road, as I glanced into my wing mirror and said, rather proudly, "Nobody's following us, Mike."

At which point I felt Ambyr, in the back seat right behind me, throw her arms around my neck, whispering in my ear, "Thank you. I know that was hard." Then I felt her lips on my neck, followed by an outburst from Lucas:

"Hey, hey, hey!" he protested. "You two are okay, like, in *theory*, but that's it. Bad enough it took you so long to get out here, but I don't wanna have to actually *look* at it, for fuck's sake."

"Then look out your window, snot," Ambyr said, without moving. "And watch your mouth."

"Oh, no, sis," Lucas said, obeying her first order by speaking into the window. "We're not home, now—I get to talk any way I fucking want to."

"Yeah?" Mike laughed. "I wouldn't let Clarissa hear you say that, kid."

"Exactly," Ambyr piled on. "And maybe you can talk like that when you're working—but around anybody else, you cut the cursing, okay?"

"Oh, *man*," Lucas whined. "I knew this whole thing was a bad idea . . ."

CHAPTER TWO

THE VARIETIES OF APPETITE

{i.}

Lucas, as always, was right, in some fundamental way, although it did not seem so at the time. The ensconcing of our two guests at Shiloh went off without a hitch, Clarissa welcoming them with a warmth I had only known her to ever show to Diana and myself; she continued to have visions of my taking over the farm one day, and Ambyr and Lucas' presence only seemed to elaborate them, giving her a sense of calm and enjoyment of the future that she had long gone without. "What do you expect?" Mike would rightly say to me later, when we were alone in the JU-52. "You not only look like you're becoming the gentleman farmer, now, but you've shown up with a ready-made family. Hell, she was even glad to see Ambyr's damned cat . . ." This last fact was especially noticeable, not least because Tommy, instead of stalking little Terence—whom I suspect he could have killed—immediately made friends with him: perhaps the oddest couple that Shiloh had ever seen.

Perhaps. As Lucas crashed in his new room that afternoon, Ambyr and I visited Marcianna, making sure that she was all right during the storm, which finally passed over just before dinnertime, allowing the sun to return to our little corner of the Taconic Valley. During the tail end of the rain, Ambyr and I caught a little sleep inside the rocky den, then hitched Marcianna up to her leash and took her for her evening constitutional down by the brook beyond the road. Our nap had restored every ounce of Ambyr's sexual energy, at least for the time being, which I was rather afraid to respond to in front of Marcianna. My worry was that it would set off that strange chirruping that had been so troubling; but, much to my surprise, it did not.

There remained the rather ticklish question of how our work hours were now to pass; and it was Lucas who answered it. After dinner, when we withdrew to the JU-52 and tried to consider what might have happened to Derek, Ambyr was at one point standing near me, listening to me recapitulate my theory of the kind of person who would likely have lured Derek away.

"It makes sense," Ambyr said gravely. "Especially when you talk about the way he looked at those pictures in the house. Derek never showed that kind of feeling or—what's that word?—*fascination* with his *own* mother, even when she was around. He definitely missed that part of life." She put a hand on my back. "Not that we all didn't," she went on, slipping her hand under my shirt.

"Whoa, no!" Lucas declared yet again. "Unh-unh. If I can't swear in the house, then at *least* you guys can't get up to that kind of bullshit when we're working. Please, I mean, I just fucking *ate.*"

I turned and murmured in Ambyr's ear, "He's probably right. Best to stay focused."

"I guess," she replied, withdrawing her hand. "But you let him *talk* to you like that?"

"*What?*" Lucas defended. "You should hear how they talk to *me!*"

Mike chuckled a bit. "He's right about that, Ambyr . . ."

"Hmm, this is going to take some adjusting to," she decided, pursing her lips and lifting one eyebrow. "Okay, so—anything more we can get from the note?"

"Not much, I'm afraid," Mike replied, as he finished running off an enlargement of a photograph he'd taken of Derek's parting message. "Except the overall tone—the happy sound to his voice. *That* is a little confusing . . ."

"Uh—maybe because it's *bullshit,*" Lucas said, leaping to his feet to examine the note as Mike pinned it up next to a picture of Derek that he'd gotten off Ambyr's cell phone. "I still say somebody had a gun to his head, or something pretty close."

"I don't think so, Lucas," Mike answered. "There wasn't any sign of a struggle: no trace evidence that Curtis Kolmback could see, which isn't definitive, granted, but on top of that, Derek packed his stuff up very carefully and deliberately, and neither of you heard a sound. Does that sound like he was taken away against his will? He may have been conned by whoever was waiting for him, but I don't think there was any force involved. Not at that stage of the operation, anyway."

"No," Ambyr said quietly, sitting atop one of the desks. "No, it sounds like there wasn't. Which doesn't make *me* feel any better . . ."

"You can't look at it that way," I said to her gently. "Remember, his decision is not a judgment of how either you or Lucas was behaving toward him. The main thing to keep in mind about these people is that they're very good at appealing to exactly the thing that each kid was looking for. The one thing both of you *can* think about is just what that weak spot was, for Derek. We know that he missed a maternal presence in his life—his mother, according to everything you've said, rejected him in favor of her other children because of his . . . difference. And, Ambyr, you simply could not have filled that gap. So the question is, what, or who, could have? As the years wore by, what kind of fantasy did Derek contrive that spelled the dream situation for him? It's not so easy as wanting another mother—we saw that in the way he admired Diana's image. There was a real longing there, too, meaning a romantic longing."

"Yeah," Mike said, nodding. "Wasn't that the first thing he said when he saw the picture? Not that she looked like a nice lady, but that she was beautiful?"

"Indeed," I answered. "He was a little—and maybe more than a little—in love with the image. So what does that tell us? I don't expect any answers tonight . . ." Which was a good thing, because Lucas was already looking a little heavy-lidded, the effects of a long day and dinner with Clarissa kicking in. "But as you think about it, try to imagine: who could have dangled what in front of Derek, to make him take a leap like that? Okay?"

Ambyr just nodded rather blankly, saying, "Yeah. Okay." Lucas had now begun to nod off, and Mike had to approach him and shout:

"*Okay*, Consulting Detective?"

"Hmm?" the kid answered, snapping to it. "Absolutely. Heard every word. I'll think about it. But now . . ." He began to stumble toward the hatch. "I'm thinking about goin' to fuckin' bed . . ."

He managed to get himself to the floor of the hangar without incident, and I guided Ambyr down the steel steps, then toward the farmhouse, walking behind her trudging brother.

"I'm so . . . fucking . . . *tired*!" Lucas protested to the sky.

"We're outside, now, Lucas," Ambyr said. "And other people can hear you."

Lucas just threw a hand in the air in acquiescence. "Right, right," he called. "Me talk pretty right now. And you two feel free to get back to your disgusting behavior . . ."

Ambyr locked one arm around my neck and put her free hand atop my left as it worked my cane. "Are you coming up?" she asked, moving her lips along my cheek, then kissing me.

"I don't know," I answered. "Not yet, anyway. Mike and I still have work to do and then I've got to make sure that the crazy girl is okay for the night."

"Mmm, I'll be asleep by then, you know."

"Yeah." I stopped before we reached the porch, and Ambyr languorously slipped around in front of me, eyes closed and smiling. "Ambyr, try not to be insulted, but—this case: Mike and I are used to working all hours, when we're on something like this."

"Understandable," she decided. "But will you do me one favor? Will you at least come in and kiss me before you go to sleep, whenever it is, to let me know you're okay?"

"I can do that."

"Okay," she said. "Now—you've got to help me get used to the house and the stairs just a couple of times. I'll get it pretty fast, but I need that much."

I guided her up to her room—which was the master and best bedroom in the house, the place where Colonel Jones and Jenna Malloy had slept, and where Clarissa and Diana had lived for so many years, but which had become unbearable for my great-aunt after Diana's death—and saw her to her bed, making sure she knew just where the bathroom was and how to get to it. If she woke up disoriented and startled, I said, she only had to knock on the wall to her left and Lucas would hear her, as that was where his room was. I lingered a moment on that old iron bed frame, surrounded by wallpaper patterned after some of the wildflowers that could be found in the fields of Death's Head Hollow, and watched Ambyr drift off to sleep, her hand tight and then less tight in mine. Moonlight suddenly swept in from the west and played across her face and body; and it was painfully apparent to me that I had never been so lucky in my life, or seen a woman of any age so beautiful. She hadn't suddenly changed, or become more physically striking; but that face, even as she slept so deeply, bespoke every horror she had ever been through, as well as the relief that she was now enjoying. And my own worst experiences, along with my own sense that there might now be hope, caused our two souls to cry out in harmony, even if one of us was deep in slumber. And that was a form of human interaction, indeed of beauty, that I had never before experienced . . .

When I returned to the hangar, I found Mike waiting. He eyed me critically as I approached, although he was also smiling, half out of skepticism and half out of happiness. "You tell her the truth yet?" he asked, handing me a cigarette and a glass of Talisker. I lit the one and sipped the other, shaking my head as we began the climb up into the JU-52.

"You heard them," I said quietly. "Lucas is in denial and she's guilt-ridden. And they're putting their faith in *us,* in case you didn't know."

"I did not," Mike said, nodding uncertainly. "But that's an incredibly frightening thought . . ."

"Tell me about it," I answered. "And you expect me to pile on by telling them that we actually think that Derek is a *member* of the throwaway organization? No, thank you."

Mike continued to nod and smoke, then downed the whole of his drink. "Well," he decided at length, "nothing like beginning a relationship in an air of duplicity."

"No," I mused quietly. "There isn't. And speaking of duplicity, did you talk to Gracie today?"

"That is entirely different," he answered. "If Gracie and I were to get involved, L.T., believe me, it would have to be very serious. Her family, unlike mine, is pretty traditional, so—" He glanced over to find me staring back at him in slight disbelief. "Ah," he realized at length. "Right. Point taken: different kind of serious, that's all." He paused for a moment before adding: "She's everything you've been looking for, isn't she, L.T.? All those others, all those 'appropriate' women—and *this* is the one." I could only nod in reply, because the truth of his words scared me so much. "And if it doesn't work out?" he continued.

"Oh," I replied, smiling. "I think we both know the answer to that . . ."

For the next several hours, Mike and I fixed our minds on two central issues: first, after turning the White Monster around, we weighed the question of Derek's disappearance from the point of view of his willing participation in the throwaway scheme. Mike noted that I spoke especially bitterly about the city and those who were taking the kids in, that night, to which I said that I thought the reasons behind such bitterness should have been obvious, especially to him: the run-in with Melissa Ward from MSNBC had brought all my old issues about being effectively exiled from the city of my birth to the surface, as had the thought that a brainless operator like her was allowed to not only remain there, but to become celebrated as an ace crime reporter. Mike told me that he of course realized all that; but he also reminded me that our impending trip to New York could not be an exercise in vengeance, that it was still entirely possible that we would find that the evil in the case resided somewhere other than down south; that, indeed, some of the kids might actually have found happy homes in the city and its suburbs. I continued to realize that my reasoning might be as flawed as he was suggesting (although he was only suggesting it), but I also insisted that the trip offered the best shot of settling the issue; and so we pushed on:

The second issue we had to cover was less a problem than a plan. Once Monday arrived, we would have to call the offices of Roger Augustine, the man whose name appeared on the certificates of authentication that Donnie Butler had carried in his bag along with the enormously expensive Hall of Fame jerseys that it had, apparently, never occurred to him to sell, although he must have known their value. Mike had already researched Augustine enough to know that he'd been a Bahamian by birth, one who'd distinguished himself by stellar years at the University of Pennsylvania's famous (many would say infamous) Wharton School of Business, and then by having become a U.S. citizen and rising young star at that rat's nest of financial machinations, Goldman Sachs. Indeed, Goldman had eventually sent Augustine back down to the islands, to oversee Caribbean operations for the company; and one could only imagine how very lucrative *that* posting must have been.

For us, however, Augustine possessed more interesting personal details: first, a pronounced and highly publicized interest in basketball, and second, a wife, Ethel, a senior VP at Goldman, whom he'd married when they were both in their early forties. Yet the couple had apparently never had any children. Mike's preliminary research had not been able to explain this crucial detail: Augustine was a thorough extrovert, whose office, as we discovered in an article in *BusinessWeek,* was covered with pictures of him posing with celebrities and basketball players (along with, tellingly, children's charity groups) at Knicks games in Madison

Square Garden and at the NBA finals in various parts of the country. But the article stayed carefully away from the issue of family, which seemed to indicate, regarding a married man who worked with kids, not a choice but a problem. The couple had enough money to try every form of artificial insemination and surrogacy available. Apparently they had not; nor did any of these details explain their failure to adopt.

Further frustration awaited on Monday morning. Cleverly disguised calls to both Augustine's office and, once we had unearthed the number, to his home told us that the man was returning from a vacation with Ethel in the South Sea islands, though no assistant could say just where: they were sailing—or, fairer to say, their crew was powering them—from place to place on their eighty-foot Ocean Alexander yacht, which displayed about as much taste as did the Augustines' New York City base, a wraparound penthouse in one of the tallest buildings in Trump Place, overlooking the Hudson. Yet these basic facts—the location of the Augustines' penthouse, combined with their jobs and ideas about vacationing—did tell us a few things about the couple. And as we continued to research them that morning, while Ambyr and Lucas got a second long night's sleep, we began to fill in still more details that would prove helpful; indeed, by the time the Kurtz siblings appeared at the plane to once again sit in on our classes, adjusting to their lives at Shiloh quickly, it more than once seemed, as Mike and I wedged our Augustine probe in around our other duties, that we might be on the verge of some kind of breakthrough; but each time, the answers simply raised more questions. Did Ethel Augustine even know, for example, that her husband had taken Donnie Butler on as some kind of "ward," a word that has covered almost as many sins as has the label "foster child"? Was Augustine living a dual life, or was Ethel in on playing the kind of perverse games with an adolescent to which so many are drawn, as part of the search to forestall age by stealing years from young people? Or, finally, was the whole thing innocent, as Mike continued to say, and had the Augustines simply taken Donnie in out of kindness and their own need for a child, which Fate had for some reason refused them?

To understand any of this, we would have to first understand the nature of that refusal; and, with the application of fairly relentless pressure, even that problem soon cracked. I told Mike what I could, in terms of profiling: that it was extremely unlikely that so extroverted and successful a man as Augustine would have risked his entire career and reputation by keeping a boy lover secreted somewhere in the city on a semi-permanent basis. More probably such a character would work out whatever inner tensions might have been driving him to such liaisons by becoming a serial employer of young prostitutes, or even a serial killer, one who used murder to tie up all loose ends after each sexual encounter. Such a character would hardly have needed or wanted to use some throwaway-child organization in so far-flung a place as Burgoyne County: moneyed as New York had become, there were still plenty of emotionally and financially endangered and credulous boys in the city itself from whom to choose.

"Curtis will be sorry to hear that," Mike chuckled Tuesday night after classes, as he studied a photocopy of one of the pictures of Augustine in his office at Goldman. "Assuming he ever comes out of those woods, and hasn't made it over into Massachusetts by now. He *did* want this to be a serial killer, the boob . . ."

"There's still no word about him?" Ambyr asked, after she and Lucas had joined us. She was, for some reason, more anxious about the tech than any of us: a fact that I chose to dismiss as some instinctive big-sister reaction, for it was impossible to even hear about Curtis without feeling sorry for him, despite his faults.

"No, not a sound," I said, watching her type notes into her Braille-equipped MacBook. A lot of blind and limited-sight people had abandoned Braille in recent years, with the rise of dictation software and talking books, but Ambyr had stayed with it, determined to be as literate as she'd been when she'd had her sight. "It's a definite concern," I continued, staring at the new pictures of Roger and Ethel Augustine that Mike had put up beside the morgue shots of Donnie. "But unfortunately—"

I was interrupted by a startling yet familiar and welcome sound: *"Ah-ha!"* Mike suddenly shouted theatrically, causing the nearby Lucas to not so much jump as suddenly levitate from his slouching spot. *"Ah-ha-ha-ha!"* Mike burst out again, laughing this time.

"Christ on a cracker, Mike!" Lucas said. "You wanna warn people, before you pull that shit?"

"Sorry, kid," Mike answered, suddenly spinning on his desk chair to tap a search into his desktop computer. "But you can't control a eureka moment!" Whereupon he stopped typing, took one of the photos of Roger Augustine, and threw it under a powerful workbench magnifying glass. He lowered the thing to the right height above the picture, smiled wide, and said simply, "Yeah . . . Whoa, yeah . . . !" Then he returned to his computer and kept slamming away with his fingers.

Mike's mood, I knew, meant that he had laid hands on a genuine clue; so, helping Ambyr toward the H-shaped grouping of desks that was Mike's center of operations, I asked, "How good?"

"Oh, good," Mike said, more evenly, but still excited. Even Lucas had climbed down to see what was happening; then Mike typed a certain sequence onto his keyboard, and the image from the magnifying glass was transferred to his big monitor. He zoomed in on one spot that showed only Roger Augustine's elbow against a marina full of the kind of giant power yachts that he owned, enhancing the resolution of the image as much as possible.

"What the fuck are we supposed to be looking at?" Lucas asked, squinting. "The dude's *elbow*?"

"No," Mike said, never even tempted to mock the kid. "What's *behind* his elbow . . ."

Lucas remained mystified. "A boat. A *big*-assed damned boat, okay, but so what?"

"It's *his* boat—Augustine's," Mike said calmly, turning to his laptop computer.

"Awesome," Lucas droned sarcastically. "Like I need a reminder of how much more fun his life is than ours."

"Lucas, shut up," Ambyr ordered, herself sensing the importance of the moment.

"Thank you, Ambyr," Mike said, although his mind was only half on his politeness. We all waited in silence for what seemed a very long time, but couldn't have been more than a few minutes, before a new page from a site that I recognized—that of the Department of Health and Mental Hygiene in New York City—flashed up on his laptop: whatever Mike was onto, it was something very specific, indeed. Finally, he spun around and said, "Son of a bitch. Son of a fucking *bitch* . . ." The shit-eating grin on his face only widened when he saw our expectant faces. "All right, L.T.," he announced. "I am the master—even you'll have to admit it." He turned to the magnified image again. "His *boat*: every pirate's wet dream, especially in the parts of the world where our friends Roger and Ethel insist on going. Which struck me as kind of weird: I mean, why not just cruise around places that are known to be safe? And that's one of the parts where this gets really good, but later. For now, just look at that baby. What do you see?"

Lucas shouted impatiently, "We see what you just said, Mike, the back of a honking big boat!"

"That's right," Mike continued. "The *back*. But, since the two people who can actually *see* the picture are too dense to get my point—Ambyr, maybe you can tell me what I'm driving at?"

Ambyr considered the matter for just an instant, then smiled in that knowing way of hers: "The *name*—the name of a boat is always on the back."

Mike beamed with pride. "Thank you. That's right, the name of a ship or a boat is always on the stern. So, L.T., if you're finished looking at the *boat,* what else do you see?" I squinted at the monitor, and spied a single name, *KRISTIANO,* which I spoke aloud. "Yep," Mike agreed. "That's the Bahamian spelling of the name, by the way: a *boy's* name. Now, that also struck me as weird. Boats and ships are almost always given feminine names, or the names of places, behaviors, or events. *Or . . ."*

I was already nodding. "Or the name of a child," I said, remembering the site that Mike had called up on his laptop and glancing at it. "They had a kid, and you've found the birth record."

"Would you expect anything less?" Mike crowed.

I half-heard him. "But something happened to that kid—something that was all but censored from the mainstream media. It's the only thing that makes sense with his profile. And it must have been bad—intimate and bad, yet in the end not quite provable, or they *couldn't* have kept it private. Unnatural death—sudden infant death, maybe, although I doubt it. Too much suspicion about SIDS, these days too many cases that turned out to be murder, or even serial murder, by women. So there's one other thing: accidental death in the home—no grounds for charging anyone. Correct?"

"*Fuck* you!" Mike said suddenly, still smiling. "This was *my* big moment, L.T., and you just went stepping all over it with your Sorcerer of Death bullshit!" Then he got himself back under control, looking to Ambyr and Lucas. "But he's right. That's the short story." Mike turned to the laptop again, moving fast from window to window and file to file, the changing light and colors of each reflecting differently on his face: "First things first: a birth certificate was issued listing Roger and Ethel Augustine as the parents—ten years ago. Baby Augustine was immediately named Kristiano—it'd been Roger's father's name. No complications, healthy kid, went home from Lenox Hill in good order. Soon as Ethel was back on her feet and able to use a breast pump, a nanny was hired, also a Bahamian. An old Augustine family friend, one that they were helping get a green card. But they couldn't prove a motive for her, so she never got into any trouble."

"Motive for what?" Lucas asked.

"Okay—next step," Mike said, turning to hit a key on his desktop so that its monitor filled brightly with the image of a short newspaper story. "Archived away in the *Daily News*—the *Times* and the *Post* didn't even report it—I found this little piece about an infant falling from a window at 799 Park Avenue into a service alley about a year later. Apartment was described as a penthouse, but it's one of those bullshit postwar condos where there's like eight apartments listed as penthouses, so who knows. What's for sure is that it was at least a twenty-story drop for a very tiny kid—gotta hope the little guy passed out before he hit the deck."

"I don't get it," Lucas declared. "Even *I* know that Park Avenue isn't by the river."

"I don't suppose it's crossed your mind that they could have moved, kid," Mike said, making Lucas grow annoyed with himself for not having considered it. "Don't sweat it," Mike continued generously. "The obvious gets by all of us, sometimes. Anyway, the baby fell, a brief investigation was conducted, but, like I say, no charges were filed. Some pretty interesting questions were asked, though. The Augustines' lawyer originally said the couple had been out of the apartment at the time, but when the nanny contradicted them—being as a green card isn't worth doing four years in Bedford Hills for criminally negligent homicide—and said that actually it happened on her day off, the couple said maybe they *had* been there, after all. And that's where the investigation lost focus, at first, and then was abandoned altogether—even though no window guards had ever been installed in the apartment. The managing agent claimed that their office had *tried* to put them in after the baby was born, but that Ethel Augustine had refused on 'aesthetic grounds.'"

"Hunh?" Lucas noised.

"She thought they were ugly," I threw in. "But Mike's about to tell us why that wasn't the actual explanation for all this . . ."

"How *did* you know?" Mike answered, growing further pleased with himself. "The story ended with two more facts that were left alone, apparently by both the media and the cops. One, *Roger* Augustine was in fact *not* home, but in his office, when the fall occurred; two, Ethel Augustine, their lawyer said, could answer no questions on the subject, because she had gone into a severe depression that 'psychiatrists' had diagnosed as 'sudden-onset bipolar disorder.'"

During this brief retelling, I had turned to the spot in the JU-52 where a picture of the Augustines was pinned alongside the shot of Donnie Butler on a slab in the morgue; but as Mike reached his latest conclusion, my head snapped back around. "That's impossible. You can cycle rapidly in and out of mania and depression, but with a woman Ethel Augustine's age, any competent psychiatrist would have told you that she must have been ill for a long time. It may only have been *recognized* when the baby died, but the lawyer's repeating what some unnamed doctors said about 'suddenly' becoming bipolar? It might sound okay to reporters, but it's a smoke screen."

"Correct," Mike said. "And like all smoke screens, it serves a purpose. Remember that Indian woman a couple of years ago in Queens, L.T.? Baby fell out the window, the same circumstances: at first it was called an accident, then it was blamed on the lack of window guards. Then the mother was reported to be acting 'strangely,' and finally they did arrest her for second-degree murder, because *she* couldn't afford a pricey legal team that could plead a nonexistent mental disorder. Take away Ethel's job and the lawyers, and she would almost certainly have been cuffed, too. Instead, they found these unidentified shrinks to say that she'd 'suddenly' become bipolar. And that was that, because *nobody* wants to piss off any big shots in the sectors of the city's economy that the town now depends on: finance and real estate. Don't get me wrong, I'm not saying that Ethel definitely threw the kid out the window, like the woman in Queens; just that they never bothered to find out."

Lucas had a look of immediate comprehension. As always, he exhibited no horror at the grimness or shock at the corruption involved in the tale—although Ambyr clearly did—but spoke with eager anticipation: "Yeah, yeah, okay. So the mom offs the kid, *maybe,* and then they move to a new apartment. So what's it all got to do with the boat?"

"The point of the boat," Mike said, "is this: they named it after their son, which might seem like a nice tribute. But then, getting back to my very first point, they go cruising this eighty-foot monstrosity down in waters that are not safe, that are known not to *be* safe: not even fishermen get a free pass, there, and the International Maritime Organization is constantly telling private yacht owners to steer clear, because it's no man's land: you've got the Chinese and everybody else arguing over those artificial islands, national navies gone rogue, and a half-dozen other things, most of all pirates. So why go? Why wrap yourselves in a big fat slab of meat and then walk right into the lion's den?"

I had already been pondering the same question: "Guilt. And not just guilt about the fall—at least I strongly doubt it. Guilt about something more." I took a couple of steps over toward the picture of the Augustines, and stabbed my cane at Ethel's very attractive, smiling face. "She didn't want a *baby*. She wanted a *kid*. There's an enormous difference, obviously; but maybe not so obvious to women like her. In the end, of course, she got what she wanted, even though the suspicious death of Kristiano meant they would never be able to adopt legally. But what the über-rich want, they get; yet as so often happens, both she and Roger found that 'having is not so pleasing a thing, after all, as wanting.' All of which ended . . ." I touched the picture of dead Donnie Butler ". . . here."

Mike tore at his hair in further exasperation. "Goddamn it, L.T., I swear . . ." Then he pointed at me, his eyes burning. "That was *my* summation, you incurable killjoy—and don't think I don't know that you ripped that 'having' and 'wanting' line off from *Star Trek,* bub!" His face sank and he tossed up some papers. "Ah, fuck it. He's right, guys, that's exactly where the facts lead."

Lucas nodded, in a self-consciously sage way. "Straight back to the wisdom of Mr. Spock . . ." he determined somberly; then, glancing at the rest of our stunned faces, he protested, "What? *I* know something about the classics, too, you know."

"It's where the facts lead," I judged, trying to ignore him and get back on track, "but it's not yet where we can *prove* that they end up. And we won't be able to do that until we confront Augustine." I pulled out my watch, popped it open, and glanced at the little calendar dial. "Their leviathan should be coming back up the Florida coast, by now, if what we were told is accurate. Figure they're not working those twin Caterpillars too hard, maybe twenty knots average: they could be home in a couple of days. Parked right outside that demon village they live in . . ."

Lucas shook his head hard. "L.T., what the *fuck* are you mumbling about?"

"What I am mumbling about, Lucas," I told him, "is that we need to be ready to head south in as little as—" Then I noticed the actual time. "Damn! Is it really that late?" Mike and Lucas both whipped out their cell phones, and confirmed that it was indeed well past nine p.m. "Jesus, I forgot to feed Marcianna, she must be having a shit fit. Gotta go!"

"Hey!" Ambyr called, latching onto my hand. "Not without me, you don't!"

"Oh, definitely," Lucas said, in wide-eyed disbelief. "Let's all keep our fucking priorities straight, I mean, we've only had a major break in the *case*, after all!"

"Leave it, kid," Mike said. "We've done all we can do, for now. Besides, isn't it your bedtime?"

"Why, you gonna read me a story, Mikey?"

Now, there was one diminutive by which you did *not* refer to my partner (as many people in New York City law enforcement had learned to their misfortune), and Lucas had just used it. Grabbing Ambyr's hand tighter, I pulled her out of the hatch as the first of the loose objects in the JU-52 began to fly. "Come on," I said, guiding her down the steps. "Before things get really ugly. I've got some meat thawed in her cooler up by the gate."

"Good!" Ambyr replied, throwing herself around me as I lifted her onto the concrete floor of the hangar. "I could use some time away from those maniacs." She leapt up, wrapped her legs around my waist— somehow knowing just how to adjust her weight so that my prosthesis would not give way—and kissed me as her hair flew in to cover both our faces. "You've been so busy, I was beginning to think you didn't love me anymore, Mister-Doctor-Man . . ."

We made our way up to Marcianna's enclosure less quickly than I had originally planned, and we lingered inside far longer than I had intended; and when I finally did return to the hangar and the JU-52, after having walked Ambyr back to the house and made sure that Lucas was, indeed, crashed for the night, I found Mike sitting at his desk with an extremely grim expression on his face. I assumed this was due either to his having to pick up after his latest skirmish with the kid or to my having taken off so abruptly after his presentation; further inspection, however, revealed that he was genuinely troubled.

"Have a good time?" he said to me, in neither a humorous nor a scolding voice. "Good," he went on, never waiting for an answer. "Don't bother sitting down—we're leaving."

"Leaving?" I checked my watch again. "Mike, it's past midnight."

"Don't I know it," he answered, strapping on his .38 and pointing at the desk drawer that held my Colt, silently telling me to arm myself, as well. "Our presence is requested. By Mitch, this time."

"And where are we going?" I asked, having gotten my holster on and slipping my jacket over it as I followed Mike out the hatch.

Mike stopped halfway down the steps, waiting for me to finish locking up. When I turned to him, he glanced downward as he said, "It's Curtis Kolmback. He's up on the ridgeline above the school. Phoned in to say he'd only come in if we brought him. Mitch is on the scene, but Mangold, Grimes, and Donovan are also on their way." Then my partner let out a long, mournful sigh and continued his descent. "So let's go. Maybe if we can get to him first . . ."

{ii.}

B y the time we reached the huge parking lot outside the sprawling, Eighties-era brick structure that was the Morgan Central School, another crowd of law enforcement vehicles had assembled, although this one was, significantly, smaller than that which had descended upon the Kurtz house. Even more notably, there were no media trucks present, and heavily armed Special Operations Response men at both the entry and exit drives to the lot were making sure that such remained the case: because Curtis, for all the crap he'd taken from everyone from Ernest Weaver right on up to Nancy Grimes and Frank Mangold, was ultimately one of their own, and this was not going to turn into the kind of media circus to which we'd been subjected at the Kurtz house.

Mitch met us as we parked. "Let's move fast," he said, handing me his cell phone as we rushed toward and then into the school building. "The number's already punched in, just hit send. I'd rather have you guys on your way before Frank and Cathy get here, and that won't be long."

"Any idea why Curtis wants to see us in particular?" I asked, as we passed by the usual innocent signs of youthful life on the school's painted cinder-block walls—bulletin boards full of artwork, athletic scores, and standardized-test schedules—then reached a wide double door that led out onto the main soccer field in the back, where most of Mitch's troopers were collected.

"None at all," Mitch answered, his voice still very grave. "But I don't like it. He sounds plain old panicked, although that could be the fact that he's lived on nothing but stream water and whatever a guy like him can catch up there for the last three days. But I don't think that's it."

"So how do you want to handle it?" Mike asked, as the line of the woods drew closer and Mitch's people began following in an anxious phalanx behind us.

"Well," Mitch said, considering it. "Make the call. We'll figure out how many of my guys who have night gear we need to coordinate with you, depending on whether or not he's calmed down some. But I don't want you going up there alone."

"I know the feeling," I said, lifting Mitch's phone and hitting send. We all halted as I put the phone on speaker, and after just a couple of rings, Curtis' voice answered:

"Major McCarron," he said, plainly terrified, "I told you, I won't talk anymore unless it's to—"

"It's all right, Curtis," I said. "It's Trajan Jones, I'm just using the major's phone."

"Oh—Dr. Jones." The poor guy breathed a little easier. "Thank God. I'm sorry to drag you into this, but—I don't know who to trust, other than you and Dr. Li."

"Trust?" I said. "Curtis, what's wrong?"

"There's somebody after me," he whispered, either because he suspected he was on speaker or because that "somebody" was close by. "I think—I think he's trying to *kill* me. That may sound crazy, but just in case I'm right, there are things I want to say—and only to you two."

"Can you give us some idea of where you are, Curtis?" Mike asked, glancing at me with a look that said he had little desire to head once more into the forest at night.

"Not that far," Curtis answered. "I've been trying to make my way down, but every few minutes—well, it seems like I hear a bullet pass or hit nearby, but I haven't heard any gunshots! Maybe I'm starting to lose my mind—"

"No, Curtis," I said firmly. "Trust me, you're not. So just give us a better idea of how to find you, and we'll come in. And don't worry, we're armed, so you'll be safe." To which Mike rolled his eyes, knowing how little protection we could actually offer on our own.

"Okay," Curtis answered. "I've gotten myself wedged into a stone formation, pretty much straight up from the middle of the main soccer field, I can see it from here. Just head up from there a few hundred yards; I'll hear you coming. But I won't move until then, I'm well protected, now."

"All right, Curtis. Meanwhile, try to get calmed down. We're going to get you out of this."

"Thanks, Dr. Jones." He clearly believed me, which was a burden of its own. "I'll be waiting."

I hit the bright red symbol that ended our call, then handed the phone back to Mitch, who said, "You really think it's true? Somebody's taking shots at him, but he can't *hear* them?"

Pulling Mitch aside with Mike, in order to make sure that none of the troopers could hear what might be deeply disturbing information, I said, "He's right, Mitch—I haven't told you this before because, well, I wasn't sure just what was happening, but somebody was taking potshots at us the night we were up on my aunt's mountain with Gracie Chang, just before her little 'accident.' He was using a .308—with night vision and a suppressor."

Mitch considered that fact silently, then slapped his Stetson against his leg. "God damn it, Trajan. I wish you wouldn't keep things like that from me."

"Yeah, well," I answered, "if you liked that, you're going to love this." And at long last, much to my own relief, I told him the true story of what had happened between Mike, Curtis, and me on the day of the tech's disappearance. "I'm sorry, Mitch," I concluded, "but I didn't know what to make of it, and I couldn't risk getting bogged down at the Kurtz house, just then. Not to mention that Frank was on the damned warpath, looking for Curtis. So I dummied up. I really do apologize."

"No, I get that one," Mitch answered, a little to my surprise, as he put his hat back on. "There's been something not right about this whole business from the start. I just wish you'd have given me the chance to help you out earlier. Which you're *going* to do now." Then he turned around, whistled at his troopers, and a few of them—who wore dark gear and upturned night vision headsets, and presented .308 Savage 10FP rifles with suppressors and black graphite stocks—came forward. One bore binoculars that glowed with the distinctive green light of night equipment, and he handed them to Mitch. "Let's see if we can't spot that rock formation he's talking about from here," Mitch went on, moving to the soccer pitch's midfield and beginning to scan the mountainside. He drew a blank, however, after which he handed the things to me to see if I could do any better.

Luckily, I could: at just the spot Curtis had indicated, less than a quarter of a mile above the playing field, a stony bald spot glowed white in the binoculars' green field. It was hard to see, but it was there; and when I pointed it out to Mitch, he caught it, too. After that, we devised a plan: Mike and I would move straight toward the location, going slowly in order to give Mitch's men—who would be moving fast to flank us on either side, at enough of a distance that they wouldn't blow the situation, but still close enough to offer us cover—time to get ahead. Then, as we neared Curtis, I'd use Mitch's phone to contact the fearful tech, and try to get an idea of his exact location.

Mike and I paused at the woods' edge as Mitch's men dashed on in, their goggles lowered. I had the pair of glowing binoculars around my neck, but that didn't console Mike much. "I ever tell you how much I hate the goddamned wilderness at night, L.T.?" I just glanced at him wearily. "Well, it's fucking true." He double-checked the cylinder of his .38, snapped it closed, made sure he was carrying additional rounds, then took a deep breath. "But fuck it. Let's get this done . . ."

And with that, we once more left civilization behind in the search of some fragment of truth that would allow us to push the case further along toward a solution. Even I, who had no undue terror of the forest at night, was realistically nervous, just then. Yet Curtis could, potentially, blow the case wide open; and we simply had to know what he did. Which did not mean that we had to abandon caution altogether, however: once we were about a third of the way to our destination, I hissed at Mike, and whispered that we should spread out a bit, and start moving behind whatever cover we could find. I had spent enough time, if not in this exact location, at least in similar spots in the Taconics to be able to gauge our progress fairly well; and when the grade of the hillside, the time we'd been walking, and the glow of the few lights in the school behind us told me that we couldn't be more than twenty-five yards from our goal, I signaled to Mike to stop, and pulled out Mitch's phone to call Curtis.

He answered quickly. "Dr. Jones? Are you close? There's an awful lot of movement out there."

"Don't sweat that, Curtis," I whispered. "It's some of Mitch's men, getting into position to cover us. We ought to be to you in just a few minutes, we're straight downhill from your spot."

His voice got even more edgy: "I can try to meet you when—*Jesus!*" His sudden outburst needed no explanation. Both over the phone and echoing through the woods, I had heard the unmistakable sound of a high-velocity bullet ricocheting off rock. Mike immediately got down low behind a very large fallen tree trunk, and I got my back up hard against an upright oak that, I hoped, was wide enough to shield me. "Dr. Jones!" I heard Curtis cry out loud. "That hit the rocks just above my spot—I'm not crazy, someone really is trying to kill me!"

"I know you're not crazy, Curtis. But you still didn't hear a report before the shot hit?"

"No," Curtis said, which was both good and bad news: even a suppressed rifle will emit an audible noise, especially in the deep woods at night, where any small sound is greatly magnified. Thus our phantom shooter was still working from a considerable distance; but he was also trying to maneuver his way to an effective angle without descending the hillside and risking discovery.

"All right, then," I said, still trying my best to sound reassuring. "McCarron's men all have night vision equipment; it's likely they've got a better idea of where he is than you do. So hunker down and sit tight, we'll be there soon."

"Please hurry," Curtis murmured. After I'd hung up on the poor fool again, I heard Mike whisper:

"*We'll* be there soon? What are you talking about, L.T., we don't even know where this fucker's shooting from! Leave this to Mitch's guys, for shit's sake."

But I was already scanning the hillside above us with the night vision binoculars, trying to find anything I could that would allow us to proceed. "I'd like to do that, Mike, but we still don't know what's what, with these guys—I know Mitch is okay, but Mitch isn't here, and who knows that one or more of these other guys doesn't have orders to silence Curtis *and* the shooter? So we have to—"

And then a sudden, fortunate realization: not having a head mount, I wasn't holding the glowing binoculars tight enough to my head, and that would mean that a small amount of the green light that they projected into the ocular lenses would be reflecting off my own eyes and face amid the darkness. I ducked suddenly, and sure enough, just as I did, a big chunk of the oak that had been offering me cover was torn away, just above the height where my head had been. Thinking fast, I let out a loud cry of pain, one that brought Mike at a run; but I quickly grabbed his shirt and pulled him to the ground beside me, seething, "Get down, Mike, you idiot!"

"Idiot?" he said, quickly determining that I was okay. "L.T., you fucker, I was trying to help!"

"And I appreciate that," I said, shutting off the binoculars and letting them dangle around my neck. "But I was bullshitting, I want him to think he got one of us, though I don't think that was his purpose. No, he meant to scare us off; but now, if he believes that one of us is wounded or dead, we can work around in a circle that way"—I pointed to my left, where the trees were more densely grouped—"and get up to Curtis."

"Oh yeah? And when did you become such a tactical expert?"

"I'm not—but I'm beginning to understand this guy better. He's fine, if he can see a target clearly. But on the move, like we were in the Prowlers, or in crowded woods, he seems less proficient. I don't think he's ex-military, which will help when we flesh his profile out a little more."

"Oh, great," Mike said, as the pair of us, crouching low, made for the thicker trees uphill. "Glad to know that I'm sticking my neck out for another one of your goddamned profiles . . ."

Despite Mike's initial anxiety, once we'd gotten another fifteen yards up-hill amid a stand of very thick pines, both of us began to breathe a bit easier: we'd be very hard to spot in that location. In addition, the ground beneath our feet had begun to show stone beneath the thick, dead pine needles: a sign that we were approaching the rock formation in which Curtis was hiding. Using only hand signals, now, Mike and I pushed our luck by pressing on another fifteen yards; but when even the pines began to thin on the emergent rock below us, I decided we'd better pause, get some cover behind the last of the good-sized trunks, and contact Curtis again.

"I hope you're close, Dr. Jones," he said, as soon as he'd answered my call.

"We are, Curtis," I replied, keeping my voice even quieter than it had been. "Look to your right and a little downhill—can you see the beginning of a long stand of pines?"

There was a pause, and then he returned: "I—I think so. There's a very dark patch, it's close."

"Okay—that's where we are, but I'm not sure we can move uphill very much farther. Any chance that, if you head down from your position, you can use the rocks you're hiding in for cover? The shooter's above you, so if you stay low enough, the angle they offer should prevent him from being able to hit anything *but* the top of those rocks."

Curtis breathed deep, seeming to have found some confidence. "Okay," he said, "On my way."

There was nothing for Mike and me to do, now, but get even lower and wait for some sight or sound of Curtis; it seemed, at last, that we were on the verge of the kind of revelations for which we'd long hoped. Realizing as much, even Mike could let out a little chuckle. "I never would've believed," he said. "I mean, when that poor little schmuck took off from the Kurtzes', I just thought it was funny: tearing off his tech suit like he was Superman, disappearing up the hill in his T-shirt and chinos, the back of his balding head bobbing around like—"

I was on the verge of sharing his amusement; but then Mitch's phone rang: "Curtis? What are you doing?"

"I'm lost, Dr. Jones!" he whispered, panicking again. "I'm standing—"

"Standing?" I had suddenly recalled Mike's precise words with horror: I rose up behind my pine, caught sight of that white T-shirt and balding head, and called out, "Curtis! Get down! *Now!*"

"Why?" Curtis answered, from his spot just above us to our right. "I must be close, I can—"

But that was all. Mike and I were close enough to hear a bullet searing through the forest night, and then the terrible sound of bone and flesh giving way. "Curtis!" I called, moving toward the place where I'd glimpsed him.

"L.T.!" Mike warned without moving. "What're you doing, get the fuck back here!"

"No, Mike," I answered as I ran. "He doesn't want us! He had one job, here, and I just pray—"

But that prayer, like so many in the case, was to go unanswered. In a few seconds I came up on Curtis' body, lying facedown in the soft undergrowth of the woodland floor short of the pine stand that had offered Mike and me cover. He'd been hit in the center of the back, the shot shattering his spine and, I found when I turned him over, taking away part of his chest. His eyes were closed, indicating that he'd lived for just a few seconds after being hit; which only magnified the horror of it all. Mike soon ran up behind me, mumbling an oath very quietly, and then we both just stood there for several minutes, trying to absorb what had happened. As reality sank in, I shouted down to Mitch, telling him that he could now order his forward units up the ridgeline as fast as possible, and join us where we were without concern for his men's or his own safety. This he did in short order, making his way through the hillside in a manner that reflected his own childhood of exploring these mountains by day and night; and when I moved to meet him, he knew from my face that something very bad had happened.

"Curtis?" he asked, hoping against hope. "He all right?" All I could do was shake my head grimly and lead him the short distance to Kolmback's body. As he saw the mess that had been made of the unfortunate tech, Mitch's face grew pained, and he removed his Stetson to kneel by him. "My God," he murmured. "My God, what's happening . . ."

"Bastard almost got Trajan, too," Mike said quietly. "Although he seems to think it wasn't—"

"It wasn't a kill shot—we can be sure of that now. He just wanted to scare us away from Curtis' position. I thought he wouldn't have an angle, if Curtis came low to meet us, and he wouldn't have had; but Curtis got lost, then panicked and stood up. Mike had reminded me: Curtis' balding head and T-shirt. They would have glowed like flares in a night scope. *Why* did I tell him to come out . . ."

Mitch shook his head. "You can't blame yourself, Trajan. Look at this wound."

I followed the order, and suddenly realized how out of proportion the bullet's damage had been: an ordinary round fired from a suppressed rifle simply couldn't have done it. But another kind of projectile, one favored by the worst of hunters as well as by many snipers, would; and so I wasn't surprised when I heard Mike say:

"You're right, Mitch." He examined the body more closely, as we steadily found ourselves surrounded by most of Mitch's troopers from below, who were gazing on the scene in shock and anger and hanging on every word. "A ballistic tip," Mike continued. "Had to be."

"Yeah-uh," Mitch droned sadly. "God damn it, I hate those bullets. Bad enough when people use them hunting. They explode inside the animals, but sometimes there's no exit wound, so no blood trail to follow. Things die in pain for no reason. Poor old Curtis, though . . . was no deer or bear. Just a little guy without much to him. But—" Mitch attempted to steel himself and get back to business. "They *do* fly awfully straight, those tips. So people just keep using them . . ." At last rising, Mitch tore his walkie-talkie from his belt and spoke to his men up the mountain, telling them to be careful but to press their pursuit. After detailing the troopers still below to bring up a stretcher, he ordered the men around us to form a second wave with their flashlights: there was no need for secrecy or subtlety, now, he said, and they all knew just what a blow the unknown sniper had struck at law enforcement. The men proceeded up the mountain with no fear, each with a Glock in one hand and a waving Maglite in the other, fanning out to cover as much ground as they could.

Mike and I went back down the hillside with Mitch, behind two troopers who had appeared with a folding stretcher and were bearing Curtis' body back to the school. Mike had already agreed with Mitch about a ballistic tip being the cause of death; but I wasn't finished with the topic:

"It's not just amateurs who use them, though, is it, Mitch?" I said, trying to focus harder. "You know as well as I do that a lot of snipers love ballistic tips. The bigger the mess they make of a suicide bomber or a guy laying an IED, so much the better, and I have no problem with that. What I *don't* like is this: you've got somebody on the loose and apparently unpursued, until now, and he's at least proficient, maybe even good, with a police-issue suppressed weapon." Mitch's face grew pained as we reached the soccer pitch and he struggled with the idea: it was one thing to concede the hasty error of a fellow officer, such as had (supposedly) occurred at Fraser; it was entirely another to admit that someone in law enforcement might have been responsible for the calculated stalking and shooting of an FIC tech. "Come on, Mitch," I insisted fervently, as we moved back through the now eerily innocent halls of the school to lay Curtis' body out in, of all places, a science lab, until Ernest Weaver arrived. "Gracie Chang visits us, and she gets run off the road. Curtis Kolmback is seen doing nothing more than talking to us, and he ends up dead—how long before somebody decides that even a troop commander in the Staties is expendable?"

I'd finally succeeded in stunning my old friend, and he plainly wanted to answer me quickly—but the burden (and chance) of doing so was suddenly taken from him: "Just what in the *fuck* happened up there?" It was a new voice; and as we turned around, a figure slid off of one of the laboratory countertops farthest from us, where he'd been seated: Frank Mangold. He strolled over to Curtis' body, actually looking somewhat remorseful. "So," he said quietly. "I guess you two doctors got a better idea, now, of what it's like when you try to play on too many sides."

"What the hell are you talking about, Frank?" Mitch said.

"Come on, McCarron—these two haven't been dealing with us straight from the start. I don't know just what it is, but there's something going on here that I don't know about. And after this?" He indicated Curtis' body. "You can be damned sure I'm going to figure it out."

It was bizarre, even more bizarre than Mangold's behavior in Albany had been. "Mitch," I eventually said, shaking my head to clear it of Mangold's insanity, "this isn't serving any purpose. We've told you all we can about Curtis' disappearance: that he was God damned scared because Frank, here, was looking for him—I assume you don't deny that, Frank?"

"No, I don't deny it," Mangold answered, those piercing eyes going wide. "I was looking for him to confirm that you people were working to cover up what was actually happening in this case."

"Yeah, fine," I said. "You take that statement for what it's worth, Mitch—but the fact is, you two need to have a serious conversation with the ADA, and Dr. Li and I shouldn't be part of it. What you needed from us, you've got: a professional sniper using ballistic-tipped .308 bullets killed Kolmback, after it became apparent that he was having a hard time toeing the party line."

"And what line *was* that?" Yet again, Mangold's confusion seemed utterly genuine.

Nevertheless, it made Mike explode impatiently: "That's *your* fucking job, Frank! How should *we* know what the party line is! We were brought in by Steve and Pete, to give some advice; and then we were hired by the Kurtzes to represent them in the Franco boy's disappearance—and that's *it*."

Mangold was about to answer, but Mitch stepped in. "Frank," he warned simply; and the sincerity of his tone—combined, of course, with his size—was enough to make Mangold show his palms and back off. "Okay, boys," Mitch went on. "If you're telling me that all you heard Curtis say was that he was afraid of getting questioned by Frank, then we'll leave it at that. I've never had reason to doubt you before. Come on—I'll make sure you get out okay."

We didn't really need Mitch's escort on our way out of the school, but it was a chance to discuss one more thing with him out of Mangold's hearing: the fact that Curtis had been the tech present at all five of the throwaway death scenes.

"You think you're surprising me, there?" Mitch said. "I'd noticed it; and also noticed, for a while, that the guy was carrying something heavier than he could handle, which only started with the fact that he was on all five scenes. But I think it was more than that—way more . . ."

"Yes, it was," I replied. "And trust me, Mitch, when he broke for the woods, we were doing our best to try to get him to at least tell *you* the truth, and protect himself. But he'd gone too far down whatever road he was on, and his inner conflict was simply too severe."

"Goddamn it," Mitch said quietly. "I hoped we might get out of this year with nothing more than that scandal at the FIC lab. But this . . . this is something much bigger. Obviously."

"I'm afraid so." We reached the front doors of the school and pushed on out into the night. "But it's this insane talk of Mangold's that bothers me the most," I went on. "You must know, Mitch, that Mike and I aren't involved in any secret plot to lead the investigation in the wrong direction."

"Yeah, I know," Mitch answered quickly, with a certain nod. "And Frank's probably just talking out of his ass—he's frustrated, not that we all aren't."

"And his little rat's cage of a brain naturally turns to the kinds of things *he's* done," Mike tossed in. "When he was down in the city, along with up here. But what amazes me—what I guess amazes us both—is that he really doesn't seem to be involved in this bizarre scheme he's imagining."

"Don't be so quick to believe that," Mitch answered. "I've known Frank a long time: the guy could perfectly well be faking, just to cover his tracks and make sure that you two don't suspect—oh, shit, here they come . . ."

Emerging from a nearby, unmarked sedan with state plates were Cathy Donovan and Nancy Grimes. They moved toward us, creating their usual impressions: Donovan the handsome, well-dressed hit-woman of county government, Grimes in a lab coat and, on this night, holding up an outstretched hand that was apparently intended as a serious warning to us to halt our progress, but which came off, characteristically, as more comical than intimidating. But we couldn't afford to be dismissive: Donovan was striding with an even greater air of deadly earnest and inscrutability than usual, in the face of which even Mitch halted and, after removing his Stetson, inclined his head.

"Director," he said. "Ms. Donovan. I'm assuming you know every-thing, by now."

"Indeed," Cathy Donovan said, smiling just perceptibly. "And were these two of any help?"

"They were," Mitch answered. "And put themselves in harm's way to do it. But they've confirmed what you must have heard: a long-distance .308 round with a ballistic tip. A kill shot. Curtis had been marked down in somebody's book, and probably a long time before he ran off."

Grimes appeared ready to launch into one of her bumptious indict-ments of Mike's and my participation in the case, but Cathy Donovan anticipated her colleague's intention and laid a slow, silencing hand on Grimes' wrist. "All right, Mitch," she said, with a slight smile that might even have passed for alluring, under other circumstances. "If you say that the good doctors had nothing to do with the cause of Curtis' breakdown, that's good enough for me—and that *is* what you're saying?"

"Yes, ma'am," Mitch answered, with another inclination of his head. "That's what I'm saying."

"And you'd stake your reputation on that?" Nancy Grimes added, gra-tuitously.

"I don't know that anybody's asking me to do that," Mitch said to her, with a good deal less deference. "But yeah, if asked, I'd stake my reputa-tion on it—*Director*."

Cathy Donovan's smile only got wider, which was not a good sign. "Nobody's asking you to stake anything on anybody," she said, still with that brilliant self-control and impenetrability. "We know Curtis was murdered, and we thank the good doctors for telling us a little more about how."

Mitch replaced his Stetson, while Mike and I each mumbled, "Good night, then," vaguely; and we all started back toward the Empress. But I knew that it had all been far too simple, and was therefore unsurprised to hear Donovan's voice call to me again:

"By the way, Dr. Jones—I understand things are going well with your protection of the Kurtz family. Or rather, what's left of them."

We stopped, half-turning back toward them, each of us surprised at the topic; but in Donovan's eyes, I already detected far too much aware-ness. "They are," I said, trying to sound sure of myself. "Far better than if we'd left them to that pack of media jackals at their house."

Donovan's head tilted judiciously. "Oh, of course. No one questions the—*nobility* of the move . . ." Then the coyness suddenly became tinged with an air of threat: "And if your protection bleeds over into something a bit more romantic in nature, well, who could blame either of you? She's a very pretty girl, after all, and you've both faced—*challenges*. There must be a great deal of mutual understanding between you."

Every drop of blood in me began to boil; and for the first time since I'd known Cathy Donovan, I could see by the expression on her face that she realized she might have gone too far. Whatever expression was on mine as I involuntarily began to move toward them, even Nancy Grimes lost her stupid, smug smile, as she took a half-step backward. "I'm sure I misunderstand you, Assistant District Attorney," I said, with quiet viciousness. "Otherwise, it *could* sound like you'd sent someone to trespass on Shiloh without a warrant—a serious offense, one that I'm sure your boss would be interested in."

But Donovan regained her composure in a quick, even remarkable, instant: "There's been no trespassing. Only gossip. People do gossip, you know, Dr. Jones. How does it get started? Who ever knows. But it's out there. So just consider this a gentle reminder about the kind of ethics that, I'm sure, *your* bosses at SUNY would be interested in hearing about."

She had me checkmated; and all I could do was very quickly ask, "Are we done here?"

"By all means, Doctor," she answered. "You gentlemen have a good night, now."

Mike and I turned to make straight for the car, while Mitch exchanged a few more words with the two women before joining us. By the time he did, Mike had the car started and I was lowering myself into my seat. "What the hell was that all about?" Mitch asked in a hushed voice.

"You heard her, Mitch," I said evasively. "Gossip. She's trying to make us believe that she's put the squeeze on one of the hands up at the farm, or some such crap. If she had anything else, trust me, she would have used it."

"Come on, Trajan," Mitch said urgently. "*Gossip?* I thought we were done hiding things. If it's none of my business, fine, but if I need to know about it, if only to protect you—"

"It's nothing, Mitch," I said, finally in the car and speaking out the window. "I'm sorry I reacted the way I did. And, just to prove my point—Mike and I are going to be leaving soon, to collect some information downstate that may help lead us all to whoever's at the root of this case.

If I was enjoying some high romance on Shiloh, would I take off like that?"

Mitch pondered the question. "The girl's not going with you?"

"Absolutely not. The kid, Lucas, is; and that should give you a hint about our plans. But I really can't go into it any further, and I have to ask you to keep even that much to yourself. Though you'd be doing me a favor if you'd occasionally drop in on Clarissa and Ambyr while we're gone. Maybe assign their cousin Caitlin to patrol in Surrender, too."

That got a dubious smile from the head of Troop G. "Pete Steinbrecher's not the only one who knows just what your aunt thinks of cops, Trajan."

"Don't worry, I'll be asking Pete and Steve to perform the same duty," I answered, as Mike began to back the car away from the collection of official vehicles. "And I'll get Clarissa on board with the idea—somehow."

"Okay, but—" Mitch walked with us a few steps as we moved forward toward the exit lane of the school's parking lot. "Just as long as *you* know that *I* know you're not telling me everything . . ."

I simply smiled and shrugged back at him. We rolled slowly to the parking lot's exit lane, soon passing the Special Operations Response officer who was posted there. All done up in his black riot gear, the man could barely give us a small salute as we passed, while also being sure to keep his AR-15 at the ready. Mike lost no time in putting the school several miles behind us, then let out a burst of air that sounded as though he'd been holding it in since our departure.

"Holy fucking shit, Trajan. I don't even know where to start with all that."

"We can't," I answered, trying to get my own feelings under control. "Not yet . . ." As we pulled into Surrender, I looked up at the statue of Colonel Jones with a new sense of dread. "We have to consolidate all we now know, and that's going to take particular single-mindedness."

"But *who* is this sniper working for?" Mike almost shrieked, as we pulled onto Death's Head Hollow. "All we know for sure, now, is that this shit is even more tangled than we thought—I mean, fuck the scorecard, we can't even tell which players are wearing what uniforms. I hate to say it, but—what you told Mitch back there, about the trip to New York. Right now, it really *is* the only way we're even going to begin to clear any of this mess up."

"Yes," I said, mulling it. "And we're not even fully prepared for *that*.

Not yet. We have a couple of days to try to gain some clarity, before the Augustines get back. We need to put that time to use. We need a fresh perspective—but from where? Damn it, there must be—wait a minute." I considered one aspect of the ordeal we'd just been through, one which my rage had prevented me from seeing: "What Donovan just insinuated, about Ambyr and me. Mangold—he didn't know about it. If he had, he certainly would have been the first to try to get a rise out of me."

"True," Mike answered. "But remember what Mitch said about him being a consummate bullshitter. Anyway, so he wasn't the first to score points, so what?"

"So *what*? Mike—we've got a fucking sniper wandering these hills, one we've been speculating works for the BCI; yet Frank Mangold may know nothing about it? Or about the information that that agent has been collecting by maintaining surveillance over Shiloh, even over Ambyr and me?"

Mike nodded once or twice; then, as he got my meaning, his mouth fell open. "Hang on. You *do* realize what you're talking about, right? About senior members of the BCI maybe being kept in the dark, while junior officers are made use of. And the only way that happens—"

"The only way that happens," I finished for him, "is with very senior authorization. This is no plot hatched by Donovan and Grimes—that's why they've never looked even a little worried, it's not *on* them. It can only come from someplace higher, and no, not from the DA, before you suggest that. The BCI is a *state* organization, Mike; you want to screw around with that chain of command, you have to have serious weight behind you. The kind of weight that—"

"The kind of weight that Indian Bill was talking about. That savage son of a bitch was right—this is bigger than we ever *have* known. Fuck... L.T., I'm not so sure we can get into bringing down a governor, much less tangling with—"

"Easy, easy..." I let silence return inside the car for a moment, hoping it might bring calm, as well. "It's not going to come to that. Our concern is this case, that's all; so we stay on course. Our planning has been thorough: everything that we've proposed so far fits the context of the Augustine couple, and the possibility that they may in turn lead us to others like them is also sound. We just have to execute our next moves correctly, and fill in a few details. Right now, like I say, it's just our perspective that's hazy; we've reached that point in every case where we *need* something, something to provide us with another viewpoint, maybe a little distance—" And then, all in a rush, a feeling so terrible that I could feel it draining the blood from my face consumed me.

Mike saw it right away, and quickly asked: "L.T.? What happened, your hip again? You wanna finally hit the damned hospital, like I've been telling you to do?"

I had felt a wave of pain, all right, but I dared not explain its nature or extent, not even to Mike; not yet. "No," I soon whispered, trying to master the storm inside me before my partner could guess the true nature of what had happened. The image of the house at Shiloh had finally come into view, and it betrayed no signs of alarm or tragedy; and there was both reassurance and awful confirmation in that fact. "No, I'm okay, Mike. Just—a twinge, there, for a minute. It's fading. Let's get back; there are things that I—that *we* need to do . . ."

I was lying to him, of course, something that broke the investigator's code and for which I despised myself; yet I knew that I would have to dissemble even more blatantly, in the hours before we left for New York City—in the hours, that is, that it would take to make me absolutely sure of the notions that had finally caused me such pain in the car . . .

{iii.}

Upon making sure that all was well within the house—that everyone was sleeping soundly and had not met with the kind of ugly fate that had befallen Curtis Kolmback—I made my way not to my room but to Marcianna's enclosure, consumed all the while by the thought that at any point the phantom who had been behind first the bloodshed and near-tragedy up on the mountain the night we visited the charcoal kilns, then Gracie Chang's wreck, and finally Curtis' murder, might now be stalking my alter ego. This fear largely faded when I saw Marcianna come bounding to the gate after I called her; and I realized that, if the creature roaming our stretch of the Taconic range had intended to kill her as a way of warning us (and specifically me) off the throwaways case, he likely would have done so already; and so I considered her, at least for now, safe.

But the easing of my fears about Marcianna did not similarly put my mind at rest about other issues, issues that kept me in the rocky den that was my companion's home that night, smoking and wondering until close to dawn about dark questions meant for dark places: and Marcianna's den—which I had modeled on photos of *kopjes,* those lonely formations of rock that rise suddenly and mysteriously from the African savannah to offer shelter to a wide variety of animal life—was an all-too-perfect place for such ruminations. Marcianna, of course, had done all she could to revive me, by urging me toward our usual forms of rough-housing; but when it became clear to her how very troubled and spent I was, she lay down with a groan and offered me her side as a pillow.

I awoke to the thunderous sound of Marcianna purring deeply beneath my right ear, which was flat against her chest; and, looking up, I saw Ambyr, dressed in that same midnight blue Chinese robe, stroking the lightly spotted white fur of Marcianna's chest and throat. It was an unexpected sight, to say the least: I had no idea, in my sleepy state, how Ambyr had even gotten into the enclosure, much less navigated the deliberately awkward passageway that led into the den. Yet it was also an amazing surprise, to see the two great beauties of my life together, Ambyr whispering to Marcianna as she moved her hands up and behind the rounded, furry ears, Marcianna pushing her head up and into those delicate hands to urge Ambyr to scratch even harder.

"What . . . ?" I mumbled, transfixed by the sheer wonder of the sight. "What's happening?"

Those opaque violet eyes turned on me, and Ambyr smiled, never having looked so beautiful. "Well," she said softly. "Somebody's finally awake. She puts up with a lot, Trajan—*you* were snoring."

"Was I?" Trying to sit up, I made it only to one elbow. "I was awake. Most of the night . . ."

"So Mike tells me," Ambyr said, giving Marcianna a last brush and then moving my way. "That was a horrible story—really horrible . . ." Her remorse seemed genuine enough. "And you really think the guy is still up in the hills?"

"Unfortunately," I said as she sat astride me, placing my arms around her after she'd undone her robe, revealing that she was naked beneath it. "They could catch him, if they wanted to," I breathed. "But somebody clearly doesn't . . ."

"But he won't get to Derek, right?" she said, even more earnestly. "Promise me that."

"I can't promise anything, Ambyr," I said. "But we'll do what we can."

Then I remembered something far more elementary: "Say, how did you get in here, anyway?"

"Shhh," she noised, moving her lips to my ear as she started to undo my clothes. "Some detective *you* are—Mike let me in, he said you needed me. And you do . . ." As if on cue, Marcianna very carefully withdrew from beneath my head and then wandered out the entrance to the den, neither angry nor jealous, but simply curious to see what the day held. "I can't believe that you spent the night here, and didn't come to me," Ambyr went on. "After a night like that . . ." By now our bare torsos were pressed tight to one another, and in another moment Ambyr had the last of both my clothes and her robe removed. "It isn't healthy, Mister-Doctor-Man," she went on. "That's what we're here for, after all, or have you forgotten—to *comfort* each other . . ."

It seems self-serving to say that no man, given the circumstances that prevailed that morning, and coming off of so long a term of painful deprivation, could have resisted the remarkable girl who had swept into my life so forcefully; yet it's true. Intellectual evaluations would only come later, however, when the passion between us had subsided and we lay on the den floor, protected atop my outstretched clothes. The easing of our mutual hunger then allowed such cogitations to slip back into my mind; and one in particular sparked the rest: *Derek*, it kept repeating; and when that was done, *Context, you idiot!* My eyes shot open, as in a rush I began to quickly put together some of the pieces that I had been helpless to make full sense of the night before.

Maintaining control over that assembly, however, was vital: "I'm sorry you're so worried about Derek," I said carefully. "You must have known him since he was just a kid, hunh? Maybe always."

"No," she murmured simply, letting her lips linger on my neck. "They only moved next door a few years before I got sick, so he was—God, I forget—six or seven, maybe? And it's funny: no matter how much I know, in my head, how he changed when he got older, I still mostly see him the way I did then: following me around like a lost little puppy, wherever I went." *Of course*, I mused silently. "Always helping with things, always trying to be cheerful. In a way, he was my friend before he was Lucas', because it took Lucas a while to adjust, and to learn not to make fun of him. After that, they got to be like brothers, but . . . Well, shit, you know. I just can't stand the idea of him being in danger, because of that— because of how I still see him . . ." *Because of context*, I reflected; *because of your perspective.* Then another rush of ideas shot through my cranium, sparks that were fanned into flame when Ambyr went on: "Oh, by the way—speaking of Mike, you'll never guess where he is, right now."

"He'd better be in that plane working," I breathed heavily, trying to laugh a little.

"While you lie up here taking advantage of the poor blind girl?" Ambyr replied, able herself to laugh quietly. "He is not. He's in Albany, helping Dr. Chang move back into her apartment from the hospital. Seems like, without telling any of us, he's been slipping off for early morning visits to Albany Medical to see her—and it also seems like maybe she's starting to take him seriously. Now . . ." Ambyr moved her head up to kiss me and speak into my lips. "I wonder where he ever got that idea?"

"He watches too much TV," I told her; and was not entirely shocked to receive a sharp slam into my chest for my trouble.

"Don't be a jerk," she said, smiling. "You know perfectly well that he got it from you."

"That's right," I said with a nod. "From me and Marcianna . . ."

And that time I really paid: after jabbing me in the ribs, she sat up on her knees and began to squeeze my hips with her thighs, tight enough to cause a sharp pain on my left side. "I warned you," she said, smiling a little sadistically. "Remember which one of us has got two good legs, and—" But I had already grunted in pain, loud enough to bring Marcianna back into the den in a confused state. "Oh, I get it," Ambyr went on, hearing those big padding paws and the accompanying panting. "Call your secret weapon in, hunh? Your *protector*? Pretty lame, buster."

"Yeah, well, so am I," I said, at which Ambyr suddenly threw herself on me and apologized genuinely, though she couldn't help but keep laughing as she did. And then the chain of all my electric shocks suddenly became completed: Ambyr's mention of Mike's activities had put the last piece of the solution to my dilemma in place. "Wait!" I said suddenly, causing even Marcianna to turn. "Ambyr, you just said that Mike's gone to help Gracie—did he say anything else about it?"

Ambyr raised herself again, sensing that I was serious, and shrugged. "Just that he might pick her brain a little about the case."

"That's what I thought," I said, full of new determination and trying to sit up; but Ambyr was having none of it, and kept her legs locked on me. "Come on, Ambyr, I beg of you—I think I may have just had an epiphany about the case."

"Tell me you love me, and then tell me what it is," she insisted, although she had already sensed enough earnestness in my voice to cause her to begin to gather her robe.

Her requests, seemingly innocent, were wrenchingly hard for me: the first brought me directly back to my crisis of the night before, almost dispelling the out-of-time experience we had just shared in the den; while compliance with the second was, at least for the moment, dangerous. However, as I always had with Ambyr, I pushed danger aside, and did as she asked on both counts. In response, she faced me with an expression that was somewhat difficult to decipher: she seemed happy to let the first statement stand, but the second she could not but question.

"I thought you said that was a terrible idea," she observed, tightening her robe as she stood up. "Back when Mike first suggested it."

"And it was," I said. "Back when Mike first suggested it. Now? It may be just the thing."

"Trajan," Ambyr said, with apparently real concern. "Are you sure it will be safe?"

"Frankly," I answered, securing my prosthesis, dusting off my outer garments, and then getting into them, "I'm not sure anything to do with this case is safe, anymore." I grabbed her by the hand and pulled her toward the den entrance, as Marcianna gleefully ran beside us, anticipating some sport in the grass of the enclosure. Once out in the glaring sun of morning, however, I only shouted down to the hangar, knowing that at least one person would be there: "Yo! Lucas!"

The kid soon shot out, obviously having leapt from the hatch of the JU-52 to the ground and still not having gained his balance, focused as he was on a half-eaten banana. "Yo!" he called back.

"Get hold of Mike, I don't have my phone!" I told him. "He'll be at Gracie's, so call his cell, and tell him to get his ass back here *now*, that it's four-alarm important!"

"Right!" Lucas said, disappearing again to head for the phone in the plane.

"I hope you know what you're doing," Ambyr said, smiling as she clung to me on our way down to the gate. "He'll kill you for cutting his romantic day short."

"No, he won't," I said. "He'll want to, but his ego will take over pretty quick . . ."

Once at the gate, Marcianna was disappointed to see us exit without her, but I explained that we'd be back for our usual *walk* (a word she knew well) that afternoon, and then took her breakfast from the cooler and tossed it over to her. She had been too worried to eat the night before, but now, with the worry seemingly gone, she snatched up the bit of beef studded with supplements and trotted back toward the high grass to consume it.

Over the course of that day, I had to do something that I had known from the beginning was inevitable (although I had never suspected, even in my worst-case scenarios, that it would become necessary in the way and for the reasons that it did): I had to separate Ambyr and Lucas from the main thrust of the investigation. Nor could I tell them why, or even attempt to lie: the first would have been calamitous, and the second Ambyr would almost certainly have detected, precipitating an even greater disaster. So I simply let them know that the discussions I needed to have, first with Mike and then with others yet to be selected, were ones to which they could not be privy, because of academic ethics. Lucas howled in protest, claiming, quite fairly, that he had not come this far only to be shut out at a key moment. I continued to tell him, however, that Mike and I had to observe some professional principles, not just as investigators, but as teachers.

"But I *still* don't get it," Lucas said, making his last stand as he stood with Ambyr on the porch that evening after dinner, while I got ready to head up the hill to the hangar. There, Mike was already waiting, having just returned from Albany and dinner with Gracie but not yet knowing why. "I mean, okay," the kid went on, "they're your students, but *I*, at least—and don't you whack me, sis, you know I'm right—*I've* been around this case a lot longer than they have, and I've sat through the courses for like, weeks! So *I* can't listen, just because one of *them* might say something *they'll* be sorry for?"

"You're not always speedy, kid, but you do get there, eventually," I answered. "Yeah, that's about it. Our jobs at the university are still our main concern—we can't play around with that. And the students won't be given enough information to screw with: they'll give us perspective on a *hypothetical* case. We need it, and there's nobody else we can get it from."

"But . . ." Lucas simply wouldn't surrender. "If it's just *hypothetical*—"

"Give it up, baby brother," Ambyr said, before the kid could argue further. "If it's going to help the case, and help Derek . . ." She flicked her cane toward my backside. "Go ahead, baby. I'll keep this one's big nose out of it—just do what you have to do."

Making my way up into the JU-52, I found a none-too-happy Mike, who began quizzing me on what idea could be so important that it required not only his cutting his romantic evening short, but the Kurtzes' being excluded from it, as well. I fell into the pilot's seat and, at long last, outlined for the first time my complete plan to follow his suggestion, made in jest early on in the case, that we use selected members of our classes as sounding boards to gain additional insights. I saw his face fill first with the involuntary pride I'd expected, then watched it change to a much deeper confusion.

"Hang on a second, L.T.," he said, starting to rub at his hair. "When I brought that idea up, as I recall, we were at a little bit of a dead end. But we're not, now. We know what our next moves are, and they all lead in the direction you wanted: straight south, to the big money in the big city."

"They may, Mike," I replied evenly. "But they may lead in other, less welcome directions, as well. Besides, even if the idea of heading south is confirmed, our record in that kind of showdown isn't exactly great: 0-and-1, unless I'm missing something. You don't think maybe we could afford to bounce our next moves, along with our overall speculations, off of some pretty exceptional minds, and gain some valuable perspectives on the case?"

Mike had to think about that one. "So," he eventually said, after lighting a pair of cigarettes, handing me one, and tossing a fairly thick file in my lap with affected nonchalance, "when you say 'exceptional minds,' I assume you're not talking about our students generally?"

"Of course not," I answered, picking up the dossier that Mike had apparently been waiting for this or some similar occasion to reveal: **UN-NAMED CASE TO DATE,** read the cover. "What the hell?"

"Well," Mike said, his pride returning again. "I figured you'd come around to this idea, sooner or later. I'm not a hundred percent sure about why *now,* but I've kept this going. It's the full notes on the whole thing—*if* it were being told as a hypothetical story. If you really want to pick some of their brains, then this'll bring them up to speed. And before you ask . . ." He opened the file and took out a USB flash drive that lay atop its contents. "The digital version. Up to date, and ready to transmit."

"Now for the tougher question," I said, seriously enough that Mike's smile faded. "If you've got this hypothetical version, I'm assuming you have a parallel *real* version, somewhere?"

Mike's concern became mixed with confusion. "Of course—but you don't want—"

"Just get it, Mike, and let's begin." He went to his main desk and fetched the second file as I stood up, pulling on my cane and the wheel of the plane hard: there was no turning back now.

"I'm not so sure I'm with you on this step, L.T.," Mike said as I joined him in the cabin. "I mean, this *was* always supposed to be a *hypothetical* exercise, right?"

"This case was always supposed to have been a lot of things, Mike," I said. "And absorbing what I think we're going to have to absorb as a result of this exercise is going to be very tough—for both of us." He wanted to ask more questions, but I held up my hand. "It'll be a lot easier if we just let it unfold once and for real, trust me. So let's start going over the names, and come up with some kind of a competent and discreet bunch . . ."

For the rest of the night, or at least until the early morning, the still-befuddled Mike and I went over the various lists of all those SUNY students who had been recently enrolled in our respective classes. Mike retrieved copies of their photos, given to us at the beginning of every semester by the school, and arranged them on a desk that was vacant (or rather that, with a crashing sweep of Mike's arm, was made vacant); and from there, the weeding process began. At each step of the way, we considered experience, variety of interests, sense of humor, and above all, reliability, while studying the faces before us; and as we did, photos went sailing away onto the floor at an alarming rate. As a final consideration, we had to ask ourselves whom we simply could not carry the project off *without*. In this category, there were at first only four names (not a bad thing, for security's sake), all of them women, in keeping with the ratio of who was going into criminal science, at the time: there was Colleen Burke, the shy but sharp Bostonian, who had worked at that city's crime lab; Vicky Ferrier, the deceptively beautiful blonde from California; Linda Walker, the quiet, no-nonsense black woman from the Bronx, whose insights would, we hoped, override her close geographical proximity to the case; and Mei-lien Hsüeh, Mike's favorite, the soft-spoken exchange student from the forensic sciences school at the Kunming Medical University in Yunnan, China.

"So—these four," Mike said at length. "You good?"

"I don't know . . . I just wish we had *one* guy. You know my feeling: too much homogeneity, of whatever kind, isn't ideal. And I wouldn't mind just a *little* more testosterone in the mix, though the Thought Police could probably get me fired just for saying that."

"Well—hang on," Mike answered, sifting through the photos on the floor. "Did we discuss—you know, the Latino kid, he was a standout in a couple of my courses, why didn't we . . . ?" At length, Mike held up a photo, which I recognized instantly:

"Frankie Arquilla!" I said, nodding. "We eliminated him on a technicality—he hasn't finished my advanced profiling course yet. But otherwise, yeah, just what I mean: brilliant, sensitive under the facade, and very funny—"

"Well, L.T., for fuck's sake . . ." Mike shook his head and put Frankie's picture on the desk. "There's what, one or two classes and a test left on that course? Not to mention that he's in Arizona, around where at least some of these throwaway kids' parents supposedly disappeared to? Might come in handy. So do you think that maybe we could let him slide, on the damned technicality?"

Realizing that I'd been a bit of an idiot, I nodded. "Yeah. I think so . . . Okay, that's our five."

"Yep. There certainly isn't a *better* group we could come up with. Now, just one more point . . ." Turning from the pictures to face me, Mike became very serious: "L.T.—just so we're straight with each other, this is the first time since we became partners that you've asked me to do something without giving me the full list of reasons why."

Badly mauled as my emotions were, I still tried, at first, to evade: "What do you mean, Mike? You *know* the reasons why: we'll gain valuable time if we just cut to the chase with them, and—"

"I'm not asking," he continued as if he hadn't heard me, his voice more sympathetic, now. "Because I know you won't tell me. *Yet.* All I'm saying is that I know you're pretty conflicted about this. I think I can guess why, but just promise me one thing: now that you've finally found some real happiness, here, and maybe I have, too; you won't go sabotaging our entire situation by taking on the powers that be over one case—a case that might not be worth it."

Once more, I was reminded of why Mike's and my fellowship had lasted so long. Stumbling badly in my attempt to answer his correct reading not only of my mind but of my heart, I finally said, "I know the dangers, Michael. But 'not worth it'? You and I both know that we made a deal a long time ago: maybe with the devil, maybe with some god, maybe just with the idea of justice as we understand it. But it is, in fact, the deal that we honor above all others. So—if this thing plays out safely, fine; if not, hey . . . we'll still be able to look ourselves in the mirror."

He nodded once, smiling grimly. "That's what I was afraid of," he said; but, having no wish to press the issue, he then turned to the photos again. "Right—so what do we do?"

I steeled myself: "We send out an e-mail to this group tonight, and stress that it is highly confidential, as it involves a real case. We ask them to go online before our classes tomorrow—I'd say noon, our time, but that's too cruel to Vicky. But she'll be *compos mentis* by eleven or so, which means two p.m., our time. Fine. We discuss the matter face-to-face. They're either all in, or all out."

"Why?" Mike indicated the pictures. "What if we can get, say, three out of the five?"

I shook my head. "Not good enough. The group's small enough, already, and even more importantly, the other two will know something's going on. We can't predict what's about to happen, or how public it's going to get. So far as they will know—unless and until they all agree—this is just an extra-credit opportunity we're offering to the five of them, in light of their continued exceptional achievements. Then, if they come on board, I figure it'll take them a day or so to go over the material. At that point, we'll have a nice synchronicity of all things: classes ending, our getting ready to go, Clarissa pulling the funding together from her bank, and the Augustines getting back from their cruise. And one more thing: they have to decide if they're in or they're out immediately. We can't let them think it over outside the conference."

"You afraid one of them will leak it?" Mike asked.

"Not intentionally—but they might ask an acquaintance, a relative, or a boyfriend or girlfriend for advice. We can't have that. They need to be ready right on the spot with answers."

"Don't worry," Mike answered. "Knowing this group, ready is one thing they will be . . ."

{iv.}

And the next day, we made sure we were ready, as well. At two p.m. Mike and I were side by side at the instructor's table in the JU-52, my partner having made sure that our webcam would get us both into frame in front of the black backdrop without any need to crowd ourselves. I'm not sure that some of our "guests" fully appreciated the gravity or the possibilities of the moment until they saw the pair of us together and facing them, along with how few of their own number had received invitations; when they did, the expressions on their faces indicated simultaneous uneasiness, respect, and varying degrees of excitement. We got greetings out of the way, and then Mike went straight to work, laying out the ground rules: none of them would have to do any further work (meaning take finals or write term papers) in our classes, although the job that we were asking would run beyond the end of the summer session. In addition, my partner said, they would all be granted highest marks in those courses simply for participating, while those of them that were receiving their degrees at the end of the session could expect particularly effusive job recommendations from both of us. This, it was plain, got the interest of all five fully ignited; but they were a canny group, and they figured there had to be a downside coming soon. As usual, that job was left to me:

This was not, I explained, an offer being made to each of them individually. They had all been picked for particular reasons, and that, combined with certain matters of security regarding Mike's and my own position within SUNY as well as our profession, dictated absolute secrecy. So, before any details would be released, the five of them would have to decide, on the spot and as a group, whether they were in or out. For their part, the candidates asked for a few moments to discuss the matter among themselves, a request we had anticipated: but the same basic rule applied: we didn't want them phoning anyone for advice about the offer. I told them that we would leave the "room," virtually speaking, for fifteen minutes: the sound in our system would be shut off, but we would leave our screens on, and they would be expected to remain visible if unheard as they talked. Then Mike and I pushed our chairs back and had a smoke as we watched the monitors.

"How do you rate the odds?" Mike asked eventually, studying the quintet. "Four to one?"

"Really? Who's your holdout?"

"Mei-lien, actually. And it's not because she isn't into the idea. But Chinese culture, dude, you do *not* deviate from the plan. Only bad things come of it."

"How would you know, I thought you were an American." I exhaled smoke and then shook my head. "No, they're all into it; and if they decide not to do it, it won't be because of anybody's culture. It'll be because it's a crazy fucking idea . . ."

Ten smoky minutes later and our sound was restored, after which the first to speak was Linda Walker, perhaps because she was the oldest of the group, perhaps because she was a genuine New Yorker and accustomed to putting things plainly:

"We all want to do it, obviously," she said, her enthusiasm tightly controlled. "And we're all honored by the opportunity. But there's just one thing."

"Just one?" I said.

"If this is, like you say, a real case," Frankie Arquilla continued, his big, powerful frame leaning forward toward his computer screen, "we're not gonna be *liable* for what we say, are we?"

"This is the only reservation," Mei-lien added, as softly as ever. "But it is an important one."

Mike and I gave each other a quick glance, then just as quickly turned back to our students. "What would make you think that there'd be any question of *your* liability?" I asked.

"Well, we *do* get MSNBC, even in Boston, Doctor," Colleen stated, quietly and evenly. "And the other networks, too. There's been quite a bit of—chatter . . ."

"And we're not utterly dense," Vicky added, smiling. "Even if some of us *are* blond and from California. A case that's achieved national attention? It could be dangerous."

"True," Mike said, before I could answer. "So, no: your names will never be mentioned."

They all glanced at one another on their computer monitors one more time, and exchanged nods. "Okay, then," Vicky said. "Looks like we're in."

"Good!" I replied, making no attempt to hide my enthusiasm. "In that case, Dr. Li will immediately transmit the case file—" Just then I caught sight of the second folder Mike had brought out the night before, the cover label of which I had not read; but its corresponding flash drive bore the same single word that was on the cover, scribbled with a Sharpie: *Cheetahfucker.*

I leaned over so that I would not be visible to the others as I whispered, "*'Cheetahfucker'?*"

"Hey, you know I always use code words for our cases, L.T.," Mike answered, smiling.

"But 'Cheetahfucker'?" I pressed, a little ticked off. "Will *they* see that?"

"Well, sure, I mean, the digital file's keyed to that password," Mike answered, still smiling at the students. "It was Lucas' idea, actually. I can change it now, but it'll take a few minutes—"

But I just shook my head. "Lucas' idea, my ass . . ." Remembering our students, I turned back to them, regaining my composure. "I beg your pardon—just clearing up the details of security. Dr. Li?"

"The case file is a little long," Mike said. "Don't bother trying to open it right off, it's encoded—I'll send the, uh, password in a separate e-mail, which will come from a second IP address, using a deliberate variant on a common junk mail subject heading: 'Russian Mail Order Husbands,' it'll say." All five students laughed: a good sign. "So keep checking your spam files."

"You'll have twenty-four hours for your evaluation," I said. "Then we'll meet again, same time."

Four of them looked taken aback; and Linda said, "That's seems like a tight schedule, Doctor."

"Perhaps, Linda," I answered. "But ask Colleen, who's actually worked in a crime lab. She seems less shocked—how long do profilers and techs often have to catch up on a case, Colleen?"

"Less than that," the quiet, scribbling Colleen agreed. "Sometimes . . ."

"Indeed. So it will be good practice for you all. Until tomorrow, then." I searched their faces rather sternly one last time. "And above all—surprise us, ladies. And, of course, gentleman . . ."

"Fuckin'-a-*right*." Frankie stacked his books with each of his next syllables: "Gen-tle-*man!*"

At that the screens began to go black; and, with the sudden realization of what we might have let loose on our little world, I simply sat back as Mike grabbed the laptop on the desk and began to transmit data to our five new advisors: our own little Privy Council, as we would come to call them.

"Is there any way," I mused, "that this could be both the best and the worst idea that we've ever come up with?"

"I don't know," Mike chuckled. "But we'll find out—and I'd say sooner, not later . . ."

The following twenty-four hours passed in a bizarre combination of hard work and emotional turmoil. Final classes were taught that same afternoon in a very relaxed atmosphere, my only real focus of hard judgment being how the five invited to become our Privy Councillors behaved around the rest of our students when participating in the ordinary debates of the day; but each was very smooth, never giving a thing away. On this unique note, the summer semester ended, Mike and I trying to behave as if we shared the collected groups' senses of relief at the coming time off. When all the screens had at last gone black, we turned at once to the tasks left to perform, that day and the following morning. Above all, we had to come up with a group of prioritized questions upon which we hoped our Councillors might shed at least some light when we met next. First, we would want to know if the five students had been able to detect any trace of duplicity in Derek Franco's behavior during the case prior to his leaving home; and if they *had* sensed such duplicity, had they gone on to postulate some kind of active role for the young man in the throwaways scheme? Would they conclude, as we had, that he had been a part, rather than a victim, of the circle that was responsible for procuring the kids and indoctrinating them for their journeys south?

The next area of focus would, we hoped, grow quickly out of the first: we would ask the quintet to put together a preliminary profile of the person directly above Derek, the person who had apparently made such lavish promises to him, as well as to the other dead children. This was a matter that had absorbed my particular attention in recent days, while Mike had been assembling his summary of the physical evidence for our case file. The profile that I had assembled had gone into two separate digital folders, one of which I showed to Mike and was perfectly prepared to share with our students. Its title had been of my partner's contrivance, going back to when we'd been discussing the last line of the script of *The Maltese Falcon:* "The Dream Stealer." It would offer an excellent test of the students' intuitive abilities, by determining if they, first, had detected the importance of the person in question, and, second, could add any valuable details to the profile, such as to what entities, if any, that person might in turn have been answering. But the second file I did not show Mike, even though I knew that it, too, would show us just how far the students had pushed their speculations. Yet it would also place an enormous strain on my own resolve; and I was praying that I would never need to reveal it. So it remained stored on a flash drive tucked safely into my vest pocket . . .

For two very tired minds, all this represented an excellent series of exercises to test the aptitude of the Privy Council. Now we needed to eat a calm meal and get some sound sleep: and with these concerns in mind, Mike finished locking away all the materials we'd used that day, while I went down into the hangar to defrost some meat for Marcianna. But there, waiting for me, was Ambyr, removing any hope that the evening would go as restfully as I'd planned. She stood very still just inside the hangar, listening to the sound made by my feet as it changed from the creaking of the steel treads to the shuffle of my prosthetic leg against the concrete floor, moved by my nagging hip.

"Clarissa," Ambyr began haltingly. "Clarissa sent me up to tell you guys to knock off for the night." She attempted to get a firmer grip on her emotions: "You know, for two guys who were trying to keep a secret, you were talking awful loud, up there . . ." It was a strange moment for me; and much would depend on what she said next: "You cut us out of this step, Trajan. You actually believe that Derek is *part* of this whole thing . . . After all we've been through—why?"

"Ambyr," I said gently, moving toward her but getting no reciprocal advance. "You've really never suspected it might be possible?"

She began to nod slowly, tears coming to the curtained violet eyes. "I guess I did. But it sounded like you guys have a lot more than suspicions."

I gently put a hand to her cane arm. "We'll know more tomorrow. Then we leave for New York. I didn't think Lucas should know while we're on this trip. He'll have enough to deal with."

"And me?" Ambyr asked, finally turning her face up to mine. "Why not tell me?"

"For your own sake," I lied. "If it turns out to be untrue, why make your suspicions worse, even for a day or two?"

She nodded, then wrapped her arms around my neck. "Oh, Trajan," she whispered. "Could I really have done that bad a job?"

It was hellish. "I—don't know" were the lame words I finally found;

then, to repair them, I added, "I mean, I don't know if *anyone* could have made up for what his family did; I just don't know if that's a hole that can be filled." *But it would have made him an easy kid to manipulate,* I mused.

"Yeah," she answered, sniffling tears away. She moved her face around to kiss me tenderly, even gratefully, for saying what I had aloud. "I appreciate that. And you did right, I know, not telling Lucas. If Derek *is* involved, baby brother will be a basket case."

"Very true," I said, returning her kiss and holding her tightly, tightly enough, I prayed, to make everything that had happened, that was going to happen in the coming days, simply cease to be real. Such are the moments that are the most self-deceptive, when we believe that we can remove a passionate love from space and time: two forces that will always reassert themselves . . .

"I assume you're going to feed the crazy girl?" Ambyr eventually asked, holding my face in her hands gently. After I'd tilted my head slowly up and down within that sweet grasp, she lightly moved her fingers down to my chest. "Okay—I'll go down and tell them you're on the way, baby." And then, with that lightning-swift change in tone of which she was such a master, she whispered into my ear: *"But don't you ever lie to me again . . ."* She brought her head back around to kiss me again, her voice softening once more: "Remember that I've had about enough of being lied to, and about enough of being used. Got it?" Then she turned away. "I'll see you at dinner," she said, smiling in that devilish way of hers; then she raised her voice to call out, "You too, Mike!"

Mike's head popped out of the JU-52. "Hmm? What's that? Oh—see you at dinner, Ambyr!"

Once she was starting down the path to the barns, Mike descended the steel steps. "Whew," he whispered. "I thought maybe *I* was gonna catch it, too."

"Were you listening to that entire exchange?" I asked, as I cranked up the microwave.

"Well, what the fuck did you *expect,* L.T.? I tried not to, but it's very quiet in this place; and I wasn't going to come down and get *my* ass kicked. Besides, what're you worried about, you're golden."

"Thank you, Michael, as ever," I said slowly, pulling the warm meat from the oven.

"Seriously—she's nuts about you. But she's tough, too, and you know why as well as I do. But take it from one who knows—you two are solid.

You've just forgotten what it's like to be in a relationship, not that you were *ever* in a relationship with a woman that's got her kind of class."

I paused before leaving the hangar. "You really believe that?"

Mike laughed. "Trajan, for fuck's sake, look at your record: that crazy nightmare who was your last girlfriend, all the nightmares before that, when all you were really looking for was somebody to give you a little fucking comfort and empathy after all those lousy years of goddamned pain." He shook his head. "And *unlike* all those nutjobs in the city, this girl *knows* you, L.T., she's *been* in your hell. At the same time, though, she demands real respect. And it freaks you the fuck out."

As he walked over to me, I just stood there, a bit nonplussed. "How the hell do *you* see all this?"

"I see it, asshole, because I've watched all of it happen, since way back. *Anybody* would have seen it, except you. Look, go feed your other girlfriend—but don't take too long. Sounds like we'd better not be late for dinner tonight." He clasped my shoulder with his free hand and grinned. "Plus, it sounds to me like you're gonna get lucky, on one of your last nights of real freedom . . ."

On that note, I turned and left the hangar at a very slow pace, making my way up to Marcianna's enclosure in like manner. I followed Mike's advice, though, and didn't spend long inside the fence: just as much as was necessary to reassure Marcianna that everything between us was all right. Then I returned to the farmhouse, went to my room, washed up some, got a fresh shirt on, and finally made my way down toward the dining room, where the others were already assembled. Clarissa, Mike, and Lucas appeared to be having a jolly enough time, while Ambyr was clearly waiting for me to get there before she relaxed entirely. Once I had and she did, dinner passed very pleasantly for us all; a slightly unreal atmosphere, given what the coming days held in store.

"All right," I eventually said, levering myself upright with my cane and the grip I had on the table once the last postprandial drinks had been consumed. "I think that's about it, for tonight—"

"*Ah-ah-ah,*" Clarissa warned. "I'm afraid I can't let you off quite so easily, nephew. The rest of you, scurry along to your rooms. I need a brief word, Trajan."

My heart sank a little at the thought of what might be coming. Mike said good night to everyone, and Lucas did likewise; then my spirits lifted a little when Ambyr slowed as she neared me, paused by my side, and folded the fingers of her right hand tight into mine, letting the top of her head brush ever so lightly against my cheek.

"I'll see you later?" she asked.

Clarissa was deliberately staring down at the table to afford us a moment, so I tilted my head over and kissed Ambyr's cheek softly, a move she returned with that desperate hunger of hers. "Of course," I said; then she followed the others, long since having learned to navigate the stairs and halls.

My great-aunt indicated the seat next to hers. "Park it, nephew." I did as told. "Trajan," she said quietly. "I wanted to make this very clear, but not in front of the others—*don't screw this up.*"

I couldn't help but chuckle, a bit exhaustedly. "Which 'this' do you mean, Clarissa?"

"Not the Kurtzes—you know they'll be welcome here, for as long as it takes. But this case. I can *just* finance your trip to New York; but you and Mike have *got* to maintain your incomes. So don't let anything jeopardize you with the university. Do you understand what I'm saying?"

"We're aware, Aunt," I said, chuckling again and rising back up. "It is constantly on both our minds. And we wouldn't want you to have us on those terms, believe me." I kissed the top of her head. "We're walking a very thin line—don't think we don't know it."

"Yes," she replied. "You certainly are . . ."

Touching her hand as she nodded once or twice, I began the long walk toward the staircase, knowing how difficult what she'd just said to me must have been for her, and how very true it was: Shiloh, however it may have looked to outsiders, was a relatively small farm, and, like all small farms, it was a shoestring operation. Every mouth fed had to belong to a contributing body, and Clarissa was already stretching things for Ambyr and Lucas. Such were all unpleasantly hard truths; and recapitulating them inside my head was a process that bore down on me with increasing weight as I made my way upstairs and into my room, where I barely had time to get my clothes and my prosthesis off before, without realizing it, I fell into a deep sleep.

I was brought around by a feeling to which I still hadn't readjusted: a powerful warmth along the whole of my body. I became conscious of it even before I was fully awake, for it utterly invaded the dream state that I had achieved. It was Ambyr, of course, herself naked and holding tight against the back of me in the bed. I rolled over sleepily, finding that I was much more rested than I would have thought possible, considering the hour or so that I believed I'd been asleep.

"What time is it?" I whispered to her, seeing darkness outside.

"Four a.m.," she replied, beginning to move those tender yet strong hands all over me. "You've been out a long time—so have I. Doesn't seem like it, does it?"

"No," I answered, rolling over toward her. "But that's a good thing. We both needed it."

"Yes, sweet one," she whispered, touching her lips to mine, as a warm breeze that had begun to blow in the afternoon kicked up once again through the window. Her embrace became tighter, her kisses more determined, and each of us simply faded away into the night.

The night, where in the distance, for reasons I was once again unable to explain, Marcianna began to issue that strange chirrup of hers . . .

{v.}

At the appointed hour on the following day, throughout which a heavy, humid but quiet rain fell, Mike and I locked ourselves into the JU-52, using the usual interior hatch mechanism. Then we sat at the desk once again and the screens opposite us came alive with the faces of our Council. Mike had so configured our laptop that just by slapping the space bar we could mute any sound we might be making, and I asked him, after he explained this prudent measure, to pull the framing of our camera shot back farther than it had been the day before, to allow me to be seen when I began inevitably pacing behind our desk: I knew that the subjects under discussion would require my most focused thinking, which always occurred when I was unencumbered by the pain of a chair.

"Good afternoon, all," I announced, touching the hard copy of the case file that lay on the desk between Mike and me. "I trust you've had time to go over the materials thoroughly."

"Yes, I think so," Linda Walker said, taking the lead again, with the somehow always-imposing backdrop of the faded, dirty yellow brick of the Bronx project in which she lived clearly visible through the window before which she sat.

"One question though, Doctor," Frankie Arquilla noted, double-checking his printout. "Why 'Cheetahfucker'?"

That set the others laughing a little, which was another healthy indicator: because, quite contrary to the grim moods that are often displayed by television shows, humor during the process of a murder investigation is a quality necessary to the preservation of sanity; and so, instead of discouraging the reaction, I smiled and tried to join in it. "That is Professor Li's idea of funny," I said to them all, smiling. "Due to the fact—"

"Due to the fact," Mei-lien Hsüeh cut in softly, her accent taking the hard edges off many of her consonants, "that five years ago, you received a permit to keep a cheetah, one that no refuge would accept due to feline leukemia, on your great-aunt's farm." She held up a copy of the permit. "With respect, sir, it is a matter of public record."

"Well done, Mei-lien," Mike chuckled. "How did you find time to dig that up?"

"It took very little time, Dr. Li," Mei-lien answered. "And was easily downloaded."

"Well, then," I pronounced. "The bar has already been set rather high, in terms of research—"

"But why do you even *have* a cheetah, Doctor?" Vicky Ferrier asked, those West Coast features full of puzzled concern. "I mean—aren't we supposed to be *discouraging* private ownership of exotic animals?"

"We are," I said, trying to move quickly past it; to which end I related, in as few words as possible, Marcianna's history. "So you see, Vicky," I concluded, "it was either bring her here or watch her get a fatal needle in her vein. And I couldn't bear the second option. But yes, if I were to find out that, say, Frankie, was hiding a tiger in his Arizona apartment, I would have to report him."

"Okay," Mike added. "So much for the cheetah fucker—for 'Cheetah-fucker,' sorry. What were your general reactions to the rest of the case?"

"Just one more thing about the materials," said Vicky—the sole member of the Council who had graduated that summer—as she looked through her own notes. "Was it really necessary to send us the links to those porn clips without identifying them? I mean, that was some disturbing stuff."

"Exactly the point, Vick," Mike answered. "Would you have believed they existed, without seeing them? And would you have watched them, if you'd known what they were?"

Vicky drew in a long, sad breath as she looked up. "Probably not," she conceded.

"And remember," I added, "that's just what's publicly available on *free* sites; the stuff that can get you arrested if you subscribe to it is far worse, as you'll likely learn during your career. But it's important that you understand how large the—*market* for such things is. As well as the market for such children. In addition, you needed to know why the Patricks were such easy prey for the state. I'm sorry if you thought we meant to offend, Vicky, but—"

"No, no," Vicky answered, waving me off. "I get it. But, *man . . .*" She shook her head and flicked a long strand of golden hair behind her ear. "Pretty tough to take."

"Indeed," I told her. "So—anybody else with an initial comment?"

"Well," Colleen said softly, her hand never seeming to lift from the business of taking notes, "I'd like to point one thing out: somebody involved in this case has been playing pretty fast and loose with the law, Professors. And it looks to me like it must be somebody high placed."

"Okay, Colleen," I replied, inwardly glad to hear her say as much. "Explain."

She shrugged. "I just don't see how the ME alone could have suppressed the theory that this tech who got killed, Kolmback, put forward, about Shelby Capamagio being murdered by a serial killer. Medical examiners can't shut up a whole department—not unless they *want* to be shut up. No, I'd say his own superiors tried to discourage Kolmback as soon as he had the idea, probably right after the Kozersky girl died; yet they were simultaneously *discouraging* any other theories that were being put forward. The whole thing doesn't appear consistent: they allowed the idea of a serial killer to get loose, but wanted no actual proof of it. So, in effect, they were deliberately trying to *prevent* any actual solution from being reached. But getting back to Kolmback, the head of the FIC, this Nancy Grimes, seems to have pulled him in tight and kept him isolated, by making him the tech at all five crime scenes. Kolmback probably thought that it was a step up, at first; then, by the time he figured out that he'd been made part of a plot to hide a scandal that most people don't even know about, and that his bosses were determined the public would *never* know about . . . it was too late."

Both Mike and I breathed a little easier: she had hit on all cylinders, which meant that they had indeed done their homework. "Impressive, Colleen," I said. "Particularly in your analysis of the seemingly contradictory aims of law enforcement, which I believe will be clarified, among this group. Anything more—anybody?"

"Yeah," Frankie said, half-lifting one hand. "Since at least some of these 'runaway parents' seem to be coming to my part of the U.S., I gotta ask: what is *up* with that? 'Throwaway children'? It's really, officially recognized as a category of homeless kids in New York State? That is *crazy*."

"Check the Arizona Department of Child Safety, Frankie," Mike said. "See if it's there, too."

"I did," Frankie answered, looking mildly insulted. "It ain't, Doc. They got *throwaways* just like most states, but that's just another name for kids who've been chucked outta their houses."

"Correct," I replied. "An entirely different category."

"Right," Frankie said with a nod. "But 'throwaways'? Nothing."

"How deep did you dig?" Mike asked.

"Doc." Frankie's indignant look spread into a confident smile. "This is *me*, Frankie Arquilla—"

"Oh, Jesus," I heard Colleen breathe in annoyed familiarity as she scribbled on.

"You *know* I am the master of research," Frankie continued, either not having heard his classmate from Boston or pretending that he hadn't. "I checked all through their Web files, I called them, I even went down to the nearest office, hit up somebody I deal with there sometimes. And they never heard of it. *Nunca*."

"I suppose they *may* have been telling the truth," I answered. "It hasn't been officially recognized in some states—but the mere contention should give you an idea of exactly how desperate the New York authorities are to keep this case from involving that subject. Even the explanation that a serial killer of children was at work would be preferable—if indeed any explanation had to be officially endorsed—so far as our governor is concerned."

"And then there's *that*," Linda said, a little reluctantly. "One of us, at least, might like to get a job in New York State, someday, or even with the Feds—and you imply at one point, with supporting evidence, that the cover-up might extend that far. It's not that I doubt it; in fact we may have more facts to support it. But are we sure our security measures are good enough?"

"We should be fine on that score, Linda," Mike cut in, nodding quickly. "Skype's encryption protocols are already fairly good, although technically hackable. But I've backed them up with some of my own."

"Okay—what else?" I asked, getting impatient and uncomfortable in my chair, then standing to begin pacing. "Let's open with the theory that the deaths were all suicides: any argument?"

Vicky cleared her throat, her rather dazzling blue eyes locking with mine. "No, we can't find any reason to argue with that, Doctor. The only one that might be open to question is the mummified boy—"

"Whose death does not form a part of the core of this case," I said quickly. "As harsh as it may sound, his importance lies elsewhere."

"We understand that, Dr. Jones," Vicky volleyed, with a peculiar sense of warning. "And we'll return to it. But there are immediate questions about the circumstances of his death that we found striking. First of all, mummification: we've never heard of that process being involved in a modern case, and certainly not as a tool for some frame by law enforcement."

"Though we oughtta emphasize that we've heard of state bureaus doing frame-ups with kids' *bodies* before—right, Collie?" Frankie teased.

"My name is *Colleen*, Frankie," she said, still quietly, but with some annoyance. "And I'm from Boston, remember? There aren't many kinds of frames that I *haven't* heard of. But this one is new."

"Yet 'new' is often the rule, in this racket," I added. "And so, Vicky—do you have a point?"

"Only that you seem to have been so preoccupied, maybe understandably, with the boy's condition, with the BCI's using him, and finally with your *own* plan to use him to defeat that scheme, that, well . . ." Her face became very quizzical, but something more, too; it was just a touch, I was sad to see, disillusioned. "It never occurred to you to dig any deeper? Into why a kid would choose that method of suicide, assuming it *was* a suicide? Or into his background and circumstances? Maybe contact his family?"

"We were split on this one, by the way," Linda added. "While we understand how Vicky and Colleen felt, Frankie, Mci-lien, and I also got why you pursued the course you did. You knew that the BCI would have had the name of the boy and his contact information, and you assumed, or at least the three of us assume that *you* assumed, that the county law— Sheriff Spinetti and Deputy Steinbrecher—would get hold of it, too, and pass it on."

"Correct, Linda," Mike said. "*Or,* Spinetti and Steinbrecher would find out about the kid *before* the BCI, which would have been even better."

"Hmm," Vicky noised, still more than a little judgmentally. "And did they do either thing?"

"Not yet," I said, somewhat elusively. "But if you've learned something that can speed that process, we would of course be anxious to hear it."

"We have and we can," Colleen said, flipping a few pages in her notes to check and earmark something. "But we'll get back to that . . ."

"And you may not be as anxious to hear our opinions as you think," Vicky added.

"No?" I slowed my pace, then came to a stop and locked onto Vicky's sapphire stare again. "Look, no cat-and-mouse games, here, any of you: if you have something to say, let's hear it."

"Well," Colleen replied, "we need to do that by moving to a different topic, one that we think is very basic to how you have conducted the case, and to how officials in your state have responded. But Mei-lien is going to take it from here for a bit."

"Thank you, Colleen," Mei-lien said, as gently as ever. "Yes, and so, I must turn our attention not to the dead children that are being referred to as 'throwaways,' in this case, but to the three living examples: the Kurtz family. The young woman, Ambyr, and the two boys for whom she has served as guardian, Lucas Kurtz and Derek Franco. First, if I may be allowed to review, you made the boy Lucas a part of your investigative team: we all understand what you hoped to gain from that, from having so young an agent monitoring his peers in the locality, and advising you of their habits. And we have agreed that it was a safe decision. Also, as I have already told my colleagues, I come from a different part of the world, where childhood has a different meaning, and where children are often employed for such purposes. So it was perhaps less shocking to me than to them."

Which was why, I now saw, they were letting her take the lead. "That's very understanding of you, Mei-lien," I said, despite a feeling of growing unease. "Next?"

"Next, yes, there is Lucas' sister, Ambyr Kurtz. You decided to involve her, as well, for reasons that are somewhat more . . ." Mei-lien searched hard for a tactful word: ". . . *complex.*"

"Though we agree that it was another good move," Frankie added. "So was bringing her and Lucas to your farm, where they'd be safe from the law, along with the kind of media crap that they got a look at that morning when you held your—*briefing.*"

"Delighted you agree," I said, ever more concerned about the meeting's shifting initiative. "But where is all this recapitulation going? Because it *does* have a purpose, I'm sensing."

"Yes, Doctor," Mei-lien answered. "It is simply that we are attempting to approach these subjects tactfully. However, our first concern centers on the member of the rather unusual Kurtz family about whom you at least made your uncertainties clear in the dossier."

"Derek Franco," I said, perplexed: for if they knew we'd been clear about Derek, what was it that they thought, perhaps even knew, we'd been *un*clear about?

"Yes, Doctor," Mei-lien replied. "You present two possible scenarios for his behavior between the time that you, Dr. Jones, first met him, and the night of his disappearance. The first is that he was simply terrified of anything that could lead to a further disruption of his life with the Kurtzes, and so he wished to keep his distance from you—in all ways. The second suggests that he was avoiding you because he was busy selecting likely children as targets—I believe you used the word 'facilitator'?"

"Correct, Mei-lien," I replied. "We did conclude that Derek had been playing that role. We just wanted to see if the facts we outlined led you to the same conclusion."

"Ah," Mei-lien noised with a slow, relieved nod. "I see. Well, then, we may say he was indeed acting—despite his emotional and intellectual difficulties—as this same facilitator for the throwaway-children plot. Now, concerning his disappearance: the principal questions seem to be, When did he learn the full dimensions of that same plot? And how? And when he discovered everything, did he immediately demand to be placed with a willing family? Is that why the others were forced to listen? And to whom, *specifically,* did he make that demand? These are more complex questions . . ." Mei-lien paused uncomfortably, putting her notes down. "We were very impressed by your analysis of the boy's fixation on the photographs in your house. We agree that he possessed an extreme need for a loving female figure in his life, and that, because his own mother had refused to play that role, he became vulnerable to the manipulations of other women. This seems plain. But I fear where we disagree with you—and you must forgive my presumption, here, if it is such—but we do not agree that there was only *one* woman. He had a contact, certainly—a 'handler,' is the term?"

"It is," I answered, rather rigidly.

"Thank you, Doctor." Given Mei-lien's evident unease, I wondered just how long the others would let her continue; but continue she did: "But this handler could not have been the *sole* woman involved in the hierarchy of the throwaway organization. There must—and we *all* feel very strongly about this—there must have been a *second* woman involved, one of influence: a woman who could have made Derek believe that she could fulfill his dream *on her own authority* and immediately, just as soon as he demanded it. The handler, being someone from the immediate area, and someone that Derek knew well, could not have done that, and Derek—given his own organizational position—would have known as much. But this second woman, being of significantly greater power, would, until this moment, have in fact been unknown to him, to preserve her own safety: especially because Derek's emotional instability made him a particular risk. Yet she would have had to have been able to project those key qualities at the moment of her revelation: beauty, compassion, seduction."

"Oh, *fuck*," Mike whispered in dread, forgetting to mute our laptop's microphones. "I know where this is going, damn it all . . ."

I began to nod, now feeling a complete return of all the dread that had struck me when Mike and I had driven back from examining Curtis' body. "Which means," I said, "that when Derek demanded to leave, the handler was taken out of the loop, and the usual chain of command in the organization was temporarily suspended."

"Precisely," Mei-lien said, again very relieved. "Suspended by its senior members. What we do not yet know is *why*."

There was a momentary lull; and then, blood pounding in my ears, I reached into my vest pocket, withdrawing another flash drive as I said, "You know, Mei-lien—the others are lucky to have you. I'm not certain that anyone who hasn't experienced firsthand just how brutal bureaucracies can be would have arrived at these conclusions . . ." Mei-lien only nodded slightly again as I pulled the laptop on the desk closer to me. "So: if you will all please observe your mail files, I am going to send a second document to you, one that represents my most recent profiling work on the case. It is titled—"

But before I could finish my statement or slip the USB drive into its port on the laptop, I felt Mike grasp my arm uncontestably. Without looking at me, he smiled what seemed genuinely to the students. "Excuse us for a minute, will you, people? I don't think that Dr. Jones and I quite have our—*schedules* coordinated. Talk among yourselves for a moment, but don't make any phone calls; and remember, I *am* recording this entire event." Then he slapped the space bar on the laptop and rose, proceeding immediately behind the black backdrop. I could only nod in agreement and follow; for I'd been careful to keep the contents of the second flash drive from my partner, and indeed had intended to show them to no one, until there was no other option. Thus by the time I joined Mike behind the screen, I was not surprised to see him scowling grimly.

"Give me that," he said, pointing at my hand.

"Mike—you don't even know what's on it."

"Which would be reason enough, L.T.: I've got the right to look it over before they do. But that's not the real point." Very seldom during our time working together had Mike ever confronted me so angrily: "You're not the only member of this damned partnership, asshole—and it doesn't take a fucking *sorcerer* to know what you're about to do. Jesus, L.T., this is *exactly* what I was talking about: don't, just *don't* do this, not until we've tried everything else!"

I studied him: *He hasn't got it,* I realized, *any more than they do; not all of it.* "Meaning what?"

"*What?*" he said. "Listen to what Mei-lien's saying, dude: she's calling the law out! And maybe they've got all the details right, maybe not. But please, at least let them finish it, before you send it."

"And let them look even more like they're schooling us than they already do?" I said. "Which will make them buy into all the bad habits of *forensic* investigators? Come on, Mike—there are still lessons for them to learn: as important as any, maybe."

Mike considered that for a moment, glancing at the floor and then back at me. "And you've thought the consequences through? Not just for yourself, but for *everybody* around here? Because, damn it, Trajan, I've spent five years watching you beat yourself up over how we handled that situation in New York. We move forward on this line now, with anything other than rock-solid proof, and I'll end up watching you do it for five more years. And I really *don't* want to see that."

I took a moment to pause, myself. It went without saying that his concern was warranted, even if his suspicions were incomplete; but unfortunately there stood in our way, as I had told him only days earlier, the idea of justice as we understood it. "I'll tell you what I'll do," I said, sensing that our Privy Councillors were getting restive. "I'm going to put this into the computer, and send the document along. *If* the group is clearly reaching the same conclusion, they can open it and I'll expand on the subject. If they don't . . . well, hell, I'll *still* tell them to open it and then expand on the subject. There's no other way, Mike—it's why we set this exercise in motion. But okay, I'll give them the chance to show their stuff first."

Mike took a deep breath, released it slowly, and said, "I never saw anybody so damned anxious to flirt with disaster . . ." He started back to the partition. "But I guess you're right. So come on."

Once we were reseated, Mike hit the space bar on the laptop again. "All right, people," he began. "Here's how we're going to proceed: Dr. Jones is going to transmit to you a final document, but we've got to ask that you don't open it until we give the okay."

"Then why send it at all?" Vicky asked skeptically. "Why not just tell us what it says?"

"Because we want to make sure you *have* these facts, Vicky," I replied, "along with any you've come up with yourselves. If something happens to Dr. Jones and myself, it will be up to the five of you to take this case on and make sure justice is done." Each of them grew visibly more apprehensive, at that. "We don't anticipate any such thing occurring, of course; but we leave for New York tomorrow, to contact the couple you have already studied in the dossier, Roger and Ethel Augustine. And one never knows what the results of such confrontations can or will be. I've done my own humble job of encoding the file. You'll need the password, *The Faust Dialectic*, to open it."

"*The Faust Dialectic?*" Linda said. "Didn't we—?"

"We did, Linda," I replied, "and thank you for remembering, as it *was* last year. But the concept remains as deceptively simple as it was then: basic dialectical thinking. I'm sure you already have ideas as to its application here, but hold them, for the time being, until our discussion leads us there. All right? On its way, then . . ." And at last I inserted the drive into the laptop and sent its contents firing along their way, knowing full well how terrible the consequences of the act could ultimately be. "Everybody receive it?" They all nodded in turn, still too apprehensive to speak. "Good. Then we'll go on with Mei-lien's summary."

The nervous young woman managed to recover her poise with greater speed than the others: more evidence of someone who had grown up in a world where harsh realities of the body and soul were commonplaces. "Thank you, Doctor. And so we return to the subject of the mummified boy."

"The mummified boy?" Mike said. "Mei-lien, we'll be happy to hear whatever you have to say, on that score, but I should warn you: we're really more concerned with preventing the *next* tragedy than we are with solving that one, right now. Because, as Dr. Jones has said, the mummified kid's death is not central to this case."

"Which is precisely our point, Dr. Li," Mei-lien answered. "You have been so focused on the possible dangers to the Kurtzes that you have overlooked the possibility that the mummified boy's *life* may have been a tragedy crucial to the case—despite his death already having occurred—and you have also overlooked the possibility that the story of his final days may hold critical clues to Derek Franco's fate."

Mike looked suddenly surprised: we had asked our Council to give us perspective on the moves we'd already made during the case, and for insight into what moves should come next; we *hadn't* been looking for the five to point out things that we might have missed entirely. What my partner didn't yet know, however, was that I *hadn't* missed them; especially the worst and most important of them. The keys were waiting in that last file: the tale of the mummified boy's final days, as Mei-lien had said. Yet I would, for my own selfish reasons, gladly have left that story in electronic limbo . . .

{vi.}

"In addition," our budding expert from Kunming continued, "you seem to have been determined not to repeat such errors as may have led to the attack on Dr. Grace Chang—"

"*What?*" Mike said reflexively; and there was no hint of flirtation in his voice, now. "Mei-lien—are you saying that you've actually *investigated* Dr. Chang's accident?"

"We have," she replied. "Enough to know that it was not, in all probability, an accident. And I have been in contact with her only this morning. I apologize if you consider this improper. I did not realize until I spoke to her that the two of you were quite so—*close* . . ."

Mike covered his mouth and whispered to me, "Damn, L.T., I thought *you* were the one who was going to take shit for being too personally tangled up in this thing . . ."

"Please be certain," Mei-lien rushed to say, "that our purpose is not to embarrass either of you; we merely wish to point out that your personal concerns *may* have blinded you to important clues, particularly where Derek Franco is concerned. Therefore—the mummified boy."

"Who *had* a name," Frankie said, in a manner that exhibited a kind of protectiveness for the dead youth. Glancing down to double-check his own notes, he continued: "He was—"

But I was through having the tables turned: "His name was Danny Gunderson," I said. "Fifteen years old, from the town of Essex, located in the county of the same name." As Mike looked at me in amazement, I added, "So, again, let's just drop the 'gotcha' tone, and you give us the facts that *you* know, straight."

None of them had been any more ready for my awareness than had Mike: *"Chido,"* Frankie said reflexively, smiling. "You *are* the man, Doc . . . Okay, well, Danny Gunderson lived with foster parents, as I guess you know. The couple runs a snack shop on the marina in Essex: it's a shithole, doesn't take in much, so they foster kids to 'augment their income.' Danny, though, was no boat boy: liked to hitchhike up to some pretty serious caves to the west, go exploring. About half that hitch, by the way, is on Route 22, which, if you keep going south on it, puts you in Surrender— looks like you were right about the whole copycat method thing."

"But, Frankie, how . . ." Mike began uncertainly; and then, glancing at me, he went on: "How can *any* of you possibly know all this? The cops didn't tell you, I'm assuming."

"No, they didn't," Frankie answered. "We found it all—Linda and me did."

"Yes," Linda said. "The trail began with a bunch of credit card charges: all at one spot, and all on one card—a card belonging to Ambyr Kurtz."

I had known the words were coming; but my heart still sank when I actually heard them, and I tried one last evasion: "Ambyr? She hasn't been outside Burgoyne County in—well, four to six months, anyway. Which she would need to have been, given the period required for the mummification process."

"We know that, too," said Linda. "But she *is* blind, Derek could've taken the card without too much—trouble . . ."

And that was that: I turned down to stare at the desk before me, knowing I must begin: "He didn't take it," I said quietly. "She gave it to him . . ."

Stunned silence reigned, until Linda finally noised, "Oh?" After a few more seconds, she continued, very carefully: "Well—whatever the case, the owners of the only establishment where we know he used it told me that they recalled a 'pretty slow kid' who said it was his mother's. And that place wasn't in Essex, it was at a takeout joint, China King, in Cambridge. That's in Washington County, north of Burgoyne and Rensselaer. About twenty miles up Route 22 from Surrender."

"Holy fuck," Mike murmured. "I've *been* there."

"We know that, too," Linda said. "Your card is also in their records. But it was *not* used at the same time as Ambyr Kurtz's. Danny Gunderson, however, had his own MasterCard, which was given to him according to a pattern that you must both find depressingly familiar, by now: his parents disappeared, leaving him plastic that had been put in his name, and which was guaranteed by them, despite the fact that soon they just—didn't exist. As long as the interest was paid on time, though, the credit company didn't care what Danny's circumstances were. Or, unfortunately, how the money was raised."

"You are fucking *kidding* me," Mike blurted. "The mummified boy was *also* a throwaway child?"

"That idea *never* occurred to you?" Vicky replied; and it was becoming ever clearer that, while the others were doing the talking, she and Colleen were the ones scrutinizing my partner and especially me the most, the one with her eyes, the other with her ears.

Realizing this, I flattened my tone even more: "No one said it didn't, Vicky."

"So it did?" Colleen finally glanced up from her notes quickly. "To *both* of you?"

"Immaterial to your report," I answered stiffly. "Presumably, then, Frankie gained Ambyr's credit card number through his usual mysterious methods, and the location gave you the name of the Gunderson boy, once you'd made the cross-reference at the restaurant?"

"We caught a lucky break, there," Frankie answered with a nod. "The two split the bills on their cards. And the owners remembered them, because there's just a few tables in the place, it's mostly takeout and the guys stayed for hours every time. Both of them mentioned hitching to get there. So that let us access Danny's card history. Anyway—Linda?"

"I researched the Gunderson boy," Linda continued, "and found out he was a missing child—a family he stayed with whenever he ran away from the fosters finally reported it."

"A family?" I asked dourly; but she only looked back at me quizzically. "An inter-agency police report requested by Sheriff Spinetti revealed that that 'family' consisted of one middle-aged man who was believed to be a child molester, and who lived with a *non compos mentis* mother."

"Well, well . . ." Linda answered with an appreciative nod. "That would probably explain it: Danny's body was found in one of those caves Frankie mentioned—a crevasse deep, narrow, and cold enough to protect it from predators, and to allow the mummification process. The discovery was a complete accident: a group of cavers with oxygen tanks spotted it. Now it would, admittedly, have been fairly easy for somebody else to stage the event, by cramming his body down there."

"I doubt that," Mike said, trying to get over his amazement. "There were no marks or deformities indicating that any force was used."

"Okay." Linda gave Mike that same nod of esteem, this time. "Just an accident, then. An accident that happened to occur to a kid who'd probably developed a fairly pronounced sense of risk, of disregard for his own safety. And so—case closed, at least on the Gunderson story."

I took a deep breath, then lit a cigarette. "Yes. And it is indeed a depressingly familiar tale, although the first to actually illustrate the failures of the foster care program—which is vital to understanding why the others took the path they did. So, well done, all of you."

"I've got one more question, though," Mike said, his voice betraying, or so I feared, ever deeper disappointment in my having kept things from him. "What does Derek Franco's recruitment, or attempted recruitment, of the Gunderson boy tell us that we didn't suspect already?"

"'*Suspect*' being the key word, Doctor," Colleen answered. Then she added only, "Vicky?"

And it was at last time for Vicky to deliver what she had plainly been thinking would be her knockout blow: "You must realize, Doctors, that Derek's interaction with Danny Gunderson not only offers a more complete picture of *his* activities, but of the methods used by the organization above him. For instance, the geographical profile developed by Dr. Chang—yes, she told Mei-lien about it—has to be expanded to include at least Washington and Essex Counties. Also, you can't say how many kids this group may have smuggled south *since* Derek Franco disappeared;

meaning, during the period that the Kurtzes have been staying on your farm. All of which you would have known, if you hadn't been so caught up with making your own little world up there, complete with—"

But even Mike had had enough of Vicky's tone, now: "Okay, okay, damn it. Listen, Vick—all of you—there hasn't been a minute when our personal activities have blinkered our pursuit of a solution to this case. Period. So to quote my esteemed colleague, just drop—"

I touched Mike's shoulder, however, somewhat intrigued by Vicky's words, as well as by her attitude: she'd found something, all right, but she hadn't found *it*. And there was at least meager comfort in that. "So that's your big issue with us, Vicky?" I said. "You think that Dr. Li and I have been swanning around like a couple of lovestruck boys, just attending to the case when we could find the time—I mean, between classes and romancing and all? And tell me this: has it seemed to any of you that we've done a below-par job of teaching at any point in this session?"

And with that, the initiative began to swing back: the three who had never had much interest in Vicky's accusations to start with—Linda, Frankie, and Mei-lien—became very uncomfortable, and even Colleen paused, glancing up at her ceiling as she considered the question. They all quietly answered in the negative, but Vicky, sticking to her guns, declared, "Well, whatever the quality of the classes, the quality of the investigation was slipshod—I'm not backing off that."

"As opposed to your own, Vicky?" I said, to which she nodded emphatically. "Watch out, now that you've graduated, Ms. Ferrier: tunnel vision, cognitive bias, whatever you want to call it, can get you in deep trouble, if you're overinvested in a personal motive."

"What?" Vicky's jaw dropped. "*Me?* That's been *your* problem!"

"So you've thought," I said, nodding. "But you've been wrong."

"Not if you apply the Theory of Context, I'm not," Vicky shot back. "Which, you'll remember, Dr. Jones, was the subject of my thesis." For a moment I considered Vicky's very skilled command of a hundred-year-old philosophy, and her ability to make it work regarding several notorious modern cases: context—to Vicky as to me, just as to the man who had founded the school, Laszlo Kreizler—was everything; and context was obviously what she honestly thought she was pursuing at that moment. Not the context of the killer, nor even of the victim, but context in its most elusive yet often most intriguing form: the context of the investigator, the biases that make the detective pursue some leads and underplay or flat-out ignore others. And just then it was Vicky herself who was slipping up, and handing me a rare opportunity, bitter though it was.

"Indeed I do remember," I answered. "And it was a first-rate piece of work. Which is more, I fear, than I can say for your present reasoning." I glanced around the screens. "What about the rest of you? Do you hold to this idea that Dr. Li and I have been blinded by our personal lives?"

"Well, Doctor," Linda answered cautiously, "Vicky did make a compelling case . . ."

"But I got a feeling that case ain't gonna hold up, Vicky *manita*," Frankie added.

Colleen had suddenly gripped her forehead. "*The Faust Dialectic*—damn it, Vicky . . ."

I looked to Mike quickly. He'd determined at last what I was up to, but he knew he couldn't stop me; so he just shrugged as I replied, "Okay—now would be the time to open the file I sent you."

"*The Faust Dialectic* . . ." Colleen repeated bitterly, scanning the short but crucial document within the file. "*Fuck*. At first I assumed you meant Derek—I guess we all did. But you're saying . . . ?"

I traced an invisible line on the desk with one finger—then cut it. "Yes. It refers, in this instance, to Ambyr Kurtz. *She* was Derek Franco's handler. *She* sent him, credit card in hand, to meet with Danny Gunderson, after Danny heard a rumor from a friend at Morgan Central School about the possibility of finding a wondrous new home and asked some questions—just as *she* sent her brother and Derek up this hollow to meet us. And of course, *she* was the first and perhaps the greatest of Derek's romantic fantasies, even when he was just a lonely, troubled boy. Understandably so . . ."

Several silent minutes passed, only the rain outside making any sound. The Councillors kept going over the file I'd sent; all save Vicky, who continued to stare at me. But her expression had changed, now, to reflect so much of my own heartbreak that I could barely stand to look up and smile a little at her before turning back down to the desk to suppress my own emotions.

"The best friend's big sister," she said quietly. "It's so obvious we didn't even consider it. A steadily developing confusion of surrogate mother and romantic ideal. And you're sure?"

"I am," I said simply, "for reasons that are, in part, personal, and don't need to be discussed here. It's enough, for our purposes, to consider these factors: first, the extraordinary number of dead throwaways that were either known to her or lived in her area—"

"Which sounds awfully close to statistical thinking," Linda said gently, without looking up.

"It could, Linda," I answered. "But in this case, it is far closer to proving Dr. Chang's exercise in geographical profiling: except that now we're not looking for a predator's stalking ground, per se, we're looking for an area in which a blind woman and a fairly seriously challenged kid might operate comfortably and without drawing attention to themselves; and we have that. The only mistake they made was getting a little too ambitious and contacting a kid in Essex County, then having Derek meet with him repeatedly in Cambridge. But simply on a behavioral level . . ." I had to steel myself, now: "She's manipulated almost everything and everyone in the parts of the case directly relating to the dead and missing kids themselves. There's Derek, of course, who in fact needed constant, close supervision. Then there was the way she orchestrated our own involvement with her family, by dispatching Lucas to join our team, which her own superiors doubtless thought would keep them at least a little ahead of us, and that we only circumvented occasionally and by chance, as in the case of the Gunderson boy, when I told neither Lucas nor her anything about what we were up to beforehand. And there were smaller things, too, such as her frequent and overly emphatic protestations that she wanted to solve the case, and the fact that she goes almost unmentioned in Derek Franco's departure note: there was no need to say goodbye to someone who was aiding his escape, after all. All we lack now is the why and how of the death scene stagings; I suspect, however, that the theory Dr. Li and I advanced on that subject is very close to the mark."

"But . . . how long?" Vicky was keeping her voice very quiet. "How long have you been sure?"

I shrugged, as yet unable to face her. "Does it matter?"

"Of course it matters," she said more urgently. "If you knew from the beginning, it's nothing short of—well, I don't know. But if you found out later—then how can you stand to go on with it?"

Taking a very deep breath and finally turning up to face her I explained, "I did *not* know from the beginning; and once I thought I did, I could go on because I held the image of each dead child fast in my mind. That was all that mattered, and still is. That, and . . ." I tried to steel myself: "That and one other thing—and listen to me, all of you, because this is important." I saw them all snap to it appropriately. "Each of you, during your career, is going to become personally involved with someone you suspect, even know, is part of the problem you face. The involvement may be a friendship, romance, whatever. What matters is, what do you do? Let them know, betraying the case but honoring the relationship? Or ignore the discovery, thereby honoring the case but betraying the relationship? *Or*, do you enter that worst of purgatories, by trying to honor both the relationship *and* the solution of the case?"

Vicky's gaze became slightly horrified. "Is that what *you've* been doing?"

"Strangely enough, it is not," I replied. "Nor am I asking all these questions because I expect answers—you *can't* answer them, until you get there, any more than you can sit in judgment on how I've dealt with it."

They all absorbed that, Vicky the first to speak: "Well, I guess that's commendable, in some pretty dark way. But you're really sure that you'll be able to maintain the act for the rest of the case? That you can just cut off your feelings?"

"It will be no act, Vicky," I breathed, again feeling a rise of emotion in my throat that I hoped didn't show in my words. "And I won't be cutting off any feelings. But—we do what we must . . ."

As the others went back to their reading (as much to escape the sad tension as anything else), Vicky tried hard to find something, anything, to say in the face of my despair. "You know," she eventually came up with, "you did a really amazing job on the four dead kids that you knew about. Both of you. We were all pretty much amazed by your ability to connect those dots, and to build profiles, not just of the perpetrators, but of the victims and the probable circumstances of their deaths, supported by physical evidence, without being officially in on the case. I'm—sorry, for what I thought . . ." It was her turn to try to laugh without succeeding. "Chalk it up to youth."

"No need to chalk it up to anything," I answered. "It happens to us all. Just have to watch it." She nodded appreciatively, and then, one by one, the others finished their examination of the new file, and all save Frankie turned up to stare at me with uniformly dumbfounded expressions, not quite able to tell if they were facing their familiar teacher or some kind of newly revealed monster: a look I knew well. "Okay," I said, gathering as much strength as I could. "So, in light of all this, where do we go?"

"Well," Colleen said, still looking annoyed, "there's some things we need to recalibrate, obviously—but there's a couple we don't, so we probably ought to get straight to those."

"Fine," I answered, checking on Mike, who wasn't quite done absorbing all he'd heard. I clapped a hand on his shoulder as I began to pace again, both as reassurance and telling him he needed to get his game face back on. "Such as?"

"Okay . . ." Colleen flipped through that seemingly endless notebook of hers. "There's this question of what happened in Hoosick Falls, and the suspicions of this pathologist, Bill Johnson: he implied that there was some kind of FBI involvement in this case. Which is where it gets good . . ." And a pleased little smile came into her usually unreadable features. "We've all been impressed, as Vicky says, by your theory concerning the first four dead kids being suicides: without being independent criminal investigators, you just couldn't have done it. But the question remains: why? Sure, they hadn't found the right families the first time out, but when you consider this organization, they had to have experienced that before, and have dealt with it, probably by finding better spots for any kids who came back. So what was wrong with these four? What drove them to thinking that they just had no hope?" She flipped through her notebook and pulled out several loose printed documents. "We couldn't be sure, of course. But it was another very big coincidence: recorded visits made by each of the dead kids to the Office of Children and Family Services—in Albany. An office that just happens to be located in the same complex—"

Having stopped my pacing suddenly, I turned: "In the same complex as the New York State Adoption Service," I said. Even Mike had begun to stand at the news, leaning forward eagerly on the desk. "What exactly made you think to look *there*?" I asked anxiously.

"Details," Colleen said. "And what was Dr. Kreizler always saying, Doctor?"

My answer was quick: " '*The keys will always be in the details.*' "

"That's right," Colleen continued, our expressions pleasing her. "And when we checked the files that were first opened on all four of them after their parents and then they themselves disappeared, we found out that, without explanation, they all *re*appeared at the OCFS office later—just before they died. But we *didn't* find that pattern among any other kids labeled as 'throwaways.' "

"But what makes you think that they went back of their own volition?" I asked, starting to pace again; because I had suddenly become convinced that a new element had been introduced, one that transcended the merely intellectual. "And you still haven't answered my first question: what made you think to look there, in the first place?"

"Well," Colleen began uncomfortably, "the first thing was, they went to the main office, not to the satellite office in Fraser, which you might have expected—"

"Except that there is no 'satellite office' in Fraser," I answered slowly. "So try again."

"There isn't?" Affecting consternation, Colleen flipped through her notes. "I was sure—"

But then Mike stepped in: "Hey, guys?" He shook his head and stuck a thumb in my direction. " 'The Sorcerer of Death,' remember? If I smell bullshit, he already knows which cow."

"Bulls aren't cows, Mike," I said absentmindedly, staring at the students as their silent discomfort grew. "There's something going on here that you're not telling us. This isn't the kind of brainstorm that you just *have* out of the blue, and there's no chain of evidence that gets you there. No . . . Personal experience is behind it. One of you has been through this, or something very like it . . ." I stood suddenly still, expecting a response; but each of them seemed to be waiting for somebody else to speak up. "Frankie," I went on carefully. "How is it that you know your way around the Arizona Department of Child Safety so readily? And still have a contact who you 'deal with there sometimes'?"

Frankie shrugged without looking back at me. "Just a buddy of mine."

And then it was time to risk provocation: "Old family friend, I suppose."

To which Frankie began to shake his head, smiling ruefully. "I guess I shoulda known better, eh, Doc? *El Brujo,* no shit. Okay—not a buddy of mine. My old caseworker."

I nodded, feeling rotten for putting him on the spot, but needing more. "And your family?"

"My family is—was—just my folks and me," he said, his mood darkening further. "They went back to Mexico six years ago."

I took a moment to study his expression. " '*Went* back'?"

"Okay, fine," Frankie conceded, leaning back in his desk chair and forcing a smile. "You got me, Doc. Yeah, I'm one of 'em, I'm a fuckin' throwaway kid; but in my case, it's kinda the throwaway process in reverse, if you know what I mean."

"I'm not sure *I* do," Mike said.

"Then ask Dr. Jones," Frankie laughed: the brave laugh of the injured, one I could spot from a mile off. "*Los deportados,* dude, just two more of them, that's what my parents are. But I was born here—I had to go with them, at first, but *I* was born *here*. And by the time I was fourteen, I'd had enough. It was hard to leave them, but I mean . . . You people up here, you have no idea. Mexicans are good people with a good country, but the government, *hijole* . . . Anyway, to do what *I* wanted to do, to do *this,* which I knew even then was what I wanted—" And I was reminded of Lucas' present determination to pursue the same discipline, at roughly the same age Frankie had been. "I mean, first off, I would have been living and working in war zones, which I'd actually learned to handle pretty well—but to be in law enforcement and be *independent*? You know how hard it is to do it here, just imagine it down there."

"But, I mean—you were *fourteen,* Frankie," Mike said. "How did you survive?"

"Until I got emancipated?" Frankie's black eyes now began to display the actual weight of what he was talking about. "Shit, I didn't wanna get into this. But here's the thing: this is what all these kids, these dead kids, went through. The system in this country, for kids who suddenly find themselves without any families—by no fault of their own—is just crawling with catch-22's. And at first I hit every one of them, because I didn't know shit. First up: no school without home or family, either natural or foster, and I didn't have either. So that meant work. But then the child labor laws step in—which, ideally, they should, provided the rest of the system is working right. But it ain't, you know that: the foster care program is a fucking game rigged for thieves. I had one hope: I was already pretty good at fixing computers. I used to do it for one of the big gangs down south, and no, I won't tell you which one. But they were hacking the shit out of businesses all over Latin America, working the machines so hard they'd fry 'em, and me and some other kids, we'd fix 'em, because our hands were still small." He splayed his fingers out before him, trying to rally. "Unlike the *bestias gigantes* you see now—"

"Frankie . . ." Colleen warned.

"Yeah," he said, darkening again. "Anyway, between fixing the computers and watching the hackers, that's where I got my skills. And by the time I was fourteen, I could pass for older, anyway, and so I kinda fucked with my passport records a little bit and boom!—I got my emancipation and working papers. Went to work in the repair department of a Best Buy, started making decent money, got a room down in one of the barrios here in town—but most kids like me had no shot at any of that. They were on the streets, and they had no families or skills and couldn't pass; couldn't go to school, and the child labor laws said they couldn't work even if they *had* something they could do. So what the fuck is left, Docs? I think you know: they could either go into the foster program, which most didn't want to do, or take the other open roads: become drug dealers, go to work with guys robbing houses, *or*—they just started tricking. Boys *and* girls, fresh meat brings a lot of money."

"Jesus," Vicky breathed. "Easy, Frankie."

"What? I'm sorry if you don't like the term, Vick, any more than you liked looking at the videos, but that's fucking reality. I'm not going to bullshit you, crime in Mexico gave me a way to stay straight in *this* country—I never did actually go to high school, I just got hold of one school's curriculum and the books and learned when I wasn't at work till I got my GED. And by then, dude, I was good enough to go here, to one of the best criminal justice schools in the country. A fact that we don't need to share with SUNY, I'm assuming, especially since it was when I found out that you two *maestros* had joined the online faculty that I chose Albany. I don't mind telling you that I coulda gone to a whole lot of places—but I wanted to learn from the best." There was a momentary pause, and Frankie smiled, very genuinely this time. "Don't let your heads explode about it or anything. But the point is, none of the four dead kids we're talking about had the skills or the chances I did, any more than most of the kids I grew up with down here did. They all got caught in a system that leads you in just one direction: foster care. But nobody gives a shit, from the governor on down—just make those kids disappear, man, stigmatize them, deport 'em, 'anchor babies,' all that bullshit. And bullshit is what it is . . ."

Frankie's last words, poignant as they were, had struck me like a shot. "Of course," I murmured. "Frankie—you just said it. Or part of it. 'Anchor babies.' When each of you hears that term, what do you immediately think of? The Southwest, right, and citizenship? But that's only part of what the debate's about. On a deep psychological level, these 'anchor babies' are also anchors to, reminders of, a plain fact: that the Southwest can't function without the presence of illegals anymore. People may not like it; they think that if they eliminate the anchors, Americans will be unchained, will step forward and clean houses, pick fruit, tend yards. But they're free to do that now, yet they won't. And this kind of psychological insecurity and overcompensation, it doesn't stop in that part of the country, or with illegal immigrants—there are other 'anchors,' other reminders of our social predicaments, and that's what these four kids were. When they're trying to turn New York City into a dormitory for the super-rich and make the upper Hudson into a new Silicon Valley, nobody wants to say that a lot of people are being left so far out of the prosperity that they'll abandon their own kids to survive. Yet if we, or anybody else, end up exposing the conditions behind these deaths and then tying them to models of success like the Augustines, that's a conversation that has to be had. *Anything* else is preferable—even a serial killer. It's the idea we had from the start, but all the pieces are falling in place to confirm it, now: the problematic kids, if they won't accept their secret arrangements, will be offered no help; and we will be discouraged at every turn from concluding that anything other than murder is behind their deaths. Curtis Kolmback got assigned to all five cases, not just because they thought they could control him, but because he truly wanted to believe that a serial killer was at work: he knew that right now that's what the public craves, and he saw a straight shot up to promotion and publicity. But in the end, even Curtis couldn't take it. Not when he found out the lies they were asking him to tell."

"And your experience on the mountain," Linda said, weighing the matter. "It wasn't just pragmatic: it was supposed to look ritualistic, supposed to make you think there was a twisted mind operating close by, like the kind in TV and movies. Anything, other than . . .'"

She didn't want to finish her statement, but Mei-lien, who had the most direct experience of such phenomena, did: "Anything other than an institutional attempt to quietly remove the problem of these children, and then, if they should somehow die, to create a false narrative of their deaths."

"And that was the mistake of returning to the office in Albany," Vicky added. "Which explains the arranged death scenes, *and* the suicides in the first place. Those four wanted to come back and do things legally, but they didn't know how high the whole scheme went. They were assuming that the system would sit up and listen, would reward them, and that they wouldn't have to just wait on line like every other kid. But the opposite was true: all that crap sent them to the back of, and maybe *off,* the line. And with both the legal and the illegal paths blocked . . . Yeah, suicide wouldn't seem so crazy."

"Especially since," Frankie said, "once you get a chance to live a better life, it gets ripped away again, and you can't see any way to get it back. Yeah—I saw more than a few kids I knew OD or just plain cut their wrists over that kind of depression."

"Indeed," I said, pausing for a moment with bittersweet satisfaction at just how well they'd done. But I couldn't let the sadness show, couldn't let the meeting get bogged down again. "And so . . ." I tried to rally. "The fact that they were turned away in Albany tells us what else? Colleen?"

"It tells us," she answered, never missing a beat, "that this conspiracy—and let's not kid ourselves, that's what we're talking about—reaches up pretty high, in the first place, but doesn't include everyone along every step of the way. And that's totally typical of government corruption. You pick the people you need, starting with overly ambitious types lower down—foot soldiers—and then you treat everybody else, high or low, as a potential problem."

"Yes," said Mei-lien, who had good reason to know. "It is the same everywhere."

"Good," I said. "So put that together with your belief that there are almost certainly *two* women involved: Ambyr Kurtz being one, the other must be a local official who meets Colleen's criteria. I'm assuming you have a nominee?"

"We do," Mei-lien replied. "But speculation now becomes particularly difficult and dangerous."

"Yes," I said. "And it is for precisely that reason that I wish you, for now, to keep it to yourselves." Groaning protests went up, but I held a hand to them. "No. Given the work you've done, I suspect your candidate is the correct one. But you mustn't speak about it or, certainly, write it down, unless and until something happens to Dr. Li and myself. At that point, you will present the case in full to my aunt, who will take it to the head of the state legislature. Can I rely on you for all this?"

The Councillors looked very taken aback—all save Frankie: "Don't sweat it, Doc. We got this one. You guys do what you need to do, and if we have to, we'll handle the fallout."

"Linda?" I asked, eyeing our sole New Yorker and knowing her misgivings.

But I needn't have worried. "You've convinced me, Doctor," she said.

"This is too important." She lifted one hand in the air in resignation. "So maybe I have to get a job in another state—worse things have happened. They always need criminal investigators in New Jersey, that's for sure."

"Thank you, Linda," I replied; and suddenly, knowing that the long meeting was finally coming to an end, and that I would have to face another, far more complex encounter with Ambyr afterward, my spirits began to flag, a feeling I tried not to show. "Very well, then: Dr. Li and I will be as much in touch as we can be from our hotel in New York, and we will convene again to consider the results of our little excursion when we return. I'm sorry we kept you all so long—"

"No hay pedo," Frankie assured me; then he gave me a small grin, one that indicated he knew at least some of what I was about to have to go through, and was trying to offer support.

"Thanks, Frankie," I said. "And I do, sincerely, want to thank you *all*: you have more than lived up to our hopes for this exercise. You may not have bargained for as much responsibility as you've ended up with, but that's the price of real brains and real independence. You're seeing many of the things we've studied put into action, now. I can only hope it's going to assist you, moving forward in your careers. And with that said— anything else?" They each mumbled in the negative as their heads shook. Then we said our final farewells, after which, one by one, their screens went black.

All save Vicky's: she continued to scrutinize me, and I waited for her to speak, which she finally did after an increasingly difficult minute or so: "It can't be as easy as you're making it sound, Doctor. I just can't accept that."

Finally allowing myself to breathe deeply, I fell into my chair behind the desk and put a hand to one aching temple. "Ah, Vicky," I said quietly. "Of course it isn't. In fact, to tell you—" I glanced at Mike, who looked about as miserable as I felt. "To tell *both* of you the truth, this trip to the city doesn't scare me half so much as the thought of how I'll survive the time until we leave tomorrow. But you know, Vicky . . ." I tried to smile. "Should you find that you've learned too well, here, and can't get a job inside an official agency in California, you may want to consider teaching. You have the talent for it, you've shown us that much. I don't know how you feel about the Northeast, but—Dr. Li and I would be happy to find a place for you with us at SUNY. And on the occasional investigation or two."

She laughed just a bit. "Thanks. I'll keep that in mind as a last resort. No offense, of course."

"None taken," Mike answered. "We'll see how you feel about it a few months from now—assuming, that is, that Dr. Jones and I are still fucking alive to renew the offer . . ."

And then, after a few more polite farewells, Vicky was gone, too, leaving me to face only Mike's scrutiny—which was neither as hard nor as mystified as I'd expected. "It's Donovan, isn't it?" he asked. "The 'candidate.'"

"Of course it's Donovan," I said, disgusted at the thought. "Who else? Smart, good-looking, scarily ambitious, and an absolute chameleon. One with a family. When these kids met up with her, she'd have had no trouble being whatever each needed her to be: mother, big sister, friend, confidante, romantic object—she's the perfect complement to Ambyr. I just didn't see it soon enough, for Derek . . ."

Mike paused before asking the next, the inevitable, question: "How *are* you going to get through the night, L.T.?" He produced two cigarettes. "As long as the subject's been brought up."

We had by now worked straight through the dinner hour at the house, so I lit my smoke and sat back. "The only way possible: by making sure that Ambyr doesn't suspect anything's wrong. We have to keep her close, and keep Lucas in the dark. It's the only way the whole scheme will work."

"Jesus." He absorbed that, then pressed: "Just when did you really start to suspect? And why?"

"Ah, Mike," I moaned. "Do we have to do this?"

"Considering that you've been fucking keeping it from me?" Mike answered, his tone far less contentious than he had every right to be. "Yeah, we do."

I took a deep drag off my cigarette, let the nicotine do its dirty, energizing work, then said, "I don't know, exactly. I know I was alarmed, at first, by the fact that she'd sent the boys up to us in the beginning; but then I told myself to stop being so paranoid, and shoved it into the back of my mind, or tried to. The contradictory assertion stayed there, of course. No, I don't think that I was ever really *sure* she was safe. Not deep down."

"Bullshit," Mike said. "You were in love with her. You *are*."

"Which does not preclude suspicion. And as far as a specific trigger goes . . ." Pausing again, I glanced at the cigarette in my hand. "You know,"

I said, chuckling humorlessly, "there are times when I think it was something Clarissa said. The night I asked her to assess Derek."

"Yeah, well," Mike answered, taking his turn to stand and walk about a bit, brushing his hair into that 110-volt stand. "It figures that Clarissa would have been the first to make her."

"She wasn't. And she didn't," I answered, pointing my cigarette at him. "And I don't *want* her to find out about Ambyr. Not for the moment, anyway. No, it was something else, something in passing. A detail: a *key*. Clarissa asked me, yet again, if I planned to give up smoking, and didn't I think losing one leg to cancer was enough. She always manages to forget that it was the Jones genes that caused my osteosarcoma, not smoking."

"But why the hell would *that* little question push you over the edge?"

"Because Ambyr never asked it. I mean, even the biggest pains in the ass I've ever dated, when they heard that I'd lost a leg to cancer and saw me smoking, they always asked if it was a smart idea. But Ambyr never did. And it's not like she's *accepting* of things: when she does object to something, Jesus, she'll let you know in a voice that's pretty chilling. I had tried very hard to block the other things out, but when I learned the details of her relationship with Derek—which was only after he disappeared—well, it started to become pretty unavoidable . . ."

"And her credit card stuff? Don't try to tell me you developed hacking skills during this case."

"No," I answered. "That was easier—and I'm surprised *you* didn't notice it. When we were signing that authorization document at their house, a couple of opened household bills were on the table. One was her monthly credit statement. I glanced over it, and saw a couple of strange charges. Strange for her, I mean. Like that Chinese joint in Cambridge. Others, too. Didn't think much of it at the time. I tried very hard not to think much of any of the things about her that just didn't fit, *at the time* . . ." Rousing myself, I tried to become as earnest as I could: "But I mean it, Mike—no telling Clarissa or Lucas anything. Not until the time comes when it's inevitable. If it does come."

The last statement was a tactical error: "*'If'*?" Mike repeated incredulously. "L.T.—don't add being a sucker to your list of mistakes: not only will that time come, it's here, *now*. Just think about tomorrow: you're really going to go on this trip, and leave her in the house alone with Clarissa?"

"I need Ambyr to take care of Marcianna while we're gone," I answered, half-aware of how bizarre it would initially sound.

"*What?*" Mike moved my way, hands in the air. "Your fucking *cheetah*? I'm talking about you putting Clarissa's life in danger!"

"That won't be a problem," I said, trying to keep my overworked nerves in check, now. "I'm going to speak to Happy and Chick about staying here, in the downstairs staff rooms. I'll tell them to be ready for anything, but won't give them any . . . specifics. And Pete and Steve will work shifts, I know that, so that one of them will show up every day, and Mitch'll be by." That seemed to mollify Mike a bit; but only a bit, so I went on: "Besides, there is that one little issue you mentioned: her feelings for me, and mine for her. I have to think that'll count for . . . something."

Mike scrutinized me very gravely. "L.T.—did you *lie* to our little Council? Are you so deluded that you think you're going to find a way to solve this case without turning Ambyr in? Make Cathy Donovan take the fall, and save the poor, misled blind girl?"

"I don't know," I answered quietly. "I don't *think* so. But there's something else, something just as important: the *why*. What's in this, for her? The money? Getting out of this place? Is she being coerced by someone, for reasons we don't know? I need to find out, before the cops—"

"Trajan!" Mike hollered. "If what we've said and heard here tonight is true, that young woman, blind and fucked over by life in whatever ways she might have been, is complicit in a whole string of nasty—no, fuck that, of *contemptible* things! And you're considering prolonging it all, just so—"

"*All right, Mike, enough!*" I had finally exploded, after so many hours of holding my feelings back; yet as my thunderclap subsided all I could do was stand and walk toward the hatch. "I don't know exactly *what* I'm considering. But there's Lucas to think of, what his life will be like—"

"That's just bullshit projection," Mike shot back, following me down the steel steps. "You're worried about what *your* life will be like, and you're saddling the kid with it—you *know* that."

"I don't know *what* I know, Michael!" I said, clutching my temples as if to keep the conflict raging between them from cracking my skull. "Except that . . ." Pulling myself together, or at least trying to, I continued on toward the microwave and threw some frozen meat into it. "Except that I need to feed Marcianna. And I need her to be safe, while we're gone."

And then, as if on cue, Marcianna began to issue that peculiar chirrup of hers, which sounded, on this night in particular, especially alarmed, lonely, and heart wrenching. Hearing it, Mike calmed down some, soon saying, "Well, then—you'd better go, sounds like she's getting impatient."

"That's not what that sound is," I said quietly, as I went to the mouth of the hangar and Mike fell in beside me. "I figured that one out at about the same time that—*other things* fell into place. It's him. The assassin they've got roaming that ridgeline. She's been calling like that when she detects him—sees him, smells him, hears him, whatever. He's up there now, Mike, and *he's* the real danger. But as long as Ambyr's here and thinks everything is fine, he won't make any move against us; probably on *her* orders. So don't tell me it's all so simple. Because, ironically, she's our best insurance against some further outrage; but only as long as she thinks that we're not onto her . . ." I retrieved my alter ego's thawed dinner. "I'm doing the best I can with the information we have—and trying, probably failing, not to let my own feelings screw with that too much." I took another deep breath, then glanced at Mike, who appeared suddenly more sympathetic. "Anyway—I'm going to the enclosure."

"Ambyr will come up," Mike warned. "You know she will."

All I could do was nod. "I'll deal with that then. One step at a time, until we get in the car and finally go."

As I moved out of the hangar, Mike clapped my shoulder reassuringly. "Okay, kid," he said. "I'm just sorry about it all. Sorry that happiness—whatever, *human* happiness—is going to get away from you. Again. But it's not fucking over, L.T. I know what you're thinking; but if you found it with her, you can find it with somebody else."

I could only chuckle. "Okay, Mike."

"I'm serious, asshole. But for now—go take care of Marcianna. And yourself . . ."

"One and the same," I said, moving toward the dirt path to the enclosure. "And *you*—just make sure you're packed by noon, and that Gracie knows to lie low. Right?"

Only half-hearing his response in the affirmative, I was quickly swallowed up in a night that had seen steady rain replaced by an almost impenetrable fog.

Marcianna was at the gate long before I got there, her sensing of the killer above us making her anxious for company. But, as was usually the case when she detected any sort of danger (perhaps a pack of coyotes, in the past, or a black bear such as those she'd stood against on the mountain), she insisted on staying in front of me, once I was inside the enclosure; and her eyes, ears, and nose constantly searched the misty night, her spirit determined that if any harm was in the offing, it should befall her first. I picked up some twigs and branches on my way to the den, and once we were inside I built a fire, sufficient to comfort me but small enough that it didn't make Marcianna feel any more nervous. And so we sat there, as I tried yet again to work out how I was going to get through the long night to come.

Soon, though, that problem began to be solved for me: true to Mike's prediction, Ambyr appeared, finding her way into the enclosure and then the den with as little trouble as she had the first time she'd visited. She had taken great pains to make herself irresistible, wearing some kind of silver satin wrap (*expensive,* I recall thinking) that was open at the front almost to her waist, with only a pair of like-colored flats on her feet. Her freshly washed and dried hair, having passed through the mist, glistened in the firelight, and the overall effect was to make her seem a sprite that had just emerged from the forest above us. Once nearby, she sensed the heat of the fire, and heightened her allure by standing before it and turning around, the lines of her body plainly visible beneath the sheer wrap.

"You like, Mister-Doctor-Man?" she said with a smile; and it again grew difficult to conceive that she could have had so little visual knowledge of the effect she had on men; on me.

"Of course," I said, perhaps less enthusiastically than she had expected: for her own smile faded, and she slowly found her way, with my help, into my lap. Once seated, she placed her delicately scented arms around my neck and her head on my chest.

"Worried?" she asked.

"Umm-hmm," I noised, my face burying itself in her hair as my arms helplessly encircled her.

"Maybe even a little scared?" she pressed.

"Maybe more than a little," I said, as she turned her face up to mine; and in that instant, all considerations of her being anything other than the remarkably liberating creature she had always been for me simply melted. Our lips met, and I came near to believing that all I had said earlier that night must have been a mistake, untrue, a series of lies. *Not this girl,* I prayed silently, *not this one, God, please* . . . And as the moments wore on, I even came close to believing it.

Close. After what must have been a half an hour or so, Marcianna's ears went back, and she began to growl lowly. Bursting out with one of her peculiar chirrups, which reverberated somewhat painfully against the den walls, she dashed outside, there to stand and continue the call.

"Ouch," Ambyr said, touching each of her ears gently. "What's gotten into her?"

"I don't know," I said evenly. "Your guess, on that, would be as good as mine. Maybe better . . ."

Did she understand from my ambiguous little statement that I was aware of what was happening, and of her part in it? Certainly, she turned toward me in an unusual way, and seemed on the verge of explaining *some*thing. Her lips parted, she drew in a breath—but then simply declared, "Come on. We're going inside, for your last night. I didn't get all done up to roll around in the dust of *this* place . . ."

And so we stood, each playing our part without acknowledging as much to the other. I made no more hint of any awareness of things beyond that moment, but simply accepted that the night had to pass without incident. Once we were outside, with Marcianna following along and occasionally letting out that cry of hers and myself stopping every few feet to comfort her and try to reassure her about the temporary nature of any change to our usual rhythm of life that might be coming, Ambyr began to soothe her, as well, saying that she would be there if I was not, and that there was no need to feel like she'd been abandoned to her fate as had happened when she'd been a cub. Then, as we passed through the gate, Marcianna leapt up to put her forelegs on my shoulders; but it was Ambyr who literally talked her down, whispering in her ear and sending her on her way back to the den with an air of genuine peace of mind.

"Well," I said, watching Marcianna go. "That was impressive. What did you say to her?"

"Simple," Ambyr replied, clutching my arm and reaching up to kiss me. "I told her not to worry—that, even if you get sick of me, *she'll* have the rest of her life with you . . ."

It was as close as she would come to admitting that, when Mike, Lucas, and I hit the road the next day, whatever wondrous and terrible thing it was that had gone on between us would be at an end; yet it still offered no clue as to why. And that, as I'd told Mike, was what I most needed to know . . .

CHAPTER THREE

"Incurable, in Each, the Wounds They Make"

{i.}

We were in trouble almost as soon as we left Death's Head Hollow. "Ow, shit!" Mike clutched at one ear as he drove. "Lucas, what in the *fuck*—I'm barely awake!"

We had just hit Route 7 after a somber parting from Shiloh, and Lucas had announced that he would be serving as the mixmaster for our trip, having burned some CDs on Mike's laptop that morning when Mike was off "getting his oil changed" at Gracie's. It was well past noon, and I, like Mike, was still a little hazy; so when the stereo started blasting with (appropriately enough) the hard chords of AC/DC's "Highway to Hell," it was a bit much for our driver.

"I thought we agreed to compromise and listen to PYX-106," Mike complained further.

"Dude, I *am* PYX-106, okay?" Lucas said, spreading out in the back seat and donning a pair of Coyote Razor sunglasses that an older youth he knew from school who'd recently returned from his first tour of duty in Afghanistan had given him, and which imparted to Lucas an apparent sense of invulnerability. "Just without the commercials. So don't fuck with it . . ."

"Excuse me?" Mike replied in disbelief.

"You heard me," Lucas said. "Gonna be a long enough ride, Mike, but I *can* make it longer . . ."

Michael and I had planned our actual journey south fairly carefully, thinking that there might be a chance that some of our friends in law enforcement would take an interest in our sudden departure from Shiloh. We hadn't originally felt like we needed to take an absurdly circuitous route: it would be easy for anyone who cared to check Mike's speeding-riddled driving record to find out that we preferred the Taconic State Parkway to the other main arteries (the scenic but unbearably slow Route 22—about which we'd said and heard enough during our investigation—and, westward beyond the Hudson, the post-apocalyptically bleak New York State Thruway), so we figured we'd be safe simply choosing one of those alternate routes. But we soon decided that we'd better complicate our movements, due to the number of television news vans that were still lingering in Surrender and being turned back by Shiloh's farmhands every time they tried to ascend Death's Head Hollow. We chose to begin the trip with a feint, taking 22 south and cutting across Route 295, which would take us toward the Taconic Parkway and make it look as though we were sticking to our habits; then, when we hit the crossing of 295 with Interstate 90, the westward side of which headed toward Albany and the Thruway, we would suddenly take it, and lose any followers on its maze-like access road.

"Brilliant, totally genius," Lucas declared laconically, as Mike and I discussed all this. "But, moving on, now that we're away from adult supervision, there's one more important thing to discuss: where and when do we stop for beer?"

For most of the drive down 22 to its intersection with 295, Lucas continued to protest that a road trip was not a road trip without beer—"and not fucking Genesee, I want some primo shit!"—making it all the harder to discuss matters of substance; which was just as well, because there weren't many matters of substance that we *could* discuss in front of the kid. So, things devolved into one more battle of insults between Mike and our consultant, while I gave up and stared out the window for most of the way, trying not to obsess over the fact that the extraordinary happiness I'd known with Ambyr in recent days, the latest chapter of which had been a very tender parting entirely consistent with an honest relationship, was almost certainly a thing of the past. Those parts of my brain involved in the processing and manufacturing of emotions continued to fight for some way out, some way in which all the things we suspected that Ambyr had done were defensible, either because of the possibility, which Mike had long advocated, that the throwaways organization had actually placed most of its children in happy homes, or because she was being coerced in a way that she couldn't tell even me, probably to keep

Lucas safe from harm. But my cognitive brain fought back hard, telling me that I knew these scenarios were unlikely, that whatever rationalizations she might have for the staging of the four deaths we knew of, to say nothing of her manipulations of other people, including me, would prove inadequate. I even tried the habit that Mike and I consistently warned our students against, listening to my gut; but all my gut told me was that I had fallen in love with a girl who had brought me out of years of torment, however briefly, yet who was still involved in something beyond shady. Had it not been me, had it been just another actor in a different case, I would have called the behavior common enough. But it didn't feel common; not from the inside . . .

With these serpentine realities tightening on me, I didn't notice for a long while that Lucas and Mike had suspended their bickering in favor of listening to Lucas' classic rock collection; and I turned once to glance at the kid as he soaked up the ride and quietly sang along to Aerosmith's "Dream On," a song that had been released before I, let alone he, was born. A species apart, was Lucas; yet the specter of the looming heartbreak—or twin heartbreaks, if something had indeed happened to Derek—that would strike him if we could manage to prove our theories about the case and about his sister was very much of the cruel, common human world, and made me feel an increased affinity and responsibility for him. I didn't really want or need anything else to feel sick about; and so at first, I was just as glad when Mike turned down the volume of the stereo a bit and quietly said to me:

"Hey. I know what it is you're working over in your brain, L.T.—but if I might interrupt?"

"For God's sake, do, Mike," I answered quickly.

He smiled just a bit at that, then asked, in a voice that was still calm and controlled, "Could you tactfully take a look in your wing mirror and tell me what you see?" He was glimpsing as often as he dared into the rearview mirror, I noticed; and that was cause for concern. I carefully reached down to press the button that would manipulate the mirror just outside my window, hoping that Lucas would not notice the movement.

Which, of course, was an idiotic thought: having not only observed what I was doing but overheard Mike's words, Lucas shot his head around to look out the back window, saying: "What? What is it, I don't see any cops."

"Shut the fuck up and turn back around, kid," Mike said, keeping his order measured but stern. "Or better yet, sink down in your seat some. But do *not* turn your head around again . . ."

By now I had shifted my mirror to see just what Mike was talking about: "*That*," I murmured, "looks remarkably like the cruiser we saw in Hoosick Falls. And the one guy driving it looks just as remarkably like the Fed we saw there, although they're tough to tell apart."

"'Fed'?" Lucas echoed quietly, slipping down below the rear window. "As in 'federal agent'?"

"Well, given your compulsion to show him your full mug," Mike answered, "we'll know in a couple of seconds. If they figure we made them, they'll—ah, fuck, and there they go . . ."

"What, what, what?" Lucas asked, afraid to look up and out again.

"They just broke off," I answered. "At the first available turn. Thus signaling, with their usual subtlety, exactly who they were."

"Aw, *shit* . . ." Real apprehension now broke through Lucas' usual attitude: "What the fuck, Mike, am I going to have to do hard time because you're a shitty getaway driver?"

But Mike wasn't even listening to him. "Keep your eye out, will you, L.T., and let me know if something or someone just as 'inconspicuous' pulls onto our tail?"

"Already on it," I replied, my eyes on the wing mirror. "Take the Queechy Lake shortcut to 295—if it's really them, and they've done their homework, their next logical pick-up point will be that shithole restaurant on the lake, right before we head west."

"Yep," Mike answered, focused intently on both the road and his rear-view mirror. "You can sit up now, Lucas—they're gone, for the moment. And I know I should've warned you, but—any time you hear me say something even vaguely like 'Check who's behind us,' do *not* stick your sparkling little mug out the back window, got it?"

"Oh, I got it, all right," Lucas answered, finally peering up and out the rear window again. "In fact, don't be surprised when we stop for gas if you find out that I'm missing after you get back. I didn't sign up for this shit."

"We're not stopping for gas," Mike said. "We're all topped off. And yes, you damn well *did* sign up for this. What'd you think, that the other side was just going to let us cruise down to the city without following us to find out where we go and what we know? Well, we'll find out at Queechy Lake—if they're not there, maybe they're dumber than I think . . ."

The road between Routes 22 and 295, which wound around the re-markably undeveloped shores of broad, calm Queechy Lake, came upon us relatively quickly; and as Mike made the sharp turnoff and began the curving run, Lucas, his brain as ungovernable as ever, looked out and asked:

"Hey, what's a 'Queechy,' anyway?"

The question surprised me: "You've never seen Queechy Lake before?"

"No," he answered defensively. "Some of us never got the chance to *go places,* L.T. But what's it mean, if that's not too stupid a question for me to ask?"

"Not stupid at all," I replied, still eyeing my mirror. "Just that nobody can answer you. The name is an old Mohican term—never been defined."

"No shit?" Lucas said more quietly, watching the lake—which was al-ways most scenic in late afternoon—with far more respect. "So, like, this is serious *Last of the Mohicans* territory, hunh?"

When I told him it was, the kid grew silent, having a moment that seemed profound—which made it all the more disheartening when I looked up and saw what we'd feared: the running lights of an unmarked cruiser like the one we'd just avoided, coming on as the vehicle started up on our approach to an old restaurant on the lake's western edge. "Shit," I said. "Okay, windows up. And hit the deck, Lucas. Mike, don't look to the side—let me do it, we don't want them to know for sure that we've made them . . ."

"Whatever you say, boss," Mike breathed.

"Aw, *really*?" Lucas whimpered from the floor in the back. "I'm gonna spend the next five to ten years getting ass-raped because you two clowns couldn't figure out how to—"

"Shut the hell up, Lucas," I answered. "I don't suppose it's occurred to you, but we haven't actually committed a God damned crime. So stop whining."

"We haven't?" the kid said hopefully. "We're not, like, fleeing the scene of—"

"Of what? The most we could even get pulled over for is *your* presence, and since I have an agreement from your guardian saying that Mike and I represent your family, they can't even try that. We're being subtle, here, because we'd rather not be obvious about where the fuck we're going."

"Quiet, guys," Mike said, now cruising to a stop at the intersection that would put us onto Route 295. Glancing into his mirror without moving his head, my partner frowned in disappointment. "Yeah—they're coming behind us. At a distance, very carefully. Fuckers."

"It's all right," I said evenly. "Our evasion plan will still work—we just know we were right about them taking an interest, so we're lucky we worked it out. Now the problem is, how good are your driving skills, Michael? Think you can lose them at the 90 turnoff?"

"If I can't," Mike answered quietly, as we pulled out and headed west, "we may just have a problem . . ." He glanced into the rearview mirror and kept a very grim look on his face. "Because these guys seem to know what they're doing. And that calls for some—*extreme* solutions . . ."

"Meaning what?" I asked, glancing into my wing mirror and seeing that the cruiser behind us was, indeed, executing perfect shadow moves: never too close, never too far, no chance for us to see their faces or anything else, but no chance—seemingly—for us to elude them, either.

"Don't ask until it happens," Mike replied. "Which may be sooner than we'd like to think . . ."

In the end, the success or failure of our attempt to elude the car that was now ghosting ours would come down (or so I thought) to some deceptively simple maneuvers: leaving the quaint little speed-trap town of East Chatham, where the posted limit suddenly sank from fifty-five to thirty-five miles an hour, then rose again a mile or so later, Mike would have to floor the Empress, until we hit the right-hand turn onto a byway called Rock City Road, which was the first leg of the winding route one had to take to gain access to the westbound lanes of I-90 and Albany beyond. The signs for the turnoff appeared only shortly before Rock City; so, assuming we could gain some distance on our company while they were still in the speed trap of East Chatham, it seemed just possible that we might be able to vanish from their sight at that point.

"But they're Feds!" Lucas protested. "What do they care about speeding to keep up with us?"

"More than you think," Mike answered, eyeing our speedometer and struggling to restrain his right foot. "Remember, they don't actually have any reason to arrest us—so they don't want to tear through town with their blue-and-reds flashing in their grilles, then get stopped by the local cops and asked for an explanation." A demonic look crept into Mike's face. "Which gives me an idea . . ."

Lucas and I then heard a short, angry squeal from the Empress' seventeen-inch tires, and were unexpectedly thrown back in our seats.

The situation took a minute to make sense of, because it was in fact so senseless—but Mike had evidently decided to rocket through the last half of quaint little East Chatham, speed limits, our own careful planning, and anything else be damned.

"What the fuck are you *doing*, Mike?" Lucas shouted.

"Being smart," Mike said, as the speedometer rose up to seventy and the far side of town quickly came into view. "I may not be sure if I can lose these Feds at the turnoff, but I *know* I can lose the local boys. And, if our friends decide to keep up and hit it this hard, the local cops'll figure we're racing, and nail the driver who's trailing. So hang on!"

Incredibly, it all played out as Mike had predicted: by the time we reached the point where the speed limit returned to fifty-five, we must have been doing seventy-five; and when our tail moved to keep pace, out of nowhere appeared a local cop. The cruiser behind us flashed the red-and-blues in its grille, but the cop couldn't see them; and even if the unmarked car had flashing strobes in the rear, the cop wanted an explanation for what the hell was going on. But by the time the mysterious agents in the cruiser had broken off to give it to him, we were already on Rock City Road.

As we made our way along the short stretch of road to I-90 West, the sound of Lucas laughing out loud as he bounced around the back seat in relief gave the situation a touch of the surreal. It was not an entirely unwelcome experience, although, for my part, I would not be truly relieved about things until we'd pulled onto the interstate and found that no new cruiser had picked up our trail. When that was precisely what happened, I let myself take some amusement from the lunatic in the back, although I still had questions:

"I don't really get it, Mike—those guys must've ID'd our plates, at least, and contacted the state patrols ahead."

"Maybe they don't want the State Police in on this," Mike answered, very evasively.

"Mike? The car's plates *are* still in place, right?" He began to fidget badly. "Mike? *Right?*"

He waved me off with a look of guilty annoyance. "What the hell, L.T., I'm not stupid enough to take the plates *off*." Yet his voice was far from relieved; and before I could get another question in, he began to mumble, "Oh, man, I've done something bad . . . really bad . . ."

Lucas managed to say, "What're you talking about, Mike, you were the dog's balls, dude—" before I got my hand up to tell him to keep quiet; then, figuring that Mike was anxious enough for the three of us, I tried to keep my voice very even as I said:

"Okay, Mike—what did you do that was so bad?"

"Well," Mike said, struggling. "Not *that* bad; I mean, we did get away, and we haven't been picked up again. Yet. Which I think means it probably worked." He took a deep breath, then gave out with the real story at last:

"Okay—so, ever since law enforcement's video surveillance became so constant after 9/11 and the Patriot Act, people have been figuring out legal ways to obscure their license plates. The cheapest way is to put a curved plastic lens over them, so that the number can only be read from head on—which eliminates speed cameras, and all the other passive stuff. But it still makes you visible to cops on your tail, because obscuring *that* view can get you into serious trouble. Some people with more extreme feelings, though, have come up with infrared LED strobes, which defeat the onboard cameras in cruisers; and some *real* diehards have been tinkering with sequenced strobes that cover the whole spectrum, and—at least in half-light or darkness—blind cops in pursuit to plate numbers. And I got to fiddling with that a while back, while we were considering going to New York in the, whatever, the abstract—I even built a set and put them into the Empress' plate frames." He reached down to a toggle switch that he had, without my ever noticing it, installed in the far left-hand corner of the car's dashboard, and shut it off. "I'm guessing that, even though it isn't totally dark yet, what with the leaves on the trees and the shadows . . . well—it worked . . ."

Lucas burst out in more triumphant laughter, making it impossible for me to speak. "Holy shit! Mike, you are a badass, G, why the fuck are you working for the *law*? Criminal genius!" He grabbed Mike's shoulders and started shaking him. *"Gang-sta!"*

"Lucas!" I was finally able to say. "Stop screwing around. Mike, that's still a serious offense, and you know it: you can't use lights to obscure your plates, that's why they made all the gangbangers take those neon plate rings off their Escalades."

"Yeah, but this is different," Mike said, knowing that he was fighting a losing battle. "According to the guys on YouTube, these lights *can* be interpreted as simple reflections of the cop's own strobes, and—ah, fuck, so maybe it's not different."

"Yeah," I answered, a bit testily. "Maybe. And I'm delighted to know that our success or failure rests with 'the guys on YouTube'—"

"Chillax, L.T.!" Lucas' voice rose above and silenced mine, after which the kid sat back. "Between that device and Mike's driving skills, man, nobody is going to know who we are or where we're going." I scowled at the kid, at which he leaned Mike's way and whispered, "It was badass, Mike, I'm telling you—you're the *shit,* dude . . ."

The statement actually brought a smile to Mike's face; and, seeing it, I started to relax a bit, myself. The strobes had, after all, worked—or so it seemed; yet when I turned to the back seat, I found Lucas suddenly puzzling with something. "What's got you, Mr. Badass?"

"There's just one thing I don't get about all this." Lucas leaned forward between our two seats, his mind having completely shifted gears once again. "It's Derek. I hate to say it, but—where in the world, even if the people were rich and desperate, would a kid like him go? I mean, it seems like this organization has got an awful lot of choices—Shelby, Kyle, Kelsey. . . . They were all smart, and all pretty good-looking—I can get why, if you had bucks and no other way, you'd be glad to go after one of them. But *Derek*? You guys don't know—I mean, you really *don't* know how much help Derek sometimes needs, and not just with shit like his homework. He gets confused, and sometimes by really simple things. Not all the time, but . . . What kind of place could *he* end up in?"

"That's—actually interesting, Lucas," I answered; yet despite the fact that the kid had indeed done some first-rate cogitating on the subject, it was impossible for me to give an honest answer. So I danced around the basics of how Derek had likely been lured away: I talked about a woman being involved, one who could read people's weaknesses and empathize with them so strongly that she could convince them to rearrange the entirety of their lives (whatever hadn't already been rearranged, that is), and then take control of their existences, thereby seeming to let them stop feeling victimized and start feeling a sense of power. With all that to consider, Lucas at last sat back silently, while I was left to sink down in my seat, feeling like a heel about not coming clean to him; but I just couldn't do it, yet. Not without knowing and being able to tell him the *why* of it all . . .

We had decided, in order to further confound our enemies, to avoid shortcuts, as well as accept the increase in trip time, by taking I-90 all the way in to its connection with the Thruway in Albany; and by this point, we were emerging from the wilds of the eastern corridor of New York and approaching the state's capital. And tonight, even this brush with fading urban greatness seemed to lift Mike's and my own spirits a bit, while at the same time giving Lucas—who had never seen such a place—a huge thrill. A spur of highway would carry us along the west bank of the Hudson, taking us within sight of the Beaux-arts magnificence of the old state capitol, along with the equally impressive and similarly styled Delaware and Hudson Railroad Building (now the administration center of our employers, SUNY-Albany), and finally to the monstrousness of the Thruway itself. But the sheer desolation of that multi-laned highway did not descend on one's spirits until the city had been left behind amid the sparse suburban bleakness of Albany's southern environs; and as we enjoyed the elevation of optimism offered by the age-old town, Lucas returned to the throwaways case, and one of its most unpleasant aspects: the actual power behind the woman I had so sketchily profiled for him.

"I mean, I get it, it's the guy up on the mountain, obviously," he said, his mind working hard. "But—does that definitely make him the guy who ran Dr. Chang off the road?"

"I believe that is where he made his next appearance, yes," I answered.

"Well, if that was him, then—then he must've been the one that drove Derek away, I mean, *somebody* had to, and it had to be somebody close by. But the woman probably wouldn't want to risk it, if she's actually so important."

I held a finger up to the kid. "Stop with your TV connections— 'must've' and 'had to' doesn't get into this. We are profiling, here: trying to build a picture of this person, and yes, that necessitates a certain amount of speculation. But we have to base that speculation on what we *know*. So let's see what kind of a picture we can paint of this imaginary man."

"Ah, yes, '*The Imaginary Man*,'" Mike said with a half-taunting smile, recalling, from my book on Laszlo Kreizler, the term that Kreizler had used over a century ago to describe early profiling.

"Yes," I replied. "Our own imaginary man. What would you say, Lucas, is the consistent purpose behind his various appearances in the case?"

"Okay," Lucas answered, picking up the challenge. "From all the sick shit that happened on the mountain, and then forcing Dr. Chang off the road—if that's what happened to her—and then murdering that CSI guy, we know one thing, for sure: he was, like, warning us—or I guess anybody—about what to expect if they pushed too far or snitched."

"Correct. Warning was certainly the predominant aspect of those events, but there are others. A knowledge of even dangerous parts of the woods, and how to handle himself with deadly force in them, even in the dark. Then, he shows deadly driving skills in an old truck. What does all that say?"

"Well, shit, that's easy," Lucas answered. "He's local."

"Correct again—all those things suggest that he's somebody local, somebody who's been hunting, target shooting, and working on vehicles since he was your age. But now, those innocent talents make him the dark creature of the throwaway organization, the one who's released to commit the ugly acts others require to discourage outside interference, most notably ours. And yet the next time we believe we encounter him, we speculate that he's involved in moving the throwaways to their points of rendezvous. That's an additional and distinct role. That involves more than force: it also requires someone who *isn't* a rogue agent, someone who's trustworthy, maybe even likable, and takes orders. And what would combine two such sides of a person?"

"Jesus," Mike whispered. "You really *are* talking about a cop, L.T.—aren't you?"

I had to give my partner a poke with my cane at that, reminding him that this was supposed to be an exercise to keep Lucas preoccupied. But as usual, the kid had heard all:

"Hey—Mike's right! If he has to do all that, he could only be—"

"Ah, *fuck*!" Mike's exclamation was quiet but no less disconcerting; and glancing outside the car, I noted that we were by now well into the stretch of the Thruway that ran south of Albany. Complete darkness, broken only by the occasional overhanging light or passing car, had crept upon us without my noticing it. But we were in the wasteland, all right; and, such being the case, Mike's alarmed curse struck a certain amount of fear into both Lucas and me.

"What, what, what?" Lucas whispered urgently. "The Feds again?"

"I'm not sure exactly what's happening," Mike replied, trying to maintain his cool. "But as soon as we left Albany, I noticed two vehicles, the ones that're behind us now, pull into both southbound lanes—meaning we can't drop back, even if we wanted to. They're driving just the way the last cruiser did, like they've done this kind of thing a lot. Only this time, it seems like they're making good and sure that if local law enforcement messes with one of them, the other one can still follow us. And there's something else, too—the way they just started moving up on us. I get the very distinct feeling they're pissed off about something. I mean, it says cops, but at the same time . . . Okay, Lucas—back down you go. And L.T., make sure your Colt's ready."

"I knew it, I fucking *knew* it," Lucas moaned, sinking down again onto the floor. "Why did I ever let my sister make me go up the hollow that day?"

Much as it distorted the truth of his own willingness to be dispatched to meet us, the question could not help but strike me at my core, and make me wonder, even as I checked the clip on my Colt, how things might have been different if Lucas and Derek had not obeyed Ambyr's instructions, what seemed so long ago . . .

{ii.}

Glancing into my wing mirror, I saw that Mike had been right about our new shadows: there were four ominous headlights strung straight across the Thruway, and although the pair in the fast lane would swing aside to allow speeding drivers to pass, they'd immediately resume position after that, blocking our ability to suddenly slow down, fall behind them, and maybe exit the highway in an effort to lose them. But as I studied the lights more closely, I also noticed several things about their arrangement and position relative to the ground that were even more ominous.

"Mike," I said slowly, "those are *not* cruisers."

"Nope," Mike answered. "Vans—*black* vans. Just figured that one out myself."

"But they have to know they'll attract the attention of whatever troopers are patrolling this stretch, staying in both lanes. All the same, they're trying to intimidate us—to say that they're willing to get ugly, if we don't keep going. It's probably just more bullshit from Frank Mangold's crew—they certainly *look* like BCI vans. But they must know the minute they try anything I'll call Mitch McCarron, and he'll have uniforms out here in a shot. So keep going—whoever these mooks are, it's a fairly safe bet that they don't know New York like we do. We'll just proceed until something happens that makes another course necessary. Or wise."

"Oh, sure," Lucas said. "Let's just roll right along, pissing our damned pants, until they let us know they want to kill us—that's a brilliant idea."

"He's right, kid," Mike said. "I don't like it any better than you do, but it's what they're trying to do—freak us out. So all we can do is refuse to *get* freaked out."

Lucas crawled back up into his seat, still keeping his head low. "But I *am* freaking out, Mike," he whispered. "So can you please tell me how I get *un*-freaked out?"

"Well, stick with what you were doing before," Mike tried. "Use your head, work shit out. After all, Lucas, these guys are just *following* us, in the end. Even if we never shake them—though you watch and see, we *will* shake them—the worst that happens is they'll end up knowing that we went to Manhattan. And that's the thing they want, for us to get out of Surrender and go there. I know it's tough, when they're being such assholes; but it's not like they're going to disappear us."

"Exactly the point." I watched Lucas uncurl as he began to trust our arguments. "So just keep your head and use it."

"O-*kay*," Lucas conceded. "If you say so . . ."

"I do. Keep your mind on the same track: keep trying to think, for instance, of where and to what kind of people Derek might have wanted to go."

The kid's face grew puzzled. "That wasn't what I said, L.T."

"Sure it was. You were trying to think of what kind of situation Derek would want—"

"*Nooo*," Lucas droned. "I said that I couldn't think of anybody who would *take* Derek. Shit, he'd go anywhere that beat Surrender, and that's a lot of places."

And with a feeling that was pretty startling, even in our situation at that moment, I realized that Lucas was right: perhaps because of my unease at having had to be evasive, I *had* misinterpreted his earlier words, and the realization of it struck me dumb.

Mike quickly grew anxious at my continued silence. "L.T.? Come on now, no Sorcerer shit—"

I began to mumble slowly: "He's right. What Lucas said before—'Who would want a kid like Derek?' Exactly; who *would*? And what you also said, Lucas: 'He gets confused.' In fact, Derek's not like the other throw-aways at all. He could be talked into anything . . . We've been wrong—*I've* been wrong." I glanced into my wing mirror, seeing the vans again, then turned to the back seat, reordering my thoughts in an attempt to reassure my colleagues and get us out of the trap into which I had arrogantly walked us. "Lucas," I said. "Pull up a map of the Thruway on your phone—I want you to find the next exit that offers us a fast way to turn completely around and head north again."

"What?" Still confused, Mike was now growing impatient. "L.T., we're on our way to New York, that's where the Augustines are, and it might be where Derek is, too—we can't turn around!"

"Yes we can, Michael. Because what you just said is both irrelevant and untrue. It's a hell of a time to realize it, but what did you tell us about those two vans—that they're taking up both lanes to prevent us from dropping back."

"Yeah?" Mike was trying carefully to follow me as he laid on more speed.

"Dropping back—or *turning around* . . ."

"Oh, fuck," Lucas moaned, eyes on his phone as he scrolled through a map page and enlarged sections of it with his fingers. "Come on, L.T., turn *around*? We gotta find out who's behind all this in New York, we have to go see that Augustine dude, and we have to find Derek!"

"Just keep looking," I told the kid. "Roger Augustine will always be there, that lead is solid. But as for the rest of it—well, if I'm wrong, we're going to find out very soon."

"L.T.—" Mike tried to calm down. "We've already figured out that these guys are following us. They want to know where we're going, to find out what we find out, or stop us *from* finding it out—"

"Got it!" Lucas shouted. " 'The New Baltimore Travel Center and Service Area.' Google Maps says we'll have to take a back route out of the place, but it'll get us back on the Thruway going north."

"Yeah, I know the joint," Mike said. "Not a bad spot to lose these guys, actually—though I'd be able to do it with a lot more conviction if I knew what the *fuck* is going on."

With Lucas still studying his phone, I turned to Mike and poked him with my cane again. "Trust me, Mike—we have to know what these guys *actually* want."

Seeing that I was in deadly earnest, Mike nodded. "And you know how, hunh? Okay—I'll trust you as far as New Baltimore. But then you've got some explaining to do, L.T."

"If I'm right, those boys back there will do the explaining for us . . ."

Soon we took the off-ramp to the New Baltimore pit stop, and made for the "Service Area" at the back, which was mainly a huge truck stop. Amid the collection of tractor-trailers, it seemed at first that Mike had been able to lose what I was now almost certain were *not,* in fact, our "shadows"; but then we came to the small intersection with a byroad that led to the Thruway going back north, to find that our antagonists had read our movements (and confirmed my suspicions), by having sent one of their vans ahead to block the way. We halted, both Mike and Lucas plainly dumbfounded.

Unfortunately, I wasn't. "So . . ." I murmured. "Not *following,* at all— *driving."*

"Meaning what?" Mike asked grimly.

"Meaning, Michael, that they're not trailing after us—they're pushing us forward. They don't want to know where we're going—they just want to make sure we keep going and get there. This whole fucking thing—it's a farce. They suckered us. Suckered *me* . . ." I pulled my phone out, and fumbled to find Mitch McCarron's private cell number.

"Oh, what the fuck, what the fuck . . ." Lucas had heard little of what I'd said, and understood less. "You guys have got your guns, right? I mean, we're not, like, helpless here, *right?"*

But just then something extraordinary, if foolhardy, happened: Mike Li got pissed off enough to start a fight. "A farce, hunh?" he said through gritted teeth. "Well, I'm not laughing . . ." He snatched his .38 from his ankle and called behind him, "Yeah, we've got our guns, Lucas." Cracking his door open, he added, "And if these guys want to fucking shoot me in front of all these fucking truckers, then they can go ahead, but I'm not putting up with this shit anymore!"

With that he shut off the car (being still sane enough to kill our lights and make less of a target of himself) and got out, eluding my attempt to grab him. I couldn't have held him back, anyway: Mike didn't often get angry enough to put his life in any kind of danger, but when he did, it was usually inspired as much by concern for his colleagues as for himself— and it almost always made him into a true wild man. Holding him back at such moments was rarely possible; and he really had had enough of being harassed by these shadowy men.

"Mike, you idiot!" Lucas called. "What are you doing, get back in the damned car!"

But Mike's words were already being directed toward the van that sat some thirty or forty feet away. He strode toward it with magnificent, foolhardy determination. *"What, you fuckers?"* he shouted, holding his arms up defiantly. "What the fuck do you want? This is still a free fucking country—*supposedly*! So all your little BCI badges and your scary-looking vans don't mean—"

I don't know if Mike even heard the first shot. He later said he did, but gunfire is not something he's ever walked into so obliviously; yet when an arm appeared on the passenger side of the van holding what looked like a Glock, and then a sharp report registered within earshot of anyone in the rest area—sending the truckers who were hanging out nearby running for their rigs, and a few of them for their own handguns—Mike just kept walking and shouting, possessed by weeks of pent-up rage that was, I knew, born of Gracie Chang's brush with death.

When the second 9mm shot nicked him in the right shoulder, however, raising a small spurt of blood that made Lucas holler in fear, Mike began returning fire wildly with his left hand. I swung my door open, drew my Colt, and started banging away at anything on the van that wouldn't result in a loss of human life: the headlights were my first targets, and they shattered, so darkening the field of fire that I could make my way around the front of the Empress and toward my retreating partner. Next, I went for our antagonists' grille and radiator, effectively eliminating them from any ensuing action on the Thruway. Yet the van's occupants did not attempt to so cripple the Empress, confirming my suspicion that their main goal was to keep us moving south; south, and away from whatever their cohorts were planning to do back north.

I got to Mike fairly quickly, and, leaning more heavily than usual on my cane, told him to get his left arm around my neck from the right side.

"Nah, I'm all right, L.T.," Mike seethed in pain. "Just get into the car, before they kill us both!"

"Forget them," I said. Several armed truckers had by now started approaching the van, guns at the ready, making our movements easier. "I don't think they're actually trying to kill us—but we've got to get back on the road, get you patched up, and come up with a new plan. The shooting may be over, for now, but we're still not out of this shit. What's the next bridge back over the river, the Rip Van Winkle, right?" Mike grunted in the affirmative as I called out, "Lucas!"

"Yo!" the kid replied, with admirable guts. He was scared, all right, but he wasn't losing it, which was good—because his next task would be his most difficult.

"You can drive, can't you?" By now Mike and I had reached the car, and I opened the back door.

The mere mention of driving caused Lucas to leap into the front seat. "Fuck yes, I can drive!"

Mike fell into the car behind the kid as I came around the back and got in beside him. "Then do it," I said, to which Lucas whooped and restarted the V-8. "We've got to head for the entry road back onto the Thruway, going south again—they won't try to stop us."

"Trajan, what in the holy high fuck are you doing?" Mike said, gripping his shoulder. "That kid can't drive—he doesn't even have a learner's permit!"

I began tearing Mike's shirtsleeve away to find a wound that, thankfully, had passed through his skin but only just grazed any muscle. "Really, Mike? That's your chief concern, right now, that he doesn't have a license?" Leaning over the front passenger seat, I opened the glove compartment and pulled out our emergency kit. "You've been clipped, there's truckers ready to turn this place into a battlefield—and your worry is that he doesn't have a God damned *license*?"

"My worry is that he's going to wreck my baby," Mike seethed.

"Don't you worry, Mike," Lucas said, adjusting the rearview mirror and then putting the car in gear. "I'm a country boy, we're *born* knowing how to drive!"

"Yeah, you *used* to be, maybe," Mike said. "Nowadays, I'm not so sure that most—" But he was cut off when Lucas threw the car into gear and slammed on the gas, causing Mike to clutch at his wound. "That's what I'm talking about, you little reprobate! A light touch, a *light touch*!"

"Whoa, I can see what you mean," Lucas judged, awed but not overwhelmed by his position. Instead, he used the rapidly emptying parking lot by the Travel Center to weave in and out of parked cars, very smartly getting the feel for the Empress' handling before he hit the highway. "It's real tight, all right—let's see what we can do to loosen her up . . ."

"No!" Mike shouted. "That's exactly—ah, fuck it, we're doomed, what am I saying . . ."

I grabbed a nearby bottle of water and then a flask of whiskey from the kit. As I opened the first, I hit the speaker button on my phone and laid it up on the rear deck, where the repeated sound of my attempt to reach Mitch McCarron was amplified by the window. "Okay, Mike," I said, opening the flask. "You down some of this like a good boy."

"What the—*ow,* fuck it, Trajan!" Mike said, drinking deep as I pressed some gauze tight to his wound. In a few seconds the whiskey hit home, and he sighed. "Whew. Better. Say—do I hear a phone ringing?"

"Yes," I said. "I'm trying to reach Mitch, and get our friends in the second van intercepted."

Mike nodded. "So," he said, "what the hell were—"

"Okay, motherfuckers!" Lucas shouted from the driver's seat, having reached the Thruway entrance. "Grab onto something that's bolted down, Lucas Kurtz is about to teach the rest of the people on this road why driving at night makes them nervous!"

"Aw, Jesus," Mike groaned. "Please, L.T., don't let him kill my car . . ."

I picked up my still-ringing phone, checked to see that I had dialed the right number, then grabbed some tape, fresh gauze, and a syringe of lidocaine from the satchel. I smeared the bandage with disinfectant and antibiotic gel, saying, "Okay, Li—get ready. Little pinch, as we say in the trade." And before he could protest, I'd pumped his arm full of the lidocaine and then taped the bandage tightly to his arm, causing him to yell and then groan deeply; but before he could let loose a long stream of invective, Mitch McCarron's voice finally came through on the speaker in my phone.

"Trajan, where the hell are you guys?" he asked.

"Exactly where you think, Mitch," I answered. "I assume the reason it took you so long to answer is that you're getting calls about us from several interested parties?"

"Yeah-uh," Mitch answered, never losing his even keel. "Who the hell is shooting at who, down there, and are you all right?"

"Mike got his wing clipped," I said. "Nothing serious—"

"Says him, Mitch!" Mike shouted. "You gonna get us some backup or what?"

"We've got units on the way to the service area, and Troop F's almost there, already. I told their commander that I've got a personal stake in this one, so he's cooperating. Just tell me what your position is—"

"Ah—I don't think I'd better do that, Mitch," I replied carefully. "You may not believe me, but I'm pretty sure that big ears may be listening to our little doings."

"Jesus—if that's true, then what makes you think they won't just track your phones? You guys know there's almost no way to stop that."

"Almost!" Mike shouted. "And that's all I'm saying about *that*."

"We'll be all right on that score, Mitch. As for our friends back there, I don't know for sure, but they're traveling in what certainly look like BCI vans."

"My God," Mitch answered. "I didn't think Frank had the guts . . ."

"He doesn't," I said. "If you ask me, he's got clearance from higher up—although, for what it's worth, I don't think his morons *meant* to hit any of us, just scare us back onto the southbound road. Mike walked himself into it, although that doesn't make it any less crazy to open fire in a spot like that. But that's as much as I think I'd better say for now. Just get after those vans—one's crippled back at the station, the other one will be following us south from here. So get them off us, will you?"

"Wait, Trajan!" Mitch called. "If you can't tell me how you're going to, uh, *proceed,* can you at least tell me what this is all about?"

"Again, Mitch, no go," I replied; then I picked up the phone, shut off the speaker, and turned to the side, keeping my voice low. "But if what I'm afraid of is in the works—well, just do me a favor, will you, and get some people over to Shiloh? This whole thing is getting real ugly, real fast."

"Okay, Doc," Mitch answered. "You be careful driving."

"I'm not driving."

"Then who the hell—"

"We'll see you later, Mitch . . ."

{iii.}

Much to Lucas' indignation, I didn't let him drive for all that long. We never saw the second black van again; I would later find out that before it even got out of the parking lot in New Baltimore, a cruiser from Troop F intercepted its crew, although those shadowy figures refused to discuss either their identities or their orders until the arrival of their superiors, who informed the troopers that a full explanation of what had taken place was above their pay grade. Inside our car, meanwhile, once Mike had dozed off in the back, I told Lucas to pull into the breakdown lane of the Thruway, where we used several of the cushions from my usual seat to get me fixed up in the pilot's spot, while the kid returned to his seat in the back. Our young apprentice was full of protests about the inadvisability of letting a one-legged man take the helm, but the truth was that he was pretty worn out, himself; and by the time we reached the long approach road that led through the chain stores surrounding the once-pretty little town of Catskill and then to the Rip Van Winkle Bridge that would carry us back over the Hudson to Route 23 headed east, the evening's stress had caused him to drift off, too.

Such was just as well, being as, while I knew a lot of indirect ways to get back to Surrender from the general area of the town of Hudson to the north of the bridge's east side, I hadn't traveled them in a long time, and needed to focus; indeed, given the terrible thoughts of what might well be waiting for us when we got back to Shiloh, focusing became doubly important. I therefore gripped the wheel as tight as I could, keeping my eyes out for route signs and trying to remember that if we didn't make it home as quickly as our covert course would allow, or if we were again intercepted on the way, all the reinterpreting we'd done in the car, all the vital reexaminations of the personalities and problems involved in this penultimate stage of the case, would mean nothing.

But solitude soon began to work against my sanity; and so it was just as well that, when the car went over a sharp break in the asphalt just at the point where the last of the county roads I'd navigated hit Route 7, some fifteen miles from the turnoff for Surrender, Mike was roused from his injury- and scotch-induced sleep. His head rolled from side to side for a moment, and then he began to scratch and rub at his hair and face, yawning and attempting to fully orient himself—a task that was only completed when he got a look at me.

"Jesus, L.T.," he said quietly, his mouth and throat dry. Then he crawled into the front seat carefully, to avoid waking Lucas. "You look worse than I feel—grab that steering wheel much harder and you'll snap it in half. What's going on?"

"Nothing," I said, hoping it sounded convincing. "Just trying to keep track of the route. It's been a slightly complicated drive . . ."

"I guess so." Mike attempted to locate some kind of moisture in his mouth and throat, and then, failing, found instead a water bottle and took a long pull. He waited a moment before proceeding, very lucidly and carefully: "Come on. L.T.—give."

"About what?"

"About *what*? First you figure out that those BCI guys—or whoever the hell they were—were actually pushing us toward New York, not following us there, which means that they wanted us out of Burgoyne County and certainly out of Surrender—"

"Yeah," I murmured. "I'm so fucking smart it never occurred to me that whoever's behind this knew just how bad I wanted payback for what we went through in New York . . ."

"I get that," Mike said, nodding. "So then you try to turn us around, and they start shooting, which pretty much proves they had orders from pretty high up on the food chain."

"Safe assumption."

"And now you're driving like . . ."

"Like my life depends on it?"

"Nope," Mike answered simply. "I've seen you in situations where your life depended on something. You don't lose it like this. You ask me, you've bottled up just about every form of anxiety that a guy can, about something or somebody *else*, and it's making you go quietly but obviously batshit." I couldn't find words to answer; but Mike soon resolved that dilemma. "It's a certain person we shouldn't mention, isn't it?" He pulled a pack of cigarettes from his shirt pocket. "Well?" he continued, lighting two smokes and giving me one. "I mean, I saw your face when we discussed her with the students last night, but—this is something new."

I shook my head, fighting to keep the words down: "Yeah. It is. Jesus, Mike, I've accepted that I'll probably never see her again, but—seeing her dead would be worse."

"You figure the sniper went after her?" Mike said, quietly. "To tie up one loose end, and to warn us off even harder?"

"Will you shut up?" I hissed desperately. "Jesus, Mike, yes, that's what I'm worried about; and if it happens, there's only one spot where he's get her—in Marcianna's enclosure, which means Marcianna's in danger, too . . ."

"Yeah. That would certainly screw with what's left of your mental balance," Mike said. I could only nod quickly in reply. "But somehow, I'm doubting any of it has happened. And if you want to know why, it's because you convinced me too good. Whoever's behind this, ultimately, on the ground they need her—the person-who-must-not-be-mentioned, I mean—they might move her somewhere, but what you're thinking about? I doubt it. Whatever's happening, she's still too useful." Having finished the water, Mike reached back for the scotch flask.

"Hey," I said, actually feeling somewhat relieved by what he'd said. "Don't drink too much more of that—whatever we find, I'm going to need you sharp."

"L.T., please," Mike said, as we finally turned off of Route 7 and onto County Route 34. "I've had maybe two shots, altogether, over an hour ago. You know me better than that."

"Just go easy." By now we'd reached the statue of Caractacus Jones. "There's a couple of Cokes in the food bin. Grab one, it'll sharpen you up." Mike did as he was told, holding his can up to the statue as I circled the town square, vainly hoping for a glimpse of Cousin Caitlin's cruiser.

"Here's to you, Colonel," Mike said, taking a deep draft of the Coke. "And to your damned riddle . . ." As Mike recapped the Coke he seemed to realize what I was doing, at which point his own expression began to look more apprehensive. We were just leaving the square and starting down the straight length of foliage-enfolded road toward Death's Head Hollow when he murmured, "Wasn't that Amazon beauty Caitlin sup-, posed to be patrolling around here?"

His answer came as soon as he'd asked the question: up ahead, at the entrance to the hollow, the flashing blues, reds, and whites of not only Caitlin's car, but several other marked and unmarked vehicles—including one that I recognized as Mitch McCarron's cruiser—were pulsing away.

"Jesus," I murmured, almost mad with fear. "We're too late. Too fucking late . . ."

"You don't know that," Mike said firmly, trying to believe it. "Mitch sent Caitlin backup after we spoke to him, that's all. No big deal. Just standard procedure, right?" His face darkened as we drew closer. "But then why's *he* here, too? And what the hell are they all looking at?"

Too drained to even try to answer Mike's questions, I slowly pulled the Empress over to the side of the road. "Mike," I said, in little more than a whisper. "I need you to drive up the hollow."

"Trajan, they're going to want us over there, we've got to stop—"

"Above all, we *cannot* stop," I answered. "Or rather, *you* can't. We'll switch seats—you take the wheel. I'll get out when we pass them, but we'll only pause for a second—then you get up to Shiloh and tell Lucas whatever you have to: say the old girl had a heart attack and I had to go with her to the hospital. Get Annabel to help, I'm guessing she knows all about this, too; give him whatever he wants, ice cream, beer laced with Ambien, I don't give a shit, but you keep him in that house!"

"Annabel knows all about it—about *what*?" Mike shook his head as I got out and he grabbed the wheel and pulled himself into the driver's seat.

"Just move," I said, getting myself back into the car.

Mike knew well enough that whatever was up was big, and I think he suspected, based on my earlier state, that something fairly terrible had happened to Ambyr, something that had to be kept from Lucas. When we pulled into the hollow, we both noted that the various occupants of the cruisers, including Caitlin and Mitch, were all gathered around something in the tall grass at the base of a big maple that had stood at the entrance to Death's Head Hollow for all of my life, and for long before that, its limbs growing outward and almost parallel to the ground. Because of this, it was a favorite climbing tree for the children of Surrender, and I had often seen them making their way out onto those limbs. When I'd been a boy, the sight had filled me with enormous envy, and I'd have given a great deal to have been able to tackle that tree; now, however, I would have given almost anything to stay away from it.

And I wondered, if my worst imaginings of the moment proved accurate, whether such children would ever play there again . . .

I got out of the car as Mitch and the other troopers turned to catch sight of us, and then sent Mike on his way. As I approached the tree through the moist grass, I picked Clarissa's face out of the cluster of officers when she turned on my approach. Her shoulders wrapped in a North African shawl, she was closer to the tree than the others, and I could see that her features were ashen. She met me several paces from the crowd and, unusually for her, embraced me very tightly.

"Again," she murmured, her still-strong frame trembling. "It's happened again—after so long . . ."

I didn't say anything in reply; there wasn't much need to. Now that I was close enough, I could see that there was a length of quarter-inch nylon cord hanging from a bough of the maple some fifteen feet from the ground. It had been cut at just about the spot that someone of Caitlin's height could have reached with her arm fully extended. She and the several other troopers parted for me, while Mitch put a hand to my shoulder.

"I'm sorry, Trajan," he said. "But don't worry—we're going to figure out what all this business means. We're going to get these sons of bitches . . ."

I didn't answer, just nodded once and took a step in front of him; and there, lying in the grass in a position that could almost have been taken for restful, if the expression on the face and the protruding of the swollen purple tongue had not been so obscene, was Derek. The nylon rope around his neck had garroted him savagely, breaking through the skin at spots. His clothes were the same that he had worn to dinner when he'd come to Shiloh: he had dressed his best, for the deliverance that had become his doom. On his chest was pinned a large piece of notepaper, its message terribly simple; indeed, its few words made the citizens of Surrender who, all those generations ago, had sacrificed the lives of two young men in like fashion to Colonel Jones' wrath seem quite eloquent:

THIS IS ON YOU—NOW BACK OFF.

I got onto my one knee by the boy, whose eyes were still open and somewhat swollen from the breaking of his neck; then I looked to Mitch. "Any idea how far away Weaver is?"

"Out of county, on call," Mitch said. "Gonna be at least an hour."

"Okay, then." I reached down, put my hand to Derek's brow, and brought it down on his eyelids. Rigor sets in faster on the eyes and eyelids than on most parts of the body—sometimes taking as little as two hours—and I wasn't going to leave the boy with that ghastly stare on the off chance that Ernest Weaver might pass up a McDonald's on his way to Surrender. Despite the slight protrusion of the dark orbs themselves, the lids slid over them easily; and with my back covering my work, I decided to finish the job by coaxing the swollen tongue into the mouth and closing the jaw. Out of the corner of my eye, I saw Mitch indicate silence to any of the assembled troopers who might want to protest; and with these small acts of respect done, heartbreaking as they were, Derek finally looked as much at peace as possible. I brushed some of his hair from his cold forehead, murmuring:

"And so, Derek—flights of angels, kid . . ."

Knowing that there was so much more yet to be taken care of, that night, I pulled myself up on my cane with some help from Mitch, and rejoined Clarissa. There was no real point in my hanging around and joining the wait to see when Weaver would show up and pompously pronounce the already obvious cause of death; there was, on the other hand, every point in getting back to Shiloh, and getting Mike down to the scene to do what he could before some FIC tech made a hash of the whole thing. Whatever time and caffeine hadn't done to burn the small amount of scotch from his body, the sight of Derek would, and he'd be sharp. So, after reintroducing myself to Caitlin, I turned to Mitch and asked if Ambyr and Lucas' cousin could drive my great-aunt and myself back up to the farm. My thought was that his cousin's presence might help Lucas with the shock of Derek's death; but surprisingly, Clarissa protested rather firmly that she'd rather walk, glancing my way to indicate I'd better not argue the point. I wasn't certain how far I was going to make it up Death's Head on foot; but, going into my pockets for a cigarette, I discovered that the ever-reliable Mike had at some point slipped the scotch flask into my jacket pocket. Thus armed, I figured I'd be okay, although I didn't want to take a snort until we were out of sight of the uniforms.

We'd only gotten about a hundred yards up the hollow, however, before Clarissa stopped me, firmly taking hold of my arm and then my hand. "Bad as that was, Trajan," she said rather desperately, "there's more to come. Get a good grip on yourself."

With those words, my insides took a momentary dip, and I went for the whiskey flask without opening it. *"Marcianna . . . ?"* I said, in what was scarcely a whisper.

Clarissa's grip loosened just a bit, and she frowned at me. "*What*? Your God damned *cheetah*? That's what you're worried about, right now?"

"It's the only thing in question," I mumbled, finally sipping the whiskey.

But Clarissa quickly grabbed the flask from me. "Your pet is fine! Jesus, Trajan—here! I found it in the master bedroom." She shoved a small piece of paper into my hand: a sheet of inexpensive white stationery likely purchased at Target, I quickly conjectured. When unfolded, it revealed yet another simple message, written in a delicate, neat hand that wavered just a bit as it warned:

We have the girl.

I suppose Clarissa was waiting for some kind of deeply emotional response; for tears, at least; all I can be certain of is that, when what she in fact got was a small, bitter smile, it caused her to slap me across the face, I think as much to bring me to my senses as to punish me.

"It's all right, Clarissa," I said, scarcely even feeling the sting on my cheek. "Nothing will happen to Ambyr. But who did you leave at the house?"

"I was able to get Happy and Chick to come up," she answered, perhaps a little surprised that I'd guessed at her move. "And they're armed, don't worry."

"I'm not worried," I said. "*They're* armed, *I'm* armed, everybody in this damned *county's* armed—and yet the only shooting in this case has been on the part of law enforcement. 'You cannot escape it, in this country . . .'"

"Trajan, I will slap you again," Clarissa said, "if you don't start making sense. Don't you understand—they've taken Ambyr!"

"I understand that Ambyr's *gone,* Clarissa—trust me on that." I finally got a cigarette into my mouth, where I left it hanging for a few seconds as I looked back at what little we could see of the pulsing cruiser lights. "And I understand that Derek's dead," I whispered. "I understand that he never stood much of a chance—and how shitty that was . . ." I shook my head hard, at which Clarissa pulled out her lighter and put it to the butt in my mouth. "We've got to get Mike down here, fast. Which means we've got to get back to the house." Then I drank the last of the Talisker in a few big pulls.

"Do you need to get drunk?" Clarissa said, as we turned to start walking again. "Is it that bad?"

"Don't worry—that was just for my hip. No, I won't get drunk; but let's go. And on the way, I'll tell you a little story. About a girl; a girl who, intentionally or not, left breadcrumbs behind her . . ."

"I've already said that I'm not going to talk to you," Clarissa warned, "if you're just going to babble like an idiot. What the hell are we going to tell Lucas, Trajan? What the hell has happened to his sister? And what the *hell* do these people want from us?"

"'*These people*'—that's complicated, Aunt . . ." We kept on moving through the unique blackness that was the lowermost part of Death's Head Hollow at night, with the sky increasingly obscured by a canopy of interlacing trees that, despite their extraordinary beauty during the day, could take on a brooding, even threatening air in the dark, one that brought to mind every bit of the misery that the old cart path had seen in its earliest years. "But," I went on, "I can say that each of them hungers for the same results: power, success, *more*. Indeed, their common and basic urge is just that—they *crave*, Clarissa, and with a voraciousness that is frightening . . ."

At which point, some might say at long last, the terribleness of Derek's death, of Lucas' sudden aloneness, and of Ambyr's supposed disappearance hit me extraordinarily hard: my words caught in my throat, as my body shook and my eyes welled up. Clarissa had chosen that same instant to light one of her Camels, and she was able to make out my features in the glow offered by her lighter; upon which she hooked her right arm tight in my free one, being careful not to let her own steps interfere with those of my prosthesis. When my voice returned, I said, with an unsteadiness that belied any professional detachment, "I can only tell you as much of it as I know, Aunt. You may not credit the story, until I can prove it; any more than you will believe me when I say that I'm beginning to understand what old Caractacus meant, when he came to Surrender that last time . . ."

{iv.}

As the hours of that wretched night wore on, Lucas entered a dissociative state of the type that can all too easily become long term and lead to severe personality disorders. That much of a preliminary diagnosis I was able to reach on my own, despite my closeness to the boy, and it was admittedly an obvious one; but it was later supported by Clarissa's personal doctor, as well as by a psychologist from Fraser, the pair of whom came to Shiloh in the morning (such were the strings that my great-aunt could still pull, vestiges of an age that would doubtless pass with her). The kid remained in the master bedroom at Shiloh, eyes fixed on the emptiness around him, all of his sister's belongings having disappeared with her. This last struck even Clarissa as a strange feature to characterize a kidnapping; and perhaps even so young and tortured a mind as Lucas' could see it. Yet if the thought did occur to him, he made no more comment on it than he did on anything else. He just sat in an easy chair by the room's westward window, immovable as stone and hysterically silent, staring at a single, indefinable point in the abandoned chamber until the lines under his eyes became bags so terribly discolored that he looked as if he had taken bad blows in a fight; and in this, of course, his outer body was only revealing his inward reality.

There was perhaps some danger of Lucas' withdrawing so far into himself that the person he had been would become splintered and finally obliterated, given that the death of his best friend—his effective brother—and the disappearance of his sister had followed the desertion of his parents far too quickly. Yet I had been through a lot with him, by now; and his ability to face down several moments of risk and danger with something that transcended precocity proved that his coping mechanisms had been developed to a point that I'd seen only in a few young people, or even adults. For the most part, I'd observed such strength among those stricken by chronic and painful illnesses, cancer (especially given my own experience) among them; yet I knew that the "disease" of Lucas' life—desertion—brought with it psychic costs as great as any physical malady, when it occurred so repetitively and brutally; and so I could not dismiss the danger of real harm, whatever my own feelings about his ability to rebound.

We got at least some encouragement when, in talking not only to the generalists present but to a pediatric psychiatrist in Albany whom Clarissa managed to get on the phone mid-morning, a consensus was reached that the period of Lucas' newfound stress had likely been too short for there to be serious risk of transition to a fugue state (a kind of amnesia, encompassing not just events but the entire persona) or other personality disorder. Furthermore, we agreed that if we could somehow spark a response in him, a response that would end his almost inhuman determination to retreat into himself, we could stave off the seeds of chronic depression, bipolarity, and even schizophrenia that too often grow out of such cases, particularly in adolescents.

We decided to take shifts monitoring our young friend—each of us staying for four or five hours at a time in the bedroom with him—and await some sign that would allow us to ward off what was, to me, the ultimate danger: the psychopharmacologists who, if we took Lucas to a hospital, would try to jerk him back to reality with drugs. And through the hours of waiting and hoping, each of us—myself, Mike, Clarissa, and even Annabel—clung ever more tightly to the belief that Lucas trusted us enough to come back, and to reassemble the pieces that had always made him so unique, and such a fighter for so much longer than should ever have been his lot. Yet our role was not simple attendance: we also needed to be on the lookout for that unknown thing that we'd all, professionals and caring friends alike, agreed might assist or trigger his process of return. And not long after the conference call, I stumbled on it. After we'd talked to the pediatric psychiatrist, I returned to Marcianna's enclosure, where I'd spent as much of the night as I could in her company. I fed and hung out with her for just a few minutes, then returned to the house and headed up to the master bedroom, where Mike was keeping watch in an armchair just inside the door, using his iPad to go over the few trace results he'd been able to obtain from Derek's body the night before. I slowly approached the west window, and noticed that, off in the distance, Marcianna had again started to issue that particular chirruping that I knew was inspired by the killer on the ridgeline. I made no mention of it, as I leaned down to stare into Lucas' terribly hollow gaze—

At which point something remarkable happened: each time that Marcianna let loose her high, somewhat desperate call, Lucas' eyes—so motionless and dead, to that point, even their blinking having been reduced to an absolute minimum—reacted. It was not a dramatic movement, just the barest beginnings of a twitch; but it was real and unprecedented, all the same. In order to confirm the observation, I retreated to where Mike was sitting, and quietly asked him to take a look and judge whether I was simply seeing something that I wanted to see; but he soon confirmed that this was the first example of response we'd had in over twelve hours.

Which was good enough for me. Breaking a long-standing edict concerning the farmhouse, and trusting to all the training concerning Terence that I'd given Marcianna, I returned to the enclosure, where my companion was racing toward the gate at full speed, seeming to know just what I had in mind. Once inside the gate, I leaned down to clip her retractable leash on her collar, then took her somewhat boxy skull in both my hands and lifted her eyes to mine.

"You have to behave, today, girl," I said. "And above all, you have to help the young one . . ."

All such admonitions, Marcianna told me through the purposeful manner in which she began to walk several steps before me toward the house, were superfluous: she knew her job, and she knew its urgency. Swiftly and without games we reached the house, Marcianna stepping onto the porch as though she had simply been waiting for someone to let her do her job. Which was the moment, of course, when I heard Clarissa's voice:

"Oh, no you don't!" she decreed, rushing out from the back of the house with Terence yapping at her heels. She adjusted her volume, if not her urgency and anger, in consideration of the patient upstairs. "Not in my house—we've had this discussion, Trajan." Emerging onto the porch, and being forcefully reminded of just how big Marcianna was (for she hadn't stood next to my other self in years), Clarissa snatched her noisy little furball off the floor and clutched him tight. "We agreed, damn it—if you want to keep that animal, okay, I gave you that pasture out of the goodness of my heart. But we agreed then that she was never, ever going to come inside—"

"*Ssh*, Aunt!" I whispered, pointing up. "What are you trying to do, make things worse?"

"What are *you* trying to do?" she whispered back; then her pair of doctors appeared, walking confidently toward the porch until they saw Marcianna, at which point they seemed to realize that there were important matters they'd forgotten to discuss just inside the house, though still close enough to observe the fun. "I've just been learning about traumas like Lucas's," said Clarissa. "What in the world makes you think that having a wild animal suddenly in his presence will do any good—"

"Excuse me, Clarissa." I let her catch her breath, after which she proceeded to finally quiet the bit of snow-white business in her arms by feeding him a couple of the dog treats: "Willing as I have been to consult with those other gentlemen," I went on, "I must remind you that I have degrees in both psychiatry and psychology, and that I specialize in predicting what behaviors will result from which stimuli. And I'm telling you this—not fifteen minutes ago, Lucas registered ocular reaction to the sound of Marcianna's voice. Understand? It's not at all uncommon for kids in his kind of trouble to shut out the human world and accept only interaction with another species—and I'm willing to bet that she'll provide the jolt that none of us have been able to. This is critical, damn it: otherwise, we're eventually going to have knock him out with drugs, to prevent a psychotic break due to self-imposed sleep deprivation. All of which is a long, stupid way of telling you that *he needs her.*"

Clarissa kept scowling suspiciously, but soon said, "You're *sure* you saw it?" I nodded. "And this 'ocular reaction'? What's so special about that?"

At which point I got unexpected help: the psychologist from Fraser. "Actually, Clarissa," he opined, stepping forward, "it would be significant. If it's prompted by one stimulus, as your nephew is saying, it would show that something has broken through the boy's determination to punish himself with sleeplessness. As we've discussed, sleep deprivation is one of the most acute forms of torment, and if there is even a chance—"

But by now Clarissa had turned on the poor man slowly, at which he dummied up, excusing himself quickly. "Well," my aunt said. "Now that *everyone's* been heard from . . ." She put a finger inches from my nose. "*Anything* goes wrong, and all bets are off. Do you understand, Trajan?"

"Got it," I said, stepping forward and then into the house, with Marcianna moving very carefully beside me. She glanced around at the place with, unusually, very little curiosity: she truly believed she had a job to do, and she wasn't going to brook distractions. We took to the stairs, which were a new experience for her, but she mastered them as she did everything; and in a few more seconds, we were standing outside the master bedroom, from which Mike had emerged to meet us.

"I heard most of the conversation," he said. "You sure about this, L.T.?"

"No," I replied, taking a deep breath. "But she is."

" 'She is'? Trajan, you *do* understand that you could just be reading a lot into the situation."

"Yeah, but I don't think so. Listen, keep going over that material of yours, will you?" I indicated his iPad. "There's got to be something we're missing . . ."

He nodded halfheartedly; and with Mike thus engaged in the hall, I opened the bedroom door a crack, one that Marcianna widened with her muzzle and head, as determined as ever to reach her goal. I decided to let her out on a fairly long lead, so that she could stand in the middle of the room as I followed at a discreet distance. She opened her mouth and seemed to chirrup, although she made no sound. Her worried air heightened, and her gaze remained fixed on Lucas, who never turned. For a moment I thought that the attempt had turned out to be what Mike had said, me reading a whole lot into things that were, in fact, disconnected. Then Marcianna tried a little harder, and a softer, quieter version of the cry that she'd been making for so long got out of her . . .

I looked immediately at Lucas' eyes; and what had been a mere flicker of movement earlier suddenly became more pronounced, and visible even from where I was sitting; then, at a second, more insistent chirrup, his terrible death stare finally began to break. He allowed only his eyes to quickly glance in Marcianna's direction, permitting me, in turn, to let more of the nylon lead out. Marcianna maintained its tautness, straining to reach the boy; and finally, when she was just a few feet from him, Lucas' head moved very slightly. I didn't want her to bound up onto him in that way that she was used to doing outside, where she'd learned that his young body could withstand her roughhousing. At length, however, I let her bring her face just up to his.

Her muzzle touched Lucas' arms, neck, and cheeks, before she committed to that ultimate token of intimacy, the brushing of her own nose against his. Lucas' eyelids fluttered, then blinked several times, and ultimately he turned to stare into the golden orbs before him. Finally, he moved: his head lifted to allow Marcianna to nuzzle into his neck, and she began to purr loudly. After that, the kid lifted one arm slowly, and stroked the side of Marcianna's neck. This went on for several seconds, until the boy put his two arms around her neck, buried his face in her fur, and began to heave just audibly with gentle sobs. Marcianna then licked at his arms, and before long, the two seemed to have joined in a ritual of horrific sorrow.

There was no way to *tell* Mike what was happening; so I let more of Marcianna's lead out, this time to allow myself to back up to the bedroom door. Silently opening it just a crack, I beckoned my partner in, stopping him when only his face appeared so that we would not upset the delicate emotional balance of what was taking place. Immediately, Mike smiled; and, thinking that Lucas and Marcianna would be all right on their own for a moment, I carefully crept halfway into the hall, so that I could whisper to Mike without being heard within.

But he spoke first, saying, just audibly, "That's unbelievable. Unbe-fucking-lievable . . ."

"Yeah," I agreed, unable to embellish his assessment. I nodded at the iPad. "Anything?"

Switching gears, Mike said, "Maybe. Just maybe. Didn't you tell me that Meisner kid had a Dodge truck with all-terrain tires?" I told him I had. "Well, here—" He pointed to an image of moist, bare ground near Derek's body. "In case you're wondering, that's an all-terrain tire track. Could be a coincidence, of course, lots of people have them—"

"*Coincidence,*" I answered bitterly as I pulled out my phone and once more dialed Mitch McCarron's number. When he answered, I quickly said: "Listen, Mitch: I need to know whatever address you people have on record for one Kevin Meisner, here in Surrender."

"We don't usually do that, Trajan," Mitch said dubiously. "But if it's connected—"

"It is," I said. "Text it to both Mike and me as soon as you can." I hung up quickly.

Mike studied me. "You sure you want to go down this road, L.T.? I hate to think what's at the end of it. Not just because it's dangerous; I don't want you to be the next one who ends up half-catatonic in that bedroom."

"It's the lead we have, Mike—time and caution, we can't afford. They'll be on the move soon, I'm betting . . ." I held down a rush of emotion. "In the meantime, I'm going to try to talk to Lucas."

"So soon? L.T., maybe give him a little more time—"

"We don't *have* time," I answered. "Not if I'm right. Let me know as soon as you get that address; I'm shutting my phone off . . ."

Without waiting for a reply, I crept back into the bedroom. Lucas' sobbing had died down, and his embrace of Marcianna had turned into short petting strokes of her head and neck. When I reentered, he quickly hid his face in her neck again, which was a sign that he was cognizant of what was happening around him, and no longer withdrawing into a reality of his own making.

"She needed to see you, Lucas," I said, as gently as I could. "Wouldn't be kept out of the house, and didn't even think of going after Terence. Just came right up here to make sure you were okay." This brought neither a positive nor a negative response from the kid; he just stayed with his face in her neck, stroking the top of her head. "So: do you think maybe I can leave her with you for a little while?" At that, the petting stopped, and he put his arms tight around her neck, as if to agree to such a plan. "Because I have to go somewhere, Lucas. And I want you to know where . . ."

This was the big moment: I knew that there was a remote danger of losing him to his flight from reality once more, but I had to take the plunge, because the kid needed to rest. "You may not believe me, Lucas, I don't know, but I'm going to tell you anyway. Ambyr—" At the mere mention of his sister's name, Lucas made an insistent little moan of denial. "I know, but listen, Lucas, you've got to get some sleep. Otherwise the doctors will stick needles in your arm to *make* you sleep."

That idea, at last, brought a small but hugely significant return of his true self: into Marcianna's fur I heard him mumble, "Fuck *that* . . ."

I had to smile. "Yeah—fuck that is right. So I'm going to leave Marcianna here. Maybe you two can get some rest on the bed together." His head shook. "Or just stay right here and take a nap, but you need to sleep. And I know you don't want to hear it, but I don't think you'll sleep until you do: Ambyr's all right. I'm going to see her now." He didn't look up at me, but there was a palpable sense that some enormous weight had been lifted from the kid. "Okay," I said, standing. "You two take care of things here. Lucas, I'm leaving her lead right here on the chair—" I placed the retracting case on the arm of his chair, and was startled when he snatched it right up. "You're in control, now. I'm trusting you, Lucas, because I know I can." I put my own hand on Marcianna's neck. "I'll be back *soon,* girl—you two look after each other, okay? And Mike's just outside, if you need him."

I retreated a few steps, making sure that everything was indeed okay, which it seemed to be. I therefore turned and put my hand on the door-knob and began to open it—but then I heard the same muffled sound of Lucas' voice, speaking into Marcianna's neck:

"L.T.?" He paused, gathering strength. "I don't know what I'll do if we can't get Ambyr back."

"I know." There was no point in even trying to bullshit him. "Me neither. But listen, Lucas—I know where you are. I know what it is to wake up in pain, and to have a huge chunk of your life just . . . taken away. But we'll make it, kid—either way." He said nothing more, so I left the room.

Mike had been joined by Clarissa and Annabel in the hallway, and they were all staring at me anxiously. "He talked?" Mike asked. "You actually got him to talk?"

"It wasn't me, Mike." I turned to my great-aunt. "Marcianna's going to stay with him in there while I'm gone, Clarissa. I trust we don't have to debate that."

"We don't," she said. "But *you*—Mike's told me what you intend to do. Are you certain?" She put her hand to my face. "You've been so happy, damn it all. You'll lose that, and for what?"

I shook my head, glancing at the floor. "Not my decision. Annabel, I think it would be a good idea to have something simple ready for him, either before he goes to sleep or when he wakes up. Do you mind?"

"Of course not, Trajan," she answered, worry in every word. "It's no trouble."

Annabel's concern made the reality of what I was entering into strike hard; but all I could say was "Thank you." As I turned to go, one last thing occurred to me: "Mike, I'm going to need the car keys." Without a sound, my partner tossed them my way: a sign that he was more anxious about me than anything else, including his baby. "Okay, then . . ."

I'd gotten halfway down the stairs when Mike whispered, "One more thing, L.T.—"

"Don't worry, Mike," I said, patting my side, where the shoulder holster I'd been wearing since the night before remained. "I've got my Colt." I kept on walking. "Let's just pray I don't lose my mind and use it . . ."

{v.}

Every city or town has a lousy neighborhood, a wrong side of the tracks, or, as in the case of Surrender, a hollow in which you just don't want to find yourself. Often, when poverty alone doesn't suffice, ignorance and rumor amplify the wretchedness and dangers of such places, simply to satisfy a basic psychological requirement: the need of most people to feel superior to some group, tribe, or ethnicity that resides, not in the next town or city or county, but very close by, providing a constant and comforting sense of superiority. In Surrender, Death's Head Hollow had fulfilled this role, until its rescue by Caractacus Jones. Thereafter, it fell to another road to become Surrender's joy and nightmare: Fletcher Hollow, a title that could scarcely seem more picturesque, calling to mind as it did an era when respected craftsmen made their living creating arrows of quality. But in modern times, Fletcher Hollow became a blacktopped thoroughfare, one that ends at the highways that head to the central and western towns of the county. Not that much of anybody ever took advantage of it: for there was always the possibility that one's vehicle might break down on the dark, sinister hollow, leaving the unfortunate motorist prey to those who live in the decaying mobile homes along its length.

Up this same Fletcher Hollow, where a quick text from Mitch had told me that Kevin Meisner resided, I was now propelling the Empress, accounting for at least some of the fear that had marked the warnings of those family and friends I'd left behind. Mike and I had visited the area several times before, while advising Steve and Pete on other cases; but it was still never an easy journey to make. What it *was,* I realized as I made my way up the blacktop, was the perfect place from which to conduct an operation such as that involving the throwaway children: not just because it was an area in which even the informal law maintained by the other residents of Surrender did not hold sway, but because it was so unthinkable that its inhabitants could imagine a criminal scheme of such proportions, or be able to establish the contacts that had placed the children in homes of the kind to which we had learned they had gone. The key to this seeming paradox, of course, was that they had not done so alone; but just how many people with power, other than (presumably) Cathy Donovan, had aided them? This was just the first question that now needed answering. I also wanted to know what had made the four dead throwaway children return: we had the suggestion of a reason—the return to the state adoption center, indicating anything from abuse to desperation—but I wanted specifics. And of course, lurking over it all, there was the question of Ambyr: the question of *why.* Certainly, money would have been an incentive; but money means as many different things to as many different people as walk the Earth. And I wanted to know just what had been so important to her that she had manipulated as many people as she had . . .

Afternoon might as well have been twilight on Fletcher Hollow, due to the complete lack of any local industry that would have the road clear of low overhanging branches. Dogs, cats, goats, and chickens roamed the blacktop freely, as did children forever soiled both by the mischievous activities they got up to during the daytime hours that they were supposedly being homeschooled, and by the pall of smoke that continuously hung over the road, produced by piles of burning leaves, brush, and human garbage. The sight of the Empress was as unwelcome that day among the adults who stood like ghouls watching it pass as it had been those other times that Mike and I had come into the hollow, an effect that had nothing to do with who was in the vehicle, but with the fact that it was so plainly an unmarked official car. Enduring the continued glowers of the adults along the road and the increasing taunts of the children in it, I kept my eyes on the decrepit mailboxes that stood on posts to either side of me. Eventually, the correct number came up, and I slowed to take a left-hand turn into what turned out to be a long, ominous driveway. I passed by several ill-fed Holstein cows, the same breed that Clarissa kept, that were wandering and searching through fields along the road, their udders painfully swollen. But there was not a calf in sight: the latter had likely gone to other farmers before they, too, became too starved to sell. So the aimlessly searching mothers were left to provide a strange counterpoint to the mystery I was pursuing.

As I drove slowly on through the overgrown driveway, I was given no reason to believe that I was not approaching yet another dismal mobile home: the place that Latrell had referred to as "theirs," meaning that there would likely be several opponents, at least, to greet me when I arrived. I didn't doubt for an instant that their orders included a command to do away with anyone who in any way threatened the operation; so I double-checked my Colt, making sure the clip was full as I swallowed my mounting fear. Then, finally, the driveway reached what was obviously its end—

And I was shocked to find a nineteenth-century farmhouse, its grounds well manicured and shaded by several enormous maple and oak trees. The clapboarding on the house was well maintained and had been painted fairly recently, while the black tin roof, obviously a recent addition, also showed no signs of deterioration. But what was perhaps most surprising about the house was its size: I could not judge the exact number of rooms from the driveway, but there were certainly many—space enough, perhaps, to house a way station for young people on their way to new and promising lives. Could this truly be the nefarious headquarters, the existence of which we had posited ever since Latrell had spoken of it?

I did not have long to consider such questions. On the left-hand side of the driveway, about twenty-five yards short of the house, stood an old barn, which appeared to have been transformed into an elaborate and, judging by the number of vehicles outside it, thriving garage. Most notable were a series of well-maintained trucks: yet I looked in vain for one that sported all-terrain tires with the tread that Mike had identified. Then, as I pulled closer, I got a better look inside the concrete-floored barn itself: replete with a hydraulic lift and work pit in its center, three or four large, rolling cases of Craftsman tools, and welding tanks, it was a motorhead's dream. But my attention was soon drawn from such details by the sight of several men emerging from the gaping doorway of this state-of-the-art yet wholly unexpected workshop: each of them carried the inevitable can of Genesee beer in one hand, and I recognized one of their number to be Kevin Meisner, whose truck, I now saw, was parked up by the house: a red Dodge from the late Nineties. Yet it was far from a beater, as had been described by the witnesses at the scene of Gracie's collision, and bore no white cap. The latter could easily have been removed, of course, but I began to have my doubts when I saw the last man to come out of the garage:

It was Bass Hagen, who told the others to stay back as he approached me, which did my courage no good: if he was an enforcer of some kind, I was in deep trouble. But I pulled the Empress to a halt and rolled down the window, encouraged by the genuinely amiable smile that I could now see beneath his mustache. He never hesitated, but came right up to lean into my window.

"Well, Doc," he said. "I guess we've got one hell of a mess."

"I guess," I answered slowly. "And are you part of it?"

"Of this business?" He pointed to the house. "Shit, no. But I'm looking out for Ambyr." He leaned in closer. "Are you?"

"I'd like to." He offered his enormous hand at this, and I shook it.

"Okay. Then you gotta know she never meant any of those kids harm. She's done a lot of good, good that the state couldn't." He glanced at the house. "Wish to fuck she'd told me about it, though."

"As do I, Mr. Hagen."

He looked back at me. "You been awfully good to them—to Ambyr and Lucas. So I'm assuming you're not actually planning to use that—" He pointed at my jacket, where the outline of my holster would have given my Colt away, even if the butt end of its grip hadn't been slightly protruding into plain sight.

"That's never been my intention," I answered. "But—well, Fletcher Hollow . . ."

"Yeah-uh," he chuckled. "You ain't wrong, there. *This* place is a little different, though."

Just then there came some indistinct shouting from the garage, to which Bass turned to listen. "*What?* Yeah, I know the clock's running, God damn it!" He glanced at me again. "Okay, then, Doc. I'm gonna trust you to do what's right." I only nodded in reply, and Bass pointed farther up the drive. "She's up to the house. Listen, though—I know this whole business ain't gonna be easy on you, but try not to be too long. Because I ain't too sure how long she's got to get outta here. Okay?"

I nodded again as he stepped away, a look of genuine sympathy on his face; and then I slowly urged the Empress on, farther into this most peculiar of mysteries I'd come on in a long time—which, given the circumstances of recent months, was saying quite a bit. Pulling the car alongside Kevin's truck, which was parked at the very end of the driveway near what was plainly the door to the house's kitchen, I got out and took a long look around the neatly kept grounds. A rubber tire swing hung from a bough of one of the trees on the lawn, each of which must have been more than a century old; and as I walked among them, not at all certain of what I was or should be doing, I saw that the grass eventually rolled away and down into the small brook that had created the hollow. It had been dammed up, at one point not too far downstream, to create a clear, inviting pond, in which two kids—maybe eleven or twelve—were swimming and splashing, their laughter inaudible until you reached the crest of the lawn.

"What in the world . . ." I murmured—and was startled when an unlikely young voice answered:

"You're the one who's here to see Ambyr?" I turned to find myself faced with yet another kid, this one maybe a little younger than those in the pond. She was pretty, with fair hair and bright blue eyes that were so appealing that I didn't immediately notice a large birthmark that crept around from her lower scalp and partway into one cheek, just below the jaw. "Nice place, isn't it?"

"Indeed," I answered. "Do you live here?"

But she ignored the question: "If you're ready, I'll take you on in."

"Okay," I said; then she took my hand and led me toward the house.

She pulled the screen door open, revealing the kitchen of the house: it was large, and whatever quaint details had been left untouched were overpowered, visually, by the complete replacement of its appliances, its countertops, and its fixtures. Though not a particularly well-thought-out renovation, with steel and granite that did not match the house at all, it was an expensive one: *precisely like the Kurtz kitchen,* I remember thinking. But that renovation had been paid for by the state; other, more sinister money had been behind what I was seeing.

"Ambyr's upstairs," the girl said to me, as I took all this in. "She said you should go right up. See you!" And with that, she was back out the door, leaving me to enter what would once have been the large dining room of the house, but was now some kind of kid heaven: there were two widescreen televisions, the first showing Disney Animation's *Big Hero 6,* the other hooked up to an Xbox 360, on which was paused what looked like the latest edition of the gaming phenomenon *Call of Duty*. Scattered around other parts of the room were iPads, cell phones, and other electronic equipment, along with half-finished sodas and bags of various snacks.

It was all a far cry from Fagin's crumbling, filthy headquarters in *Oliver Twist*; and yet, one could not help the feeling that there was some kind of connection to be drawn between the two. As I made my way through the next room—probably the parlor, in its day, but now converted into a place where adults clearly took their ease, with slightly larger televisions than the kids used, and very plush La-Z-Boy chairs positioned before them—and then put one foot on the wide, center-hall staircase, I became ever more disoriented and even afraid.

"Where in the fucking world *am* I?" I murmured,

"Trajan?" she said, that remarkably keen hearing having caught either my footsteps, my barely audible voice, or the sound of my cane. She approached slowly from the right side of the upstairs hall, and finally appeared: dressed, now, as I had never seen her, in expensive jeans and a dress shirt that was tied just above her midriff, with her hair held up in a flip on the back of her head by a barrette—and her white cane nowhere in sight. She was sweating, and had clearly been working hard at something that I guessed at with a single word that knocked my insides loose: *packing*.

"Come on up," she said, her voice very serious. "But be careful of a couple of the steps, they're steep . . ."

She headed back to resume her work, clearly feeling that time was pressing hard; and I followed along, wishing with all my soul that this inexplicably pleasant world into which I'd walked was in fact the nightmare that it suddenly felt like; but, knowing it wasn't, I quickly typed a text message into my phone, although I didn't hit send yet. Not yet . . .

I found her in a large bedroom, appointed in a manner not unlike the one in her home, save that each piece of furniture and each detail of decoration was obviously far more expensive. Moving to the bed, the frame of which was built of solid oak in a very handsome Mission style, with a white lace spread that had obviously been hand-worked, I saw several piles of clothes: designer clothes, to judge by the looks and the labels. These had not been bought locally; indeed, the closest place that they could have come from was the large collection of designer outlet stores in Manchester, Vermont, a place that drew in many a New Yorker on their way north for vacationing in summer and skiing in winter. And the perfect place, I realized, to make contact with wealthy families who were seeking children to join them, as well as to carry out the hand-overs of such precious merchandise . . .

"This is very nice stuff," I commented, my voice already taking on a bitter edge as Ambyr continued to fold the pieces up and carefully place them in a couple of leather Cipriani trolley cases and tote bags. "I'd almost think it belonged to Shelby—but of course, she's dead."

"Don't, Trajan." Ambyr shook her head with a look of gratifyingly genuine pain on her face. "If you start off being mean, it's only going to take up time."

"Oh?" I noised, my tone only getting worse. "You in a hurry to get someplace, Ambyr?"

"Yes," she answered, still with great self-control. "And there's things we have to talk about."

"Really?" Her manner had begun to enrage me. "You think so?"

"Stop it, Trajan."

"*Stop* it?" I growled. "I haven't even started it, yet!" I moved around the bed as quickly as I could and grasped her by the shoulders, ready to shake her. "Your brother is back at my place, in a very serious dissociative state that's kept him up for almost sixteen hours, his mind ready to snap because Derek is dead and *you* disappeared—and now I show up here in fucking Wonderland, with you packing, and you ask me not to take up *time*?"

She remained limp in my grasp, apparently having expected some such reaction. "Yes—I do. There's a lot I need to explain, and I don't have long to do it. So can we just move on?"

I was ready to do almost anything to bring her around—kiss her, slap her, scream at her—but then I studied the expression on her face more carefully and saw what I was dealing with: genuine compartmentalization disorder. Not the kind of phenomenon that pop psychologists like to blather about, but a deeply narcissistic syndrome in which separate realities simply cannot and will not be integrated in a person because of psychic deformities caused by trauma in childhood—trauma that, in her case, I understood only too well. I had been one of those realities, fully genuine for Ambyr during the time that we had spent together; but I had only been one, and now, with both herself and the operation that was centered on this strange house in apparent danger, she was existing in another.

"That's it, then, isn't it?" I said, releasing her. "All we've been through, all we've shared: an episode. Pleasant, maybe even loving, but most of all necessary; and now the necessity has changed . . ."

"I don't want you to remember it like that," she answered, her pronounced detachment never breaking despite her words. "It meant so much to me. So much . . ."

"Ambyr, please. I've studied too many patients like you. And there's not a damned thing that I can say or do right now that's going to make you come back to me—you're just not in that world, anymore. I might as well be . . ." I stared at the clothes on the bed, as she returned to the task of packing them. *"Dead."* Then, trying to summon what strength I could, I continued, "So let's talk about the things that *do* matter: the things I need to know. Obviously, you're the handler, the woman involved in this operation that we've long since determined must have been convincing most of these kids that it would be okay to take off with a family of rich strangers."

"Yes," she said, nodding as she began to tear up a bit. "How long have you known?" She was trying to keep the conversation on a path of practicalities, to avoid the kind of emotional distress that might actually force her to face who she'd been and what she'd done.

"With certainty, for the last week," I told her. "I'd had moments of suspicion several times before then, but that was when all the pieces began to fit too precisely to avoid, when I really couldn't explain it away, anymore. Although God knows I tried. I was only confused, ultimately, about one detail—your accomplices. But I began to figure that one out, too, the night that Curtis Kolmback was murdered. She's not quite so clever at it as you are, old Cathy Donovan. Tell me: was she giving you orders, or vice versa? I mean, who actually decided that Derek—" At the mention of the dead boy's name, Ambyr drew in a sharp breath, and leaned onto the bed for support. I could have gone to her, I could have offered her comfort; but in her present state of mind, it would have been fruitless. "I'm sorry if the mention of his name bothers you that much." Then the ice flowed in my veins full force: "Responsibility for a life is a terrible weight, isn't it?"

"I was never responsible for Derek's life," Ambyr said, her voice taking on that lethal tone that it had on just a few other occasions. "I never

wanted to be responsible for *anybody's* life. Nobody's but my own. I was tricked into everything else."

"Actually, I was speaking more about his death," I said, matching her manner. "Or do you contend that you didn't consistently tell him that, if he put you in touch with other throwaways, one day you'd come up with a new home for him, too?"

"You believe I'd do that?" she said, with astonishment that was either real or a very good act; I simply didn't know, anymore. "He just assumed it, and then, later, he started to get impatient, in that way he always did: so pigheaded, so self-centered, so fucking—"

She caught herself just in time, but I knew where she'd been going: "So fucking *retarded*? You can say it, Ambyr, nobody else will hear you."

"Except that I want you to know—" she said, with what, again, seemed genuine emotion. "I want you to know that it was the others who decided he had to go, without telling me. But you're just not listening, are you?" She zipped up one bag and tossed it on the floor. "Anyway, like I said, there are other things we've got to talk about. Mainly one thing—Lucas."

I had stupidly hoped that the one thing we really needed to talk about was *us*; and when it wasn't, my injured pride only took fuller control. "Okay," I said, my sarcasm transparently wretched. "Let's talk about Lucas. Or rather, let's talk about where you're going, first, and about why you can't take Lucas with you."

"Stop asking questions that are pointless," she said, growing increasingly irritated with my attitude. "I can't take him with me when I'm going to be one step ahead of the law."

"And how do you know that's what's going to happen?"

She threw more clothes into another bag. "Because, baby," she said, matching my sarcasm, "you're going to tell them. If you haven't already."

I was a little awed by her insight; but I wasn't going to let it show. "Okay. Let's say I am—you certainly don't seem to be *packing* for a life on the lam. More like an ocean cruise, I'd say."

"*I earned these things*," she answered, the same warning in her voice. "And I'm keeping them, damn it. As for Lucas—imagine what'll happen if I take him with us and we get caught. Juvie, almost for sure. The best that it could turn out is that they'll stick him in some lousy foster home somewhere, and I don't want that."

I nodded slowly, pulling out a cigarette. "Admirable—but what *do* you want for him?" I struck my lighter hard, lit my cigarette, and took a long drag, blowing the smoke in her direction.

Just then a honking came from below, and it didn't take a genius to tell what it was about: her ride was getting impatient. Ambyr moved to the window and stuck her head out, calling, "I'll be down in just a few minutes, Kev!"

The more it hurts, the less you show it: the same lesson I had learned as a boy, and countless times since. "Ah, yes—*Kev*. The young man who had a crush on you, but in whom you had no interest. He must love you a great deal, to have pimped you out to an old cripple just to keep this operation safe—"

"*Trajan!*" Ambyr shouted. "I can understand how you feel, but there is just no time, we've gotta talk about Lucas!"

"Not yet, we don't," I said firmly. "I want to talk about just how this operation has worked, and how you could have allowed four kids to die in what I suspect was this very house without calling it off. Or did Donovan rule that out? Maybe threaten you with jail if you didn't conceal the suicides?"

"*Stop it!*" Ambyr suddenly cried, clapping her hands over her ears; and as I watched her crisis in action, I realized, with some damnable satisfaction, that there must in fact have been real feeling for me, in there; but prod and poke and torment it as I might, it simply wasn't going to get out. "I can't do this," she went on after a moment. "I've got to worry about getting out of here, and about what's going to happen *to* Lucas!"

At which the sound of a screen door slapping shut below became audible, to be quickly followed by hard, fast steps on the stairs. In seconds, Kevin Meisner appeared at the doorway, looking somewhat surprised to see that some incident of violence wasn't taking place.

"Everything okay, Ambyr?" he asked, catching his breath and nodding at me, in a none-too-friendly manner, this time. "I heard shouting."

"It's fine, Kev," Ambyr answered, straightening up and looking dead at him. "I'll be down as soon as I'm finished."

"Okay," Kevin replied, a bit anxiously. "But if we're going to drop those three downstairs off and then keep going, we need to move."

"I know," Ambyr said. "I won't be long, I promise."

Kevin started away from the door, giving me what I took to be a warning look, one that I answered with a small smile and a blasé salute of the two fingers that held my cigarette. After he'd disappeared, I said, "The young man still places great stock in your honesty, it seems. Perhaps I should have a talk with him. I don't suppose it's ever occurred to you, Ambyr, that you're now doing just what your parents did—running out on everybody you professed to care about."

"This is different."

"Is it? Maybe so far as I go it is. But there is, as you say, the matter of Lucas, who's now on the verge of being thrown away twice. And he knows it."

"Yeah," she said, hoping that we were finally getting to her point. "And I need to know—"

"Not quite yet, Ambyr. The exact nature of this operation: I need details."

Again disappointed to be put off, she replied, "I can't tell you *all* the details. You have to go to Donovan for that."

"I will," I said. "But, sticking to your part: the few blanks left, like how you got in touch with all those rich New Yorkers. These clothes you're packing for your desperate getaway tell me that, I think. But two points I have to know, for the sake of my own God damned sanity. The first is Derek—what happened? Why did he have to die?"

"I told you, *I don't know.* I had nothing to do with his death."

"Actually, you said you had no responsibility for his life, and then that you weren't told at the time of their plan to kill him. You must have been, since. So why? Just because he was getting so insistent?"

"*I don't know!*" she repeated, trying to keep her voice down, this time. "Nobody here knows."

"So—Donovan again? She seems to take the responsibility for *all* the evil acts."

"And she should," Ambyr answered. "She ordered that Dr. Chang be driven off the road, she was behind Kolmback's murder, and Latrell's killing, too. But you need to believe one thing: I loved Derek, I really did. No, I didn't want to be his damned mother, and yeah, he could get me good and mad, but I did love him, and I tried as best I could—"

"By involving him in a criminal conspiracy?"

"Look, *he* found out about what we were doing," Ambyr answered, her determination renewed. "And *he* wanted in. We had another kid doing it, a kid we finally found a place for—and Derek wanted in. He'd heard

Kevin and me talking, and Derek basically blackmailed us into letting him be our next contact with the kids. And he was good at it—being the way he was, it kind of put the kids at ease, made them trust him."

"Yes," I said. "The old Judas goat ploy. You must have been very proud."

Now she was tearing up for real, the drops from her eyes falling on the profits of her enterprise. "And so, even though it made me nervous, we kept going, provided he absolutely never told Lucas anything. And unlike Lucas, Derek knew how to keep a secret."

"Then why is he dead? We found a note pinned to his chest—"

"I know what it said. Kevin saw him hanging there, on his way to get me; I couldn't look, though, when we left. But I don't know what it meant. You and Mike will have to figure that out."

Studying her, I realized that, insofar as it was possible for her to tell the truth, anymore, she was. "All right," I said at length. "Let's say I buy that. What about the others—Kelsey, Kyle, Shelby, Donnie. What happened to them?"

She sighed, then relented. "Yes. They all happened here. Nobody in this place was involved, or anything. It started with Kelsey, and after that, I don't know, it was like a *germ,* or something. But each one that came back, they heard about the others, about going to the adoption center, and thought it would be different if they tried it. But it wasn't. So—copycat, right? It happens with teenagers all the time. Not for these reasons, but ..."

"And what were those reasons? I mean, the reasons they came back here?"

"You want every one?"

"I do."

Closing up the last of her bags and setting it on the floor, she turned and sat on the bed, facing away from me and into the light that was coming through the room's wafting lace curtains. "Kelsey—she got raped. Pretty obvious, I guess you think, but we'd actually never had it happen before. It was the guy who owned all the horses, the guy who was going to give her a career in that business—that was his price, he told her, and why the hell did she think he'd paid so much money for her, anyway? Dirty fucking pig already had a wife and three grown children, *and* another young girlfriend on the side. Didn't matter. So—Kelsey came back, but her folks wouldn't have anything to do with her. She didn't much want to go back there, anyway, so I told her she could stay here until we found her a new family. But she tried the legit way, and then . . . As for Kyle, well—we never were too sure what happened with Kyle. He couldn't talk about it. Just said the people he'd gone to turned out to be—weird. Maybe there was something sexual—he did mention something about them wanting to give him baths, treat him like he was a five-year-old. But whatever it was, he was awful ashamed of it. He didn't even last a week, after the state said no . . ."

Ambyr stood and tried to stretch upward; but she seemed to lack either the strength or the will for the motion, leaning instead on the window frame. "And Shelby, well . . . You know all about Shelby. Took an awful lot to drive *her* off—and the one thing it took, her new 'dad' managed to try: drugs. Her actual parents being such meth heads, she just wasn't ever going to go there, everybody knew that. Sex? Hell, yes, she would have screwed anybody to get what she wanted, and did. Screwed the husband, just to get more *things* out of him. But it got just as out of hand as it had with that stinking PE teacher of ours, Mr. Holloway. Anyway, the husband, her new 'dad,' he tried to get her into cocaine, partly because *he* was, and partly so he'd have a way to control her. But she pitched a fit, the wife found out about the whole thing and—back she came. We told her, just like we told the other two, that we'd find another place, but—I don't know. Like I say, it was almost like it'd turned into a virus, by then, that they were catching from each other: hopelessness, especially when they couldn't even become fosters. And then came Donnie. Donnie, he should've been fine. Those people, the Augustines, the ones you hate so much because them and their friends have ruined your city, they were actually okay. Really sad, really guilty about what'd happened to their own boy, and how it meant that they'd never be allowed to adopt. And so they took Donnie, and stuck him in a nice prep school up near where they live, and he turned into the star of the basketball team again, but . . . The kid missed home, and I don't mean North Briarwood, either. He missed the playground in Fraser. I think, really, that he just missed *any* playground. Started hanging out in some he found in New York, and before long—well, the Augustines were people who had to worry about appearances, obviously. And Donnie started fooling with drugs, started getting a little out of hand, a little too much *street,* which is kind of—ironic, or whatever, when you consider how much Mr. Augustine admired the pro players who'd come from places like that. But they started cracking down on him: curfews, no going to playgrounds, no being . . ."

"No being himself," I finished for her, the four stories having melted my icy blood in a way that Ambyr had been unable to do. "So he eventually decided to come back to the playgrounds he'd known, and to punish the Augustines on his way out the door."

"Yeah," Ambyr said softly, turning to me and sensing the change in my voice. "That's about right. We told him not to try the state, told him how it had been for the others. But he went. Then we told him he had to stay here, and not go to the basketball courts in Fraser. We knew he'd talk—you know how boys get on those courts. We said we could find him another family, one that would really accept him. But he just couldn't wait."

"No. He couldn't." I began pacing, taking all these terrible yet somehow utterly believable facts in. "So we were right when we speculated that, after they'd been thrown away, then accepted into worlds they'd only dreamt of—which became their worlds, if only for a time—and were then thrown *back,* they simply couldn't live with the memory. Not if there was so little hope of anything to follow, legal or otherwise."

Ambyr smiled, in that knowing way of hers. "Yes. You were very knowledgeable about that. But then, you've lost, in your life. Tell me, Trajan—when you dream, do you still have both your legs?"

The question was so shockingly insightful that it took me an instant to absorb its mournful weight. "Always," I murmured at length.

"Well—there you go."

I stubbed out my cigarette on my shoe and pocketed the butt, using the opportunity to dispatch the text message on my phone. "Okay, then—just two more questions: first, the one I was going to ask before: did you always just assume that you could leave Lucas on my doorstep, when trouble came? I mean, even before you met me?"

She just shrugged and nodded in resignation. "Yeah. I did."

Hard words to hear; but I had to push on: "Thank you for that bit of honesty. Which leaves only the final issue: why involve me at all? There had to be other places you could have used as an emergency drop for Lucas—your cousin and your uncle, for instance. Why send the kid up the hollow to become part of our team? And why, having done so, was it necessary for you to seduce me so completely?"

"Is that what you think I did? I'm sorry if you really do. I know what 'seduce' means—I looked it up in the dictionary, once. It means convincing someone to do something you know is wrong. That wasn't what I was trying to do. At all."

"We can get to that," I said, with a wave of my hand. "But why Lucas? Why get your own brother involved in our work?"

Ambyr let out yet another sigh, rubbing her face for a moment with both hands. "That—is something I really do have to apologize to you for. I lied about it, when we first met."

"I'm assuming that," I answered, my voice hardening. "But *why*?"

"Because . . . Because, like I said then, I knew how *good* you were. You and Mike. I'd read about you, see; and I knew that our partners in law enforcement would do what they did: try to make up a series of teenage murders. To protect themselves, to protect the image of the state and this fucking asshole governor, all in an *election* year. And I thought that if you guys came in, you'd definitely figure out the truth, or as much of the truth as you needed to know to finally get the stories of the throwaways out and public. Once you figured out they were suicides, I figured, you wouldn't stop, you'd just keep pushing until you had enough to make them all believe it. Make the world believe it."

I was stunned into silence for very long seconds, eventually saying, as confidently and directly as I could (which was tough): "And we did. We will."

"Yep." And then Ambyr's voice attained a newfound passion that bordered on pride: "Because people need to know about it. But that's not all. What we've been doing here, it has to go on. Yeah, I'm going to be on the run for a while, who knows for how long, but wherever I am, I'm not going to stop. That's the most important thing of all. All these kids who wake up one morning to find out that their families have just disappeared without a trace—somebody has got to help them. And who's going to? The state? We've seen that answer. No kid in his right mind wants anything to do with the foster system, the way it's run—but they've managed to fix things so that kids can't go out on their own, either." Her words were becoming chillingly reminiscent of Frankie Arquilla's. "Child labor laws, parental consent for school, all of these things that were set up to protect them, they're all working backwards, now. The throwaways can't help themselves, and the people who are supposed to help them just put them into shitty situations. Have you ever even been to any foster homes, Trajan?"

"Yes," I said, nodding ruefully. "And I know what they are, most of them. Monthly check farms: ways to pull in state money without doing much if anything for the kids themselves."

"Exactly." Ambyr reached back, undid her barrette, and let that wonderful sandy hair, the scent of which I imagined I could make out, fall down her back. "So it's not really so complicated—if I can help, I figure I have to. And if I can make a living, not off the state, but off the families we place the kids with, well . . . I figure that's okay, too. You're completely focused on the four who died, Trajan, but do you know how many we've placed that're happy, now?"

"No. Obviously. How many?"

"Well—" She checked herself. "I'm not gonna tell you that, just in case. But it's a lot. A *lot*. And I'm not stopping, and neither is anybody else involved—which, by the way, doesn't include my uncle Bass or any of those beer-drinking motorheads you met on the way in. Though they let us use this place, and will let someone after me do it, if I get caught."

She had laid a lot out; but as I considered it all, I couldn't escape one truth: "A noble series of rationalizations, Ambyr," I said. "But against all your manipulations and lies? Tough to see them as very much more . . ." I took a deep breath. "And finally, Lucas? What am *I* supposed to do with him?"

"Well," she said, trying to brighten a little. "You said yourself he's helped you, and that he's got real talent for the kind of work you do. So it won't be so bad if he stays with you, will it? I mean, until I can send for him, someday when it's safe?"

"I—suppose it wouldn't," I said, swallowing at least part of my pride and giving in. "But on that day—are you going to send for *me*, too? Or will Kevin object?"

She smiled indulgently at my jealousy. "How many times have I got to tell you, Trajan? Kevin's *not* my boyfriend, however he feels about me. I'm not quite as good a liar as you think I am."

"You might want to tell him that. I don't think he got the memo."

"Oh, he got it. More than a few times." She leaned over, at that point, and lifted the cat carrier containing Tommy, which I had not even noticed during my brief rush to try to shake sense into her, from behind the bed. Setting the big, happy feline on the lace spread, she continued: "And I don't know if he secretly hopes that something'll happen, someday, now that we're going to be on the run, or whatever. But it isn't. It just isn't there, for me, with Kevin, and like I say, I've told him that more times than I can count. The rest is his problem. As for you and me . . . I know what I *wish* could happen. But wishes don't mean anything, in this world. So I don't know."

The time, then, had come to tell her: "You're right, Ambyr: wishes don't mean anything. So you'd better move—I alerted Mitch McCarron a couple of minutes ago. He'll be here very soon."

I suppose I expected an outburst; or perhaps I simply wanted one, as a sign that our time together had meant something; but she simply moved to the window again and leaned out of it, calling, "Kev! I'm coming down with Tommy and one bag—soon as I do, you can get the rest, okay?"

"Got it!" I heard Kevin call from below; and with the deepest pang of dread I'd yet felt, I realized that our moment together—in this room, during that summer, perhaps in this life—was over.

As Ambyr shuffled toward the door carrying one of the leather tote bags and the cat carrier, I stepped in front of her, rather desperately taking hold of her arm. "Ambyr—I can't—"

Suddenly, she shocked me by letting her head fall against my chest. "I never lied about you and me, Trajan. It was always the truth."

"It . . . just isn't anymore," I whispered.

"No, it's not like that," she said, still holding her own against her emotions. "But things have changed so much, in so little time. But maybe. Someday." She sniffed back tears as I released her. "Someday . . . And now I've got to get out of here. Because the man I love has ratted me out." She smiled that sly little curl of her lips. "So fucking smart," she whispered. "If only you weren't so fucking—dedicated, too . . ." She finally lost the last of her tears, shaking her head to try and clear it.

"Just—tell me this," I whispered. "It was real, then, wasn't it? Us?"

"I told you, Trajan," she answered. "But I'll tell you again: it was real . . ."

I stood back another step, almost ready to collapse and suddenly aware that my left hip was throbbing like a bastard. "Okay—then go. For God's sake, go now, Ambyr . . ."

She simply nodded a last time, then moved out the door, Tommy the cat meowing once or twice as his big case bumped into the doorframe. I didn't watch her go, couldn't watch her go: I had that much of a sense of self-preservation, at least. But as I heard her thumping down the stairs, I looked into one corner of her bedroom—and saw her white cane. Maybe she meant to come back for it, or perhaps Kevin was meant to bring it along with him; on the other hand—

I decided to satisfy this final suspicion: going to the top of the stairs as she reached the bottom of them, I called down to her, "Ambyr? One more thing—and it *will* be quick, I promise you."

She turned up to me, to *exactly* where I was standing, and said, "Okay. If it's quick."

I was almost afraid to put the question; but the investigator in me was taking precedence again, enabling me to ask: "Were you in fact, during the time that I knew you, still blind?"

She gave me that same roguish smile and replied, "You're the doctor—what do *you* think?"

"I think," I answered, returning her smile and glad, at least, that if we had to part enemies, it would not be hateful, "that most cases of blindness caused by anorexic hypoglycemic coma resolve within months. Sometimes sooner. A few are permanent, however."

"Well, then," Ambyr answered, moving toward the front door, enigmatic to the end. "I guess you've got your answer, baby . . ."

All I could do, as she vanished, was retreat into her bedroom and hobble about, trying to get a last trace of her scent. I kept at it even after Kevin had come and gone again, until I'd heard them collect the three children outside—Ambyr in full mother mode and herding them into the rear seat of Kevin's extended cab—and until, finally, the truck started up and pulled away. Then, at last, I allowed myself to collapse onto the edge of the bed, put my face into one of her pillows, and weep . . .

{vi.}

I cannot say how long I stayed in that room and that house, any more than I can say how long I cruised around Burgoyne County after leaving the place. Certain that I couldn't yet return to Surrender, to tell not only Lucas but Clarissa and Mike about the hard truths I'd learned (and perhaps to be informed of Ambyr's arrest), I retraced many of the roads we'd taken during the case; and at length I found myself back up at the Capamagios' old trailer in Daybreak Lane, which still had fading crime scene tape hanging loosely from its door. I don't know why that was the place that brought icy clarity to my thoughts: perhaps because it had all started there, or perhaps because I now had to imagine Ambyr's cohorts, maybe even Ambyr herself, carrying Shelby's body into the forlorn trailer, there to arrange it so grotesquely and then abandon it. Whatever the case, I finally did understand one thing, about the relationship that had inspired more hope than any other in my life, then crashed and burned so badly:

I had confused the similarity of the *traumas* that Ambyr and I had endured when we were younger with a close, even a precise, similarity of *experience*; and I'd therefore confused extreme compassion with genuine understanding. But where we had both known savage pain, before we met, for her the experience had been recent; there had been no time, first to make the mistakes and create the kind of havoc that emotional suffering inevitably drives humans toward, in the initial effort to relieve it, and then to finally grow tired of such behavior, and seek the kind of counseling that no relationship, not even a marriage, can replace. I'd had that time: time to do all the things that Mike had said I'd done, pick the wrong women, over and over, hurt them, let them hurt me, until I'd finally entered a program of psychotherapy myself. I wondered, as I walked about the overgrown grounds outside the trailer, if Ambyr would ever seek out such help. Plenty of traumatized people don't; and they play hell with themselves and others for years, often for lifetimes, whatever their other accomplishments. Certainly, I could imagine Ambyr spending years doing just what she was doing now, pursuing a noble cause, on the one hand, and using it to rationalize lying to and using those close to her, on the other: only later would she learn that methods are as crucial as goals . . .

I could take none of these thoughts home with me, of course, if only for Lucas' sake. There was, after all, a difference between being frank with the kid years down the road, and being so brutally honest at that moment that I would catapult him into disruptive, self-destructive behavior—or even cause him to slip back into his dissociative state, from which he would likely emerge only to embody just the sort of clinical compartmentalization that had come to afflict his sister. He didn't deserve any of that. The only things that would keep him on a road toward the kind of recovery that might allow him to take care of himself and others were time, the help of a therapist of his own (which I would make sure he got), and the belief that Ambyr had not meant to betray him by behaving as she had. And that was the message I would bring to the kid. Confident that this was the correct course, I got back into the Empress and headed for Surrender and Shiloh, driving like Mike: with a lead foot and an utter disregard for speed limits. I lit a cigarette, rolled down my window, and punched the stereo on. Lucas' CD was still there, ready to accompany my drive away from the late afternoon sun with a fully appropriate song: Led Zeppelin's "Fool In the Rain." All that was missing, I realized with a small laugh at the triteness of the thought, was the rain . . .

When I arrived at Death's Head Hollow, I saw no signs of any reporters: all their vans had vanished, which might have seemed strange, had I not been certain that someone from the state—likely Donovan herself—had told the press that the real story was no longer there. The assistant district attorney's ambition to rise quickly, which had been another engine of so much tragedy, required a shift of media attention to whichever of her superiors stood in her path to promotion, whom she would now, I was sure, try to implicate in the throwaways plot. It was another brilliant example of misdirection, and for now, it was fine with me: I needed time to adjust to my new reality, and to encourage Lucas to do the same. And so I headed on home—or rather, I tried to:

At one shielded bend in the road, just within sight of the hangar, the barns, and the roof of Shiloh's farmhouse—the very spot where I knew that BCI cars had parked the evening that Gracie Chang had first come to visit us—were two vehicles. The first was an unmarked cruiser with a BCI card banded to its downturned visor. It was ominous, but the second was the one that struck terror into me: it was a beat-up Dodge truck from the late Nineties, with a white cap and all-terrain tires.

"Son of a bitch," I whispered. "A fucking coincidence, after all. Or is it . . . ?"

I pulled the Crown Vic over and, with my Colt drawn, got out to examine the truck's interior. On the front seat was the thing I most feared, an open and nearly empty Pelican tactical rifle case. Only the suppressor had been left behind: a deathly sign that secrecy had been abandoned altogether. Dashing forward, I tried the driver's door of the cruiser, and found it open. Searching the papers scattered about the passenger seat, I discovered an official departmental note that was meaningless, save for its addressee: Frank Mangold.

"Jesus . . ." My mind was slipping into panic. "So Mitch was right about you, after all, Frank . . ."

I got out to look in all directions. They were here. At precisely the moment when I'd believed that I'd reached some kind of resolution about how to handle my homecoming, and been thankful, as always, that there was such a home to return *to*, everything had been thrown under renewed threat. Frank Mangold, lacking Cathy Donovan's cleverness, needed someone to blame for his own shortcomings in the case. In addition, as he'd said to me at the Kurtz house that day, someone wasn't playing straight with him, and he'd evidently decided that the culprits were Mike and me. So, to tie these ends together, he'd decided to charge us with something, anything, bringing their assassin along for backup. Not that I believed for a minute that the shooter usually drove that old Dodge: they'd bought it to try to confuse us, on the chance that we might see Kevin Meisner's truck, and pursue a red herring. Which I almost had, the night we'd met Kevin. That part of the scheme was likely more of Donovan's work, I didn't know for sure; but before long, it seemed, I would find out. That is, if Mike and I were given that long to live: for we knew Mangold's methods all too well . . .

My mind set to work, trying to figure out a plan; but I was prevented by the sudden sound of a gun going off up near the house. Not the short clap of a pistol report, but the long, echoing boom of a large-caliber rifle. Terrified, I quickly got back behind the wheel of the Empress, then heard its rear wheels growl as I slammed down the accelerator and spun them against the dusty dirt of the road. I didn't even dare think about what, specifically, the gunshot had meant: every option was too horrifying. Instead, I steered, a bit perilously, with my left hand, keeping my Colt tight in my right.

"All right, you fuckers," I said, rage cutting into my nauseating worry. "You shot first. Just remember that. Because I have *had* it . . ."

I reached the driveway in seconds, took the left-hand turn, and then raced on up to the house, not even bothering to continue on to the usual parking spot by the barn. Instead, I pulled onto the house's lovely, sloping lawn, got out, and looked around, listening carefully—

But there was nothing; no sight, no sound. I waited for a few seconds, thinking that there might be more shots to indicate who was firing at whom from where; but again, nothing. The entire situation was the apotheosis of eerie; but, my first thought being for Clarissa—who had been, after all, drafted into the case, and was the least deserving of harm—I set my cane to working hard, got up the slope of the lawn and onto the porch, then hobbled quickly through the screen door in front of me and into the living room, expecting to at least find *somebody*. But the house, like the rest of the farm, was deathly silent. I called all of their names in turn—"Clarissa! Annabel! Lucas? It's okay, it's me, Trajan!"—but still, nothing. Ignoring the rising pain in my hip, I made for the stairs and climbed them, using, by that point, almost every ounce of my strength to reach the second floor and get to the master bedroom. But the chamber was empty; even Marcianna was gone. And then a terrible thought occurred to me: hunting rifle—Marcianna—had they dared . . . ?

Going back toward the stairs and still crying out to the others—"*Will one of you answer me, damn it?*"—I still got no response. But I also found no trace of blood, not even when I checked Clarissa's bedroom and then went downstairs, stumbling once or twice as I did, to the kitchen. That comfort faded in speedy fashion, however, as I realized that the shot must have been fired outside, based on how loud its report had been, and how it had echoed up and down the hollow. *Outside,* I remember thinking clearly; *it must have come from outside, and likely higher up than the house . . .*

"No . . ." I whispered, the worst dread that I'd felt all day consuming me. "No, no, *no!*"

Bursting back out the screen door, I went to the northwest corner of the porch, from which I could just see the fence of Marcianna's enclosure. With a shock that caused a lone, wretched, tearless sob, I saw that the gate was open: *open,* with my beloved other self nowhere to be seen. "*Marcianna!*" I called from my vantage point. "Marcianna, you come here—*now!*" But she did not appear, as she had every other time I'd called her, during the years since she'd learned her name and truly acclimated to life at Shiloh. Even the few times that, for whatever reason, she'd gotten loose, she'd always come at the insistent sound of my call. But now . . . nothing.

Getting back to the ground, I left the Empress where it sat and started toward the barn, still calling her name, along with Clarissa's, Annabel's, and Lucas', as I went. But I continued to be answered by that maddening silence, which was universal: even the birds had stopped making any sound, with the boom of the rifle shot, as had the cows. It was literally, or so I thought, a *deathly* silence; and by the time I reached the barn I was becoming frantic. Finding no more sign of life here than I had anywhere else, I made for the hill to the hangar, and began to call Mike's name.

Finally, a response, from high up in Marcianna's enclosure: Mike's voice. "L.T.?" he called. "L.T., watch the fuck out! That fucker's on the loose!"

Breathing a heavy sigh of relief but keeping my head on a swivel, I started up the hill. "But where the hell *is* everybody, Mike?" I shouted.

"We're all up here," he said. "In Marcianna's cave, den, whatever the fuck you call it!"

"Are you all okay?" I responded. "What the hell was that shot?"

"Yeah," he said; and suddenly, there was a note of real trepidation in his voice: "We're all fine, but—Marcianna . . ."

"Marcianna what?" I cried, my voice warbling badly.

Mike paused before answering: "She got hit—trying to protect us."

"No . . ." Tears had already come to my eyes. Then I asked the terrible question: "Is she okay?"

"She's hurt, L.T.," Mike answered slowly. "I think it might be bad. I already called her vet—but he says he isn't coming until the shooting's stopped. The problem being, we don't know where the fuck the shooter is, or *who* the fuck he is!"

"Have you seen Mangold?" I asked, a lethal desire for revenge now in my words.

"Christ, is he here, too?" Mike answered. "No, not him—I never saw this fucker before."

"Where did he go?"

And finally, a new voice: from behind the parked Prowlers in the lean-to shed adjoining the barn, it was the sound of a human who'd descended to the level of an injured, angry animal:

"I'm right the fuck over here, Jones . . ."

He slithered out from behind the ATVs, using one of them for support. In his left hand, and pointed at me, was the rifle that, I had no doubt, had done the damage to the roof of the machine he was leaning on, to Marcianna, and to Curtis Kolmback: a Savage 10FP. He was thin but wiry, with bright blue eyes, while his face, which I suddenly realized I'd seen before, was pale from loss of blood; and the cause of the loss was easy to locate. The *de rigueur* black sniper's costume that he was wearing had been torn away from his right arm, as had much of the flesh near the shoulder and all through the hand. He was bleeding badly, but he didn't seem to know just how badly: I was relatively certain that Marcianna had shredded his brachial artery, and that, without fairly speedy medical assistance, he would bleed out in moments.

"Rare kind of hunting dog, hunh?" he said, his voice hoarse with weakness and pain. "That fucking *thing* just about tore my arm off. But I worked a bullet into her—don't you think I didn't . . ."

"Sergeant Dennis Shea," I said, immediately recalling the scene in North Fraser that night, when it had been this excuse for a man who had put a bullet through Latrell's brain.

He nodded with a pathetically evil grin. "Didn't know if you'd remember me." He kept the gun leveled at my chest, but unsteadily. "Glad you did. Your friend Dr. Li, he didn't; just carried your animal up into that cave with the others. I didn't stop 'em, they don't matter. You're the only one who does. I nail you, my bosses'll be happy. Now toss that Colt over here . . ."

I did as instructed, having absolutely no fear, now. If Marcianna was indeed dying, I had no more interest in living, myself. Not after that day, not in a world that could have caused all this to happen. But I was, as always, curious about a few details:

"So," I said, raising my right hand while I switched my cane over to my left: for more reasons than mere submission. "You're Frank Mangold's golden boy, and he's probably let you in on everything that's gone on with this case. Then you've fed that information to the people who've been placing these kids down south, the people that Frank didn't even know he should've been looking for. Got paid a nice fat fee for all you did, knowing that, when the time came, you could break the case open, and make yourself look good. But only after the Kurtz girl and her friends had gotten away, so that they'd never suspect you of playing both sides against each other."

He nodded, his wretched, pained grin spreading. "Something like that. You think you know so much, but you never figured all that out till now."

"No," I answered. "I didn't." I began to move toward him by slow increments. "So it was *you*, then—the Gunderson boy, in the Patricks' house. You put him there?"

"Right" came the answer. "On orders, of course. We almost tied the whole thing up with the Patricks. Even had Frank believing it. But you . . ." Shea began to gasp, wincing in pain, and the muzzle of his Savage drooped. "You had to do it, didn't you? Wasn't enough that you went and fell in love with Ambyr"—and from the way he said her name, I could tell that he harbored his own feelings about my departed paramour—"you had to fuck everything else up. Now you take it all with you."

"I'm not quite *that* stupid, Shea," I said, still advancing slowly. "Even if you kill us all, others know, and will take over. But tell me: is it just my imagination, or is *everybody* in this damned county in love with Ambyr Kurtz?"

"Don't you talk like that! She ain't that way, she was only with you to protect the operation."

"You sap," I answered, trying to keep his blood flowing hard with anger. "Whatever she was really doing, *you* don't know, and you'll certainly never find out."

"Think so?" he answered. Then he caught my movements: late, and a sign of his diminishing strength. "Stay right the fuck there, Doc!" he warned; but the rifle in his left hand drooped even more. "So fucking smart," he said; and there was a terrible similarity in the way he said it that almost made me believe he *had* had some intimate moments with Ambyr. "I'll find out—once I get to Mexico and meet up with her, and we ditch that Meisner kid."

"Mexico?" I let out a short laugh, despite the fact that my left hip was giving me hell again. "You chump—did she really tell you they were headed for *Mexico*?" The added weight that came from having my cane on the wrong side made me wince, I hoped not perceptibly: for the longer I remained in that configuration, I determined, the more he'd believe that it was my right and not my left leg that had been amputated. "And when you get there," I went on, "are you going to tell her that *you* killed Derek Franco? On Cathy Donovan's orders?"

"She don't need to know that," he answered, still trying but failing to level the rifle.

"Well, I'm sure you'll be very happy, then. Two liars, off into the sunset. Except that she won't *be* in Mexico, Shea—that's just some story she told you."

"You shut up about her, I said! She told me she'd be there because that's the truth, and don't you try to tell me anything else."

I could only smile mournfully. "Shea—if you know anything about her, you know that that girl has a different version of the truth for every person she talks to."

"Shut *up!*" he cried, with a renewed lethality. "Just shut the fuck up and stand there, while I figure out—" He tried to drag his rifle up onto the fender of the Prowler and point it at my head, but could only get it as far as the shaky perch of the top of the front tire. "Goddamn it," he said, his frustration revealing how far his thinking had been clouded. "They never—I never learned how to shoot with my left, damn it . . ."

"Of course not." I studied his bearing and general demeanor more closely, along with his ignorance of the fact that the main wound to his shoulder was slowly draining the life out of him. "You weren't military, Shea. They teach their snipers to at least defend themselves with either arm. You're just some dumb cop playing soldier, who doesn't even know basic wound awareness."

"Meaning what?" he said, his voice becoming desperate.

"Meaning that you're dying, Shea. If you don't get that bleeding stopped, you'll be dead in a matter of minutes. Less, perhaps."

"Yeah?" he said bitterly. "Well—you'll go before *that!*" And then he fired off another shot that sounded up and down the hollow.

But my ruse had worked: unable to get his gun to a sufficient elevation to aim it at my chest or head, he'd blasted away at what he thought to be my one good leg, tearing a nice-sized hole in my pants and ripping away a piece of the outer plastic of my prosthesis without affecting its structure much, if at all. The force of the shot itself did cause me to stumble, at first; but after that, seeing my chance, I quickly grasped the head of my cane and pulled the blade within it free, ready to move on Shea and drive the steel through his idiot's chest just below the left ribs. He began to pant and gasp, whimpering pathetically as his rifle chambered a new .308 round and he fought to keep its muzzle from falling completely; but I'd gambled on his inability to do so, and just kept moving.

"Stay back!" he cried desperately, unable to right the gun. "I'm warning you, Jones—"

"You're warning me of what, Shea?" I said, still limping my way toward him, my speed reduced by the effective loss of my cane. I could have leaned down to pick up my Colt, and finished him with that; but I was far too maddened by hate for such to be satisfying. "That you're going to kill me? You already said that, but you've lost too much blood to lift that Savage, and even if you could, you said yourself that you don't have the skill to use it effectively with your left arm. No, Shea—you're the one who's going to die, here, but it isn't going to be from bleeding to death . . ."

His whimpering grew in intensity as he realized the truth of everything I'd just said. "I—I . . . *Don't!*" he pleaded at last, his eyes on the blade in my hand.

But I was done talking to this idiot; the kind of idiot I'd dealt with my whole life—

And then another shot sounded. For a moment, I thought I had mistaken the situation, and that he must have been able to hit me, for blood was suddenly sprayed over the front of my clothes. A quick check of my situation, however, made me realize that I felt no pain other than in my hip, and that the amount of blood on me was inadequate for any wound in my own body from a rifle shot at that distance. Then, looking up, I saw that Dennis Shea's forehead had simply exploded, and that his body was quivering with a final paroxysm as it fell against and then slid down the side of the Prowler. And as it did, another figure came into view:

Frank Mangold, his Glock smoking in his two hands. There was a look that I'd never seen before on his face: anger, yes, but something more, something complex—an awareness, not only of his actions, but of his own mistakes, his own misplaced trust. He stepped forward, stared down at Dennis Shea's lifeless body, and, instead of closing the fool's eyes, raised his foot and kicked the lifeless, violated head hard, causing the corpse to collapse completely to the ground.

"You dumb fuck," he murmured, holstering the Glock as he stared at Shea's body. "All you had to do was go by the book, and you could have gone far. But you just had to cut corners, didn't you? Like the rest of your worthless generation. Can't fucking take the time to do things right, have to grab every goddamned shortcut you can. Well—this is what it gets you . . ." He turned to look at me, seeming to come back from a very far-off place. "How you doing, profiler?" he asked, picking up my Colt and handing it to me.

I sheathed my blade in the body of my cane, quickly replacing the whole in my right hand so that I could lean on it and get some relief, and then accepted my gun. "Jesus, Frank," I said uncertainly. "I never thought I'd say this to you, but I'm . . . grateful."

"Shouldn't sell people so short," he said with a quick smile. "This piece of shit . . ." He nodded at Shea's body, in front of which I could now make out a large chunk of pink brain, blown out through the hole in his skull, the bright white of which could be seen through all the blood; then Mangold produced a ballistic-tipped 9mm round. "Gave him his own medicine. Once I figured out what was happening, I knew he had to be stopped. I'd had my eye on him, I knew he was working for somebody above me—ever since he shot that black kid in North Fraser, before I'd given the order to fire."

"*You* didn't give the order?" I said, even more stunned.

Frank shook his head bitterly. "Nope. At the time, I thought he was just a go-getter, but later, when my guys saw a sniper go up your mountain, I figured out he must've done it to shut the kid up. Damn it all. He really could've written his own ticket; but nobody wants to wait anymore. Everybody wants the easy way. The *easiest* way . . ."

"And you know who he was working for?"

Mangold nodded in disgust. "Cathy-fucking-Donovan, just like you got him to say. I would've beaten it the fuck out of him, but . . . well, you came along. You played long odds, Jones—he would've killed you, don't doubt that." He shook his head, and hissed in disgust: "The fast track . . ."

"Which 'fast track'?"

Frank smiled and even laughed a little. "You know, profiler, I doubt we'll ever understand each other—I mean, did you *really* think I'd plant a dead kid's body just to frame those Patrick pigs?"

I owed it to him to be straight: "Yes, I thought so. Cops have done it before."

"Hunh," he noised, shaking his head. "Well, not *this* cop, fuck you very much. But whatever you think of my ass, one thing you can trust me on: you do *not* understand how modern law enforcement is working. Police—locals, state cops, Feds, everybody—the fastest way to the top, now, is to kill somebody. In the line of duty is always best, but if you have to do it in secret, so long as it makes the people on top happy, well, that's just fine, too. Advancement by blood—that's the ticket, these days."

I studied my old antagonist, this former enemy who had ensured that my life would go on and was now my bizarre ally; and I found myself actually taking a moment to consider his thoughts. "It sounds like the old imperial guards in Rome," I finally judged. "The Praetorians . . ."

"You know," he said, his expression brightening, involuntarily and just briefly, "I've thought the same thing. The Praetorians. Easiest way to the top was to kill somebody on orders. But they all ended up like this asshole, eventually. Makes you and me the barbarians, doesn't it?"

Mangold was dead right; but I couldn't smile at it, for I still had to face what awaited me at the top of the hill, no matter how crushing it might be. "Well—my thanks, again, Frank," I said, starting to move off. "I have to see how the—*others* are."

"You mean your *cat*?" Frank said, smiling in disbelief. "Come on, profiler, we've got people to bust. If you'll work it with me, I think we can make it quick and clean."

"And we will, Frank," I said, never breaking stride. "But I have to do this, first..."

He said nothing more, just went back to the Prowler and stood by the dead disappointment on the ground, cursing him once more and spitting hard.

When I finally reached the gate to Marcianna's enclosure, I called out: "It's okay, you guys! You can come on out, it's all over!" Reaching into my pocket, I found my own phone, and quickly located the number for Marcianna's vet. I told him that the shooting had stopped, that the shooter was down and the police were on the scene; and I was grateful to hear that, anticipating my call, he'd driven to the foot of Death's Head Hollow, and was just waiting for the all-clear to drive up to the enclosure. That left but one grim task: finally finding out what had happened to my "favorite sister."

Clarissa, Annabel, and Mike emerged. I hugged both my great-aunt and Annabel, and would've hugged Mike, save that he was keeping his .38 at the ready, not quite trusting the situation. But when he saw the blood on the front of me, and quickly realized that it wasn't mine, he at last felt safe returning the revolver to his ankle holster. "What the hell?" he asked, correctly concluding that I couldn't have shot the assailant; and on being told who had, he whistled low. "No shit... *Mangold*? World's just full of surprises, isn't it?"

"Brother," I said, "you don't know the half of it..." I braced myself. "How is she?"

"She's in there, with Lucas," Clarissa said, looking very grave. "She's alive, Trajan, but terribly weak. Did you convince the vet to come?"

"Yes. He should be here any second, in fact."

"Good," Clarissa answered. "You can't let anything happen to her, nephew—she tried so hard to protect us. I think it was Lucas she was worried about, most of all."

"It always has been," I answered with a nod. "Well—all right, then . . ."

"Stay strong, kid," Mike said, putting a hand to my shoulder as I headed in.

Within the *kopje,* Lucas was cradling Marcianna's head in his crossed legs, stroking her neck gently as she purred: not the usual, electric-motor purr of happiness, but the deep, breathy vibration that cats manifest when they are in pain. She was panting intermittently, making me wish I'd thought to bring her water—and so I called to Mike, asking him to get some. Scanning the overall scene further, I saw that there wasn't a lot of blood evident, which might or might not have been a good sign: if the damage was entirely internal, she was almost certainly in severe peril.

"Hey," I said to Lucas, getting to my knees and joining him in stroking Marcianna's neck.

"Hey, L.T.," the kid answered, in a voice that showed he'd been crying, but had stopped before I'd entered. "She's hurt awful bad . . ."

"Oh, I don't know," I said, more bravely than I felt; then I leaned down so that Marcianna could see me in her dull, half-lidded stare. "Hello, my love," I whispered, running my knuckles along her jaw just under her mouth. "I'm home; and I'm never going away again—understand?" She made a halfhearted attempt to whimper in return, but it only came out as a kind of pathetic grunt. "You just keep quiet, for once," I said. "You've done enough . . ." I scanned her body for more-detailed evidence of what had happened, and eventually, I found the wound: the bullet had pierced her left thigh, and looked to have exited somewhere on the right side of her belly. I couldn't determine just where, however, because each probe brought a growl and a weak swipe at me with her left forepaw. "Okay, okay; I get the message." I moved my knuckles to her forehead and pressed them hard.

"What're you doing now?" Lucas asked with desperate interest.

"Nobody really knows," I answered. "But all cats, when they're in pain, seem to seek pressure to the forehead. Kind of works for people, too; I've tried it, but—for cats, definitely."

Lucas nodded. "The vet gonna get here?"

"Any second."

He paused, slowly working his way up to the next question: "Ambyr come back with you?"

I shook my head. "But we can talk about that later."

"It's okay," he said. "I didn't really expect her to."

"Maybe," I said. "But you were hoping, all the same. She had reasons, though, Lucas." I glanced up at his now-doubly-pained face, and then back down at Marcianna. After a few seconds of silence, I murmured a dimly remembered quote: "'Incurable, in each, the wounds they make . . .'"

"Hunh?" Lucas noised quietly. "Who said that?"

"An ancient playwright," I answered, having already worked out my own tears.

"Yeah?" the kid asked. "What's it mean?"

"Ah," I sighed. "We can talk about that later, too . . ."

Finally, the vet appeared at the entrance, along with an assistant. He took a quick look and agreed with my diagnosis: didn't look like any bone damage, just a question of whether her internal organs had been damaged, and if so, how badly. Turning to me as the assistant prepared restraints, he said: "You sure you want this young man to be present?"

"You just try to fucking move me," Lucas declared; and while I admired his spirit, I had to warn him of realities:

"Lucas—they have to secure her, and make sure she can't scratch or bite. That's going to look cruel to you, but until they get her sedated, they've got to do it. Don't you think—"

"I'm staying, L.T.," Lucas replied, his tone still unbending.

And stay he did, as the vet and his assistant carefully bound Marcianna's front and rear legs, then expertly slipped a light muzzle over her mouth. Not wanting to shoot her with a tranquilizing gun from inside the den, they had been forced to use this method of immobilization, because the pain of the coming injection just might have made her crazed enough to do real damage. As it turned out, though, she accepted that pain with only a mild protest, and within minutes, she was finally resting for real, in a deep, deep sleep. The veterinary assistant fetched a stretcher from where they'd left it outside, and we all got her on it, removing the restraints and muzzle, in order to take her down to the hangar, where the vet could do what he needed to atop the Formica table. Lucas never left the stretcher's side, bravely enduring Marcianna's drugged appearance; I, on the other hand, had to slow up, both to try to talk to Mike and Clarissa, and because my hip was finally starting to buckle. The kid was advised to keep his hands clear of Marcianna's now-freed claws and mouth, just in case, and so he quickly ran around to the opposite side, where her long, dipping spine lay still. And all the way down the hill, he kept stroking her neck, even though he'd been told that she couldn't feel it.

"But she can," he insisted to the vet. "I know she can . . ."

There wasn't really much for me to say to the others, it turned out, as we followed along. They could all see that Ambyr had not returned with me, and that I was both in pain and enraged: in fact, so at war were my feelings—for now I held Ambyr fully responsible for what had happened to Marcianna, along with everything else she'd done—that all I could ultimately do was keep murmuring the fuller quote from Euripides:

"'Stronger than lover's love is lover's hate. Incurable, in each, the wounds they make . . .'"

Mike and Annabel understood the general meaning of my words; but Clarissa recognized the line from *Medea* immediately, as well as its specific importance at that moment. So she drew close, letting me lean on her hard as we kept descending to the hangar . . .

{vii.}

As it turned out, and more thankful for it was I than for anything I could remember in a long time, some wounds that Ambyr had made *were* curable: the bullet that had struck Marcianna had not, in fact, pierced any vital organs, and her vet assured me that once she'd been sewn up, bandaged, and shot full of antibiotics, she would begin to recover with a speed remarkable only to those who do not know cats. I had deep misgivings about leaving her again, about having her wake to find me not there; but we had things to do, yet, and I had to trust that, if she did come around before I returned (assuming I did), Lucas would continue to be enough of a comfort to pull her through the shock. The vet also agreed to stay until my return, particularly when I told him that I did not anticipate being gone for more than a couple of hours.

When Mike and I finally descended to plan our next moves with Frank Mangold, I took Clarissa along, or perhaps I should say that she took herself: she wanted to know all that had transpired, who was responsible for what, and exactly how far I now intended to stick my neck out to press the case home. Her own desire for justice was behind this urgency, I knew, along with concern for our safety—but I was also aware that she had still another reason: Clarissa was a force to be reckoned with in county politics, but she still wanted to know whom we were planning to go after, and what if any effect our plan would have on Shiloh. Told that we had our immediate sights set on ADA Cathy Donovan, she couldn't help but smile.

"Really?" she more stated than asked, seeming very pleased. "Oh, I think I'm going to enjoy this—I have never trusted that woman. But listen to me, Trajan: you've got to be sure. We can't have this boomerang on us, and more importantly, on the farm."

"Oh, we're sure, Aunt," I said. "The only question is whether or not we can get her to confess, and implicate anyone else."

I had not objected to Clarissa's coming down to the car, in part because it would have done no good, but also because I wanted to see the effect that she and Mangold would have on each other; and I have to say that, while the entertainment did not disappoint, it was surprising, nonetheless. Mangold was still by Dennis Shea's gruesome corpse, leaning on the ATV's fender and going over some messages, perhaps instructions, that he'd received from his superiors on his phone. This didn't bother me: Frank may have been a thug, but he was also far more principled, in his way, than I'd previously believed, and I didn't think that there was any purely political pressure that could induce him to let up, once he'd perceived what he believed to be the correct course of action. He didn't turn as we approached, just assumed that it was only Mike and me who were doing so. Therefore, still staring at his phone, he growled:

"Well, Jesus H. Christ, profiler, if you and your sidekick are done playing Doctor-fucking-Dolittle, maybe we can take care of some damned business." He drew a pen out of his jacket pocket and held it toward me. "Here. Take this—"

And then he caught sight of Clarissa. I'm not sure what I was expecting, if I was actually expecting any one thing at all; but certainly, I wasn't prepared for what I got. Mangold immediately quieted down, becoming, not obsequious, but very respectful and perhaps even a little intimidated, keeping my great-aunt's record of unnerving cops consistent. "Oh." Frank checked himself like a berated schoolboy and stood straight up. "I, uh— beg your pardon, ma'am. I thought it was just the two docs, here."

"I should think you *would* beg my pardon, Mr. Mangold," Clarissa said fearlessly; no mean feat, because if anyone else had referred to him as "*Mr.* Mangold," they would likely have gotten Frank's hard fist to their face. "And what's that?" She looked behind him, seeing Shea's exploded head. "Good Lord!" Clarissa immediately retreated from the sight, but lost none of her bearing. "What do you mean, leaving a body in that condition in open view, mister? We have a child on this farm, I'll have you know—would you like him to stumble on that?"

"Uh," Mangold noised. "No, ma'am."

"'No, ma'am' is right. Trajan, get a tarp from the barn and cover that thing up. As for you, Mr. Mangold, I'm tempted to report this business to your superiors. You wouldn't like that, would you?"

"No, ma'am," Frank answered, fairly humbled; then he found himself a bit and added, "But I don't think you would, either, Ms. Jones."

Clarissa, much to my surprise, simply nodded appreciatively at the truth of the statement. "All right, then." She indicated his hand, which was still holding the pen out, if far less aggressively. "Suppose you show me just what it is you intend to do . . ."

Mangold waited the thirty seconds or so that it took me to cover Dennis Shea's body, then proceeded, in a steadily stronger tone, to outline how he thought we ought to nail the case down before anyone could interfere from a very high level. The plan, adjusted by both Mike and me, was certainly bold, though it was not reckless; and whatever Frank's stated feelings about profiling, it would all come down, in the end, to my correct reading of Cathy Donovan's psyche, and how it would react to certain stressors.

We phoned the ADA's office and were told, unsurprisingly, that she would be happy to receive us, even on that unusual day and at that unusual hour. This initial stressor was augmented by a call to Mitch McCarron: after I'd changed my clothes, and Mike and I had gotten into the Crown Vic and under way to Fraser, I pulled up Mitch's private number. With the phone on speaker, my partner and I discovered that Mitch had worked his magic on the highways heading north of Surrender by calling ahead to his fellow senior officers, who held him in as high regard as I did. Mitch having relayed his information, I hung up, then turned to find Mike glancing at me quickly, shaking his head, and letting out a groaning sigh.

"Whoa, boy," he said at length. "I know where your mind's headed, L.T.; but don't you ever wonder about it, yourself?"

"Hmm?" was all I could say in reply, as I stared out the passenger window.

"I'm talking about your notorious—*detachment*. Don't you feel anything at all, even now?"

I nodded. "Far too much," I said, in a flat tone that apparently didn't meet with Mike's approval: he picked up a nearby CD case and whacked me over the head with it.

"Damn it, L.T.!" he said. "That's just what I'm talking about—it isn't right! Every time the shit gets worse, the more you sound like you're dead inside."

"What do you want me to do, Mike?" I turned to him, my voice still calm. "Go into Donovan's office in a state of emotional crisis? This isn't over, yet; and she has to think we can't touch her."

He shook his head with a sour look. "Convenient excuse—except that I've seen you like this before, you know. Shutting down. And it just isn't right."

"No," I answered, looking back out the window again. "It isn't . . ."

Not wanting to go on in this vein—for it was, as Mike had indicated, a conversation that we'd had many times—I looked back out at my wing mirror, periodically checking to make sure that Frank Mangold's cruiser was behind us. And, all the way to Fraser, it was: following just as the men on the Thruway (confederates and subordinates of Dennis Shea's, Mangold had speculated) had done: at a distance but steadily, never letting anything get in the way of his ability to shadow our movements. The thought did occur to me, since I'd experienced so heavy a dose of betrayal, by then, that he might be setting us up to take the blame for all the blunders that had occurred. But this was a passing concern: Frank needed us as much as we needed him, just then. Not for his own selfish reasons, and certainly not for ours, but to reach the goal that had been his life's too-often brutal work: getting at the truth and closing the case.

By the time we reached the Fraser courthouse, where the office of the assistant district attorney was located on the second floor of the western wing (as far, I noted for the first time, from the sheriff's office as was possible), the sun had begun to set; but there was still a great deal of activity going on around the building. I was glad to see Steve Spinetti and Pete Steinbrecher outside, giving orders to a group of their own people, as well as to some Fraser cops: whatever they were doing, it clearly had nothing to do with our case, but their mere presence put both Mike and me much more at ease. We parked and got out quickly, catching both men before they had a chance to enter their own cruisers. Their faces brightened upon seeing us, a glad expression that was quickly tempered by mystification when they saw Frank Mangold park his car, not in the building's lot, but across the street, after which he emerged to put on his sunglasses and cross over toward where we were standing.

"Boys," Steve said, as we exchanged handshakes all around. "Pardon my asking, but—what the *hell* are you doing here with Mangold?"

"Don't tell me he finally arrested you?" Pete said, echoing Steve's astonished tone.

"No, no," I answered. "We're—actually working with Frank, at this stage, Pete."

"As fucking unbelievable as that sounds," Mike tossed in dubiously.

"*What?*" Steve asked, ever more amazed. "On what? And what the hell are you all doing *here*?"

By now, Frank had gotten close enough to hear the conversation. "Above your pay grade, I'm afraid, Sheriff," he said, with his usual delicacy. Then he looked from Mike to me. "Well? Time to play charades, fellas."

"Charades?" Pete said; but almost as soon as he had, he held up his hands. "I know, I know, above my pay grade. Well, just as well—we've got to get uptown. North Fraser's busted loose again. Ever since your boy shot that kid, Inspector, we've had some kind of rioting just about every other day."

I was as perversely glad to hear this as I had been the first time I'd been informed of unrest following Latrell's death: someone needed to remember him, and if this was how they were going to do it, fine. There was only one flaw, as I told Pete: "Why don't they come downtown and tear things up? That might actually do some good."

"It might, at that," Steve said with a small grin. "But I don't think any of them wants to risk a bullet to the head like Sergeant Shea dealt out that night."

"Yeah, well," Mangold said. "You don't have to worry about Sergeant Shea, anymore, Sheriff. Okay, let's go, Doctors . . ."

Signaling reluctant goodbyes to the still-confused Steve and Pete, Mangold, Mike, and I, the oddest law enforcement trio imaginable just then, entered the beautiful if decaying courthouse, and made our way up the marble stairway, myself hanging onto the wrought iron and brass banister. The second-story hallway was deserted, save for two men posted outside the door to Cathy Donovan's office: men who, I was sure, had been among those who'd tried to block our return to Surrender via the New Baltimore Travel Center. The sight of them dislodged much of my trepidation, replacing it with anger; and as we approached, the pair of thick-necked goons glowered at Mike and me.

"We do have an appointment," Mike said, with a laudable absence of fear, himself. Yet the men made no move to admit us, prompting me to ask:

"Or perhaps you'd prefer that we shoot it out in yet another parking lot?" Both of their broad faces grew sour, which was only a red cape for my increasingly bullish feelings. "Whatsamatter, fellas? Cathy won't pay to get your van fixed?"

"Okay, okay, enough flirting," Mangold said. "They do have an appointment, boys, and you don't want to keep your boss waiting."

"Need to pat 'em down, first, sir," one of the sentries said, showing Frank proper deference.

Mangold shrugged. "Better you than me," he said, indicating that they should go ahead, which they did. Mike and I had, of course, been sure to leave our guns at home; and when the goon doing the patting reached my prosthesis, he stood up, smiling in a sickeningly smug manner.

"Gimp," he said. "Without that Colt, you're just another geek pussy, aren't you, Jones?"

"Hey, that's *Doctor* Pussy to you, asshole," Mike answered. "And—"

But I held a hand up to my partner. "And before this is over, you may wish that it was *me* who had his gun tonight, after all." The exchange thus ended, one guy laid hold of the doorknob to Donovan's outer office and pushed the mahogany portal open for Mike and me, while Mangold stayed behind, for the time being, in the hallway. A hydraulic closer dating back decades closed the thing behind us with a hiss, giving the man I'd insulted just enough time to say:

"Enjoy yourselves, ladies . . ."

There wasn't anyone in Donovan's outer office, which was an ominous sign: it meant that Cathy hadn't called in any of even her closest flunkies to witness the meeting, didn't want anyone overhearing us, even by chance. Walking past a tidy assistant's desk that'd been straightened up for the following day, we knocked on another mahogany door that was even thicker than the one we'd just passed through; yet Donovan's voice was clear enough to penetrate it: "Come in, Doctors . . ."

Inside, we found the ADA standing before one of the office's tall nineteenth-century windows, looking down at the parking lot. A lone banker's desk lamp, its green glow only slightly reinforced by some recently installed recessed lights in the ceiling—faded back, now, to a dim but perceptible level—gave the dark paneling and white paint of the room a very eerie effect, one that I was sure Donovan had spent some time creating. As for the woman herself, she was dressed, as always, in a very smart business suit, although when she turned with a smile to indicate that we should sit in the wooden chairs in front of the desk, I noted that, for the first time since I had known her, the suit's jacket was unbuttoned, revealing an extremely sexy, tight-fitting shirt that allowed us to see more of her ample cleavage than was usual. She sat when we did, leaning toward us in a way that made her attributes even more visible: an effect that I was certain was meant to throw us further off our guard. But I was beyond such displays, at that point; and even the sybaritic Mike sat stony-faced.

"Well, gentlemen," Donovan began, as cagily as ever. "We have a situation to resolve."

Going into my jacket pocket, I withdrew my usual small pad of paper, and then the pen that Mangold had given me. Clicking it once, I asked, "Cathy, do you mind if I take notes, by any chance?"

Her smile only got wider, revealing very white teeth that glowed green, given the downturned shade of the banker's lamp. "Let's not fool around, Dr. Jones. No banter, none of your usual repartee. Just put the pad and pen away, thank you."

I did as told, sliding the pad back into my jacket pocket, then clipping the pen to the same opening so that the top of it was clear of any fabric. After that, I let my jacket hang as loosely as I could.

"Now," she began, "I'm sure you can guess that the State Police have already picked up the Kurtz girl and Kevin Meisner on their way north. Apparently on a tip from you, Dr. Jones."

I stared deep into those inscrutable eyes of hers. "Apparently."

She smiled again, very seductively: a smile very similar to Ambyr's, who, I was now convinced, she had coached in such matters. "Love doesn't triumph over all, then?" she asked.

"It does not," I said, past all these sorts of provocation.

"No. But justice does. *If* it's justice." Donovan finally sat back. "I understand you like to quote Francis Bacon, Doctor." When I nodded, she said,

"What about this one: 'Revenge is a kind of wild justice; and the more man turns to it, the more the law ought to weed it out.'"

Nodding again, I said, "You've mangled it pretty badly, however. Not the kind of thing I'd expect from—" Looking to her wall, I picked out one of many framed diplomas. "A Northwestern Law graduate? Impressive." It was my turn to lean forward. "So what happened to *you*, Cathy?"

She laughed lightly, engagingly—again, just as Ambyr would have done—and took the moment to stand and remove her jacket, revealing the rest of her shirt, if it could be called that, which clung tightly to her very toned body, just two thin straps of cotton reaching over her shoulders.

I hoped Mike could keep holding it together; for the image was alluring, indeed. But he simply smiled, eyes widening a bit, and said, "Jesus. Somebody's been hitting the gym pretty hard. What do you favor, Ms. Donovan? Weights? Yoga? Or maybe the StairMaster?"

She gave him the same smile. "Good eye, Dr. Li. Yes, the StairMaster."

"Perfect," I grunted. "Once an instrument of labor punishment in prisons. They called it 'the treadwheel.' But look what it's done for you, Cathy."

By now she was getting a little weary of my using her first name, although she tried not to voice it: "Gentlemen—Doctors—we have the guilty parties in this case in custody, now. It doesn't seem to disturb you much, Dr. Jones, which I'm happy to see. I've asked you here to say that I'm ready to call all things even, from now on. The accused will make some wild accusations, against me, against others, maybe even against you two, who knows? But if you're prepared to—how should I say this . . . ?"

"To cut cards with the devil?" I asked.

She glanced at me with what seemed genuine appreciation. "Well put, Doctor. And if you'll agree to it, I can tell you that the state is ready to quash anything these two may have to say about you." Pausing to stretch her arms in satisfaction above her stylishly cut hair, she then ran her fingers through it. "Well, what do you say? It's a good deal; and I warn you, I'm by far the least powerful person you'll have to worry about, if you decide to say no."

Mike piped up bravely, still somehow keeping himself immune to Donovan's physical charms—perhaps a testament to the newfound depth of his feeling for Gracie Chang: "We know that. And we've known it for quite a while."

"Yes," Donovan replied. "Your presence in Hoosick Falls, and the pieces put together by your friend Bill Johnson. You don't want to put his job in jeopardy either, I'm assuming."

She really was pulling out all the stops; so it was time to counter. "Okay, Cathy—"

But then she snapped at me, "Doctor. I've shown you the courtesy of using your title. Do you think that maybe you could do me the small favor of using mine?"

I nodded again, smiling in what I feared was too sarcastic a fashion. "Of course, Assistant District Attorney. So, let's say we agree. You're not really leaving us much choice, are you?"

Then, with a suddenness that was once again reminiscent of Ambyr's style, her voice turned lethal, her face darkened, and she said, "Understand this: I will make it my life's fucking work to destroy you and everyone around you, if you don't agree. That means your great-aunt, whose farm subsidies might come up for review when it's discovered that a second business—yours—is being conducted on the grounds of Shiloh; it means taking Bill Johnson's license away, for sharing information with unauthorized investigators; it means—and I'm dead serious, here— revoking your permit to own an exotic animal, and ensuring that that creature, who took the life of a BCI officer today, is put down. And all of that's just for starters. Exposure of your conduct to the SUNY-Albany chancellors will certainly mean the end of your teaching careers. Anything I've left out?"

I was too angry and astounded to form words quickly; but Mike stepped in. "The dog," he said.

"What?" Donovan replied, glancing at him in annoyance.

"Miss Clarissa's little dog," Mike said. "You forgot to say that you'll come over and shoot it."

Her face now reddening, Donovan's voice became ever more menacing: "I assure you both—I am not fucking around, here. I have the authorization of people you've only imagined backing me up. Don't try my patience."

Certain that the ever-unpredictable Mike was about to test Donovan even further, I stepped in: "Don't worry, Ms. ADA; we're not prepared to see any of the things you just outlined happen."

Turning to me and altering her mood on a dime, Donovan let her face relax, and very quickly became the soul of comeliness again. "Well. All right, then. I'm happy to hear that, Dr. Jones."

"But, since we're alone here," I continued, "and unlikely to be over-heard, there are just one or two things I'd like to ask, in return for our cooperation."

She narrowed her eyes at me, just for an instant. "I can't tell you any-thing about who might be authorizing this offer, or may have authorized this operation."

"Of course not. But more personally . . ." I leaned forward. "What hap-pened, Cathy?"

Looking bewildered for the first time, she said, "What happened where?"

"To *you*, Ms. ADA," I said. "How did your life end up here? You had a bright enough start—" I again indicated the diplomas and pictures around me, which told the tale of a beautiful young scholar and athlete from, apparently, the same South Briarwood Combined School that Donnie Butler had attended, who had gone on to SUNY-Albany and then to Northwestern Law, probably on a partial or full scholarship. "How does someone with so much promise end up back here, doing this kind of grunt work for local and state officials?"

Her full smile returned. "You just don't get it, do you?" she said, echo-ing other sentiments I'd heard of late; but this time, I did get it, all right, though I wanted to hear it, too. "Sure, I had offers to go into corporate law when I got out of Northwestern, but that didn't interest me. I'd fo-cused on criminal prosecution, which is the fastest way into politics, and I know this state: I know how far someone who's prepared to work within the machine can go, and how many corners can be cut just how fast. Sometimes, like with our present governor, it's a family name that lets you do it. Sometimes, as in the case of certain other people who shall remain nameless, it's religion, or race; and sometimes, I knew, there are situations that not only don't exclude women, but require them." She began to walk behind her desk, running a finger along its surface and then picking up one of the framed pictures. "Yeah, I was quite something in high school; and I learned a lot, there. Academically, sure, but also which male teachers would succumb to what behaviors. Same thing in college: let me tell you, there are a couple of my old pre-law professors at SUNY who would be very nervous, if they heard I'd been taken into cus-tody on any kind of conspiracy charge. But that's not going to happen, is it?"

Mike, fascinated by all he'd heard and seen—for I think even he was drawing the connection, now, between Donovan's behavior and Ambyr's—asked, "And the 'glass ceiling' we keep getting told about? How'd you break that?"

But Donovan only scoffed. "The 'glass ceiling' . . . Let me tell you something, Dr. Li: the glass ceiling exists only for women who insist on playing by men's rules. And they're idiots. The ceiling isn't glass, it's steel; and if you don't know by the end of high school that you're going to have to go around and not through it, well . . . you deserve whatever happens to you."

It was a stunning explanation of her behavior; but I needed specifics. "So—and I ask this question purely academically, because we *are* prepared to accept your bargain, but—are you saying that this entire method of suppressing the throwaway-child crisis in this state was of *your* contrivance?"

"I'm not saying any such thing," she answered, causing me momentary disappointment; but then she added, "I had help. Whatever help I wanted, really. But I knew that the smaller the operation, the better the chance for security—and for success. Your girlfriend came in handy: she was idealistic enough to think that she could help these kids, and herself, too. She never realized until I came along just how the game works, and by then it was too late. It wasn't really bred into her. Which made her and that idiot Meisner kid the perfect fall guys, though they never suspected it. I was so honest with them, *so* concerned for these children that get abandoned by their families. All bullshit, of course. We just needed it to go away."

I paused before asking, "And do you really imagine it will? Given the way things are, in this state and this country right now—do you really think that other parents won't opt for leaving their kids, or one of their kids, or their only kid, behind, and simply starting over? That this little operation of yours can suddenly restructure what's happening to our society, to our economy?"

She positively beamed. "Not only don't I think so, Dr. Jones, I don't give a shit. I was tasked to solve *this* crisis. And I did, cleanly; or it would have been clean, if you two had just kept to your teaching, and that pain-in-the-ass brother of Ambyr's hadn't given you so many breakthroughs. But hey, who knew the kid had a gift for this kind of thing? Who could've known you'd take the *insane* step of including him in your investigation? Not me, certainly; but we countered it, and very effectively. It meant certain complications, of course. I didn't know that Dr. Li, there, had a history with Grace Chang, for one; but we even used that to confuse you, for a while."

"And Derek Franco?" Mike asked.

"Derek?" she asked in return; and for a moment the barest flutter of regret passed across her features. "Yeah . . . I was sorry about him. He was useful, too. But *so* goddamned retarded. I never thought he'd try to put my back to the wall." She rallied. "And I *certainly* never imagined that that little idiot Kolmback actually had a conscience. He could've had Nancy Grimes' job, one day, but . . ."

I could only remember Mangold's words: "But he wasn't prepared to 'advance by blood,' was he?" Cathy Donovan just shook her head. Maybe she realized she'd already told us an awful lot; or maybe somewhere in the primitive parts of her brain there still existed the trace of a human conscience; but she was close to being done with us. Yet I pressed one last time: "So there's no way we can induce you to tell us just who these 'higher powers' are that ordered the operation you ran?"

She smiled coyly and laughed lightly, never having looked quite so alluring. "Dr. Jones," she said indulgently. "You're not serious. Isn't it enough for me to say that there isn't a thing the two of you can do that will either induce me to provide that information, or stop the shitstorm that'll descend on you and everybody associated with you, if you don't agree to my offer?"

I sat there silently. I was satisfied with all I'd heard, now, yet there was no happiness in that satisfaction; so, I simply leaned back toward her office door, clicked the pen in my pocket again, and said, "Yes. I suppose it's enough." Calling out loud, I said, "How about it, Frank? *Is* it enough?"

And suddenly, Frank Mangold burst through the door. He stood there, sweating a bit and looking particularly bloodthirsty. "Well, Doc," he said, catching his breath. "I didn't exactly get the first part, though I got the gist. I was a little busy . . ." He held the door open, allowing us to see the two guards from the hallway nearly unconscious on the outer office floor, each bleeding from a blow to the head. Donovan's face went pale, and she immediately pulled her jacket back on. "Don't worry, Cathy," Mangold continued, taking out a handkerchief and wiping blood off his Glock before he holstered it. "I didn't hurt 'em *too* much, and they won't have more than a fat pair of headaches when they wake up."

"Frank!" Donovan shouted. "Do you have any idea of what you're doing?"

"Yep." Mangold pulled a set of handcuffs out of a case on the back of his belt. "I'm arresting you. And your flunkies. Those that're still alive, anyway. I already killed Shea"—as he spoke, Mangold moved over and slapped the cuffs onto Donovan's hands behind her back—"but he gave us a nice, fat confession, just like yours, before he went."

"You're—*arresting* me?" Cathy said in disbelief. "On what possible charge?"

"You just gave us the charge," I said, pulling the pen from my pocket. "Conspiracy, Cathy. It's all recorded on this simple little device."

"Hey, Doc, that's the high-end model," Frank protested with a smile. "Had to make sure you got every single word, in case those two gave me more of a fight than I figured. But they didn't." He lifted his head, holding on to Donovan's arm, and let out a piercing whistle with just his teeth and lips. At the sound, several BCI men stormed in from the hallway. "Cuff those two, then take this garbage down to the van in the parking lot. And don't fucking listen to a word she says."

As he turned Donovan around, she said bitterly, yet still without losing her proud demeanor, "Frank, trust me, you have absolutely no idea who and what you're screwing with, here, except your own career. Just uncuff me, and we'll forget the whole thing."

"I don't know, Cathy," Frank said, sending her into the hands of his subordinates. "It's quite a story to forget, just like that. Okay, fellas—out they all go . . ."

And it was no more or less complicated than that. Cathy Donovan, bathed in hubris, had fallen for a gimmick that she would certainly have expected, if Mike and I had been crooks, cops, or lawyers. But we were just a pair of seemingly defenseless independent criminal investigators and teachers, at least one of us an advocate of methods that seemed to have gone out of style, but which had, in the end, induced her to fall into traps that her cunning mind would ordinarily have detected at their outset.

After the outer door of her office closed with that same hissing sound, Mike, Frank Mangold, and I just stood there in that eerie green glow for a few seconds, Mike looking amazed that things had finally, apparently, been tied up, myself feeling just numb, and Mangold brushing at his hair and clothes. "Shit," he mumbled. "I think one of those pricks bled on my suit . . ." Then he moved over to the window behind Donovan's desk and looked down. "Hey—Jones," he called. "Come here, will you? Something I think you ought to see." Both Mike and I started toward the window, but Mangold waved my partner off. "Won't interest you, Li. Just the pro-filer, here . . ."

I had assumed that he wanted me to see Cathy Donovan entering the BCI wagon that would take her down to Albany for processing and inter-rogation (and wouldn't Mangold just love that session?). And, looking into the street, I did see his men emerge from the courthouse, where they attracted the attention of those local officers who had earlier been dis-patched to North Fraser but who'd stuck around, evidently fascinated to see what was going to happen inside. Watching in amazement, this group included Steve and Pete, whose faces broadened with smiles of confused happiness, after which they looked up to the window where we were standing and gave thumbs-up gestures. But then a State Police cruiser that I recognized as Mitch's pulled into the lot and up to the van, and suddenly neither Pete nor Steve looked very happy, anymore:

They had already seen what I had not. Mitch, emerging from the cruiser, opened the back door as another trooper got out of his passenger seat and stood guard. And from the cage in the back of the vehicle emerged Ambyr and Kevin, both, like Donovan, cuffed behind the back. It was hard to make out any actual words, but it was nonetheless clear that Ambyr was playing her part to the end: she tearfully insisted on something, looking inside the cruiser, and Mitch's subordinate eventu-ally went in and got her white cane, carrying it as he took her to the same van into which Donovan had already disappeared. I could just make out her final protest—"But I don't *understand*!"—before a female BCI officer guided her into the van from within and the doors banged closed on them all. Kevin Meisner, meanwhile, was taken quickly over to Frank Mangold's own cruiser and shoved roughly into its back seat, two of his men standing guard as they waited for their boss.

I spun on Frank, suddenly enraged and feeling as if, despite all we'd been through that day, he was the swine I'd always pegged him for. Not-ing my expression, as well as the balling up of my right fist, he nodded, smiled just slightly, and said, "You want to take a poke at me, Jones? Go ahead. I can take a punch, and something tells me yours won't be the worst I've felt. But you needed to see that."

"Why, Frank?" I seethed. "What possible good could come of it, of taking away any last shred of illusion I might have about her?"

"Just exactly that," he answered; and I began to get his point. "Listen, profiler," he went on, "you think you're the first guy in an investigation that it's happened to? You think we all haven't fallen for somebody on the wrong side of a case, at some point? I'll admit, most guys don't fall for it when they've gotten to your age, but that's just poor, dumb luck."

"You saying it happened to *you*, Frank?" Mike asked, having put together enough of what I'd witnessed without himself needing to have done so.

"Me?" Frank chuckled, brushing his grey buzz-cut. "Ah, shit, Li, you don't wanna know. When I was coming up, back in the city, there was this chick, this bartender . . ." For a moment an almost gentle memory seemed to soften that sallow, chiseled face. "But, yeah. She was dirty, all right. Played me like a fuckin' harp. And it helped me, seeing her get carted off. Seeing her like she really was." He shook the moment off: "Anyway—just thought I'd return the favor. You boys take care of yourselves, and for God's sake—" He grabbed his recording pen from my hand and headed back to the outer office door. "Stay the hell out of official investigations, will you, from now on?"

"Oh," I said, looking back out the window with Mike. "Absolutely."

"Yeah," Mangold laughed. "That's what I figured. Well, don't say I didn't warn you."

Mike and I watched the dispersing scene in the lot and across the street. Steve and Pete were still glancing up at us, both with expressions, less of confusion, now, than of sympathy. But when, just before Steve got into his cruiser to head off to North Fraser, he lifted his shoulders to ask what could possibly have happened, and then Pete made a similar gesture as he got into his car, I could make no move. Mike, on the other hand, made the universal sign of a telephone receiver with his right hand, and the sheriff and his deputy both nodded, finally feeling free to take care of their own business. Mangold had emerged to take the wheel of his own unmarked car, a downcast Kevin Meisner barely visible in the back seat, and with a squeal of his tires he headed off in the direction of Route 4, which would carry him down to 787 and, from there, to Albany.

Taking a deep breath, Mike murmured, "Well? You okay, L.T.?"

And, strangely enough—all the stranger because my reaction was in keeping with Mangold's intention—I found myself, if not okay, something like it. "Getting there, Mike," I said, leaning on my cane and starting out of the office. Then I stopped once, when I saw a small framed photograph of Cathy Donovan as she had been in what must have been high school or her undergraduate days: picking it up, I saw a beautiful girl surrounded by unremarkable but handsome young men, all of whose attention was focused on her; but her eyes were locked onto the camera. "Advancement by blood," I said quietly. "The easy way out . . ."

"Yeah, what the fuck was that all about?" Mike asked.

"I'll explain it to you on the way home," I answered, replacing the picture and then leaning on Mike's shoulder with my left arm.

"Easy, L.T., for crying out loud!" Mike said; but he didn't shirk the weight. "I got shot, remember?"

"Sorry," I said, taking my arm off. "Come on, let's get home. I need to see how Marcianna's doing, and I think we could both use a drink. Maybe we can dig up a couple of bottles of Talisker along the way."

"Hunh," Mike grunted. "Don't you bet on it, kid . . ."

CODA

W ithin just a few days, Marcianna regained strength enough to get up and wander, if not yet run, around her enclosure, which she patrolled with great diligence; and by that third day I even ventured to take her on our usual afternoon walk down to the stream beyond the hollow road, from which she drank heavily, still feeling a thirst that I could empathize with only too readily: the thirst that comes from recovery after an extreme insult to the body, whether that insult be surgery or getting shot. Her vet didn't believe that her wound held any long-term implications for her leukemia; although he suggested a couple of follow-up blood tests, just to make sure of that opinion. For the moment, however, on that afternoon of that day, there was nothing to do but sit on one of the rocks by the stream as she pressed her head into my arms and chest, moaning in frustration about her inability to play our usual game of chasing the little puppet on a string.

And then, suddenly, she caught a scent in the air, and turned to see, before I could detect as much, that Lucas was approaching. It was a welcome sight, and then some: other than taking several shifts watching over Marcianna as she recovered, during which he spoke only of her condition, he had remained silent since his sister's arrest. He had finally abandoned the master bedroom—indeed, he started avoiding it—and returned to his own room next door; though there were nights, when I returned very late from the enclosure, that I heard a knocking sound coming from within, and went into the master bedroom to realize that he was rapping his fist against the wall that divided them. Perhaps he was asleep when he did it, or perhaps it was just a desperate desire to hear his sister knock back, I don't know; and I left it alone, as we left him alone, to eat his meals silently in the kitchen, to walk the grounds of the farm-house, and to try to come to terms with all that had happened. Yet he would never be able to perform that task entirely on his own; and so when I saw him finally making what seemed an attempt to interact, not only with Marcianna but with me, down by the water's edge, I became hopeful.

As he approached, Marcianna let out her happiest chirrup, raising the paw on her right side alone to welcome him: she could not yet jump, and certainly couldn't get up to the kind of roughhousing that she and Lucas had been used to. But he engaged with her, to the extent that they both were able, and finally sat down and held his head and arms out, so that she could get a kick out of toying lightly with at least those parts of his body.

"Hey, you," Lucas said to her, almost sounding like his old self. "Don't go biting my head off, that isn't fair." Nevertheless, Marcianna kept rubbing the sides of her fangs against Lucas' hair and scalp. "Hey!" he laughed. "Come on, girl, that doesn't exactly tickle, you know! And I just washed my hair, damn it! L.T.!"

It was, of course, a slightly orchestrated way to establish contact with me, on the kid's part; but at that point, I'd take it, and gladly: "Come on, Lucas," I said. "She does it to me all the time, it doesn't hurt."

"Yeah, but it's fucking scary!" he replied; and the vulgarity, too, was a good sign.

"Well, you got her started, and you can stop her," I laughed. "Just give it a shot."

Lucas pulled his head up and pointed a finger at Marcianna. "Okay: we're stopping now. Got it?" Marcianna did indeed stop, simply staring at Lucas and releasing another merry chirrup. The kid sat back, slightly surprised. "Well—whatta you know?"

"See?" I said. "Not so tough to take your head out of the wild beast's mouth."

Lucas scratched at the particularly disheveled, sandy mop on his head, as he walked over to sit on a rock next to me. "Yeah," he droned. "I get the point. I'm not that dumb."

"What point?"

"It's a—a whattaya call it, a metaphor, right? You're trying to tell me I can get over Derek dying and Ambyr lying to me, not to mention my parents' disappearing."

"Whoa," I said. "Was I really doing all of *that*?"

"Yeah, you did, asshole." He caught himself quickly. "Sorry. Professor. Doctor. Whatever you're being right now."

"I suppose 'friend' is too much?" I ran my hands over Marcianna's head and neck, as she moaned for more attention.

"Okay, then," Lucas said, clearly ready, at long last, to tackle the subject. "You're my friend. And you're gonna try to tell me, based on what I've been hearing you and Mike say up in the plane—"

"You've been listening to Mike and me?" I asked, genuinely surprised.

"Yeah," the kid answered, his tone as yet noncommittal. "And the pair of you seem to think that I can learn to forgive Ambyr, someday; maybe even forget that she walked out. On us *both*."

"She didn't walk out on us, Lucas," I said. "She was chasing something, something she never got to have: a life like anybody else her age. And she honestly thought she was doing good by the throwaways, along the way. Maybe she even did, for some; we'll never know. But listen to me: don't ever question how much she cares about you. This isn't like your parents."

"Yeah?" He began to pick up pebbles and throw them back at the ground, hard. "Well, it sure as shit *feels* the same way. And it's got kinda the same effect, doesn't it? I mean, what's gonna happen to me, anyway?"

"Well, that's where it really *is* different," I answered, a little tentatively. "Your parents left you flat. Ambyr knew that something like this might happen; and she sent you up here to get involved in the case, but also— she knew it would be a safe place for you."

"How do you mean?" Lucas asked; and while he was trying to maintain his stony demeanor, there was plainly hope in his voice.

"Well—" Trying for a moment to find a subtle way of putting it, I found that there wasn't one; and so I just plowed on through: "Ambyr wanted this to be your foster home. I've talked to Clarissa about it, and we're both willing."

Lucas paused; not with real surprise, but with some disbelief, nonetheless. Then he said, very quietly: "No shit?"

"No shit. But there's conditions."

"Uh-oh."

"You have to stay in school. You can't become a fuck-up, and you pull your weight around the house."

"Oh," he answered brightly, relieved. "That's it? Well, shit—I can do all that."

"I know you can," I said with a certain nod. "In return, you'll keep working with Mike and me, and learn the criminal sciences as long as you want to. If your interests change, fine, but you have to be serious about them."

"No, no, I want to stick with what we've been doing," he said anxiously. "Then, someday, maybe I'll go to college, even."

"That's the general idea. Clarissa and I will find a way to make it work, though by then, with the training you'll have, you should be able to get a scholarship to any first-rate school of criminal justice."

A broad smile crept into Lucas' face, broader than I'd seen in a long time. "Really? Well—fuck me . . ." And then, just as quickly, the shadow loomed again: "And Ambyr?"

"What about her?" I asked, perhaps more coldly than I'd intended.

"What's gonna happen to her?"

"Well, she didn't actually kill anybody, and she wasn't responsible for staging the death scenes. Nor did she have a hand in Derek's actual death. Mangold, Mike, and I will make all that clear. She was only complicit in an illegal adoption service, or whatever you want to call it, so she'll probably get a light sentence in some minimum security joint. Be out in a couple of years."

"No," Lucas said. "What I mean is, are you gonna make me go visit her?"

"Do you want to go visit her?"

"I don't know." He started tossing his pebbles harder. "I'm pissed at her, but—she's my sister. My family. I guess."

"So, you'll give it time, and go see her when you're ready. She can't expect more than that."

"And if she tries to come back here?" he asked, very tentatively.

"Lucas," I said. "You're looking way too far ahead. Let's just try to get the next couple of steps squared away. If you want to see her, someday, or if she tries to come back, and you don't want her to, well . . . we'll handle it."

"Hunh." Lucas dropped his handful of pebbles. "How about you?"

"Me?"

"Sure." Lucas started stroking Marcianna's neck again. "She fucked you over almost as bad as she did me. Worse, in some ways."

Taking a deep breath, I said only, "I'll have to deal with it when it happens, too, Lucas. All we can do."

Lucas glanced around, sadness touching his features. "I miss Derek, sometimes," he said quietly. "And I hate to think of him . . . on that tree."

"We can have it cut down, it's on our property." A look of uncertainty entered Lucas' face, so I went on: "Seems a shame, though. Kids love to play there. And it wasn't the tree's fault."

"Yeah. That's true . . ." Standing up, Lucas took Marcianna's face in his hands once more; and it became clear to me how very much she was going to be a part of his ability to recover from his latest round of losses. "It *is* true, isn't it?" he said to her, shaking her head just a little from side to side, very gently. In return, she knocked him to the ground with a simple, happy movement of her neck, and in seconds was atop him, causing him to laugh and holler simultaneously.

And then a new voice was added to the chorus: Mike's. "Finally!" he called from the top of the pasture, where he emerged from behind some shrubs with Gracie Chang—who'd been paying regular visits to Shiloh—in tow. "We've been sitting here for ten minutes, getting grass stains on our asses, waiting for you three idiots to finish your private time!"

"Stop it, Mike," Gracie said, slapping at him. "We have not." Then she called to us, with a smile that bespoke no lingering effects of her crash, "But do you guys mind if we come down?"

I just held up my arm and smiled in return, and they made their way to us. Gracie was fascinated to watch the interaction between Lucas and Marcianna, which gave Mike a chance to sit beside me and light a cigarette. Himself watching Lucas as the kid wrestled and laughed, Mike grew obviously pleased that both our colleague and our young apprentice had recovered so much of themselves; and he called, "Don't you *ever* fucking run out of energy, kid?"

"Nope!" Lucas declared, rolling away from Marcianna and then falling victim again as she pursued him. "Come on, Gracie, try it, she's actually a riot."

"I think I'll just stay a spectator, thanks, Lucas," Gracie answered; yet she made no move to join Mike and me, meaning that something was on my partner's mind.

Mike watched Marcianna and the kid, shaking his head and letting out a chuckle. "Well," he said. "Everybody's got their own way of healing up, I guess." Taking a drag of his cigarette, he added, "So I guess you told him, hunh? About staying on here?"

"Yeah," I said. "I told him. Give me a smoke, will you?"

Fishing a cigarette out of his shirt pocket, he handed it to me and offered a light. "And he's cool with the whole thing?" I nodded in reply. "What about you—you sure *you're* cool with it?"

"Well," I sighed. "I'm sure it's the best thing for *him*. Maybe for me, too."

"Yeah?" I could feel Mike eyeing me. "And what about your—health? What did the doc say when you went yesterday?"

"He said," I answered slowly, "that whatever the 'strenuous activity' was that I'd put the affected areas of my body through this summer, I hadn't done myself any favors."

"And what'd you tell him?"

"I told him it was worth it."

Nodding, Mike tried hard to find another subject. "Hey—Clarissa just happened to mention to me, on my way down here, that you made some claim to maybe knowing what old Colonel Jones was talking about, that night he rode into Surrender for the last time."

"Yeah," I said, nodding. "I might."

"Well?" he pressed impatiently. "Share, dude—what was it?"

Hearing these words, Gracie finally joined us. "Yes, Trajan, I'd like to know that, too."

I paused, gathering my thoughts. "It's just my opinion," I answered, still watching Marcianna carefully, to make sure she didn't overexert herself. "But—I think he'd had enough. Enough of watching young people die for the plots and schemes of ambitious, supposedly responsible adults. I don't mean during the war; I'm talking about after it, first in the border states and then here. Think of those two stupid young men they sent up from town that night, a century and a half ago; then think of the kids that died before and during this case. Think of Latrell. Derek. All to preserve people in power, or to advance those who were trying to get it. 'Advancement by blood,' Frank Mangold said. Not that blood isn't necessary sometimes—the Colonel genuinely believed that slavery was a fundamental crime, which was what gave him the strength to make it through the four years of fighting. But then it ended, yet down where he was they were still lynching young men, black and white. He thought he'd gotten away from it when he came to Surrender. And those kind of crimes—the crimes he saw the night he rode into town, the kind of crimes we've seen . . . All caused by fear, ambition, corruption, and greed. And you really cannot escape any of it, in this country."

Mike and Gracie both weighed that for a long couple of minutes before Gracie asked, "Is there anywhere you *can* escape it?"

"Doubtful. Just have to fight it, that's all." I sighed, almost groaning as I did. "But you get tired. You just get so damned tired . . ."

"Yeah," Mike said. "You do." He tried to switch gears: "So how about Cathy Donovan? Will she roll on the people she was working for, to get a deal?"

"Donovan?" I said. "I doubt it. But who knows? She may fool the whole courtroom. We know she wants a career in politics. Rolling over on her bosses and claiming coercion may give her that. We can only hope that our testimony, and Frank's, *and* her recorded words, will counteract it. But, in the legal language of the day, 'we have no CSI,' no 'forensic evidence,' not on her, so anything's possible. Hell, we've seen murderers walk, without forensics. And the machine in this state is as powerful as ever. So . . ."

Gracie paused before asking, "And Ambyr?"

I shook my head. "I don't know. I just don't know anything about Ambyr, anymore. Maybe I never did. Still . . ." I tried to snap out of it, to become the criminal analyst again: "In the end, she didn't actually orchestrate the death scenes. That was Donovan's and Shea's boys. Which may count for something. And in court, she'll play the poor blind girl who tried to do something good, you can bet on that." I couldn't keep it up. "But I just—have to stop thinking about it . . ."

We all sat silently on the rocks for a moment, listening to Lucas and Marcianna and to the stream behind us; and when Mike did speak again, it was very quietly: "Well. Given all that, I'm not sure I should tell you this, but—Pete Steinbrecher just called. That's why we came down."

I could only laugh a little, blowing smoke out as I did. "Don't even tell me . . ."

"Yep. Another case. Simple homicide, says the good Dr. Weaver. Pete and Steve're not so sure."

Lucas' head had already shot up from the ground. "What's that?" he called to us, with an eagerness that was very surprising and, being so, totally characteristic. "Another case?"

"Oh, shit," Mike murmured, crushing out his butt, poking a hole in the ground with his finger, and burying all of it save the filter, which he pock-eted. "Haven't you had enough, kid?"

"No fucking way!" Lucas declared. The three of us rose and approached him, as I retracted Marcianna's lead and brought her in by my side, where she began to try to shove her head into my jacket pocket. "You know what they say, Mike," Lucas went on. "When you get into a really bad car crash—oh. Sorry, Gracie, I was just—"

But Gracie only smiled, very generously. "That's all right, Lucas, go ahead."

"Well," Lucas resumed: "Alls I was gonna say is, the first thing you gotta do after a car crash is get back behind the fucking wheel."

Mike began to shake his head, and I let the three of them go on ahead at a faster pace. "That is not the expression, you ignorant urchin," Mike said. "It's 'If you fall off a horse—'"

"A *horse*?" Lucas echoed in disbelief. "Who the fuck's got a horse?"

"Shut up and listen to me, will you?" Mike said, trying to remain pa-tient: "'If you fall off a horse, you have to get right back on again.'"

"Why the hell would you do that?" Lucas asked in disbelief. "You fall off a horse, you stay the fuck away from horses, that's what you do. You're all scrambled up in your head, Mike—nobody uses horses, anymore, and *everybody* uses cars—"

"That's not the point!" Mike finally cried. "It's a proverb!"

"Forget proverbs," Lucas retorted. "I wanna hear about this case . . ."

We kept on walking, but I maintained a nice, slow pace, because Mar-cianna had had about enough exercise for the day. "You tired, girl?" I said; to which she looked up at me anxiously with her golden eyes, her face marked so sadly and permanently by the long, black tear tracks run-ning down her face from them. "Okay," I said, finally digging out the few dog treats in my pocket that she'd been unable to reach. "God knows you've earned them . . ."

After she'd finished briefly dicing and swallowing the things, she pulled alongside close, keeping her body tight against my good leg: not for support, I knew, but simply to make sure that I knew she was there.

ACKNOWLEDGMENTS

The list of authors who have fought to reveal the endemic corruption, failure, and mistakes that have characterized modern American forensic science on the local and federal levels is finally though slowly growing longer, despite the endless mythicizing of the field in print and on screens large and small: an imbalance that should concern every citizen of this country. It would be impossible to list all the pioneering authors here, but among those who have paved the way, special mention goes to D. Kim Rossmo, happily mentioned in this book, a few of whose views—expressed in his key text, *Criminal Investigative Failures*—I might take issue with, but whose willingness to speak and teach so many more truths in the face of great odds has been unqualifiedly honorable. Similar thoughts were inspired by Michael Lynch, Simon A. Cole, Ruth McNally, and Kathleen Jordan's *Truth Machine: The Contentious History of DNA Fingerprinting*, Cate Shepherd's *Emotional Orphans*, Dennis J. Stevens' *Media and Criminal Justice: The CSI Effect*, Gary Greenberg's *The Book of Woe: The DSM and the Unmaking of Psychiatry*, and of course, the National Academies' *Strengthening Forensic Science in the United States: A Path Forward*. I'd also like to give special mention to Sarah Burns, David McMahon, and Ken Burns for their documentary, *The Central Park Five*. Anyone wanting to know precisely how it is possible for police to achieve the shockingly fallacious results through interrogation that they often do should sit down and watch it.

It hardly need be said that these are but a fraction of the sources relied on for this book; but they are a very good starting point for anyone who wishes to explore how criminal science has been so terribly perverted during its century-old transformation into forensic science.

On a personal level, the completion of this book owes much to many people, some of whom have been mentioned, many of whom have not. Of the latter, I must include my aunt and uncle, John and Kathy Von Hartz whose love and support has meant more than they may ever know; Prudence Munkittrick, who has always been a sounding board and the very best of beloved friends, and who has pursued a teaching career that fills me with pride and admiration; my mother and her husband, Francesca and Bob Cote, who've gone the extra mile; Scott Marcus, whose generosity and willingness to participate in the madness of the music room has helped provide a pressure valve; Jessica Weisner, part-owner of the Princess (ironically, for such she is, and not because of any address); my stepsister, Christine Speicher, who has always swooped in with mad, enthusiastic plans; my honored old friend Ezequiel Viñao, always stalwart; John Tobin, the last of the true St. Luke's boys, and the definition of a great New Yorker; Jim Turner, who never gives up on anybody or anything; Elizabeth Gray, whose compassion has been both consistent and sudden; and Jim Martinez, the very definition of what a banker should be, just as his brother Marcus is one of the finest GP's and diagnosticians I've ever met (and one hell of a courageous man). Thanks, too, to Michael Weinberg at Columbia Presbyterian; to Kindred Harland; and, as always, to my good friend and medical guardian, Bruce Yaffe; and speaking of "always," there is Tom Pivinski, who absolutely defines the word. A special thanks must also go to Bill Puretz, with whom I have profited from many hours of high-speed enlightenment, laughter, and affection.

To my agent, Suzanne Gluck, and to her indefatigable and indefatigably kind and patient assistant Clio Seraphim, who is every bit as wonderful as her name, my thanks for working so hard to get me through. Special thanks, too, to Eve Attermann for her wise counsel. To my L.A. hit girl, Debbie Deuble, deepest thanks as well. At Random House, this book has traveled a long and sometimes confusing road that was straightened by the brilliant and dedicated Caitlin McKenna; would that we had been able to do business long ago. And thanks to Sally Marvin for helping with the rollout, and to Carlos Beltrán for taking a sketch and making it a wonderful cover.

In addition, I must thank the other members of my Quintet on the Internet for their patience, insight, and friendship: the visionary Frank Schell, my old colleague and close friend Jon Lellenberg, Elizabeth Gray, once again; and Jamie Linville, my only literary friend in New York (now

ACKNOWLEDGMENTS | 597

London), who remained loyal when things got tough. Thanks also to my colleagues, Michael Walsh, who offered some very timely advice at a moment of deep personal trouble, and Dan Stashower, whose regular communications have reminded me that the endeavor we call writing goes up and down for us all, but must still be pursued, and Dana Kinstler, wise, dedicated, and still lovely.

Special thanks to my brother Ethan for his help managing Misery Mountain; to my nephew Sam Carr, whose affection for this place has always been appreciated; my "other" nephew, Ben, for his sketches and good humor; my niece Lydia and her husband Michael; my niece, Gabriela, wherever in the world she may be; and my last (I hope) niece, Marion, for her patient attempts to teach me to fly, which, ultimately, only resulted in my doubling down on armor. I also want to salute the Friends Seminary graduating classes of 1976 and 1977, who have re-emerged to give me support and inspiration—just as they did, so many years ago.

To the disciples of the gotcha game, let me warn in advance that this book is laced with small homages to both literature and classic cinema; I have learned from unfortunate experience that I'd better say this now. These references have nothing to do with plot, but are there for the enjoyment of those wise enough to identify them. A word about contemporary fiction: when one shrouds one's work in history, the unfortunate tendency of readers to try to identify just who in a writer's life inspired which character is suspended—return to our own time, and that tendency is immediately resumed. Let me only say that the characters in this book are, precisely like the characters in my historical fiction, an amalgam of experience, imagination, and research. I would not pause to mention this save that certain masters of the obvious are going to link certain characters to real people who don't need the hassle: obviously, this is most true of Ambyr Kurtz, who is not connected in any way (save a few admirable traits) to a certain E.R.H., who remains only a source of inspiration and admiration, these many years later.

A final word on the appearance in this book of Marcianna, an exotic animal in private ownership: some readers who do not pay careful attention to the text may interpret this as a sign that I approve of such ownership. But I hope the very opposite is clear to those who read the novel thoroughly. Marcianna was created under the careful tutelage of Big Cat Rescue's owners, Carole and Howard Baskin, with whom I have long been associated, and without whose kindness this book would not exist.

BCR is a blessing of an organization that has long fought, as have I, against the private ownership of big cats (anyone reading this book should try to support them); and what is in fact pertinent about Marcianna is *not* her appearance in private ownership, but her rescue from one of the innumerable rackets called petting zoos that overpopulate our country with unwanted adult big cats. In one such a place Marcianna contracted feline infectious leukemia, as so many cats, large and small, do in similarly filthy and abusive zoos, circuses, and animal "shelters" around the world. That Trajan Jones chooses to invest a great deal of time and money saving her from euthanasia should not obscure this fact; he has the means and, more important, the land with which to do it. But a decision such as his can apply only to individual animals who would be otherwise doomed and who, even if saved, must be kept in isolation from their own kind.

For myself, I still have my hands full with my own Siberian forest warrior, as well as counselor and fixed point, the now somewhat (in)famous Masha. She was rescued from a shelter after her own history of abuse, the effects of which she still suffers, but which have not prevented her from becoming the terror and beauty of my house and my hollow. Does one sense parallels between the two animals? Perhaps, for, as I have said, it is all a matter of mixing experience with imagination. Then, too, I have always agreed most emphatically with Joseph Méry's remark to Victor Hugo: "God made the cat that man might have the pleasure of caressing the tiger." But for most of us, it must remain the small cat and not the big that we try to rescue and caress.

ABOUT THE AUTHOR

CALEB CARR is a novelist and military historian, and the award-winning author of the *New York Times* and worldwide bestsellers *The Alienist* and *The Angel of Darkness,* as well as numerous other works of fiction. His nonfiction works include the critically acclaimed *The Lessons of Terror: A History of Warfare Against Civilians* and *The Devil Soldier: The Story of Frederick Townsend Ward.* A native of New York City, he has spent much of his life in upstate New York, where he now lives.